GRACELING

THE GRAPHIC NOVEL

KRISTIN CASHORE

Adapted and illustrated by **GARETH HINDS**

KRISTIN CASHORE

GRACE

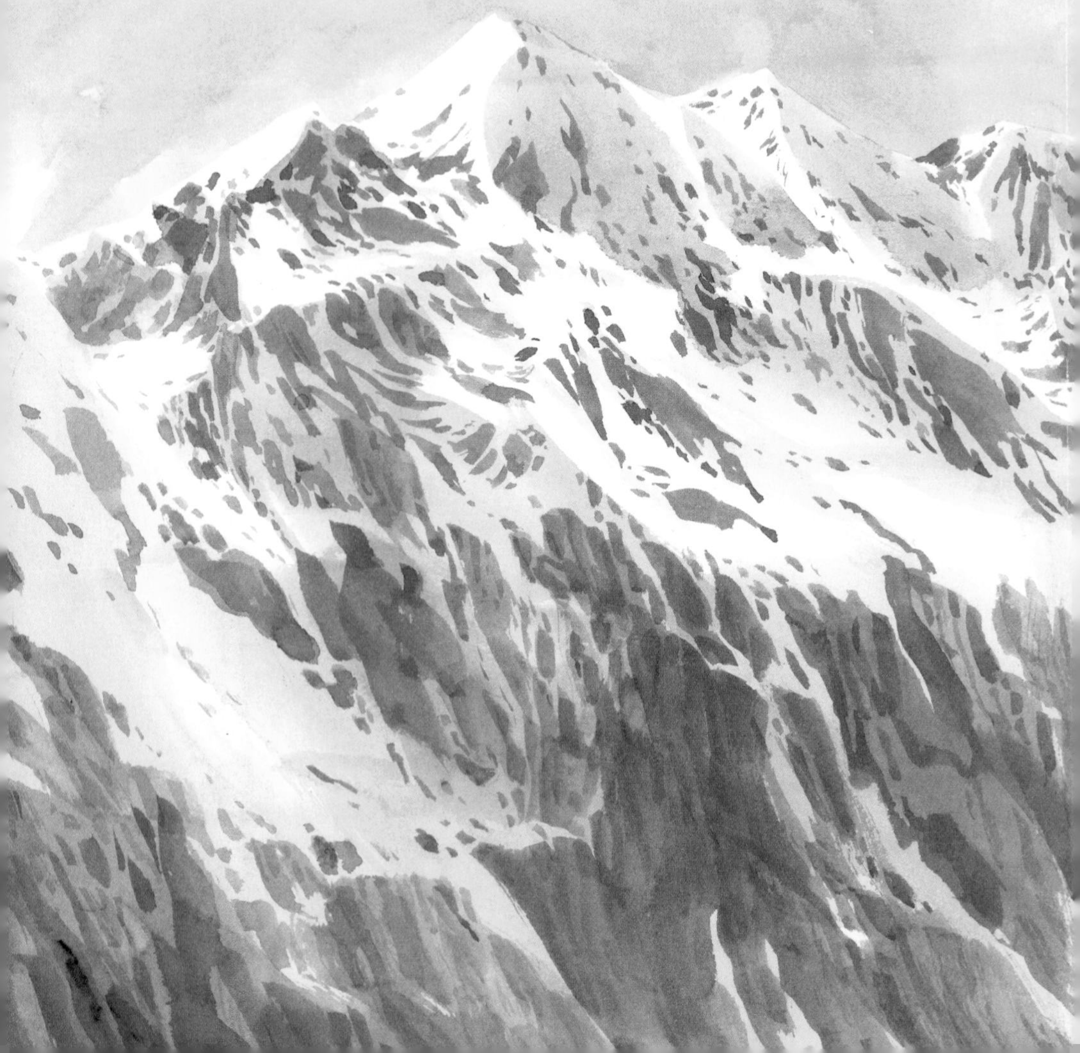

LING

THE GRAPHIC NOVEL

Adapted and illustrated by **GARETH HINDS**

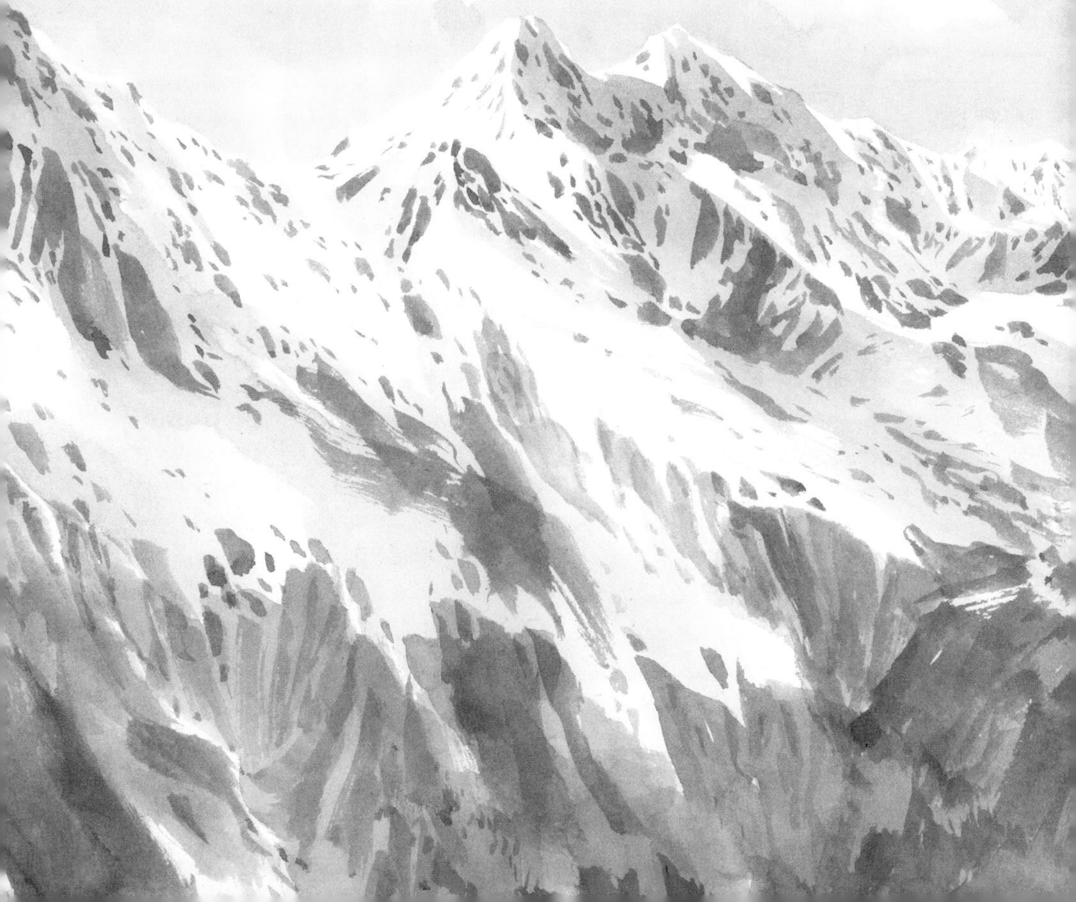

Text copyright © 2021 by Kristin Cashore

Illustrations copyright © 2021 by Gareth Hinds

Text adapted by Gareth Hinds, based on the novel by Kristin Cashore

Etch is an imprint of Houghton Mifflin Harcourt Publishing Company.

hmhbooks.com

Flatter: Frank Reynoso

The artwork was done with watercolor, ink, and digital media.

The text was set in a hand-lettered font.

Cover design by Kaitlin Yang

Interior design by Kaitlin Yang

The Library of Congress Cataloging-in-Publication Data is on file.

ISBN: 978-0-358-25042-5 hardcover

ISBN: 978-0-358-25047-0 paperback

Manufactured in China

SCP 10 9 8 7 6 5 4 3 2 1

4500827870

Dear Reader,

One day in the summer of 2012, I opened my email to find a brief note from my friend Gareth.

"Hey. I have a small present for you, but I don't seem to have your address. Please tell me where I can send it?"

Oh, how nice, I thought. I sent him my address, then forgot about it. Until one day soon thereafter, when I checked my mail and found a package from Gareth that did NOT contain a small present. It was a monumental present: Gareth had sent me a drawing.

The drawing depicted a scene from my third Graceling Realm novel, *Bitterblue.* A marble statue of a little girl stood on a plinth. The girl was crouched low, her arms transforming into wings. It was clear that the transformation hurt, for the girl's face was contorted with pain. The drawing, in pencil and charcoal on gray paper, was precise, glorious, even breathtaking. For me, though, the most remarkable and endearing thing about it was that it felt just right. The little girl in the sculpture was suffering, but she was also turning into a bird, which was magnificent, because her wings would carry her to safety. Gareth captured the spirit of the thing exactly. Today, Gareth's "small present" remains one of my most precious possessions.

One day in the summer of 2018, Gareth and his wife, Alison, were visiting my town, so I met my friends for a meal. While we were chatting, Gareth and Alison dropped another "small present" into my lap. They asked me, had I ever considered a graphic novel adaptation of *Graceling*? What if Gareth gave it a shot?

It was one of the easiest yeses of my life.

Since then, I've gotten an inside view of the massively intense process of Gareth Hinds adapting and distilling a long work into graphic form. Of Gareth deciding who these characters are, when they come from his hand; of him choosing their faces, their clothing, their landscapes; of him translating their adventures and emotions into form and color. Gareth consulted me frequently, always thoughtfully. Every time I gave feedback or tweaked the occasional bit of dialogue, it was a joy. And now he's created something so beautiful that I'm honestly a little confused when I try to figure out how this could have possibly come from the debut novel I wrote some seventeen years ago.

The drawing Gareth sent me in 2012 now hangs framed in my entranceway. It makes me happy every time I see it. If you're curious what I mean when I say that Gareth's work is glorious, that it captures the spirit of the thing exactly . . . all you have to do is turn the page.

PART ONE
The Lady Killer

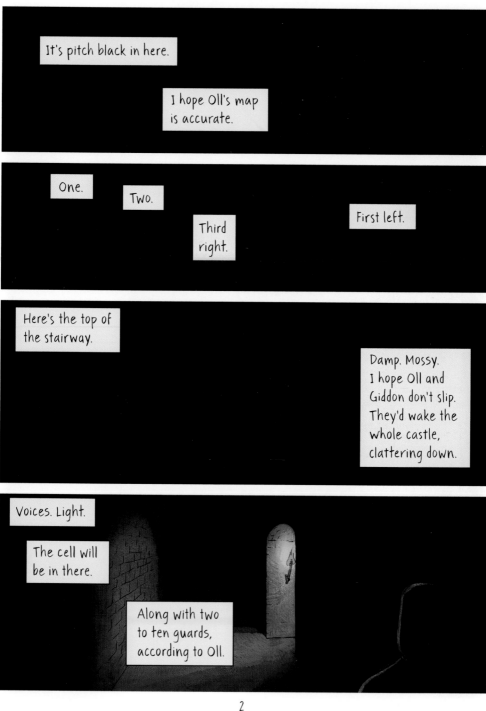

It's pitch black in here.

I hope Oll's map is accurate.

One.

Two.

Third right.

First left.

Here's the top of the stairway.

Damp. Mossy. I hope Oll and Giddon don't slip. They'd wake the whole castle, clattering down.

Voices. Light.

The cell will be in there.

Along with two to ten guards, according to Oll.

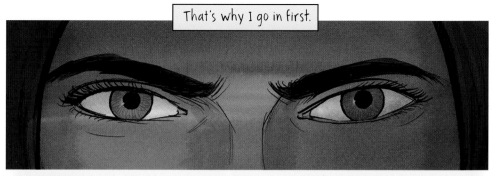

That's why I go in first.

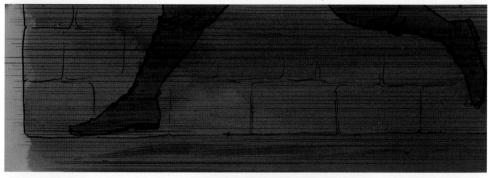

Five. Not a problem. They'll be out before they've had a good look at my eyes.

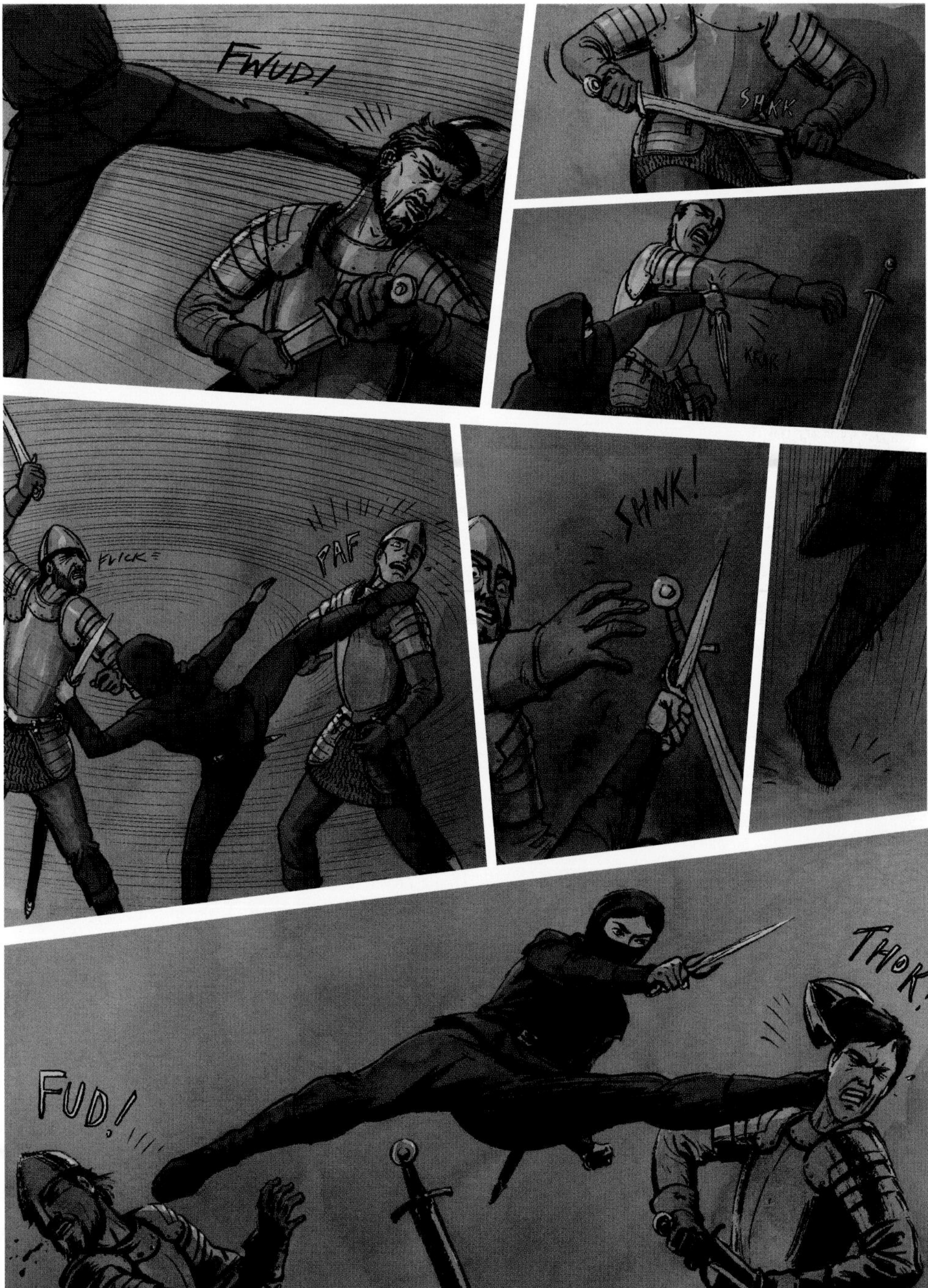

FWUD!
SHKK
KRAK!
FLICK
PAF
SHNK!
THOK!
FUD!

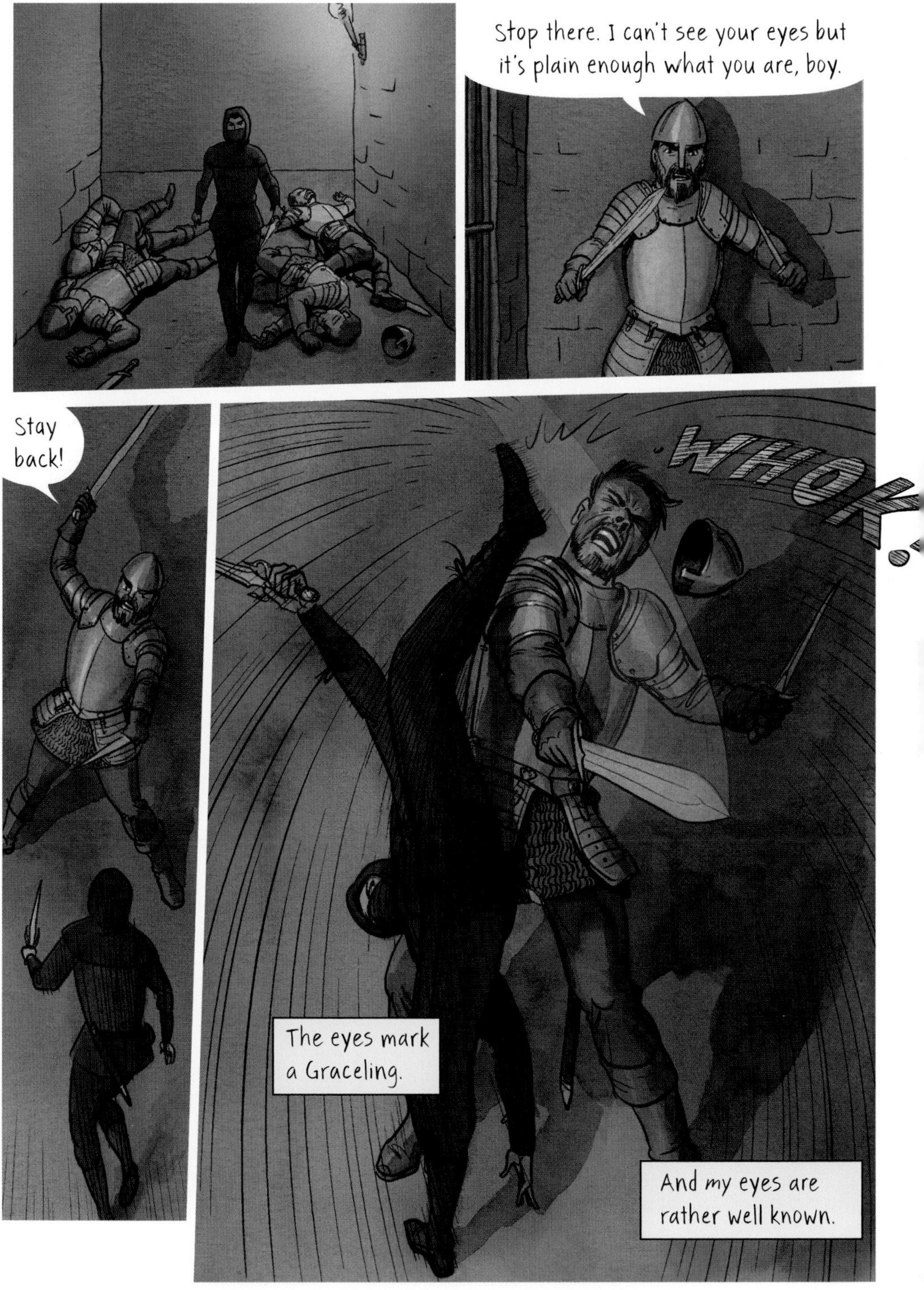
Stop there. I can't see your eyes but it's plain enough what you are, boy.
Stay back!
WHOK!
The eyes mark a Graceling.
And my eyes are rather well known.

Prince Tealiff?

CLANK

That's him, all right. The earrings mark him as Lienid.

FWEE-OOO

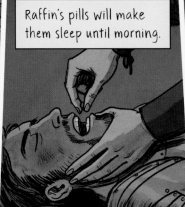

Raffin's pills will make them sleep until morning.

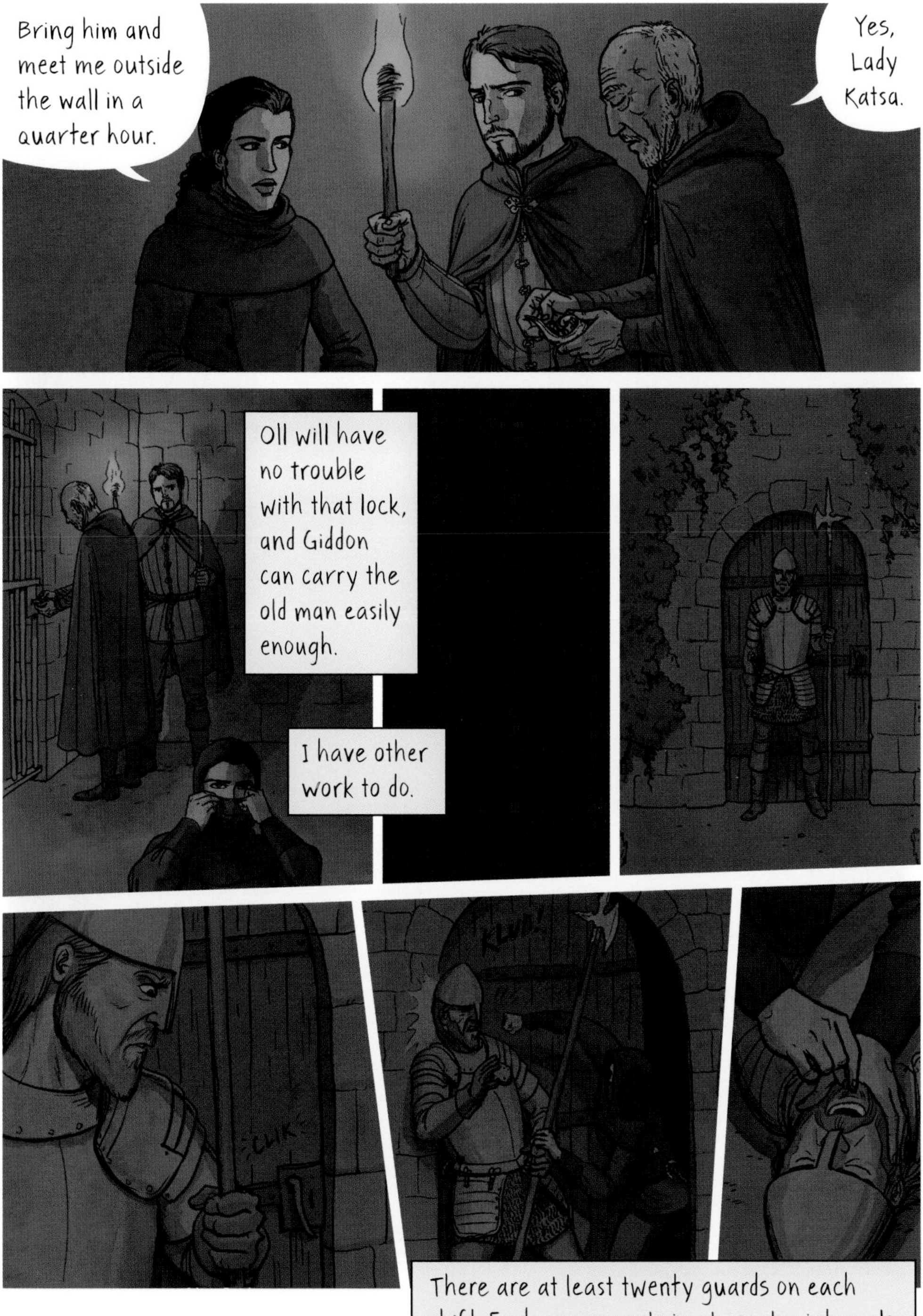
Bring him and meet me outside the wall in a quarter hour.
Yes, Lady Katsa.
Oll will have no trouble with that lock, and Giddon can carry the old man easily enough.
I have other work to do.
CLIK
KLUD!
There are at least twenty guards on each shift. Each one reports in at regular intervals.

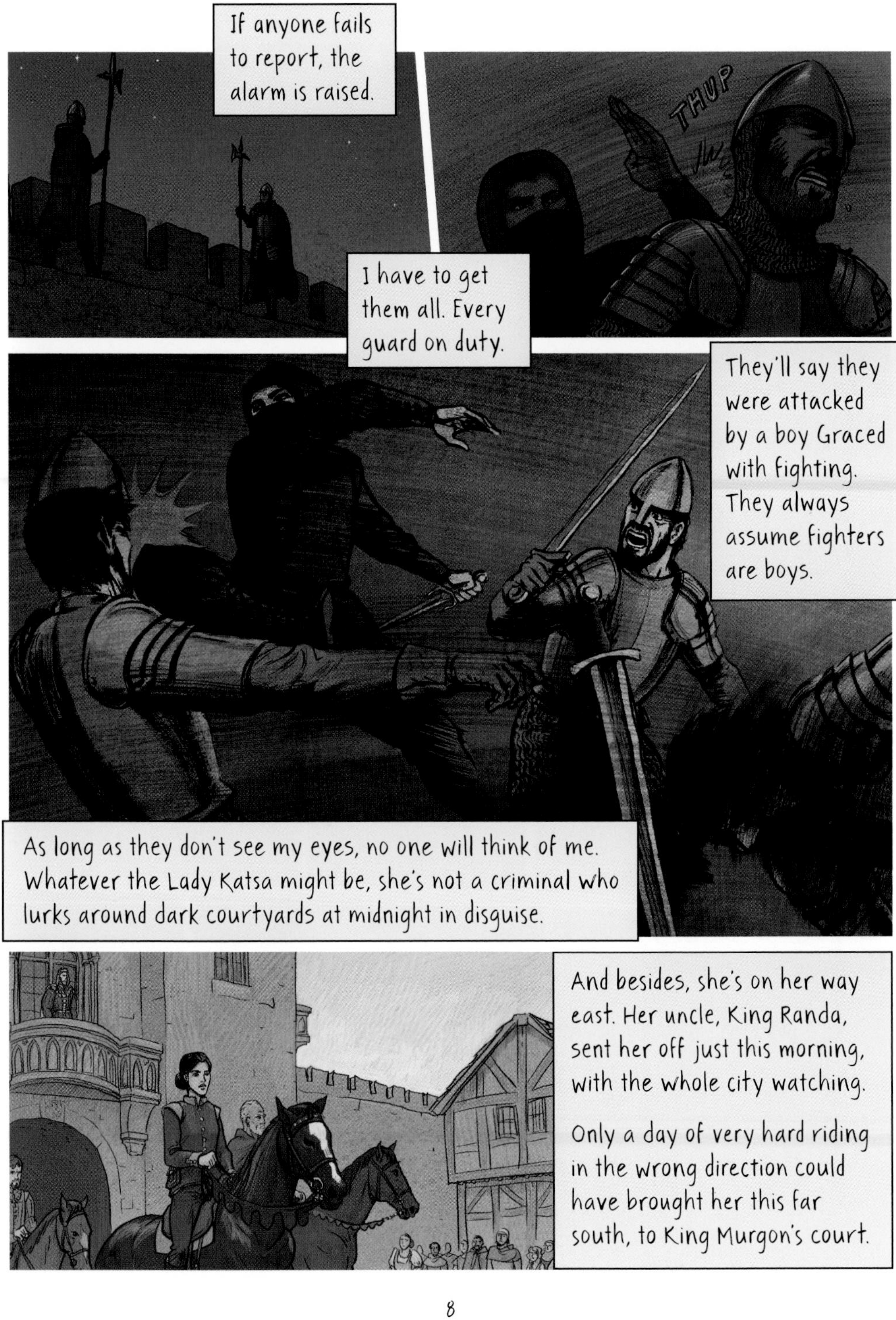
If anyone fails to report, the alarm is raised.
THUP
I have to get them all. Every guard on duty.
They'll say they were attacked by a boy Graced with fighting. They always assume fighters are boys.
As long as they don't see my eyes, no one will think of me. Whatever the Lady Katsa might be, she's not a criminal who lurks around dark courtyards at midnight in disguise.
And besides, she's on her way east. Her uncle, King Randa, sent her off just this morning, with the whole city watching.
Only a day of very hard riding in the wrong direction could have brought her this far south, to King Murgon's court.

It would be faster to just kill the guards, Giddon said.

I told him to get someone else if that's what he wanted.

TOK!

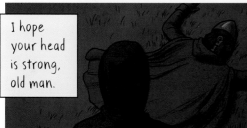

I hope your head is strong, old man.

I never want to kill by accident again.

I was barely eight when it happened.

My eyes had turned, but I didn't yet know what my Grace was.

9

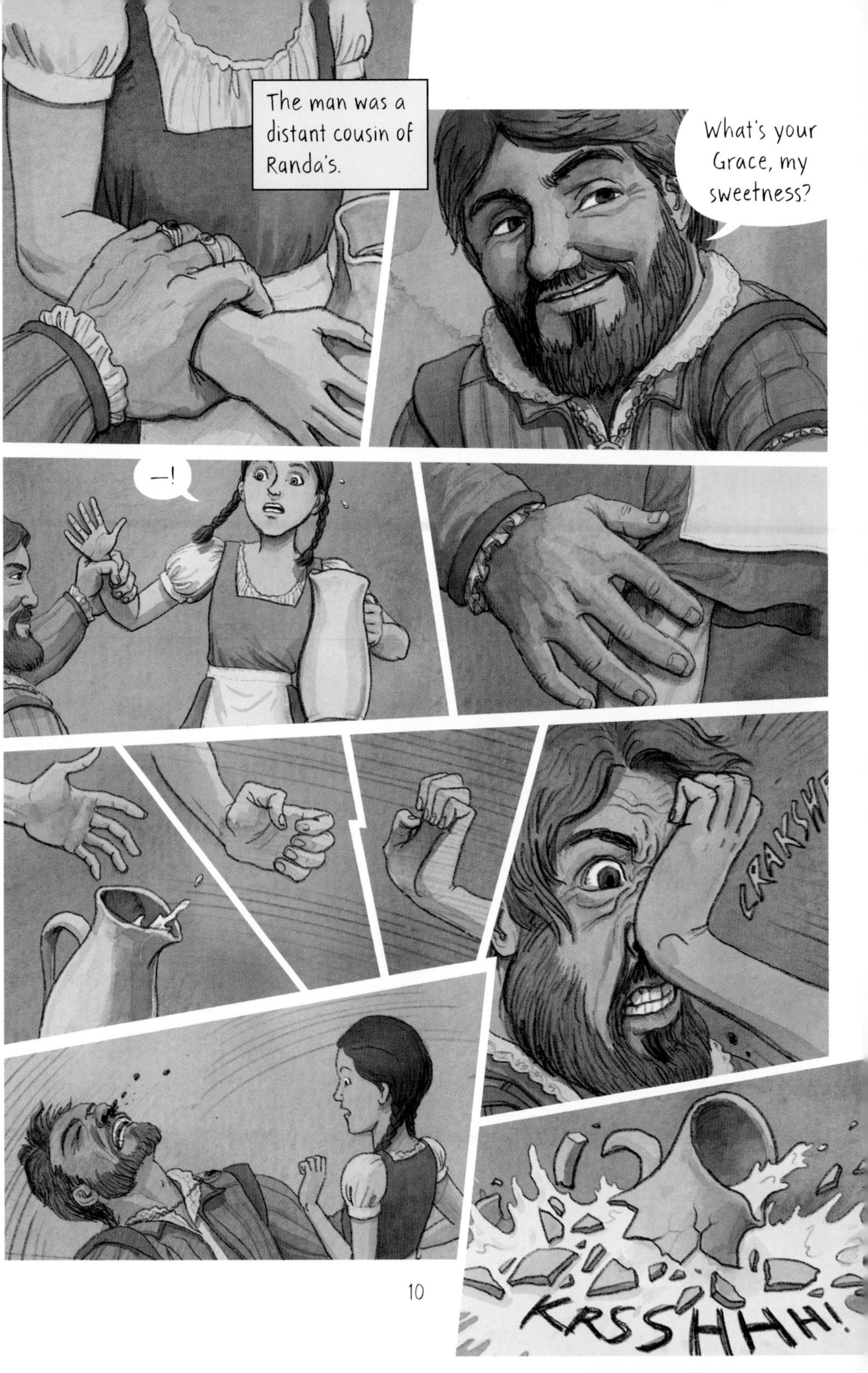
The man was a distant cousin of Randa's.
What's your Grace, my sweetness?
—!
CRAKSH
KRSSHHH!

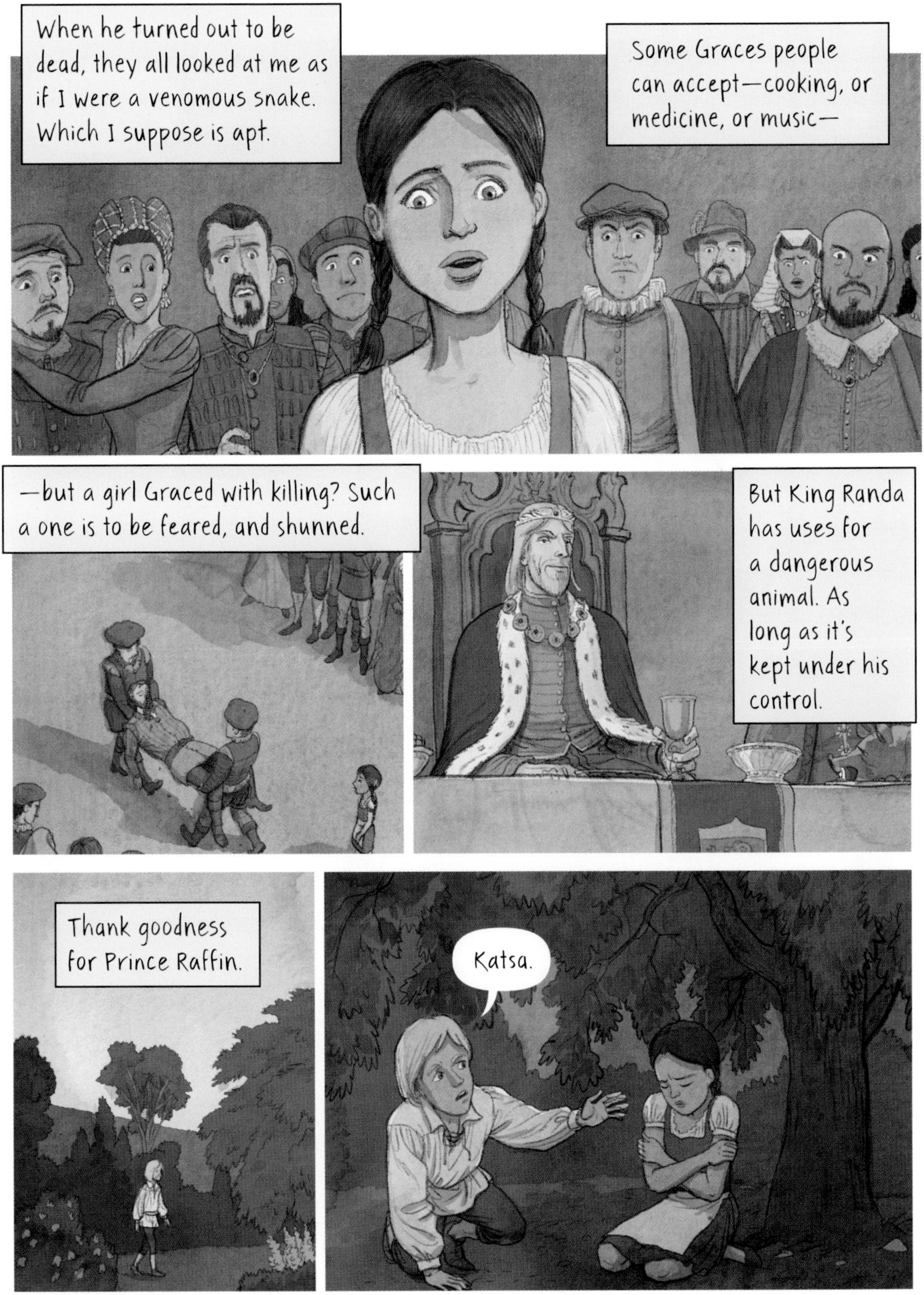
When he turned out to be dead, they all looked at me as if I were a venomous snake. Which I suppose is apt.
Some Graces people can accept—cooking, or medicine, or music—
—but a girl Graced with killing? Such a one is to be feared, and shunned.
But King Randa has uses for a dangerous animal. As long as it's kept under his control.
Thank goodness for Prince Raffin.
Katsa.

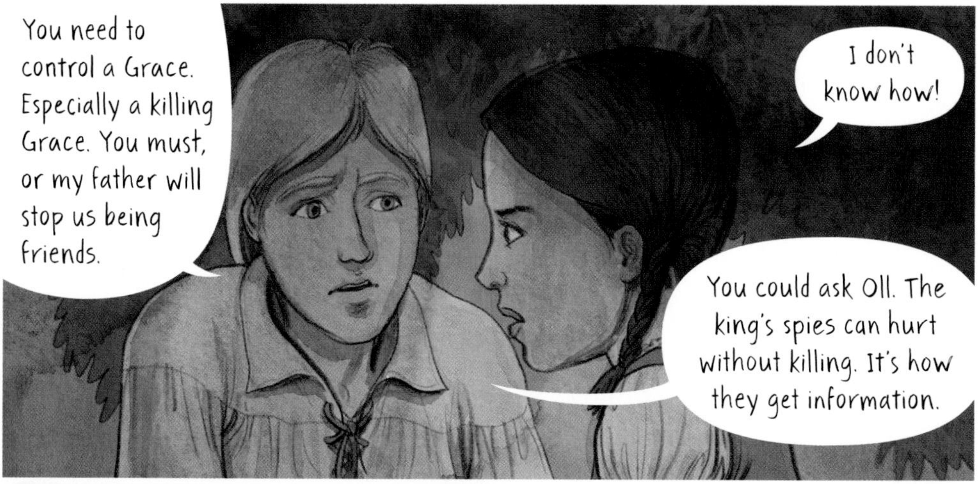
You need to control a Grace. Especially a killing Grace. You must, or my father will stop us being friends.
I don't know how!
You could ask Oll. The king's spies can hurt without killing. It's how they get information.

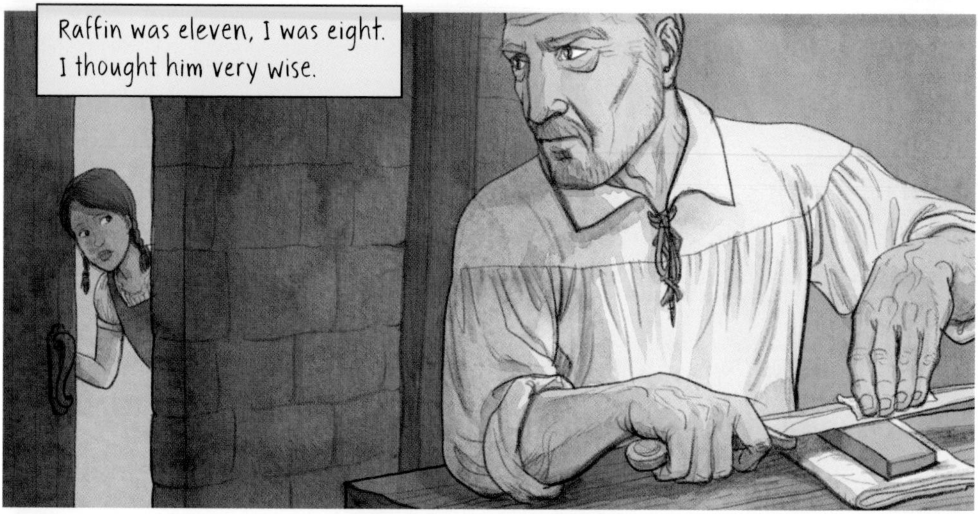
Raffin was eleven, I was eight. I thought him very wise.

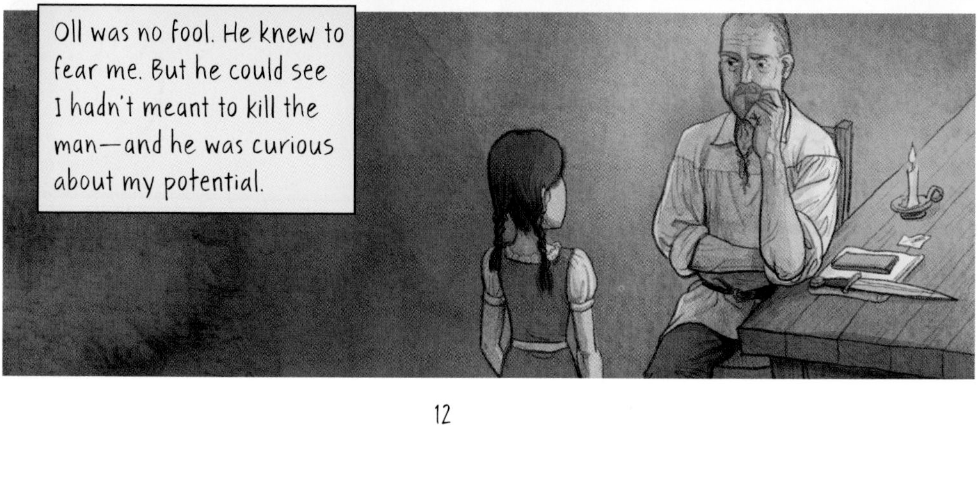
Oll was no fool. He knew to fear me. But he could see I hadn't meant to kill the man—and he was curious about my potential.

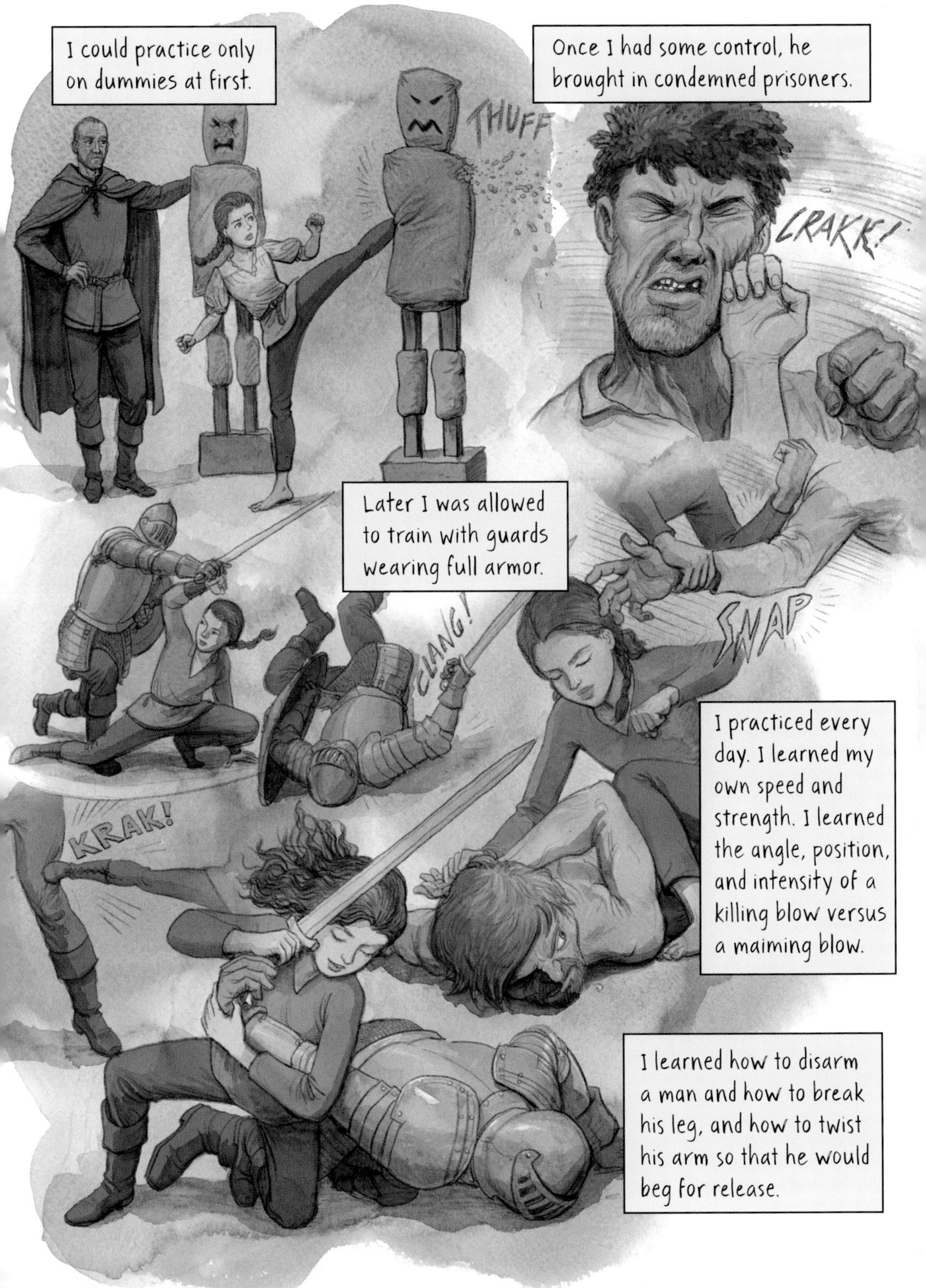
I could practice only on dummies at first.
THUFF
Once I had some control, he brought in condemned prisoners.
CRAKK!
Later I was allowed to train with guards wearing full armor.
CLANG!
SNAP
I practiced every day. I learned my own speed and strength. I learned the angle, position, and intensity of a killing blow versus a maiming blow.
KRAK!
I learned how to disarm a man and how to break his leg, and how to twist his arm so that he would beg for release.

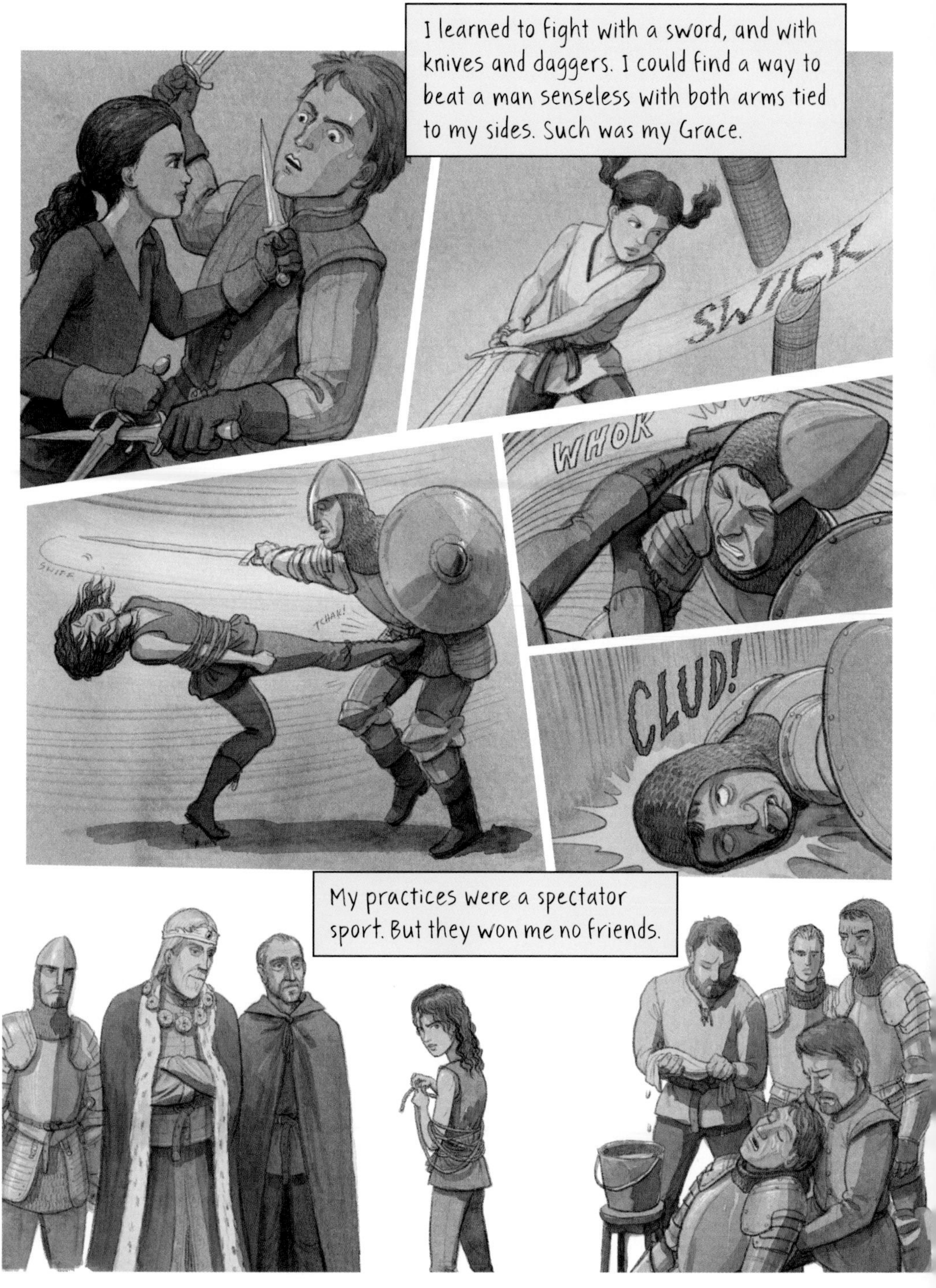

I learned to fight with a sword, and with knives and daggers. I could find a way to beat a man senseless with both arms tied to my sides. Such was my Grace.
SWIICK
SWIFF
TCHAK!
WHOK
CLUD!
My practices were a spectator sport. But they won me no friends.

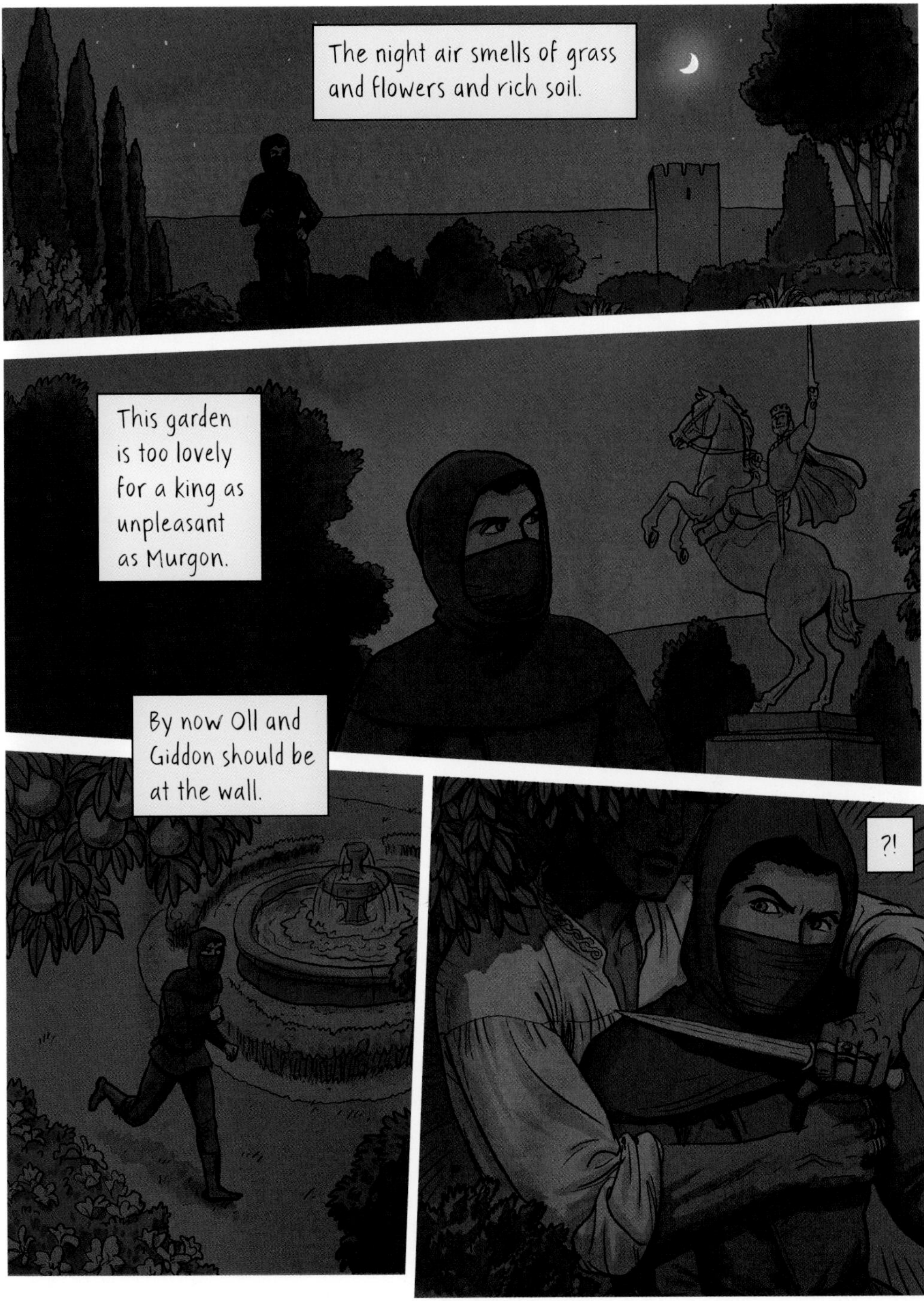
The night air smells of grass and flowers and rich soil.
This garden is too lovely for a king as unpleasant as Murgon.
By now Oll and Giddon should be at the wall.
?!

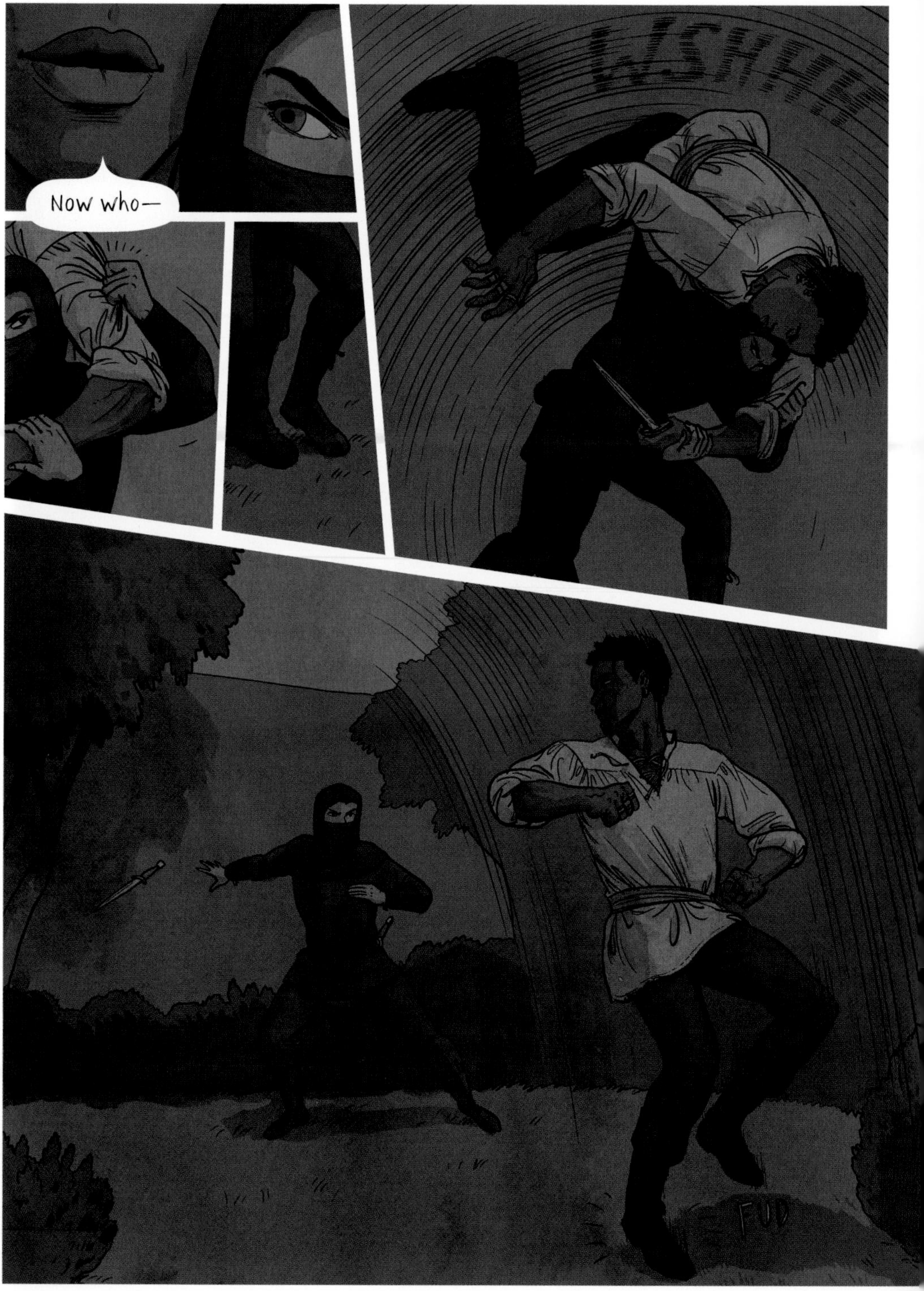
Now who—
WSHHH
FUD

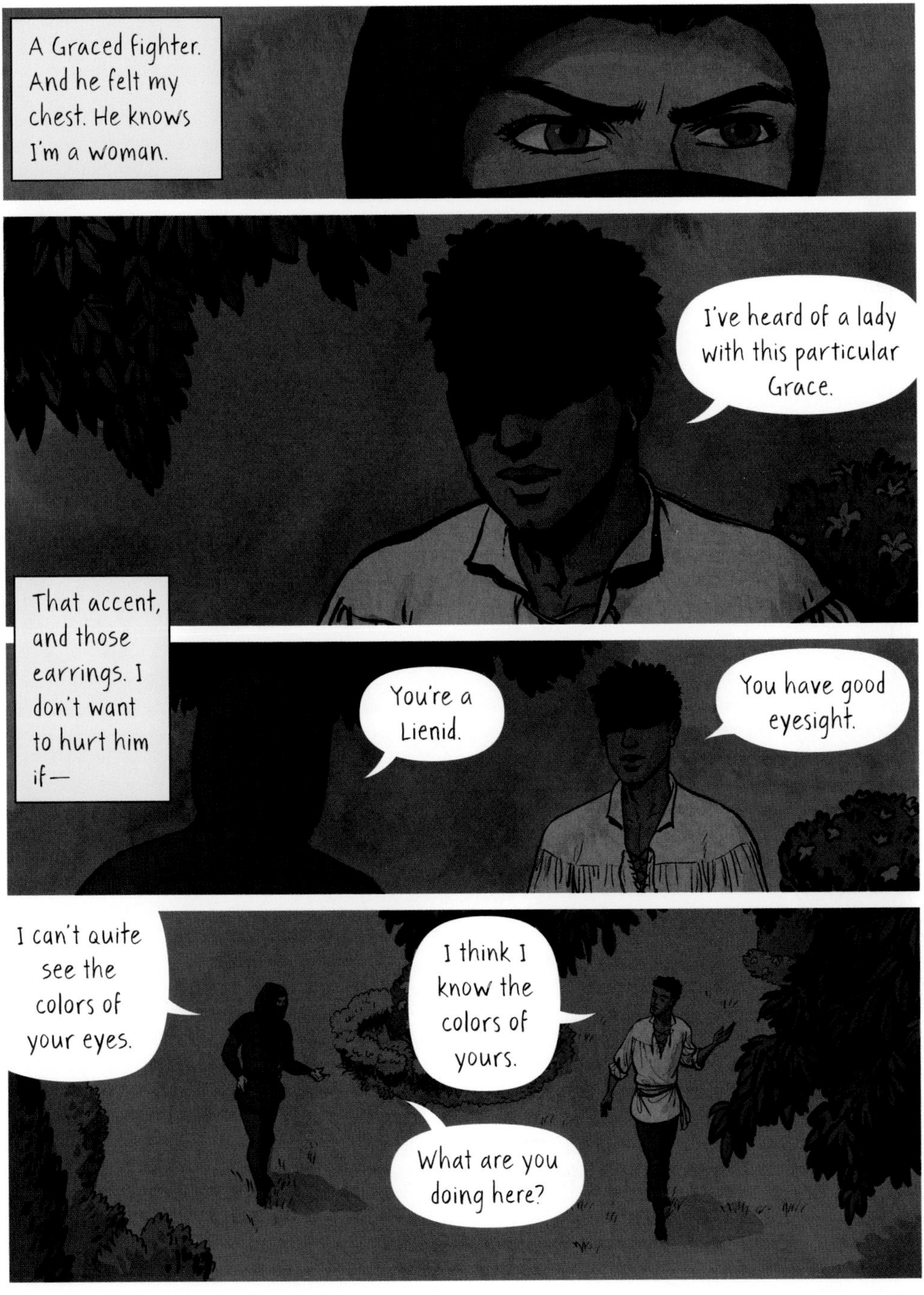
A Graced fighter. And he felt my chest. He knows I'm a woman.
I've heard of a lady with this particular Grace.
That accent, and those earrings. I don't want to hurt him if—
You're a Lienid.
You have good eyesight.
I can't quite see the colors of your eyes.
I think I know the colors of yours.
What are you doing here?

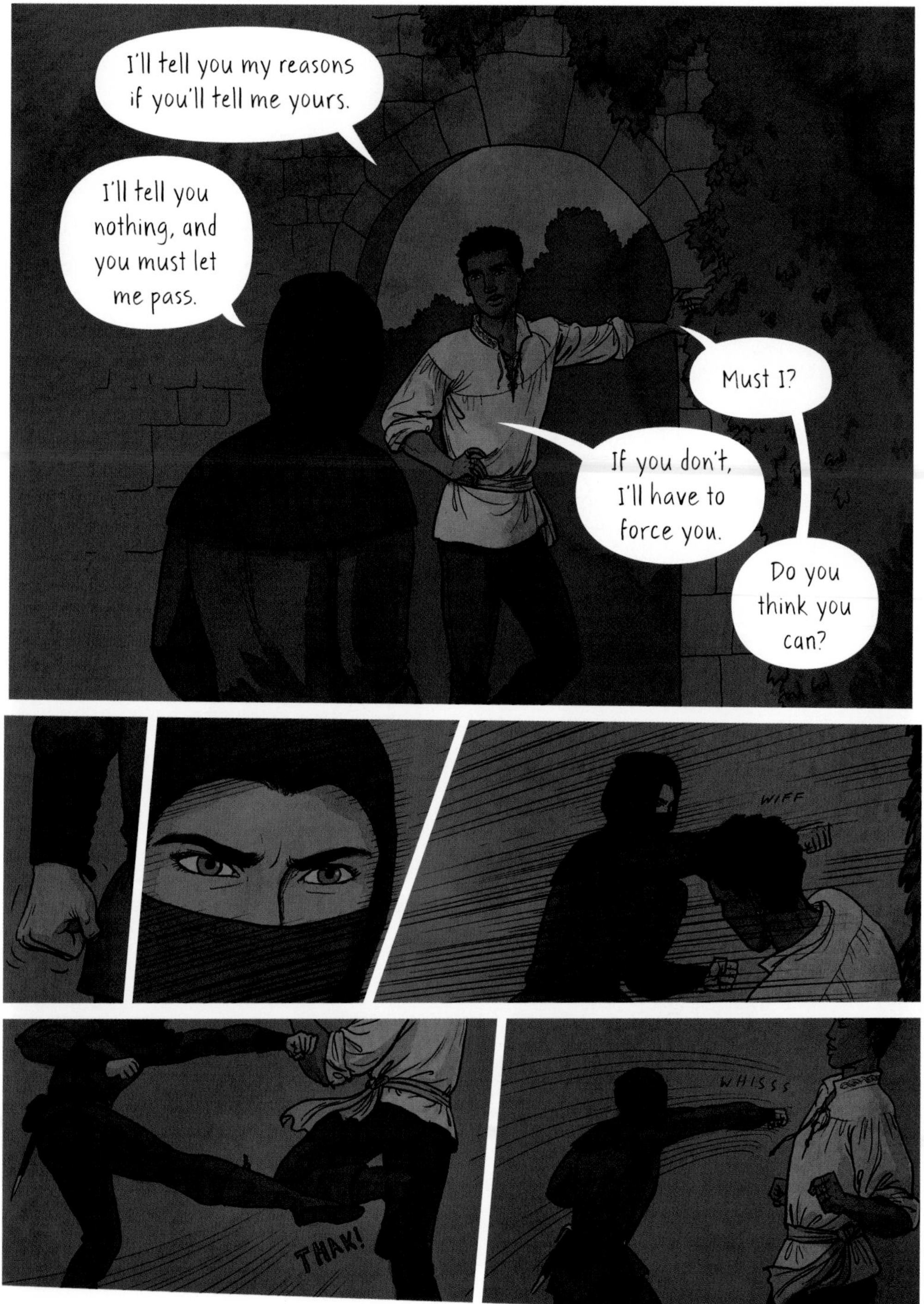
I'll tell you my reasons if you'll tell me yours.
I'll tell you nothing, and you must let me pass.
Must I?
If you don't, I'll have to force you.
Do you think you can?
WIFF
THAK!
WHISSS

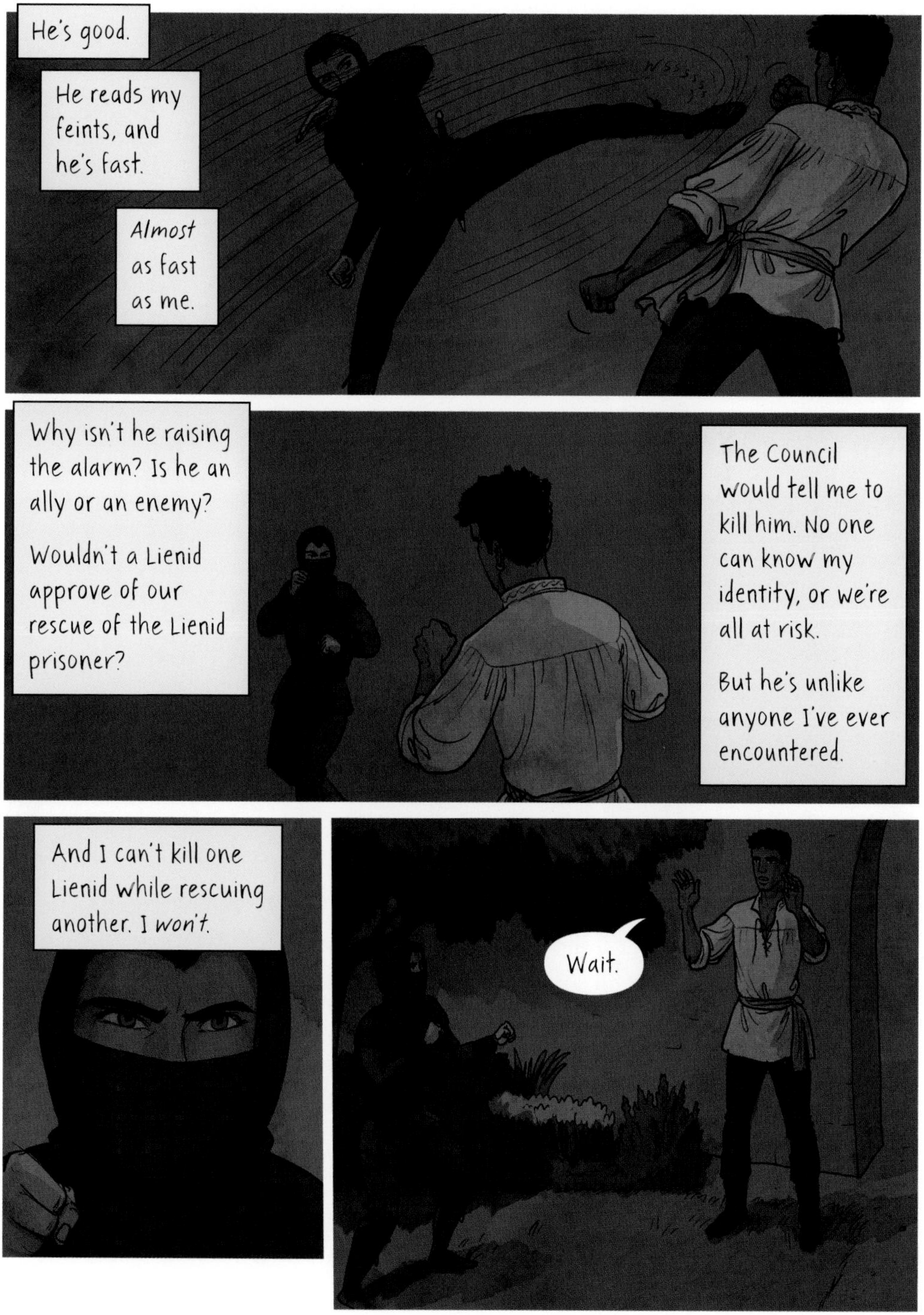
He's good.
He reads my feints, and he's fast.
Almost as fast as me.
Why isn't he raising the alarm? Is he an ally or an enemy?
Wouldn't a Lienid approve of our rescue of the Lienid prisoner?
The Council would tell me to kill him. No one can know my identity, or we're all at risk.
But he's unlike anyone I've ever encountered.
And I can't kill one Lienid while rescuing another. I *won't*.
Wait.

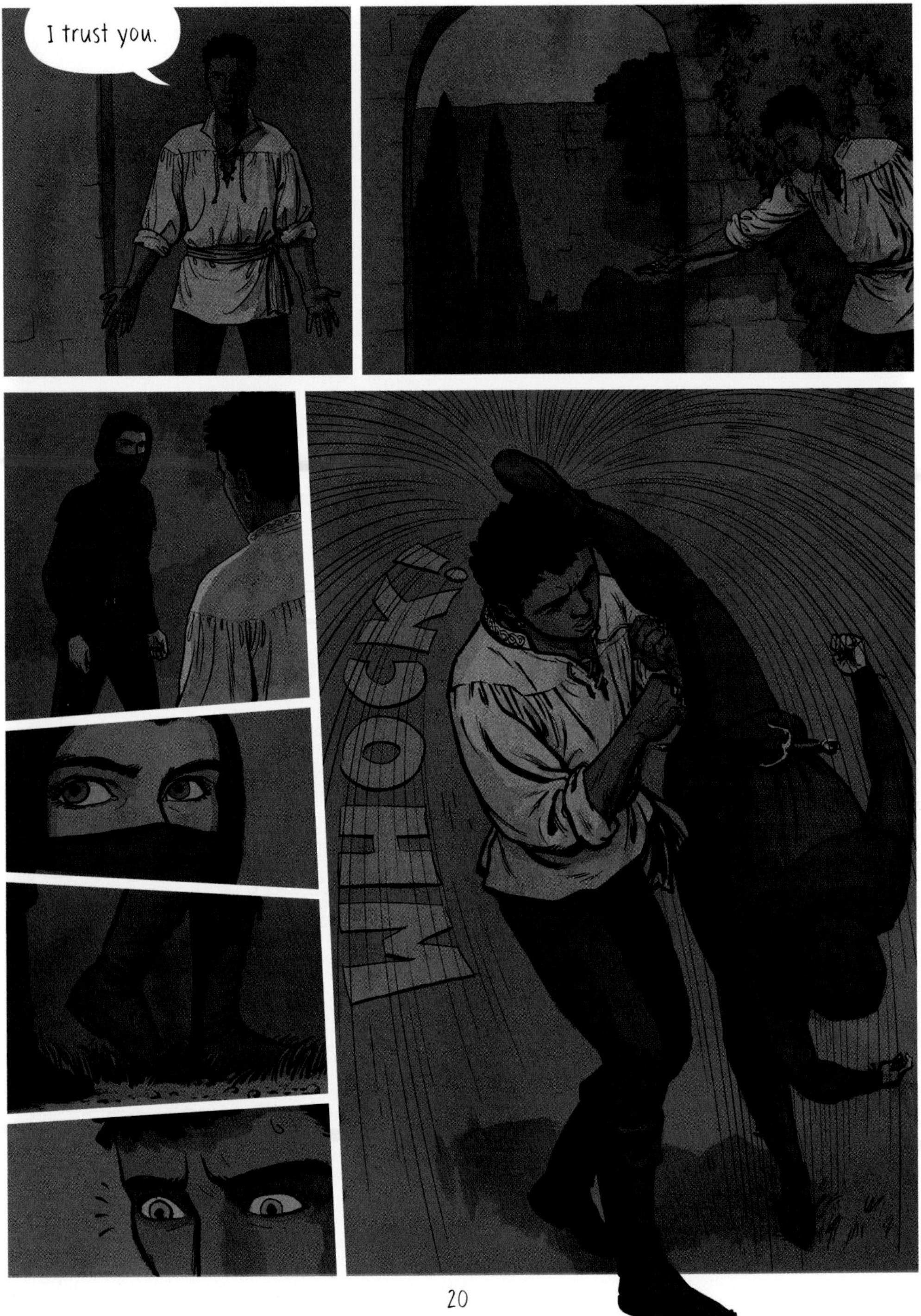
I trust you.
WHOCK!

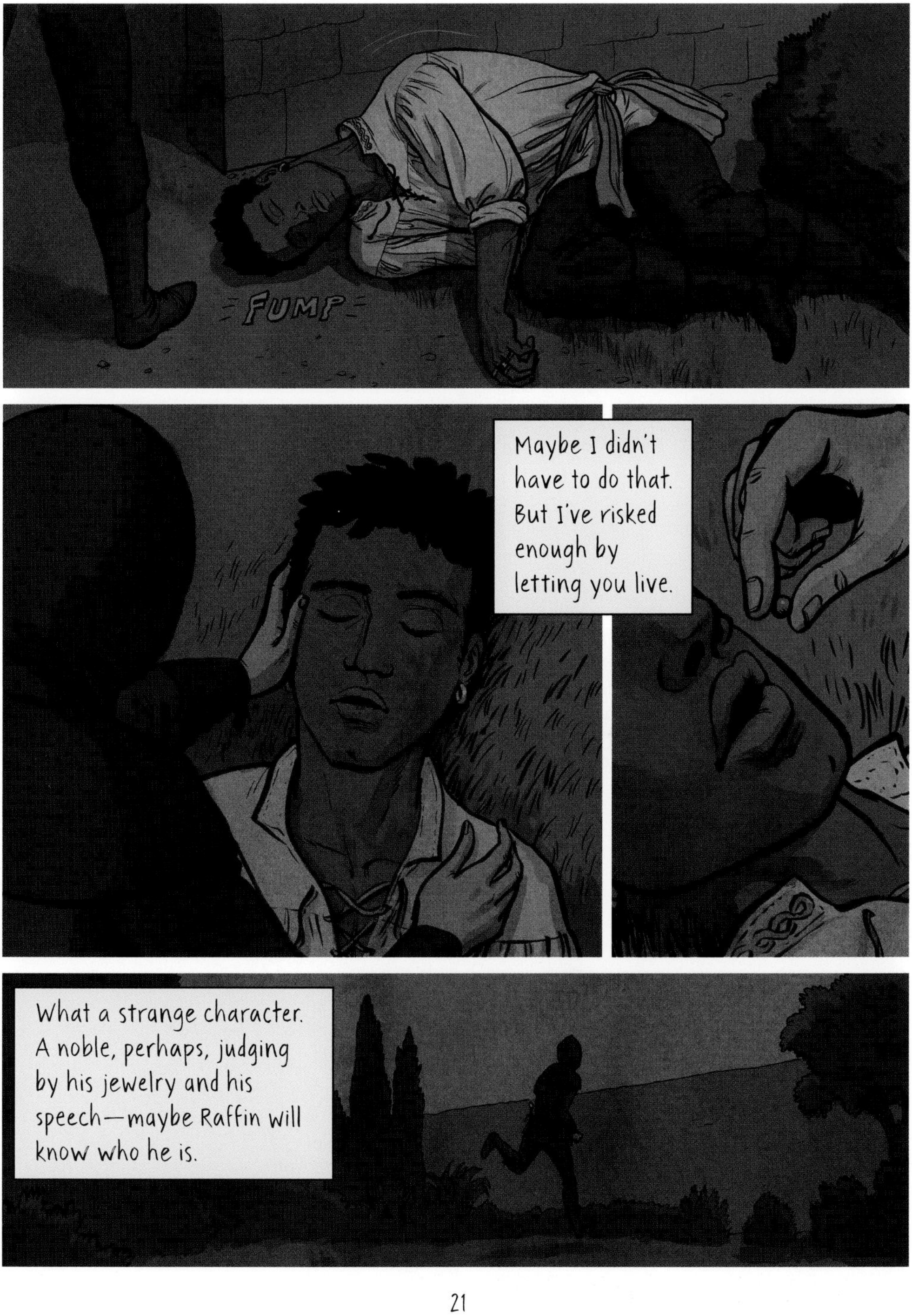
FUMP
Maybe I didn't have to do that. But I've risked enough by letting you live.
What a strange character. A noble, perhaps, judging by his jewelry and his speech—maybe Raffin will know who he is.

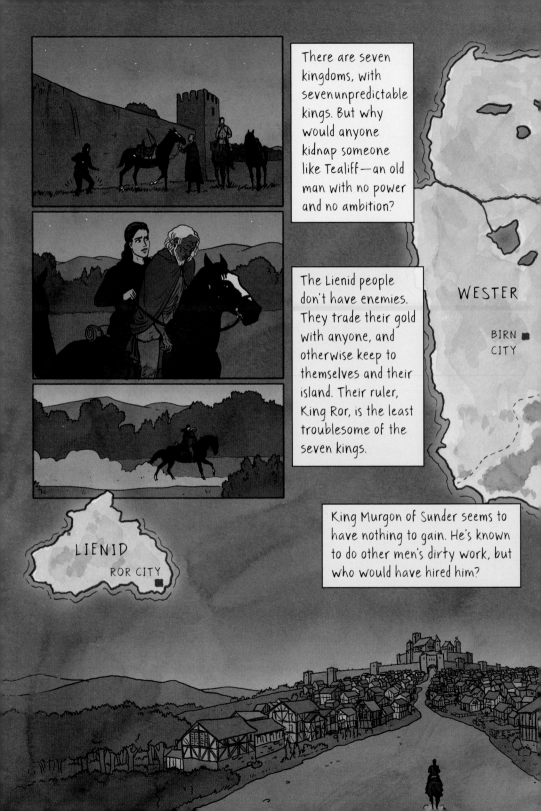

There are seven kingdoms, with seven unpredictable kings. But why would anyone kidnap someone like Tealiff—an old man with no power and no ambition?

The Lienid people don't have enemies. They trade their gold with anyone, and otherwise keep to themselves and their island. Their ruler, King Ror, is the least troublesome of the seven kings.

King Murgon of Sunder seems to have nothing to gain. He's known to do other men's dirty work, but who would have hired him?

WESTER

BIRN CITY

LIENID

ROR CITY

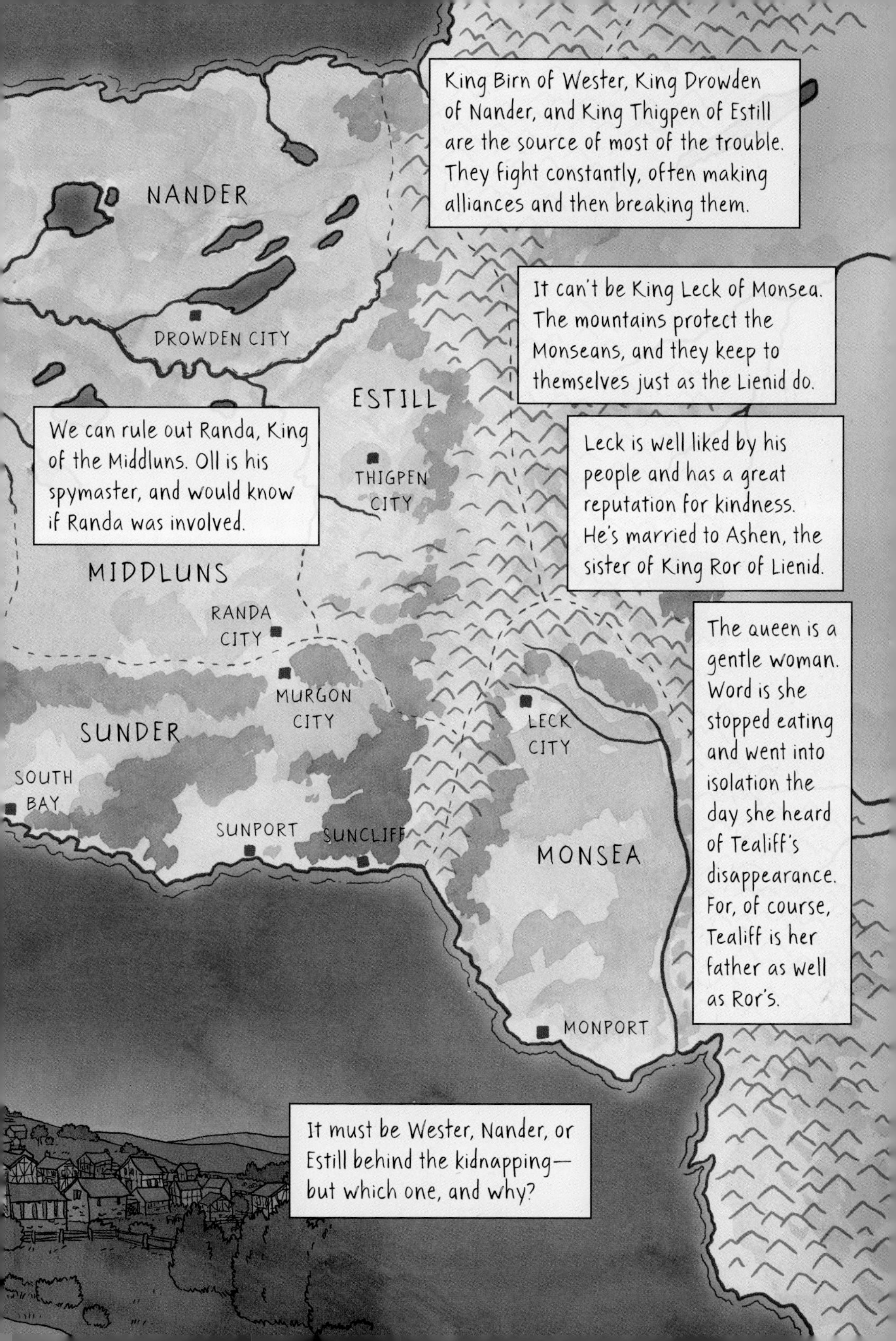
King Birn of Wester, King Drowden of Nander, and King Thigpen of Estill are the source of most of the trouble. They fight constantly, often making alliances and then breaking them.
It can't be King Leck of Monsea. The mountains protect the Monseans, and they keep to themselves just as the Lienid do.
Leck is well liked by his people and has a great reputation for kindness. He's married to Ashen, the sister of King Ror of Lienid.
The queen is a gentle woman. Word is she stopped eating and went into isolation the day she heard of Tealiff's disappearance. For, of course, Tealiff is her father as well as Ror's.
We can rule out Randa, King of the Middluns. Oll is his spymaster, and would know if Randa was involved.
It must be Wester, Nander, or Estill behind the kidnapping—but which one, and why?
NANDER
DROWDEN CITY
ESTILL
THIGPEN CITY
MIDDLUNS
RANDA CITY
MURGON CITY
SUNDER
SOUTH BAY
SUNPORT
SUNCLIFF
LECK CITY
MONSEA
MONPORT

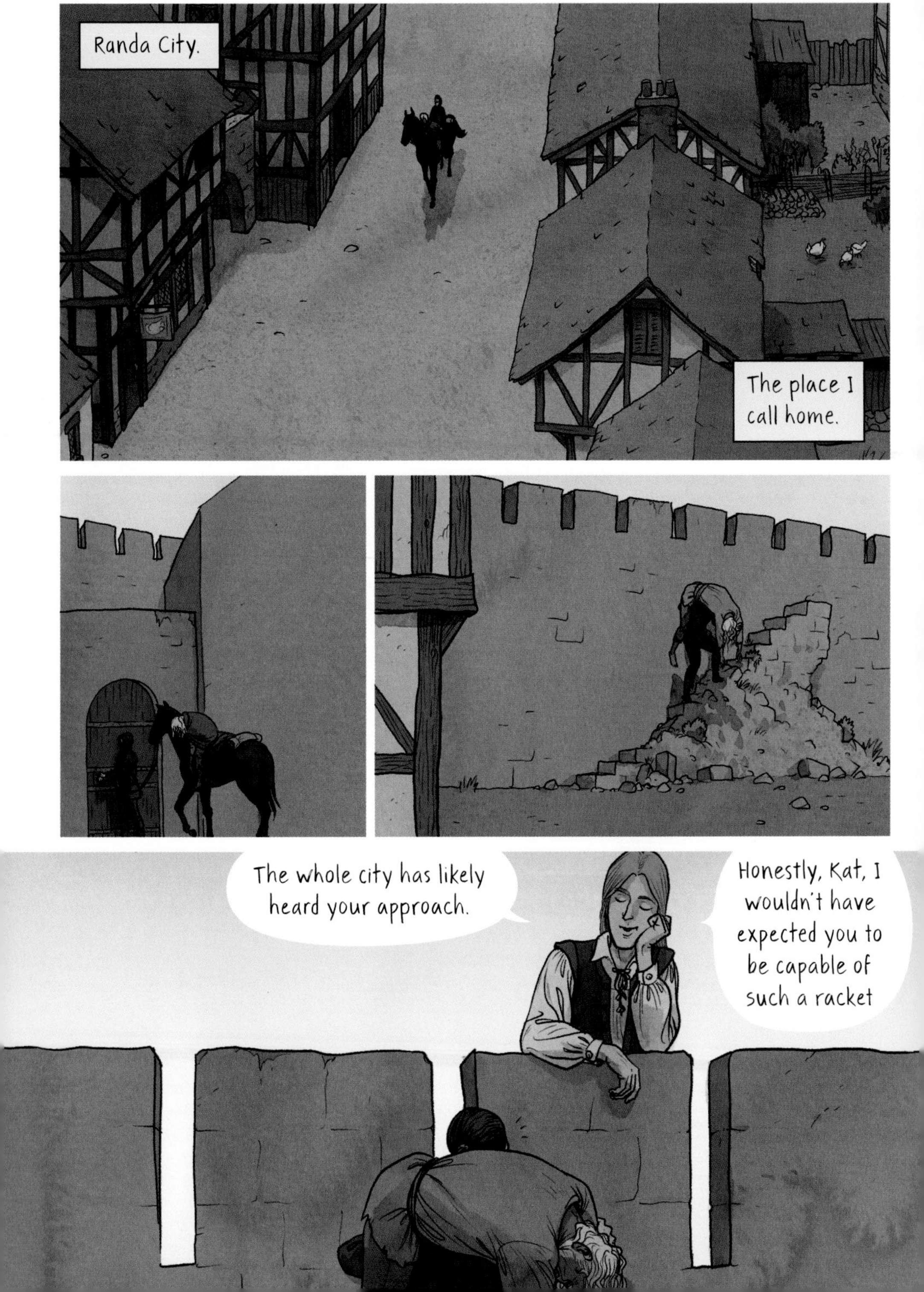
Randa City.
The place I call home.
The whole city has likely heard your approach.
Honestly, Kat, I wouldn't have expected you to be capable of such a racket

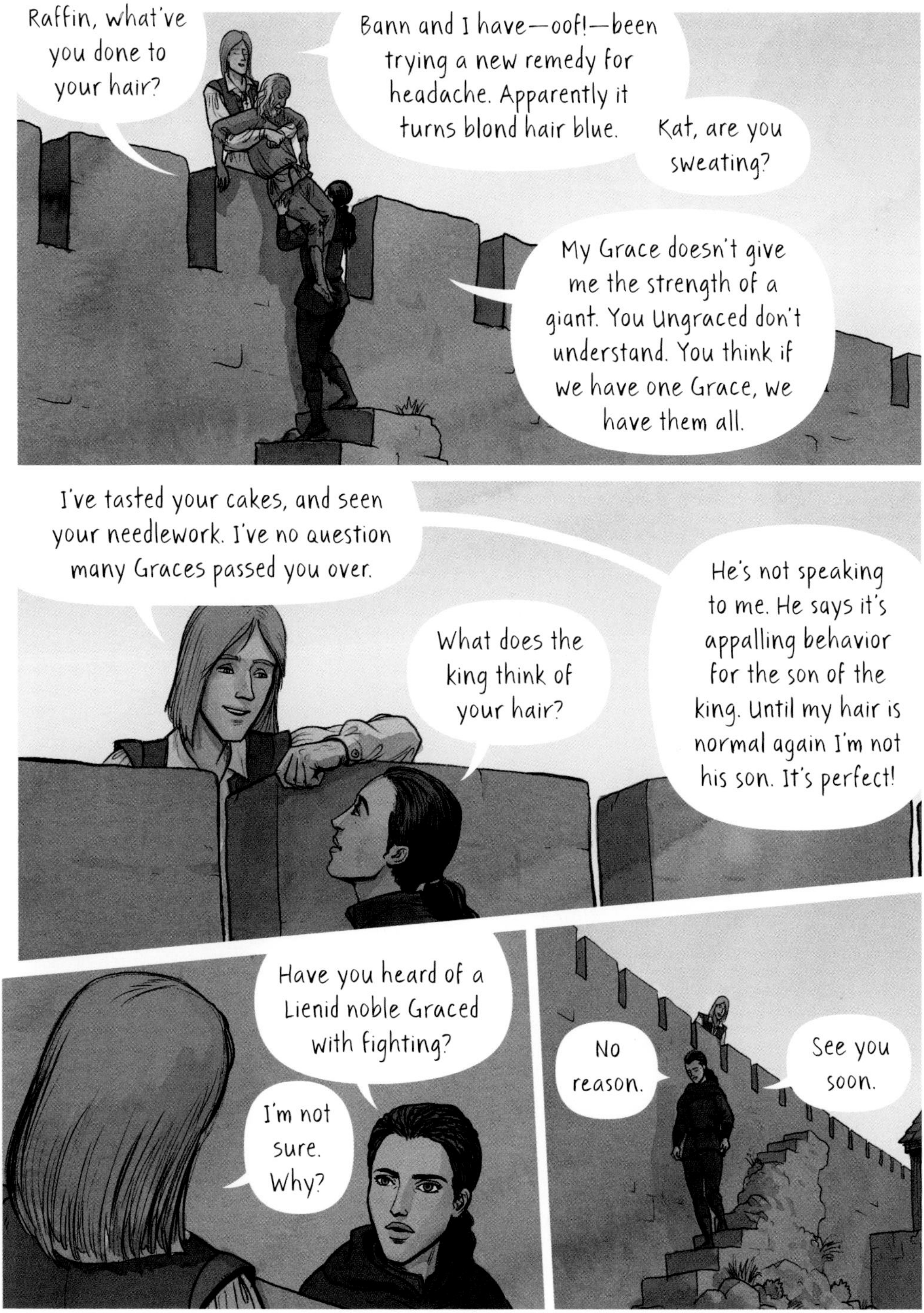
Raffin, what've you done to your hair?
Bann and I have—oof!—been trying a new remedy for headache. Apparently it turns blond hair blue.
Kat, are you sweating?
My Grace doesn't give me the strength of a giant. You Ungraced don't understand. You think if we have one Grace, we have them all.
I've tasted your cakes, and seen your needlework. I've no question many Graces passed you over.
What does the king think of your hair?
He's not speaking to me. He says it's appalling behavior for the son of the king. Until my hair is normal again I'm not his son. It's perfect!
Have you heard of a Lienid noble Graced with fighting?
I'm not sure. Why?
No reason.
See you soon.

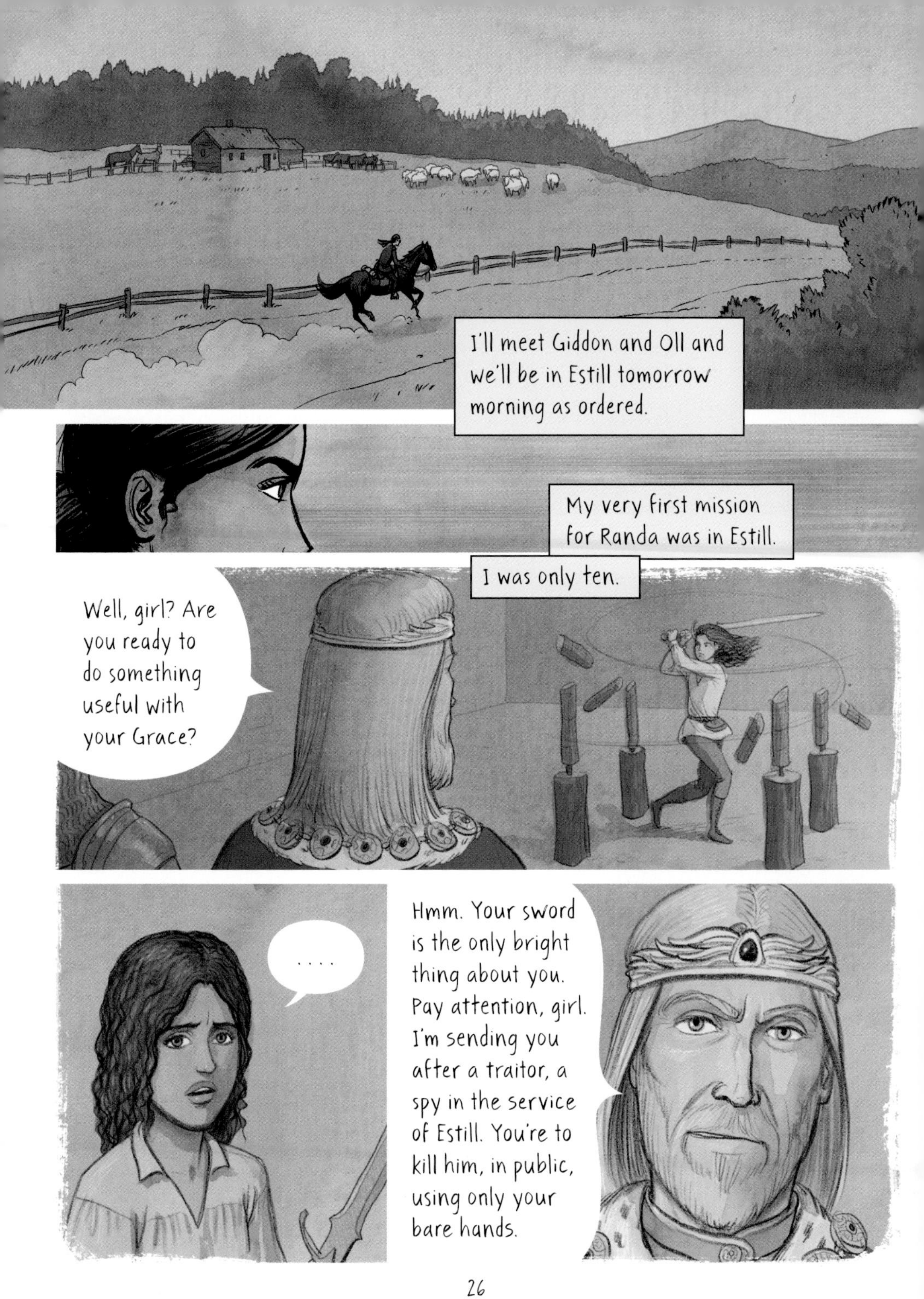
I'll meet Giddon and Oll and we'll be in Estill tomorrow morning as ordered.
My very first mission for Randa was in Estill.
I was only ten.
Well, girl? Are you ready to do something useful with your Grace?
. . . .
Hmm. Your sword is the only bright thing about you. Pay attention, girl. I'm sending you after a traitor, a spy in the service of Estill. You're to kill him, in public, using only your bare hands.

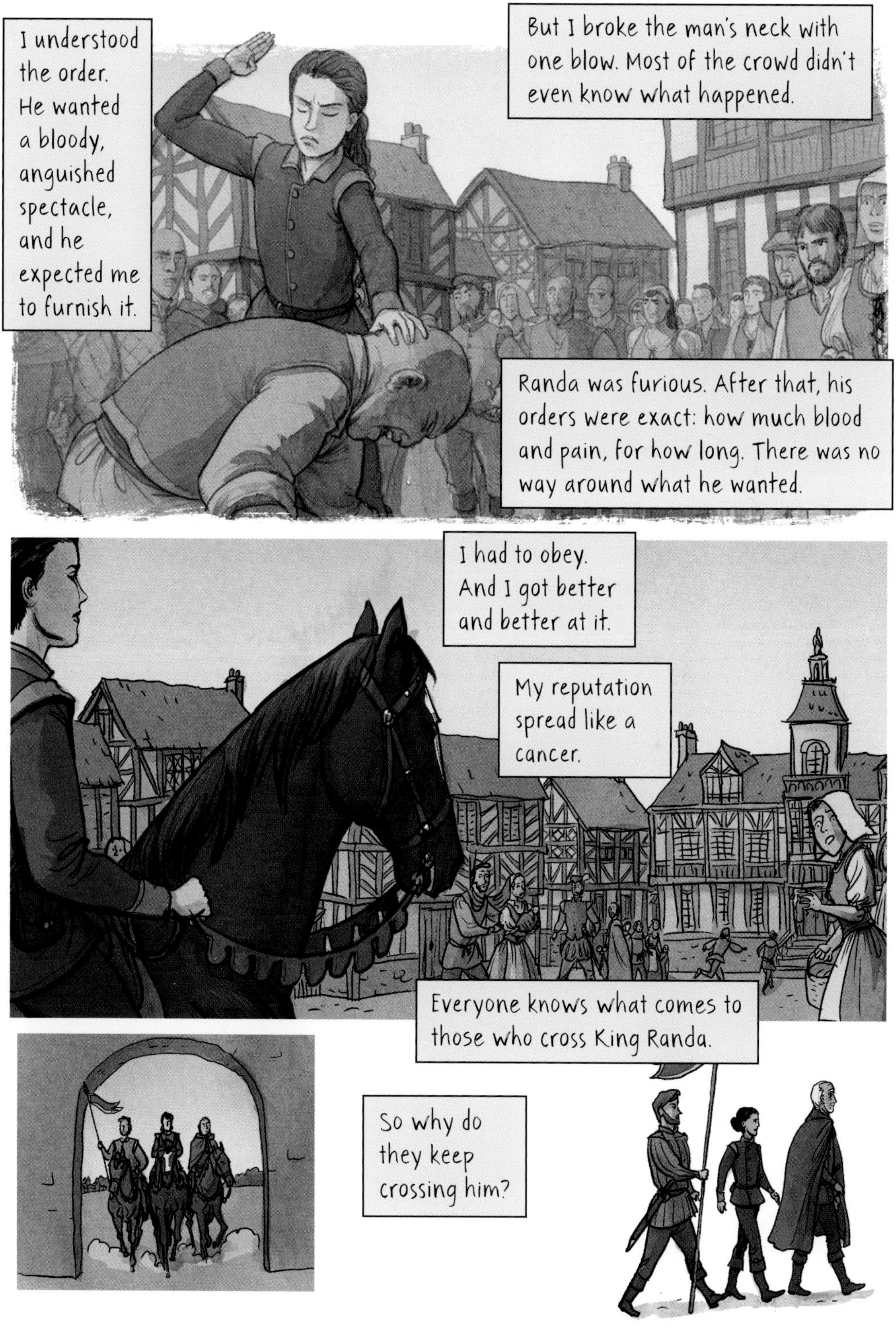
I understood the order. He wanted a bloody, anguished spectacle, and he expected me to furnish it.
But I broke the man's neck with one blow. Most of the crowd didn't even know what happened.
Randa was furious. After that, his orders were exact: how much blood and pain, for how long. There was no way around what he wanted.
I had to obey. And I got better and better at it.
My reputation spread like a cancer.
Everyone knows what comes to those who cross King Randa.
So why do they keep crossing him?

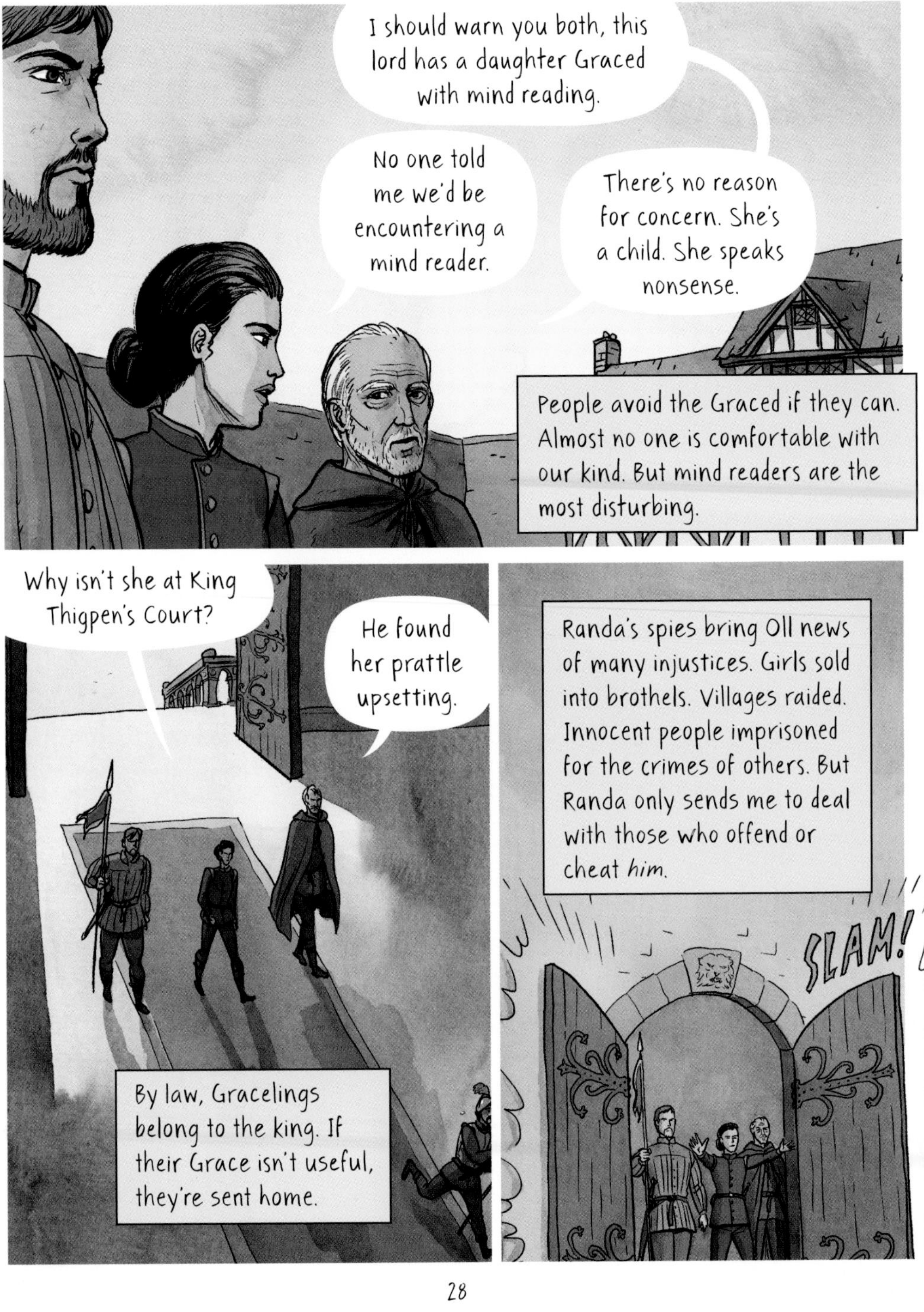
I should warn you both, this lord has a daughter Graced with mind reading.
No one told me we'd be encountering a mind reader.
There's no reason for concern. She's a child. She speaks nonsense.
People avoid the Graced if they can. Almost no one is comfortable with our kind. But mind readers are the most disturbing.
Why isn't she at King Thigpen's Court?
He found her prattle upsetting.
By law, Gracelings belong to the king. If their Grace isn't useful, they're sent home.
Randa's spies bring Oll news of many injustices. Girls sold into brothels. Villages raided. Innocent people imprisoned for the crimes of others. But Randa only sends me to deal with those who offend or cheat *him*.
SLAM!

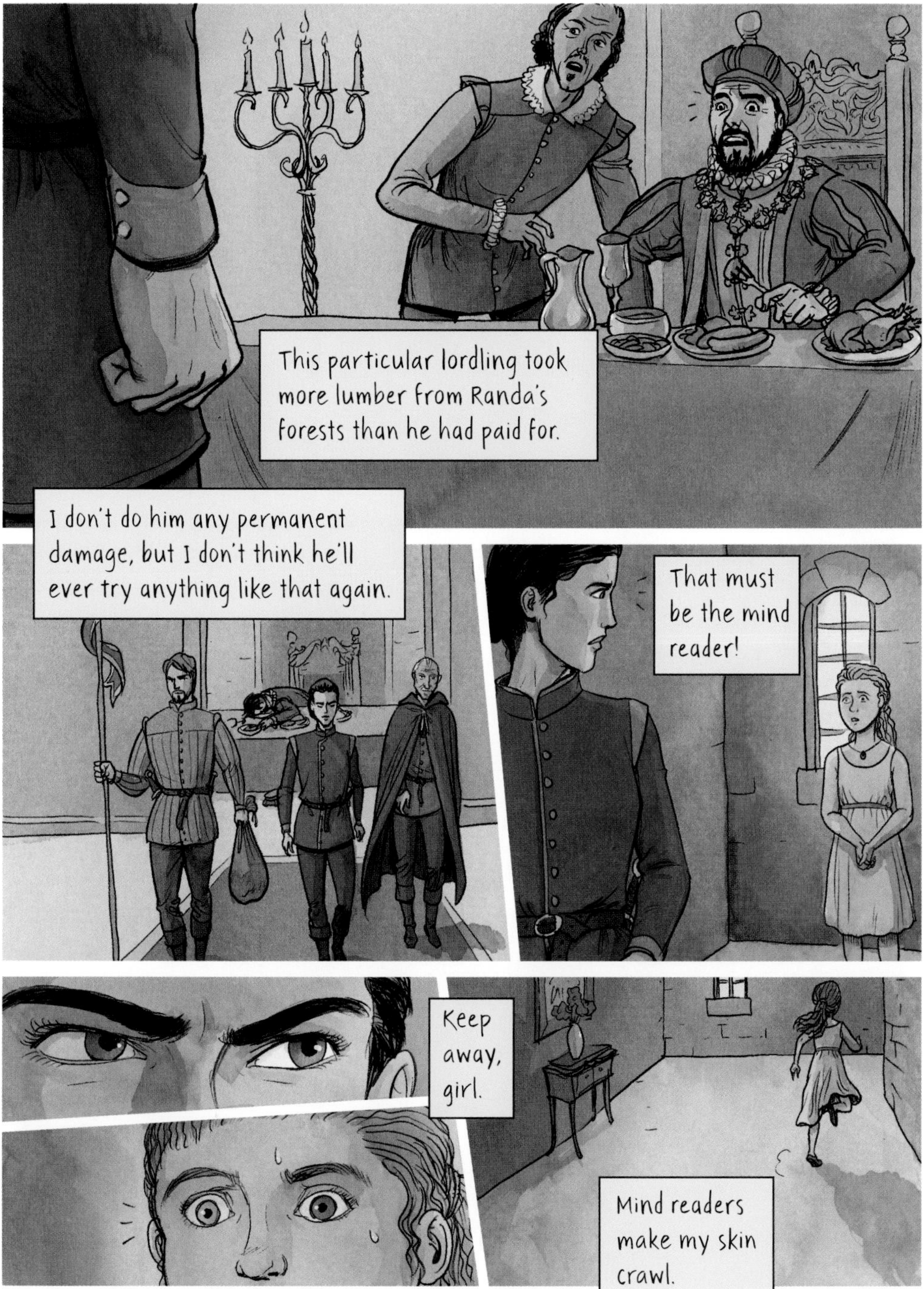
This particular lordling took more lumber from Randa's forests than he had paid for.
I don't do him any permanent damage, but I don't think he'll ever try anything like that again.
That must be the mind reader!
Keep away, girl.
Mind readers make my skin crawl.

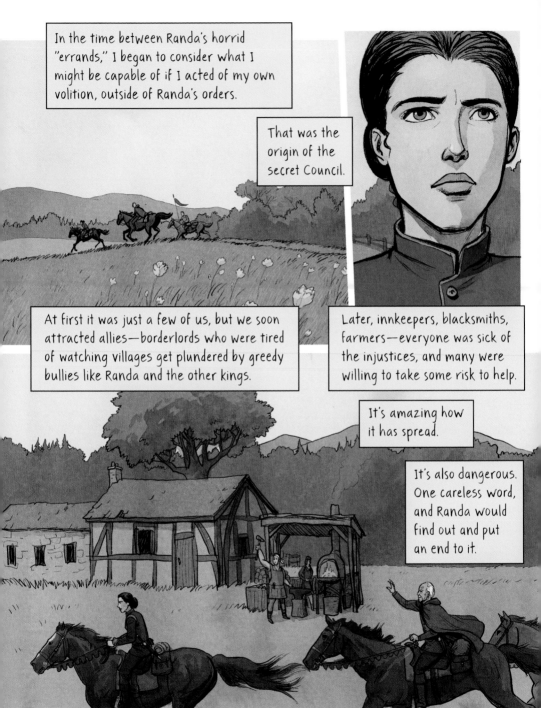

In the time between Randa's horrid "errands," I began to consider what I might be capable of if I acted of my own volition, outside of Randa's orders.

That was the origin of the secret Council.

At first it was just a few of us, but we soon attracted allies—borderlords who were tired of watching villages get plundered by greedy bullies like Randa and the other kings.

Later, innkeepers, blacksmiths, farmers—everyone was sick of the injustices, and many were willing to take some risk to help.

It's amazing how it has spread.

It's also dangerous. One careless word, and Randa would find out and put an end to it.

30

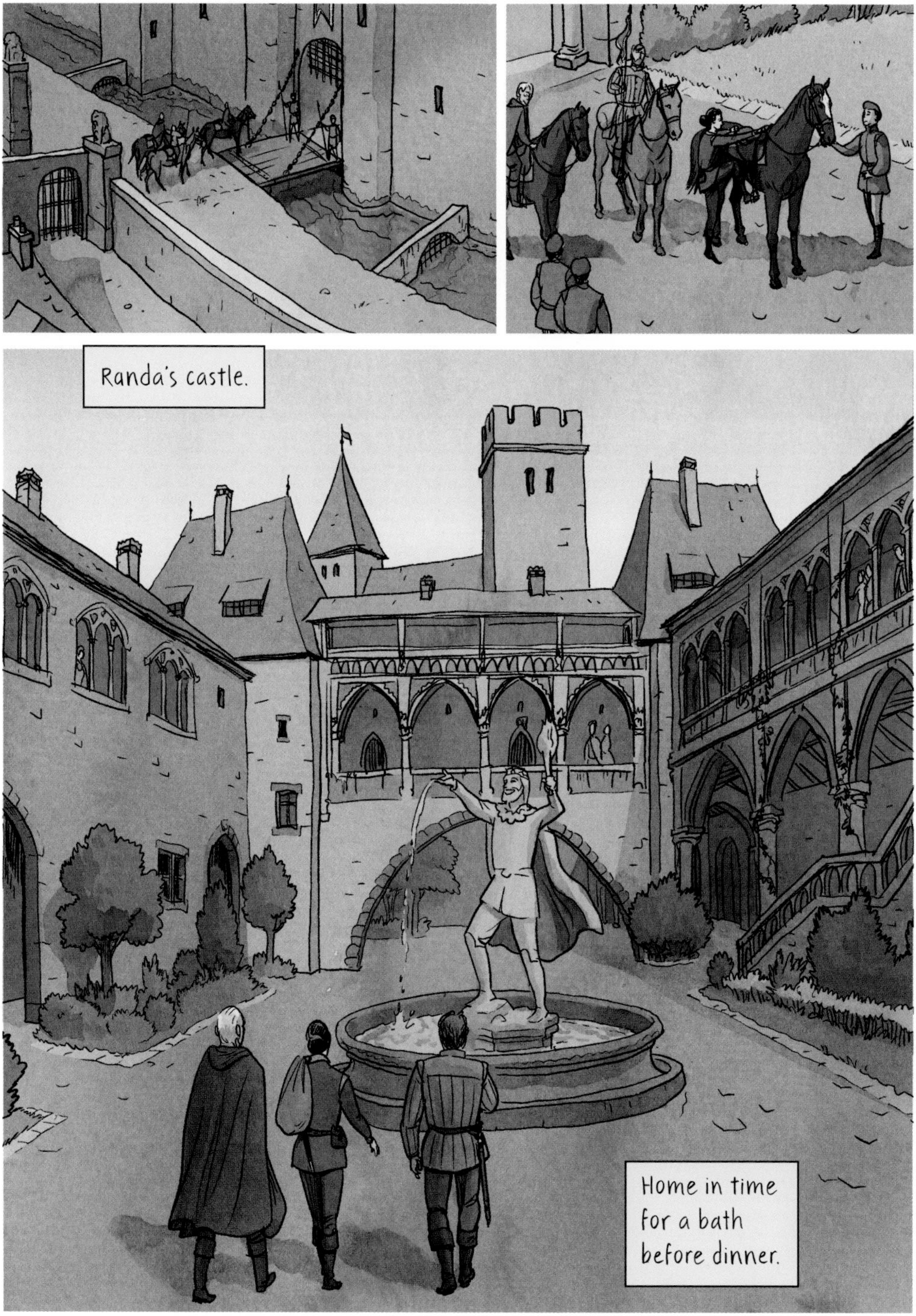
Randa's castle.
Home in time for a bath before dinner.

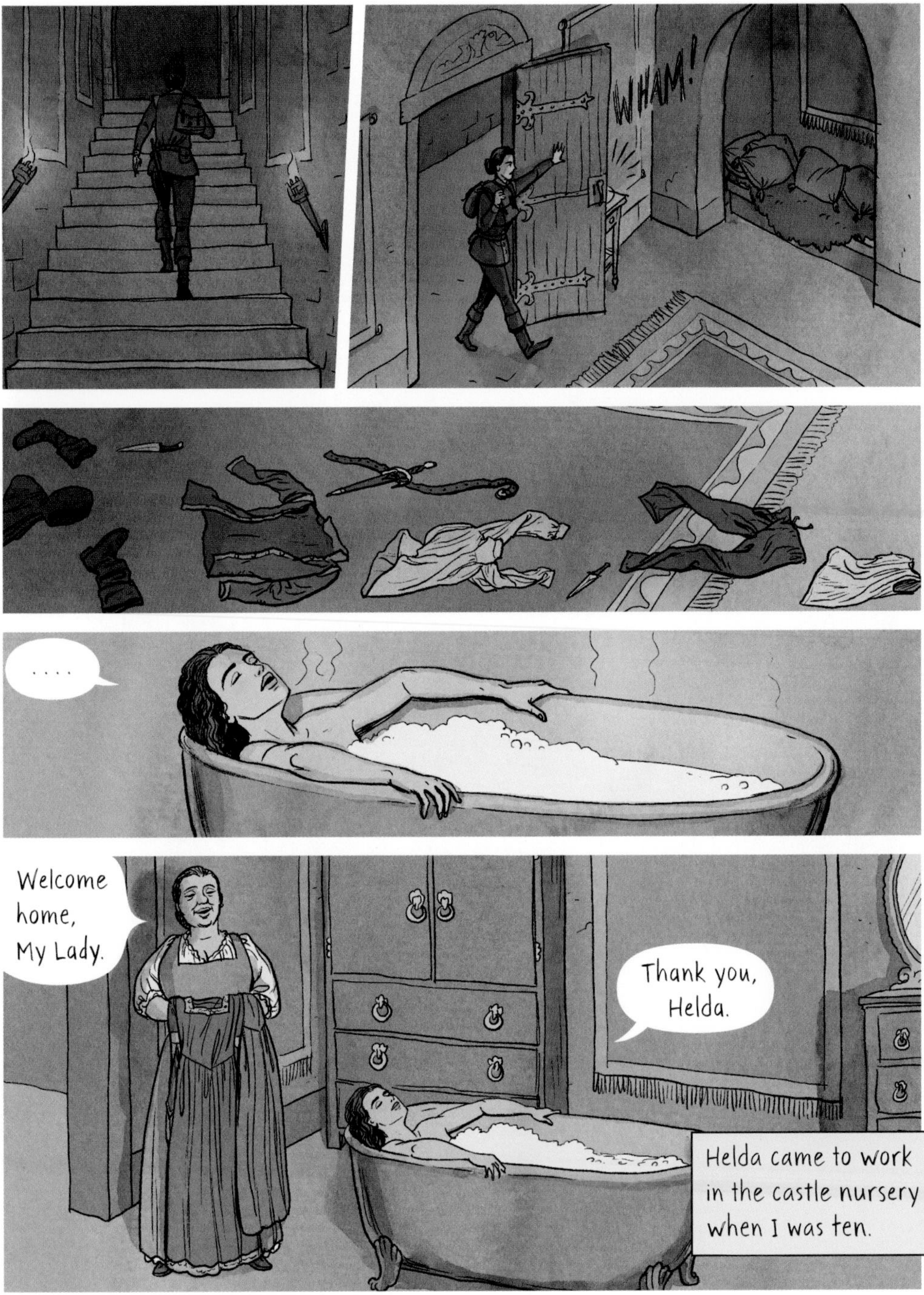
WHAM!
....
Welcome home, My Lady.
Thank you, Helda.
Helda came to work in the castle nursery when I was ten.

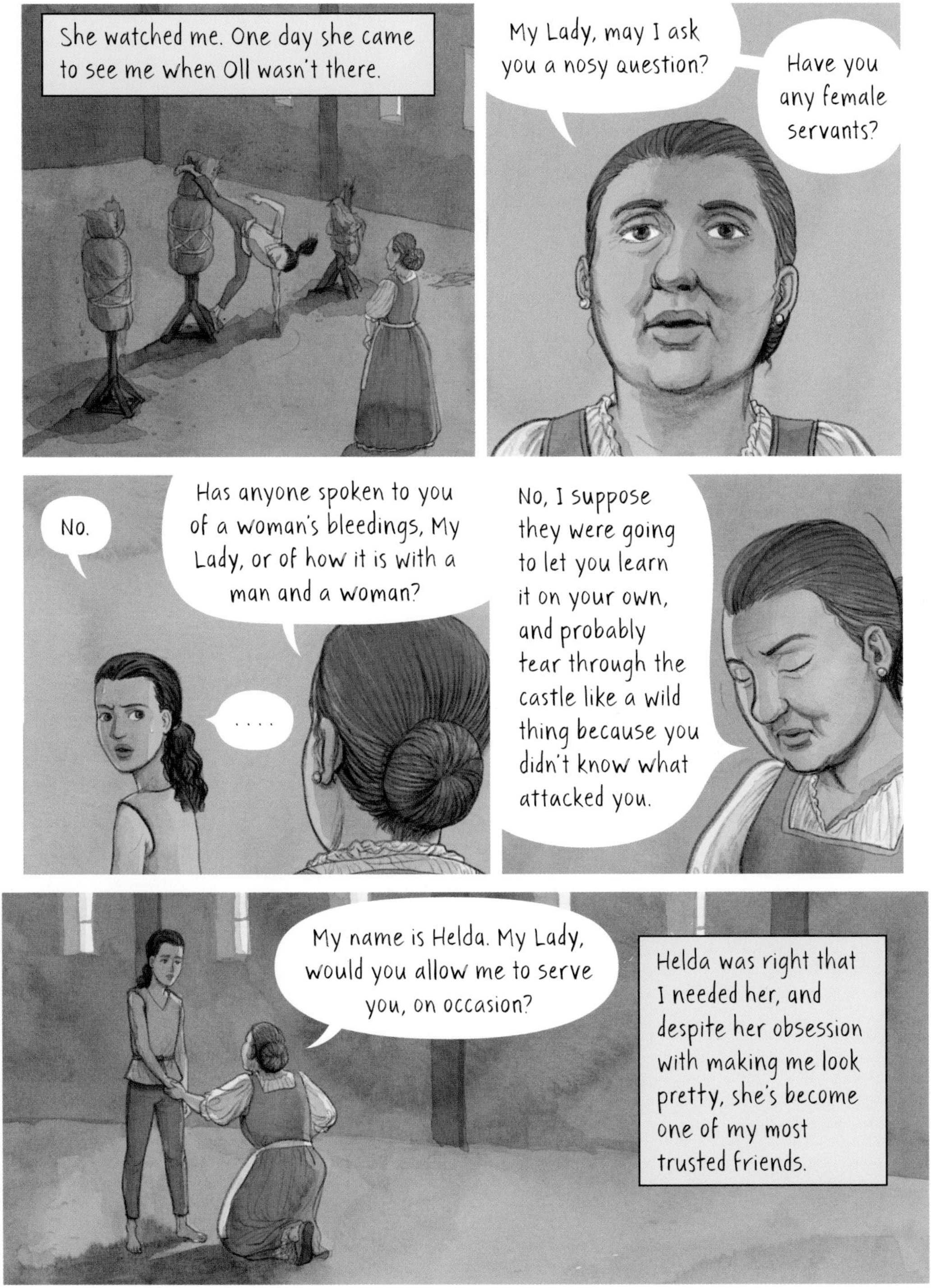
She watched me. One day she came to see me when Oll wasn't there.
My Lady, may I ask you a nosy question?
Have you any female servants?
No.
Has anyone spoken to you of a woman's bleedings, My Lady, or of how it is with a man and a woman?
....
No, I suppose they were going to let you learn it on your own, and probably tear through the castle like a wild thing because you didn't know what attacked you.
My name is Helda. My Lady, would you allow me to serve you, on occasion?
Helda was right that I needed her, and despite her obsession with making me look pretty, she's become one of my most trusted friends.

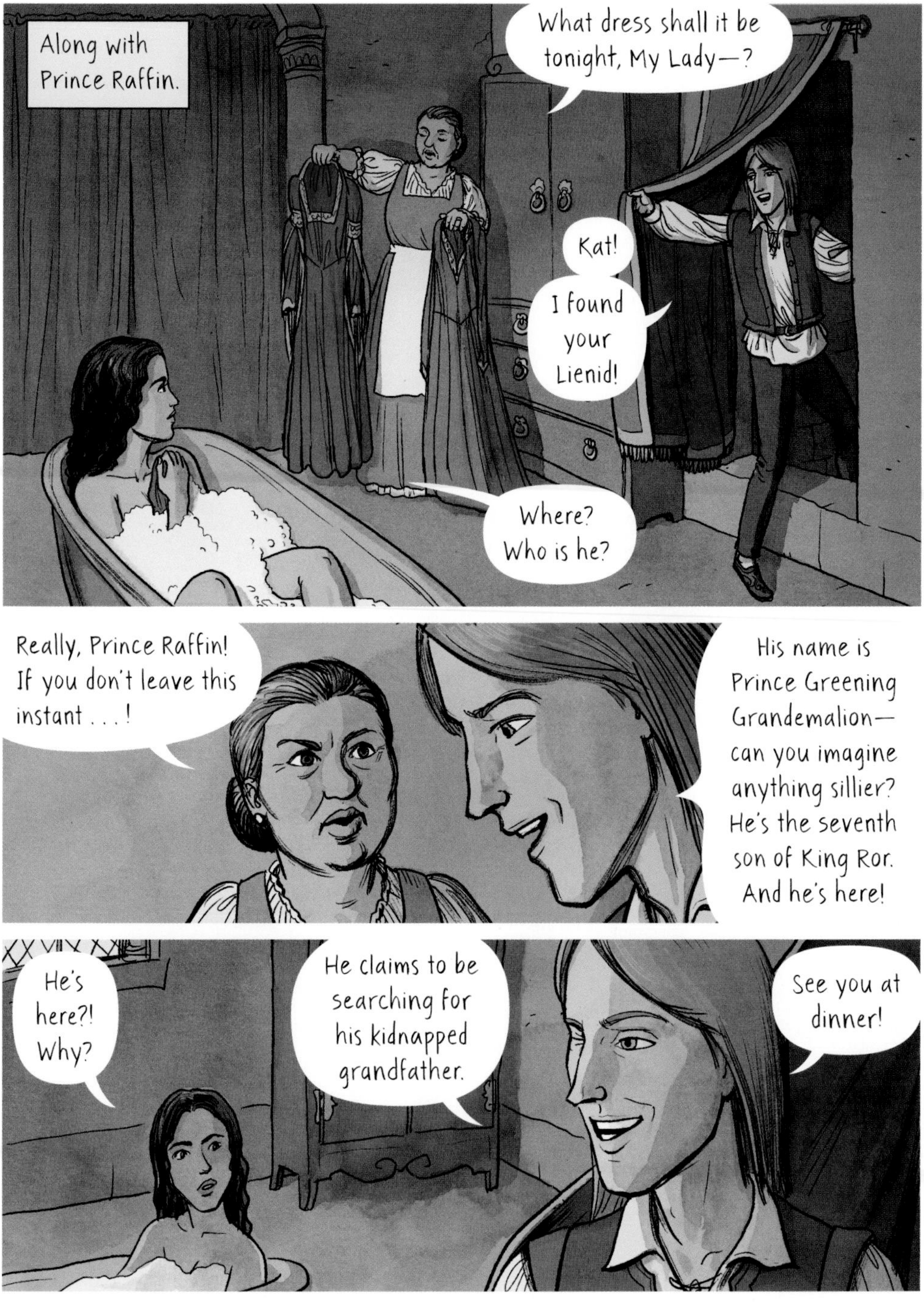
Along with Prince Raffin.
What dress shall it be tonight, My Lady—?
Kat!
I found your Lienid!
Where? Who is he?
Really, Prince Raffin! If you don't leave this instant . . . !
His name is Prince Greening Grandemalion—can you imagine anything sillier? He's the seventh son of King Ror. And he's here!
He's here?! Why?
He claims to be searching for his kidnapped grandfather.
See you at dinner!

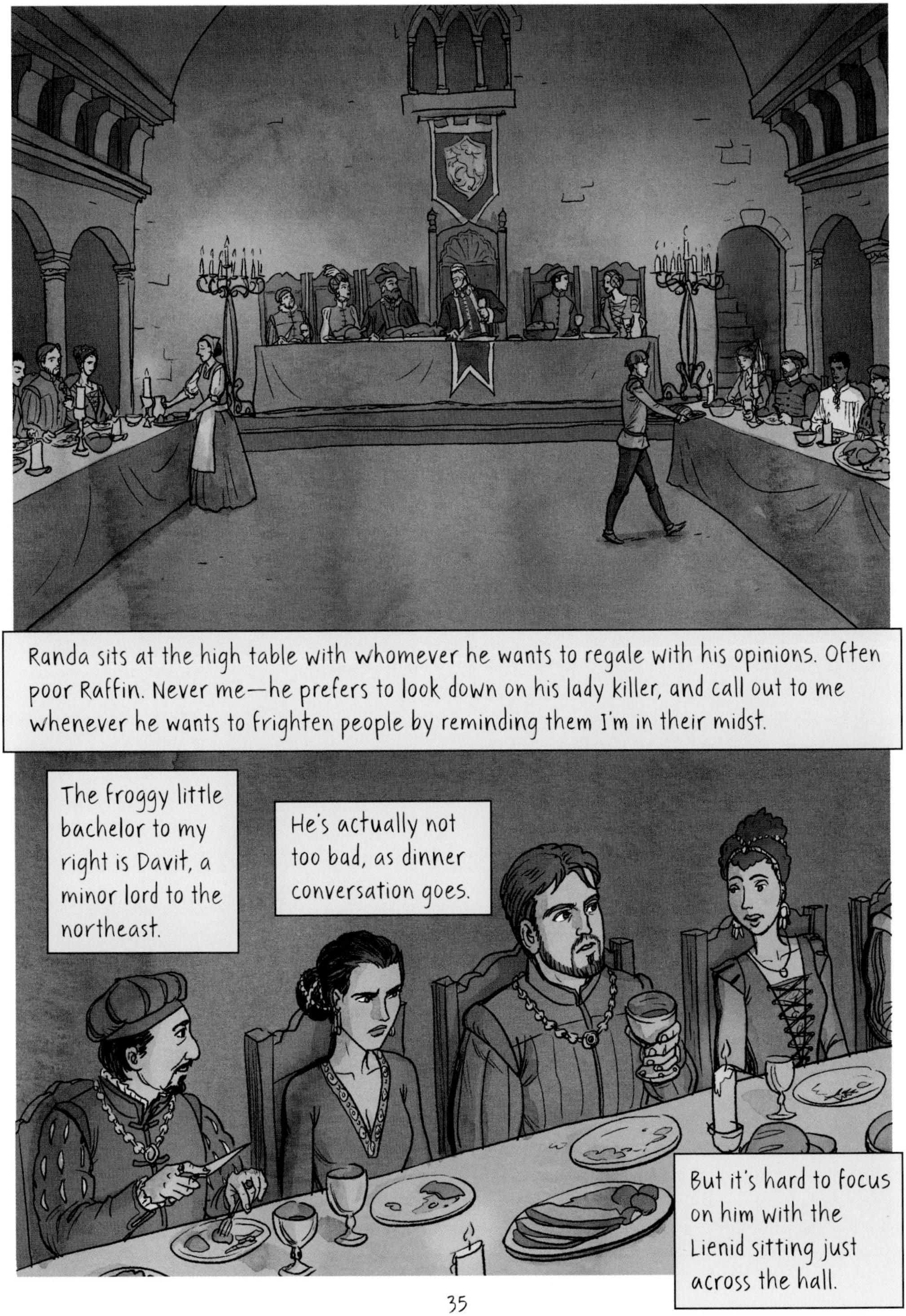
Randa sits at the high table with whomever he wants to regale with his opinions. Often poor Raffin. Never me—he prefers to look down on his lady killer, and call out to me whenever he wants to frighten people by reminding them I'm in their midst.
The froggy little bachelor to my right is Davit, a minor lord to the northeast.
He's actually not too bad, as dinner conversation goes.
But it's hard to focus on him with the Lienid sitting just across the hall.

Those eyes. Silver and gold? How did I not see them shining in the dark when we met in Murgon's garden?

My Lady, I have information for the Council.

We'll speak later. Giddon, arrange a meeting.

Mm.

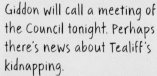
Giddon will call a meeting of the Council tonight. Perhaps there's news about Tealiff's kidnapping.

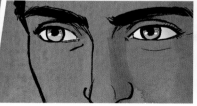

Katsa, are you all right? You aren't ill?

HAHAHAHAHA HAHA!

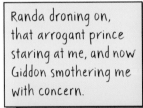

Randa droning on, that arrogant prince staring at me, and now Giddon smothering me with concern.

It's nothing. Excuse me, My Lord.

I'll go with you.

No. You won't.

HA HA HA HA!

I must get away from all these staring eyes.

I need the archery range.

37

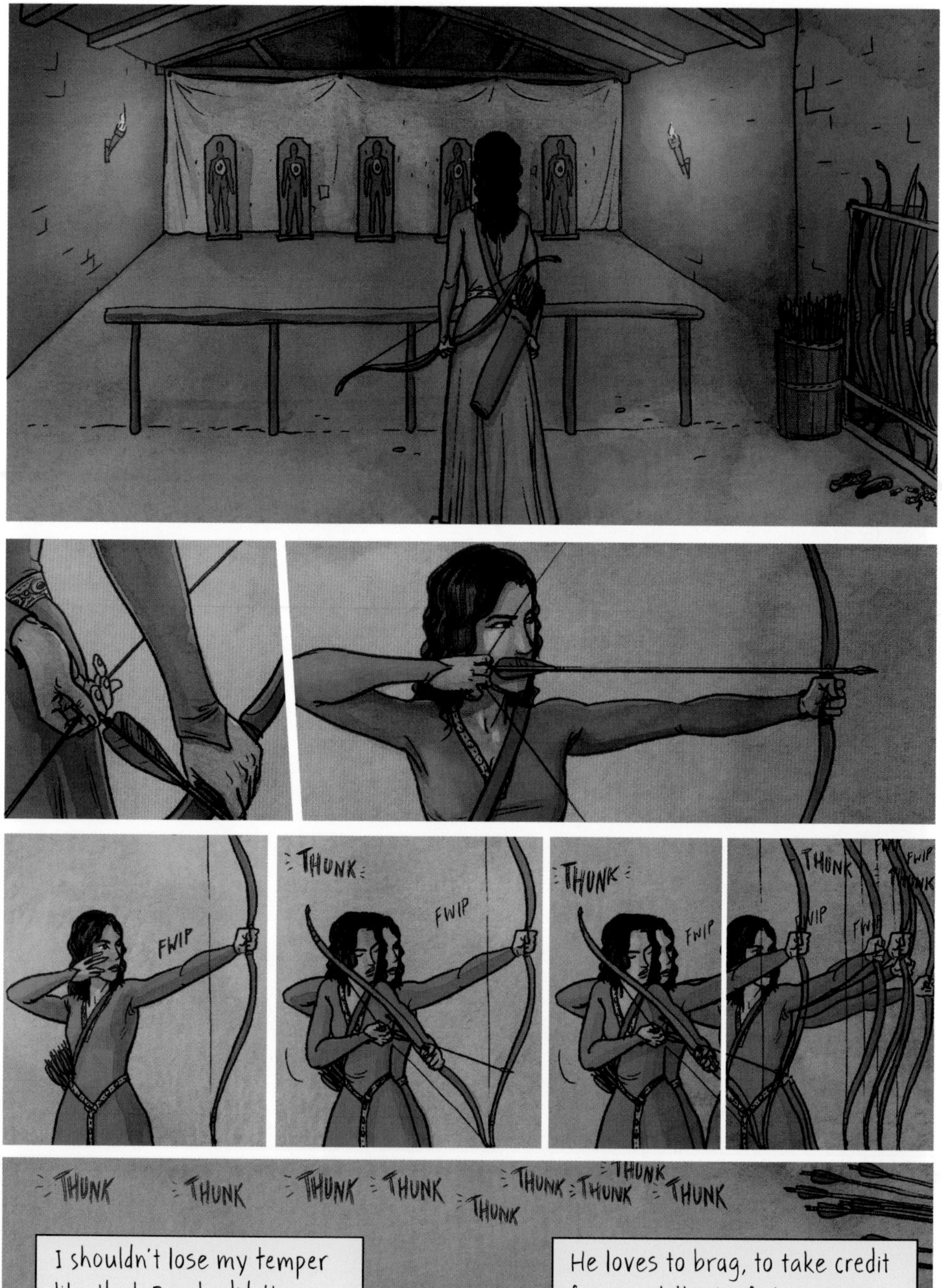
FWIP
THUNK
FWIP
THUNK
FWIP
THUNK
FWIP
FWIP
THUNK
THUNK
THUNK
THUNK
THUNK
THUNK
THUNK
THUNK
THUNK
THUNK
I shouldn't lose my temper like that. Randa didn't even say anything to me.
He loves to brag, to take credit for my skills. As if I'm just an arrow and he's the archer.

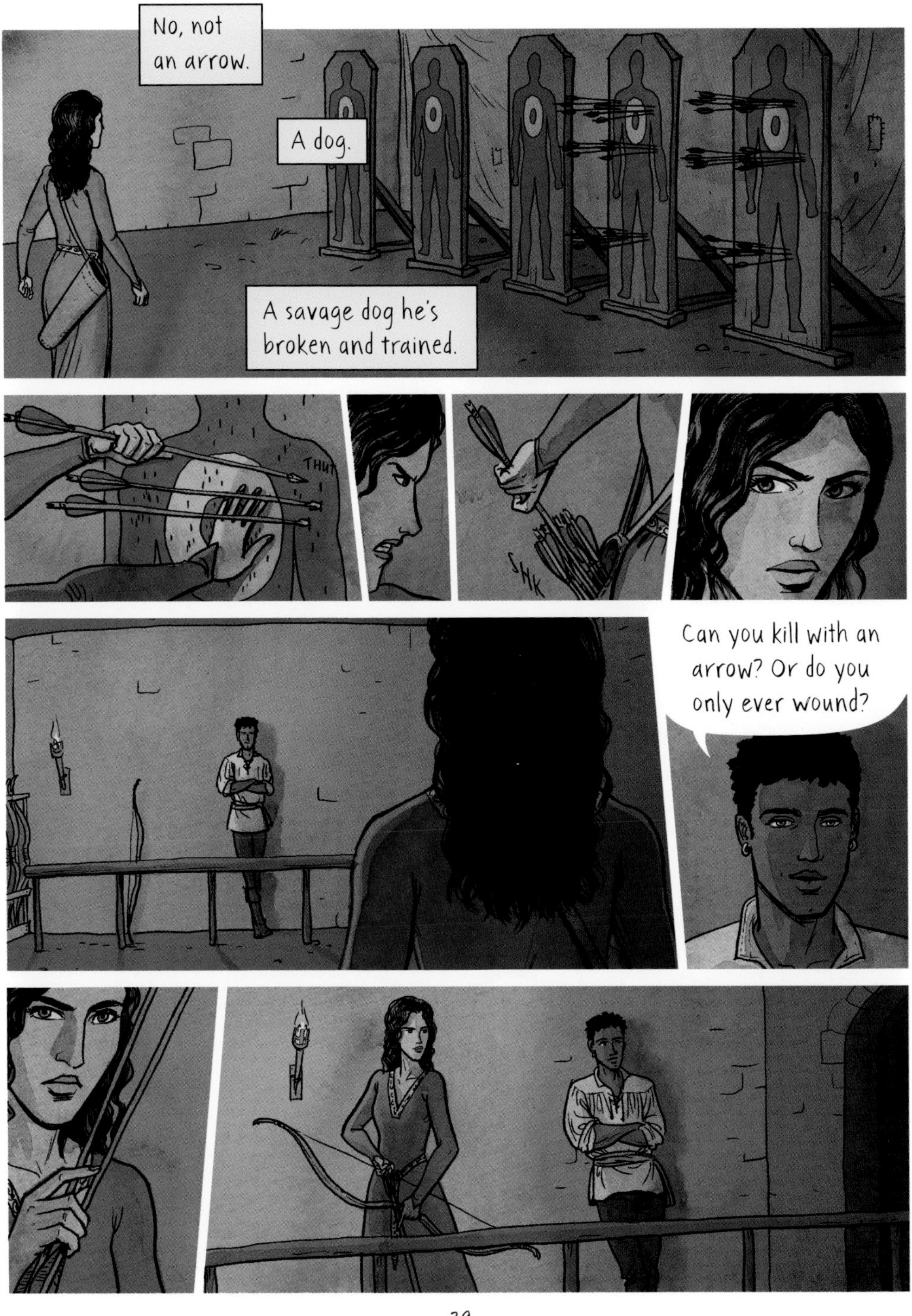
No, not an arrow.
A dog.
A savage dog he's broken and trained.
THUT
SHK
Can you kill with an arrow? Or do you only ever wound?

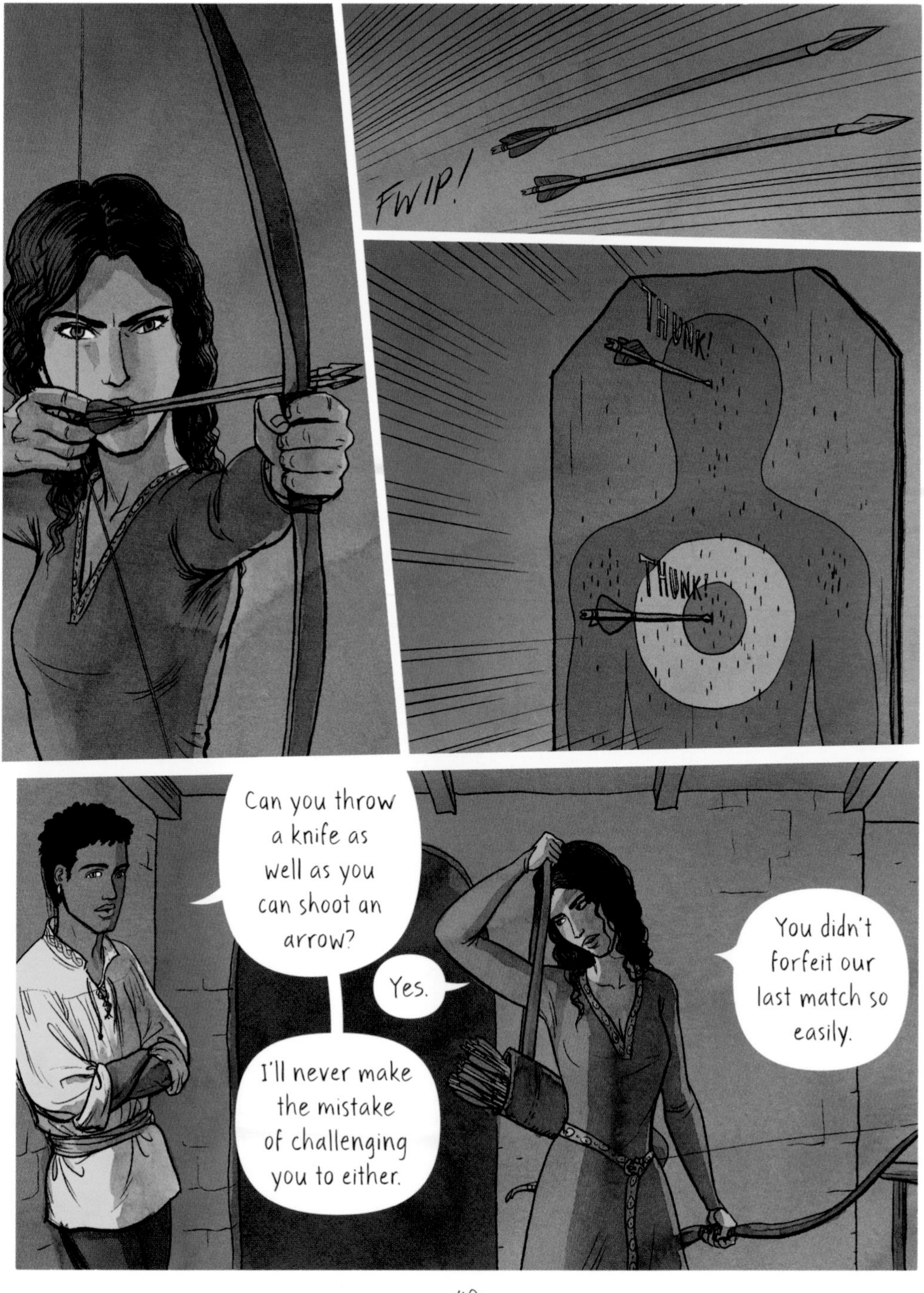
FWIP!
THUNK!
THUNK!
Can you throw a knife as well as you can shoot an arrow?
Yes.
I'll never make the mistake of challenging you to either.
You didn't forfeit our last match so easily.

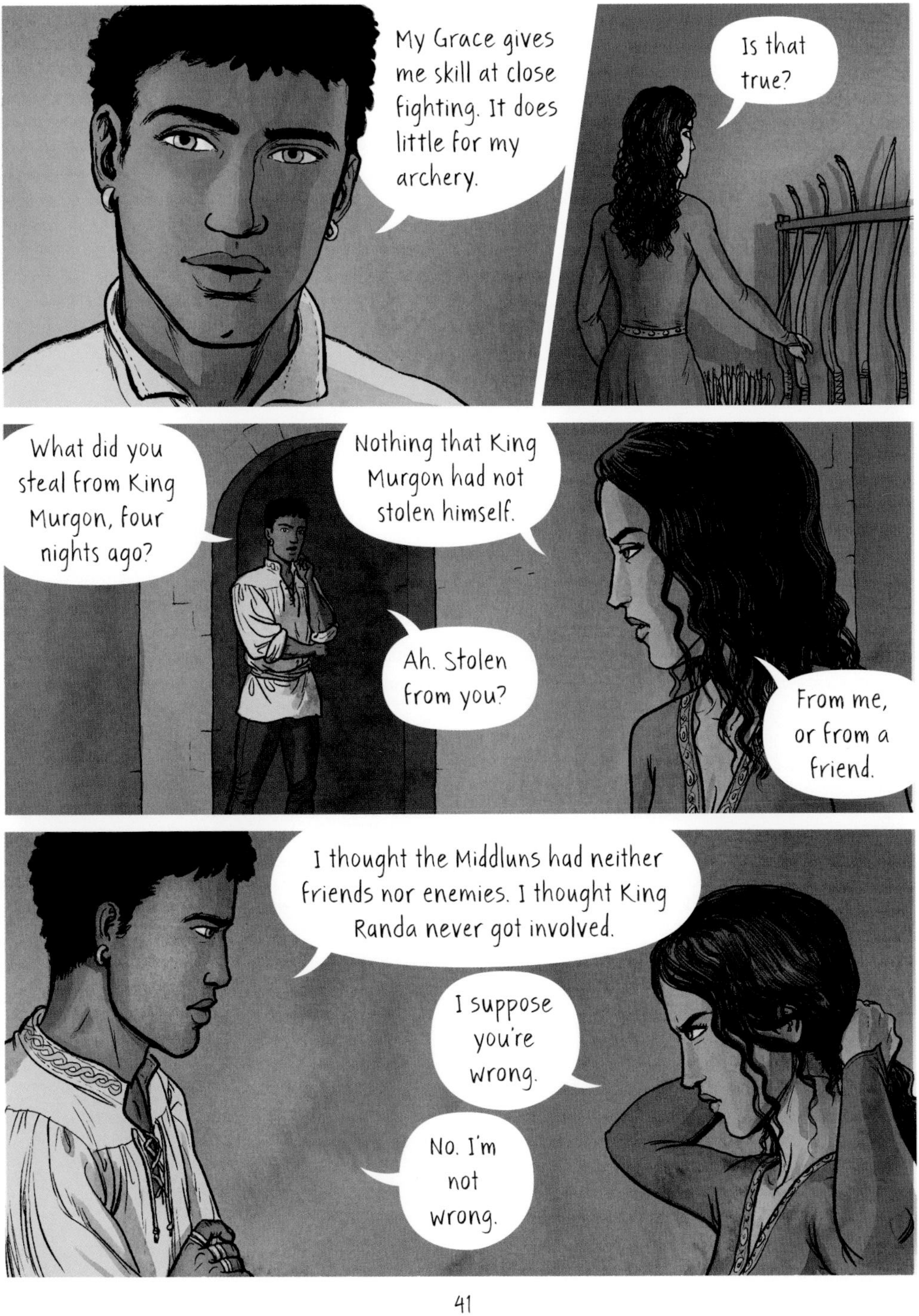
My Grace gives me skill at close fighting. It does little for my archery.
Is that true?
What did you steal from King Murgon, four nights ago?
Nothing that King Murgon had not stolen himself.
Ah. Stolen from you?
From me, or from a friend.
I thought the Middluns had neither friends nor enemies. I thought King Randa never got involved.
I suppose you're wrong.
No. I'm not wrong.

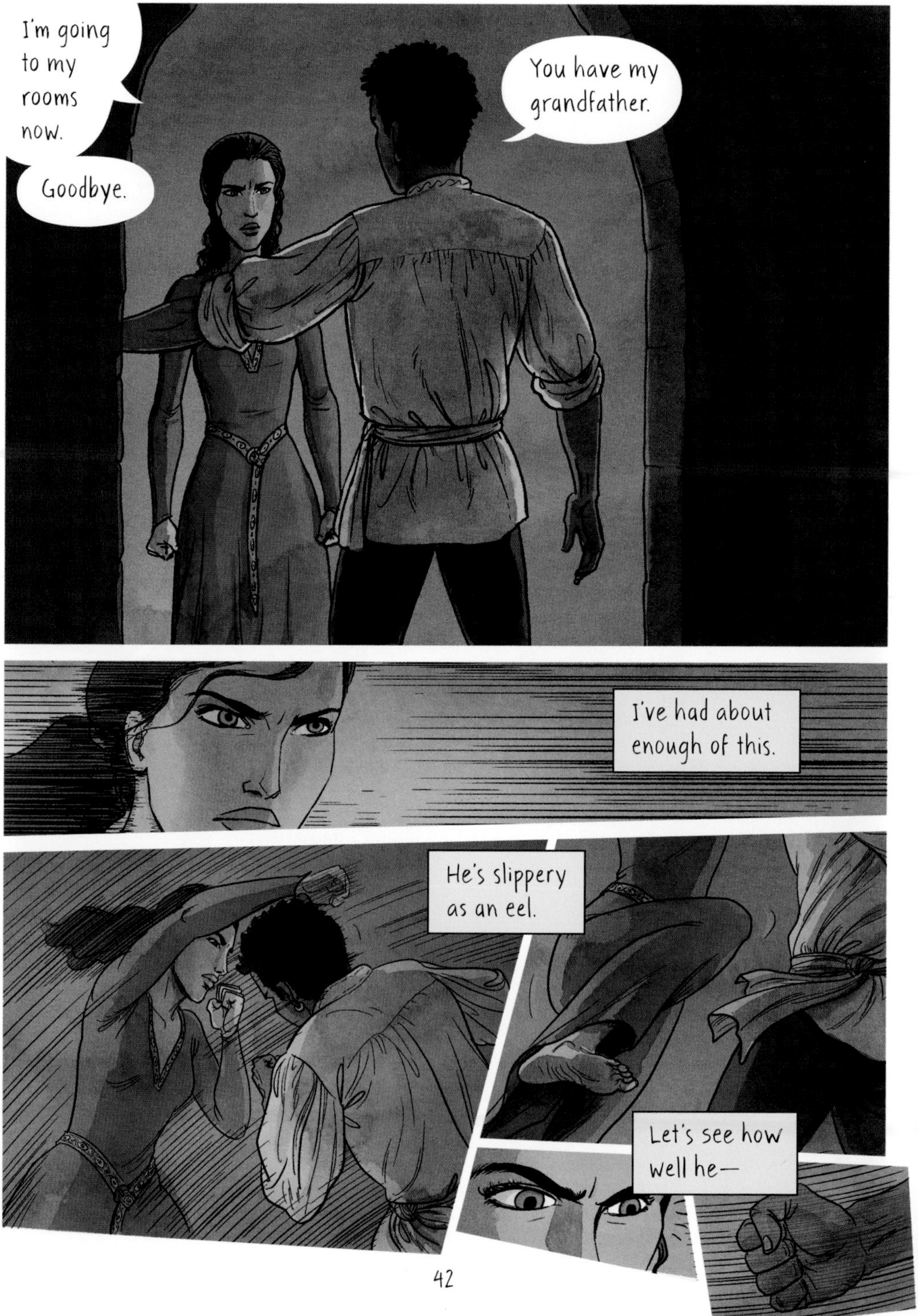
I'm going to my rooms now.
Goodbye.
You have my grandfather.
I've had about enough of this.
He's slippery as an eel.
Let's see how well he—

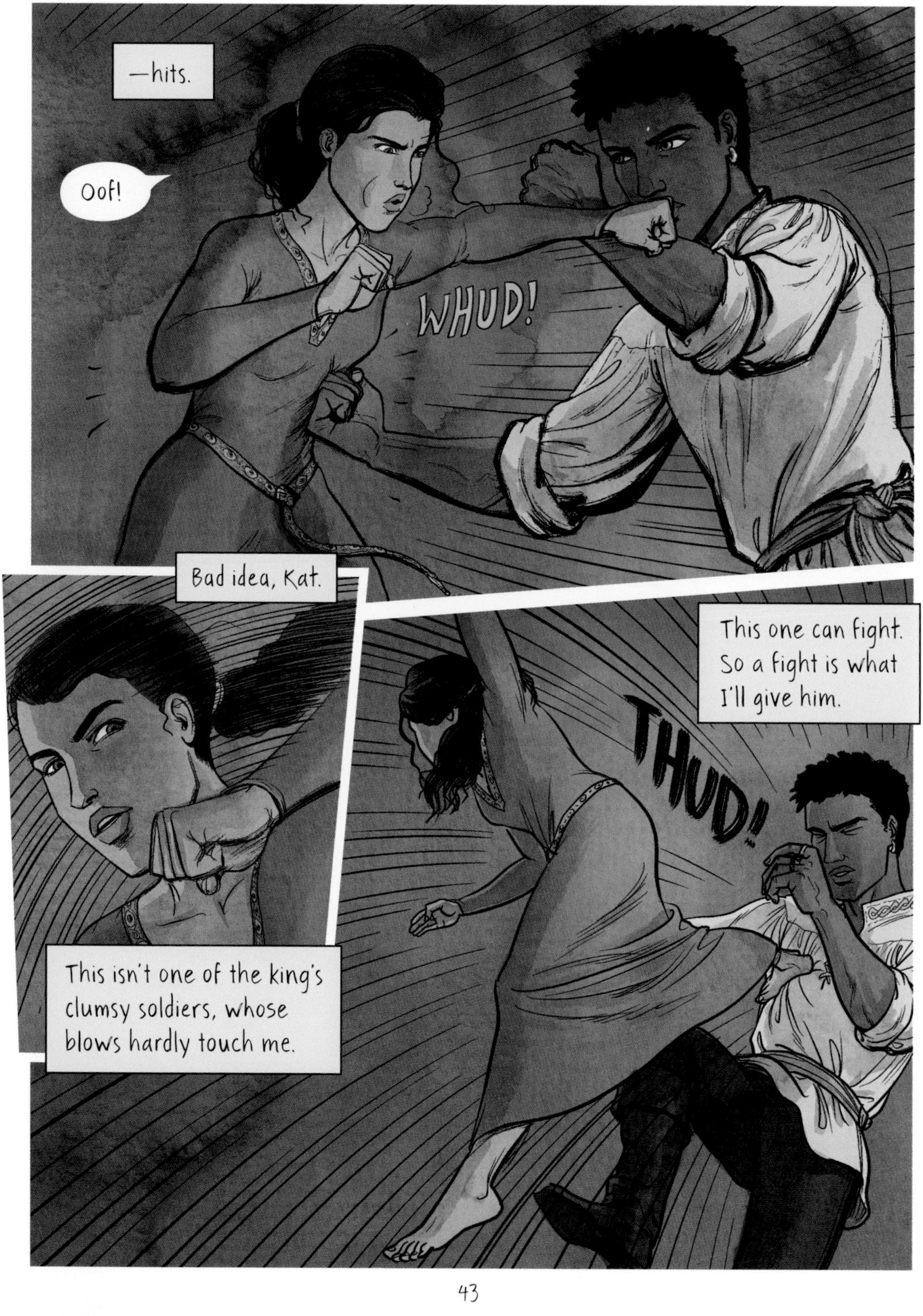
—hits.
Oof!
WHUD!
Bad idea, Kat.
This isn't one of the king's clumsy soldiers, whose blows hardly touch me.
This one can fight. So a fight is what I'll give him.
THUD!

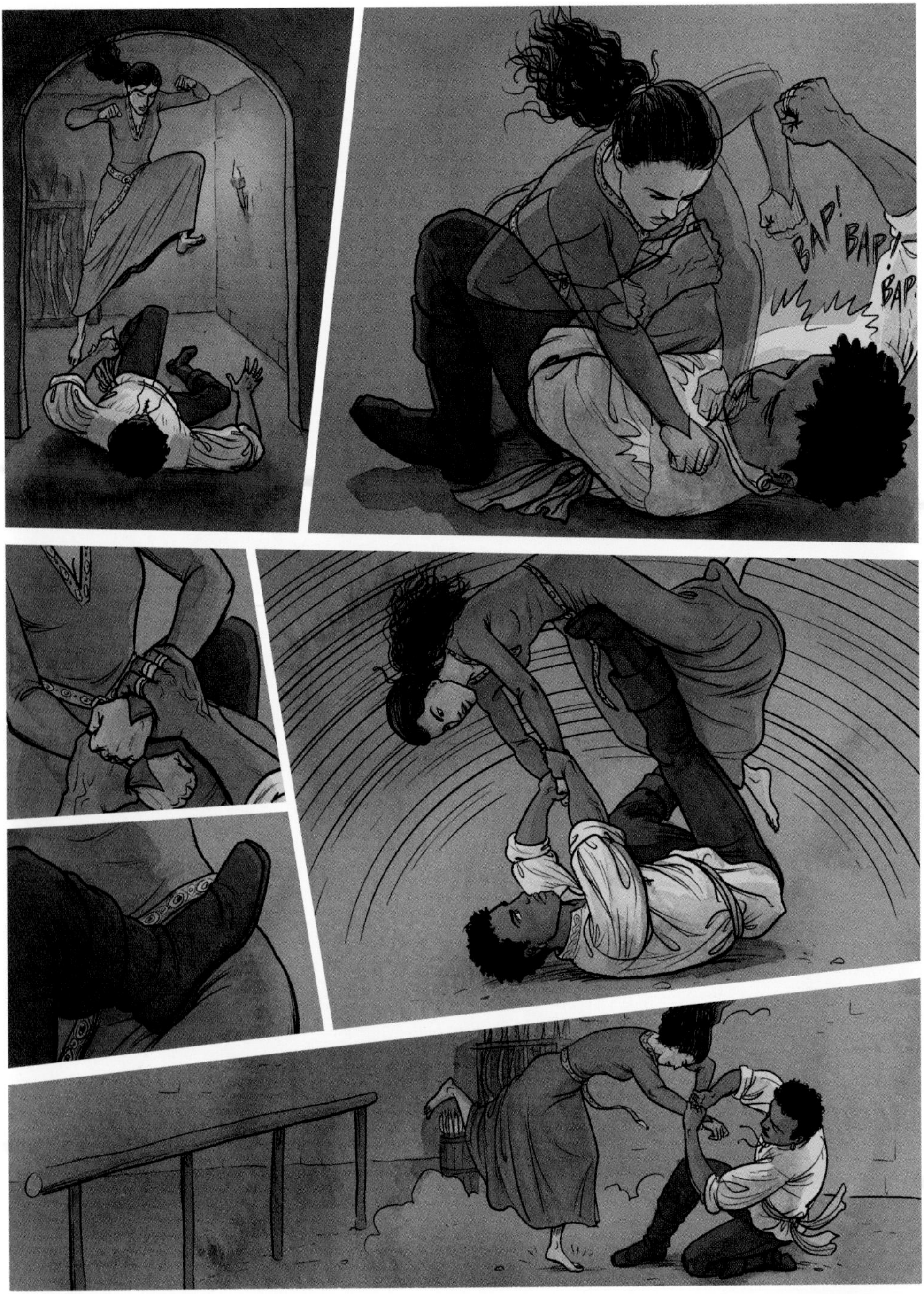
BAP! BAP! BAP!

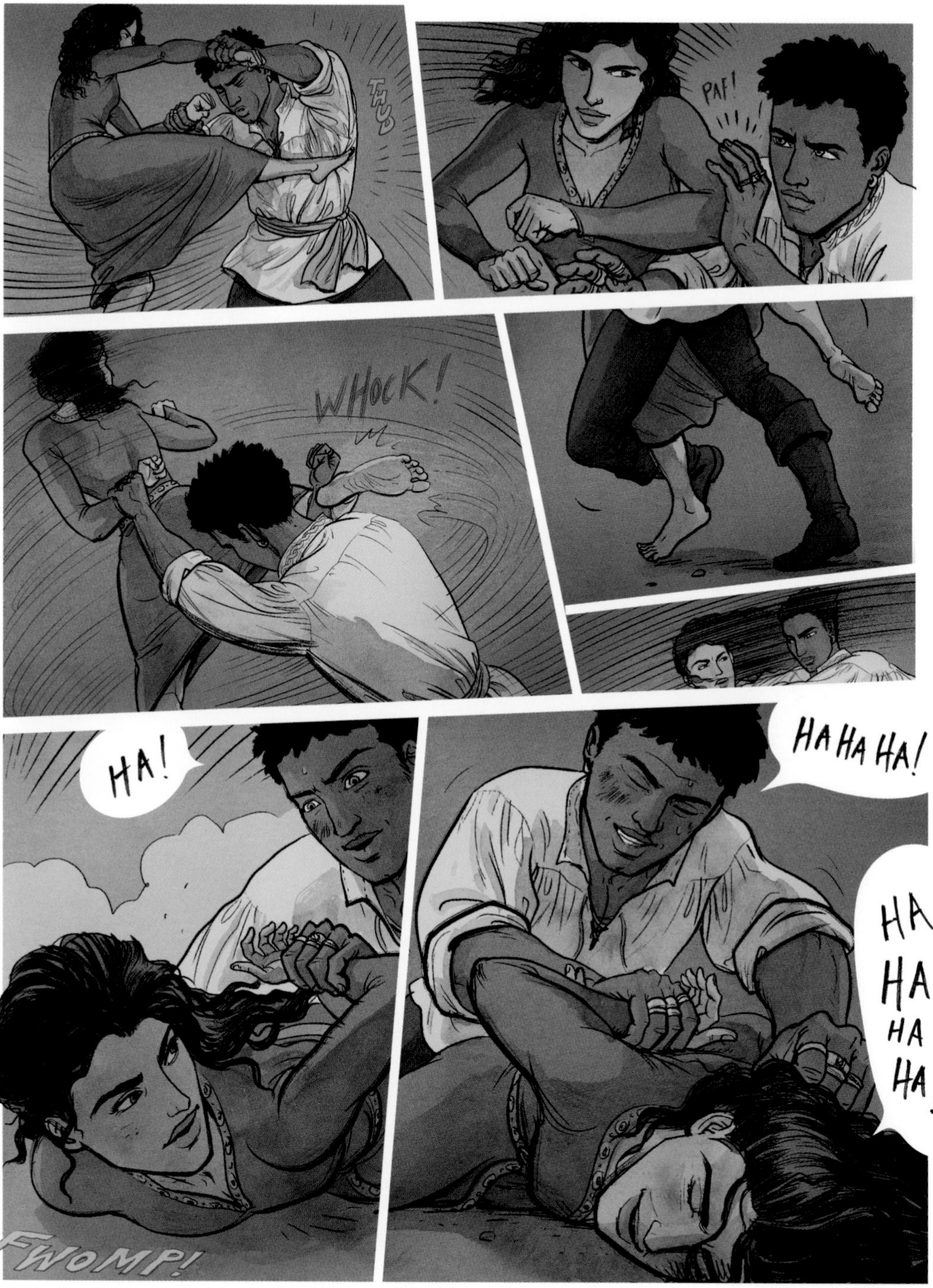
THUD
PAF!
WHOCK!
HA!
FWOMP!
HA HA HA HA!
HA
HA
HA
HA!

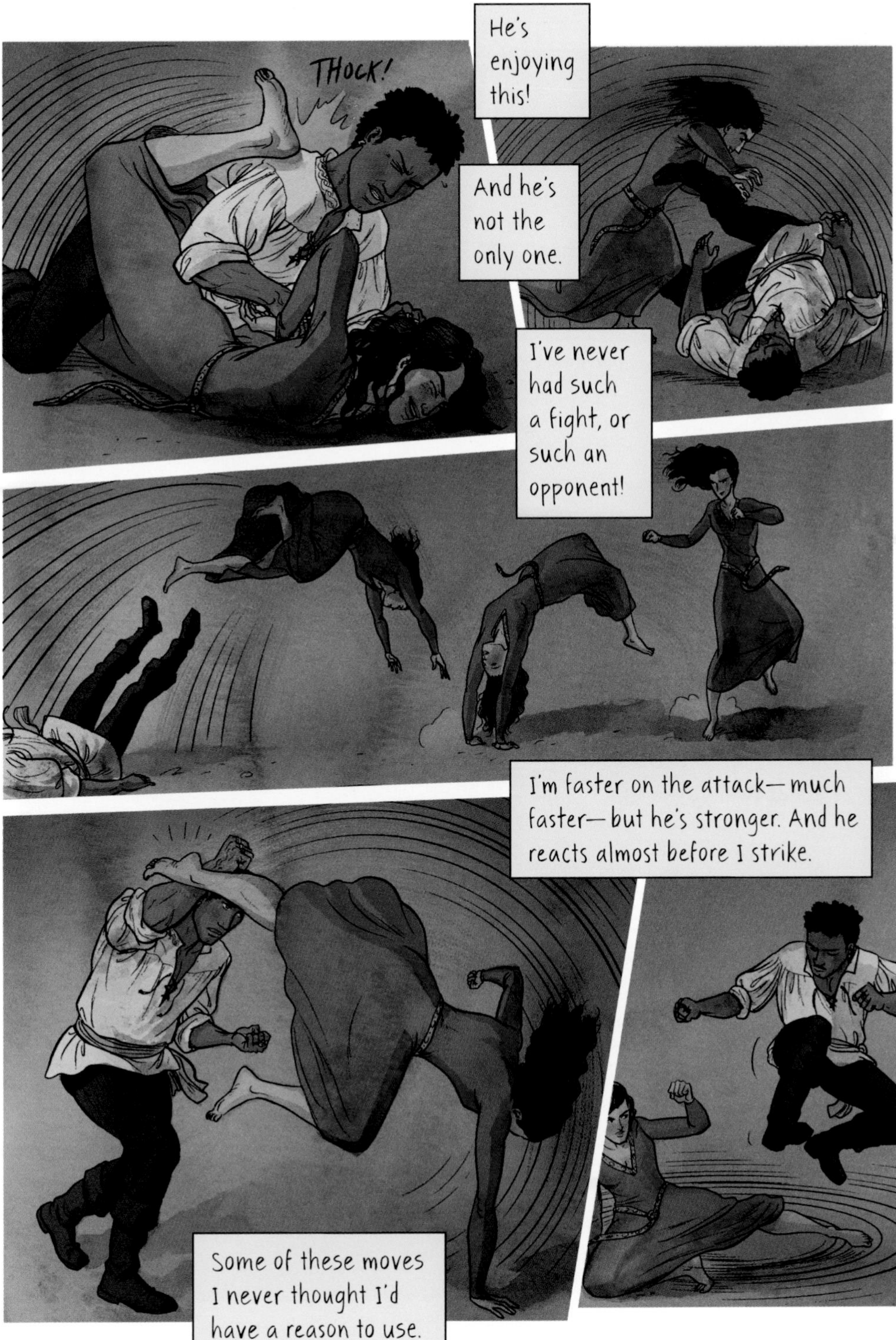
THOCK!
He's enjoying this!
And he's not the only one.
I've never had such a fight, or such an opponent!
I'm faster on the attack— much faster— but he's stronger. And he reacts almost before I strike.
Some of these moves I never thought I'd have a reason to use.

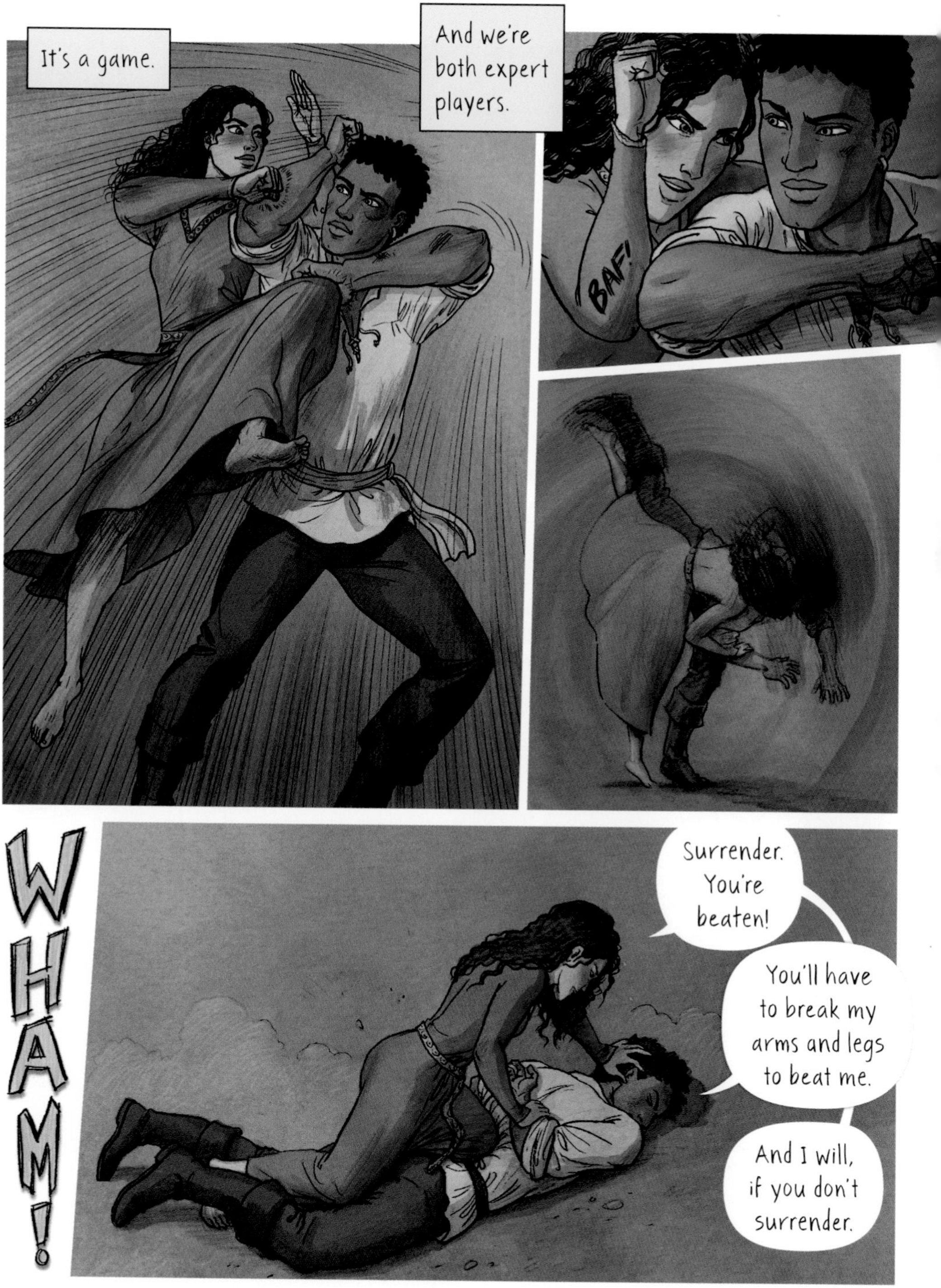
It's a game.
And we're both expert players.
BAF!
WHAM!
Surrender. You're beaten!
You'll have to break my arms and legs to beat me.
And I will, if you don't surrender.

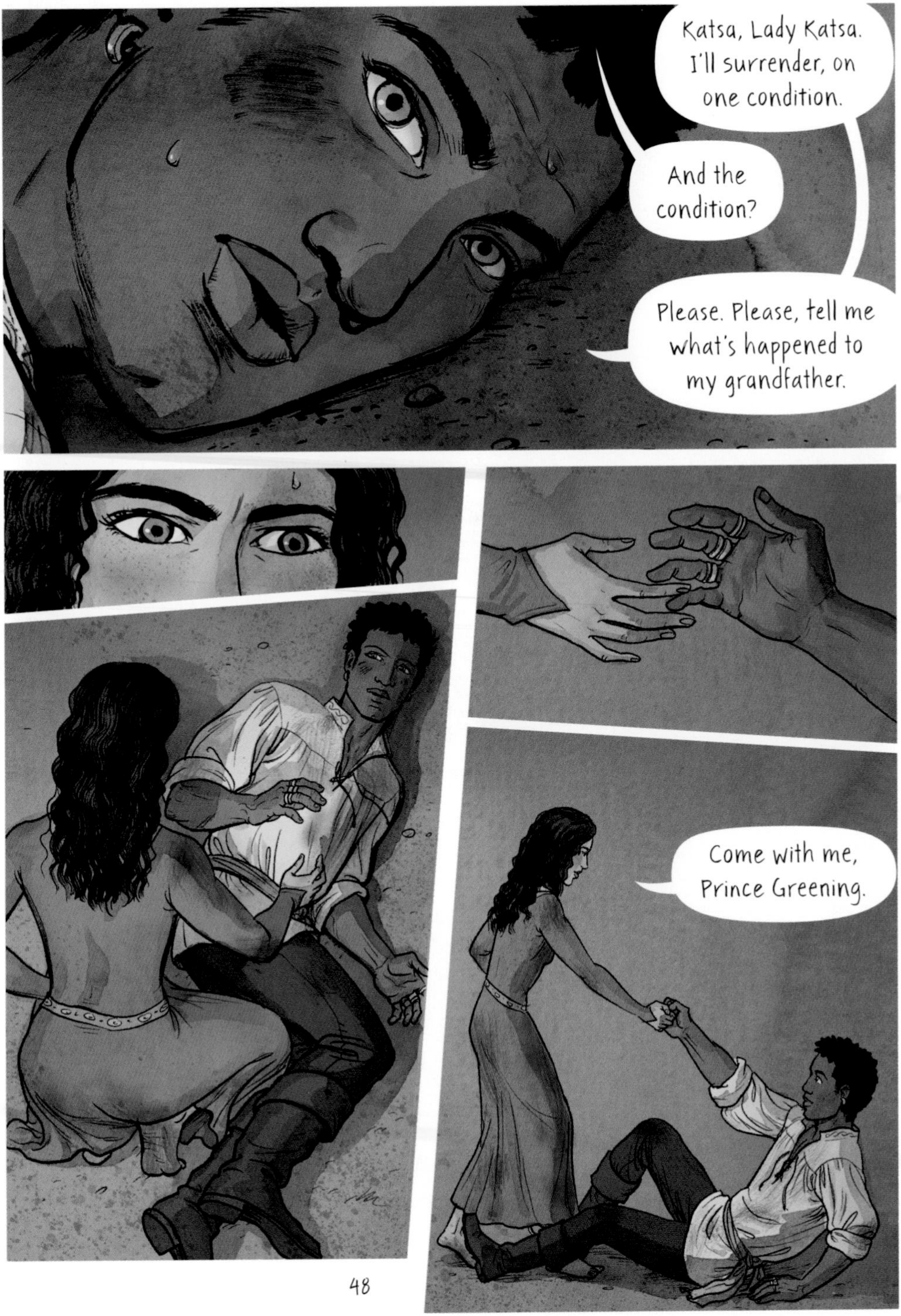
Katsa, Lady Katsa. I'll surrender, on one condition.
And the condition?
Please. Please, tell me what's happened to my grandfather.
Come with me, Prince Greening.

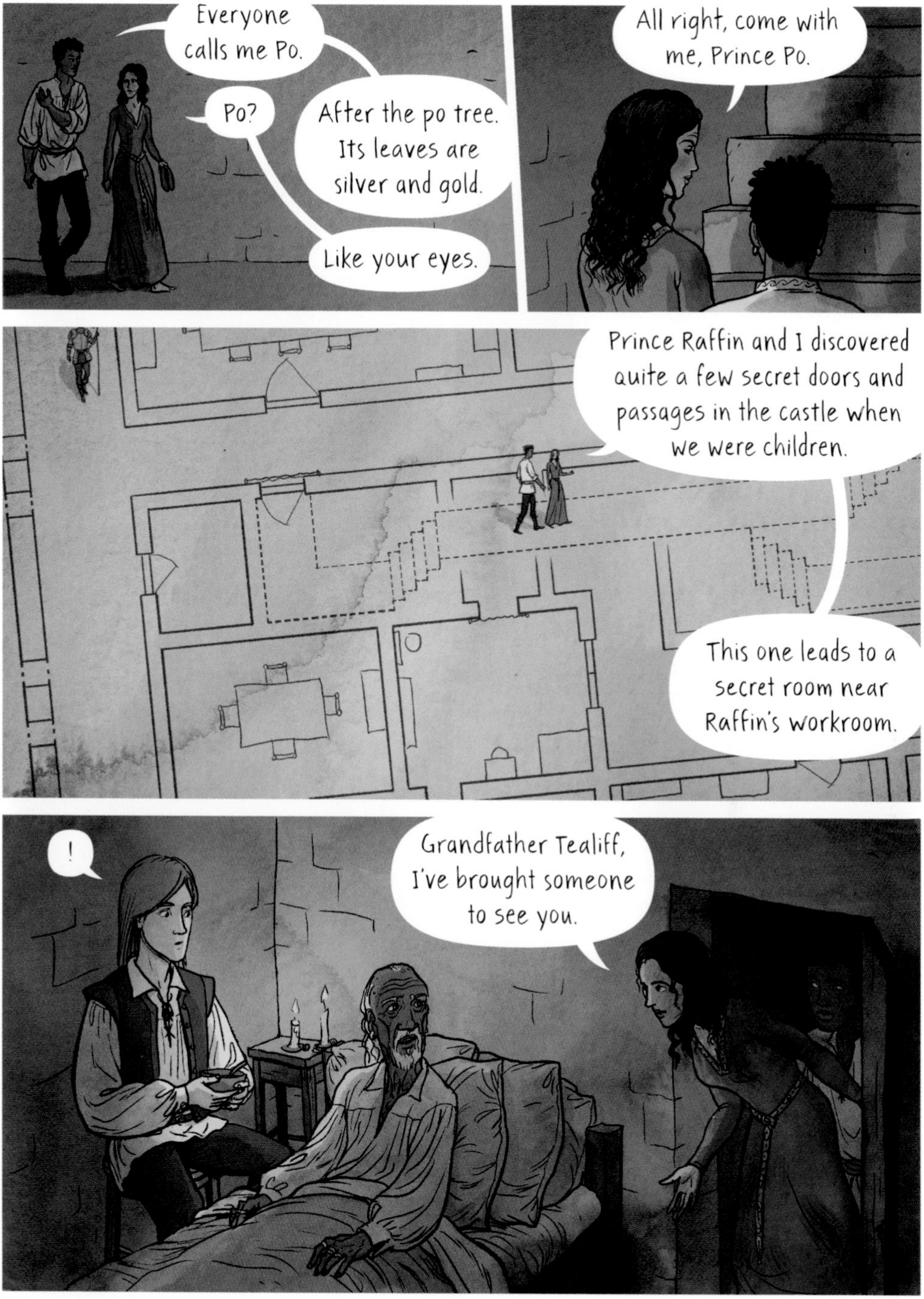
Everyone calls me Po.
Po?
After the po tree. Its leaves are silver and gold.
Like your eyes.
All right, come with me, Prince Po.
Prince Raffin and I discovered quite a few secret doors and passages in the castle when we were children.
This one leads to a secret room near Raffin's workroom.
!
Grandfather Tealiff, I've brought someone to see you.

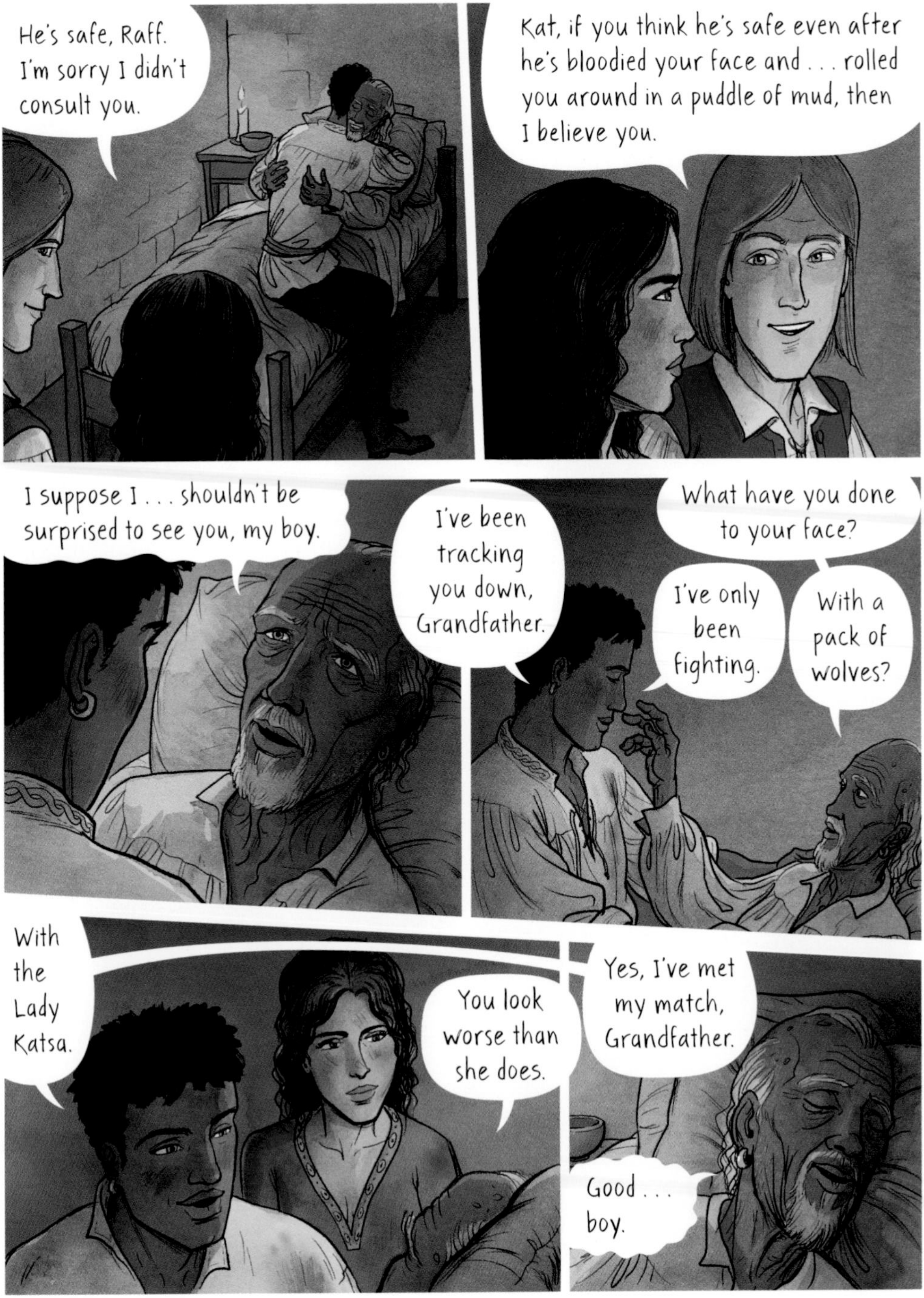
He's safe, Raff. I'm sorry I didn't consult you.
Kat, if you think he's safe even after he's bloodied your face and . . . rolled you around in a puddle of mud, then I believe you.
I suppose I . . . shouldn't be surprised to see you, my boy.
I've been tracking you down, Grandfather.
What have you done to your face?
I've only been fighting.
With a pack of wolves?
With the Lady Katsa.
You look worse than she does.
Yes, I've met my match, Grandfather.
Good . . . boy.

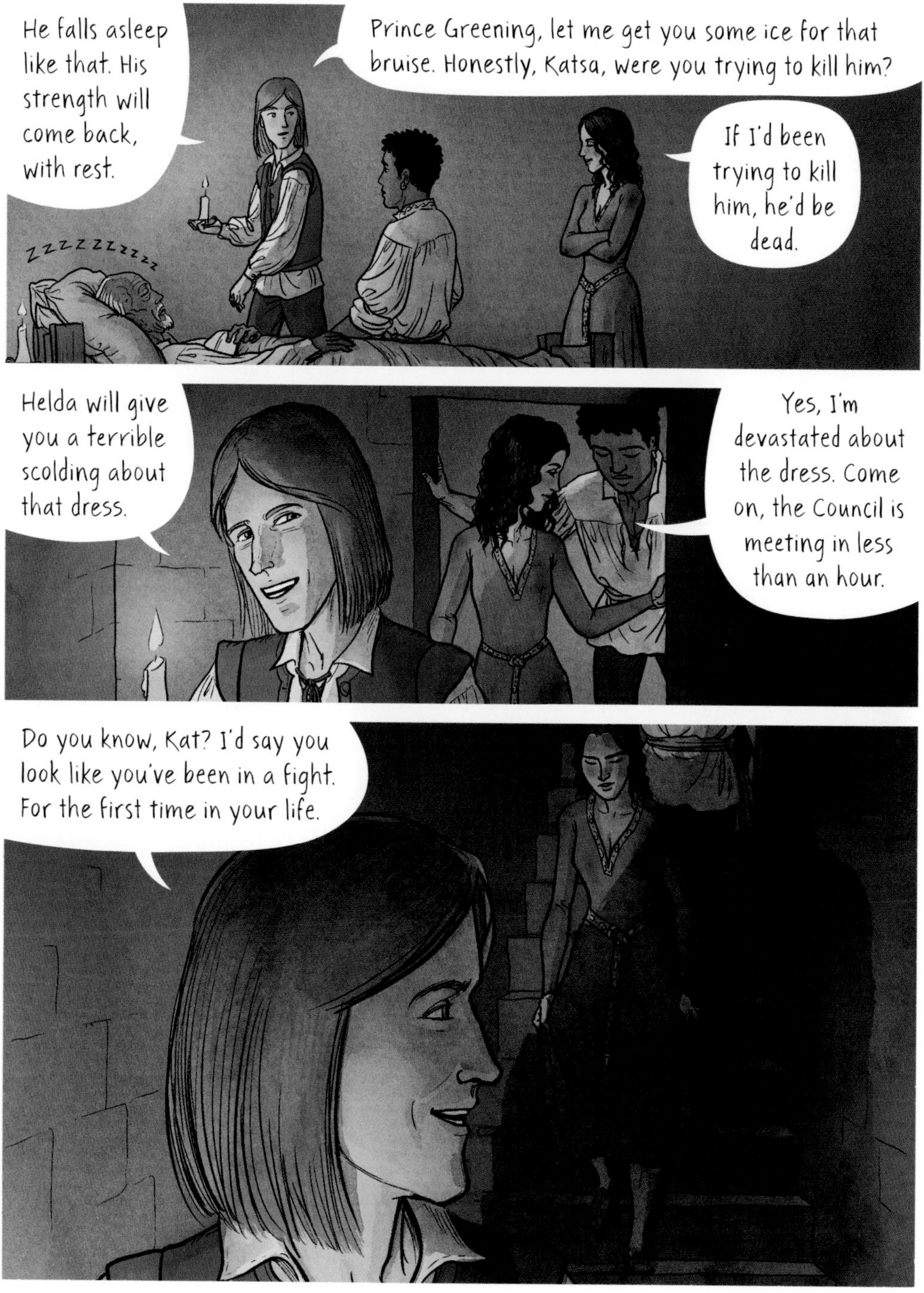
He falls asleep like that. His strength will come back, with rest.
Prince Greening, let me get you some ice for that bruise. Honestly, Katsa, were you trying to kill him?
If I'd been trying to kill him, he'd be dead.
ZZZZZZZZZZ
Helda will give you a terrible scolding about that dress.
Yes, I'm devastated about the dress. Come on, the Council is meeting in less than an hour.
Do you know, Kat? I'd say you look like you've been in a fight. For the first time in your life.

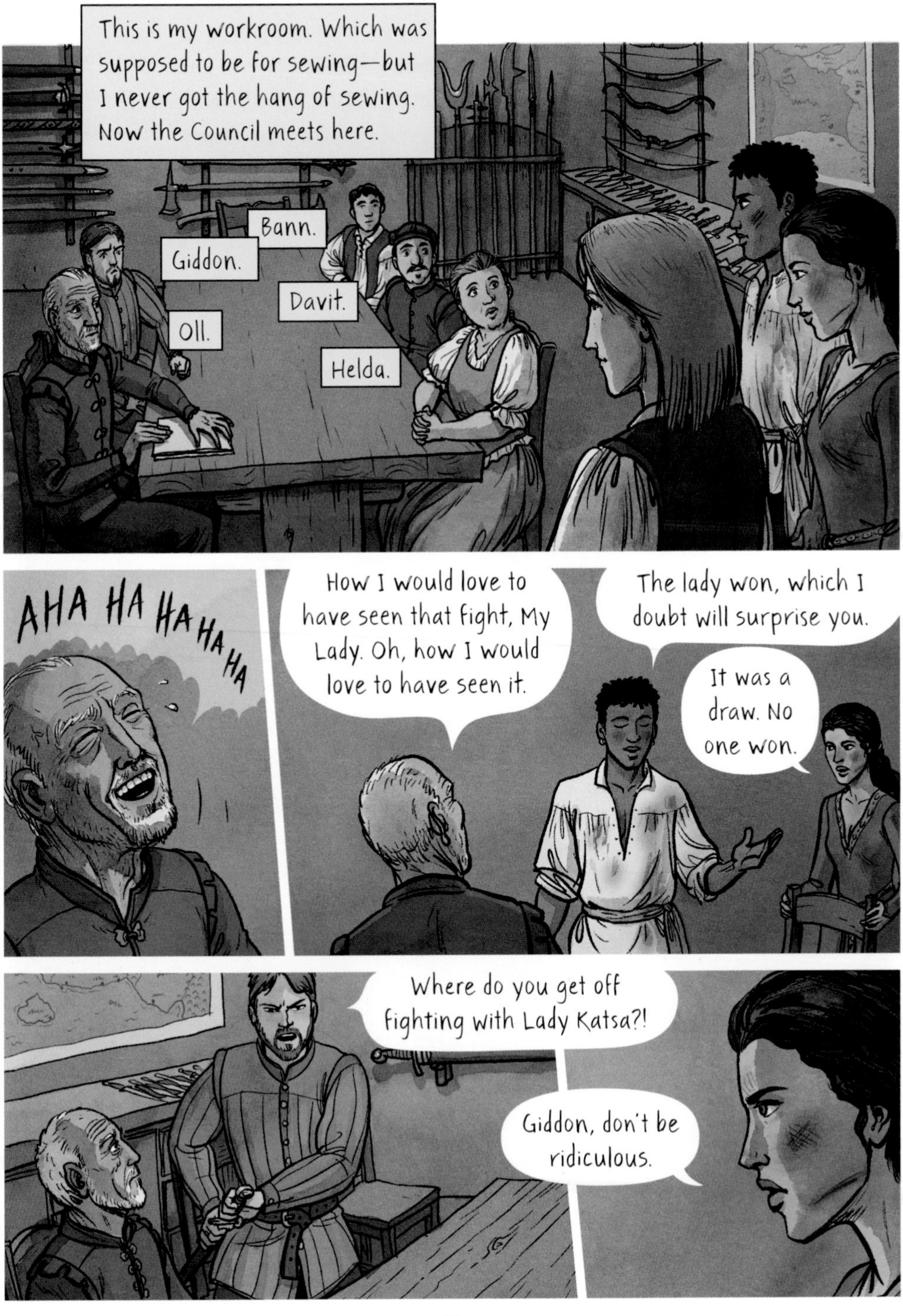
This is my workroom. Which was supposed to be for sewing—but I never got the hang of sewing. Now the Council meets here.
Giddon.
Bann.
Oll.
Davit.
Helda.
AHA HA HA HA HA
How I would love to have seen that fight, My Lady. Oh, how I would love to have seen it.
The lady won, which I doubt will surprise you.
It was a draw. No one won.
Where do you get off fighting with Lady Katsa?!
Giddon, don't be ridiculous.

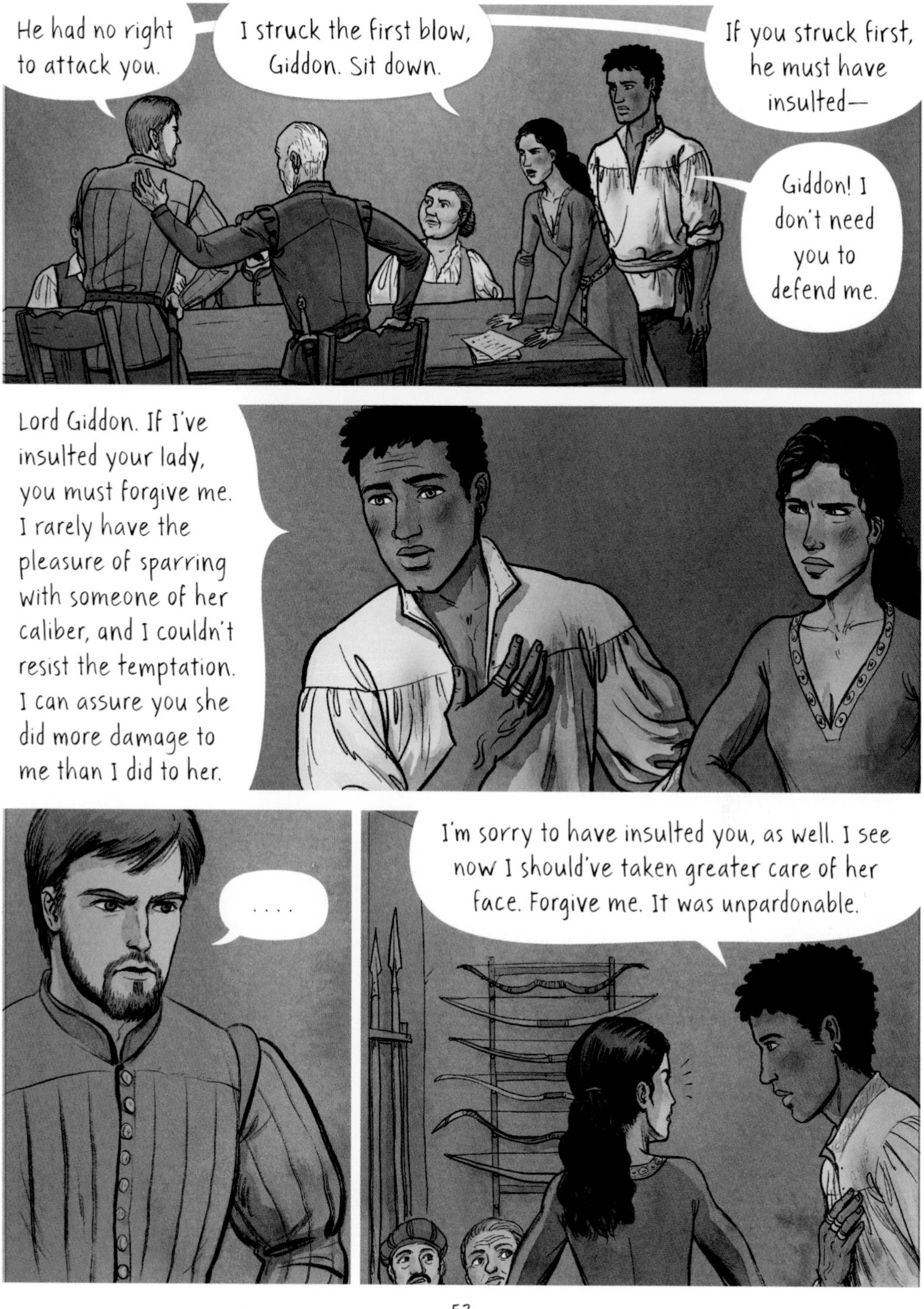
He had no right to attack you.
I struck the first blow, Giddon. Sit down.
If you struck first, he must have insulted—
Giddon! I don't need you to defend me.
Lord Giddon. If I've insulted your lady, you must forgive me. I rarely have the pleasure of sparring with someone of her caliber, and I couldn't resist the temptation. I can assure you she did more damage to me than I did to her.
. . . .
I'm sorry to have insulted you, as well. I see now I should've taken greater care of her face. Forgive me. It was unpardonable.

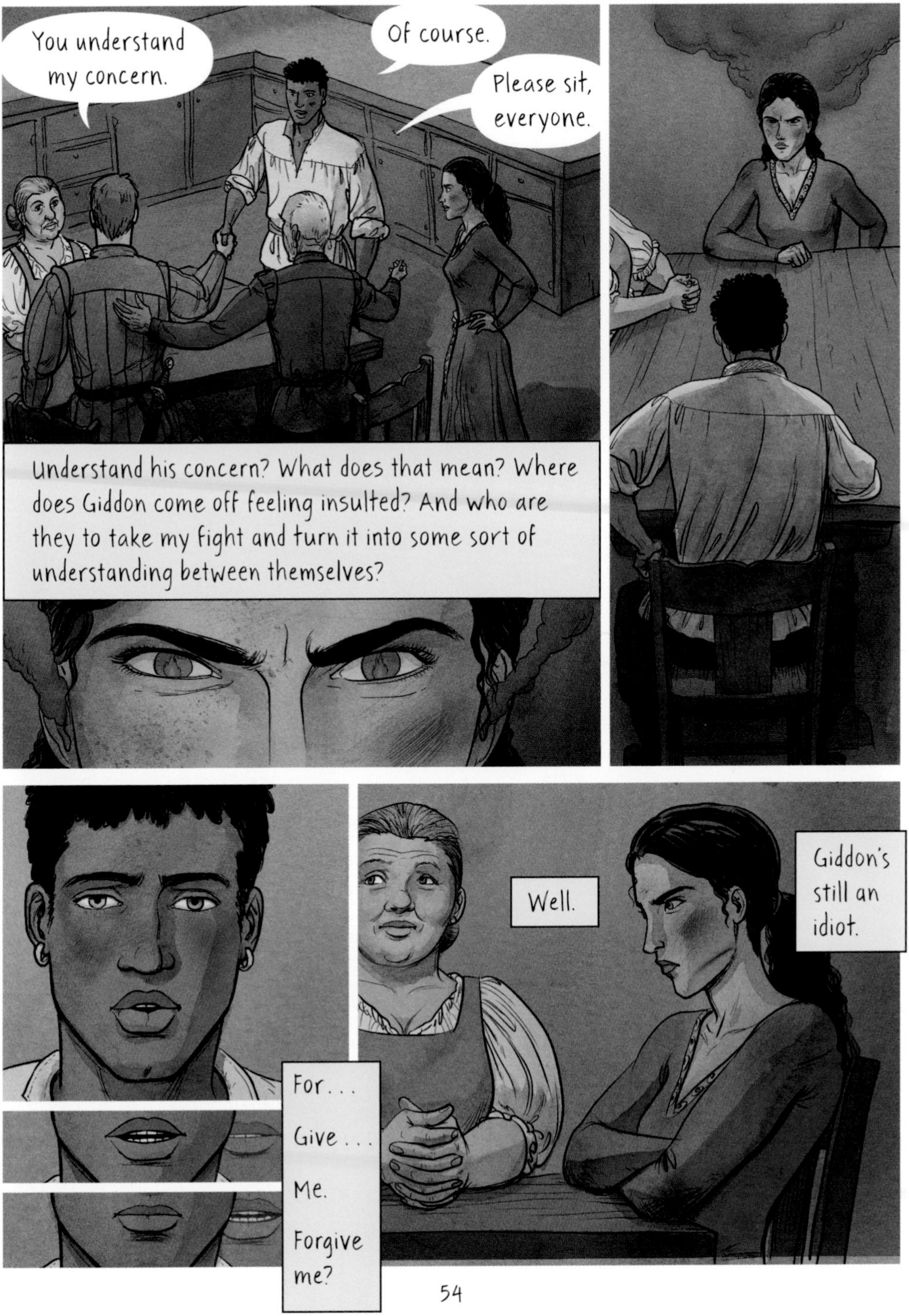
You understand my concern.
Of course.
Please sit, everyone.
Understand his concern? What does that mean? Where does Giddon come off feeling insulted? And who are they to take my fight and turn it into some sort of understanding between themselves?
For . . .
Give . . .
Me.
Forgive me?
Well.
Giddon's still an idiot.

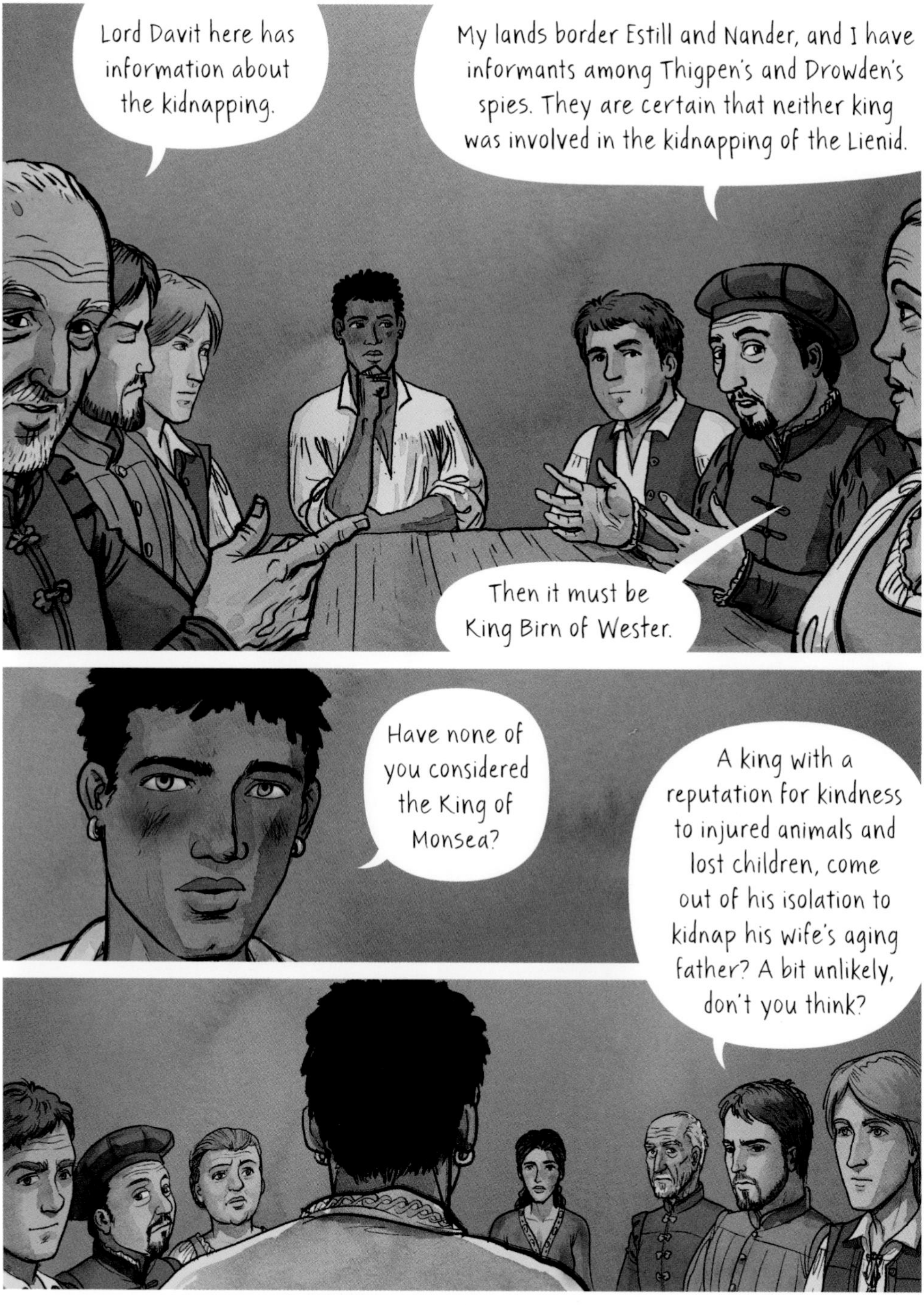
Lord Davit here has information about the kidnapping.
My lands border Estill and Nander, and I have informants among Thigpen's and Drowden's spies. They are certain that neither king was involved in the kidnapping of the Lienid.
Then it must be King Birn of Wester.
Have none of you considered the King of Monsea?
A king with a reputation for kindness to injured animals and lost children, come out of his isolation to kidnap his wife's aging father? A bit unlikely, don't you think?

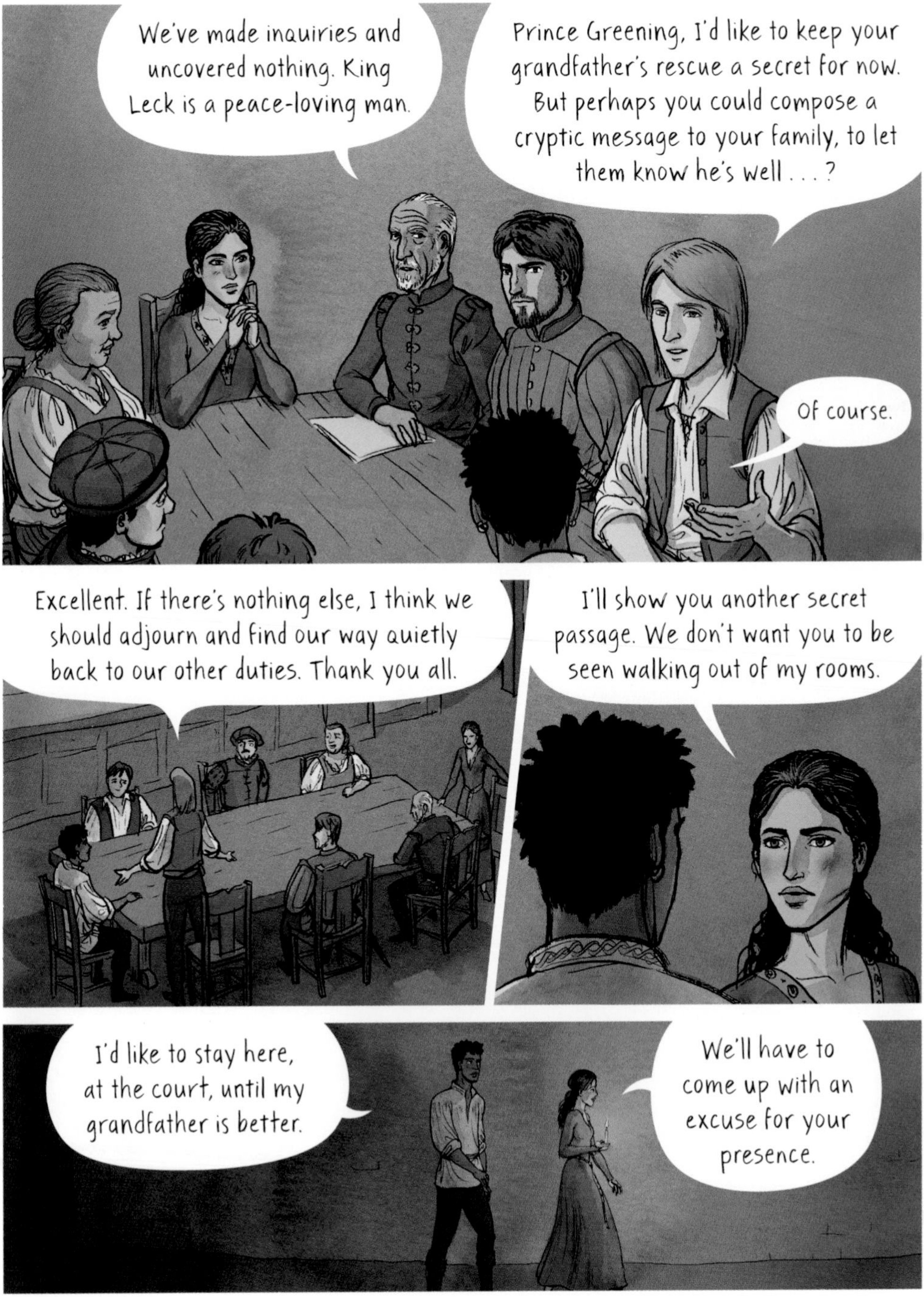
We've made inquiries and uncovered nothing. King Leck is a peace-loving man.
Prince Greening, I'd like to keep your grandfather's rescue a secret for now. But perhaps you could compose a cryptic message to your family, to let them know he's well . . . ?
Of course.
Excellent. If there's nothing else, I think we should adjourn and find our way quietly back to our other duties. Thank you all.
I'll show you another secret passage. We don't want you to be seen walking out of my rooms.
I'd like to stay here, at the court, until my grandfather is better.
We'll have to come up with an excuse for your presence.

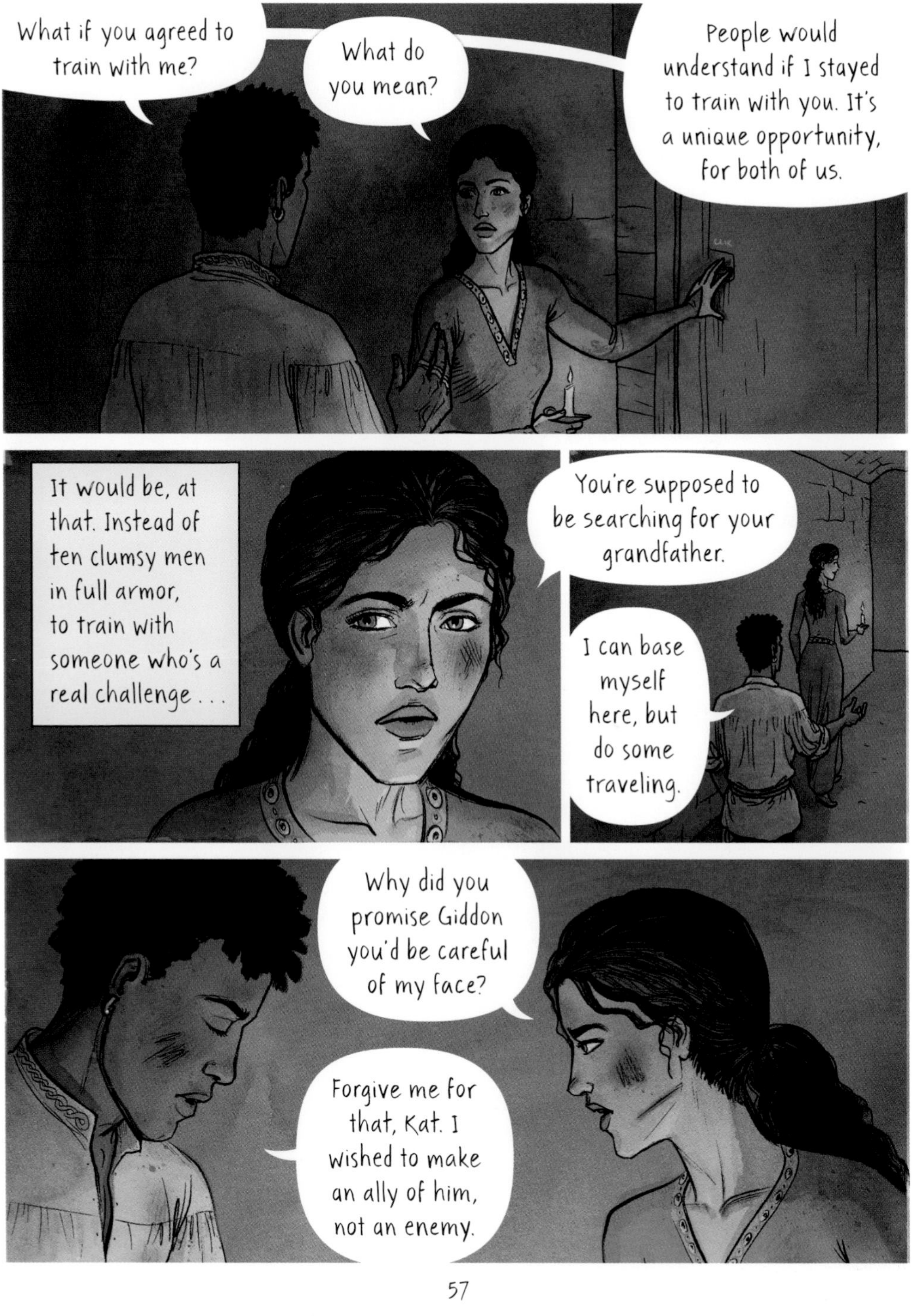
What if you agreed to train with me?
What do you mean?
People would understand if I stayed to train with you. It's a unique opportunity, for both of us.
It would be, at that. Instead of ten clumsy men in full armor, to train with someone who's a real challenge . . .
You're supposed to be searching for your grandfather.
I can base myself here, but do some traveling.
Why did you promise Giddon you'd be careful of my face?
Forgive me for that, Kat. I wished to make an ally of him, not an enemy.

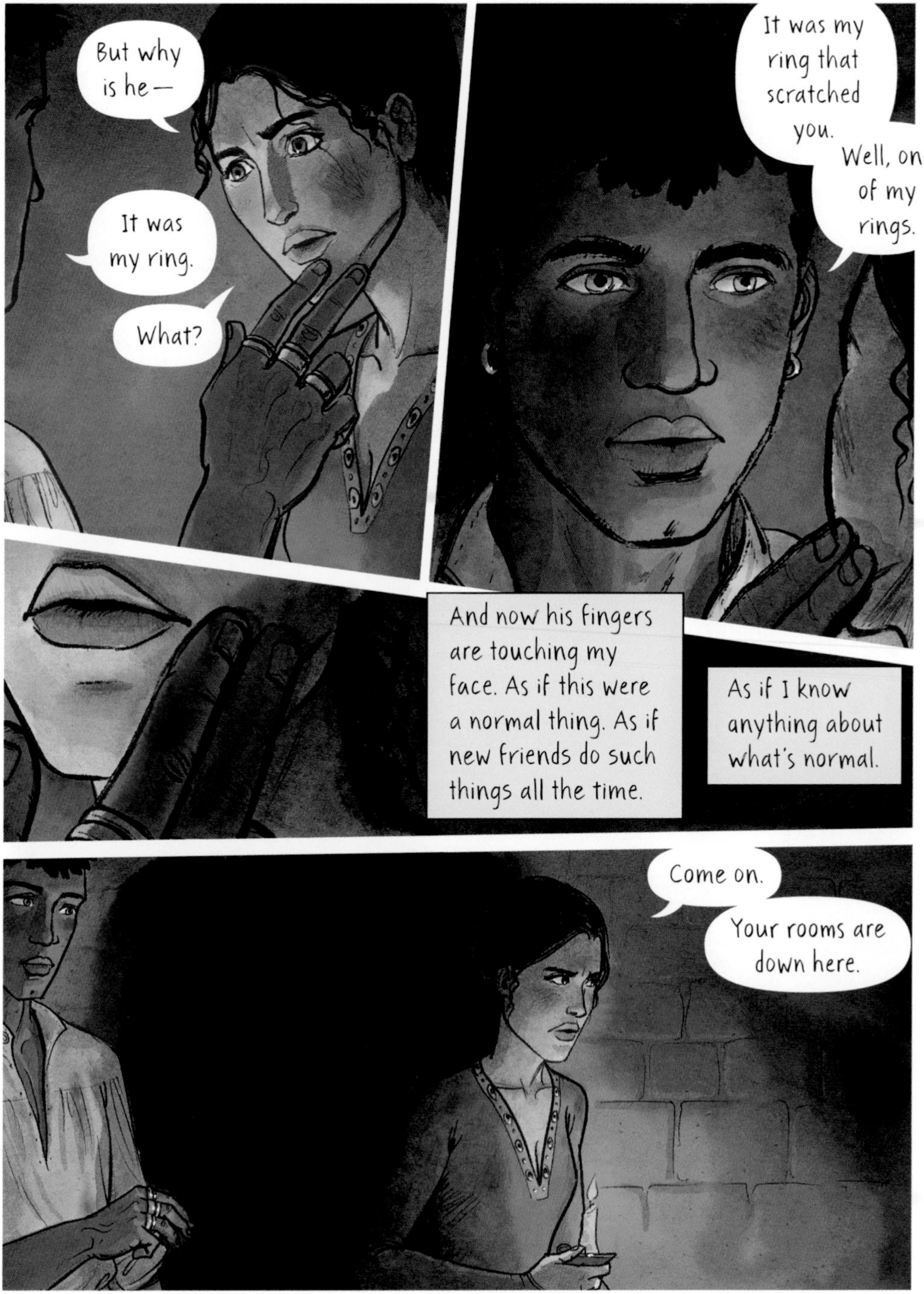
But why is he—
It was my ring.
What?
It was my ring that scratched you.
Well, one of my rings.
And now his fingers are touching my face. As if this were a normal thing. As if new friends do such things all the time.
As if I know anything about what's normal.
Come on.
Your rooms are down here.

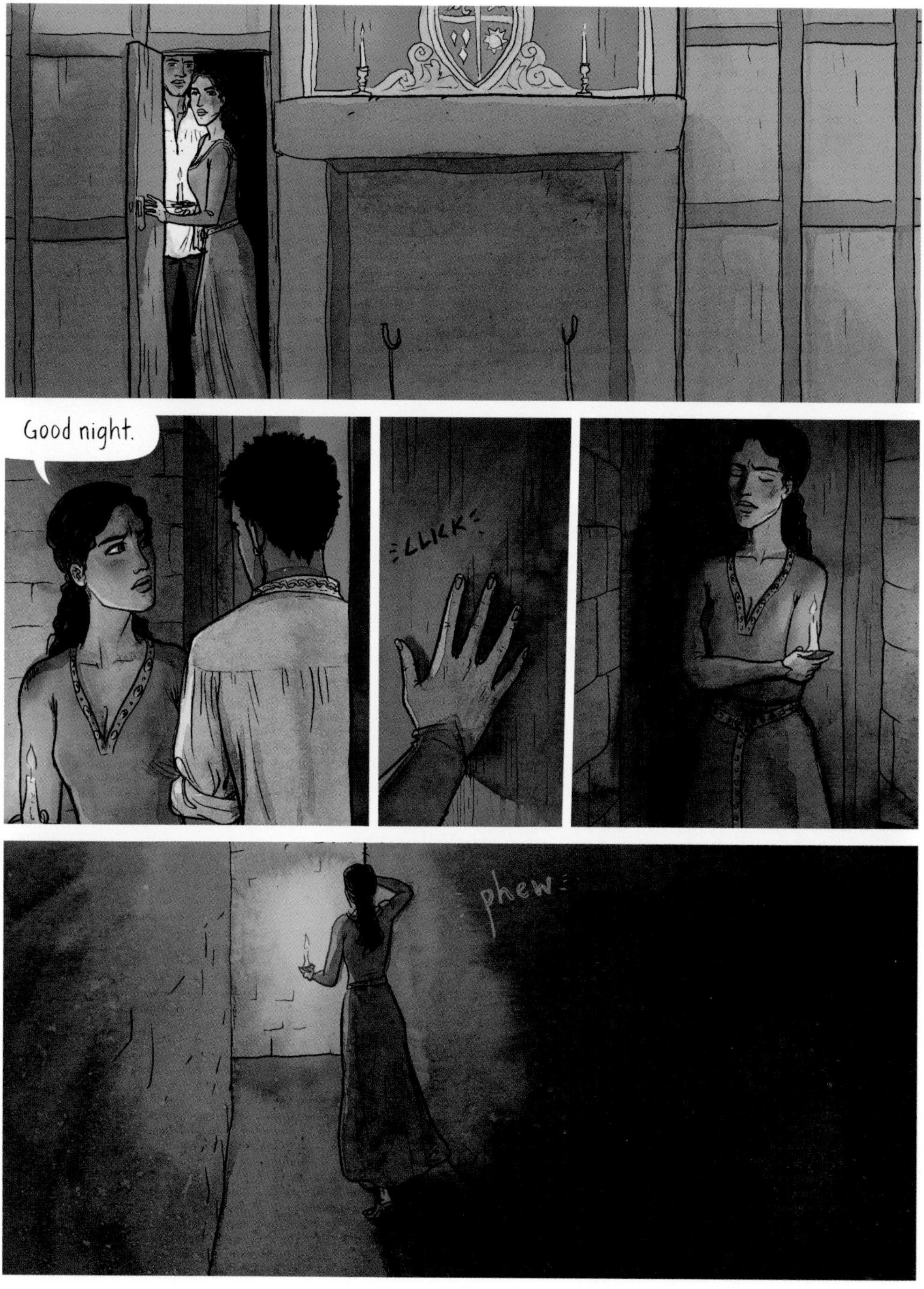
Good night.
CLICK
phew

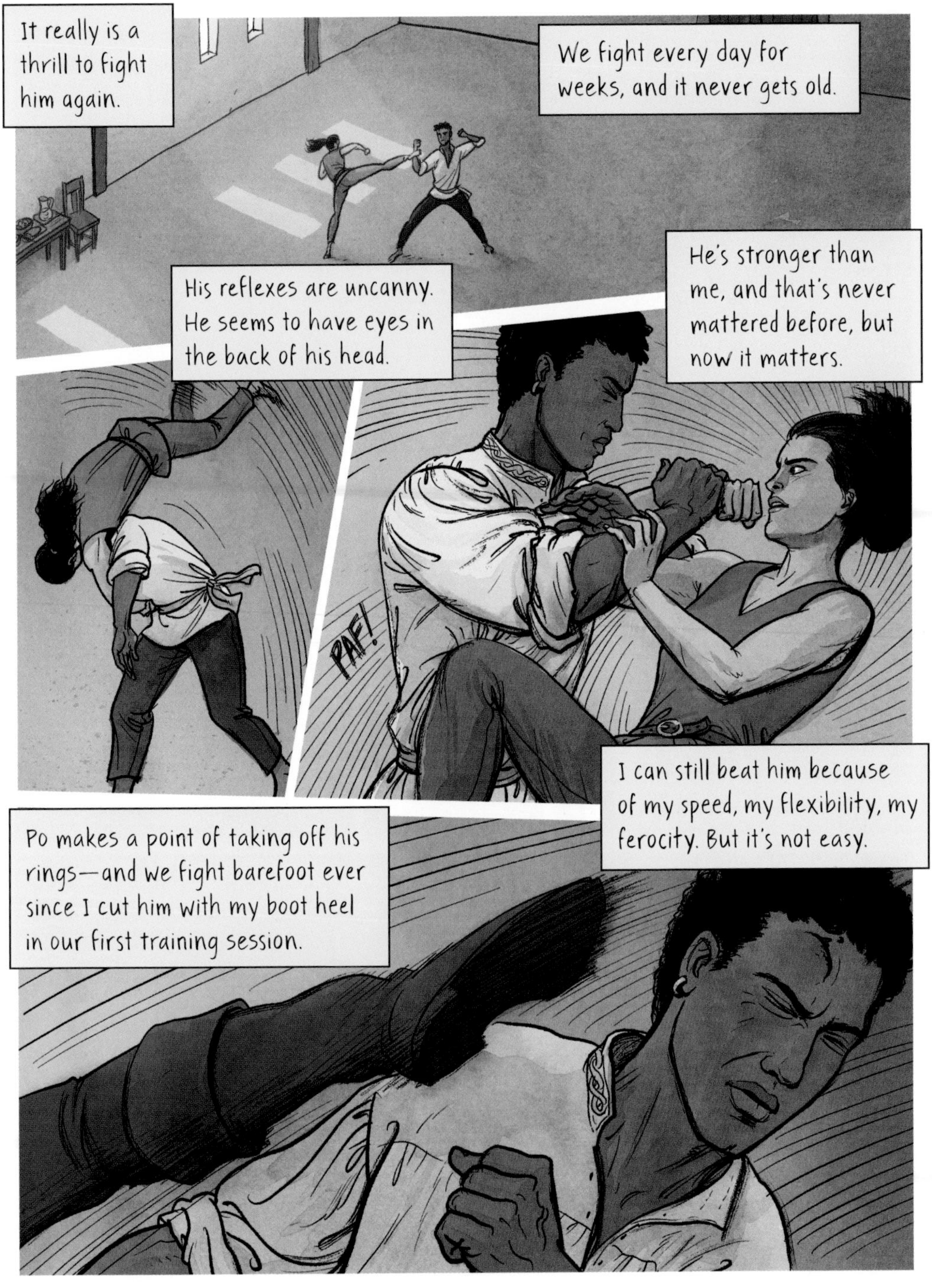
It really is a thrill to fight him again.
We fight every day for weeks, and it never gets old.
His reflexes are uncanny. He seems to have eyes in the back of his head.
He's stronger than me, and that's never mattered before, but now it matters.
PAF!
I can still beat him because of my speed, my flexibility, my ferocity. But it's not easy.
Po makes a point of taking off his rings—and we fight barefoot ever since I cut him with my boot heel in our first training session.

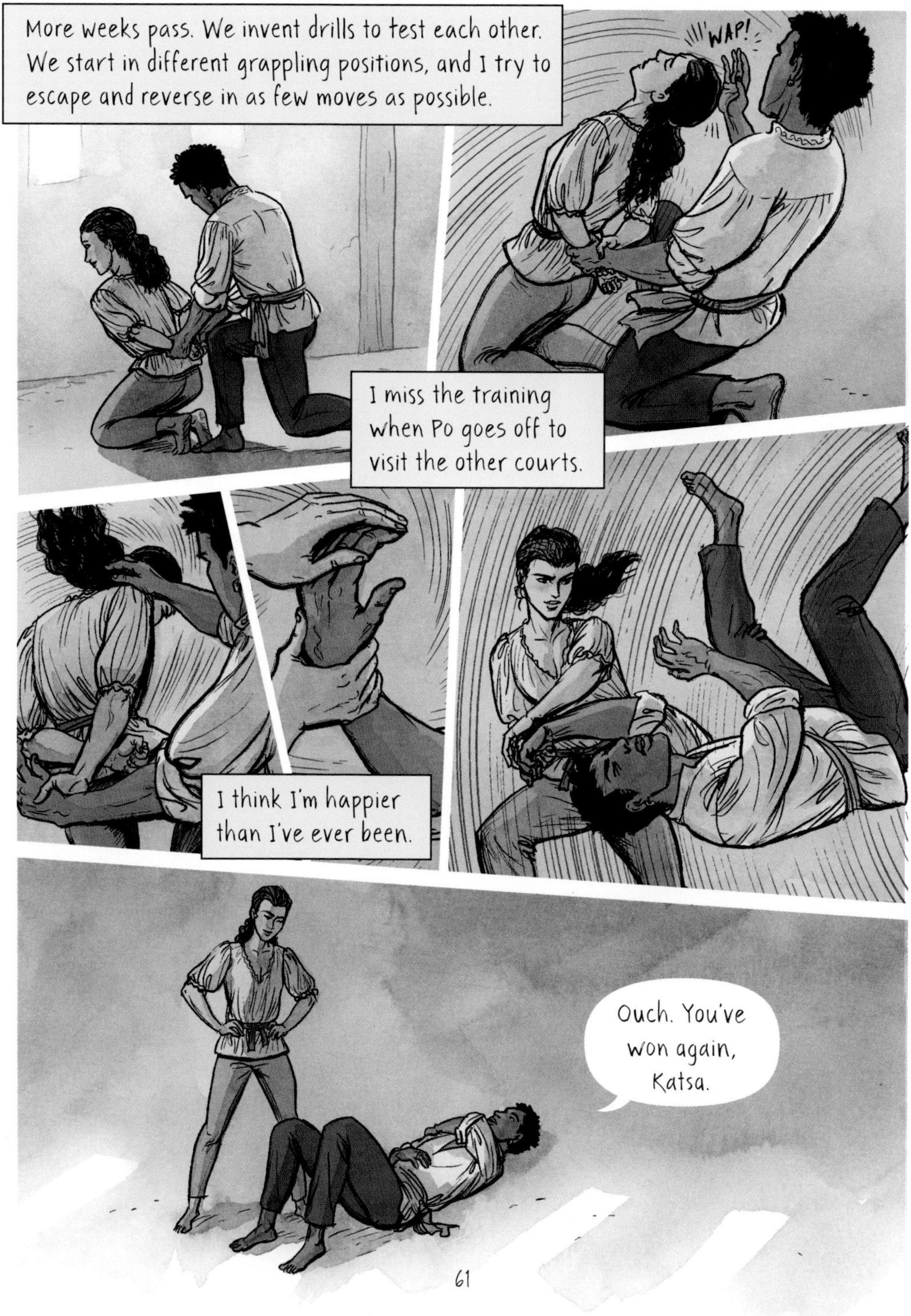
More weeks pass. We invent drills to test each other. We start in different grappling positions, and I try to escape and reverse in as few moves as possible.
WAP!
I miss the training when Po goes off to visit the other courts.
I think I'm happier than I've ever been.
Ouch. You've won again, Katsa.

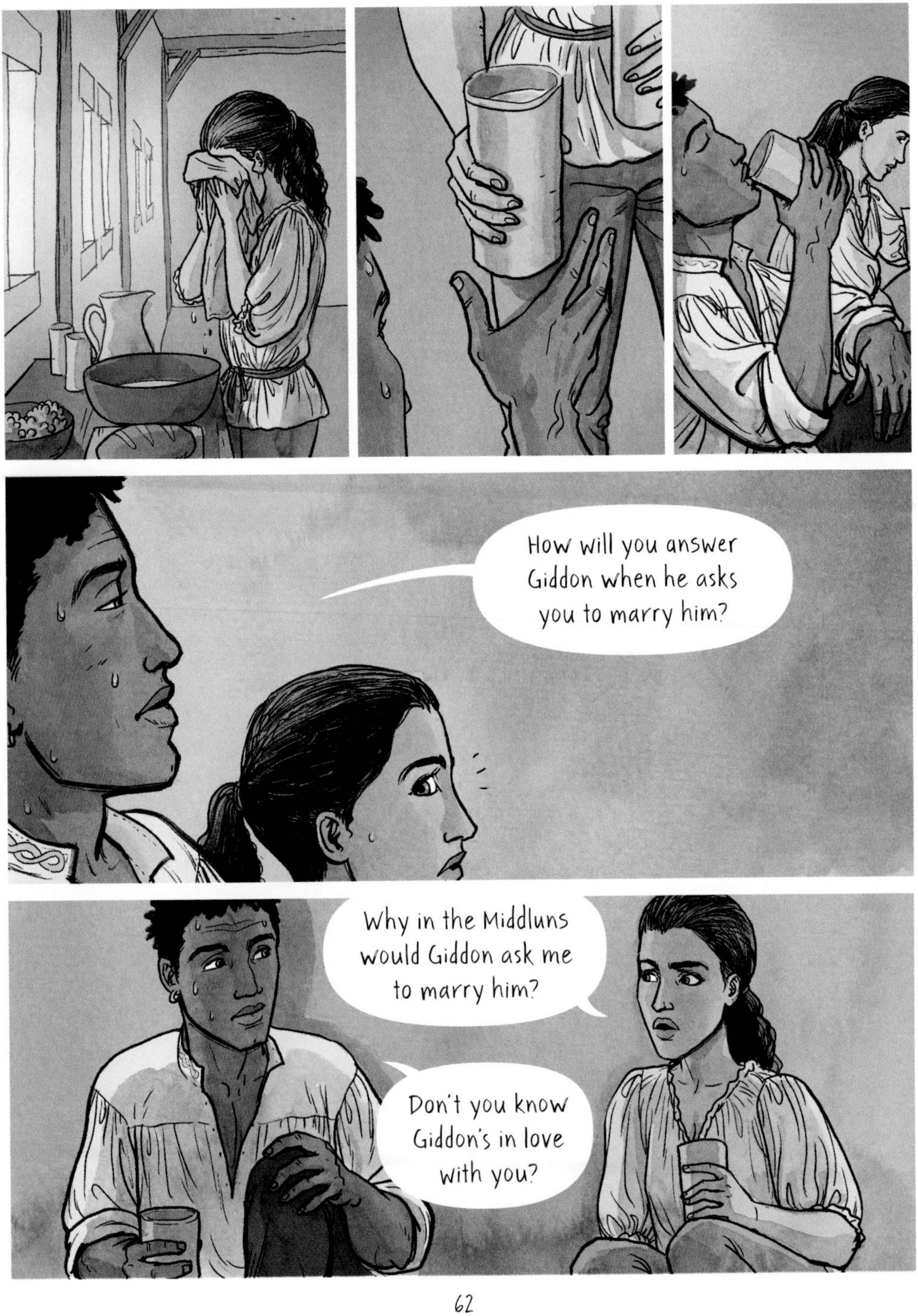
How will you answer Giddon when he asks you to marry him?
Why in the Middluns would Giddon ask me to marry him?
Don't you know Giddon's in love with you?

Don't be ridiculous. Giddon lives to criticize me.

Katsa, how can you be so blind? He's completely smitten.

Don't you see how jealous he is? Don't you remember how he reacted when I scratched your face?

I don't see what that has to do with it. And besides, how would you know? I don't believe Lord Giddon confides in you.

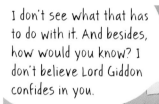

No, he certainly doesn't. Giddon doesn't trust me at all. He thinks any man who fights you as I do is no more than an opportunist and a scoundrel.

You're wrong. Giddon feels nothing for me.

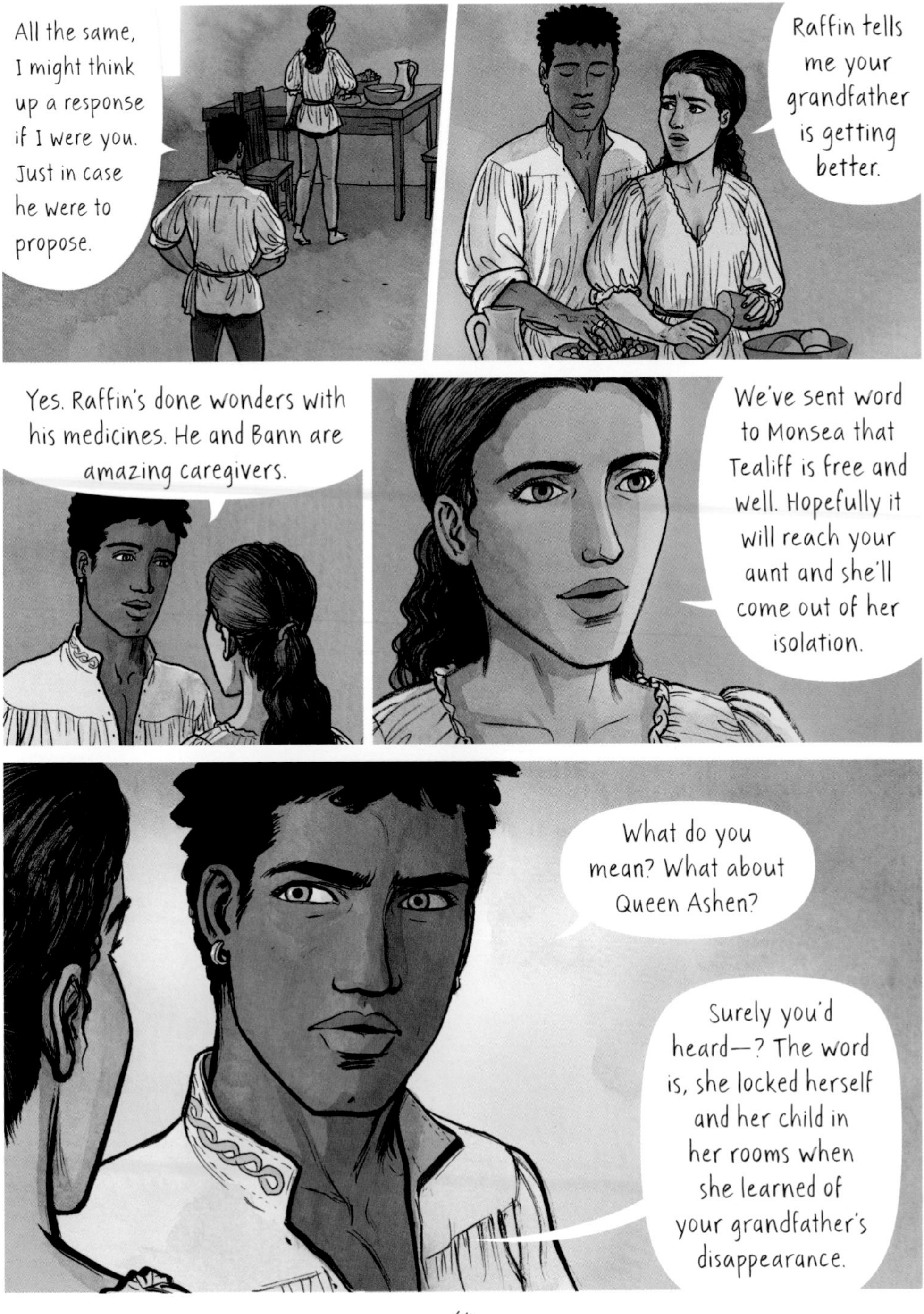
All the same, I might think up a response if I were you. Just in case he were to propose.
Raffin tells me your grandfather is getting better.
Yes. Raffin's done wonders with his medicines. He and Bann are amazing caregivers.
We've sent word to Monsea that Tealiff is free and well. Hopefully it will reach your aunt and she'll come out of her isolation.
What do you mean? What about Queen Ashen?
Surely you'd heard—? The word is, she locked herself and her child in her rooms when she learned of your grandfather's disappearance.

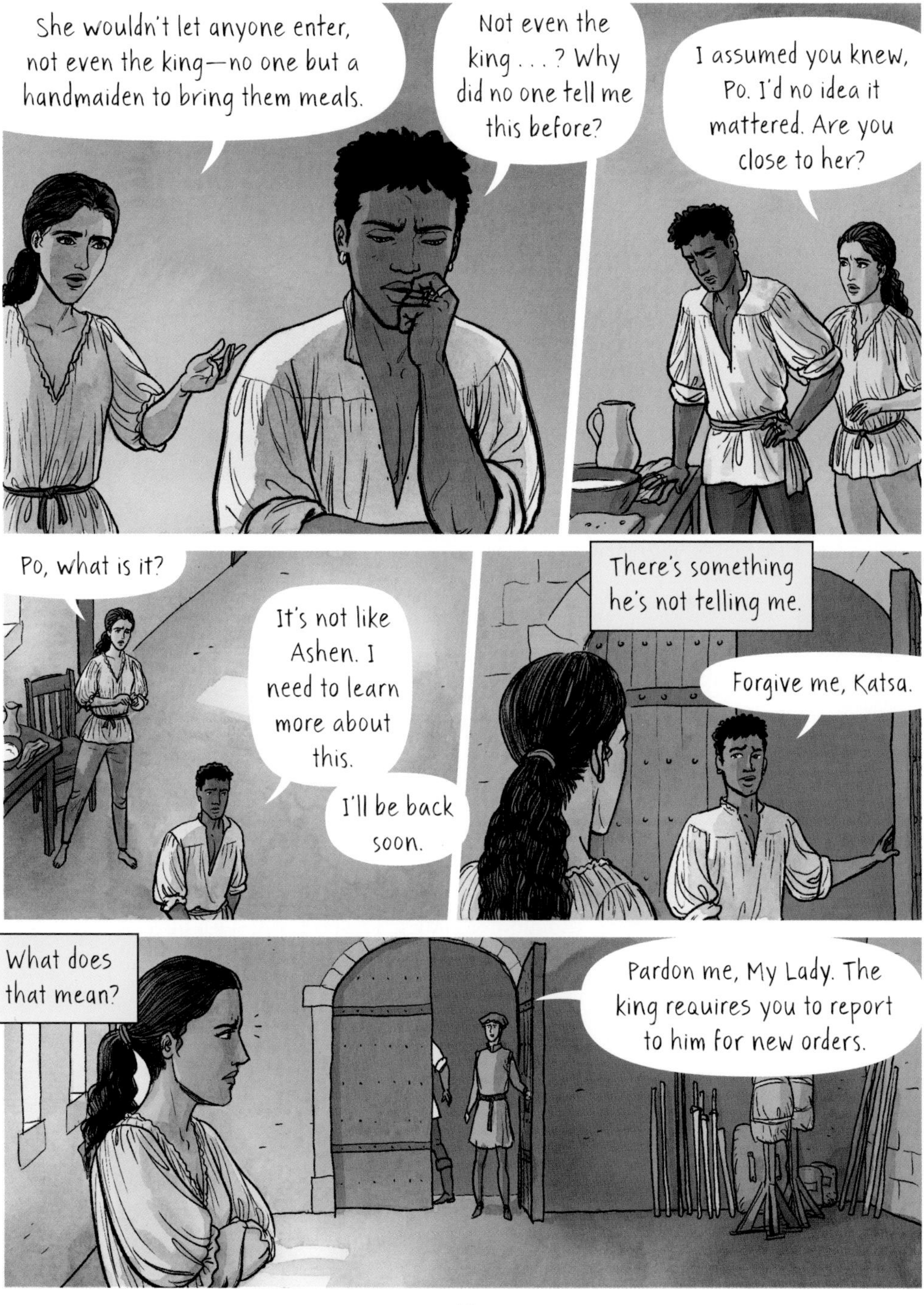
She wouldn't let anyone enter, not even the king—no one but a handmaiden to bring them meals.
Not even the king . . . ? Why did no one tell me this before?
I assumed you knew, Po. I'd no idea it mattered. Are you close to her?
Po, what is it?
It's not like Ashen. I need to learn more about this.
I'll be back soon.
There's something he's not telling me.
Forgive me, Katsa.
What does that mean?
Pardon me, My Lady. The king requires you to report to him for new orders.

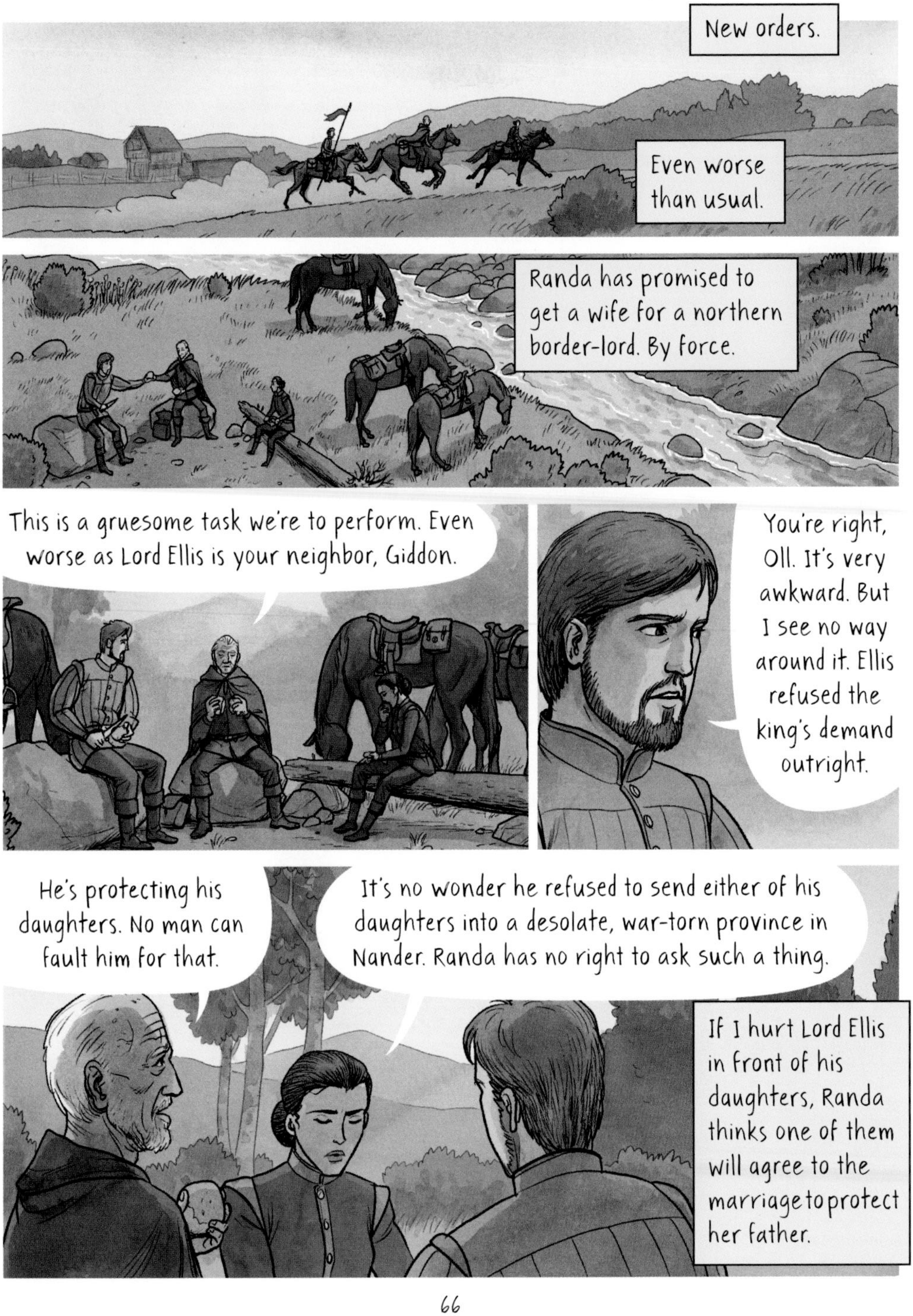
New orders.
Even worse than usual.
Randa has promised to get a wife for a northern border-lord. By force.
This is a gruesome task we're to perform. Even worse as Lord Ellis is your neighbor, Giddon.
You're right, Oll. It's very awkward. But I see no way around it. Ellis refused the king's demand outright.
He's protecting his daughters. No man can fault him for that.
It's no wonder he refused to send either of his daughters into a desolate, war-torn province in Nander. Randa has no right to ask such a thing.
If I hurt Lord Ellis in front of his daughters, Randa thinks one of them will agree to the marriage to protect her father.

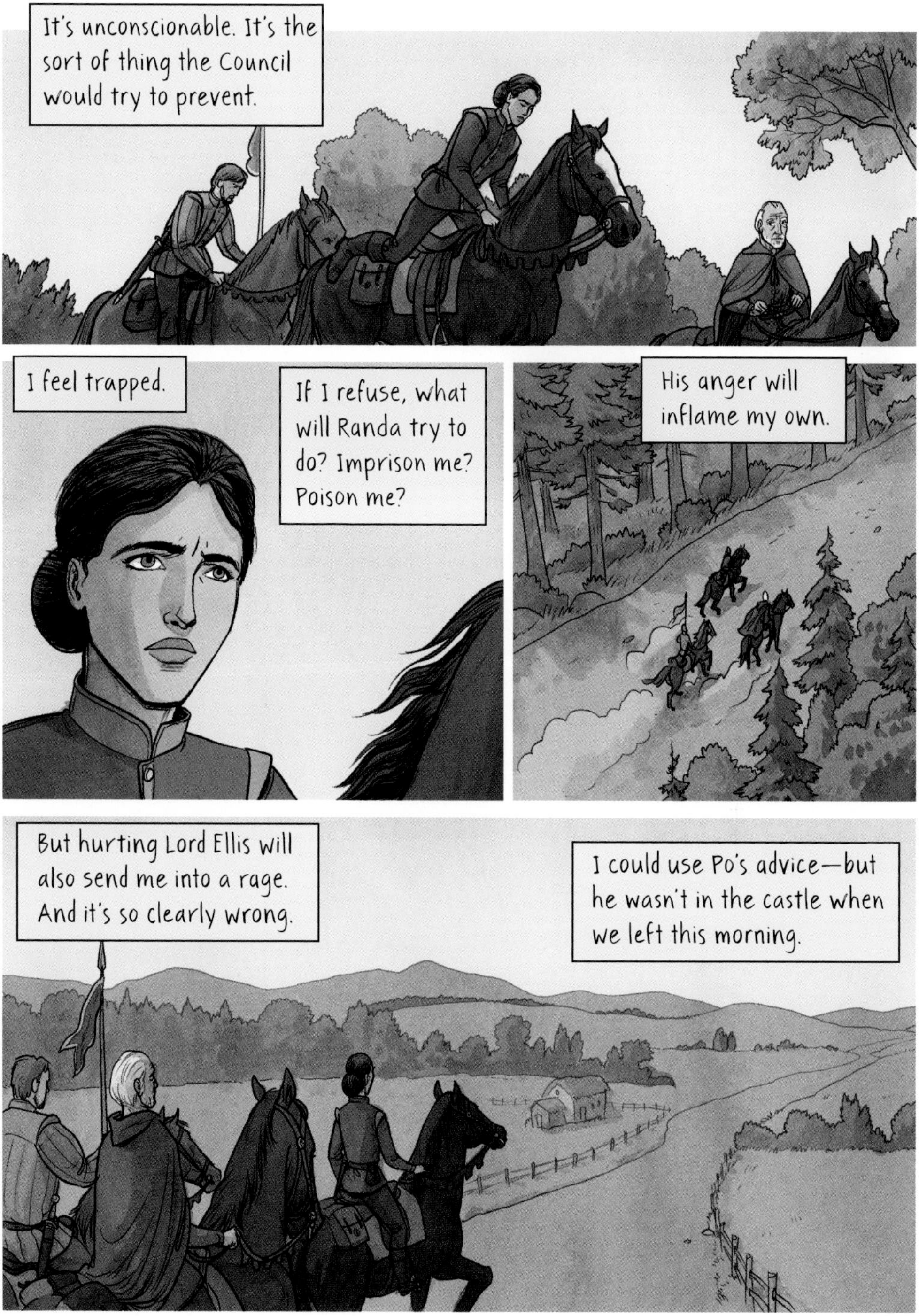
It's unconscionable. It's the sort of thing the Council would try to prevent.
I feel trapped.
If I refuse, what will Randa try to do? Imprison me? Poison me?
His anger will inflame my own.
But hurting Lord Ellis will also send me into a rage. And it's so clearly wrong.
I could use Po's advice—but he wasn't in the castle when we left this morning.

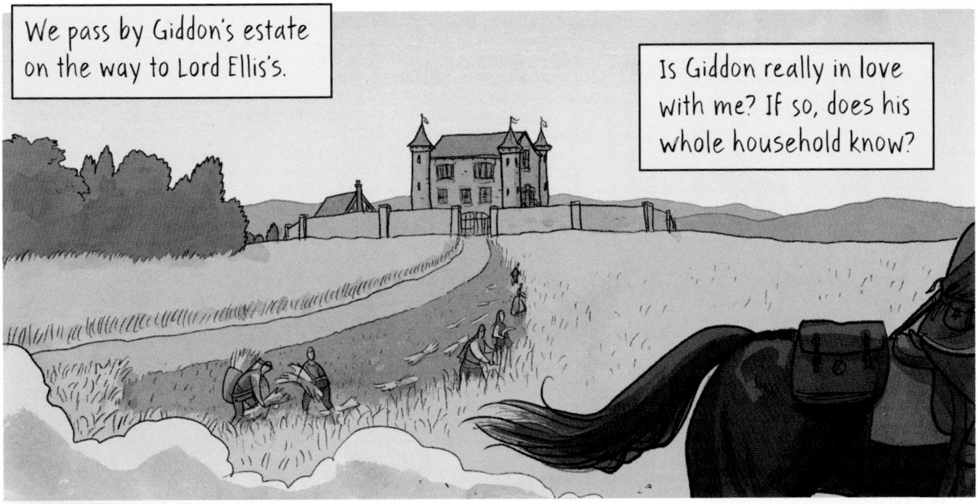
We pass by Giddon's estate on the way to Lord Ellis's.
Is Giddon really in love with me? If so, does his whole household know?

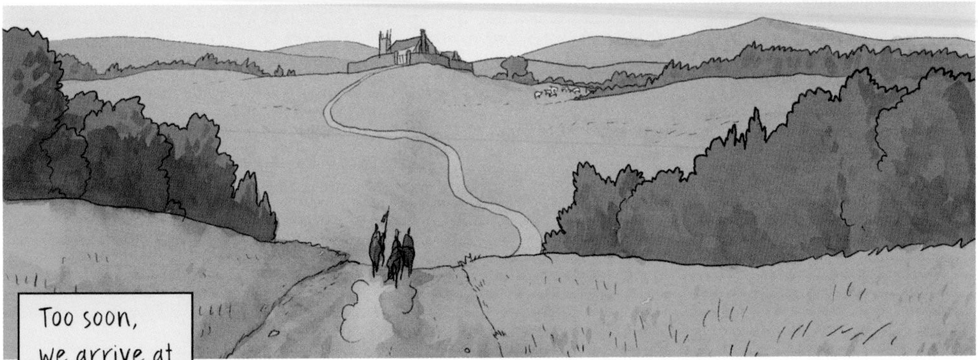
Too soon, we arrive at Ellis's estate.

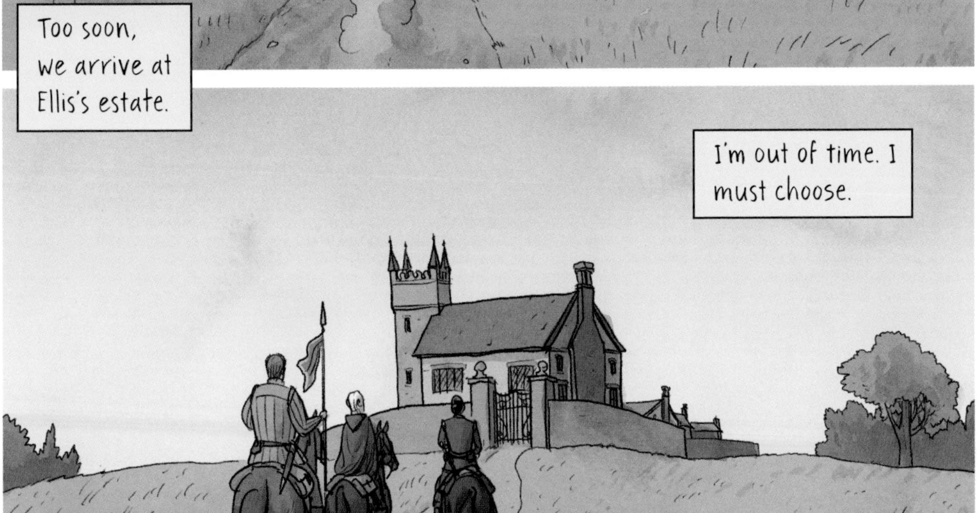
I'm out of time. I must choose.

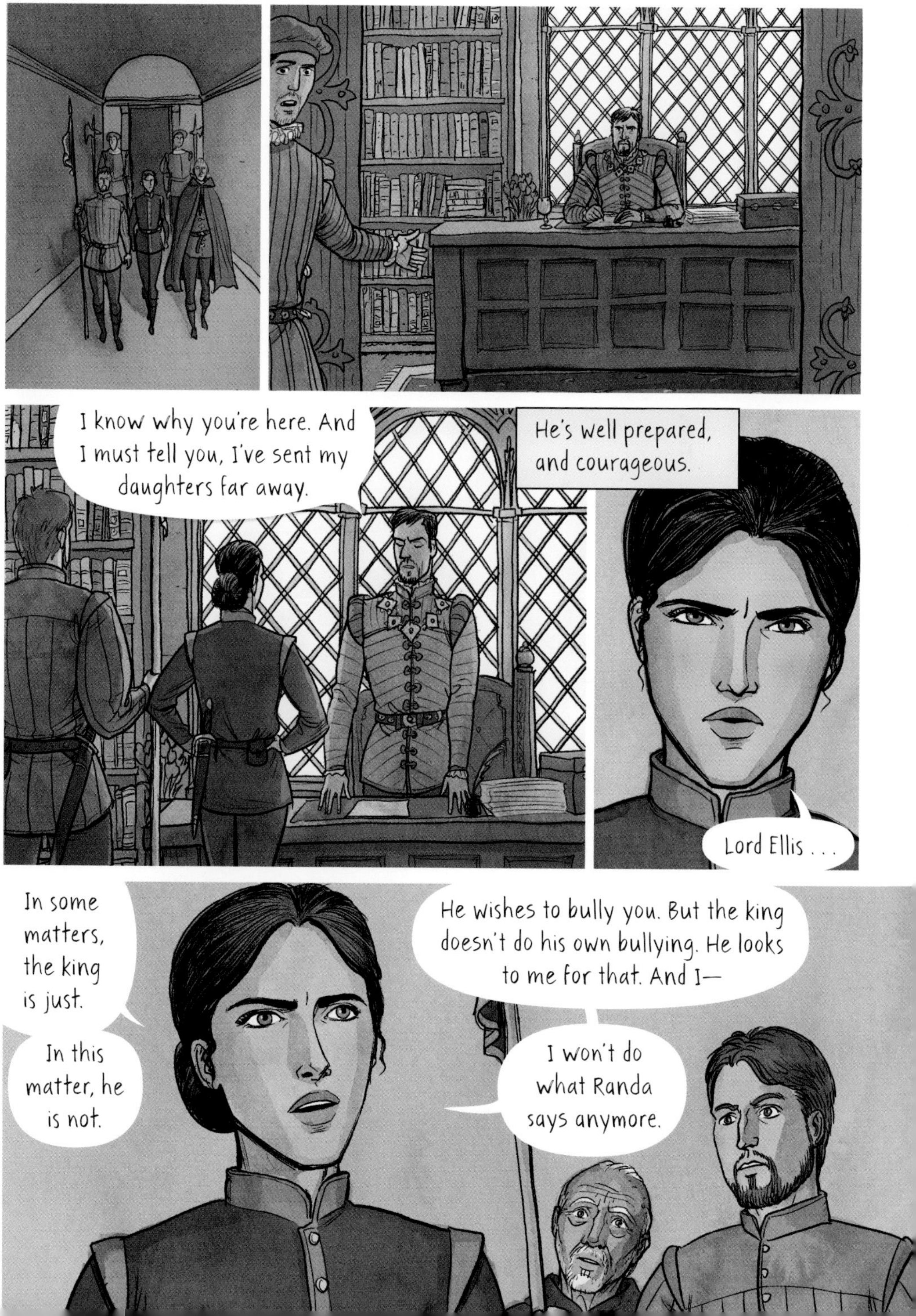
I know why you're here. And I must tell you, I've sent my daughters far away.
He's well prepared, and courageous.
Lord Ellis . . .
In some matters, the king is just.
In this matter, he is not.
He wishes to bully you. But the king doesn't do his own bullying. He looks to me for that. And I—
I won't do what Randa says anymore.

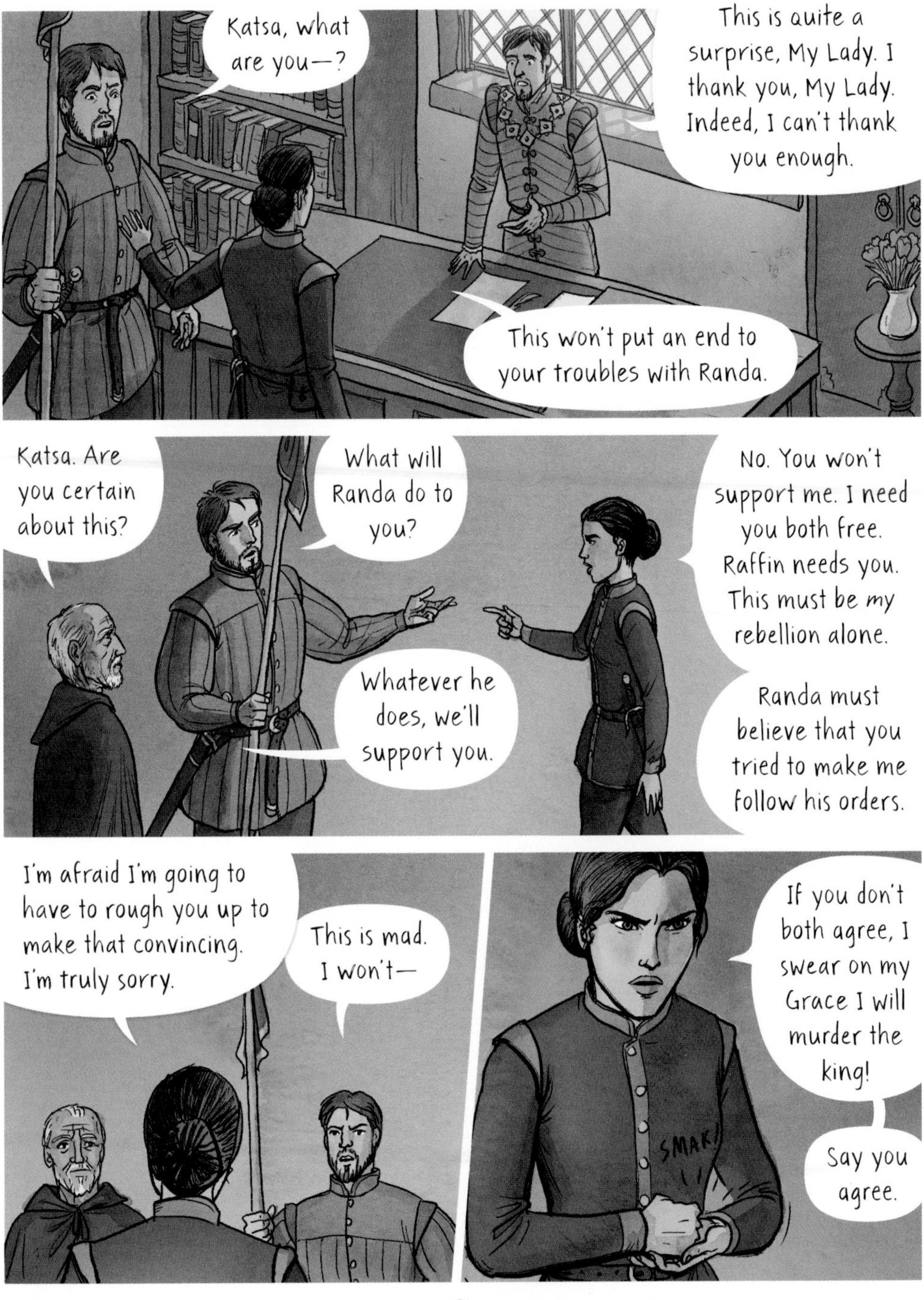
Katsa, what are you—?
This is quite a surprise, My Lady. I thank you, My Lady. Indeed, I can't thank you enough.
This won't put an end to your troubles with Randa.
Katsa. Are you certain about this?
What will Randa do to you?
Whatever he does, we'll support you.
No. You won't support me. I need you both free. Raffin needs you. This must be my rebellion alone.
Randa must believe that you tried to make me follow his orders.
I'm afraid I'm going to have to rough you up to make that convincing. I'm truly sorry.
This is mad. I won't—
If you don't both agree, I swear on my Grace I will murder the king!
SMAK!
Say you agree.

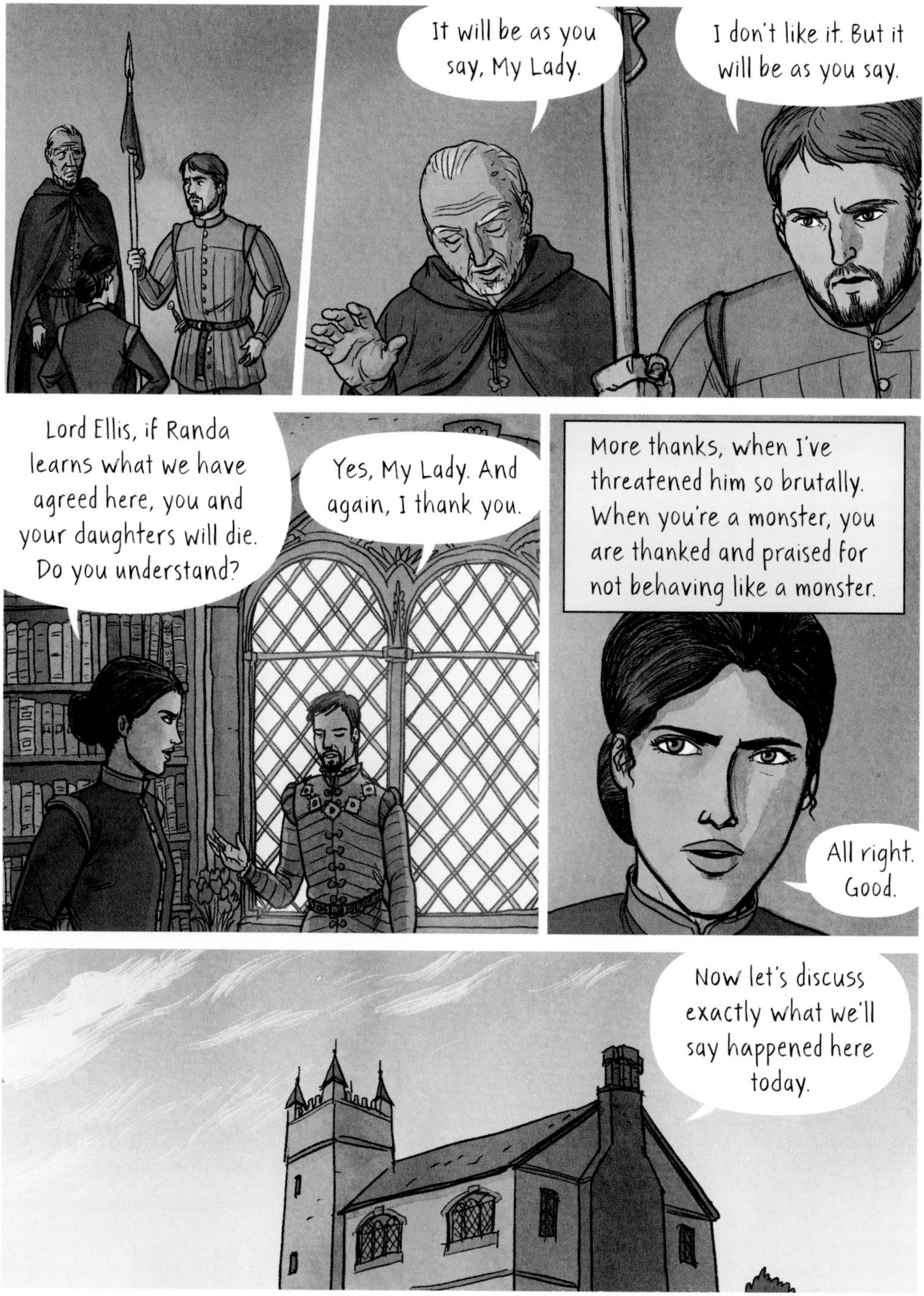
It will be as you say, My Lady.
I don't like it. But it will be as you say.
Lord Ellis, if Randa learns what we have agreed here, you and your daughters will die. Do you understand?
Yes, My Lady. And again, I thank you.
More thanks, when I've threatened him so brutally. When you're a monster, you are thanked and praised for not behaving like a monster.
All right. Good.
Now let's discuss exactly what we'll say happened here today.

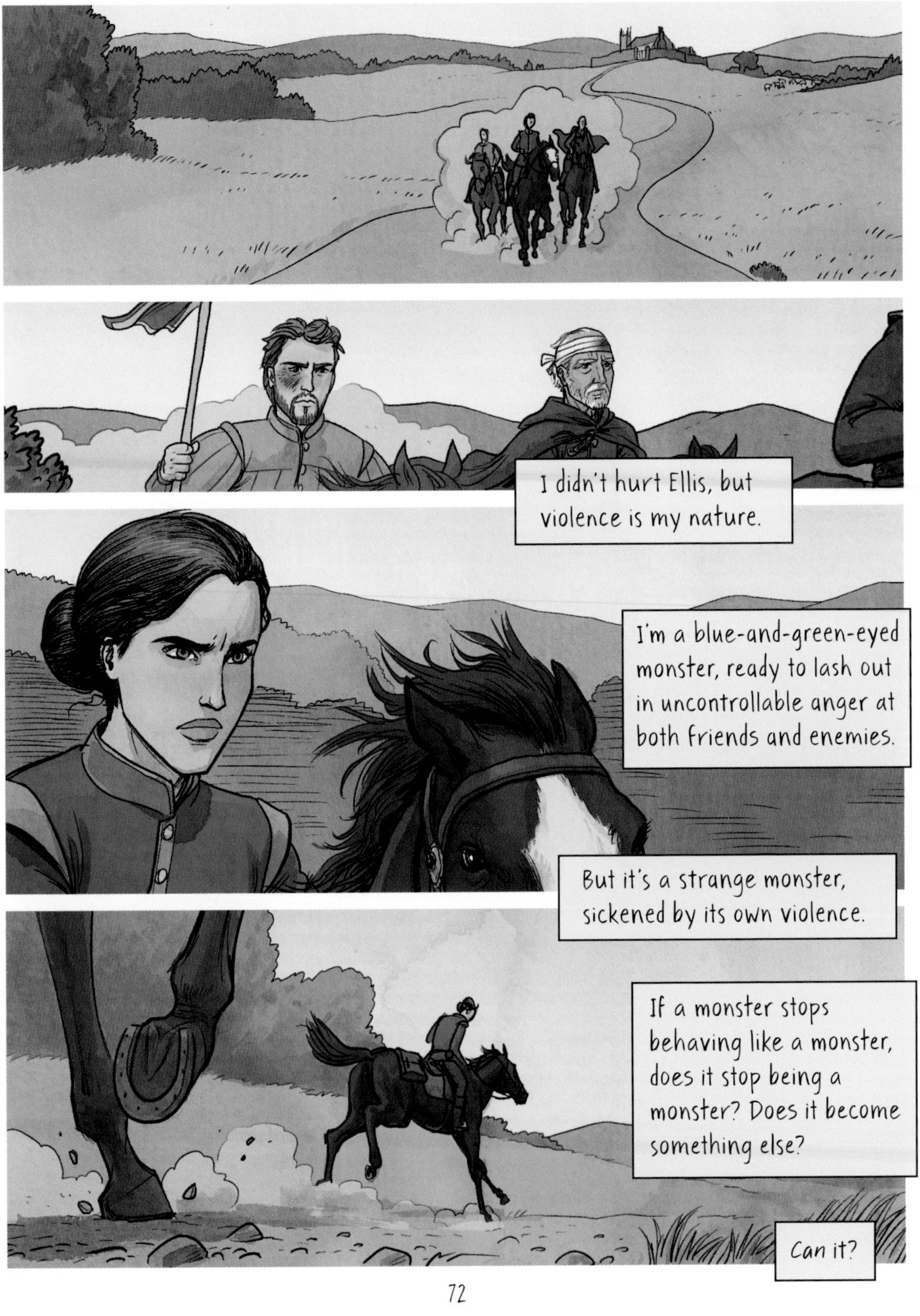
I didn't hurt Ellis, but violence is my nature.
I'm a blue-and-green-eyed monster, ready to lash out in uncontrollable anger at both friends and enemies.
But it's a strange monster, sickened by its own violence.
If a monster stops behaving like a monster, does it stop being a monster? Does it become something else?
Can it?

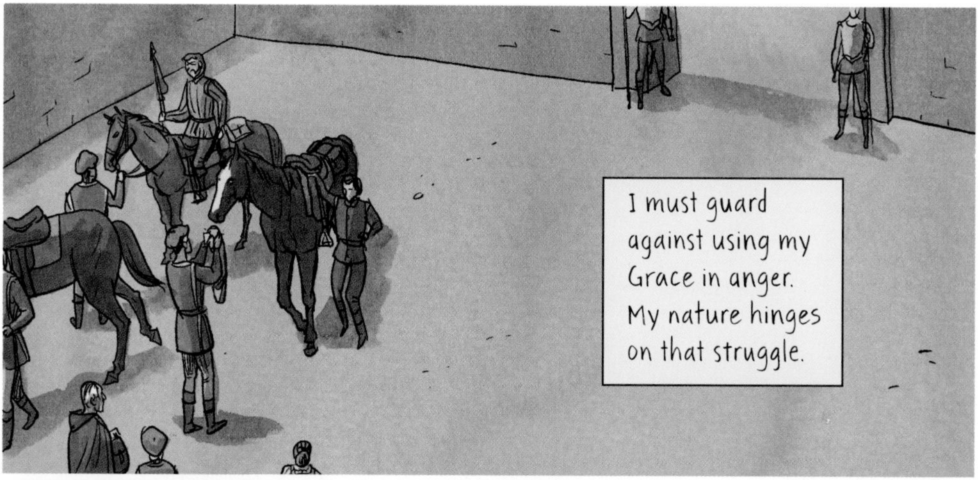
I must guard against using my Grace in anger. My nature hinges on that struggle.

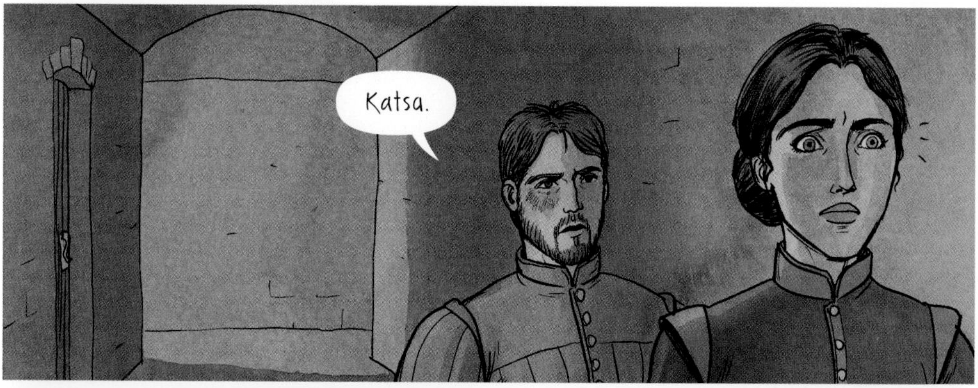
Katsa.

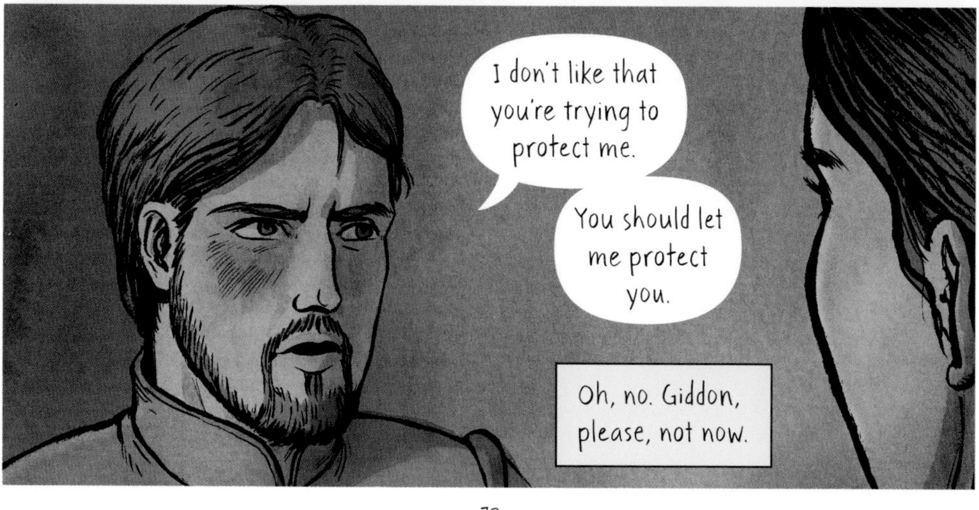
I don't like that you're trying to protect me.
You should let me protect you.
Oh, no. Giddon, please, not now.

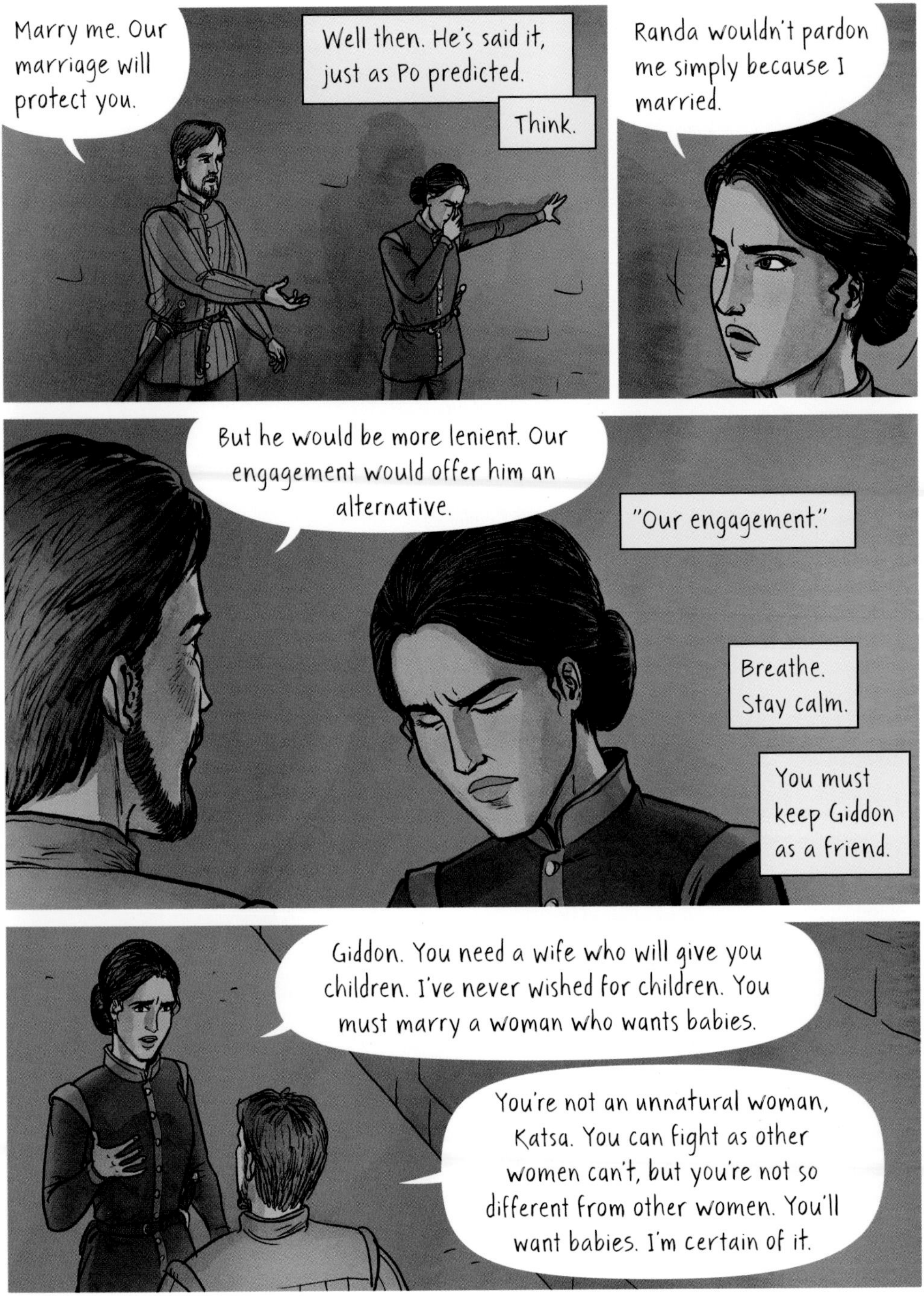
Marry me. Our marriage will protect you.
Well then. He's said it, just as Po predicted.
Think.
Randa wouldn't pardon me simply because I married.
But he would be more lenient. Our engagement would offer him an alternative.
"Our engagement."
Breathe. Stay calm.
You must keep Giddon as a friend.
Giddon. You need a wife who will give you children. I've never wished for children. You must marry a woman who wants babies.
You're not an unnatural woman, Katsa. You can fight as other women can't, but you're not so different from other women. You'll want babies. I'm certain of it.

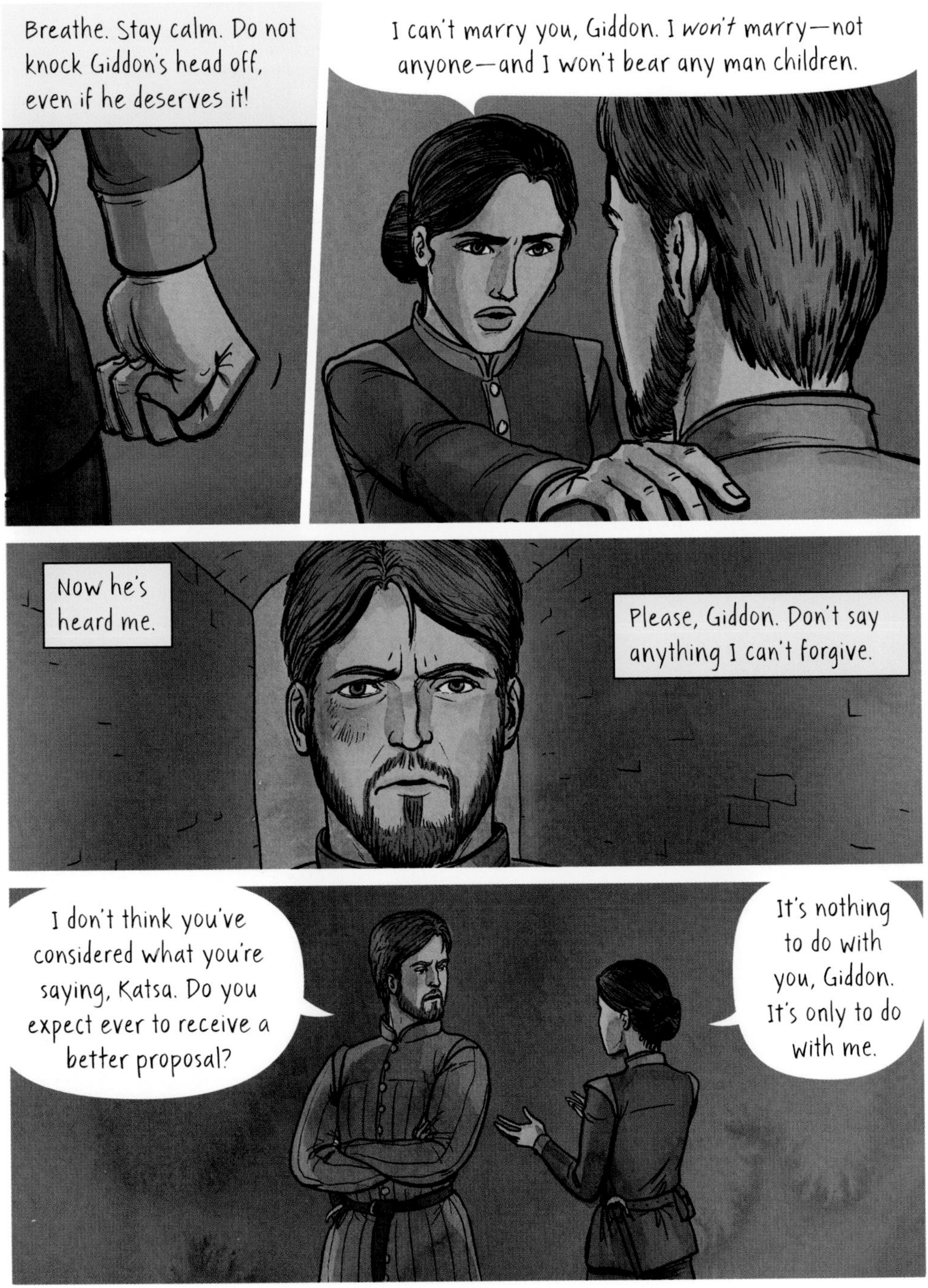
Breathe. Stay calm. Do not knock Giddon's head off, even if he deserves it!
I can't marry you, Giddon. I *won't* marry—not anyone—and I won't bear any man children.
Now he's heard me.
Please, Giddon. Don't say anything I can't forgive.
I don't think you've considered what you're saying, Katsa. Do you expect ever to receive a better proposal?
It's nothing to do with you, Giddon. It's only to do with me.

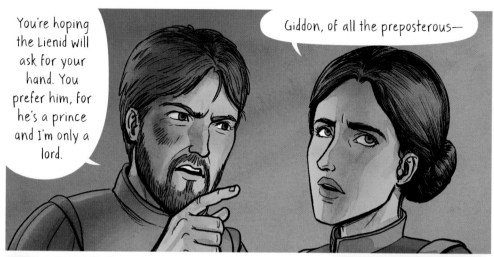

You're hoping the Lienid will ask for your hand. You prefer him, for he's a prince and I'm only a lord.

Giddon, of all the preposterous—

He won't ask you—and if he did you'd be a fool to accept. He's about as trustworthy as Murgon.

Giddon, I assure you—

A man who fights you as he does is no more than an opportunist and a scoundrel.

No more than an opportunist and a scoundrel. The exact words Po used.

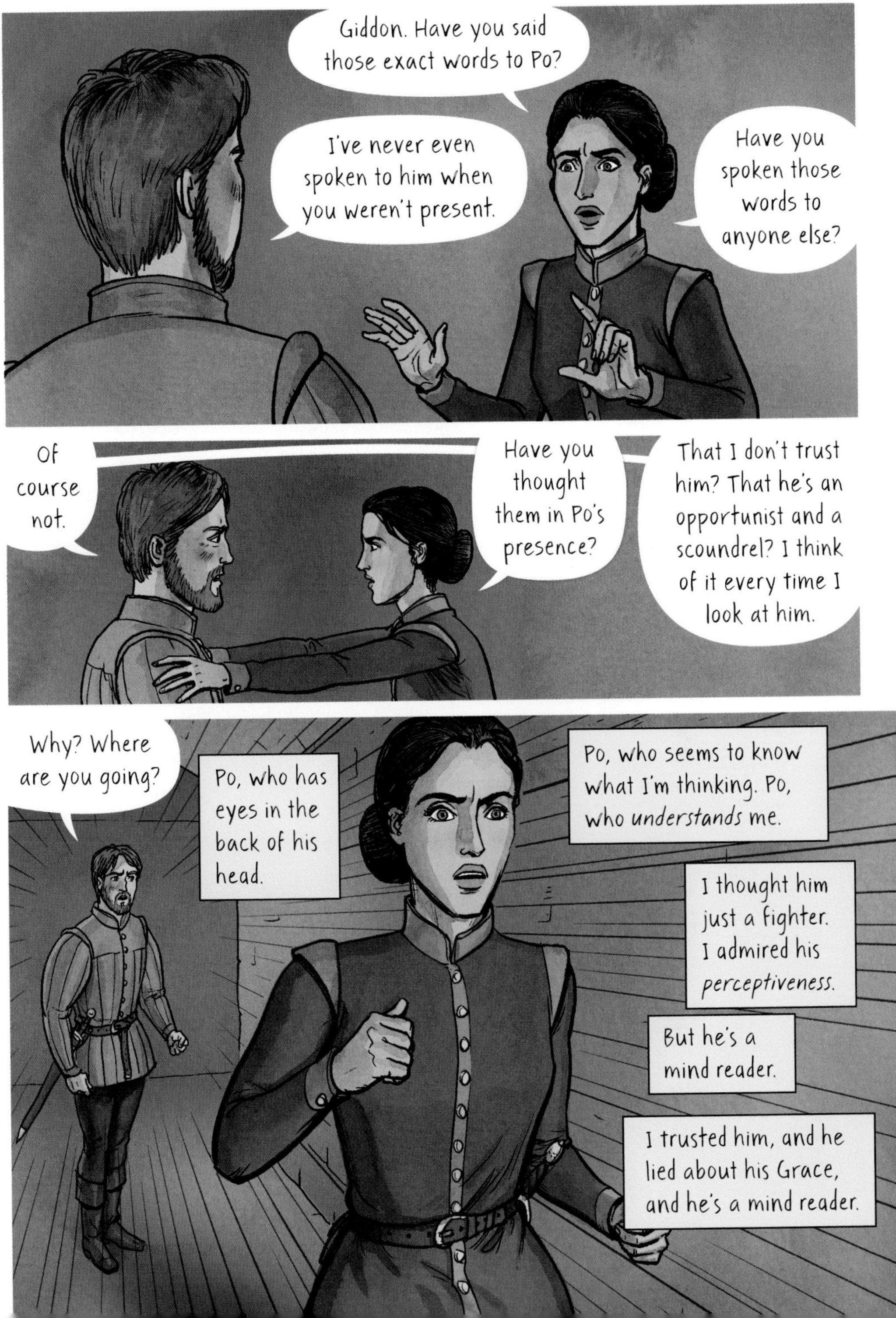
Giddon. Have you said those exact words to Po?
I've never even spoken to him when you weren't present.
Have you spoken those words to anyone else?
Of course not.
Have you thought them in Po's presence?
That I don't trust him? That he's an opportunist and a scoundrel? I think of it every time I look at him.
Why? Where are you going?
Po, who has eyes in the back of his head.
Po, who seems to know what I'm thinking. Po, who *understands* me.
I thought him just a fighter. I admired his *perceptiveness*.
But he's a mind reader.
I trusted him, and he lied about his Grace, and he's a mind reader.

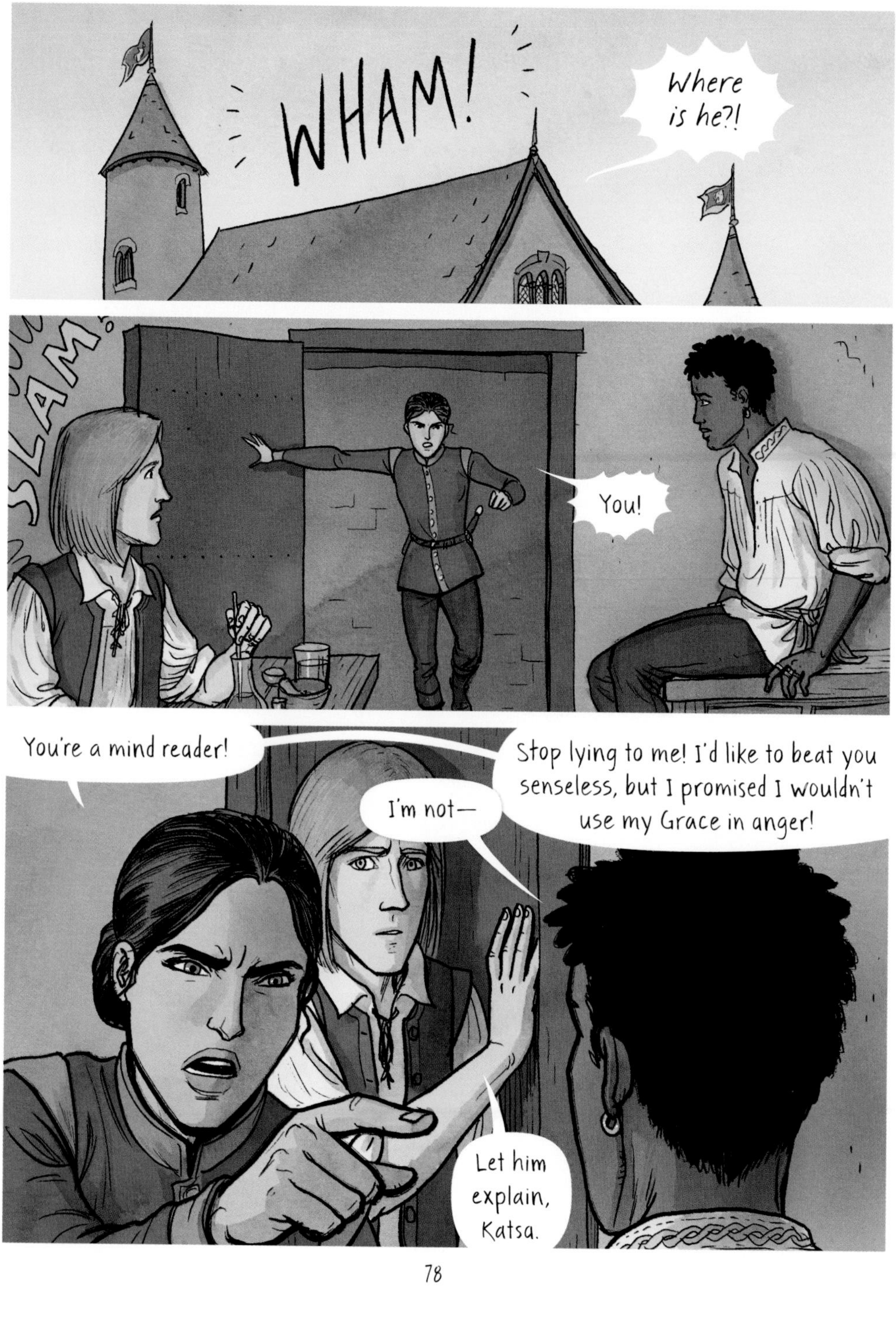
WHAM!
Where is he?!
SLAM!
You!
You're a mind reader!
Stop lying to me! I'd like to beat you senseless, but I promised I wouldn't use my Grace in anger!
I'm not—
Let him explain, Katsa.

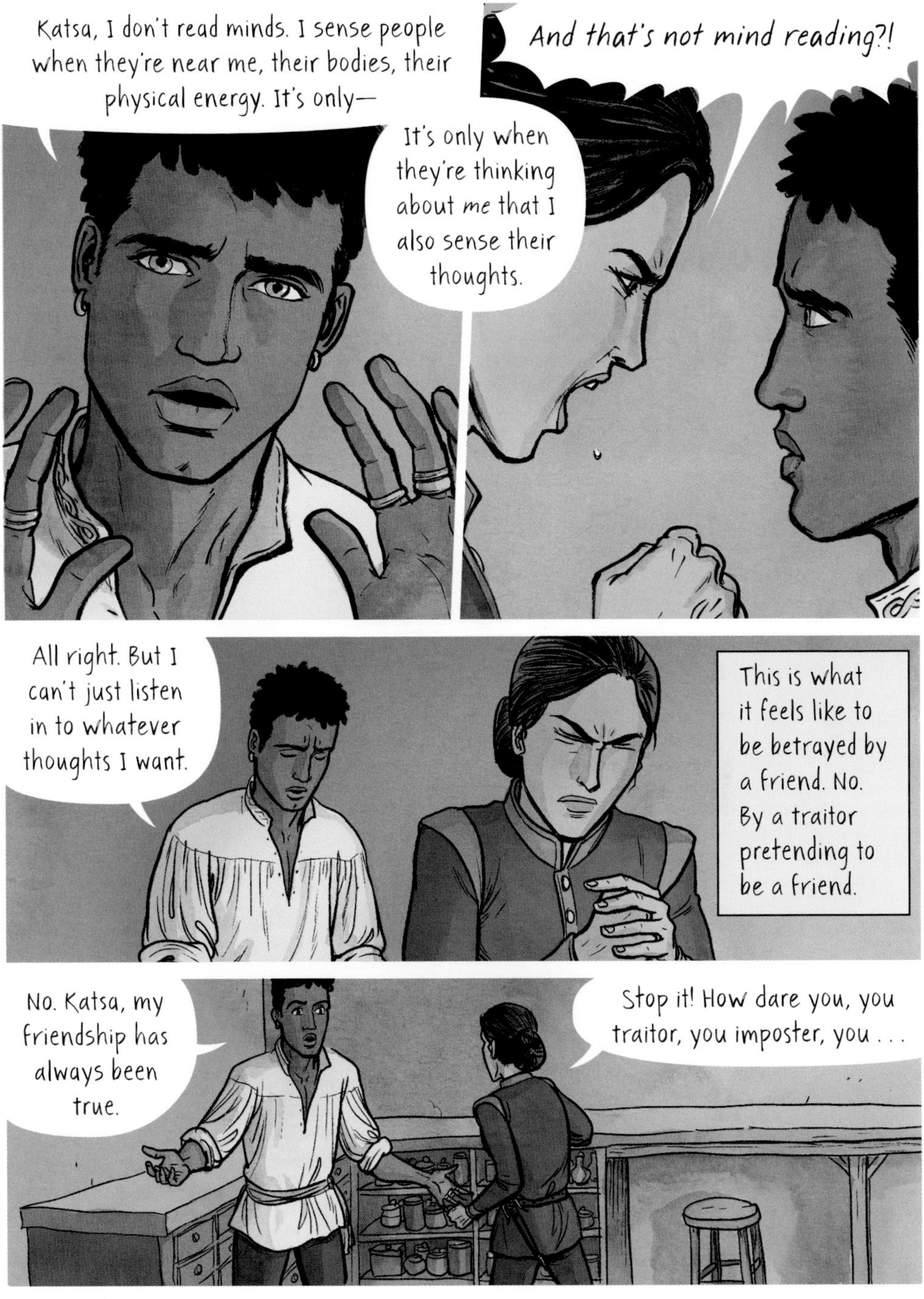
Katsa, I don't read minds. I sense people when they're near me, their bodies, their physical energy. It's only—
It's only when they're thinking about *me* that I also sense their thoughts.
And that's not mind reading?!
All right. But I can't just listen in to whatever thoughts I want.
This is what it feels like to be betrayed by a friend. No. By a traitor pretending to be a friend.
No. Katsa, my friendship has always been true.
Stop it! How dare you, you traitor, you imposter, you . . .

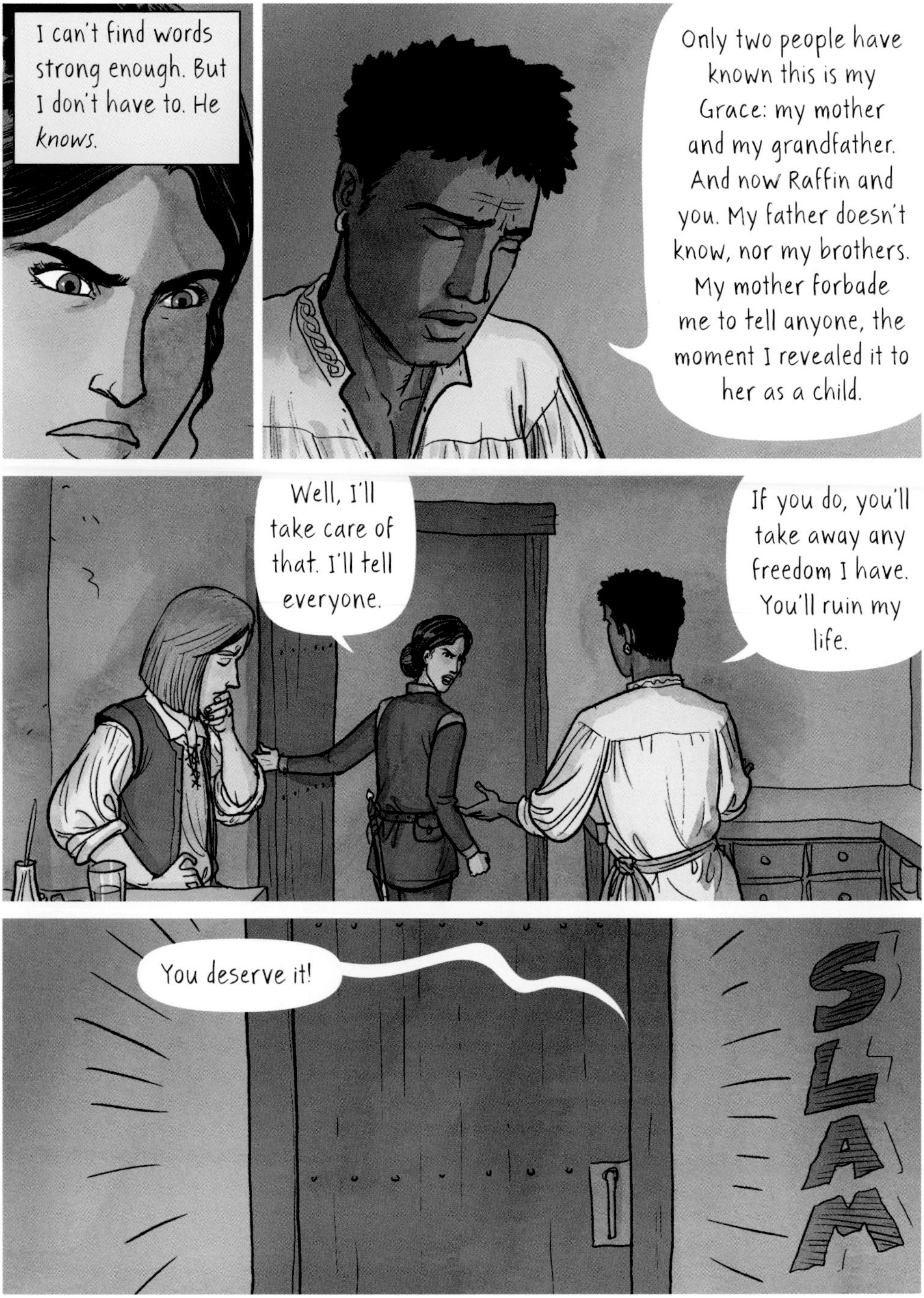
I can't find words strong enough. But I don't have to. He *knows*.
Only two people have known this is my Grace: my mother and my grandfather. And now Raffin and you. My father doesn't know, nor my brothers. My mother forbade me to tell anyone, the moment I revealed it to her as a child.
Well, I'll take care of that. I'll tell everyone.
If you do, you'll take away any freedom I have. You'll ruin my life.
You deserve it!
SLAM

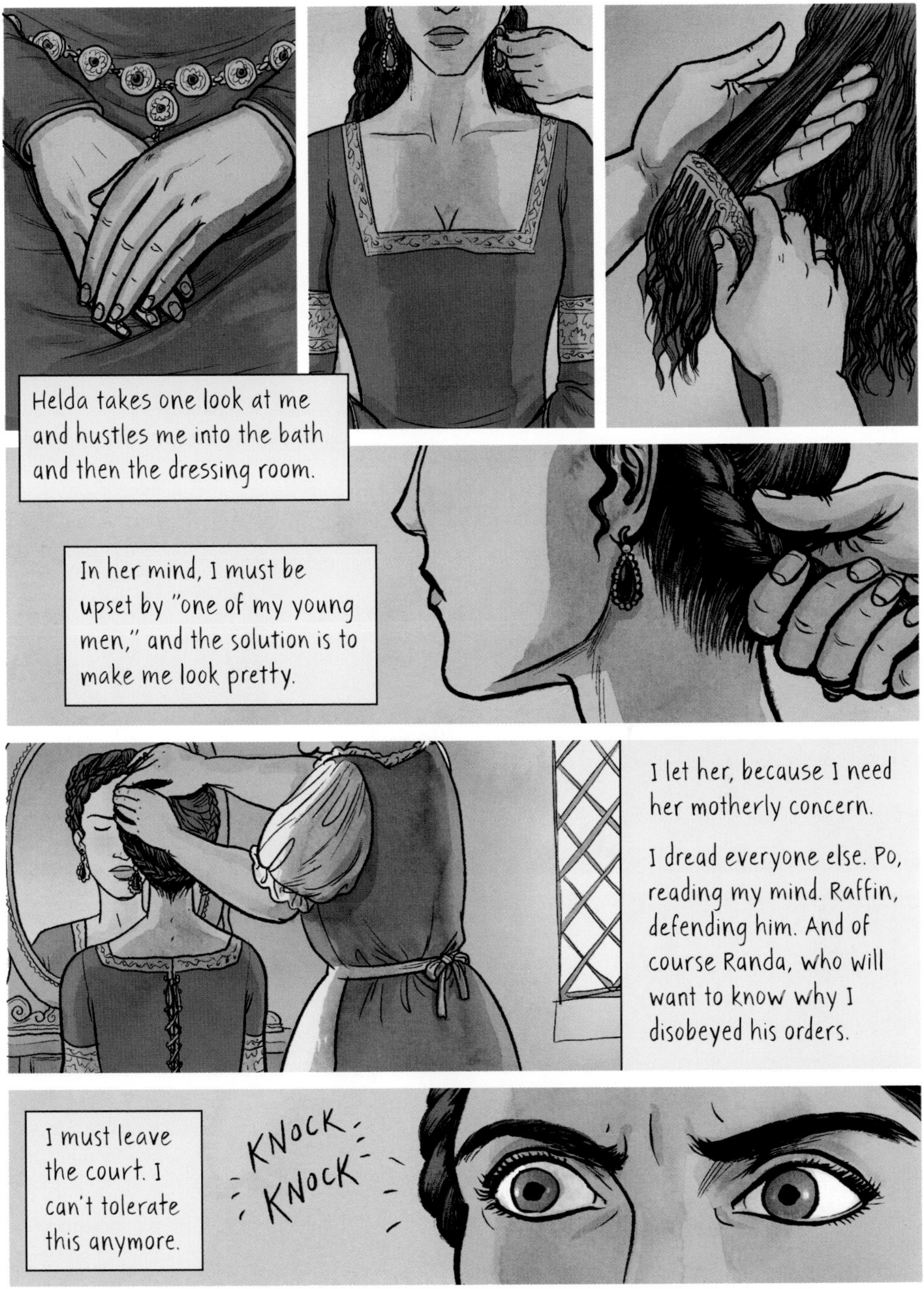
Helda takes one look at me and hustles me into the bath and then the dressing room.
In her mind, I must be upset by "one of my young men," and the solution is to make me look pretty.
I let her, because I need her motherly concern.
I dread everyone else. Po, reading my mind. Raffin, defending him. And of course Randa, who will want to know why I disobeyed his orders.
I must leave the court. I can't tolerate this anymore.
KNOCK KNOCK

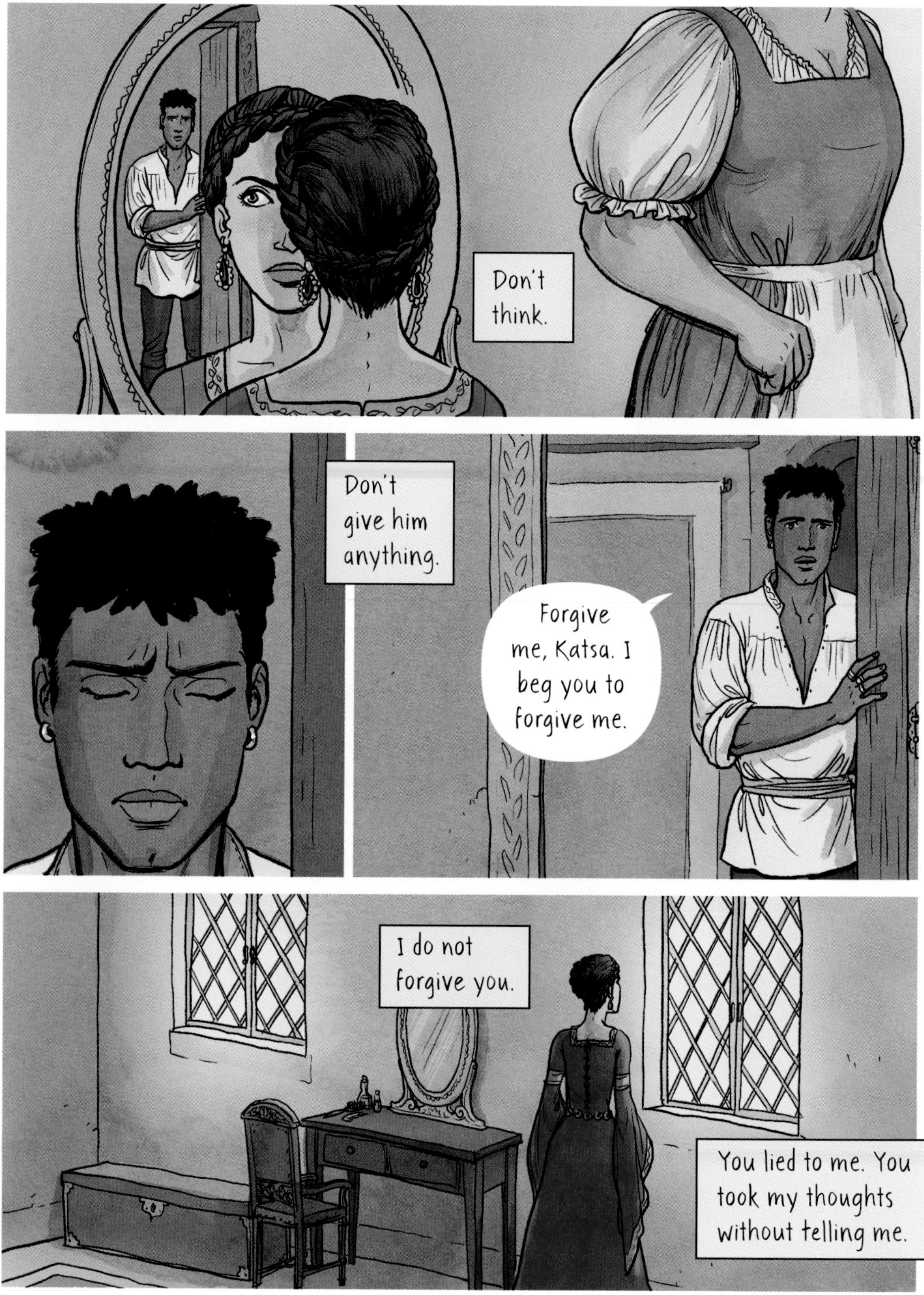
Don't think.
Don't give him anything.
Forgive me, Katsa. I beg you to forgive me.
I do not forgive you.
You lied to me. You took my thoughts without telling me.

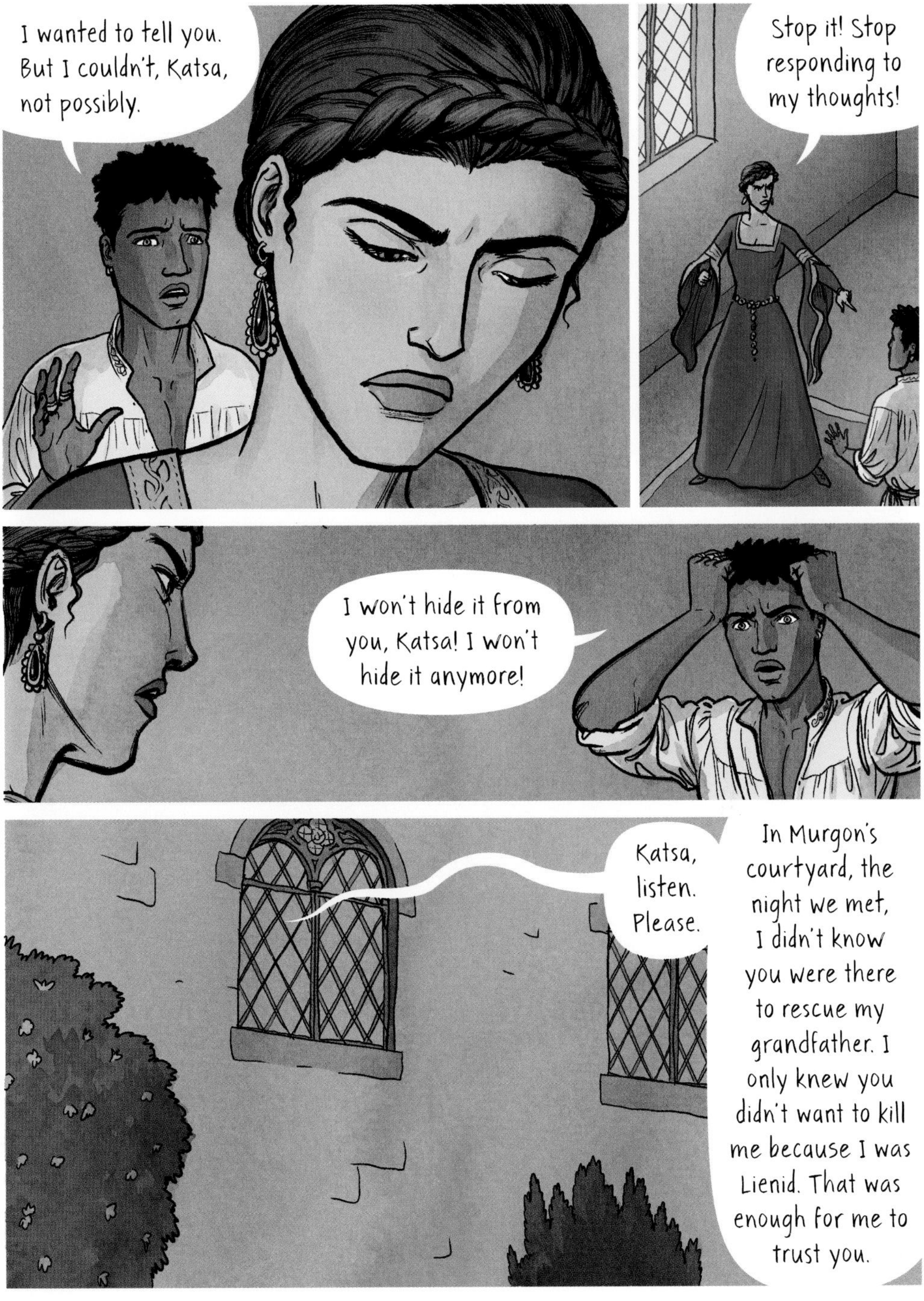

I wanted to tell you. But I couldn't, Katsa, not possibly.
Stop it! Stop responding to my thoughts!
I won't hide it from you, Katsa! I won't hide it anymore!
Katsa, listen. Please.
In Murgon's courtyard, the night we met, I didn't know you were there to rescue my grandfather. I only knew you didn't want to kill me because I was Lienid. That was enough for me to trust you.

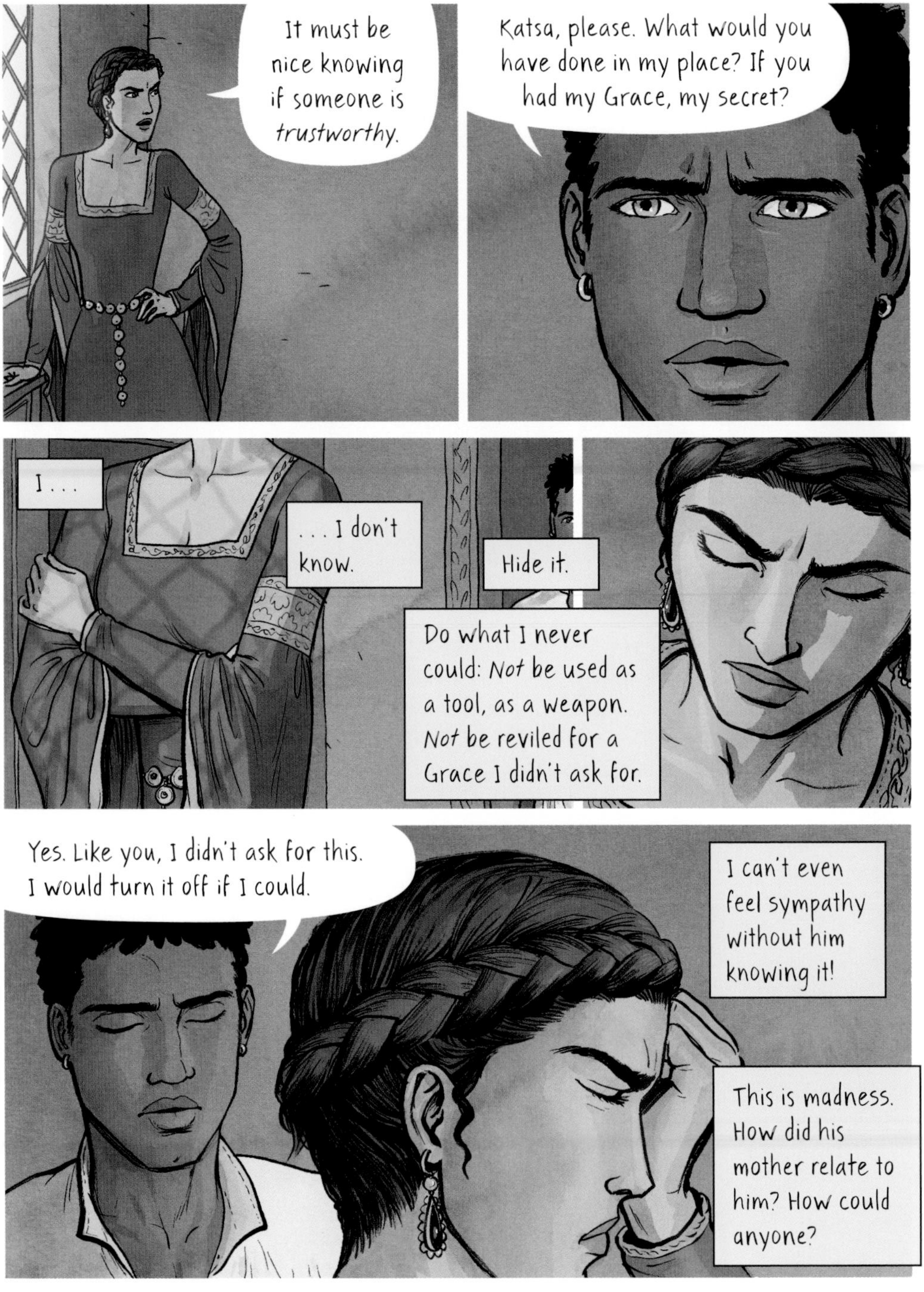

It must be nice knowing if someone is *trustworthy*.
Katsa, please. What would you have done in my place? If you had my Grace, my secret?
I . . .
. . . I don't know.
Hide it.
Do what I never could: *Not* be used as a tool, as a weapon. *Not* be reviled for a Grace I didn't ask for.
Yes. Like you, I didn't ask for this. I would turn it off if I could.
I can't even feel sympathy without him knowing it!
This is madness. How did his mother relate to him? How could anyone?

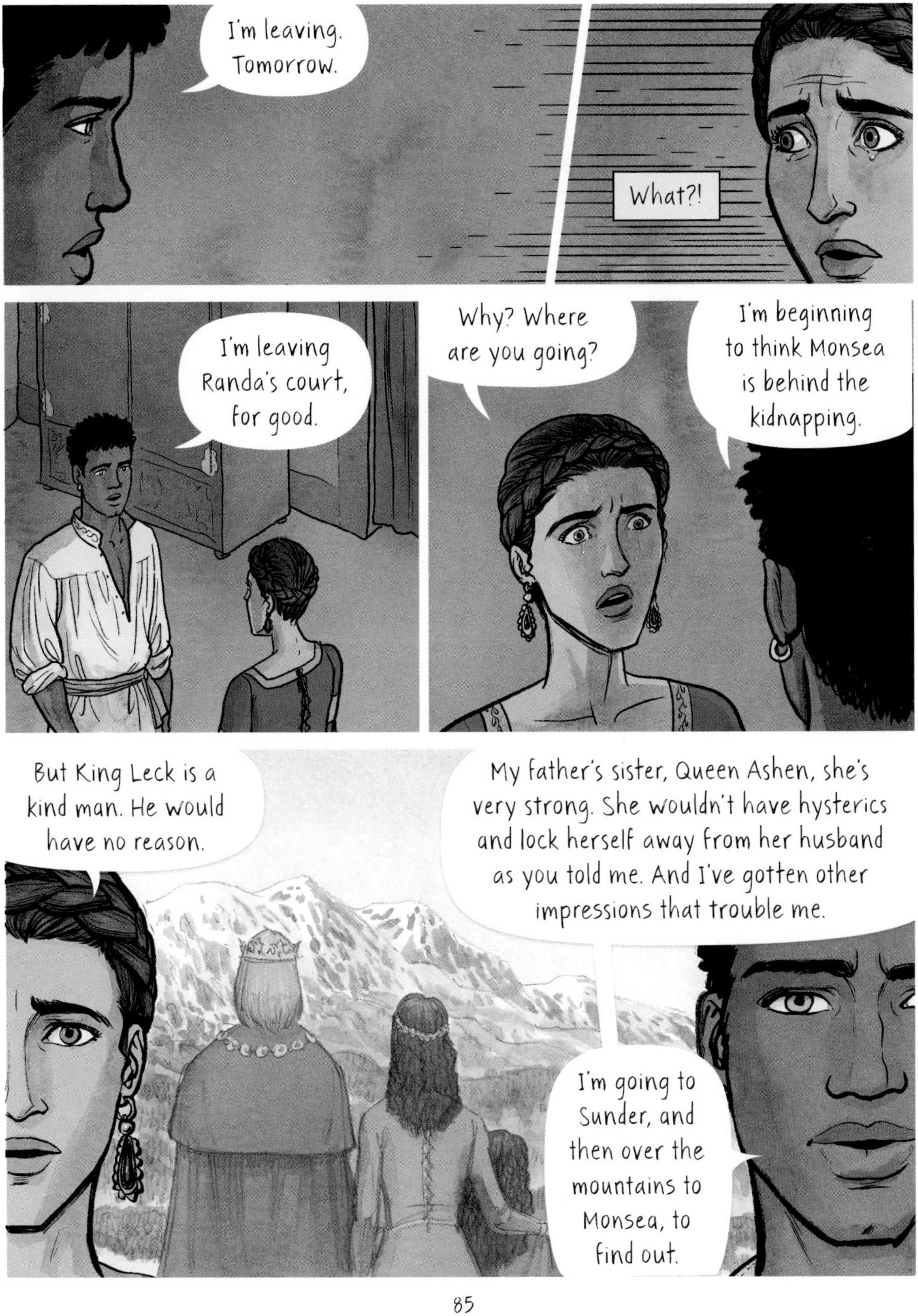
I'm leaving. Tomorrow.
What?!
I'm leaving Randa's court, for good.
Why? Where are you going?
I'm beginning to think Monsea is behind the kidnapping.
But King Leck is a kind man. He would have no reason.
My father's sister, Queen Ashen, she's very strong. She wouldn't have hysterics and lock herself away from her husband as you told me. And I've gotten other impressions that trouble me.
I'm going to Sunder, and then over the mountains to Monsea, to find out.

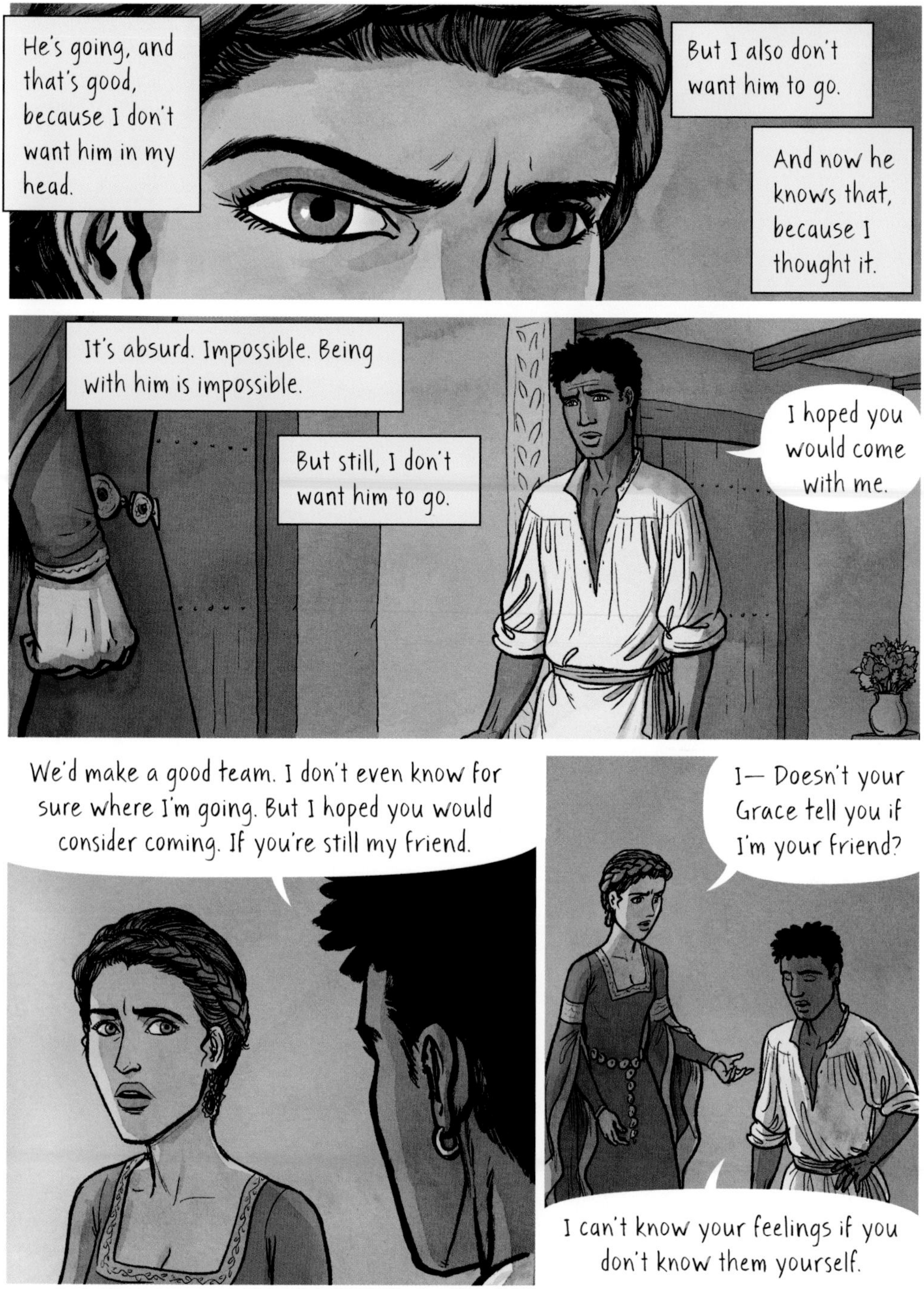
He's going, and that's good, because I don't want him in my head.
But I also don't want him to go.
And now he knows that, because I thought it.
It's absurd. Impossible. Being with him is impossible.
But still, I don't want him to go.
I hoped you would come with me.
We'd make a good team. I don't even know for sure where I'm going. But I hoped you would consider coming. If you're still my friend.
I— Doesn't your Grace tell you if I'm your friend?
I can't know your feelings if you don't know them yourself.

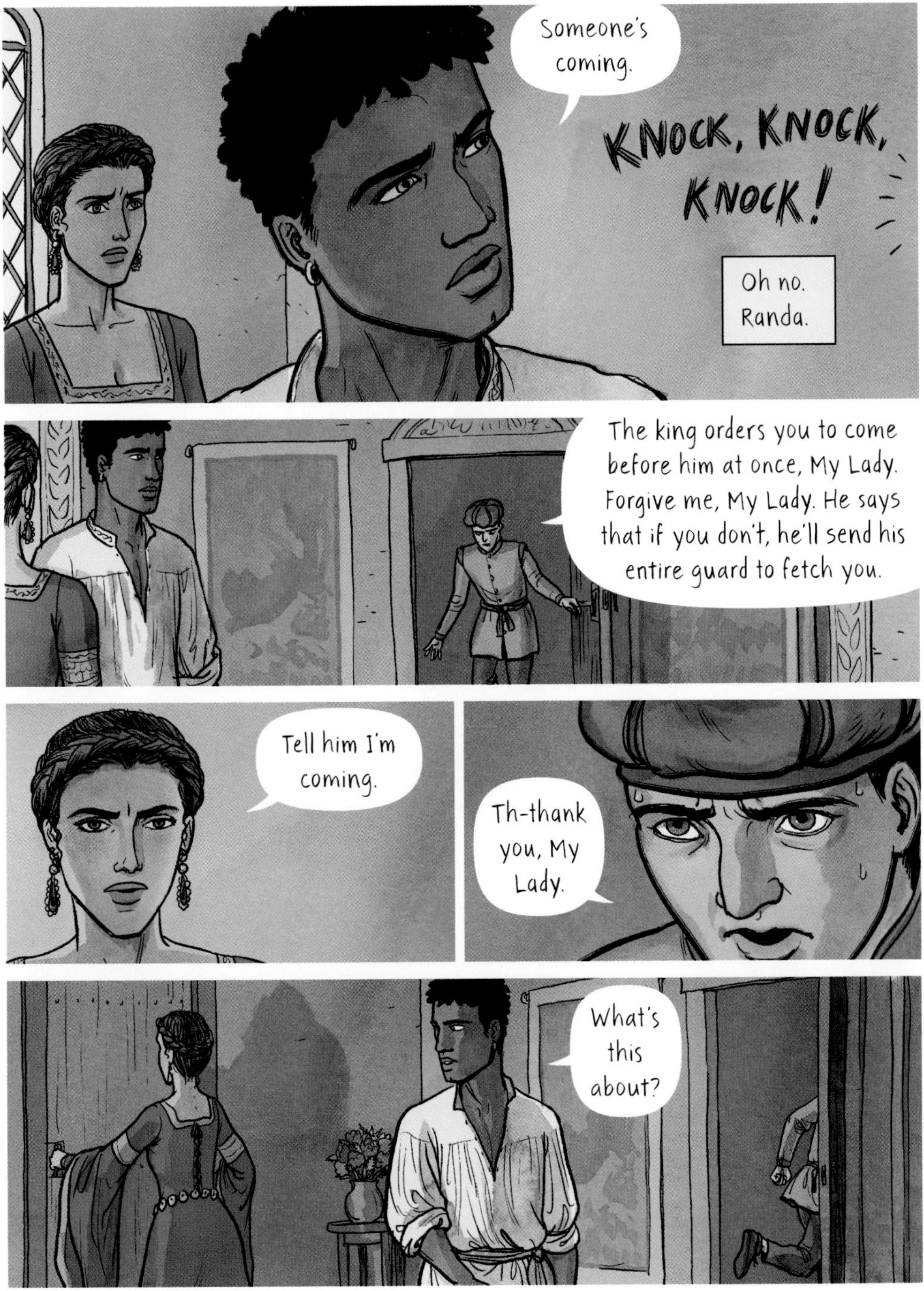
Someone's coming.
KNOCK, KNOCK, KNOCK!
Oh no. Randa.
The king orders you to come before him at once, My Lady. Forgive me, My Lady. He says that if you don't, he'll send his entire guard to fetch you.
Tell him I'm coming.
Th-thank you, My Lady.
What's this about?

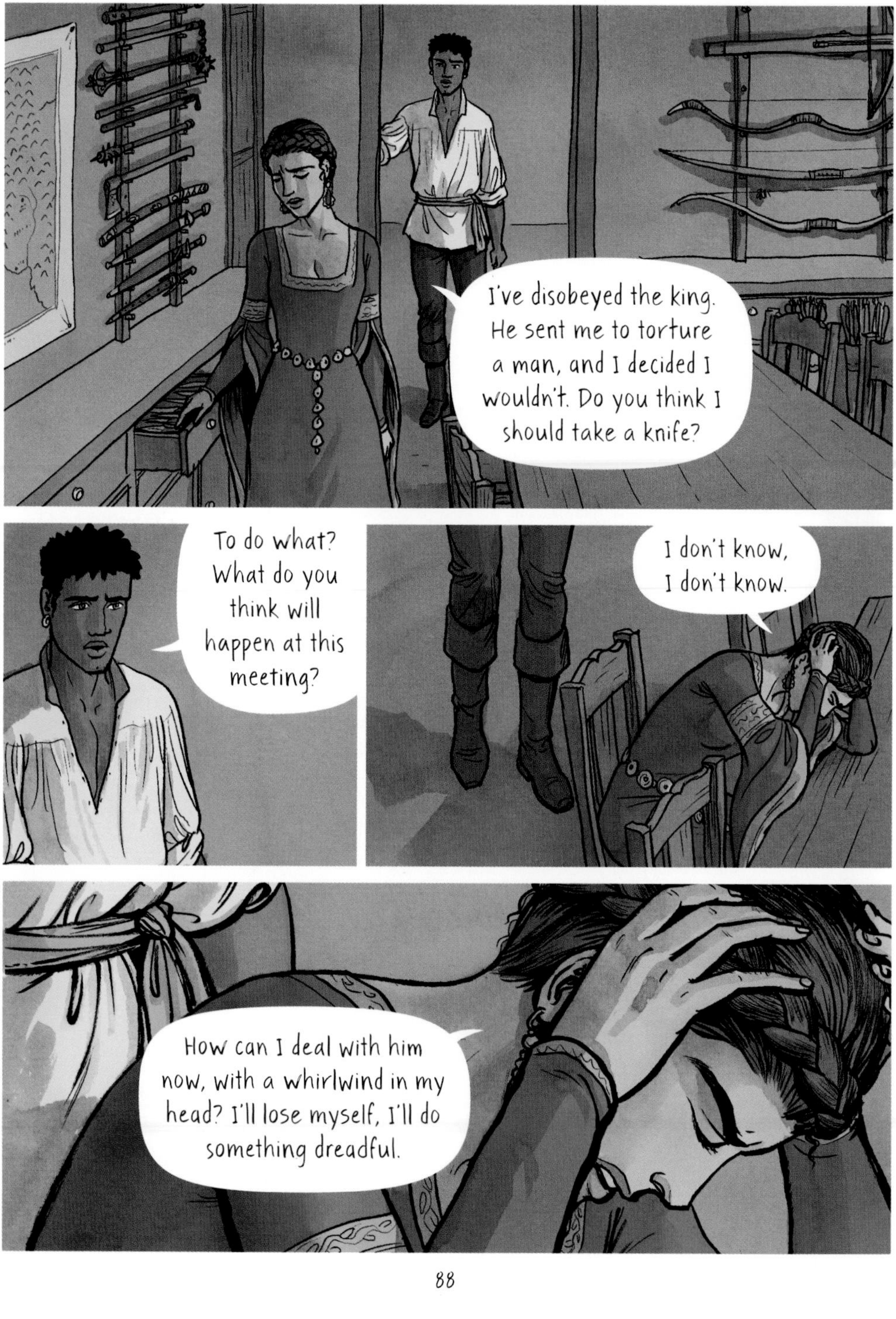
I've disobeyed the king. He sent me to torture a man, and I decided I wouldn't. Do you think I should take a knife?
To do what? What do you think will happen at this meeting?
I don't know, I don't know.
How can I deal with him now, with a whirlwind in my head? I'll lose myself, I'll do something dreadful.

Katsa. Listen to me. You're the most powerful person I've ever met. No one can make you do anything, and your uncle can't touch you. The instant you walk into his presence, you have all the power. If you wish not to hurt him, Katsa, then you have only to choose not to.

But what will I *do*?

You'll figure it out. You only have to go in knowing what you *won't* do. You won't hurt him. You won't let him hurt you. You'll figure the rest out as you go along.

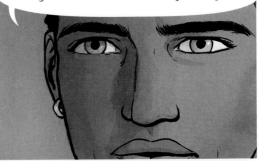

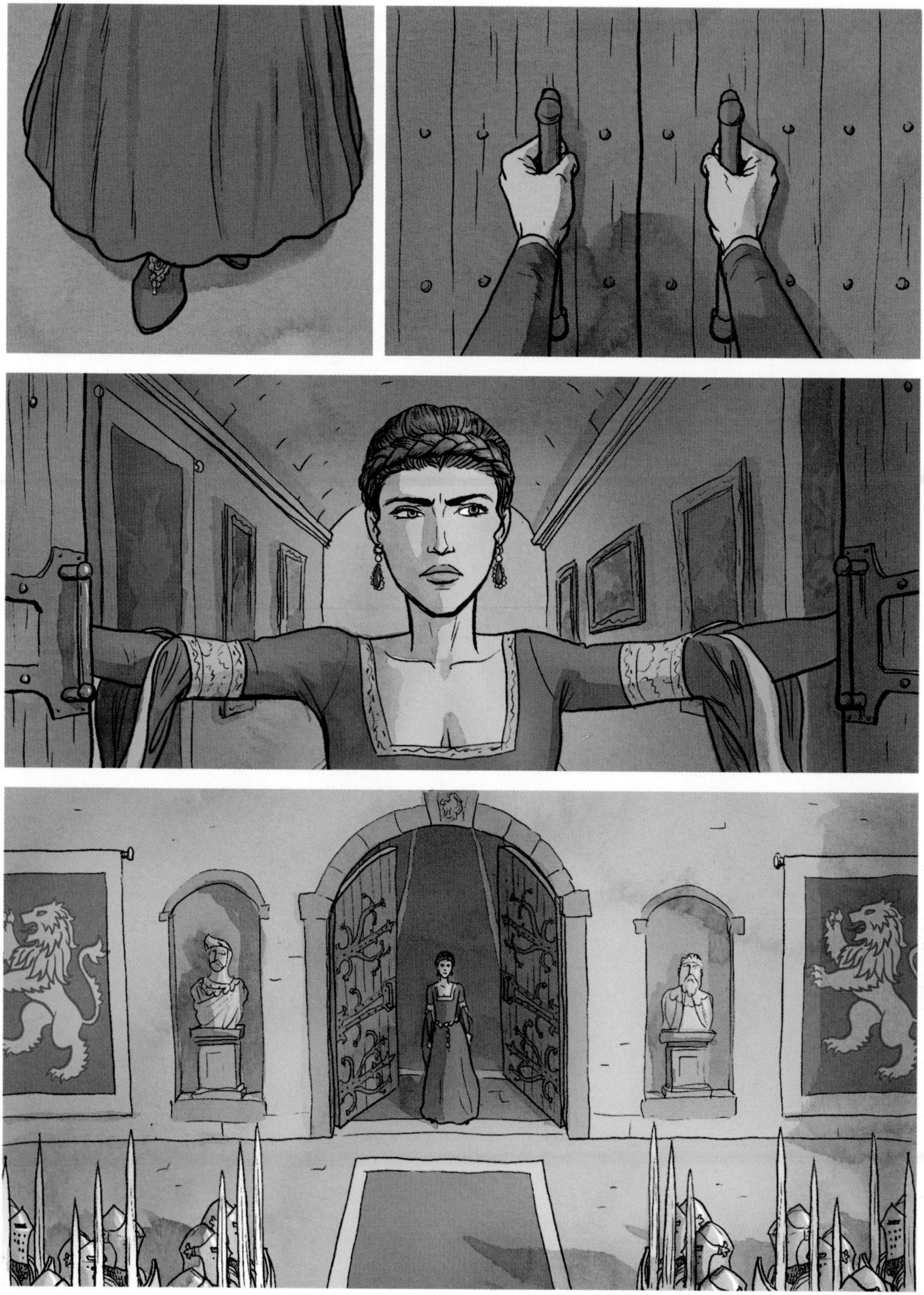

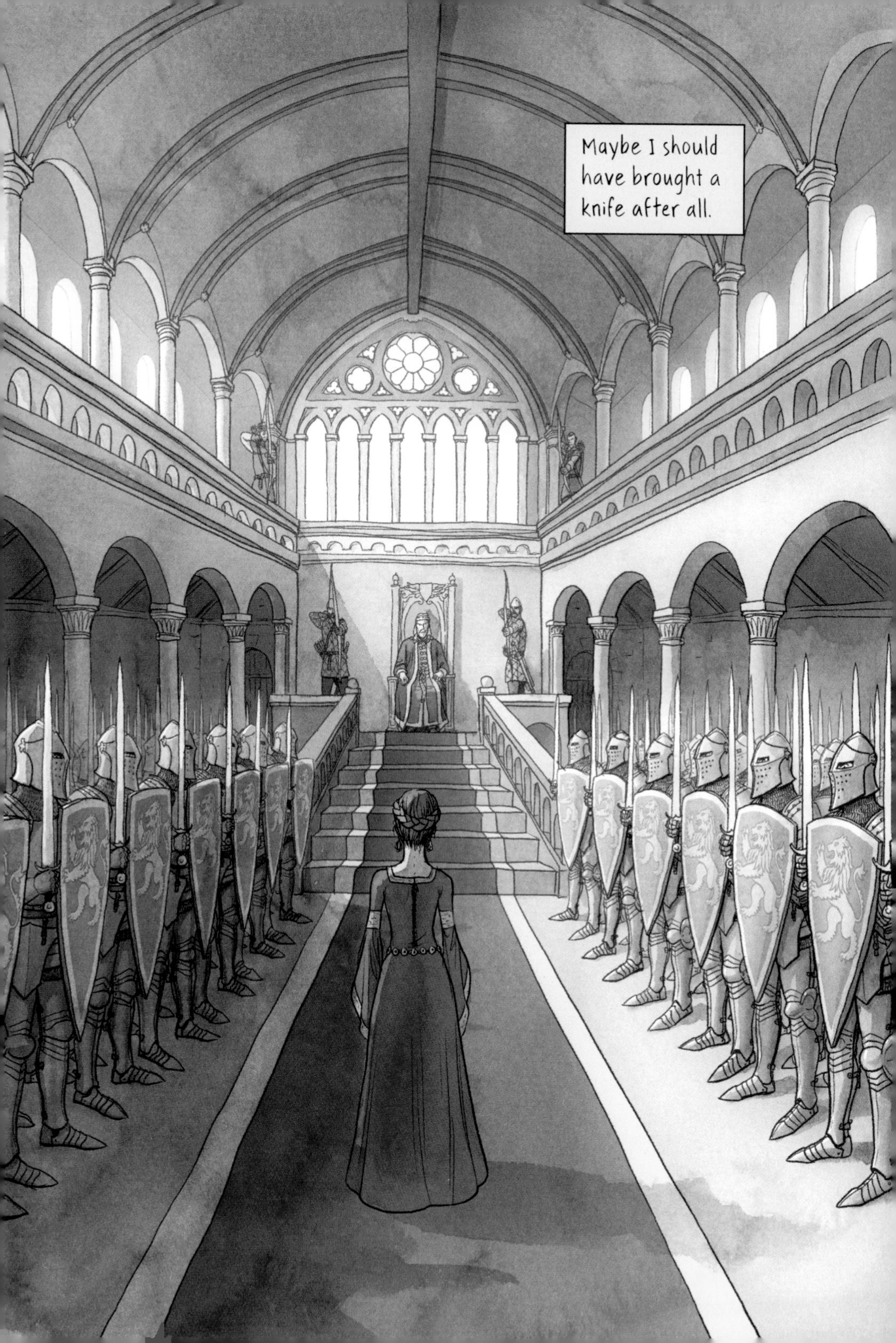
Maybe I should have brought a knife after all.

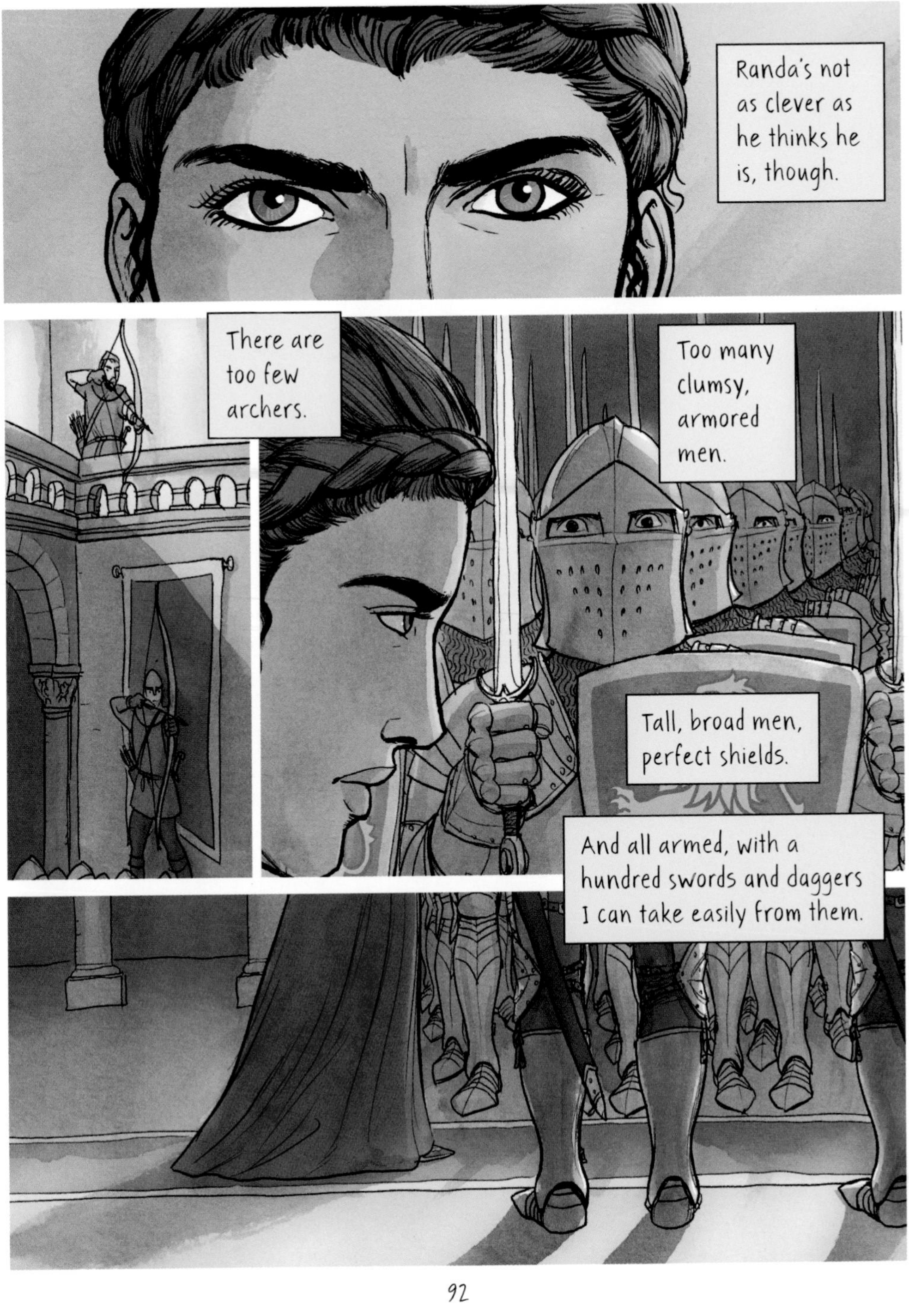

Randa's not as clever as he thinks he is, though.
There are too few archers.
Too many clumsy, armored men.
Tall, broad men, perfect shields.
And all armed, with a hundred swords and daggers I can take easily from them.

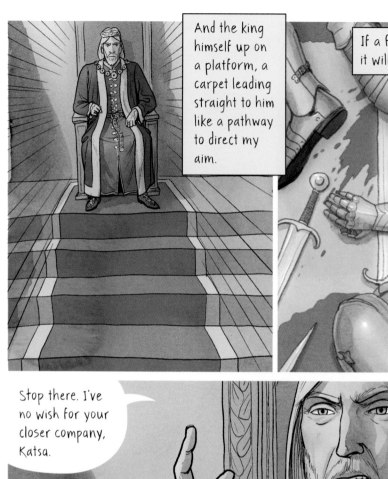

And the king himself up on a platform, a carpet leading straight to him like a pathway to direct my aim.

If a fight erupts here, it will be a massacre.

Stop there. I've no wish for your closer company, Katsa.

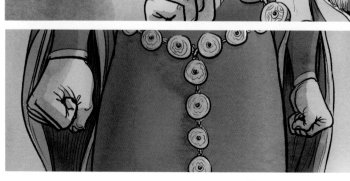

When a battalion of soldiers doesn't trouble me, why does his voice rile me so badly?

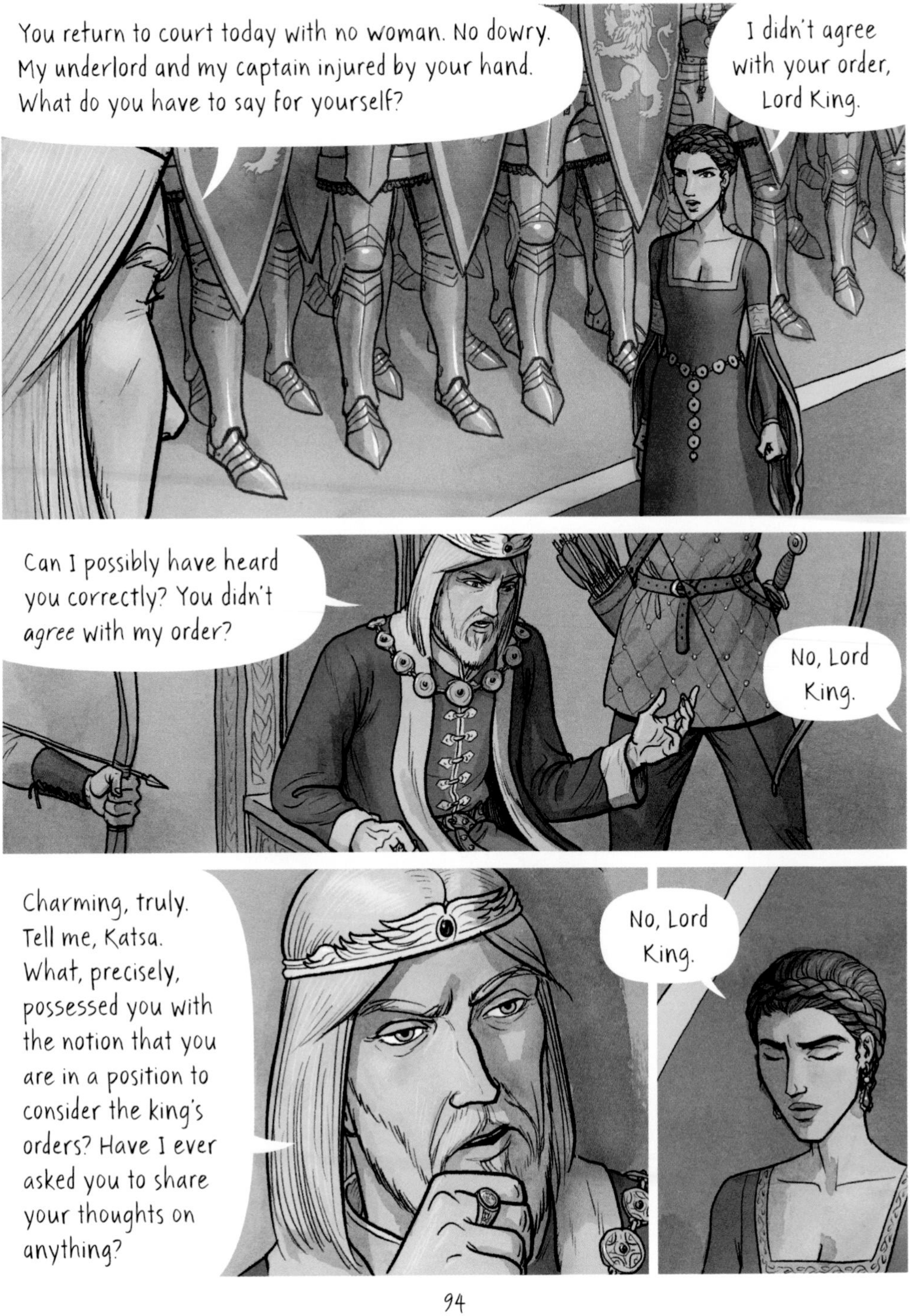
You return to court today with no woman. No dowry. My underlord and my captain injured by your hand. What do you have to say for yourself?
I didn't agree with your order, Lord King.
Can I possibly have heard you correctly? You didn't *agree* with my order?
No, Lord King.
Charming, truly. Tell me, Katsa. What, precisely, possessed you with the notion that you are in a position to consider the king's orders? Have I ever asked you to share your thoughts on anything?
No, Lord King.

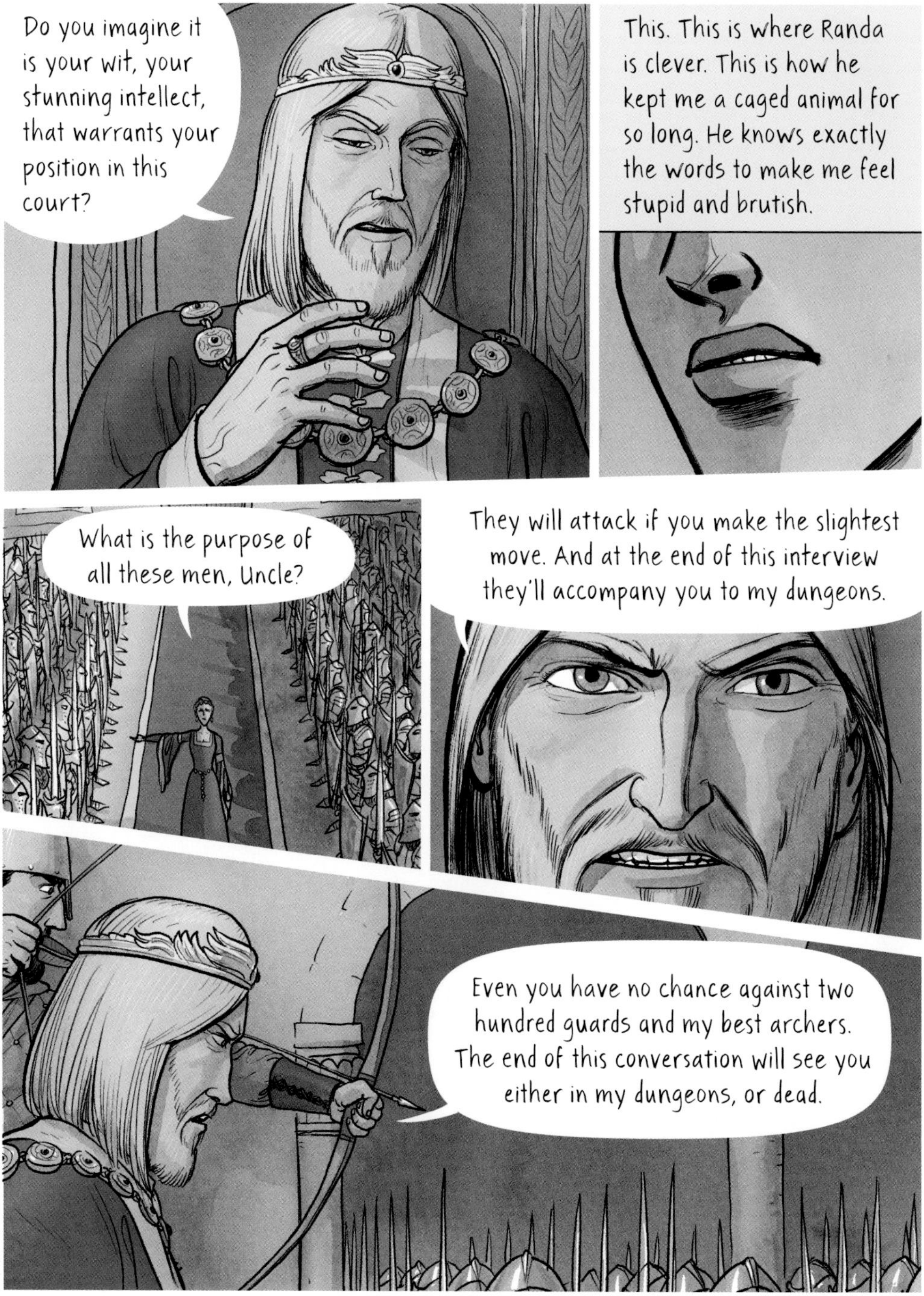
Do you imagine it is your wit, your stunning intellect, that warrants your position in this court?
This. This is where Randa is clever. This is how he kept me a caged animal for so long. He knows exactly the words to make me feel stupid and brutish.
What is the purpose of all these men, Uncle?
They will attack if you make the slightest move. And at the end of this interview they'll accompany you to my dungeons.
Even you have no chance against two hundred guards and my best archers. The end of this conversation will see you either in my dungeons, or dead.

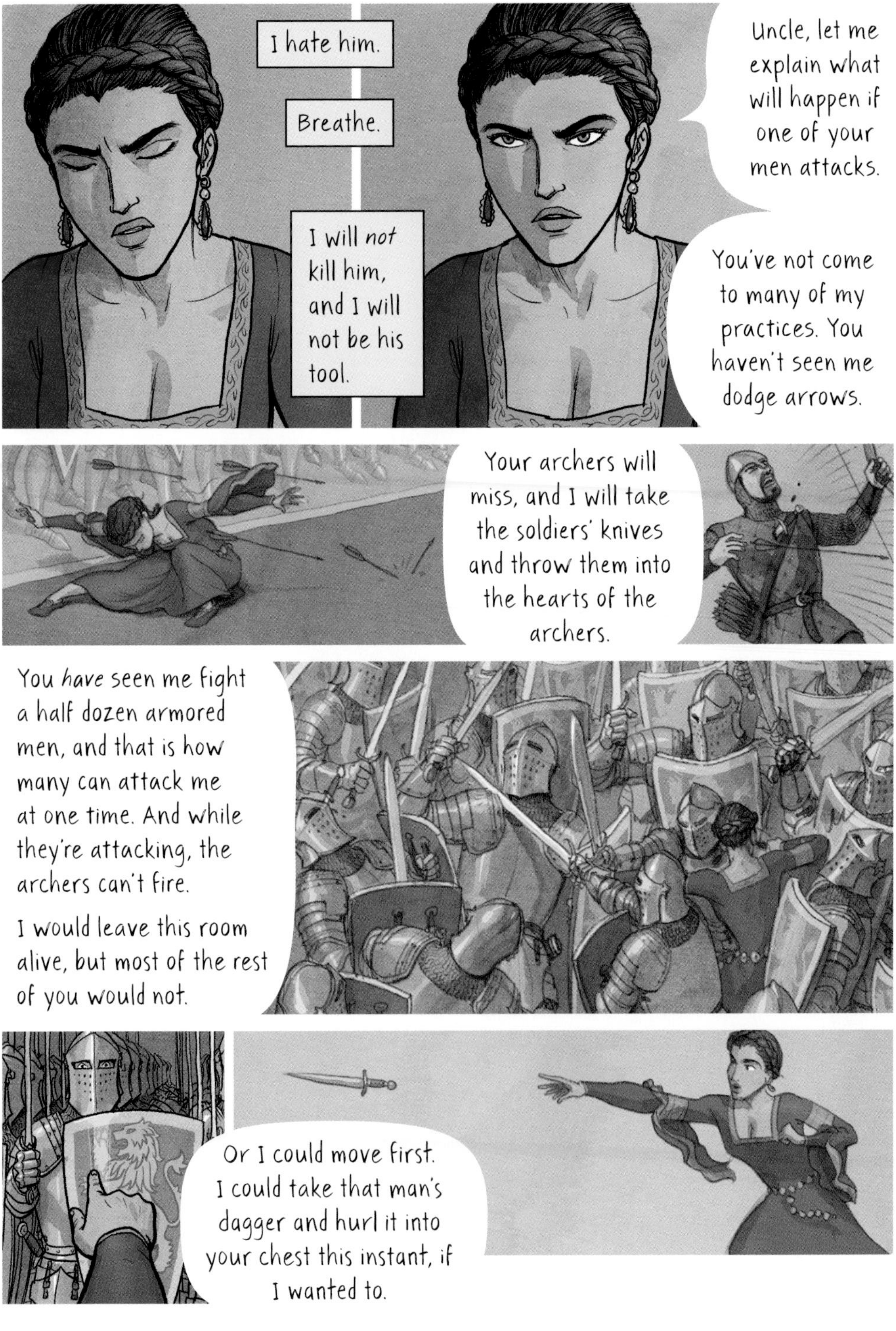
I hate him.
Breathe.
I will *not* kill him, and I will not be his tool.
Uncle, let me explain what will happen if one of your men attacks.
You've not come to many of my practices. You haven't seen me dodge arrows.
Your archers will miss, and I will take the soldiers' knives and throw them into the hearts of the archers.
You *have* seen me fight a half dozen armored men, and that is how many can attack me at one time. And while they're attacking, the archers can't fire.
I would leave this room alive, but most of the rest of you would not.
Or I could move first. I could take that man's dagger and hurl it into your chest this instant, if I wanted to.

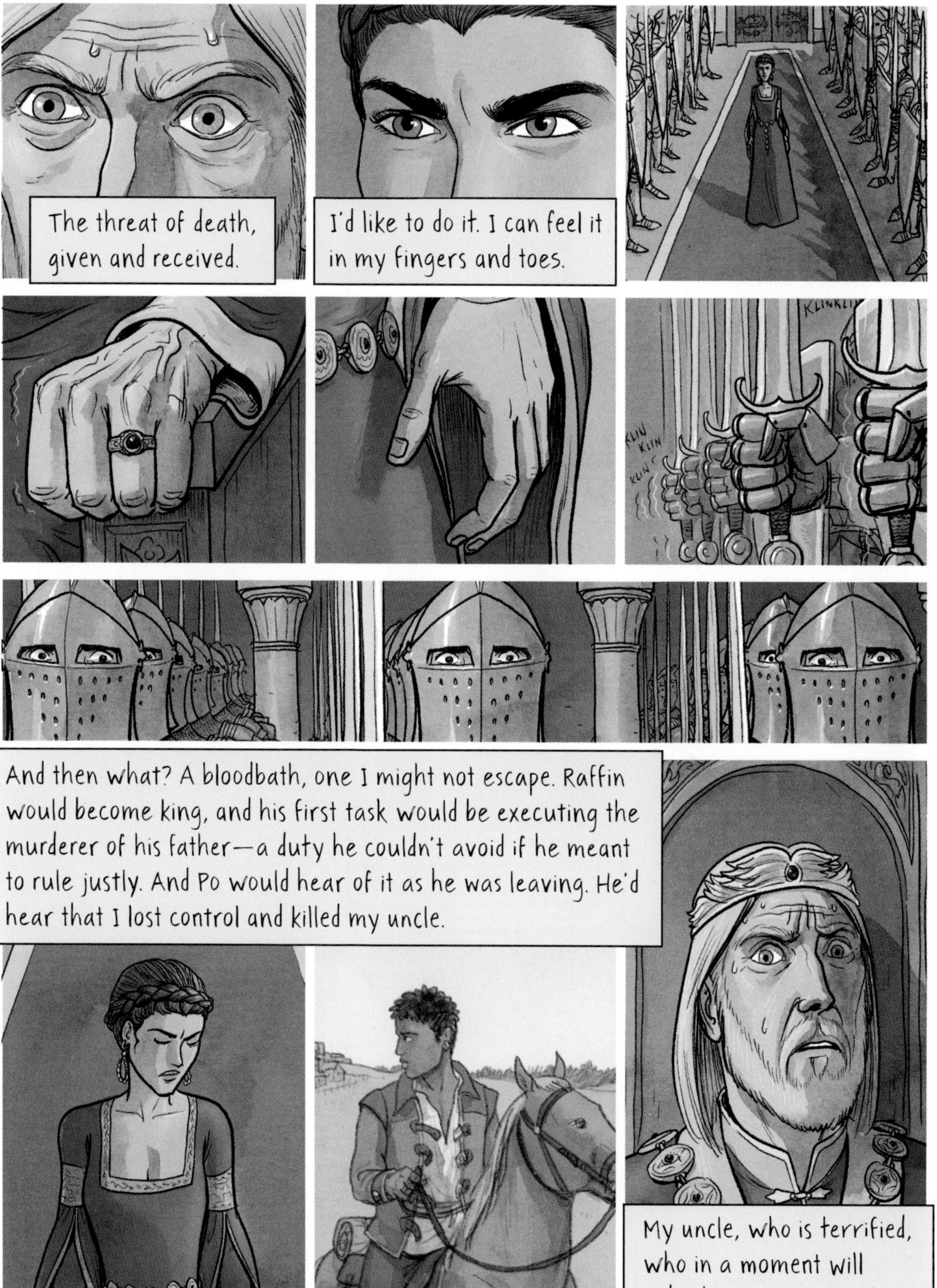

The threat of death, given and received.
I'd like to do it. I can feel it in my fingers and toes.
KLINKLI
KLIN
KLIN
KLIN
And then what? A bloodbath, one I might not escape. Raffin would become king, and his first task would be executing the murderer of his father—a duty he couldn't avoid if he meant to rule justly. And Po would hear of it as he was leaving. He'd hear that I lost control and killed my uncle.
My uncle, who is terrified, who in a moment will order his men to attack.

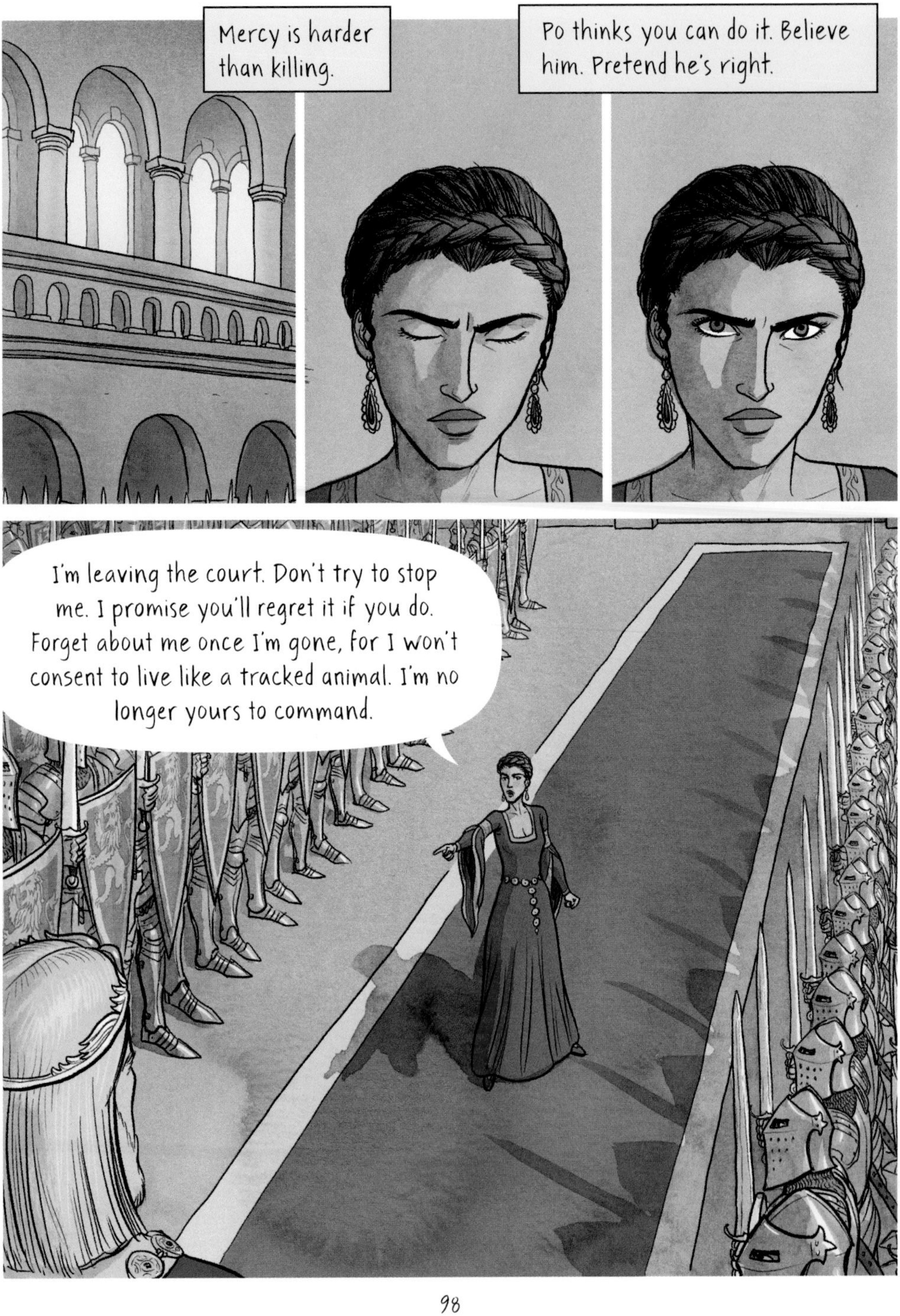
Mercy is harder than killing.
Po thinks you can do it. Believe him. Pretend he's right.
I'm leaving the court. Don't try to stop me. I promise you'll regret it if you do. Forget about me once I'm gone, for I won't consent to live like a tracked animal. I'm no longer yours to command.

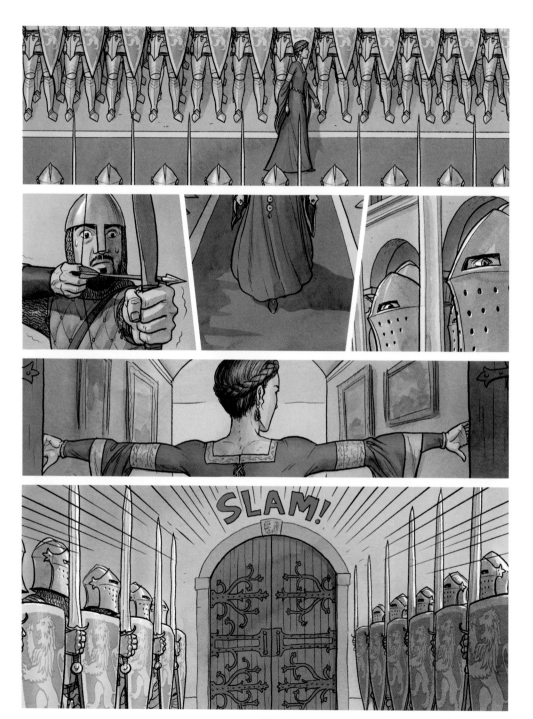

SLAM!

PART TWO
The Twisted King

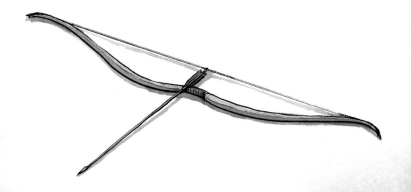

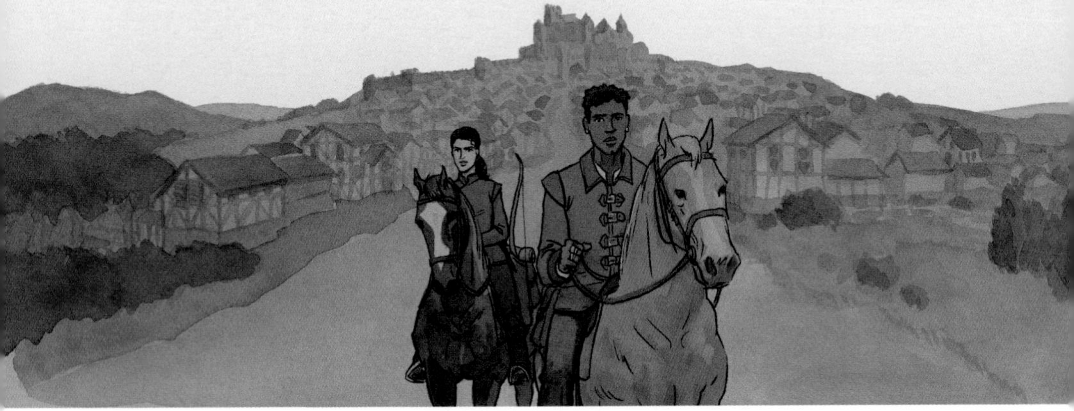

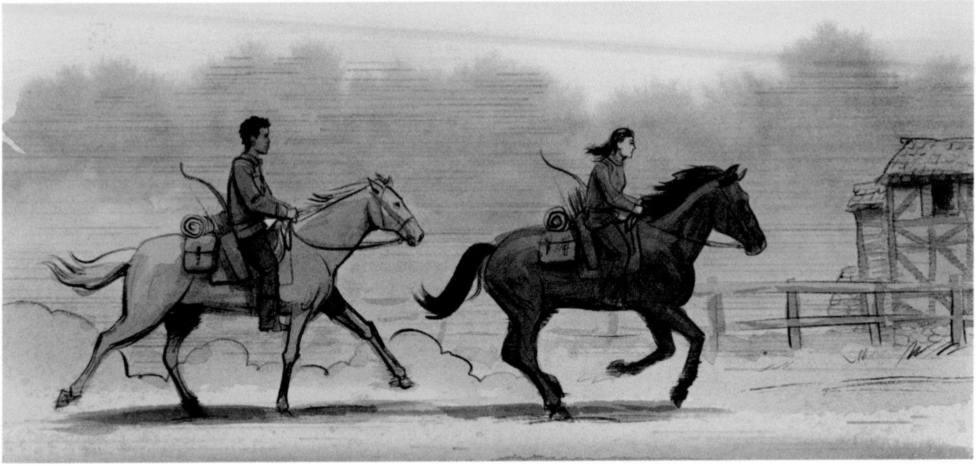

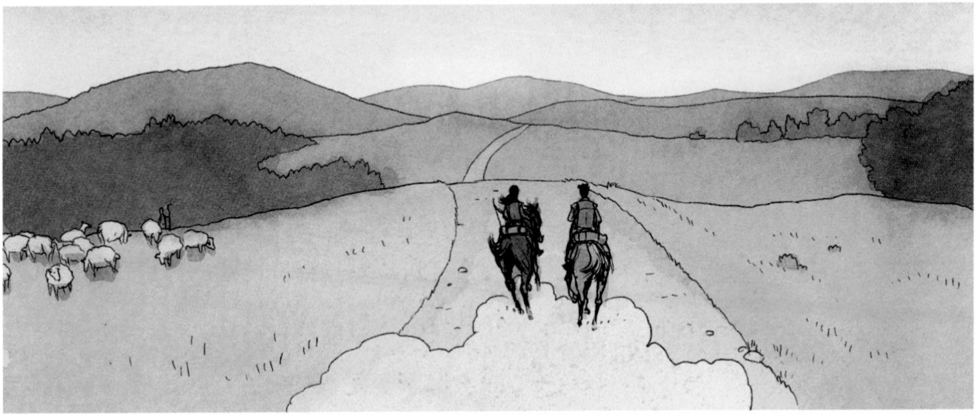

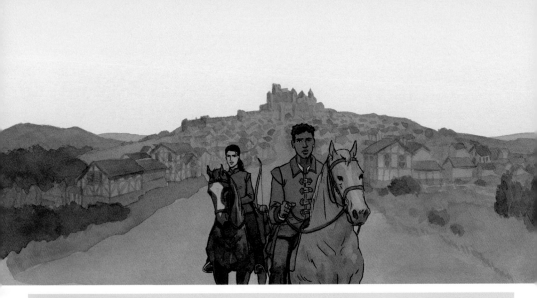

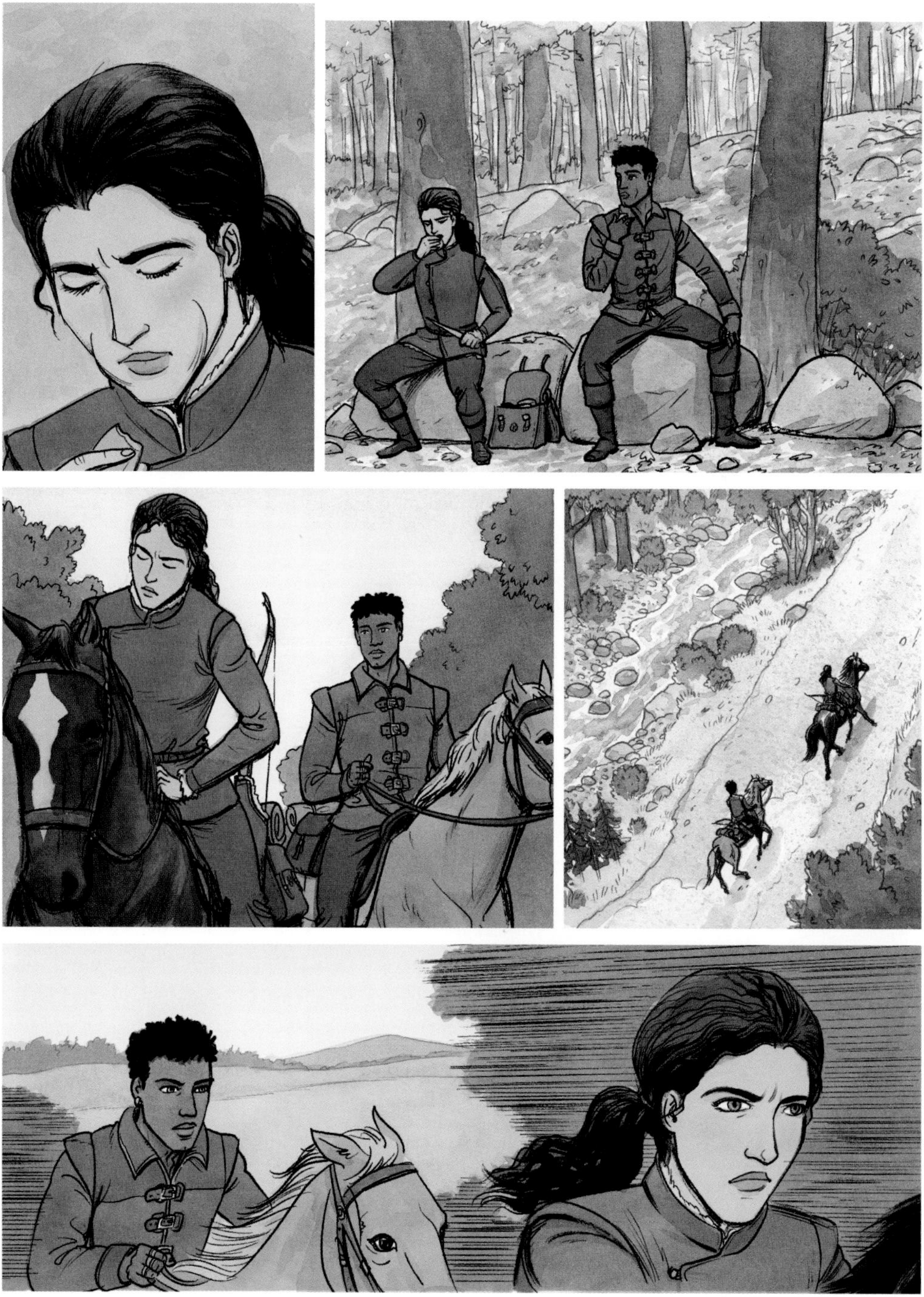

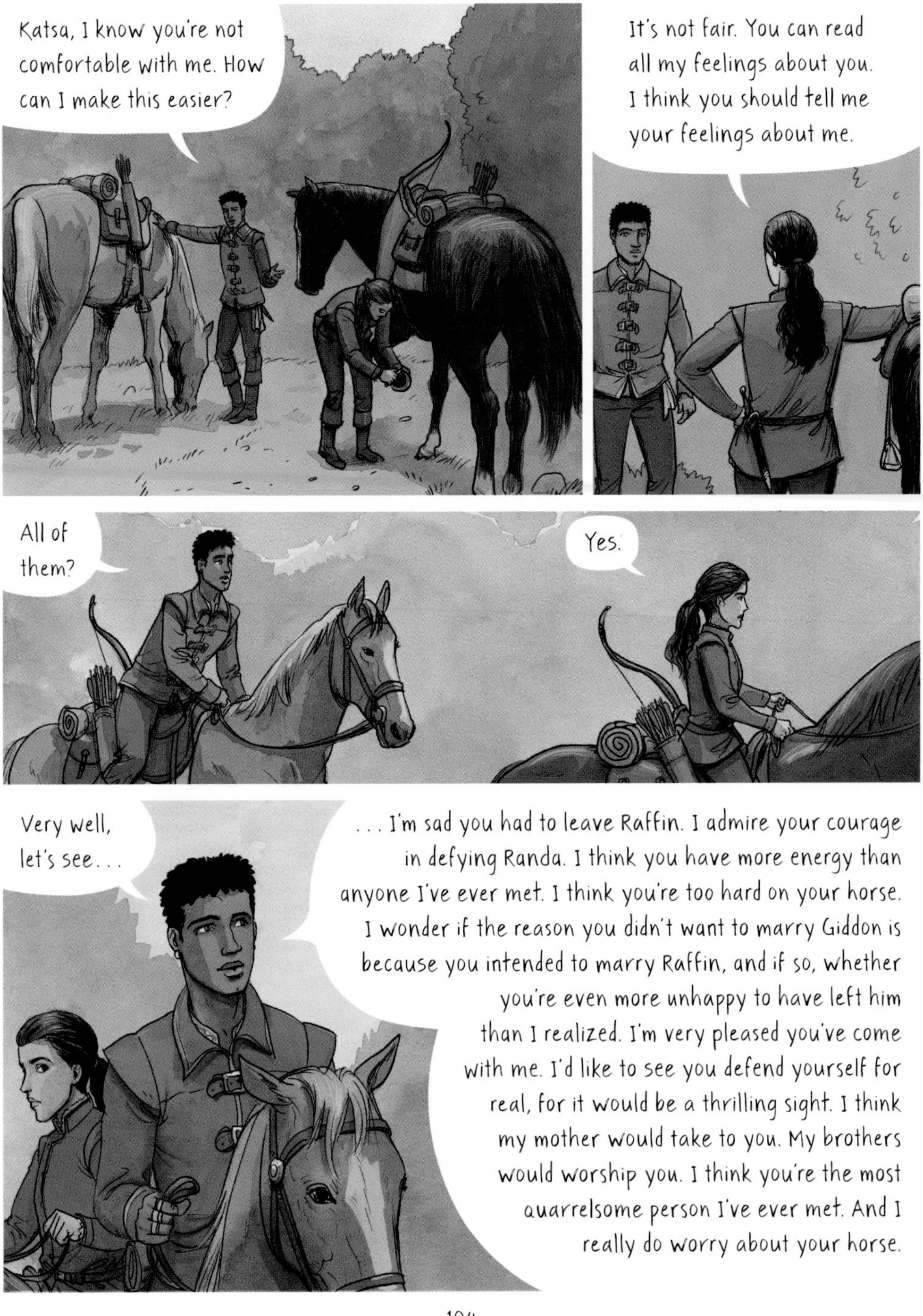
Katsa, I know you're not comfortable with me. How can I make this easier?
It's not fair. You can read all my feelings about you. I think you should tell me your feelings about me.
All of them?
Yes.
Very well, let's see...
... I'm sad you had to leave Raffin. I admire your courage in defying Randa. I think you have more energy than anyone I've ever met. I think you're too hard on your horse. I wonder if the reason you didn't want to marry Giddon is because you intended to marry Raffin, and if so, whether you're even more unhappy to have left him than I realized. I'm very pleased you've come with me. I'd like to see you defend yourself for real, for it would be a thrilling sight. I think my mother would take to you. My brothers would worship you. I think you're the most quarrelsome person I've ever met. And I really do worry about your horse.

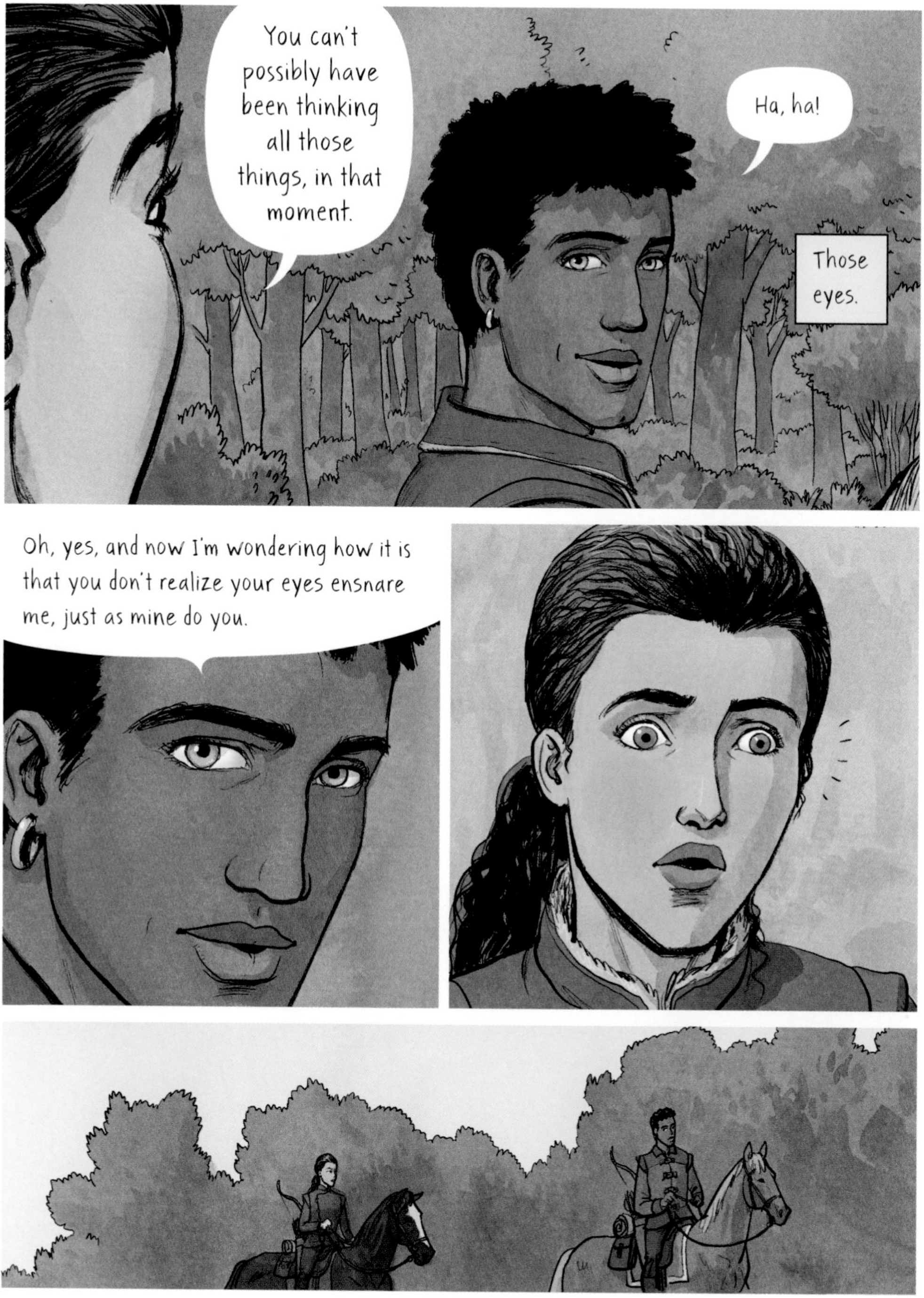
You can't possibly have been thinking all those things, in that moment.
Ha, ha!
Those eyes.
Oh, yes, and now I'm wondering how it is that you don't realize your eyes ensnare me, just as mine do you.

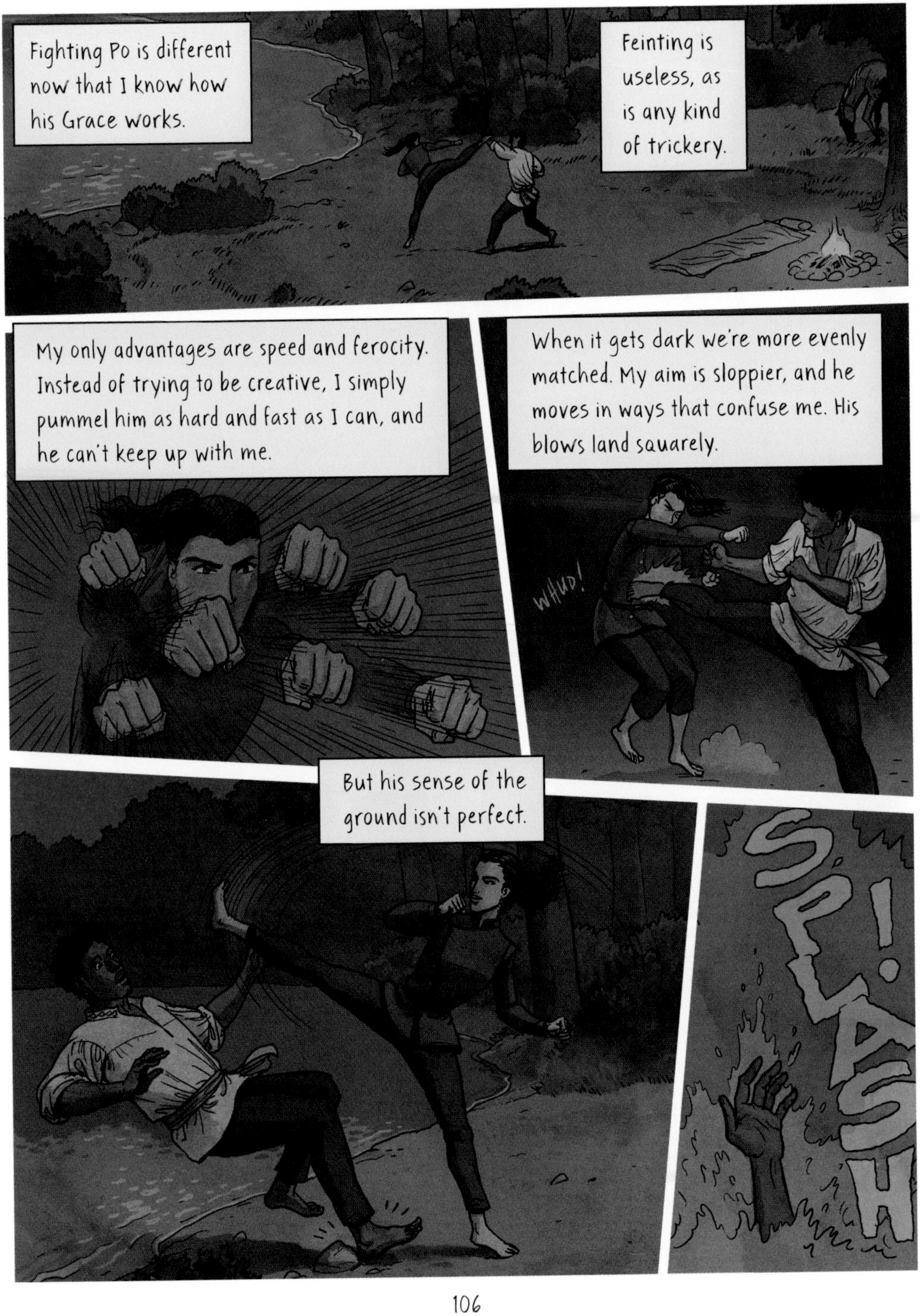

Fighting Po is different now that I know how his Grace works.
Feinting is useless, as is any kind of trickery.
My only advantages are speed and ferocity. Instead of trying to be creative, I simply pummel him as hard and fast as I can, and he can't keep up with me.
When it gets dark we're more evenly matched. My aim is sloppier, and he moves in ways that confuse me. His blows land squarely.
WHUD!
But his sense of the ground isn't perfect.
SPLASH!

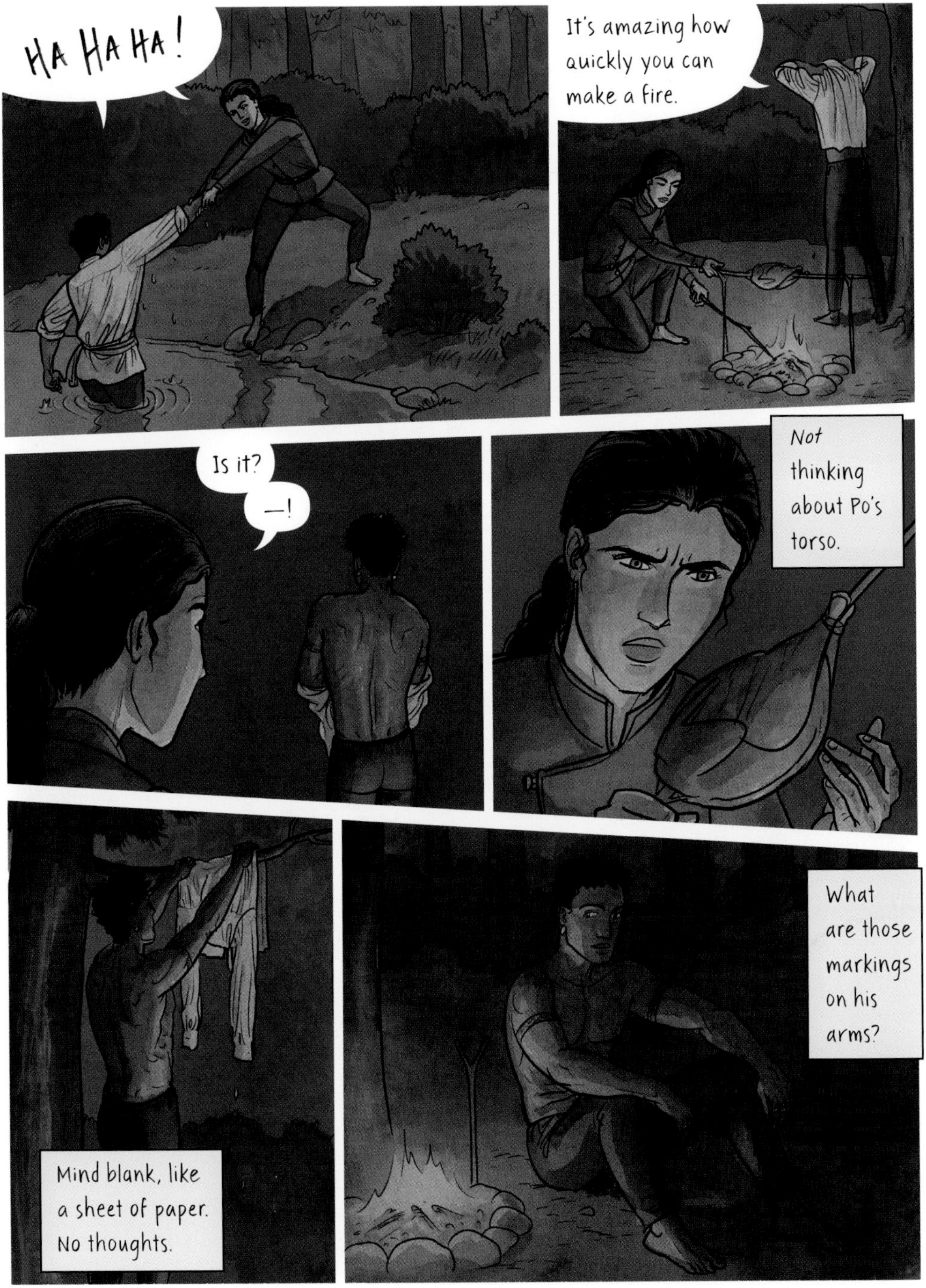
HA HA HA!
It's amazing how quickly you can make a fire.
Is it?
—!
Not thinking about Po's torso.
Mind blank, like a sheet of paper. No thoughts.
What are those markings on his arms?

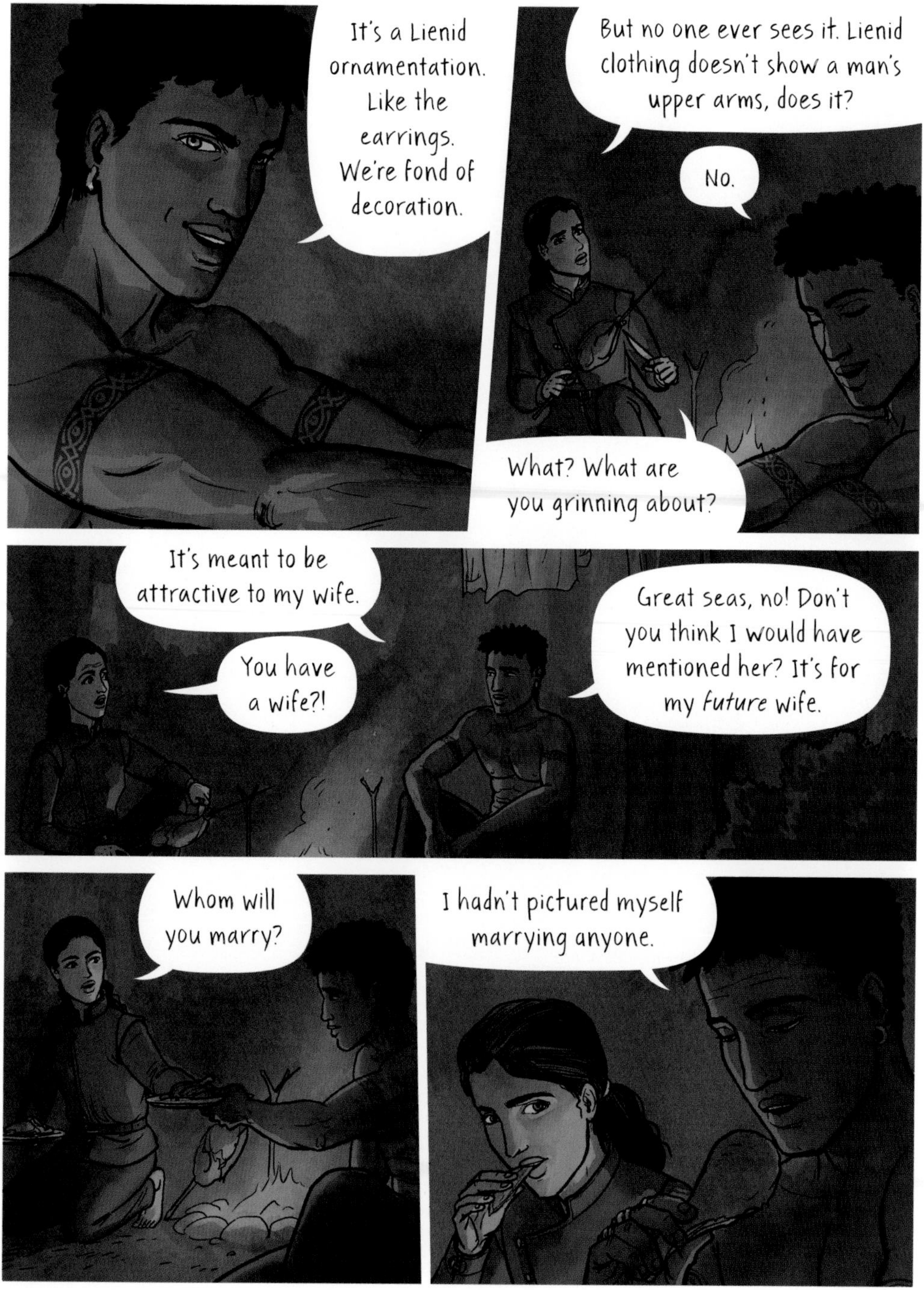
It's a Lienid ornamentation. Like the earrings. We're fond of decoration.
But no one ever sees it. Lienid clothing doesn't show a man's upper arms, does it?
No.
What? What are you grinning about?
It's meant to be attractive to my wife.
You have a wife?!
Great seas, no! Don't you think I would have mentioned her? It's for my *future* wife.
Whom will you marry?
I hadn't pictured myself marrying anyone.

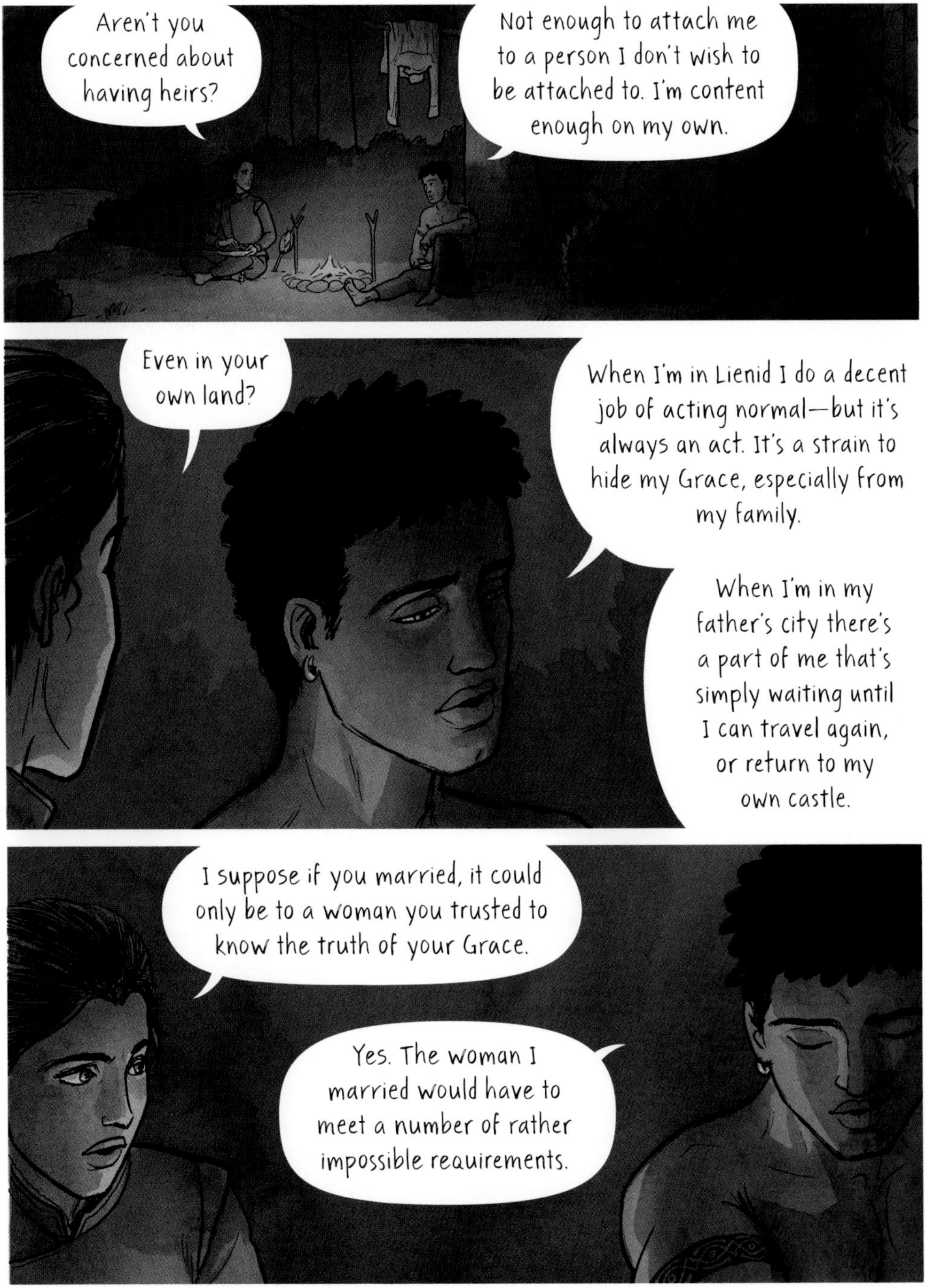
Aren't you concerned about having heirs?
Not enough to attach me to a person I don't wish to be attached to. I'm content enough on my own.
Even in your own land?
When I'm in Lienid I do a decent job of acting normal—but it's always an act. It's a strain to hide my Grace, especially from my family.
When I'm in my father's city there's a part of me that's simply waiting until I can travel again, or return to my own castle.
I suppose if you married, it could only be to a woman you trusted to know the truth of your Grace.
Yes. The woman I married would have to meet a number of rather impossible requirements.

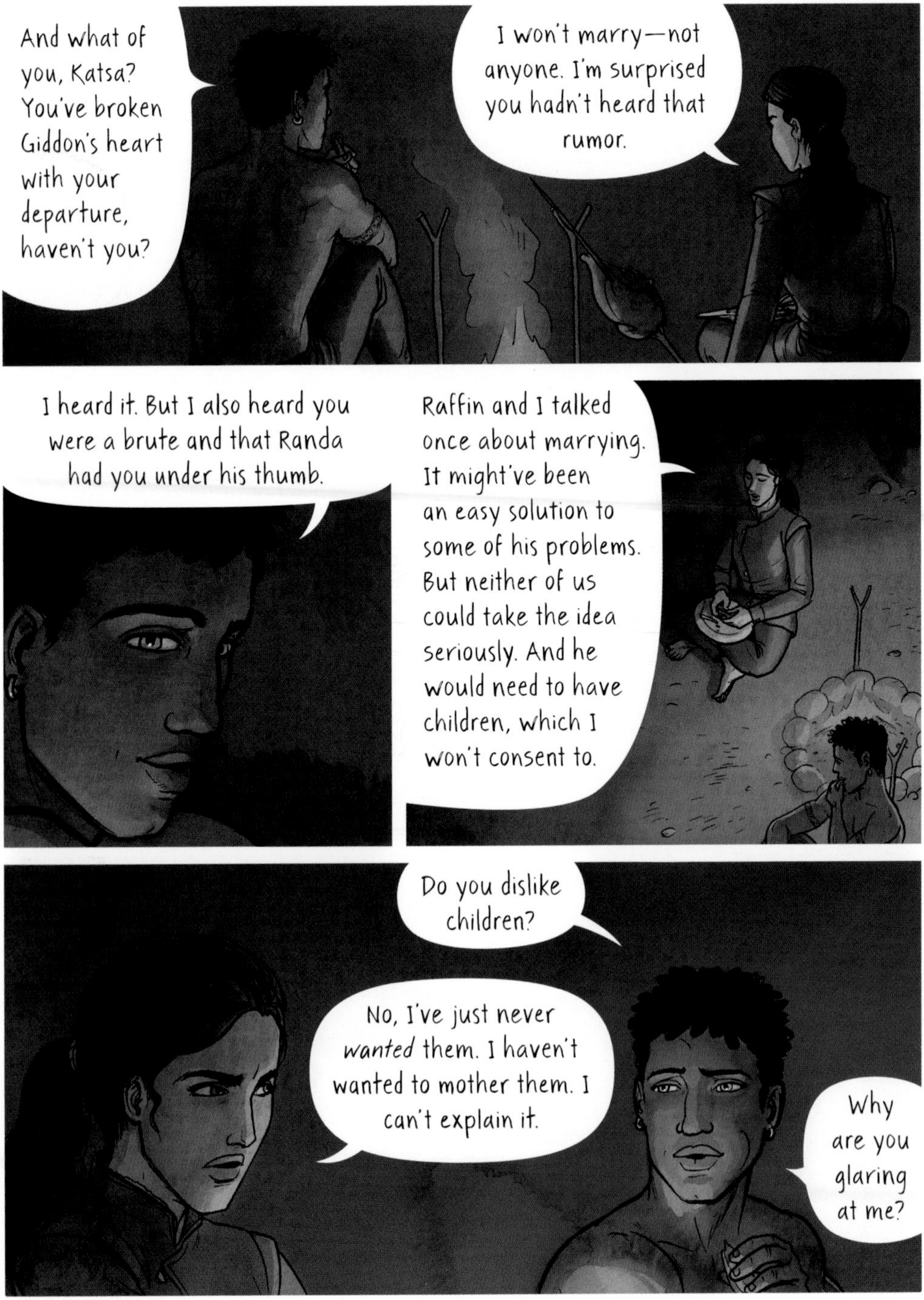
And what of you, Katsa? You've broken Giddon's heart with your departure, haven't you?
I won't marry—not anyone. I'm surprised you hadn't heard that rumor.
I heard it. But I also heard you were a brute and that Randa had you under his thumb.
Raffin and I talked once about marrying. It might've been an easy solution to some of his problems. But neither of us could take the idea seriously. And he would need to have children, which I won't consent to.
Do you dislike children?
No, I've just never *wanted* them. I haven't wanted to mother them. I can't explain it.
Why are you glaring at me?

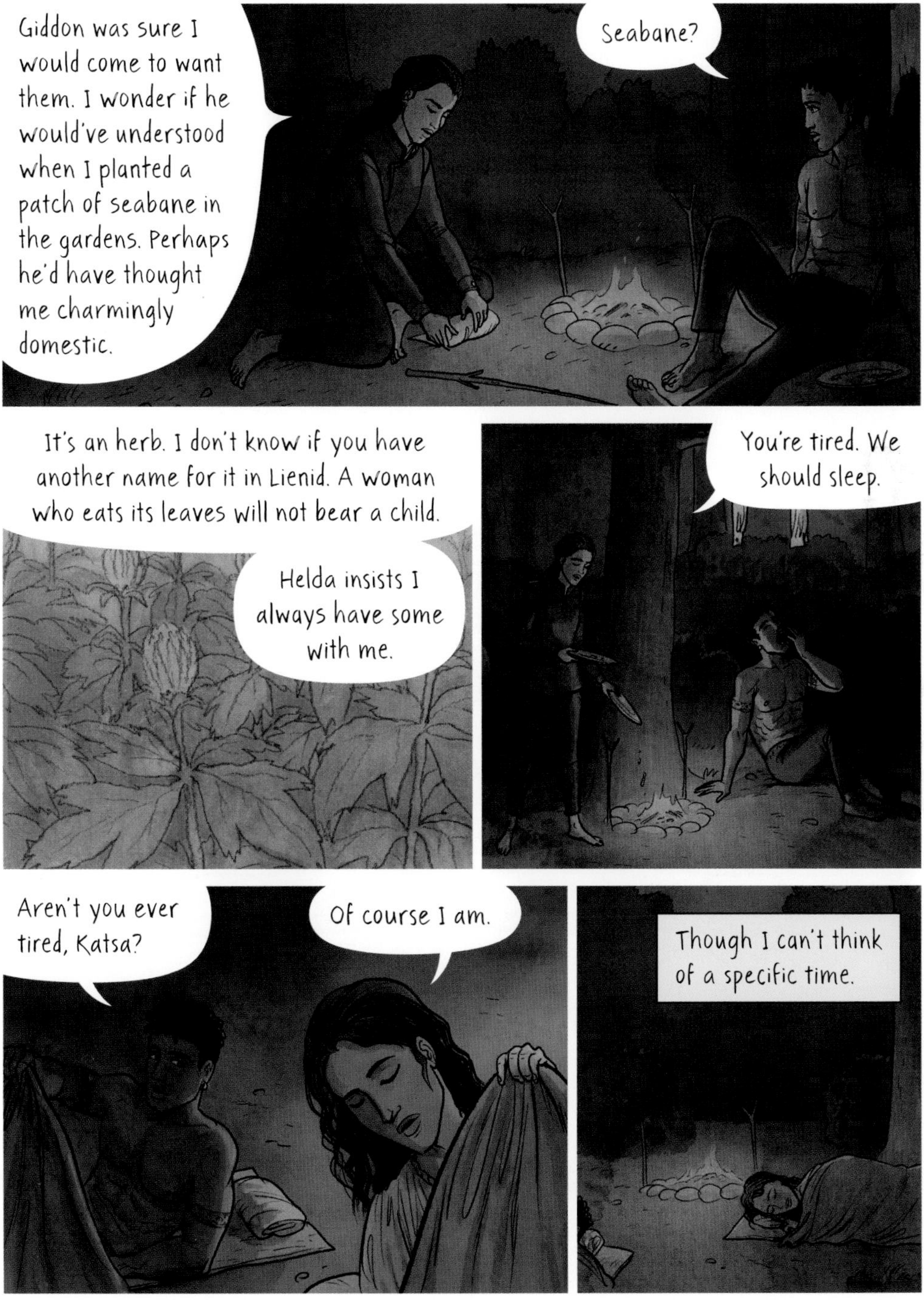
Giddon was sure I would come to want them. I wonder if he would've understood when I planted a patch of seabane in the gardens. Perhaps he'd have thought me charmingly domestic.
Seabane?
It's an herb. I don't know if you have another name for it in Lienid. A woman who eats its leaves will not bear a child.
Helda insists I always have some with me.
You're tired. We should sleep.
Aren't you ever tired, Katsa?
Of course I am.
Though I can't think of a specific time.

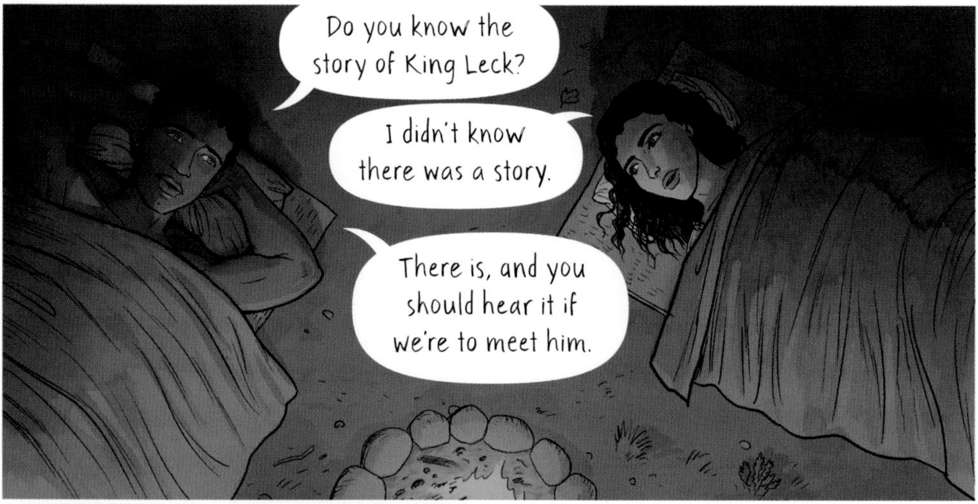
Do you know the story of King Leck?
I didn't know there was a story.
There is, and you should hear it if we're to meet him.

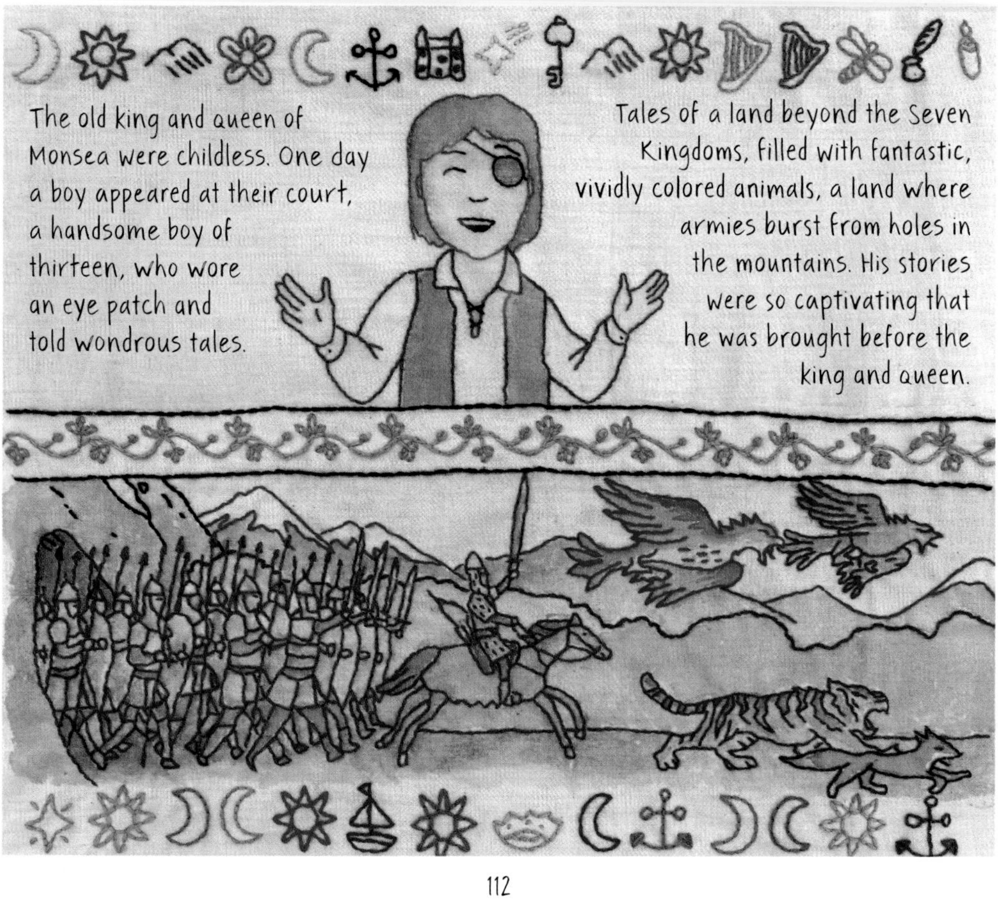
The old king and queen of Monsea were childless. One day a boy appeared at their court, a handsome boy of thirteen, who wore an eye patch and told wondrous tales.
Tales of a land beyond the Seven Kingdoms, filled with fantastic, vividly colored animals, a land where armies burst from holes in the mountains. His stories were so captivating that he was brought before the king and queen.

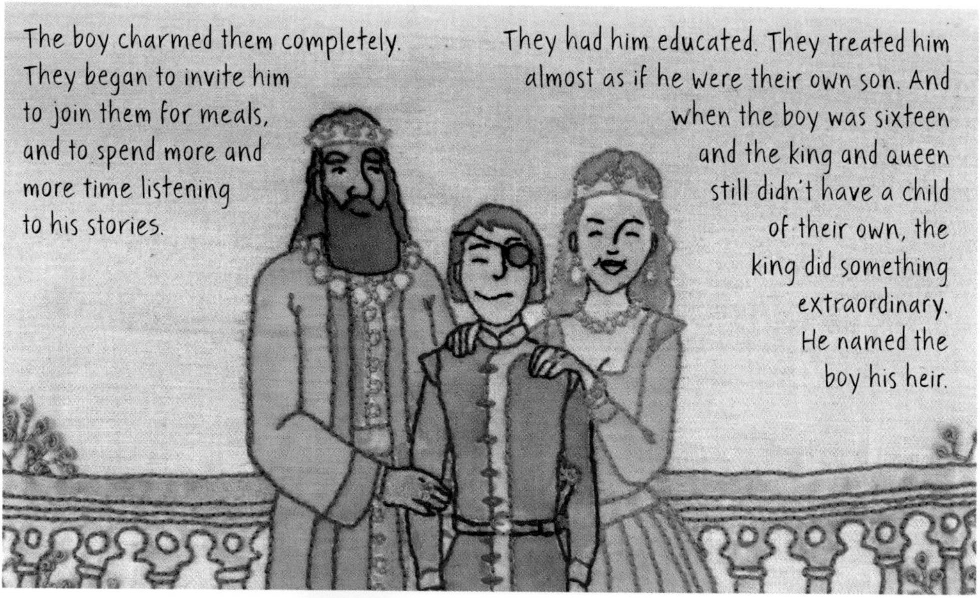
The boy charmed them completely. They began to invite him to join them for meals, and to spend more and more time listening to his stories.
They had him educated. They treated him almost as if he were their own son. And when the boy was sixteen and the king and queen still didn't have a child of their own, the king did something extraordinary. He named the boy his heir.

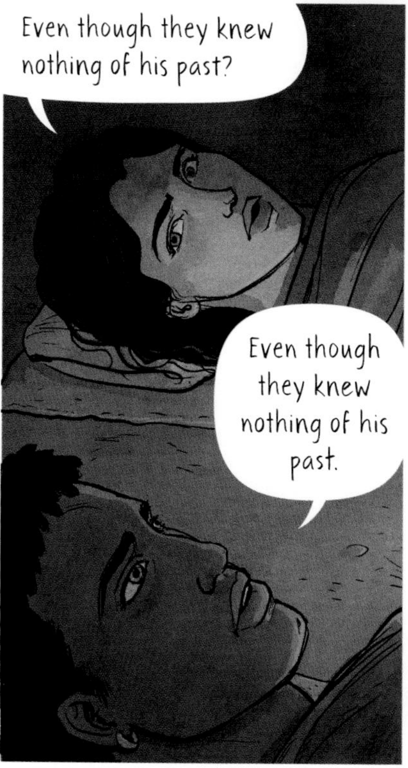
Even though they knew nothing of his past?
Even though they knew nothing of his past.

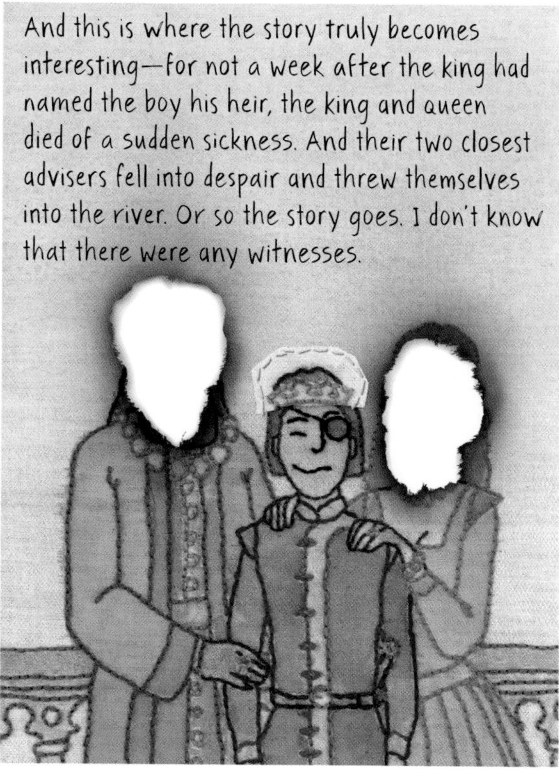
And this is where the story truly becomes interesting—for not a week after the king had named the boy his heir, the king and queen died of a sudden sickness. And their two closest advisers fell into despair and threw themselves into the river. Or so the story goes. I don't know that there were any witnesses.

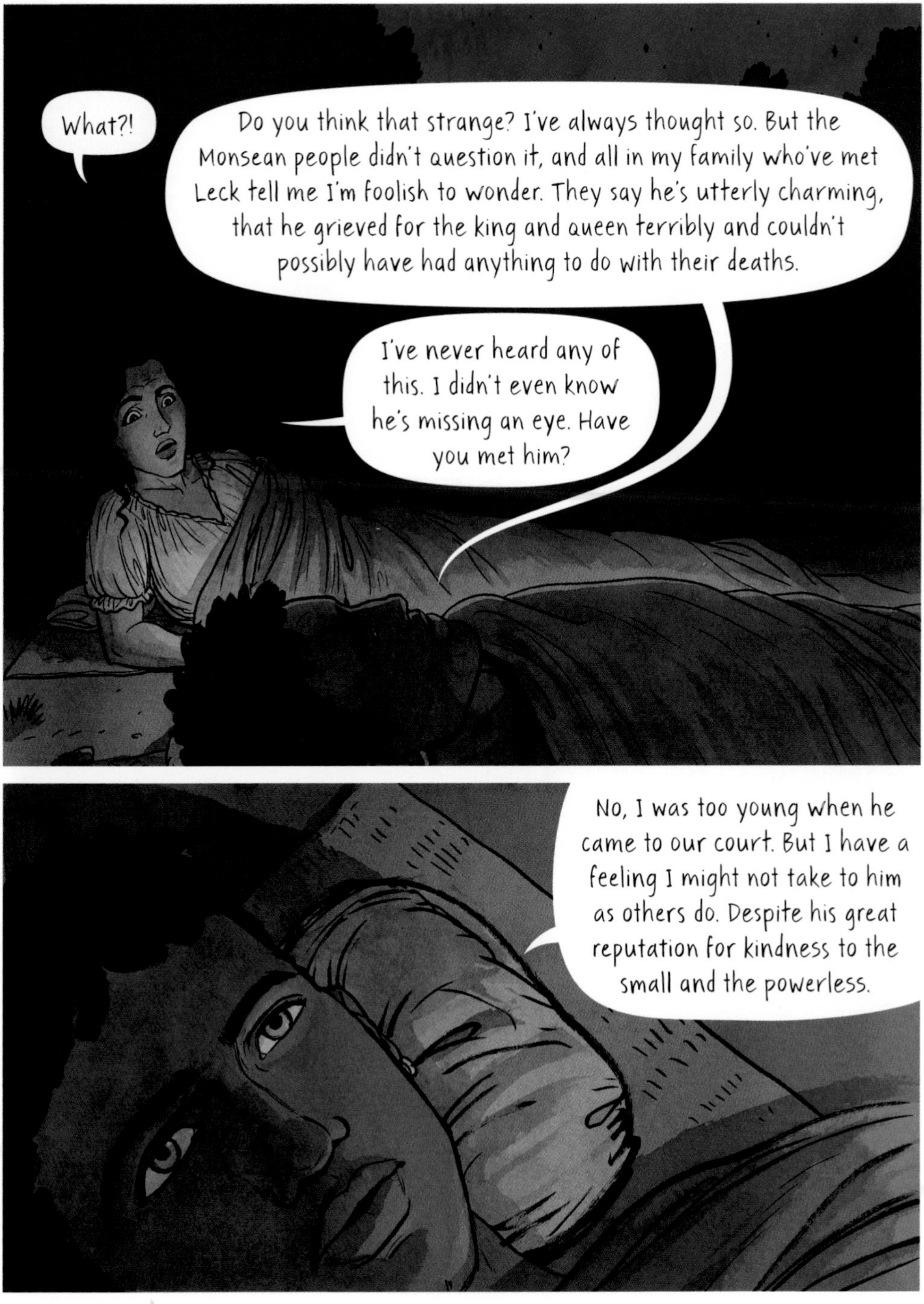

What?!
Do you think that strange? I've always thought so. But the Monsean people didn't question it, and all in my family who've met Leck tell me I'm foolish to wonder. They say he's utterly charming, that he grieved for the king and queen terribly and couldn't possibly have had anything to do with their deaths.
I've never heard any of this. I didn't even know he's missing an eye. Have you met him?
No, I was too young when he came to our court. But I have a feeling I might not take to him as others do. Despite his great reputation for kindness to the small and the powerless.

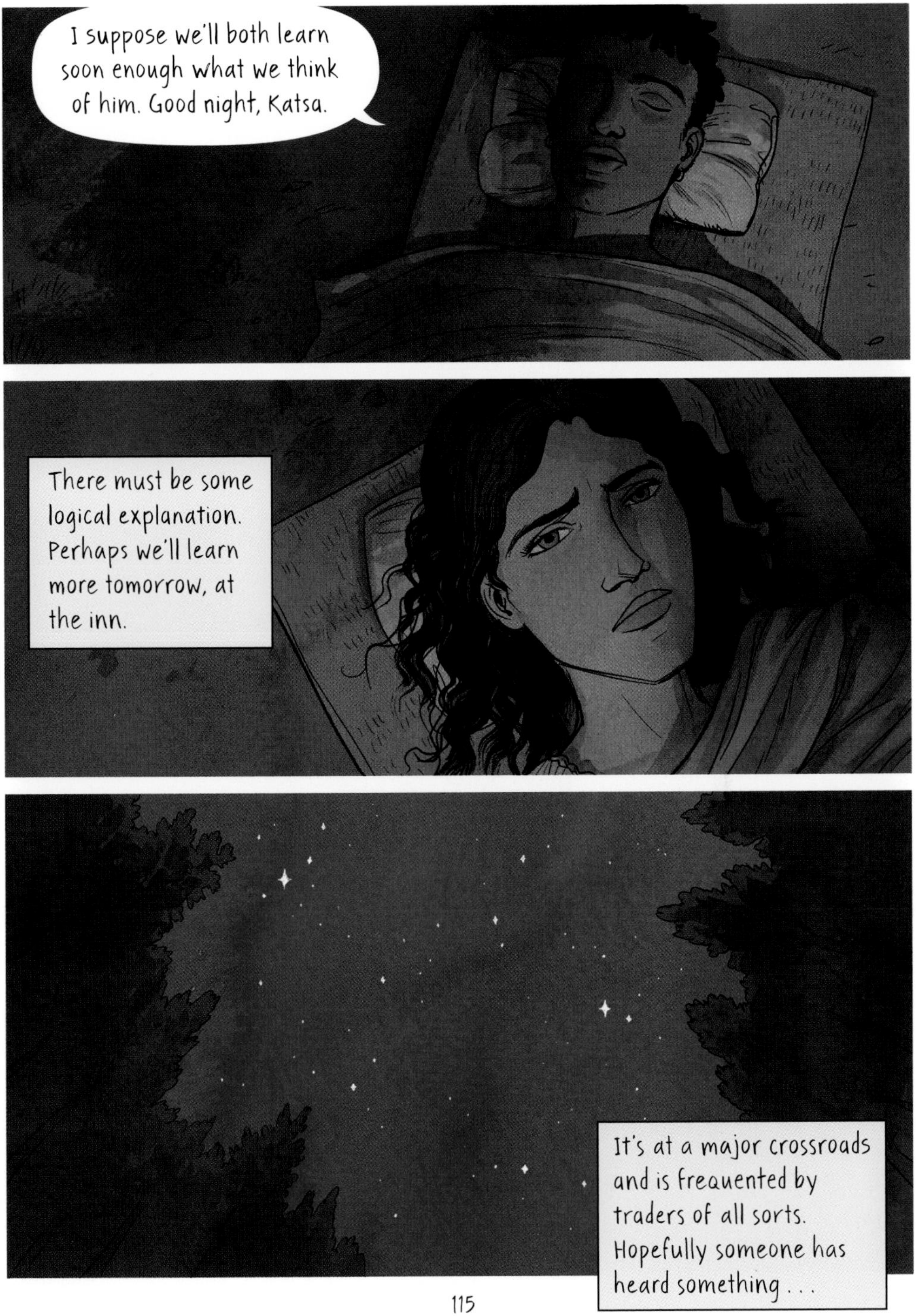
I suppose we'll both learn soon enough what we think of him. Good night, Katsa.
There must be some logical explanation. Perhaps we'll learn more tomorrow, at the inn.
It's at a major crossroads and is frequented by traders of all sorts. Hopefully someone has heard something . . .

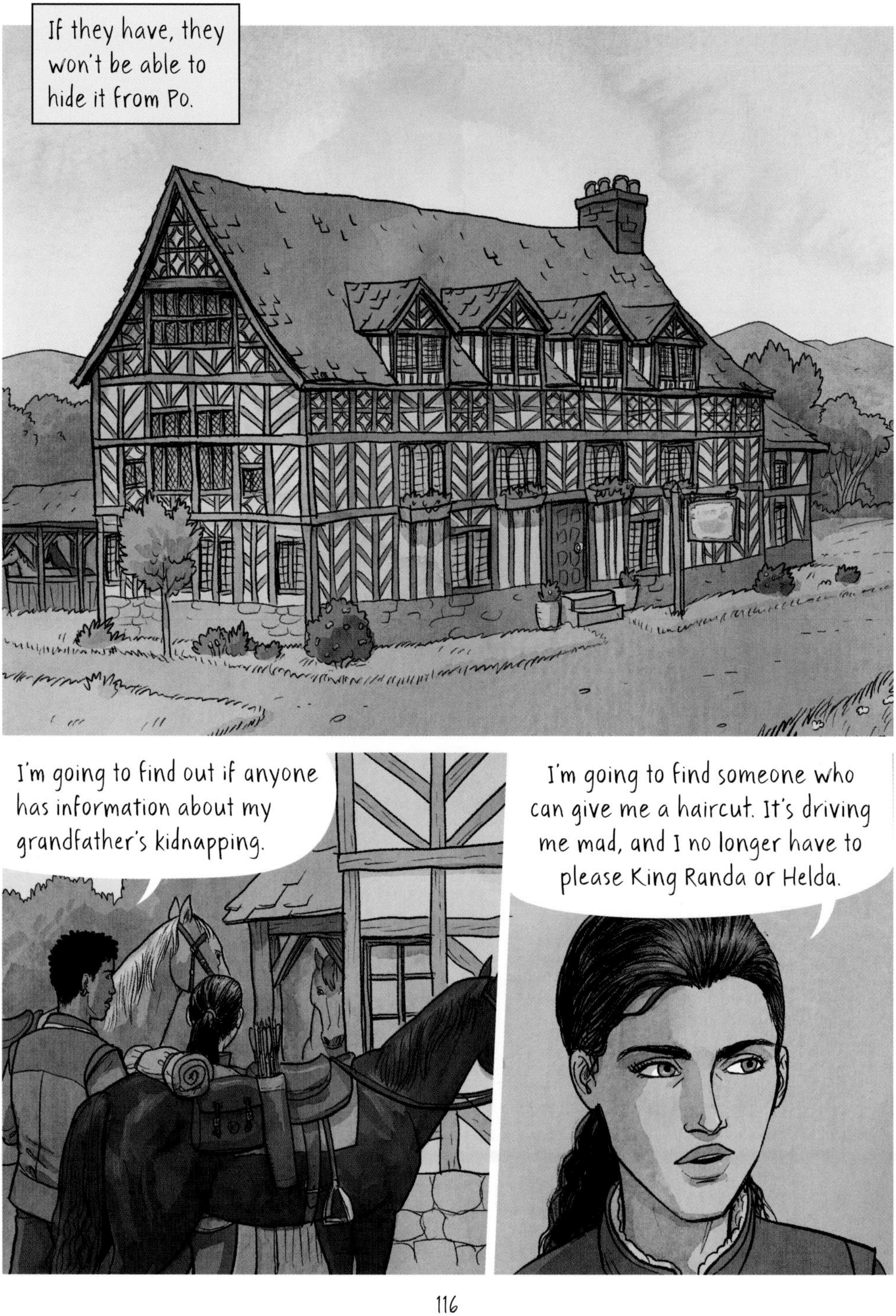
If they have, they won't be able to hide it from Po.
I'm going to find out if anyone has information about my grandfather's kidnapping.
I'm going to find someone who can give me a haircut. It's driving me mad, and I no longer have to please King Randa or Helda.

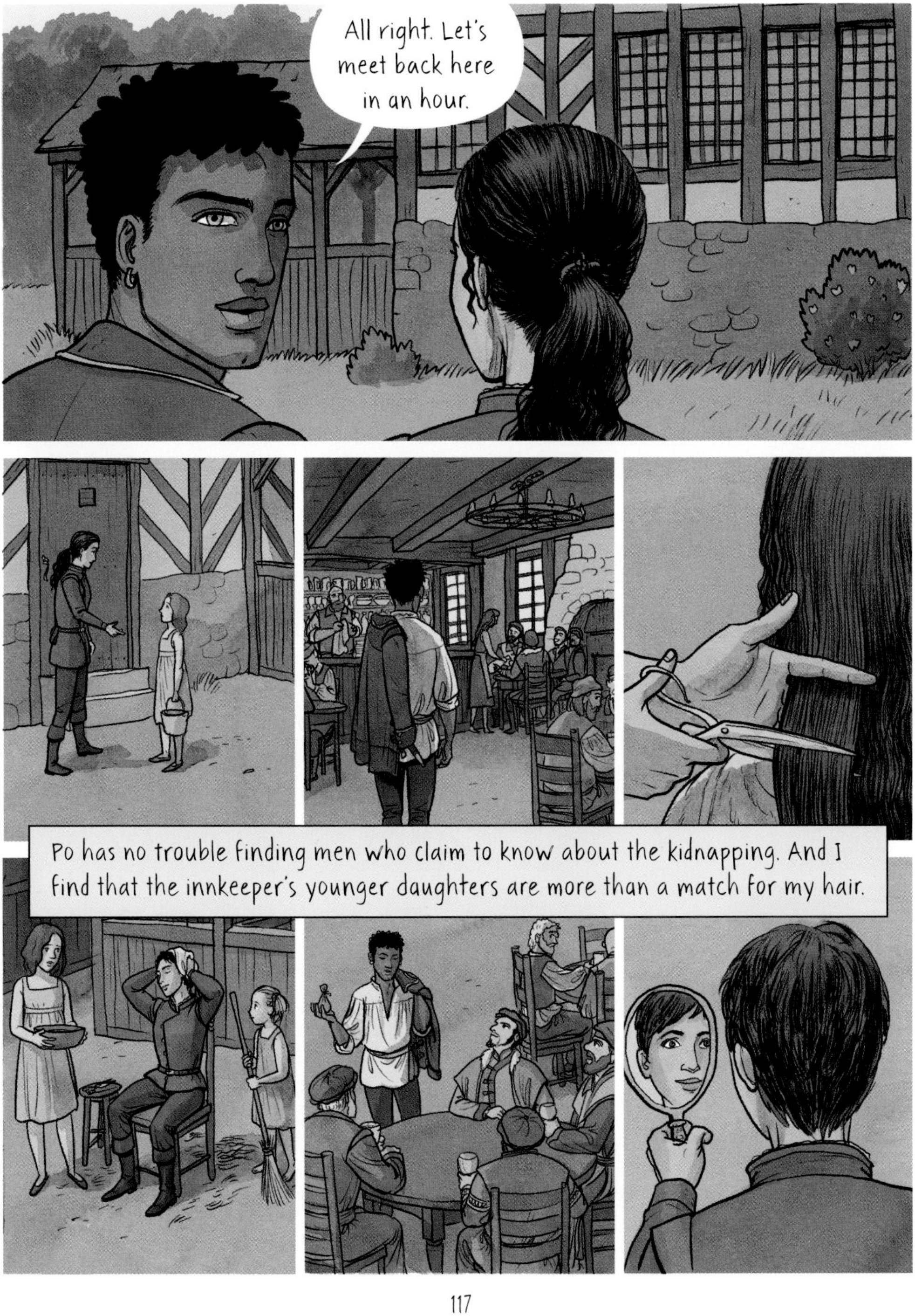
All right. Let's meet back here in an hour.
Po has no trouble finding men who claim to know about the kidnapping. And I find that the innkeeper's younger daughters are more than a match for my hair.

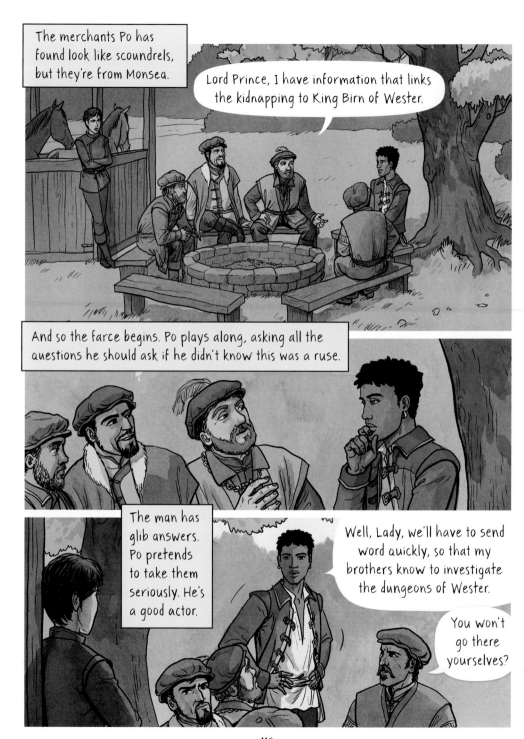

The merchants Po has found look like scoundrels, but they're from Monsea.

Lord Prince, I have information that links the kidnapping to King Birn of Wester.

And so the farce begins. Po plays along, asking all the questions he should ask if he didn't know this was a ruse.

The man has glib answers. Po pretends to take them seriously. He's a good actor.

Well, Lady, we'll have to send word quickly, so that my brothers know to investigate the dungeons of Wester.

You won't go there yourselves?

118

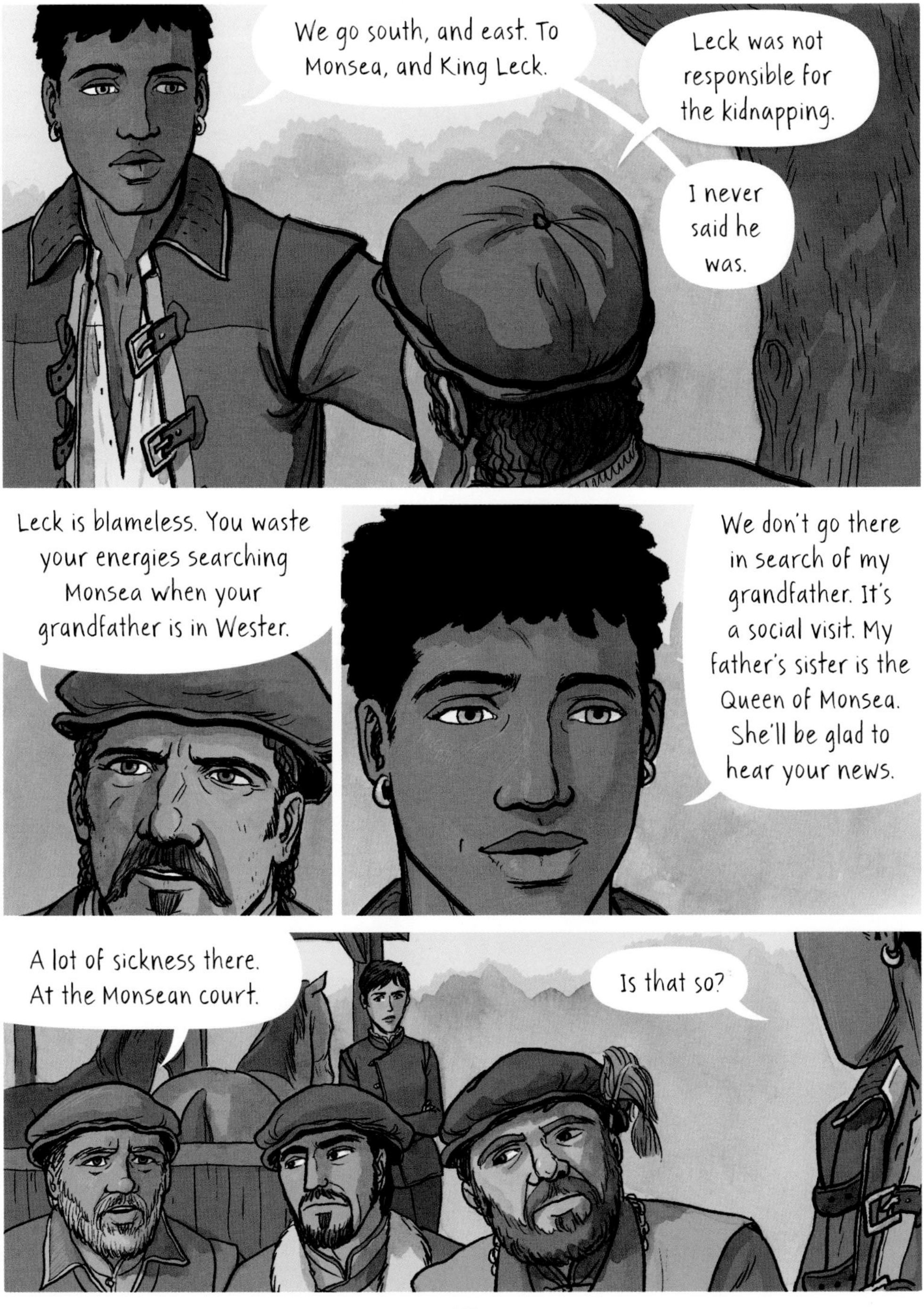

We go south, and east. To Monsea, and King Leck.
Leck was not responsible for the kidnapping.
I never said he was.
Leck is blameless. You waste your energies searching Monsea when your grandfather is in Wester.
We don't go there in search of my grandfather. It's a social visit. My father's sister is the Queen of Monsea. She'll be glad to hear your news.
A lot of sickness there. At the Monsean court.
Is that so?

I've family in Leck's service. Distant cousins. Two little girls who worked in his shelter—well, they died a few months back.

His shelter?

Leck's animal shelter. He rescues animals, Lord Prince, you'll know that.

He's got hundreds of them—dogs, squirrels, rabbits, bleeding from slashes on their backs and bellies.

Slashes on their backs and bellies.

You know. As if they'd run into something sharp.

Of course. And any broken bones? Diseases?

I haven't heard tell of any of that.

I see. And do you know what sickness the girls died of?

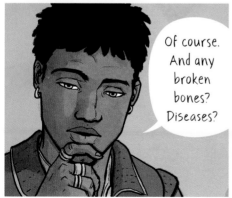

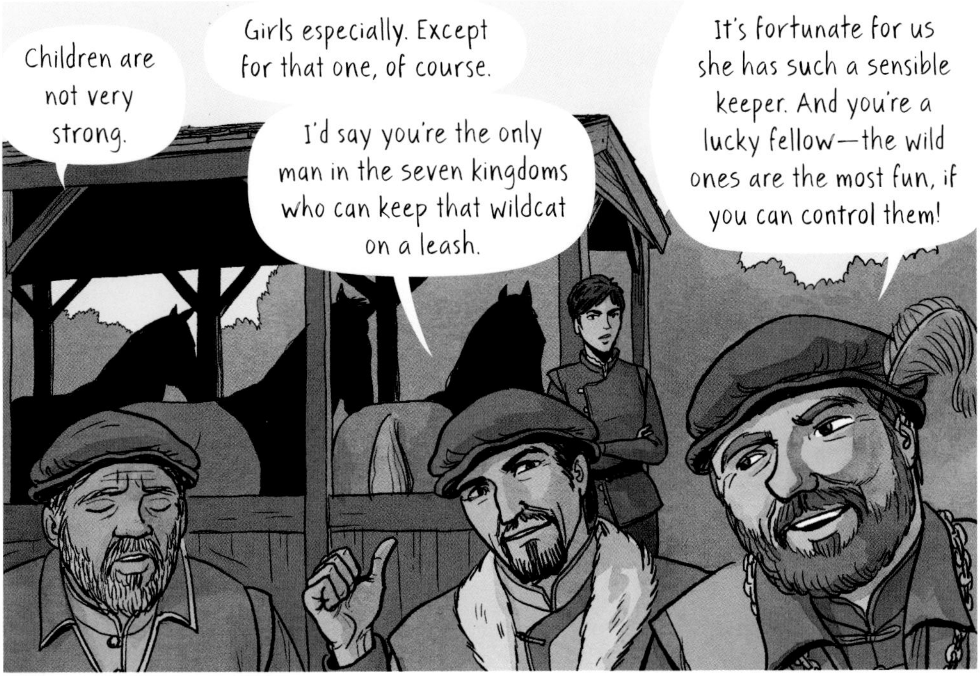
Children are not very strong.
Girls especially. Except for that one, of course.
I'd say you're the only man in the seven kingdoms who can keep that wildcat on a leash.
It's fortunate for us she has such a sensible keeper. And you're a lucky fellow—the wild ones are the most fun, if you can control them!

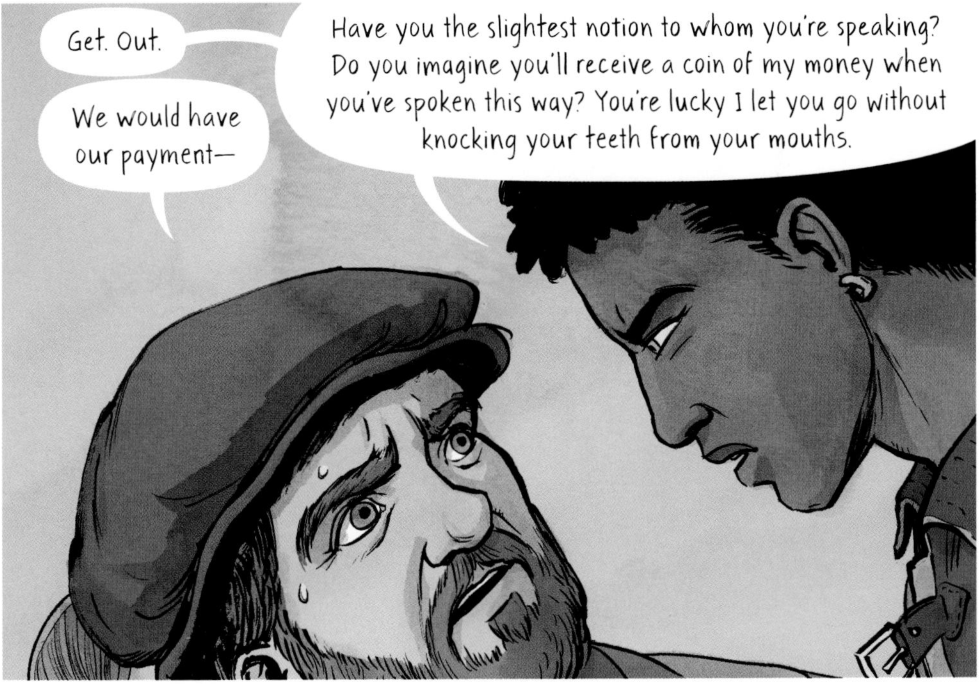
Get. Out.
We would have our payment—
Have you the slightest notion to whom you're speaking? Do you imagine you'll receive a coin of my money when you've spoken this way? You're lucky I let you go without knocking your teeth from your mouths.

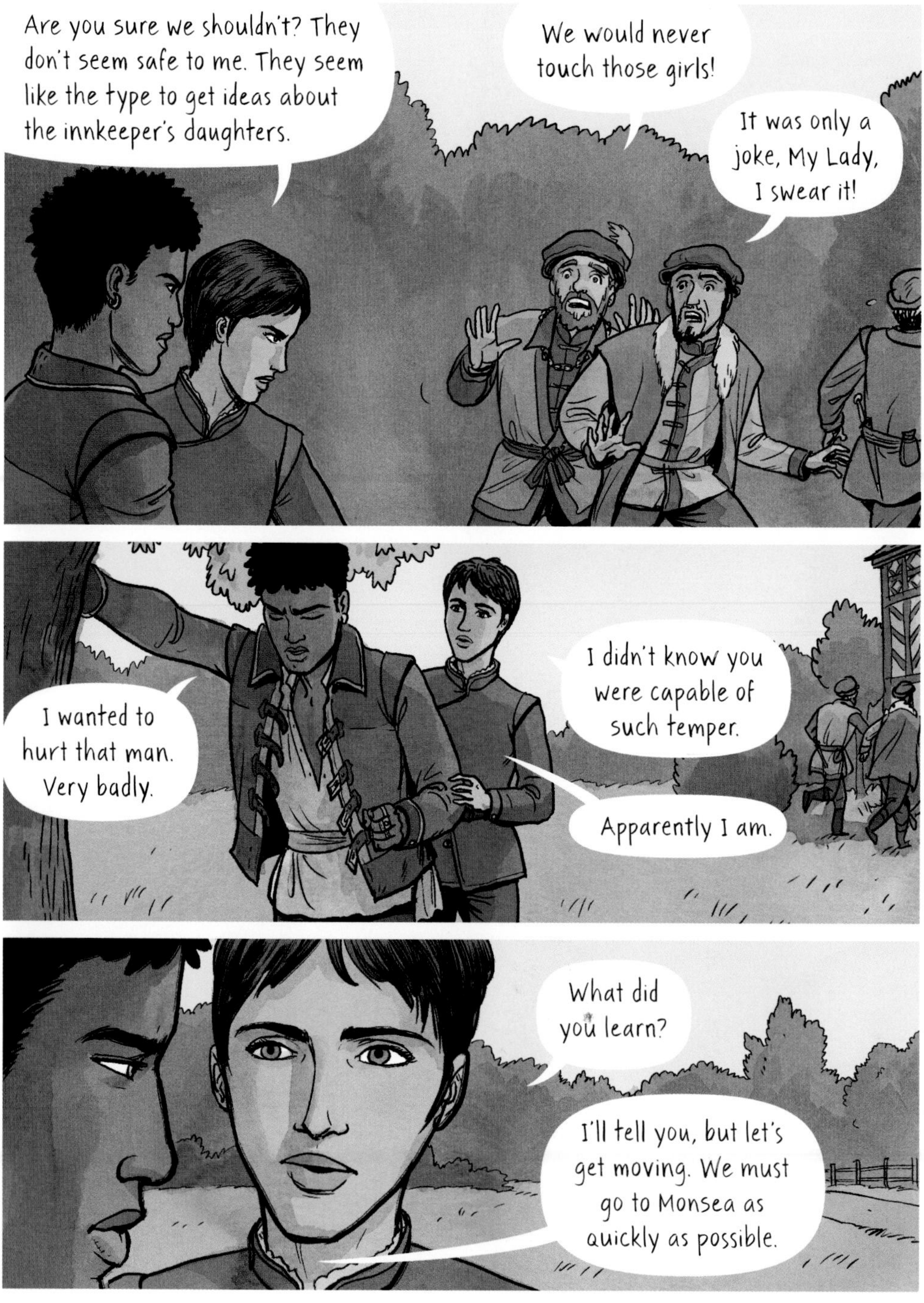

Are you sure we shouldn't? They don't seem safe to me. They seem like the type to get ideas about the innkeeper's daughters.
We would never touch those girls!
It was only a joke, My Lady, I swear it!
I wanted to hurt that man. Very badly.
I didn't know you were capable of such temper.
Apparently I am.
What did you learn?
I'll tell you, but let's get moving. We must go to Monsea as quickly as possible.

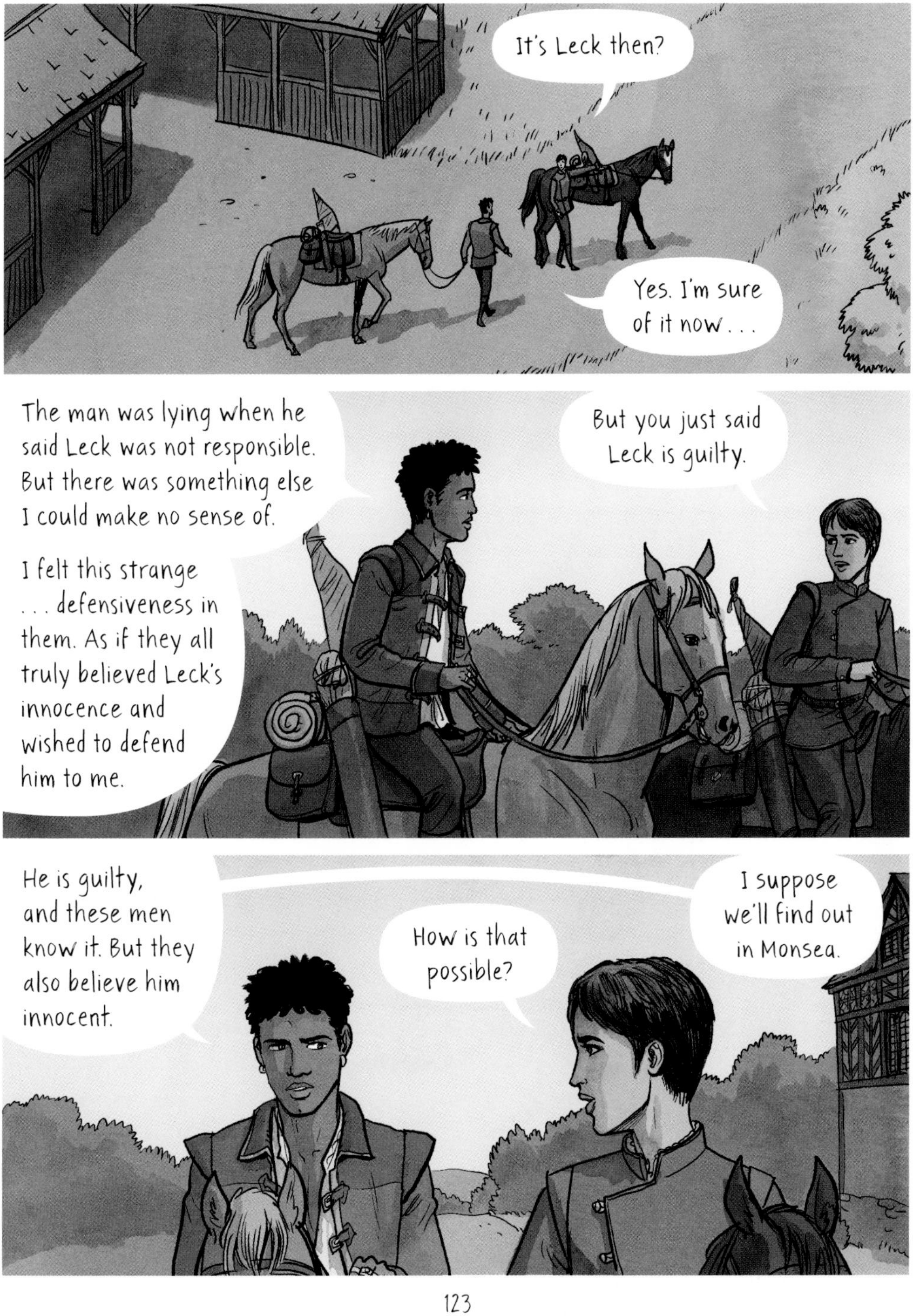
It's Leck then?
Yes. I'm sure of it now . . .
The man was lying when he said Leck was not responsible. But there was something else I could make no sense of.
I felt this strange . . . defensiveness in them. As if they all truly believed Leck's innocence and wished to defend him to me.
But you just said Leck is guilty.
He is guilty, and these men know it. But they also believe him innocent.
How is that possible?
I suppose we'll find out in Monsea.

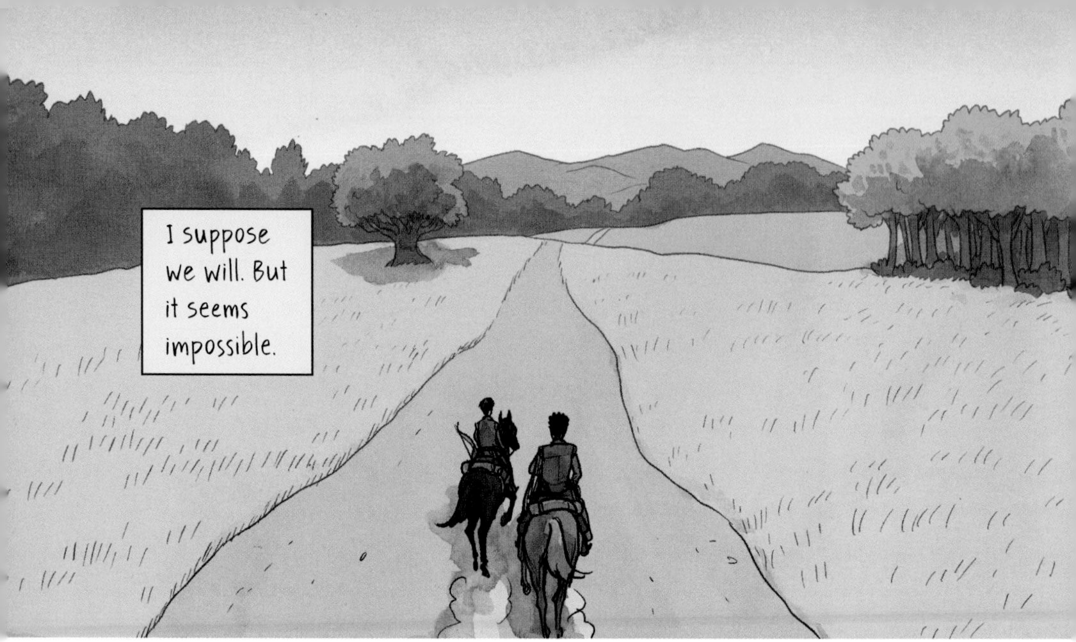
I suppose we will. But it seems impossible.

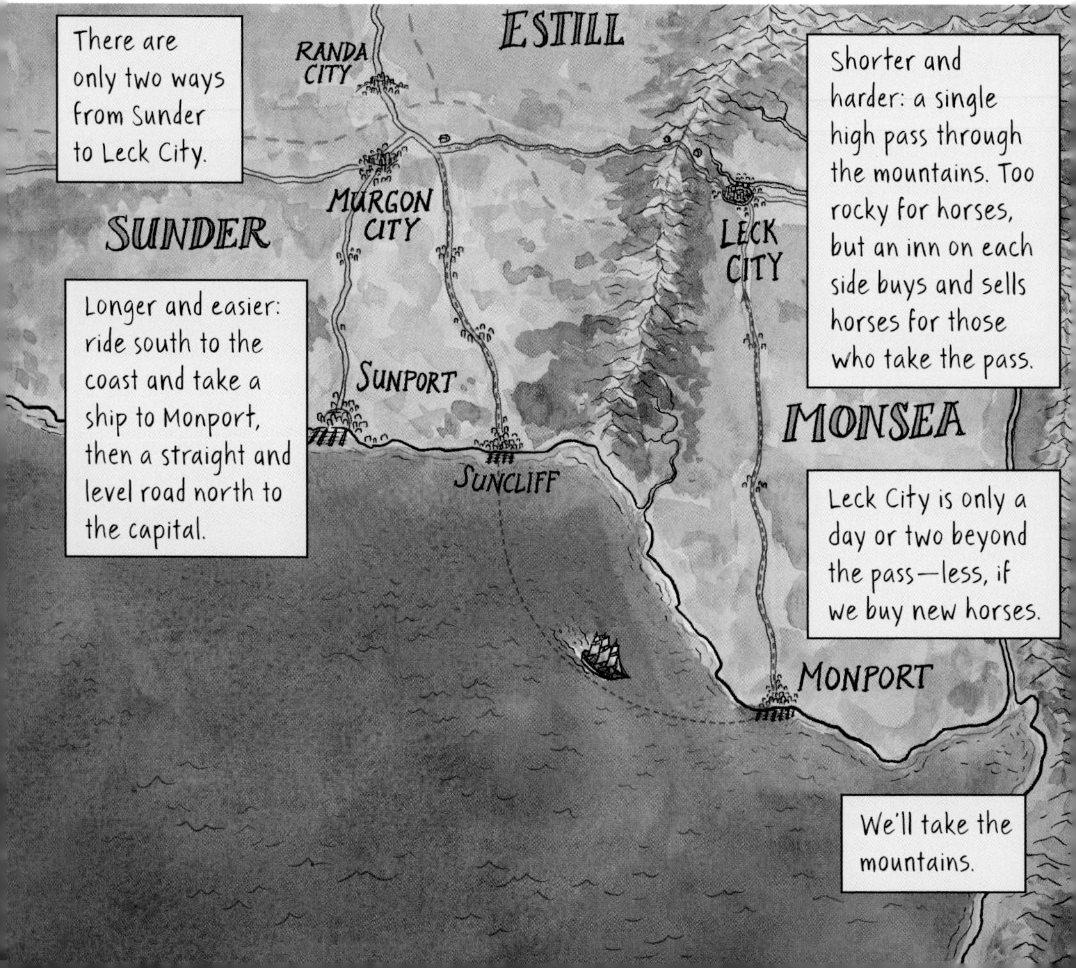
There are only two ways from Sunder to Leck City.
ESTILL
RANDA CITY
MURGON CITY
SUNDER
SUNPORT
SUNCLIFF
LECK CITY
MONSEA
MONPORT
Longer and easier: ride south to the coast and take a ship to Monport, then a straight and level road north to the capital.
Shorter and harder: a single high pass through the mountains. Too rocky for horses, but an inn on each side buys and sells horses for those who take the pass.
Leck City is only a day or two beyond the pass—less, if we buy new horses.
We'll take the mountains.

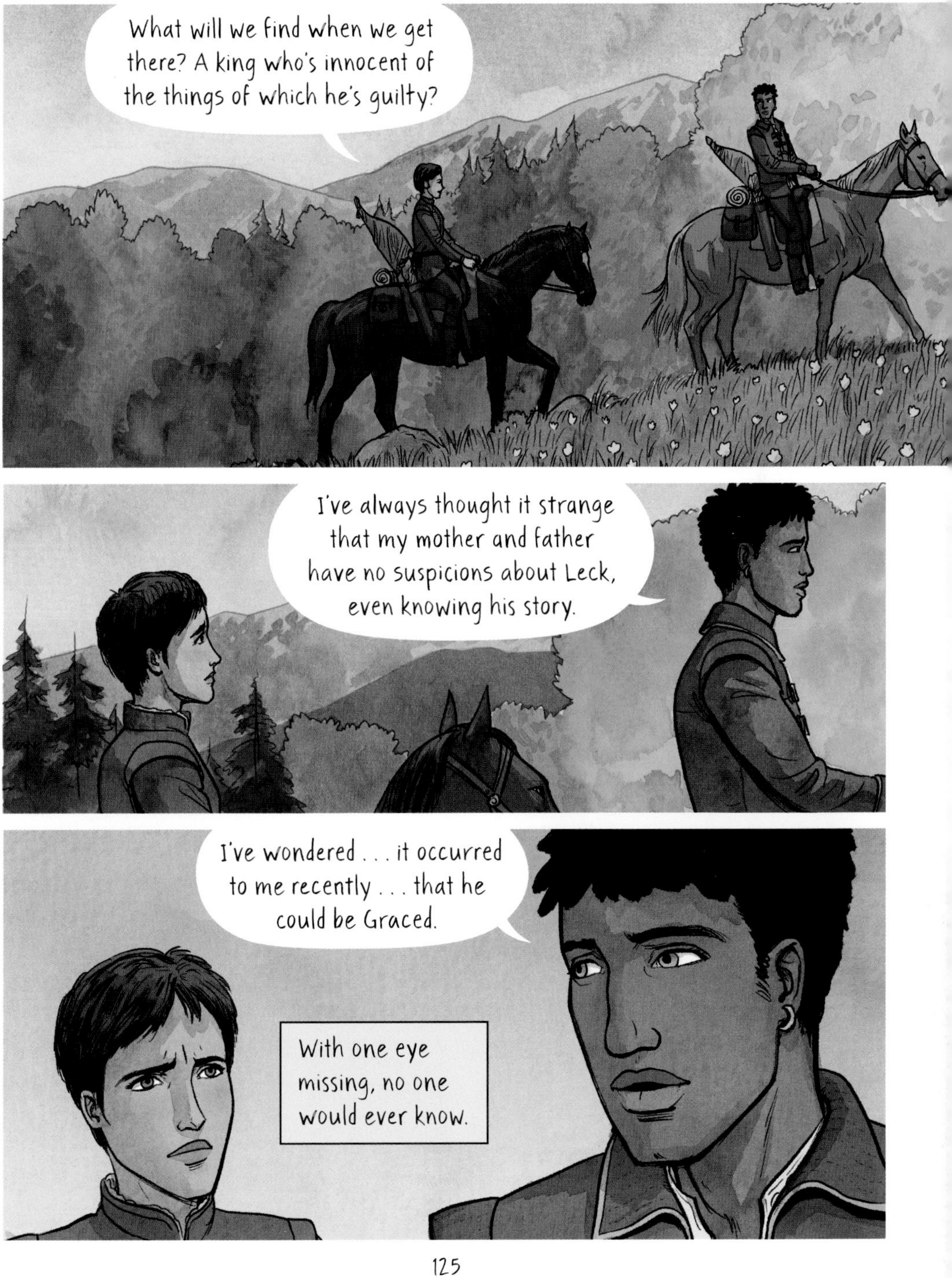
What will we find when we get there? A king who's innocent of the things of which he's guilty?
I've always thought it strange that my mother and father have no suspicions about Leck, even knowing his story.
I've wondered . . . it occurred to me recently . . . that he could be Graced.
With one eye missing, no one would ever know.

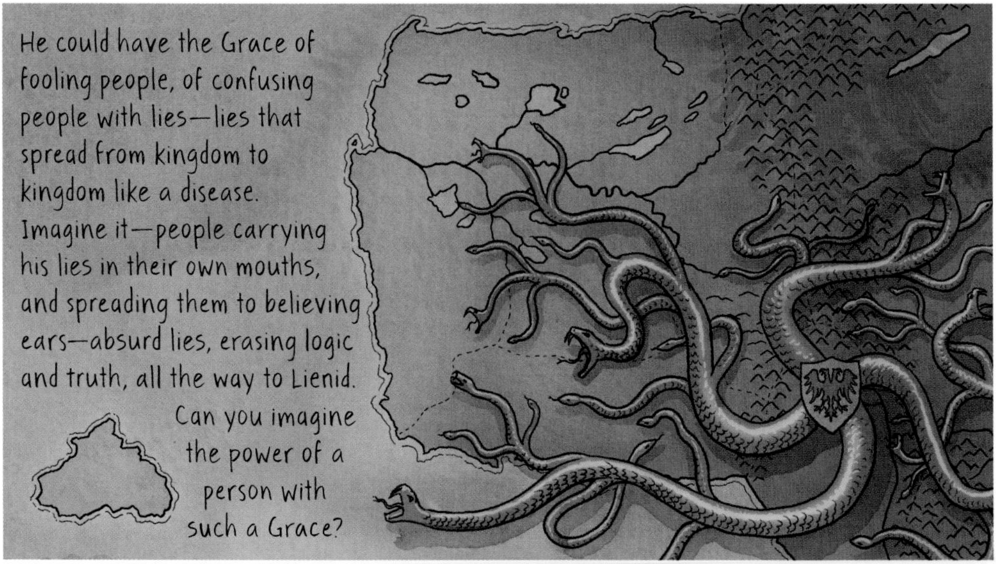
He could have the Grace of fooling people, of confusing people with lies—lies that spread from kingdom to kingdom like a disease. Imagine it—people carrying his lies in their own mouths, and spreading them to believing ears—absurd lies, erasing logic and truth, all the way to Lienid.
Can you imagine the power of a person with such a Grace?

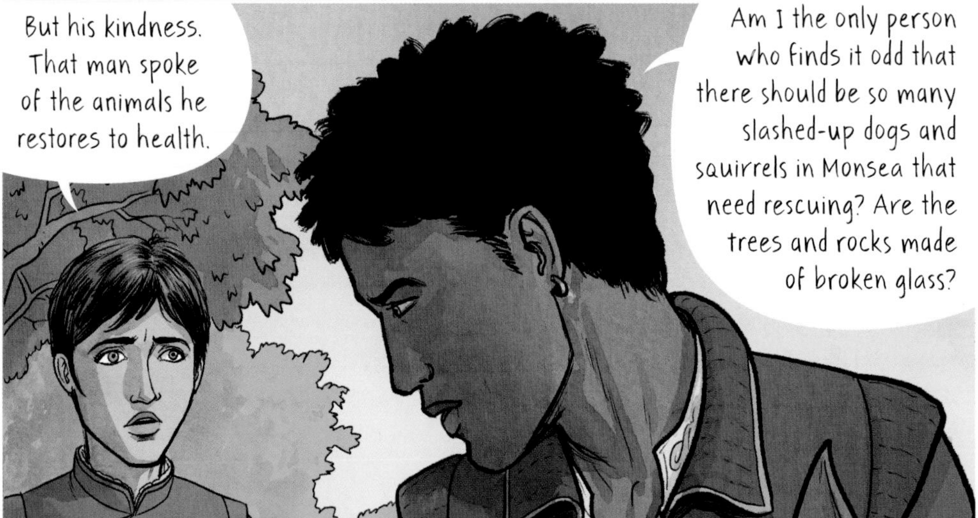
But his kindness. That man spoke of the animals he restores to health.
Am I the only person who finds it odd that there should be so many slashed-up dogs and squirrels in Monsea that need rescuing? Are the trees and rocks made of broken glass?

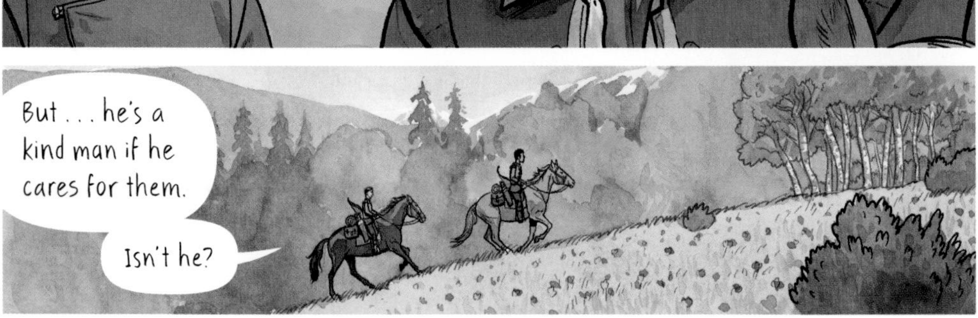
But . . . he's a kind man if he cares for them.
Isn't he?

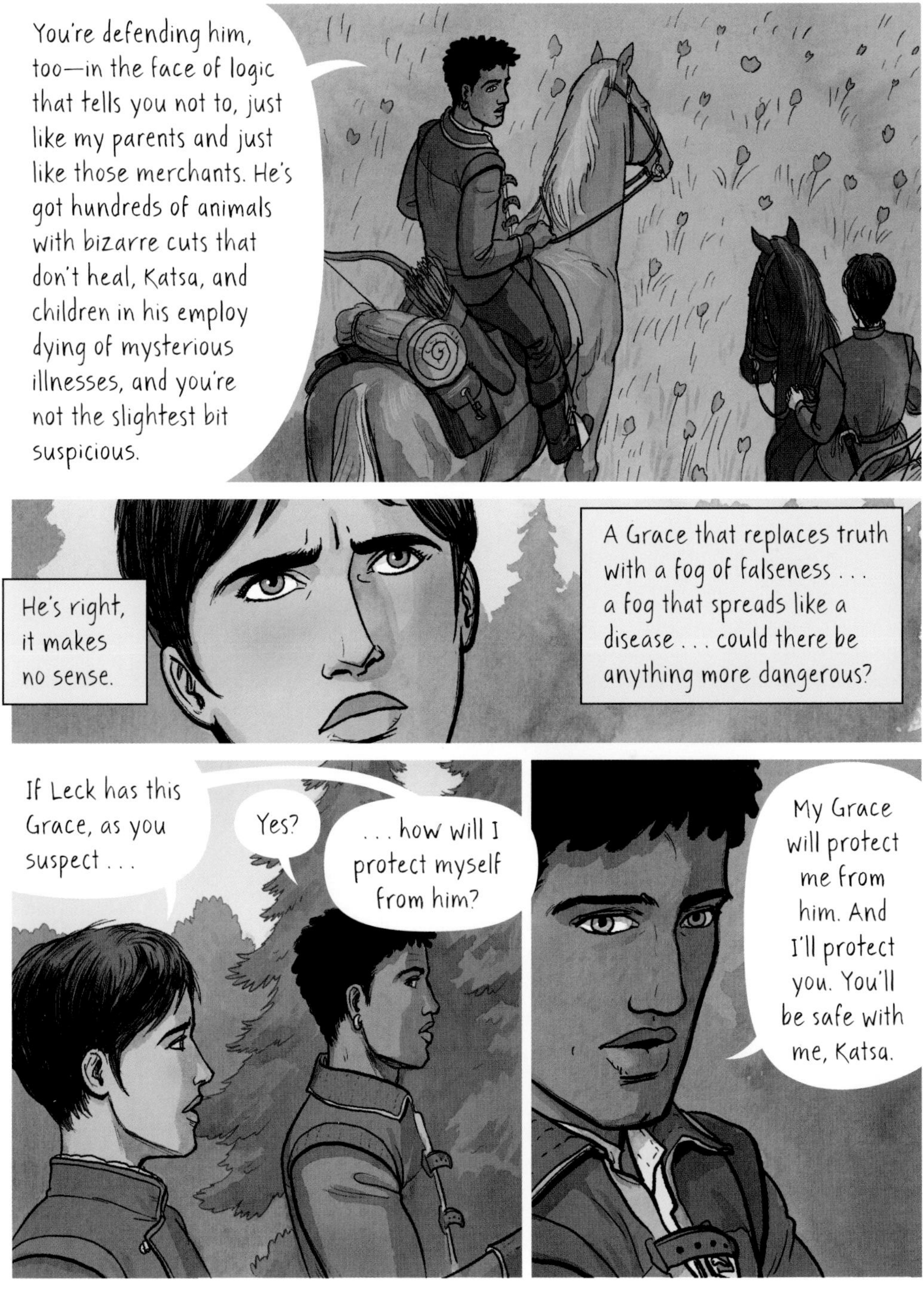
You're defending him, too—in the face of logic that tells you not to, just like my parents and just like those merchants. He's got hundreds of animals with bizarre cuts that don't heal, Katsa, and children in his employ dying of mysterious illnesses, and you're not the slightest bit suspicious.
He's right, it makes no sense.
A Grace that replaces truth with a fog of falseness . . . a fog that spreads like a disease . . . could there be anything more dangerous?
If Leck has this Grace, as you suspect . . .
Yes?
. . . how will I protect myself from him?
My Grace will protect me from him. And I'll protect you. You'll be safe with me, Katsa.

Po's Grace will protect him from Leck, and he will protect me.

He said it as if it were nothing—but it is not nothing for me to rely on someone else for protection. I've never done it in my life.

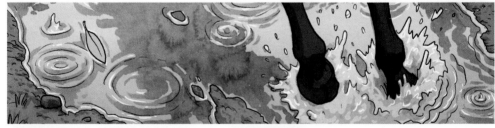

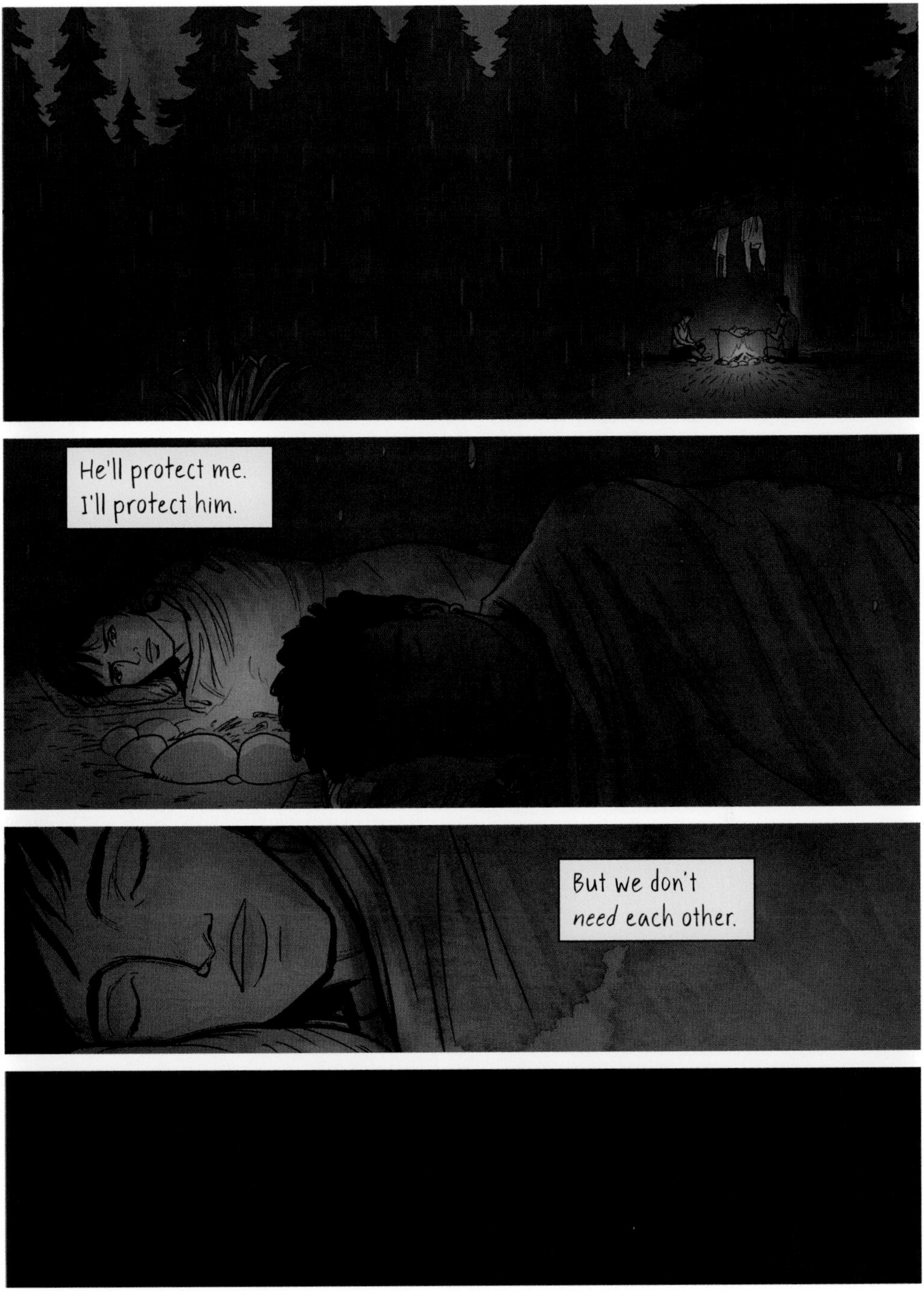
He'll protect me.
I'll protect him.
But we don't need each other.

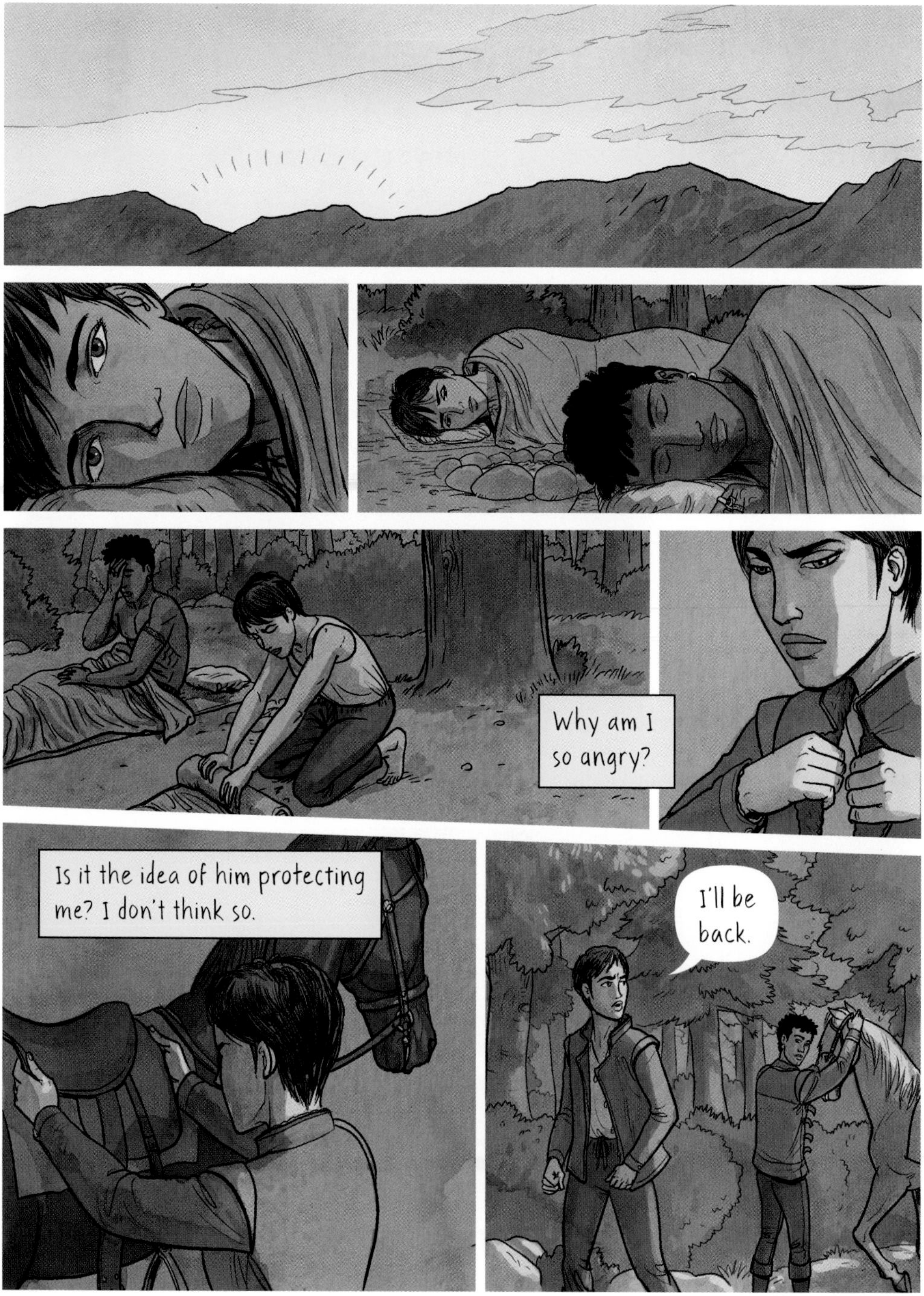
Why am I so angry?
Is it the idea of him protecting me? I don't think so.
I'll be back.

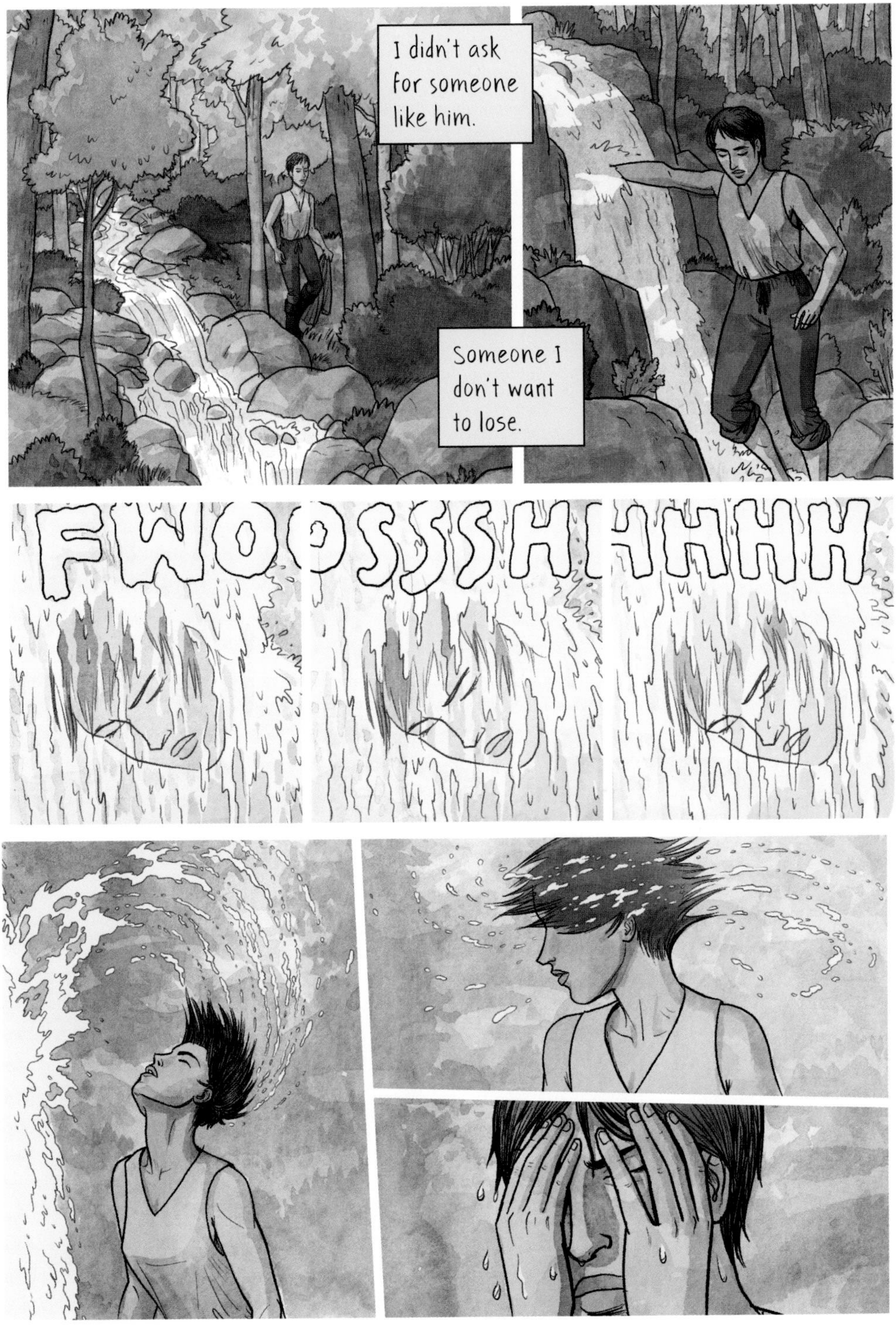
I didn't ask for someone like him.
Someone I don't want to lose.
FWOOSSSHHHHH

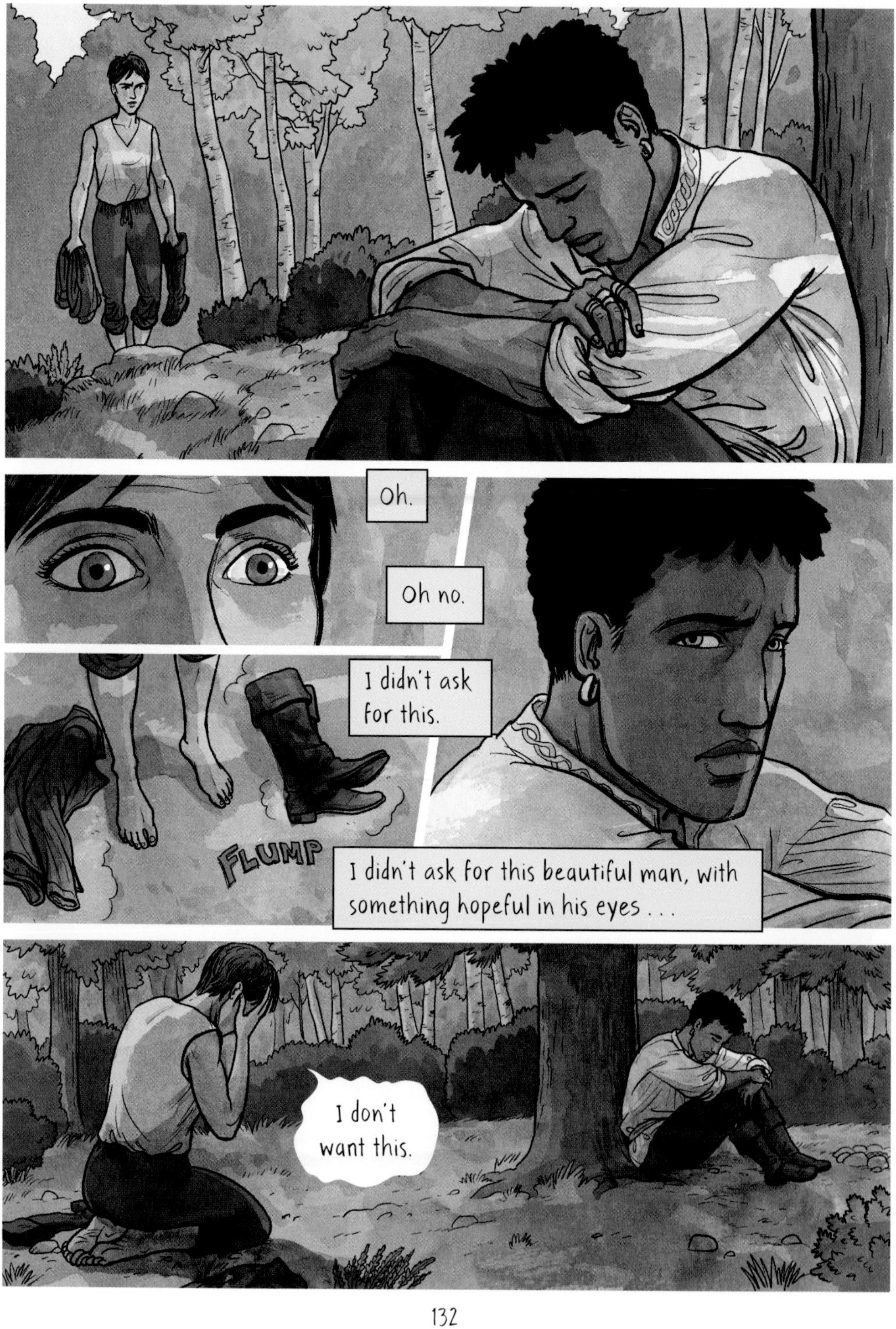
Oh.
Oh no.
I didn't ask for this.
FLUMP
I didn't ask for this beautiful man, with something hopeful in his eyes . . .
I don't want this.

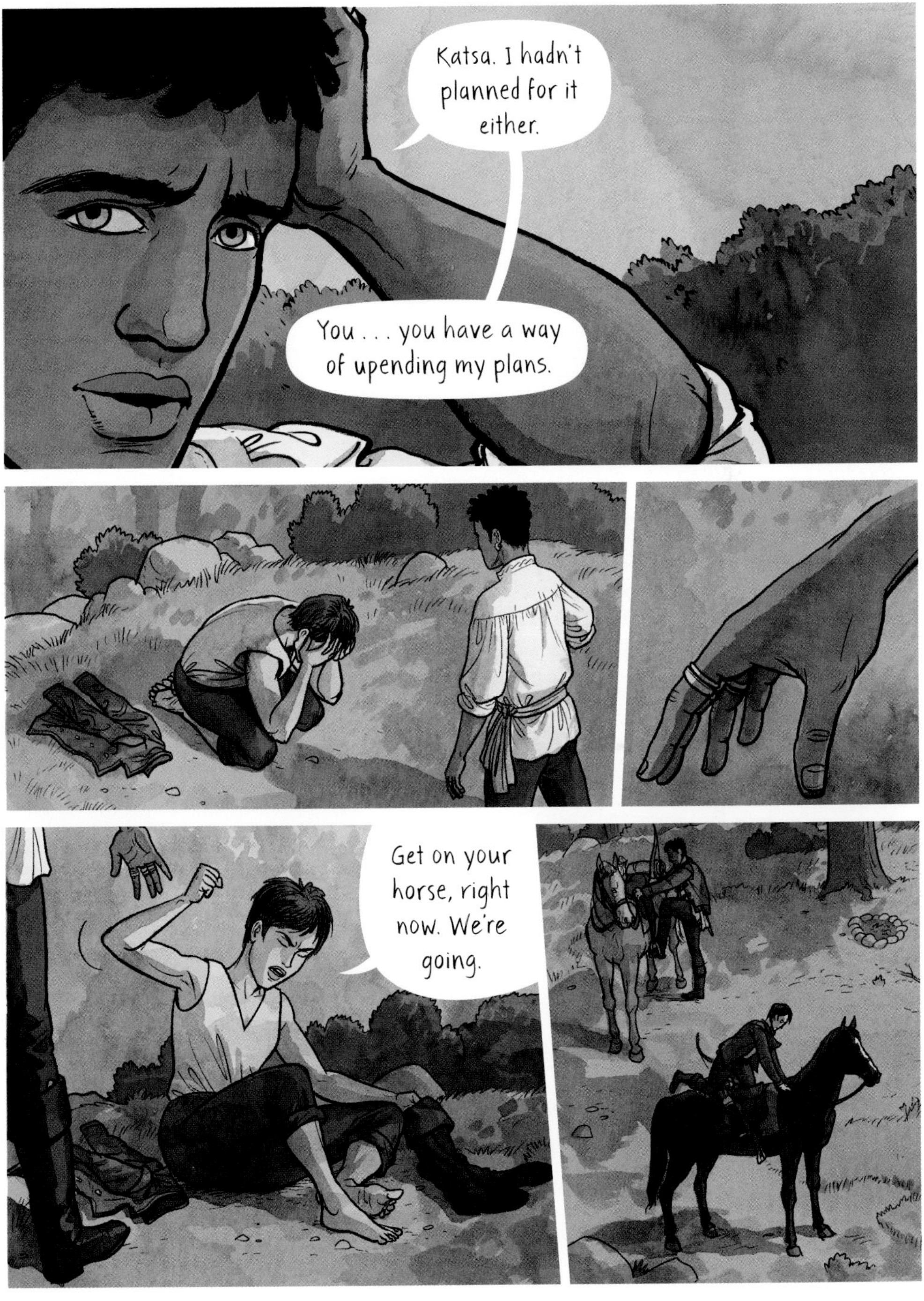
Katsa. I hadn't planned for it either.
You . . . you have a way of upending my plans.
Get on your horse, right now. We're going.

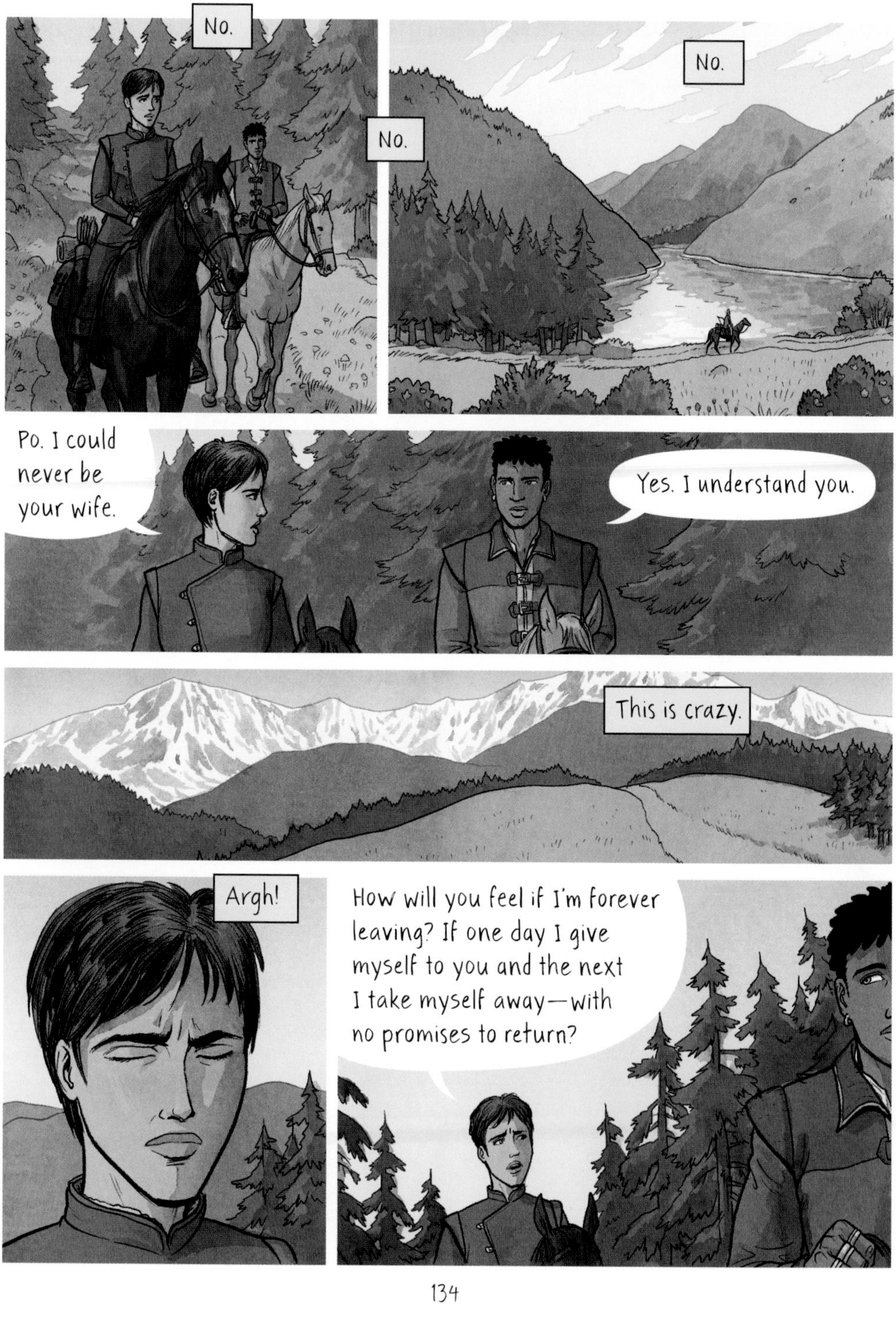
No.
No.
No.
Po. I could never be your wife.
Yes. I understand you.
This is crazy.
Argh!
How will you feel if I'm forever leaving? If one day I give myself to you and the next I take myself away—with no promises to return?

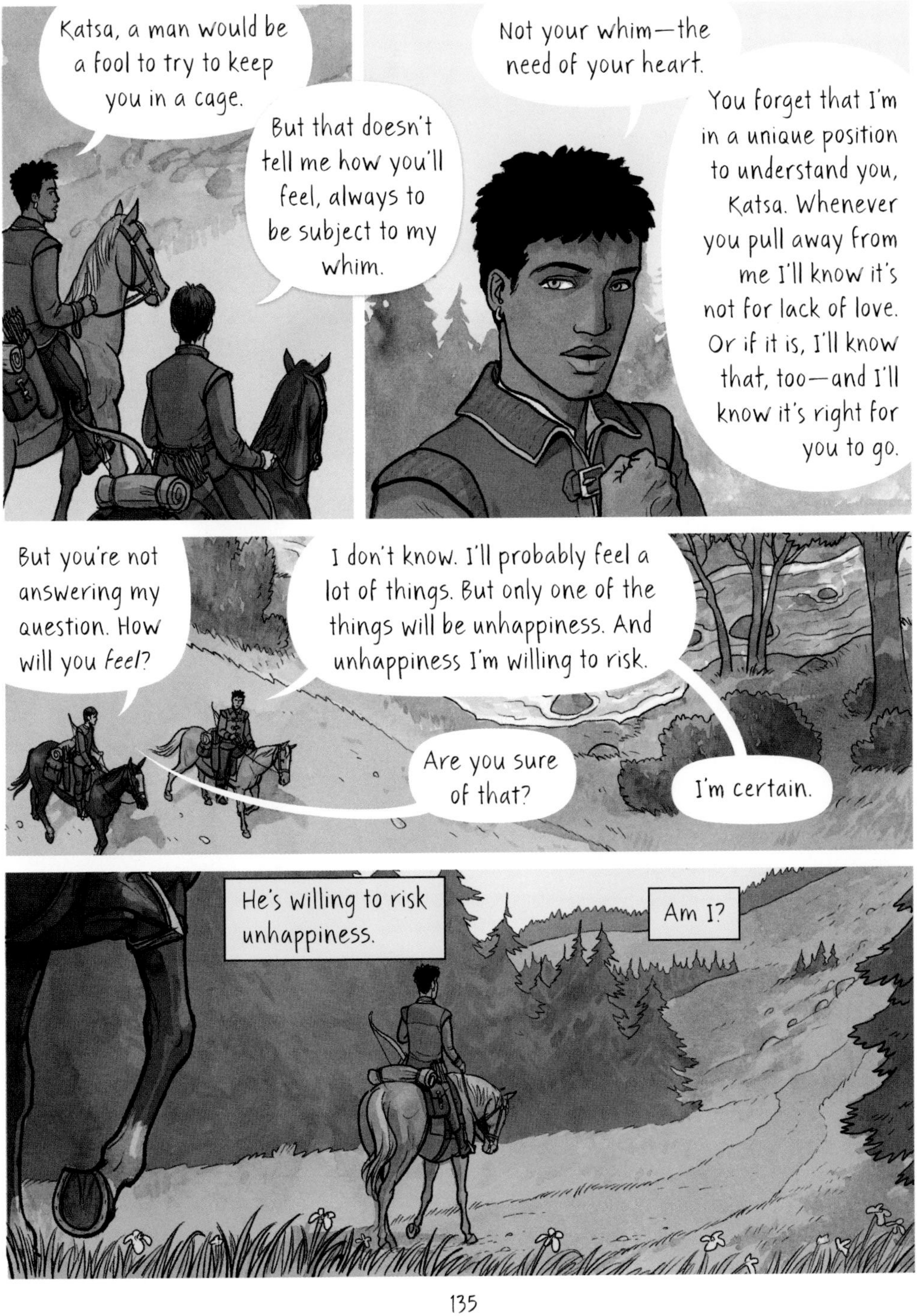
Katsa, a man would be a fool to try to keep you in a cage.
But that doesn't tell me how you'll feel, always to be subject to my whim.
Not your whim—the need of your heart.
You forget that I'm in a unique position to understand you, Katsa. Whenever you pull away from me I'll know it's not for lack of love. Or if it is, I'll know that, too—and I'll know it's right for you to go.
But you're not answering my question. How will you *feel*?
I don't know. I'll probably feel a lot of things. But only one of the things will be unhappiness. And unhappiness I'm willing to risk.
Are you sure of that?
I'm certain.
He's willing to risk unhappiness.
Am I?

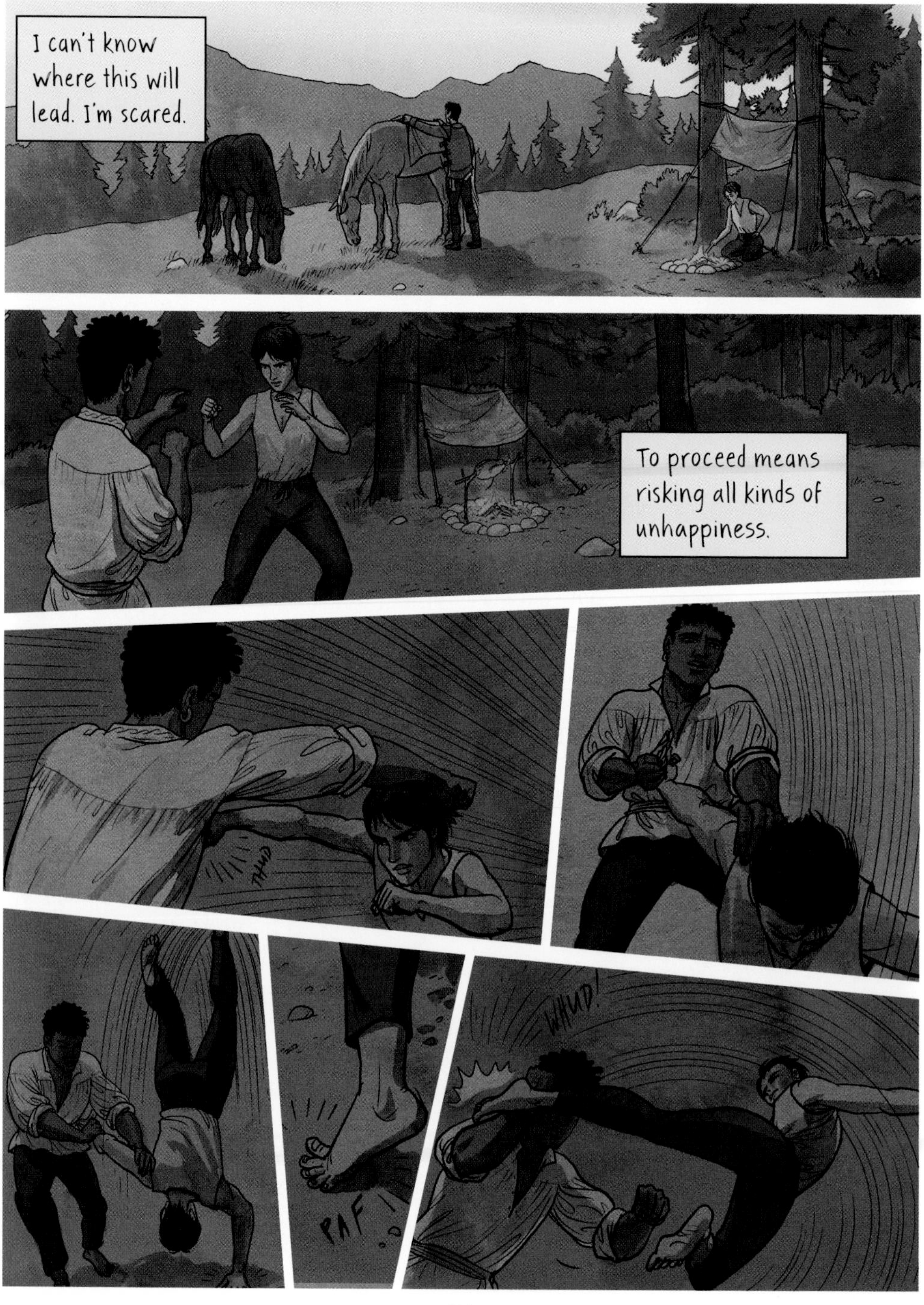
I can't know where this will lead. I'm scared.
To proceed means risking all kinds of unhappiness.
THUD
PAF!
WHUD!

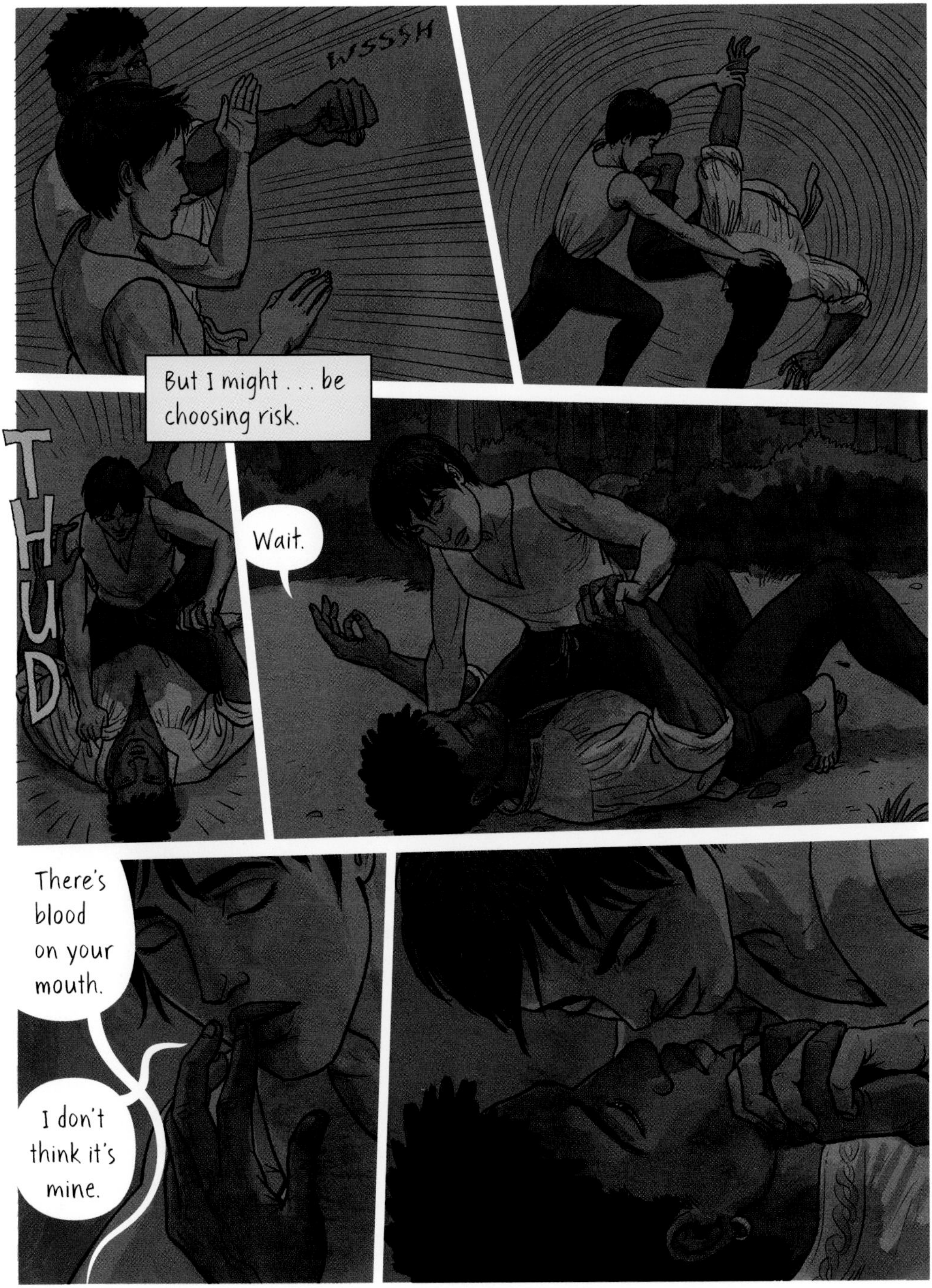
WSSSH
But I might . . . be choosing risk.
THUD
Wait.
There's blood on your mouth.
I don't think it's mine.

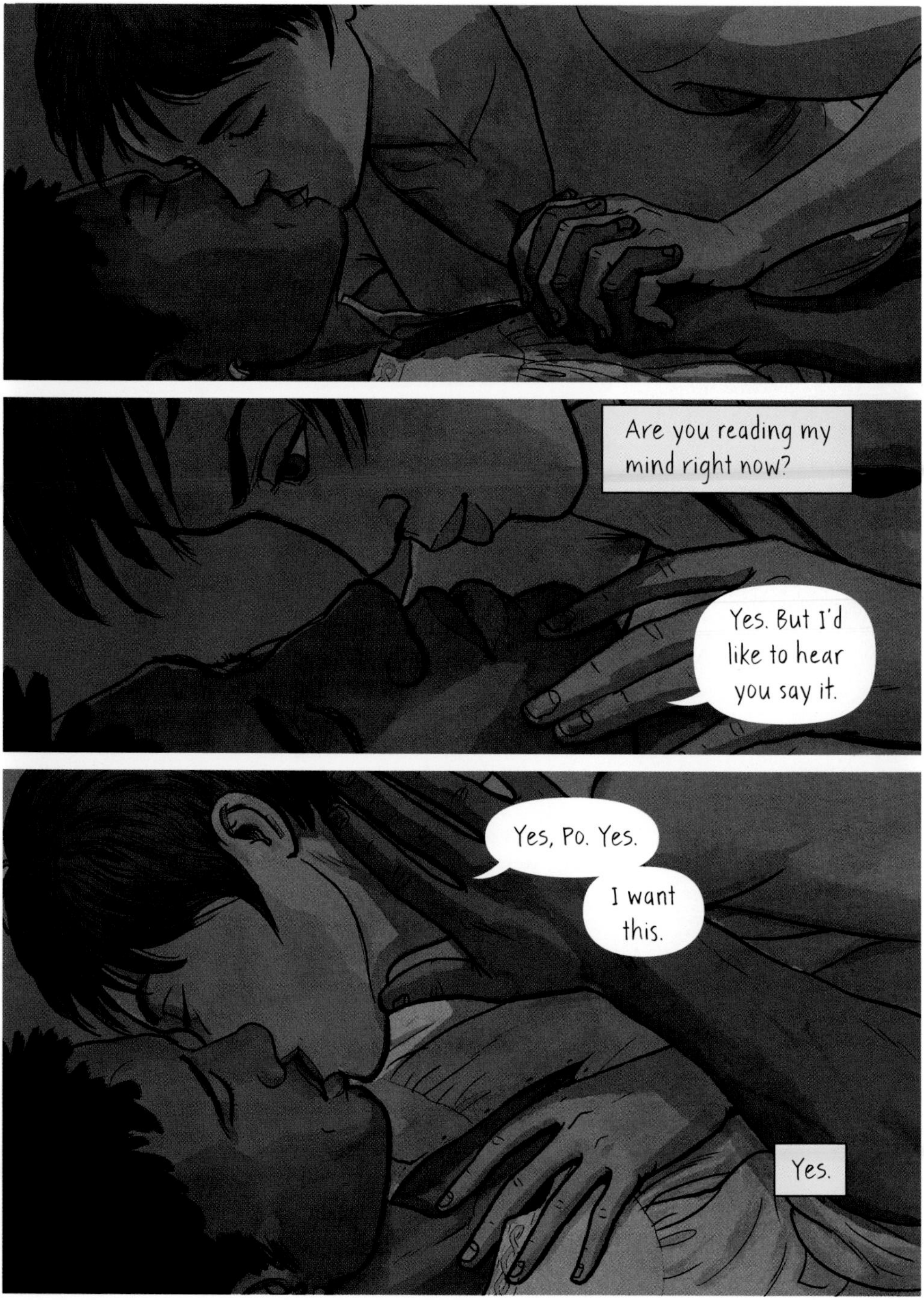
Are you reading my mind right now?
Yes. But I'd like to hear you say it.
Yes, Po. Yes.
I want this.
Yes.

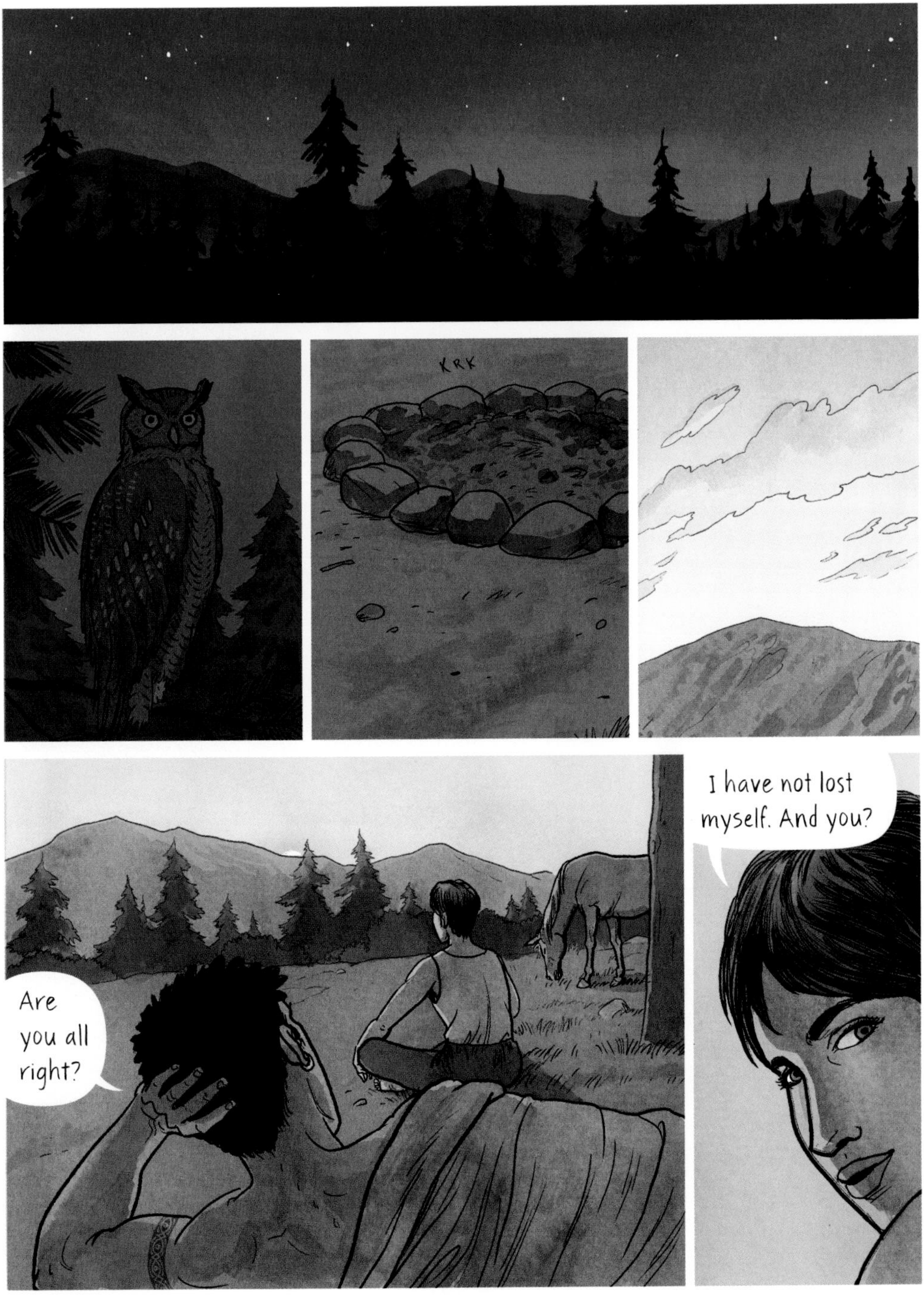
KRK
Are you all right?
I have not lost myself. And you?

I'm very happy.

This should feel strange, but it doesn't. It feels natural and comfortable. Inevitable. And only the smallest bit terrifying.

He's beautiful.

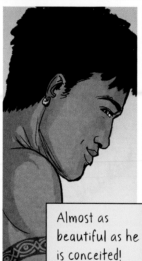

Almost as beautiful as he is conceited!

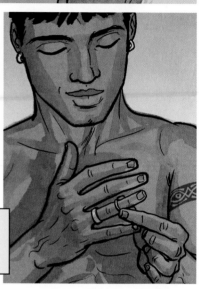

Do your rings have meaning?

Yes. Each one represents a member of my family—my parents, my grandfather, and my six brothers—and one is for my own princehood and inheritance.

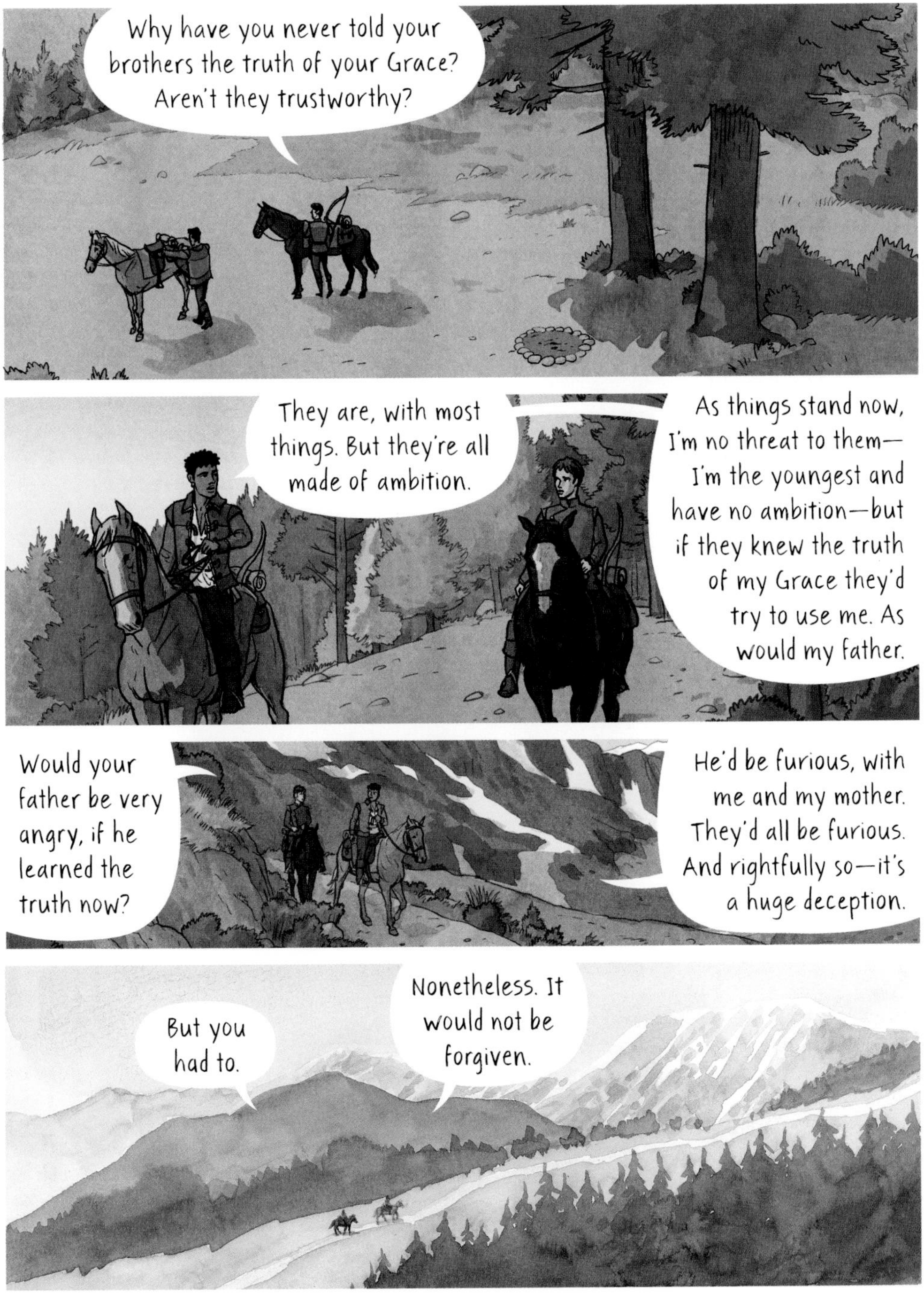
Why have you never told your brothers the truth of your Grace? Aren't they trustworthy?
They are, with most things. But they're all made of ambition.
As things stand now, I'm no threat to them— I'm the youngest and have no ambition—but if they knew the truth of my Grace they'd try to use me. As would my father.
Would your father be very angry, if he learned the truth now?
He'd be furious, with me and my mother. They'd all be furious. And rightfully so—it's a huge deception.
But you had to.
Nonetheless. It would not be forgiven.

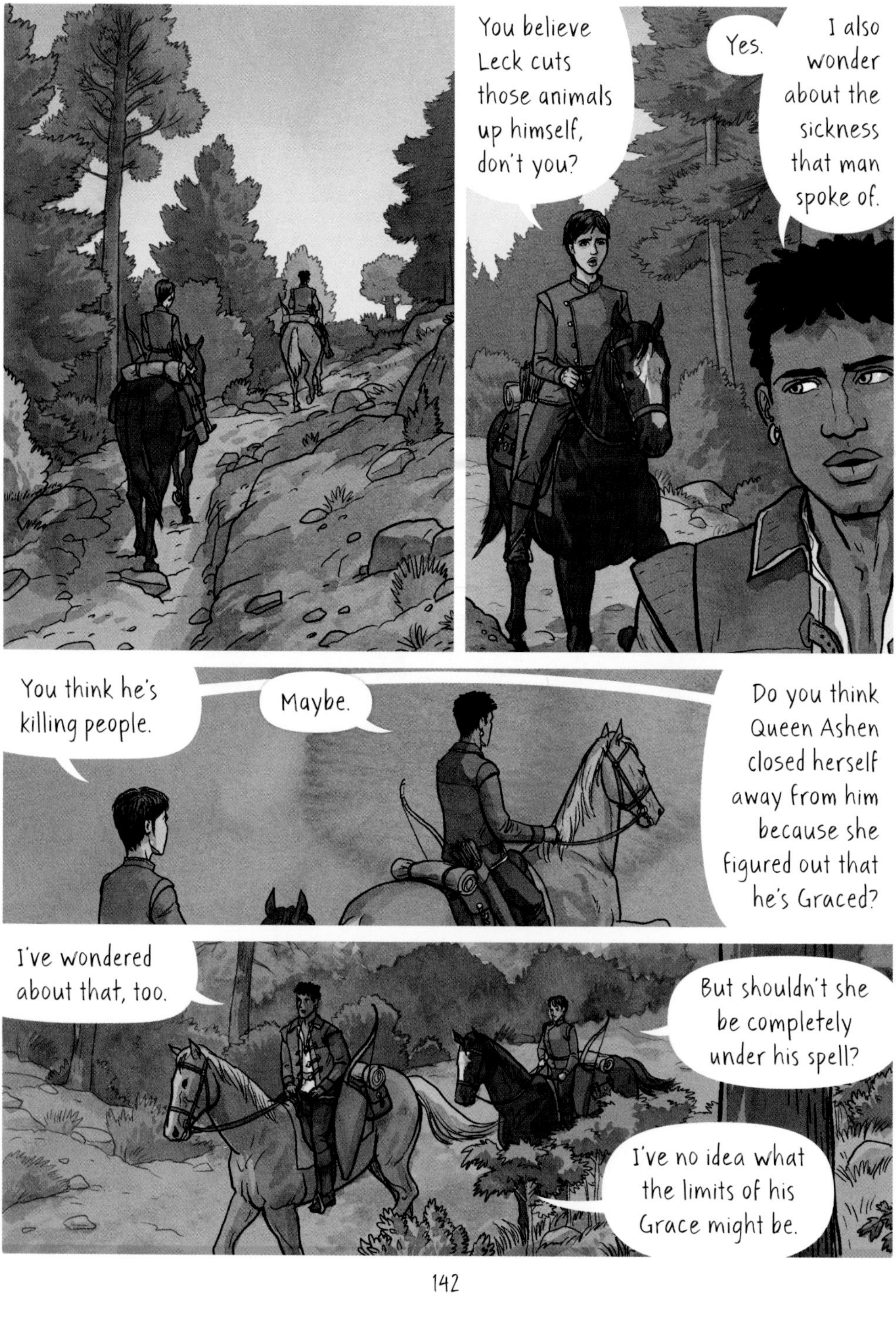
You believe Leck cuts those animals up himself, don't you?
Yes.
I also wonder about the sickness that man spoke of.
You think he's killing people.
Maybe.
Do you think Queen Ashen closed herself away from him because she figured out that he's Graced?
I've wondered about that, too.
But shouldn't she be completely under his spell?
I've no idea what the limits of his Grace might be.

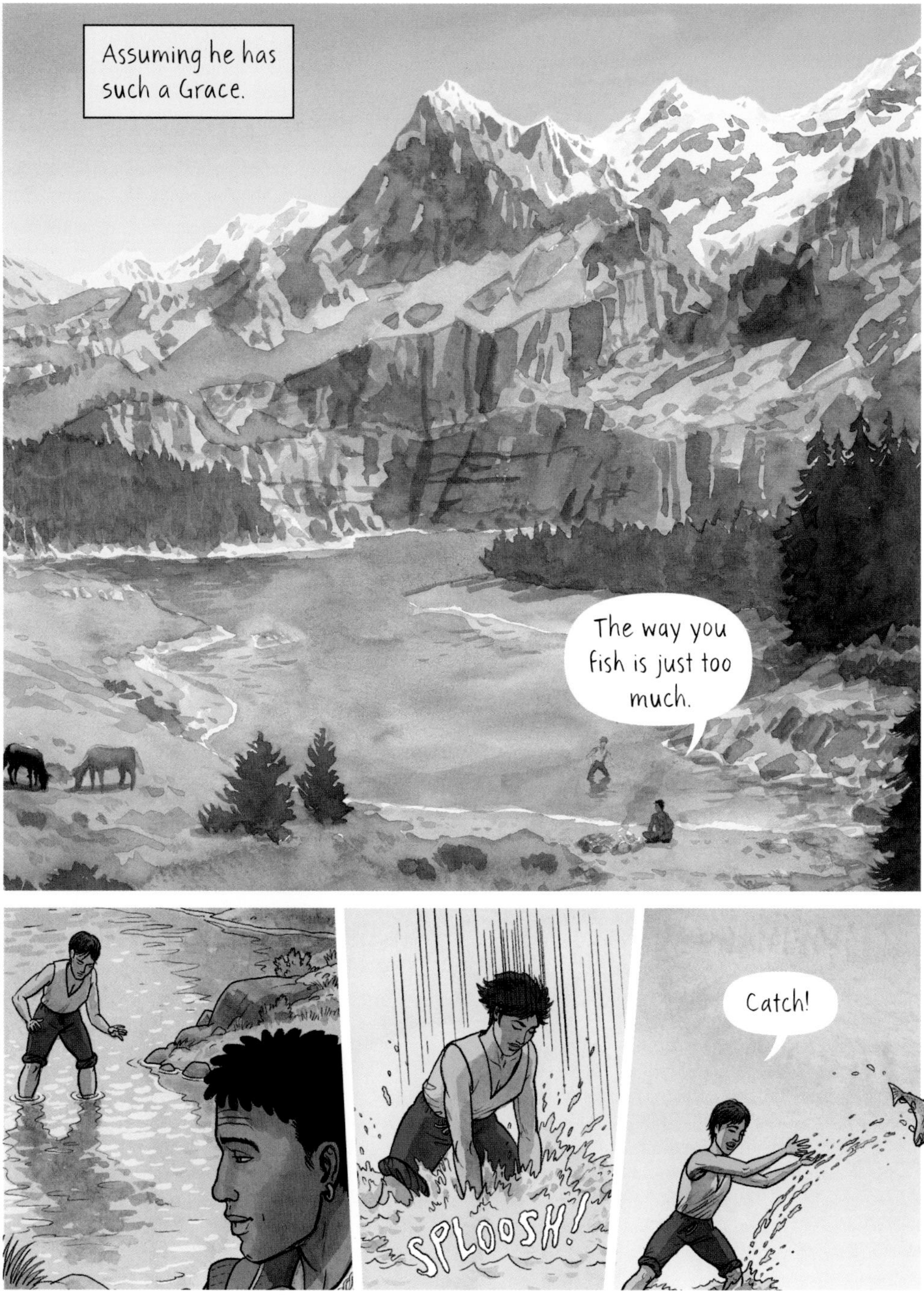
Assuming he has such a Grace.
The way you fish is just too much.
SPLOOSH!
Catch!

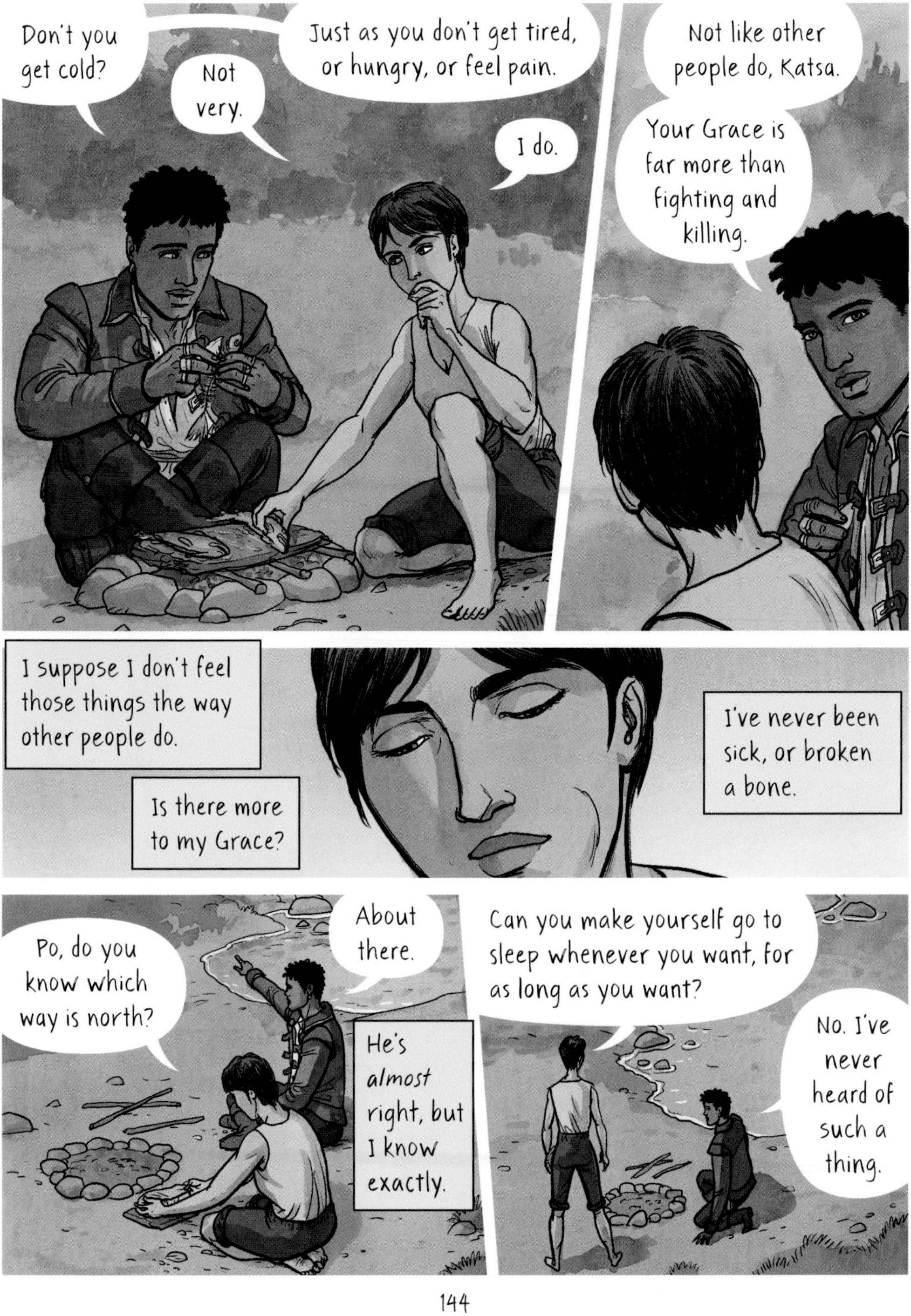
Don't you get cold?
Not very.
Just as you don't get tired, or hungry, or feel pain.
I do.
Not like other people do, Katsa.
Your Grace is far more than fighting and killing.
I suppose I don't feel those things the way other people do.
Is there more to my Grace?
I've never been sick, or broken a bone.
Po, do you know which way is north?
About there.
He's *almost* right, but I know exactly.
Can you make yourself go to sleep whenever you want, for as long as you want?
No. I've never heard of such a thing.

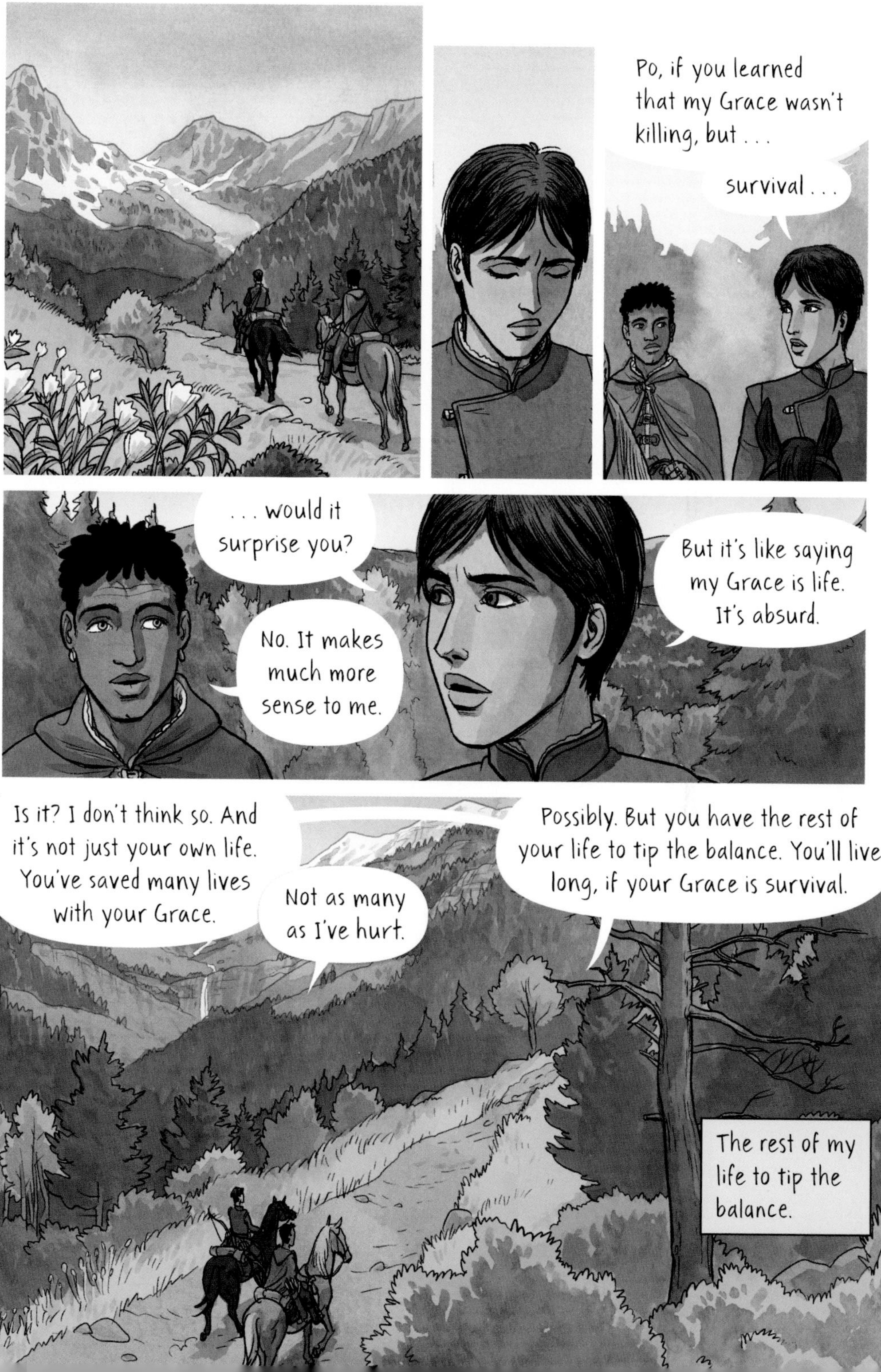
Po, if you learned that my Grace wasn't killing, but . . .
survival . . .
. . . would it surprise you?
No. It makes much more sense to me.
But it's like saying my Grace is life. It's absurd.
Is it? I don't think so. And it's not just your own life. You've saved many lives with your Grace.
Not as many as I've hurt.
Possibly. But you have the rest of your life to tip the balance. You'll live long, if your Grace is survival.
The rest of my life to tip the balance.

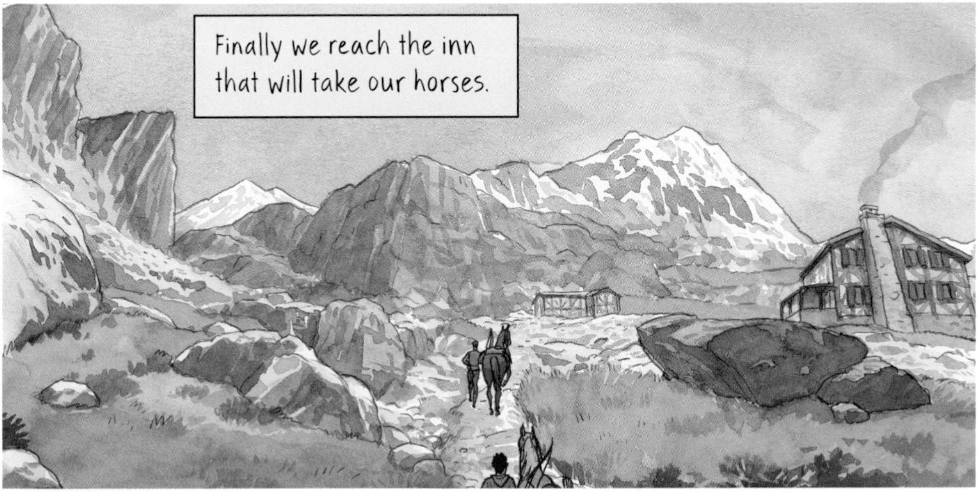
Finally we reach the inn that will take our horses.

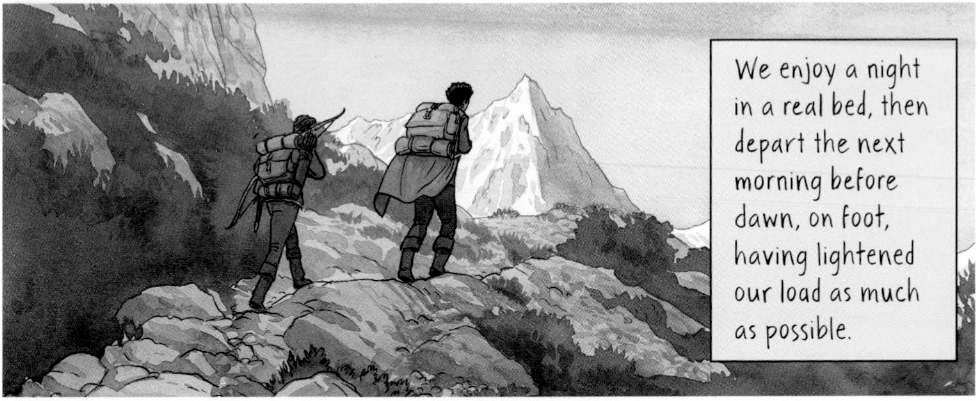
We enjoy a night in a real bed, then depart the next morning before dawn, on foot, having lightened our load as much as possible.

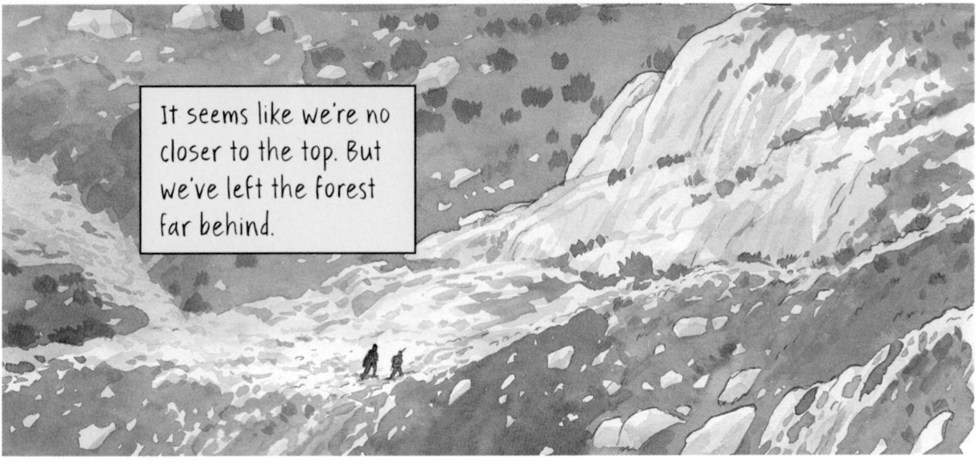
It seems like we're no closer to the top. But we've left the forest far behind.

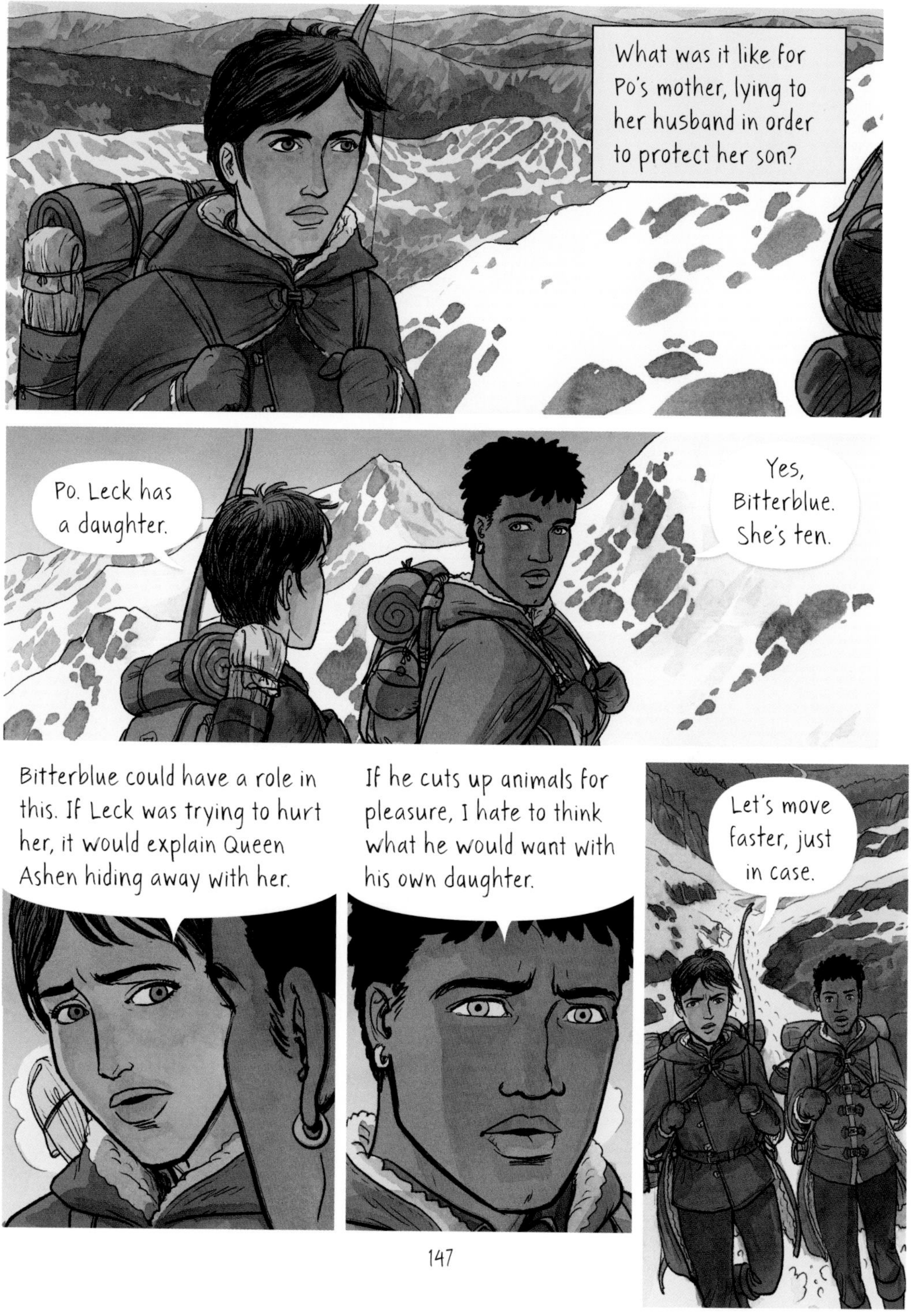
What was it like for Po's mother, lying to her husband in order to protect her son?
Po. Leck has a daughter.
Yes, Bitterblue. She's ten.
Bitterblue could have a role in this. If Leck was trying to hurt her, it would explain Queen Ashen hiding away with her.
If he cuts up animals for pleasure, I hate to think what he would want with his own daughter.
Let's move faster, just in case.

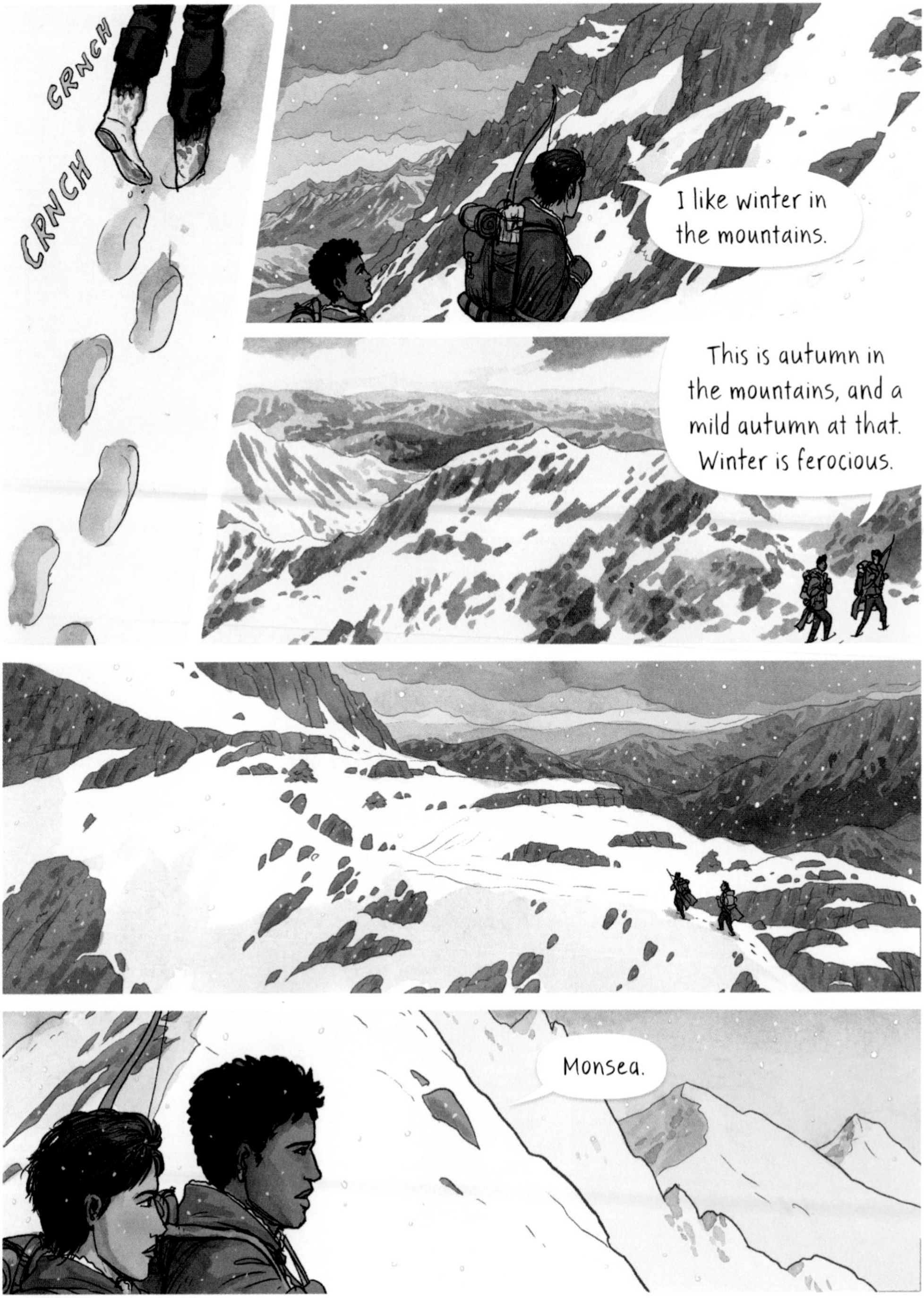
CRNCH
CRNCH
I like winter in the mountains.
This is autumn in the mountains, and a mild autumn at that. Winter is ferocious.
Monsea.

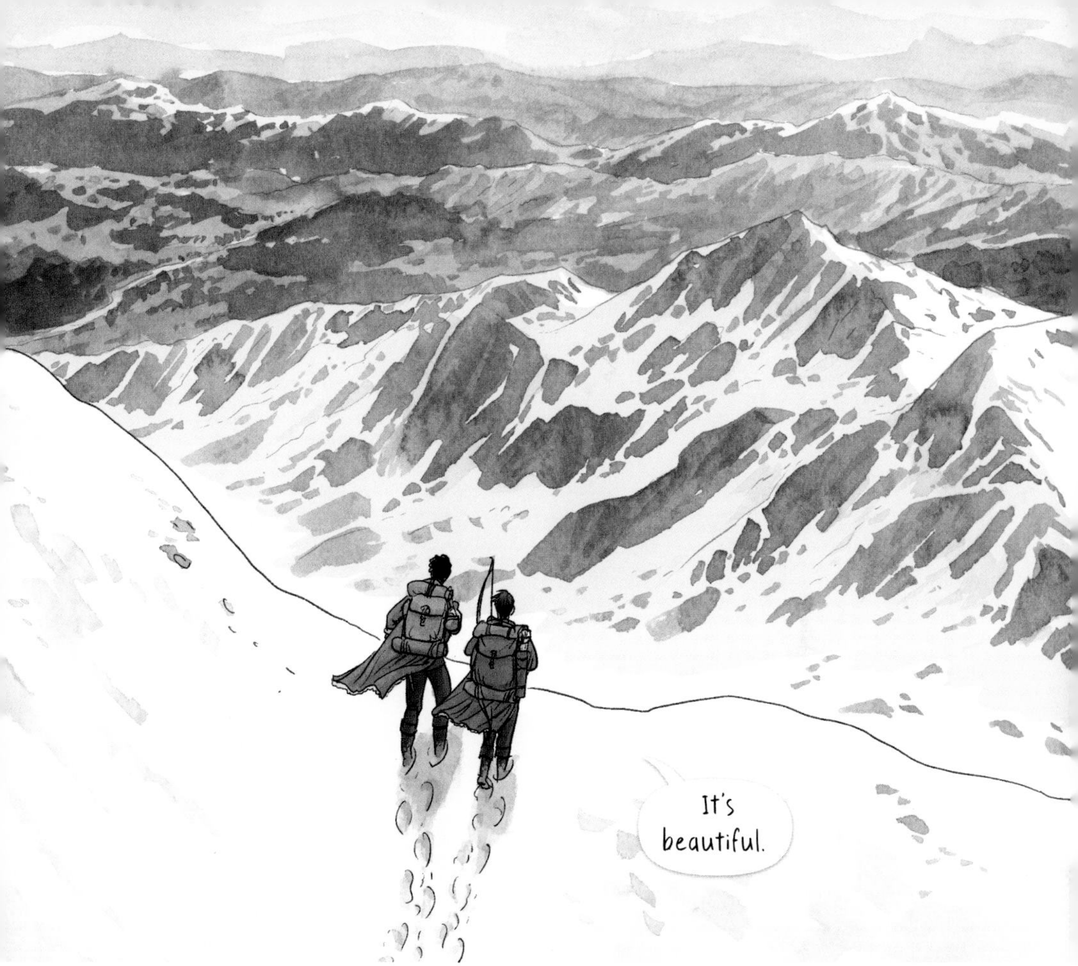
It's beautiful.

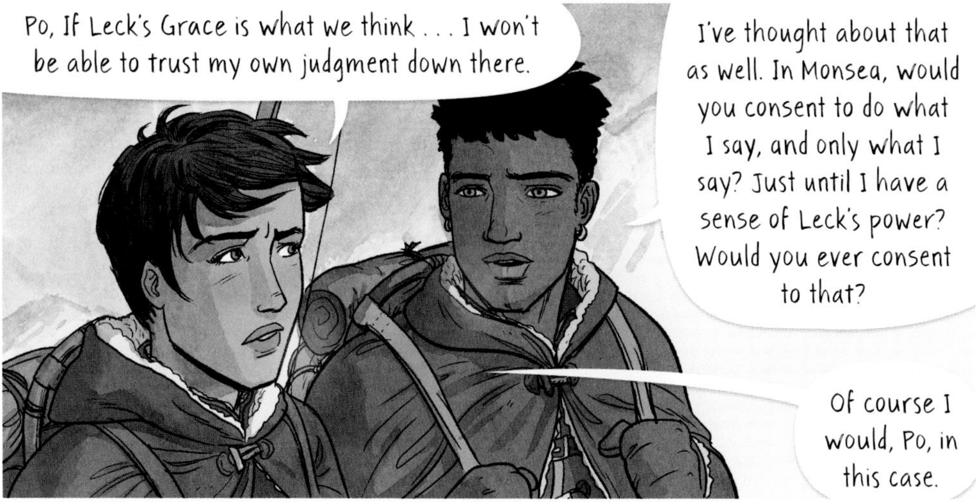
Po, If Leck's Grace is what we think . . . I won't be able to trust my own judgment down there.
I've thought about that as well. In Monsea, would you consent to do what I say, and only what I say? Just until I have a sense of Leck's power? Would you ever consent to that?
Of course I would, Po, in this case.

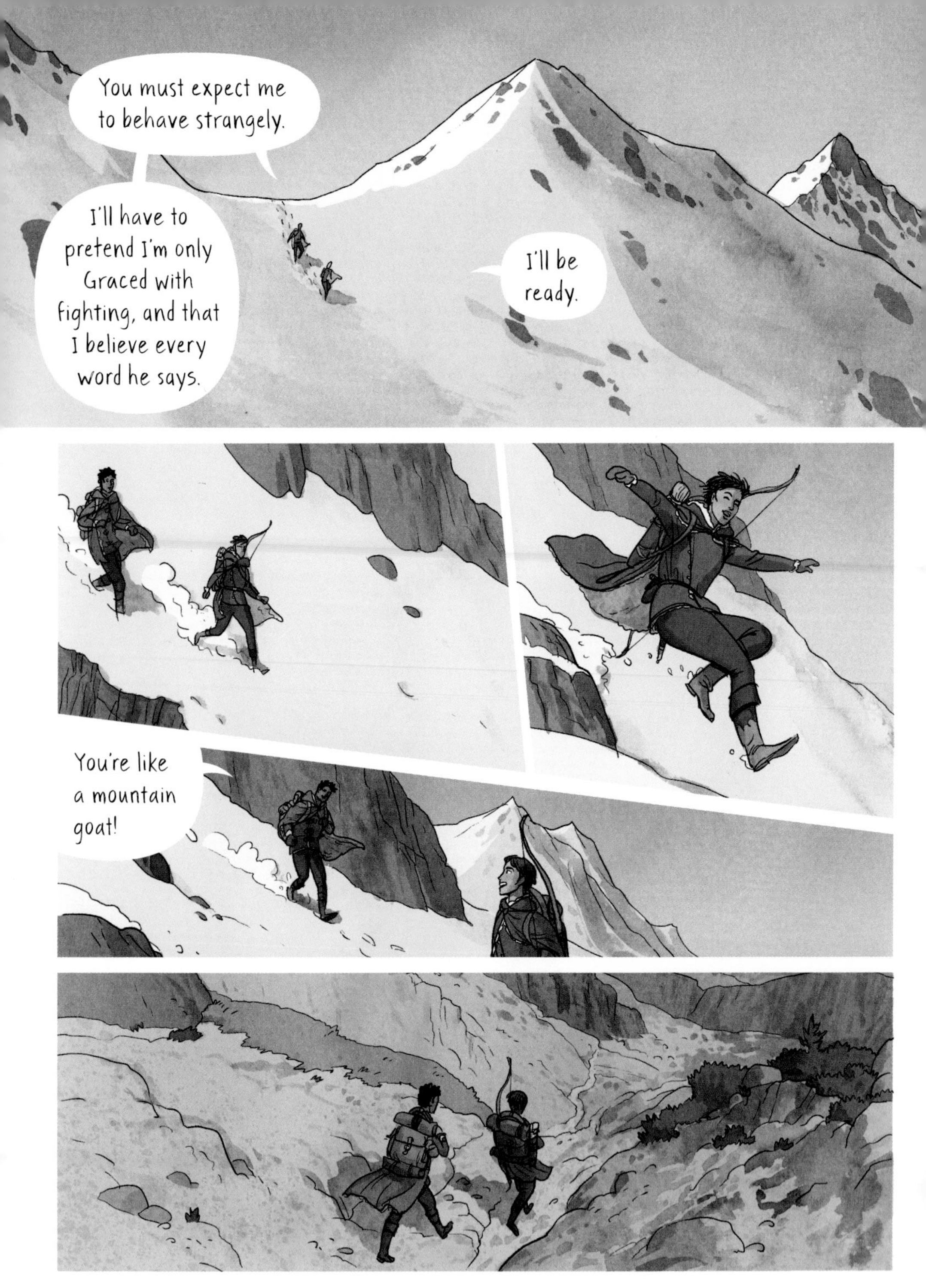
You must expect me to behave strangely.
I'll have to pretend I'm only Graced with fighting, and that I believe every word he says.
I'll be ready.
You're like a mountain goat!

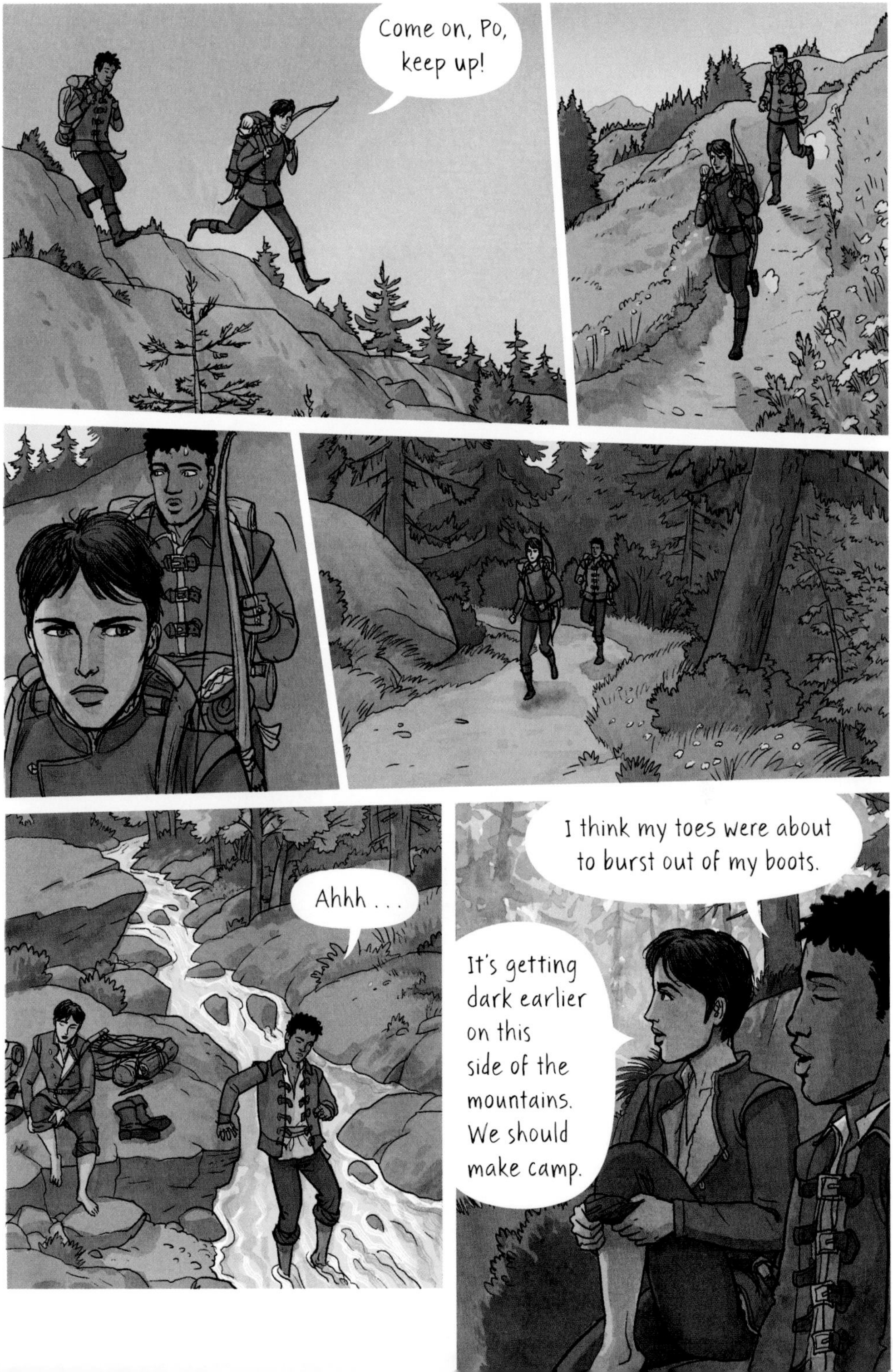
Come on, Po,
keep up!
Ahhh . . .
I think my toes were about
to burst out of my boots.
It's getting
dark earlier
on this
side of the
mountains.
We should
make camp.

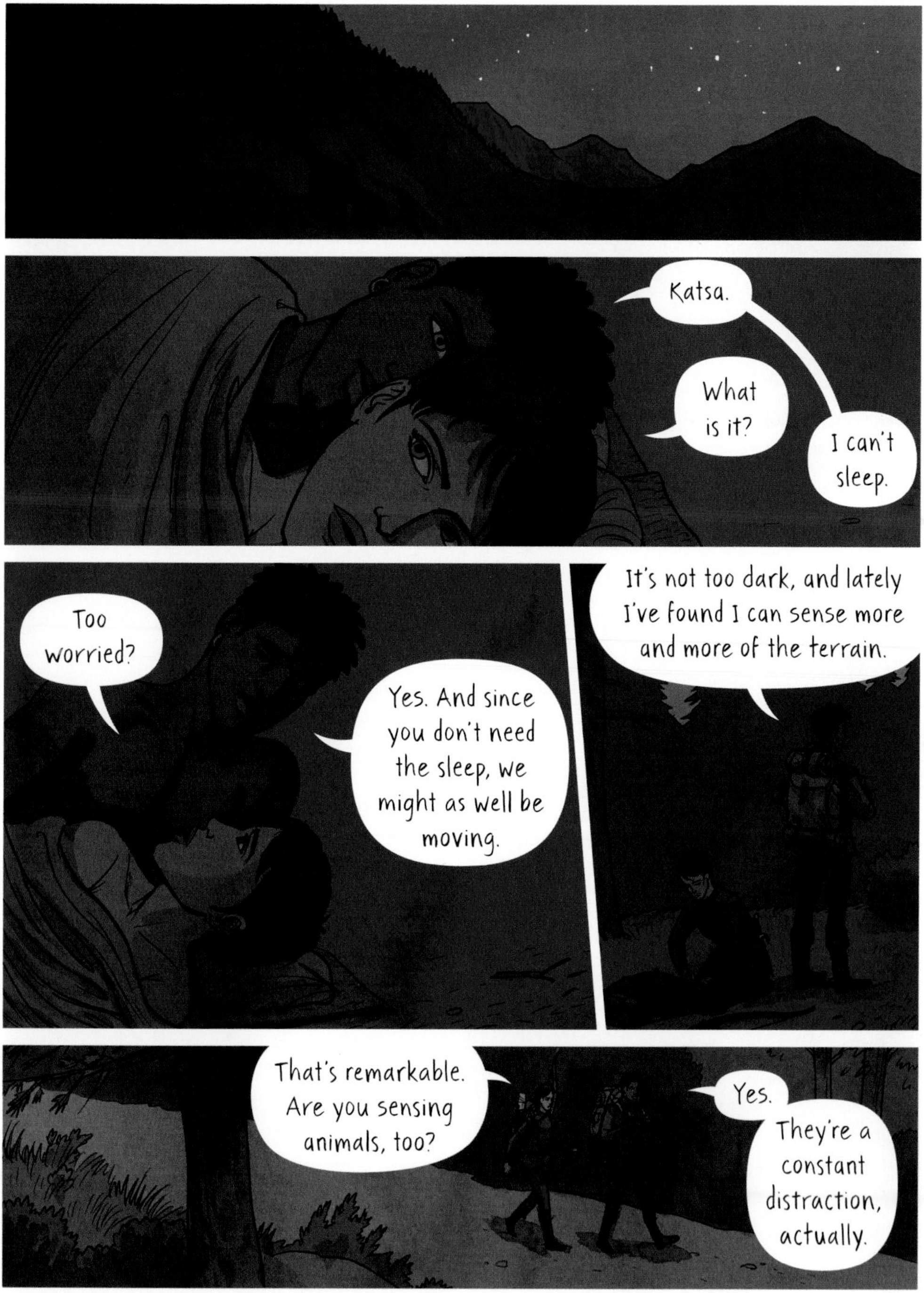
Katsa.
What is it?
I can't sleep.
Too worried?
Yes. And since you don't need the sleep, we might as well be moving.
It's not too dark, and lately I've found I can sense more and more of the terrain.
That's remarkable. Are you sensing animals, too?
Yes.
They're a constant distraction, actually.

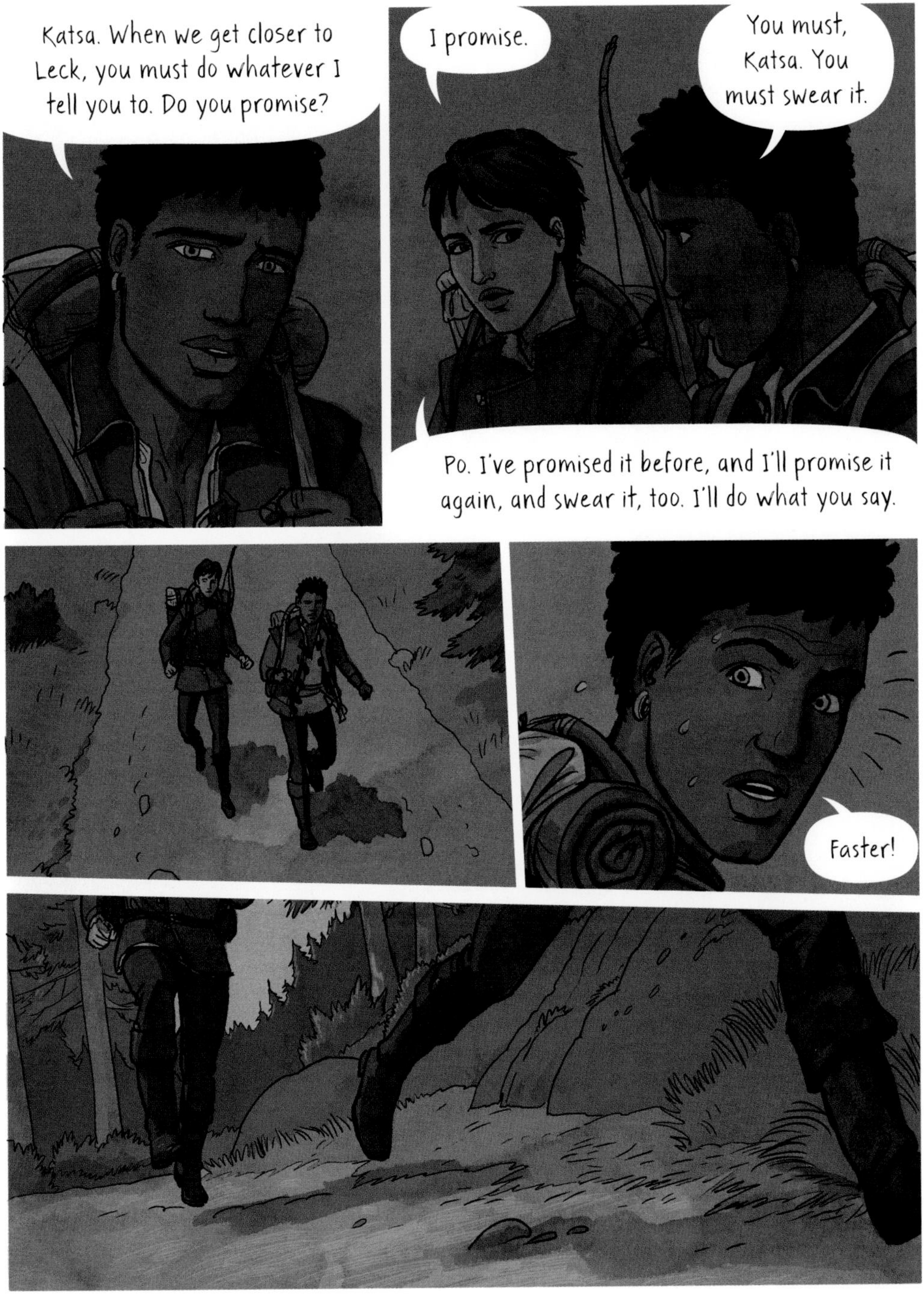
Katsa. When we get closer to Leck, you must do whatever I tell you to. Do you promise?
I promise.
You must, Katsa. You must swear it.
Po. I've promised it before, and I'll promise it again, and swear it, too. I'll do what you say.
Faster!

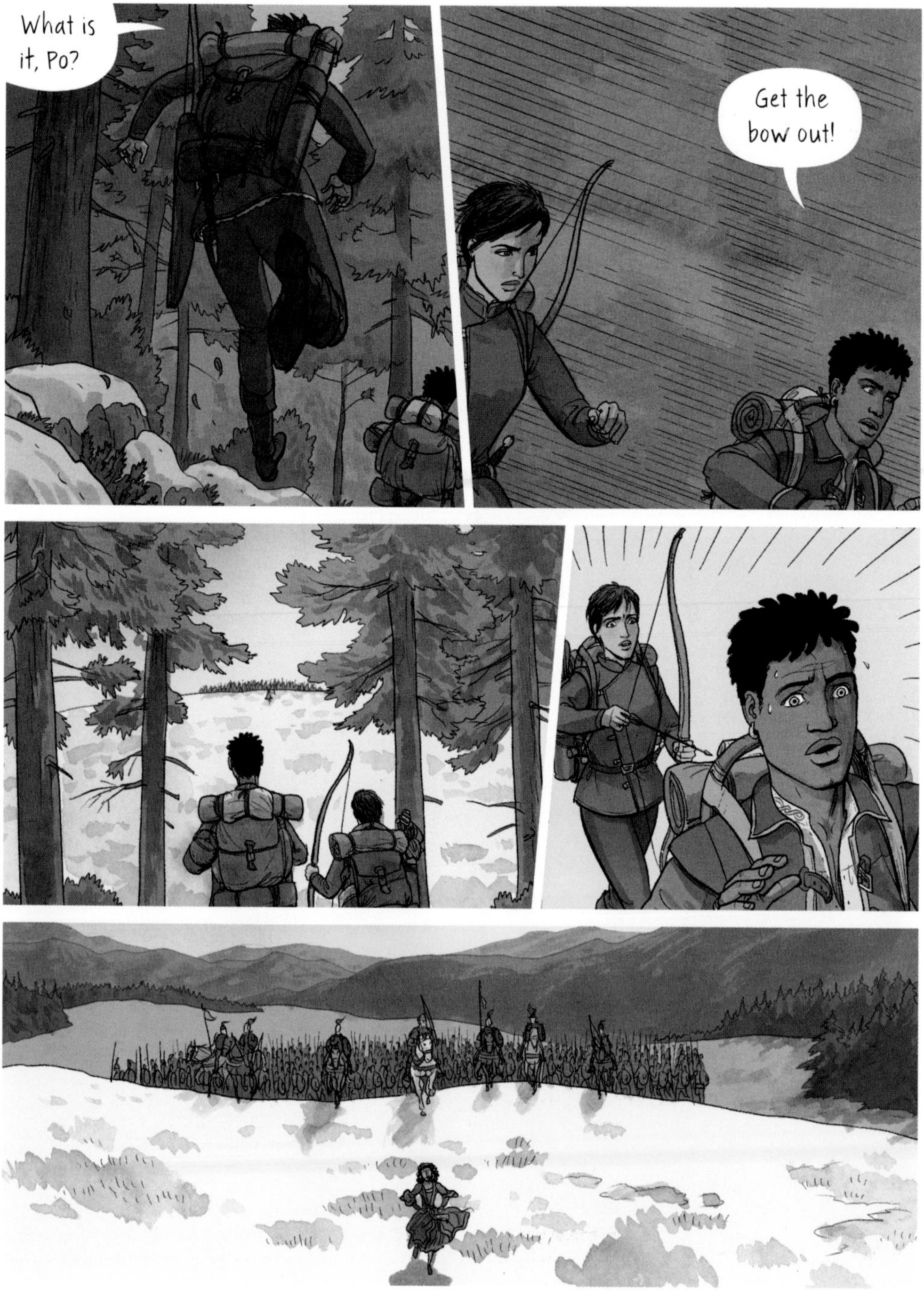
What is it, Po?
Get the bow out!

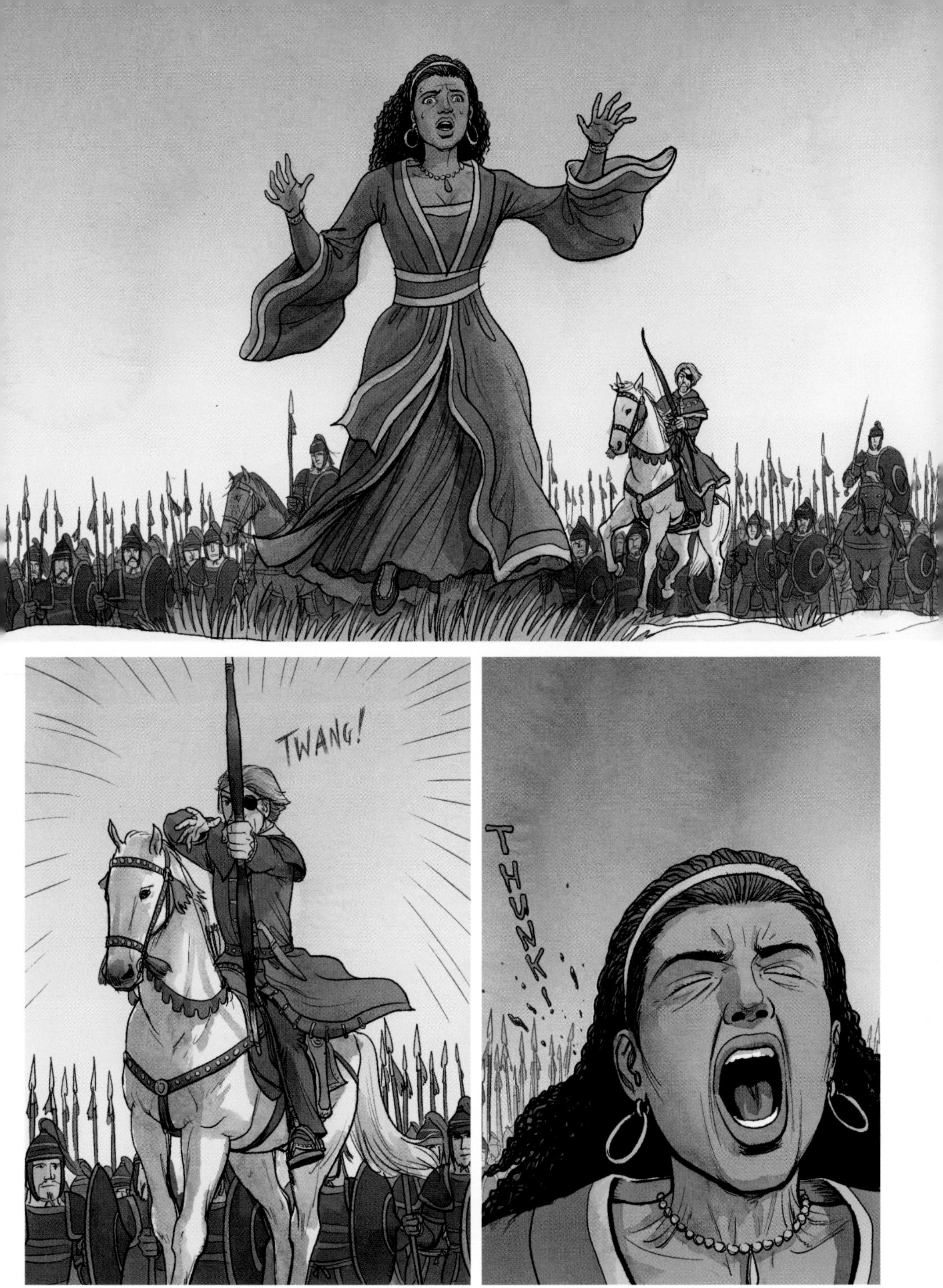
TWANG!
THUNK!

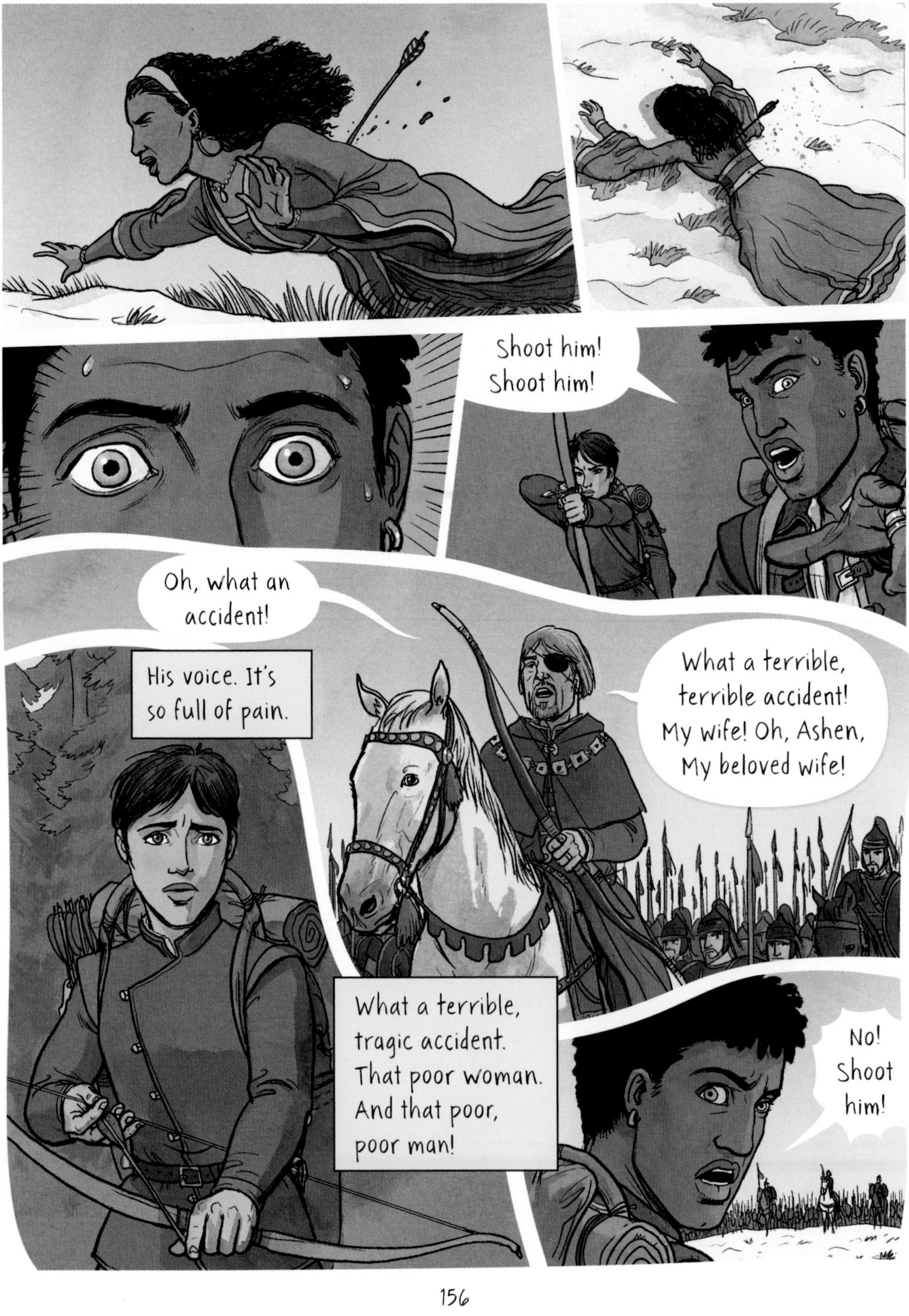
Shoot him! Shoot him!
Oh, what an accident!
His voice. It's so full of pain.
What a terrible, terrible accident! My wife! Oh, Ashen, My beloved wife!
What a terrible, tragic accident. That poor woman. And that poor, poor man!
No! Shoot him!

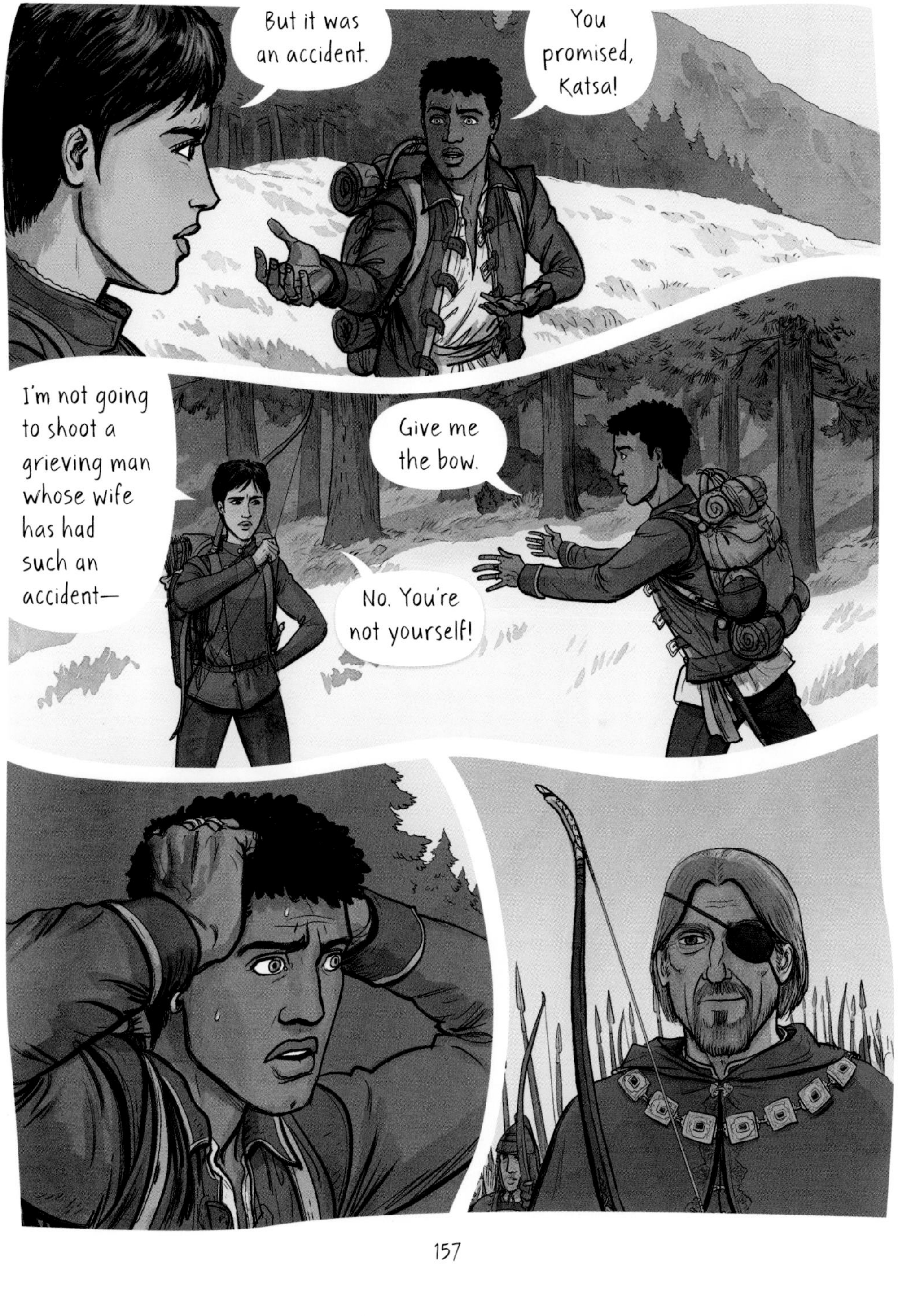

But it was an accident.
You promised, Katsa!
I'm not going to shoot a grieving man whose wife has had such an accident—
Give me the bow.
No. You're not yourself!

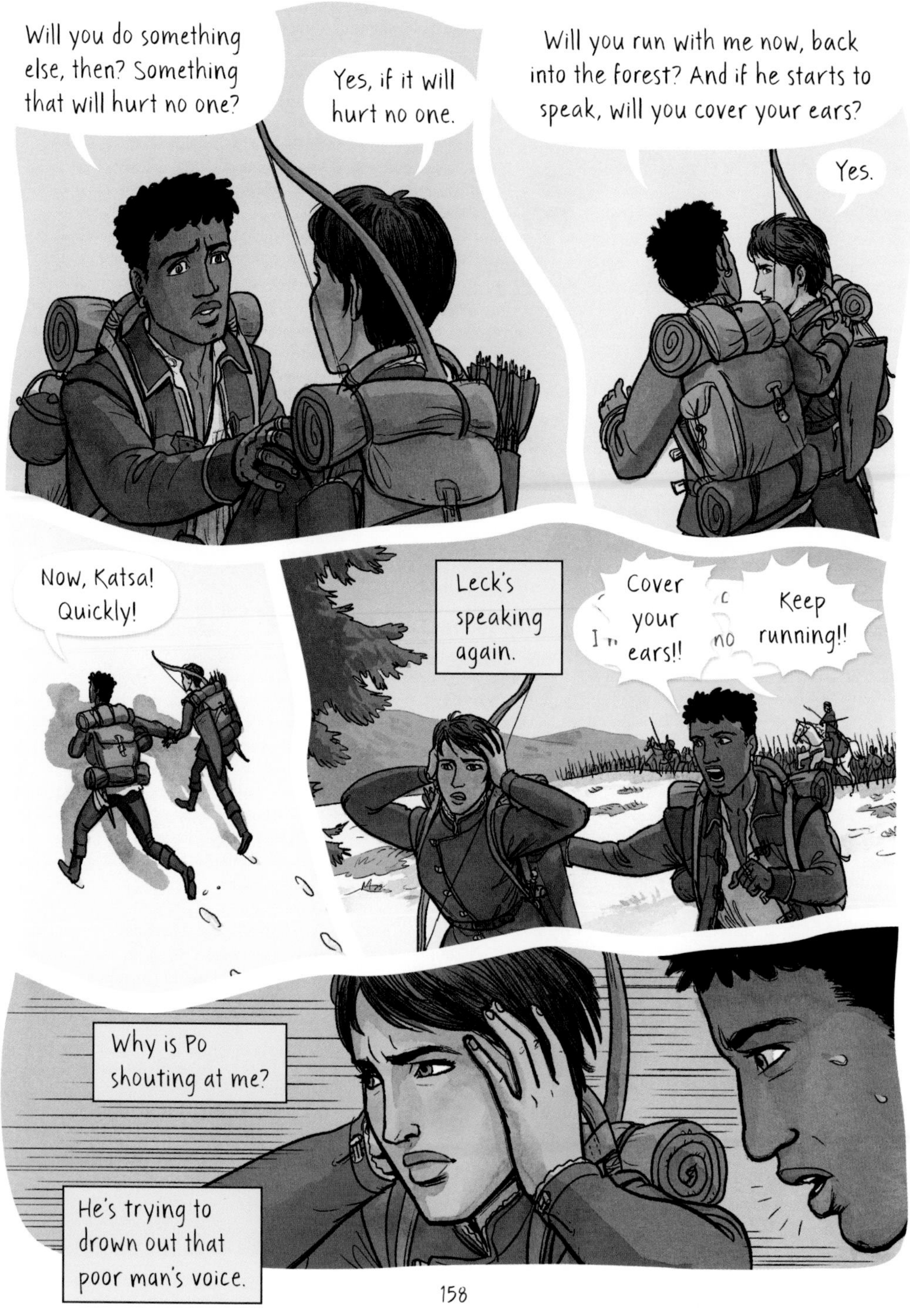

Will you do something else, then? Something that will hurt no one?
Yes, if it will hurt no one.
Will you run with me now, back into the forest? And if he starts to speak, will you cover your ears?
Yes.
Now, Katsa! Quickly!
Leck's speaking again.
Cover your ears!!
Keep running!!
Why is Po shouting at me?
He's trying to drown out that poor man's voice.

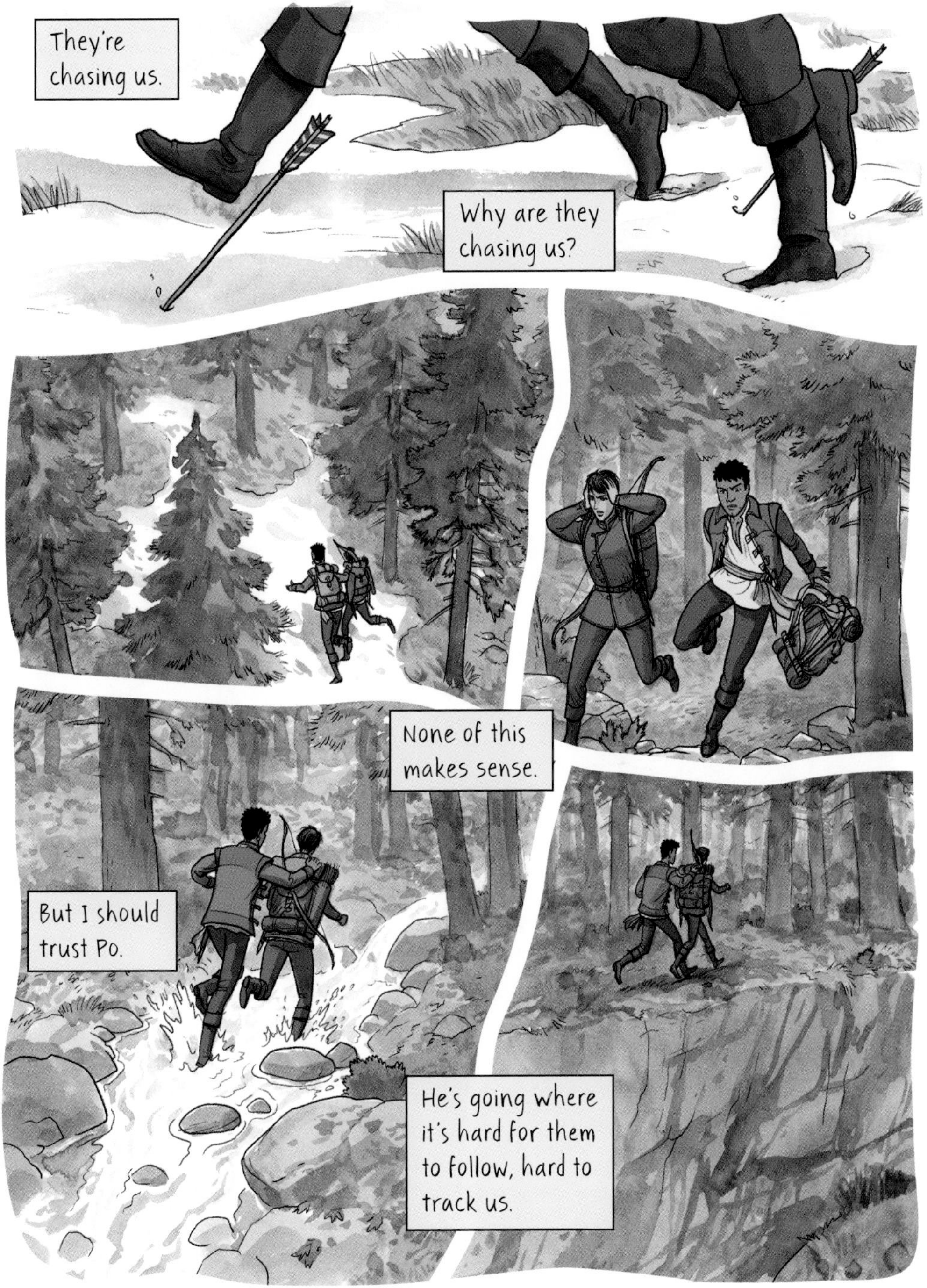
They're chasing us.
Why are they chasing us?
None of this makes sense.
But I should trust Po.
He's going where it's hard for them to follow, hard to track us.

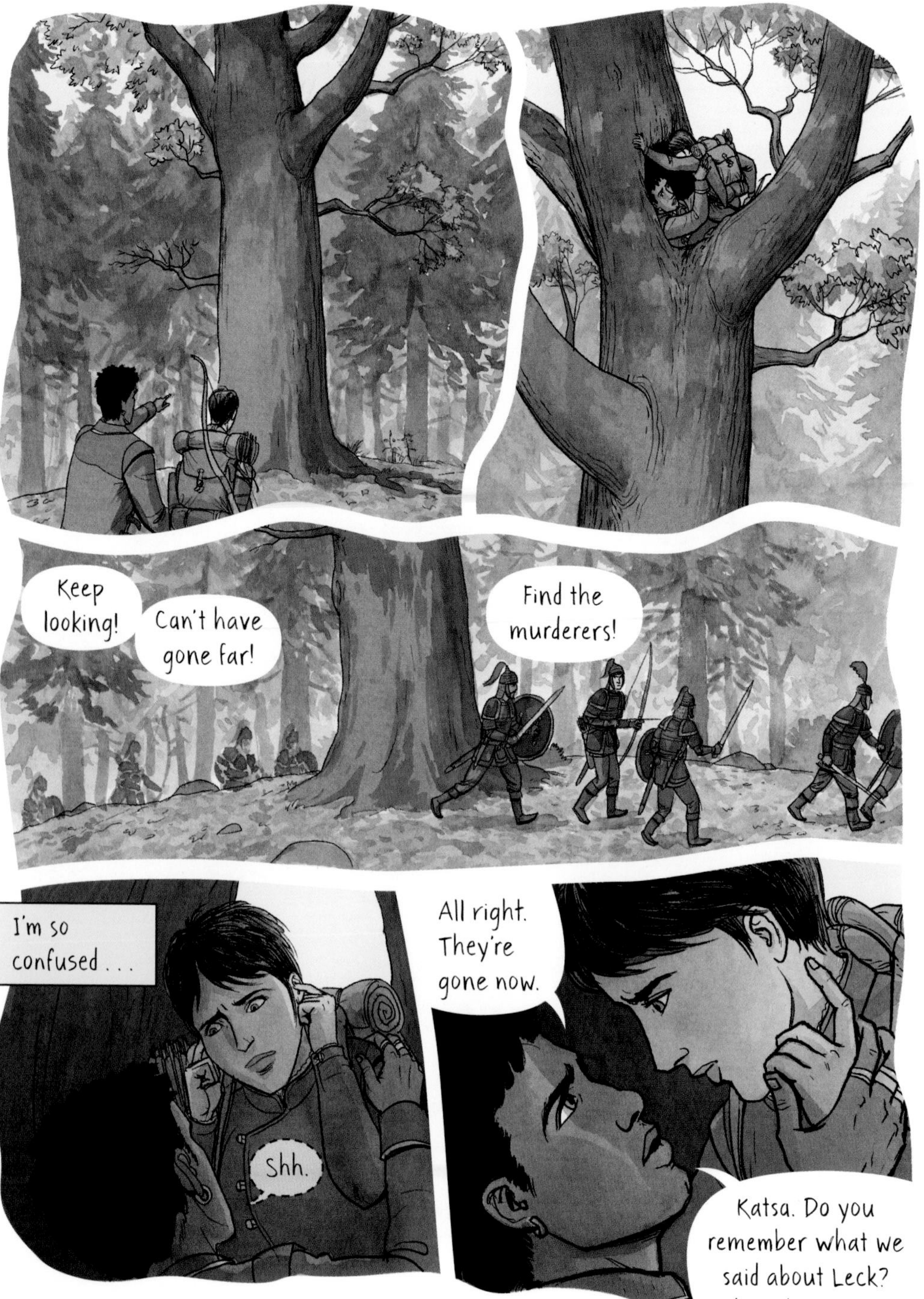
Keep looking!
Can't have gone far!
Find the murderers!
I'm so confused . . .
Shh.
All right. They're gone now.
Katsa. Do you remember what we said about Leck? About his Grace?

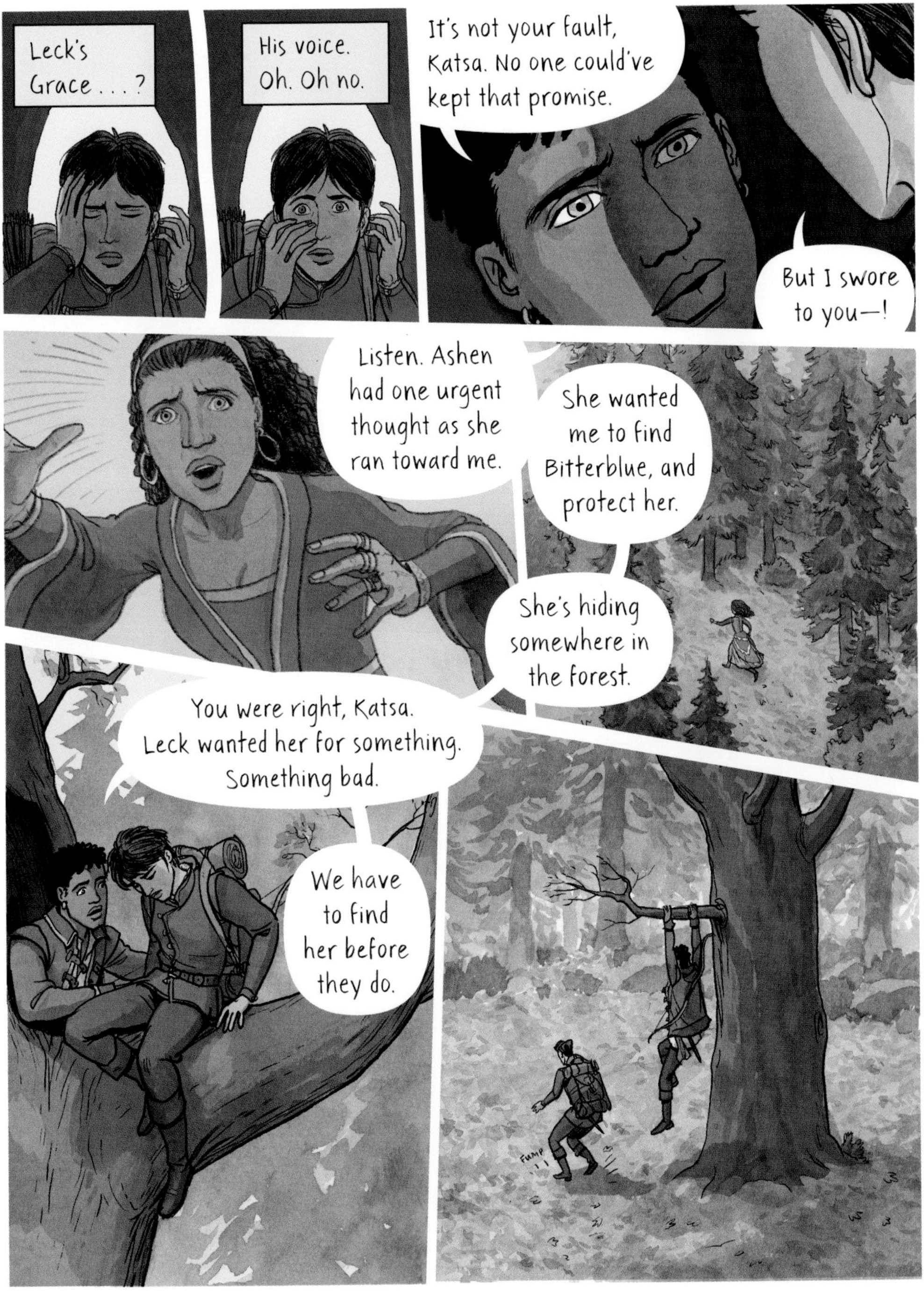
Leck's Grace . . . ?
His voice. Oh. Oh no.
It's not your fault, Katsa. No one could've kept that promise.
But I swore to you—!
Listen. Ashen had one urgent thought as she ran toward me.
She wanted me to find Bitterblue, and protect her.
She's hiding somewhere in the forest.
You were right, Katsa. Leck wanted her for something. Something bad.
We have to find her before they do.
FWMP

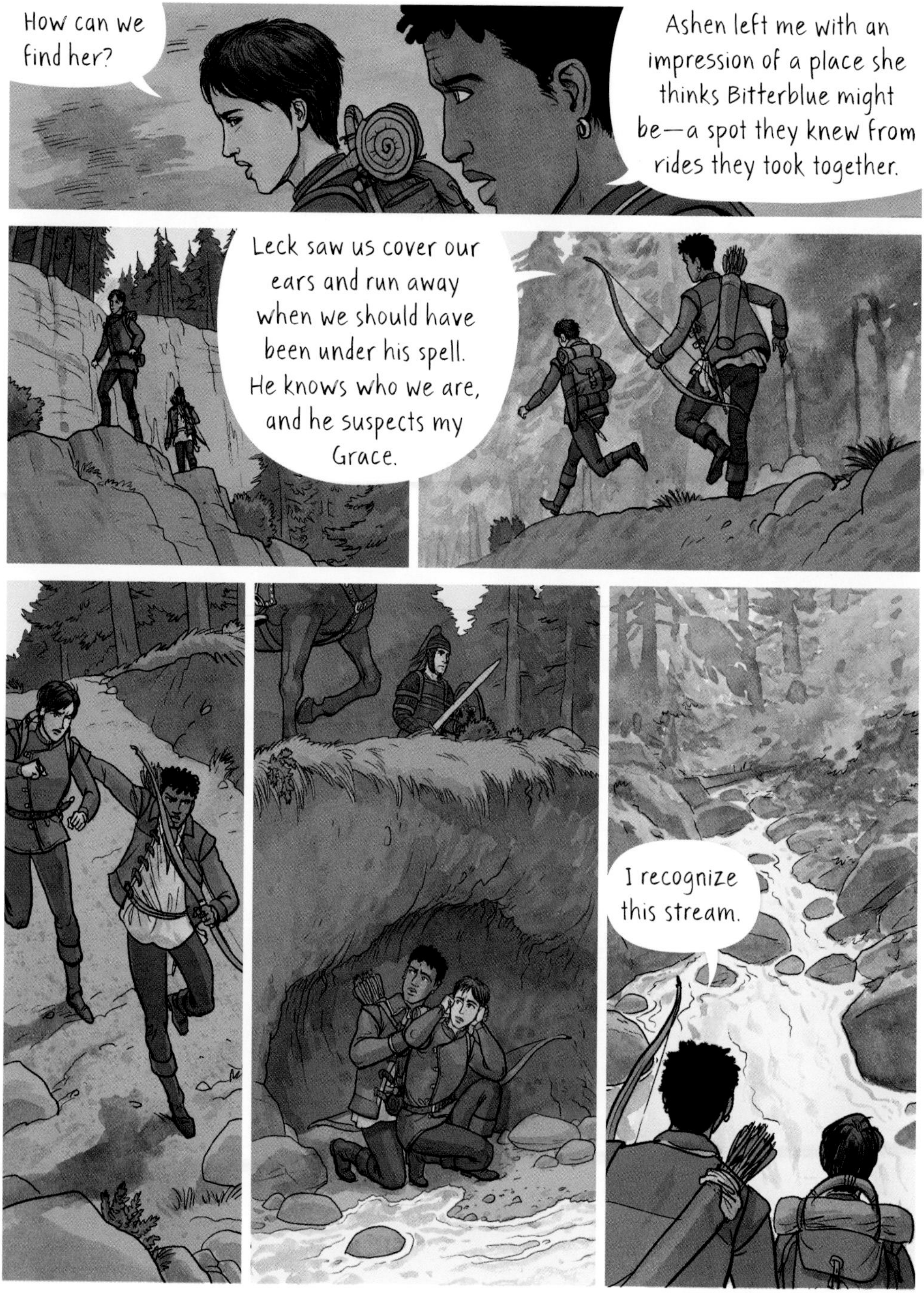
How can we find her?
Ashen left me with an impression of a place she thinks Bitterblue might be—a spot they knew from rides they took together.
Leck saw us cover our ears and run away when we should have been under his spell. He knows who we are, and he suspects my Grace.
I recognize this stream.

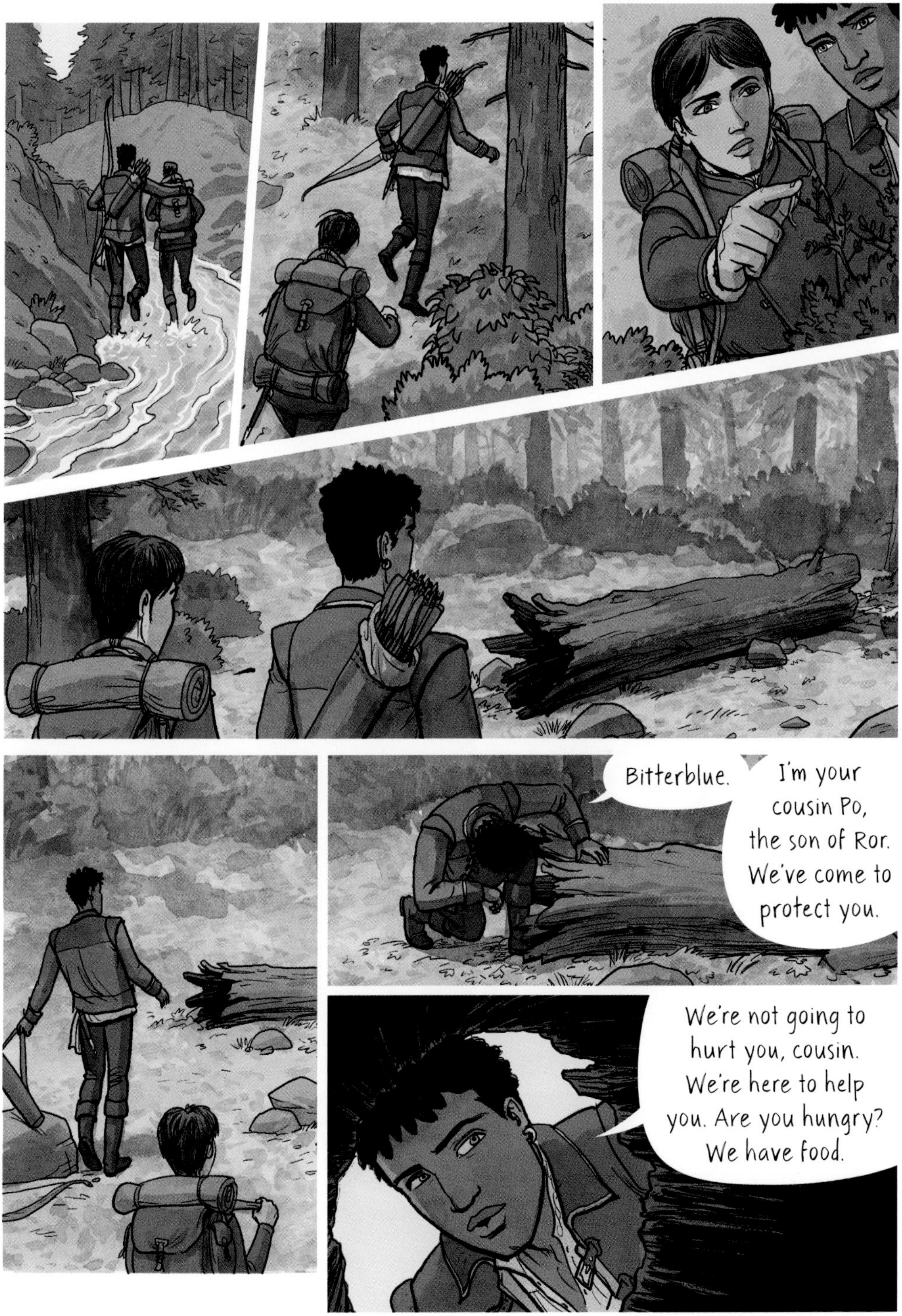
Bitterblue.
I'm your cousin Po, the son of Ror. We've come to protect you.
We're not going to hurt you, cousin. We're here to help you. Are you hungry? We have food.

Katsa.

She's afraid of me. Because I'm a man. You must try.

Take care. She has a knife, and she's willing to use it.

Good for her.

Princess Bitterblue. I'm the Lady Katsa, from the Middluns. I've come with Po to help you. You must trust us, Bitterblue. We're Graced fighters. We can keep you safe.

We know about your father's Grace.

Do you think we could break the tree apart?

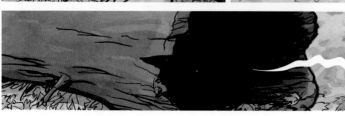

Where is my mother?

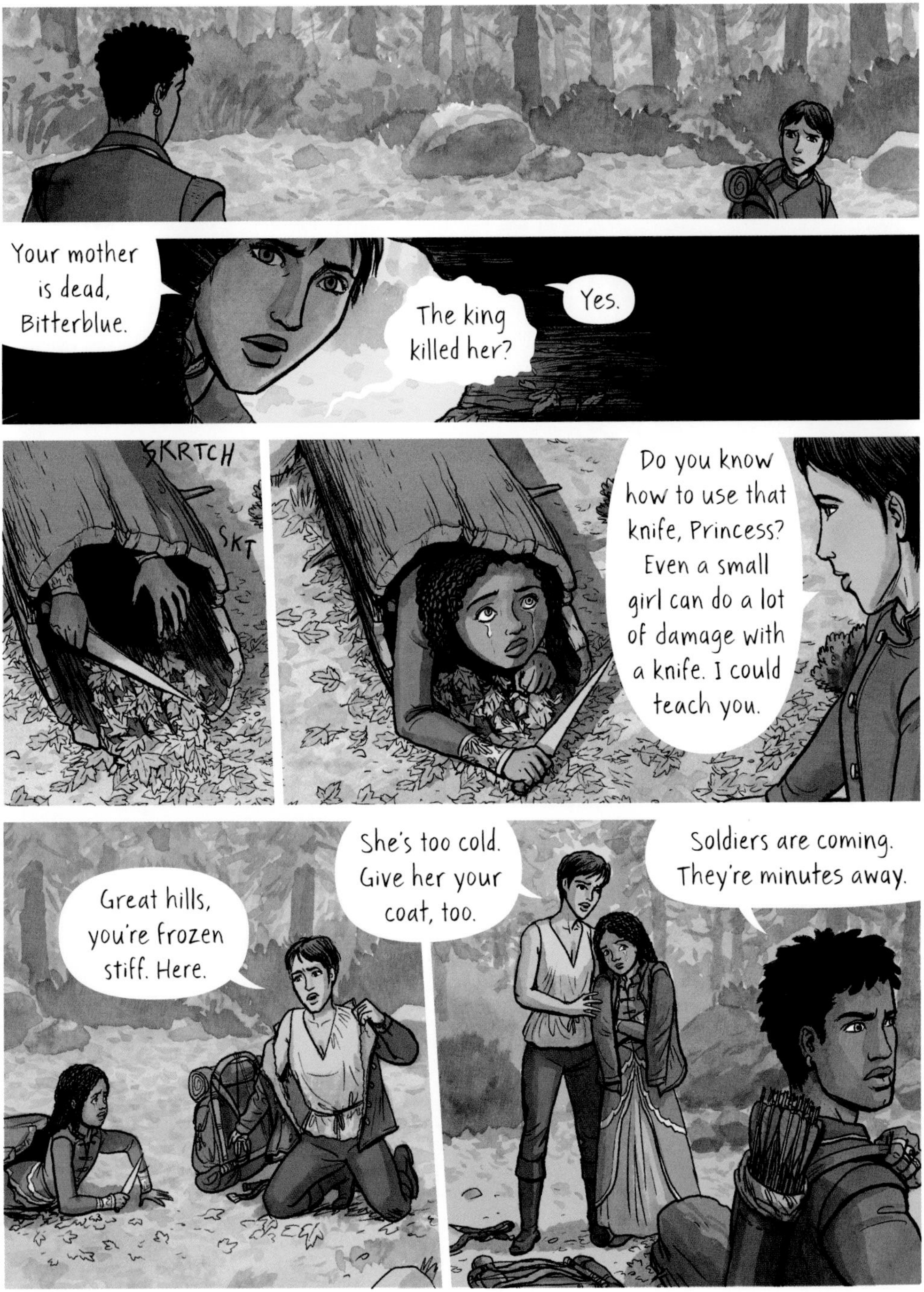
Your mother is dead, Bitterblue.
The king killed her?
Yes.
SKRTCH
SKT
Do you know how to use that knife, Princess? Even a small girl can do a lot of damage with a knife. I could teach you.
Great hills, you're frozen stiff. Here.
She's too cold. Give her your coat, too.
Soldiers are coming. They're minutes away.

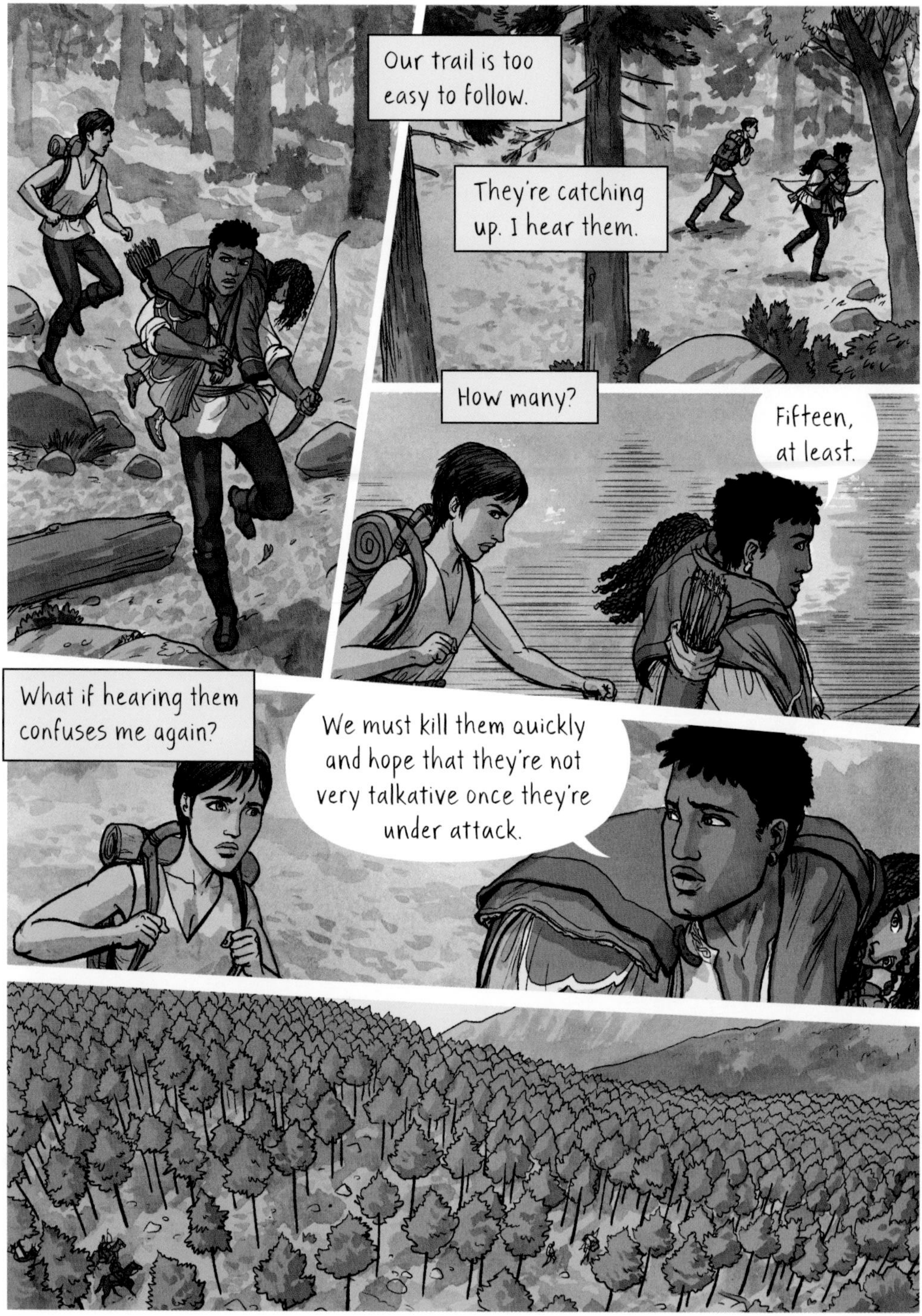
Our trail is too easy to follow.
They're catching up. I hear them.
How many?
Fifteen, at least.
What if hearing them confuses me again?
We must kill them quickly and hope that they're not very talkative once they're under attack.

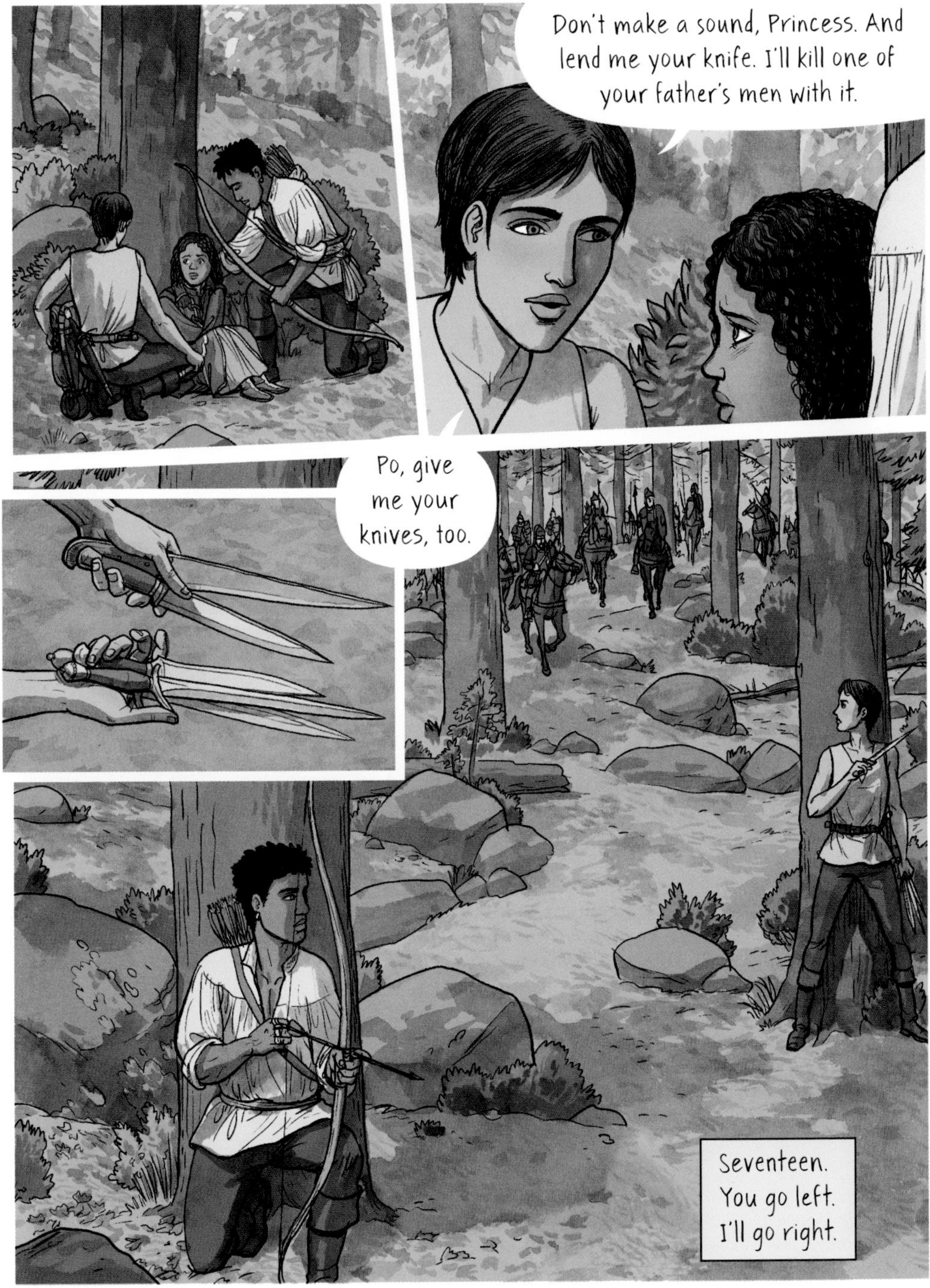
Don't make a sound, Princess. And lend me your knife. I'll kill one of your father's men with it.
Po, give me your knives, too.
Seventeen. You go left. I'll go right.

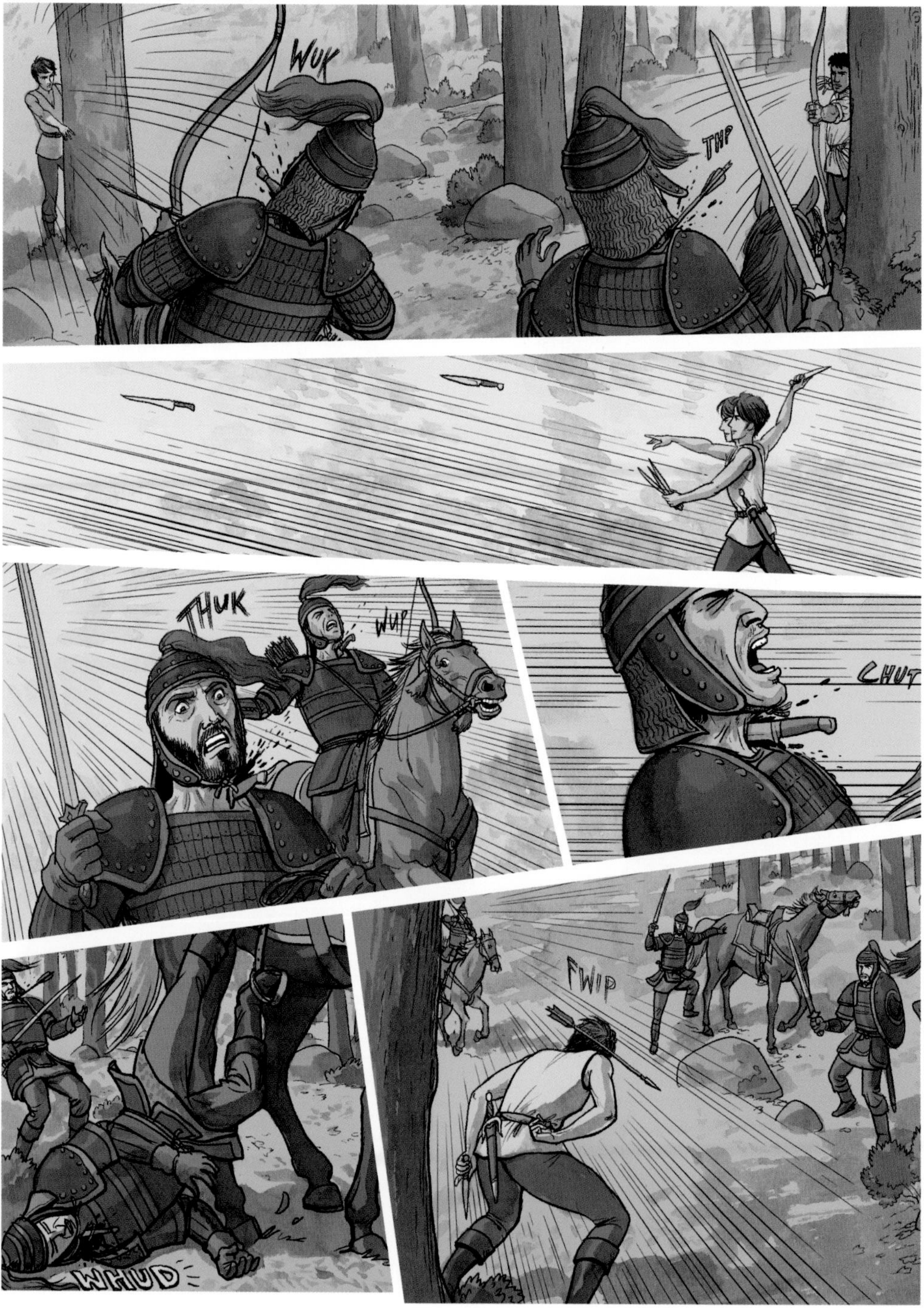
WUK
THP
THUK
WUP
CHUT
FWIP
WHUD

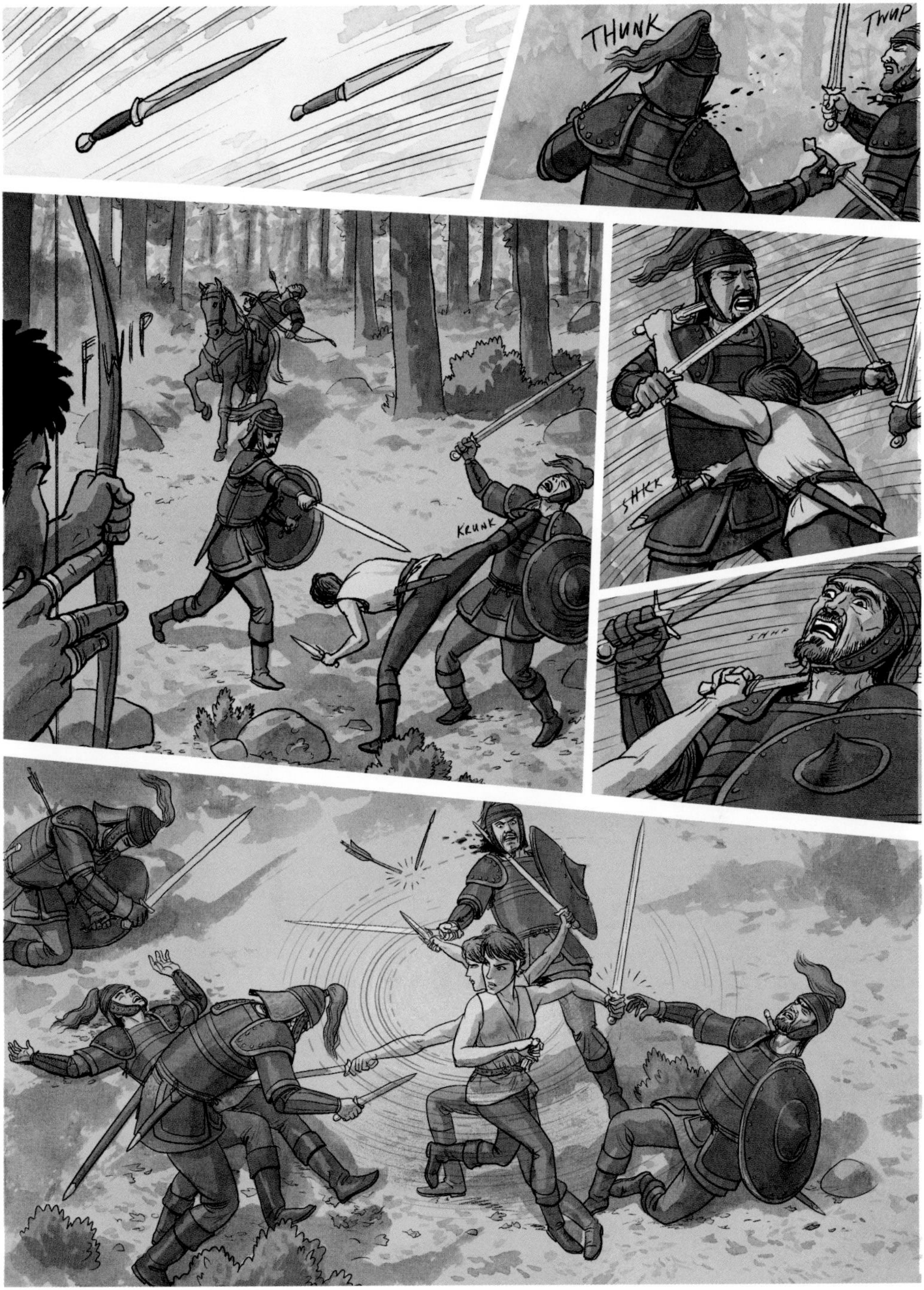
THUNK
TWUP
FWIP
KRUNK
SHKK
SHHP

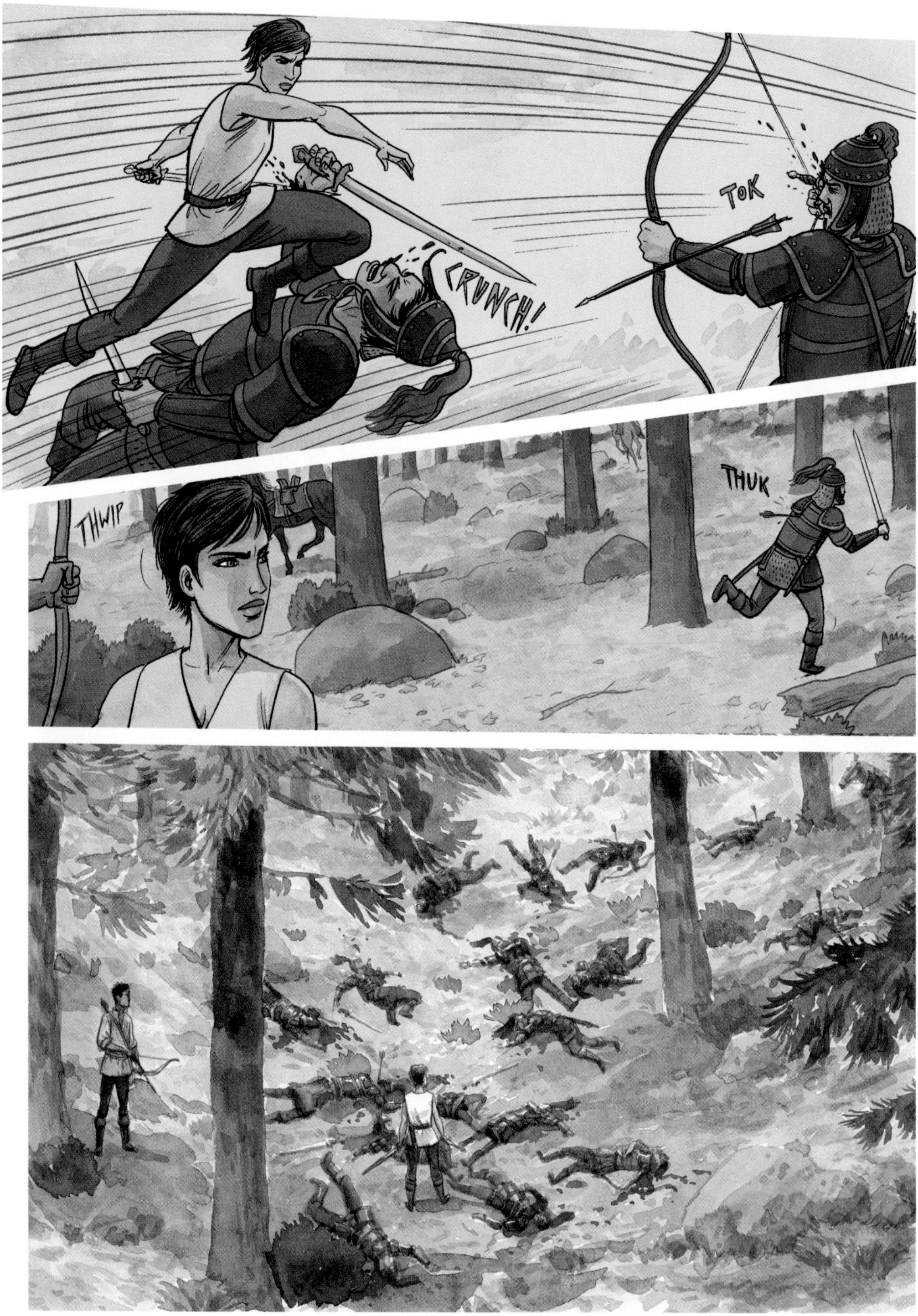
CRUNCH!
TOK
THWIP
THUK

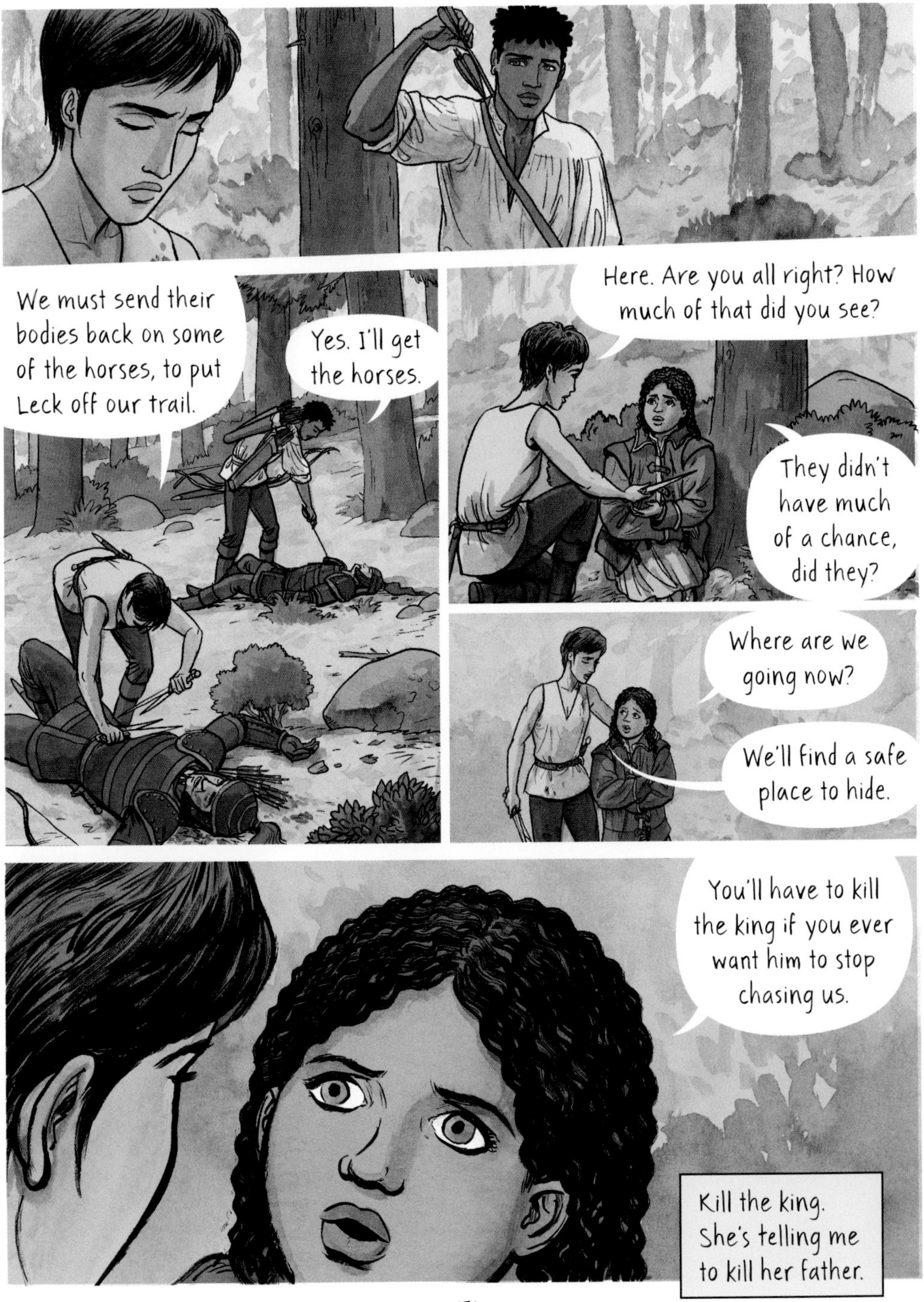
We must send their bodies back on some of the horses, to put Leck off our trail.
Yes. I'll get the horses.
Here. Are you all right? How much of that did you see?
They didn't have much of a chance, did they?
Where are we going now?
We'll find a safe place to hide.
You'll have to kill the king if you ever want him to stop chasing us.
Kill the king. She's telling me to kill her father.

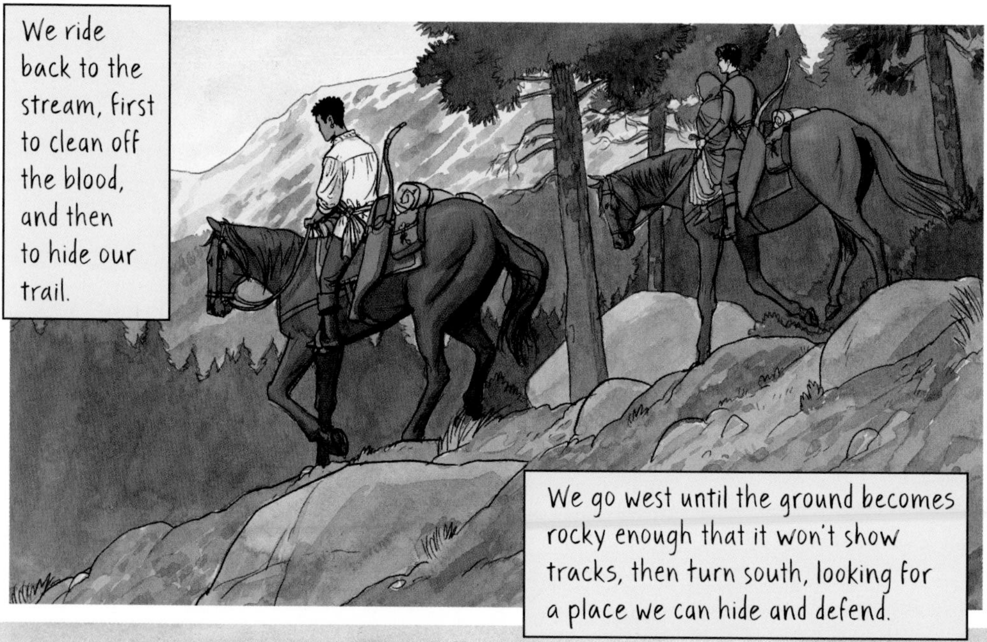
We ride back to the stream, first to clean off the blood, and then to hide our trail.
We go west until the ground becomes rocky enough that it won't show tracks, then turn south, looking for a place we can hide and defend.

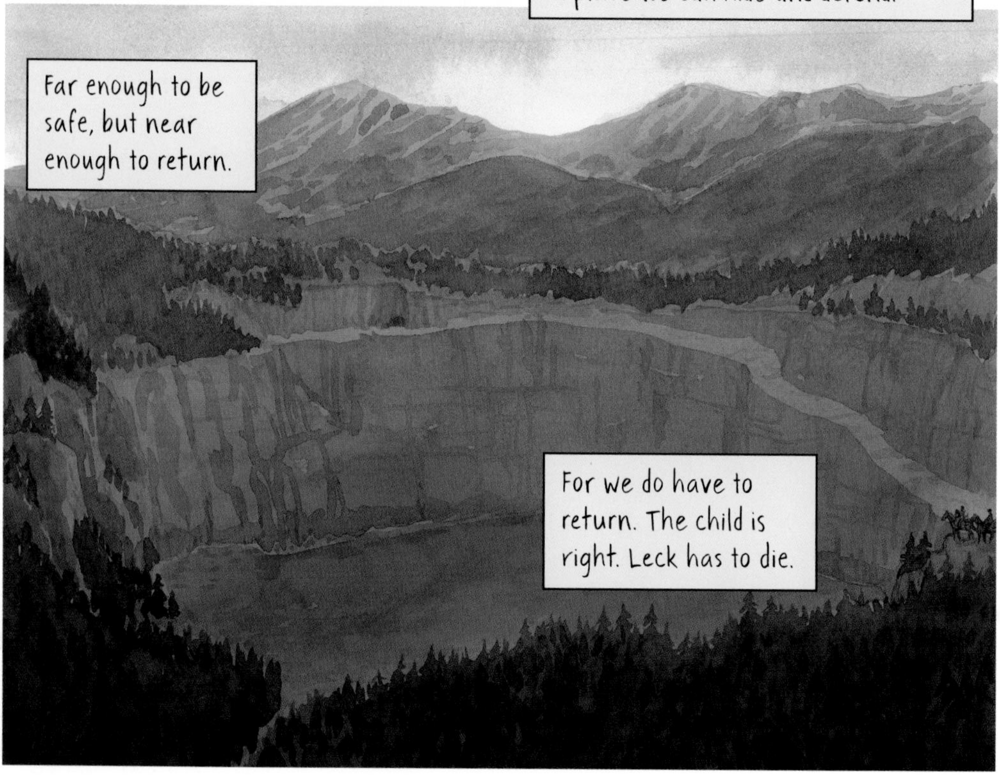
Far enough to be safe, but near enough to return.
For we do have to return. The child is right. Leck has to die.

And I can't get near him, so it will have to be Po.

Po, alone, must kill a king guarded by an army of soldiers.

This'll do. At least it'll hide our fire.

Katsa, I think I spotted some quail in the reeds down by the lake.

Sensed, you mean. Bitterblue will guess your secret if you're not careful, Po.

Slowly. Slowly, or you'll be sick.

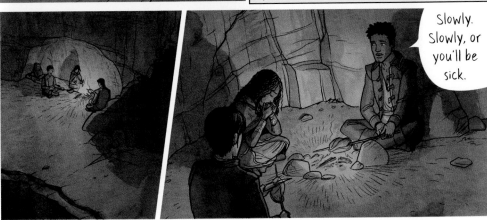

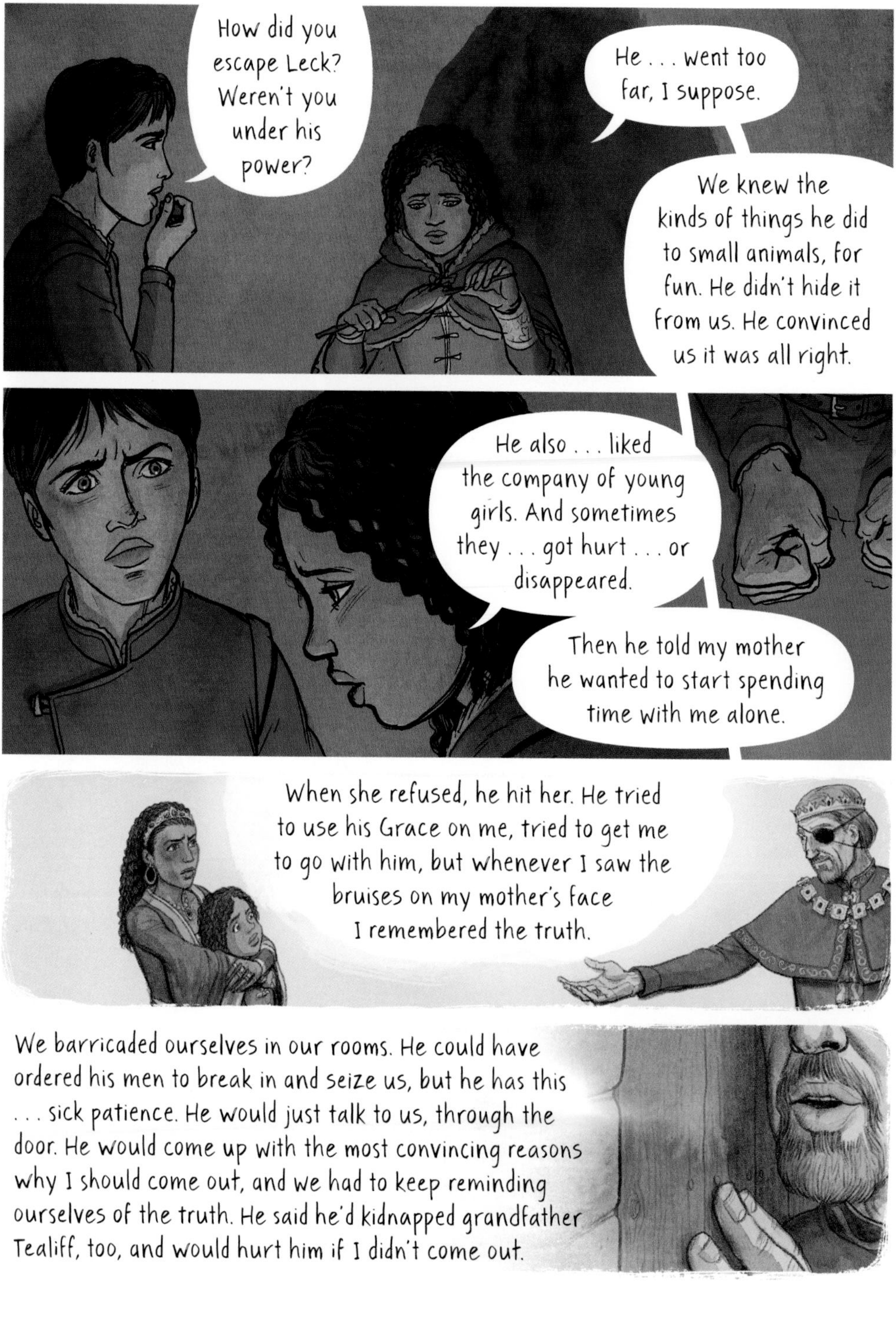
How did you escape Leck? Weren't you under his power?
He . . . went too far, I suppose.
We knew the kinds of things he did to small animals, for fun. He didn't hide it from us. He convinced us it was all right.
He also . . . liked the company of young girls. And sometimes they . . . got hurt . . . or disappeared.
Then he told my mother he wanted to start spending time with me alone.
When she refused, he hit her. He tried to use his Grace on me, tried to get me to go with him, but whenever I saw the bruises on my mother's face I remembered the truth.
We barricaded ourselves in our rooms. He could have ordered his men to break in and seize us, but he has this . . . sick patience. He would just talk to us, through the door. He would come up with the most convincing reasons why I should come out, and we had to keep reminding ourselves of the truth. He said he'd kidnapped grandfather Tealiff, too, and would hurt him if I didn't come out.

One day the girl who brought our food had cuts on her face. And other injuries, too, that we couldn't see. She wasn't walking right. When we asked her what happened, she said she couldn't remember. She was a girl my age.

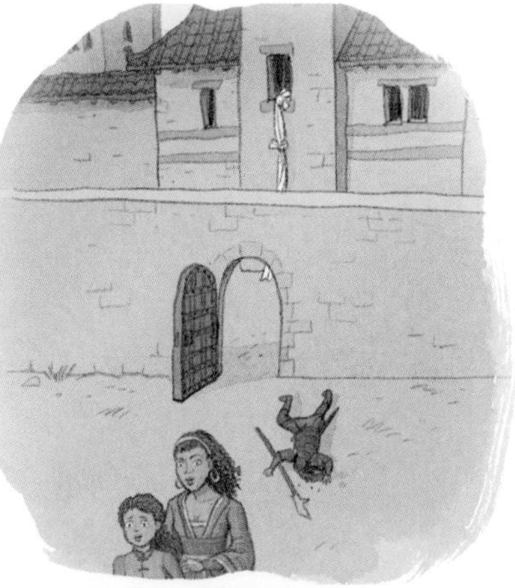

That's when my mother decided we had to escape. We tied sheets and blankets together and climbed out through the windows. I thought I wouldn't be able to do it, but my mother talked me through it, all the way down. My mother killed a guard, with a knife. We ran for the mountains.

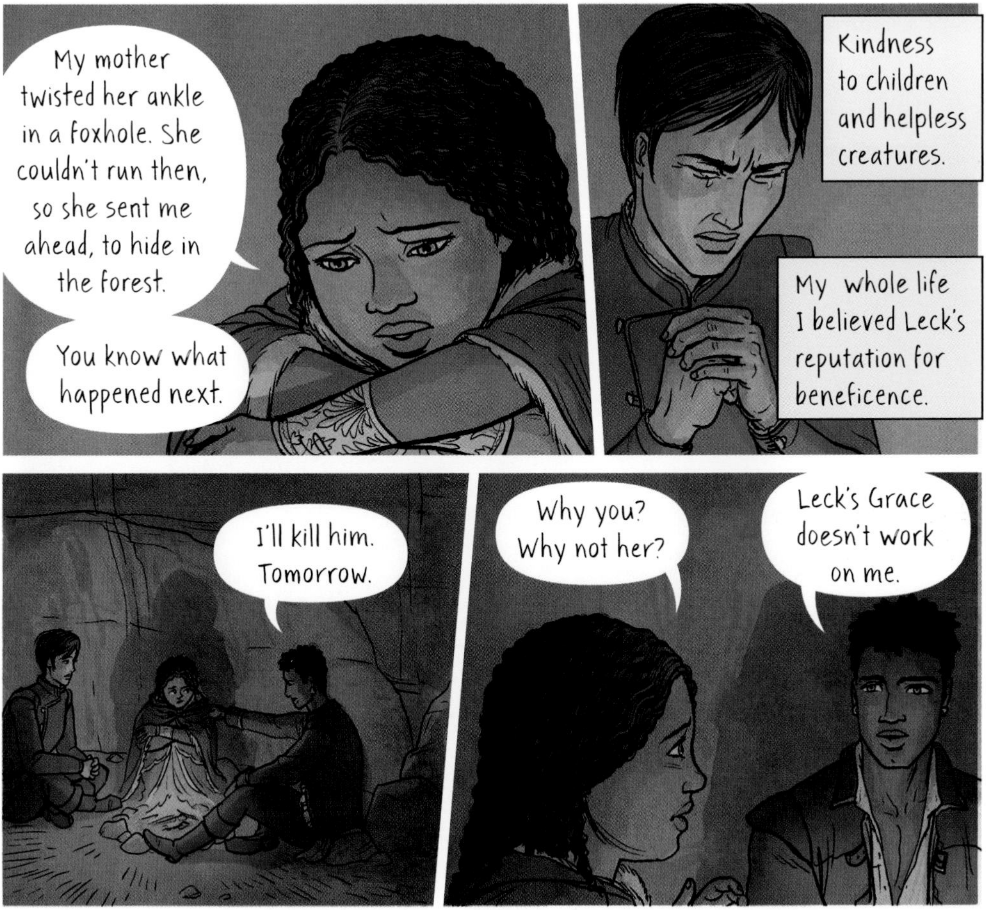
My mother twisted her ankle in a foxhole. She couldn't run then, so she sent me ahead, to hide in the forest.
You know what happened next.
Kindness to children and helpless creatures.
My whole life I believed Leck's reputation for beneficence.
I'll kill him. Tomorrow.
Why you? Why not her?
Leck's Grace doesn't work on me.

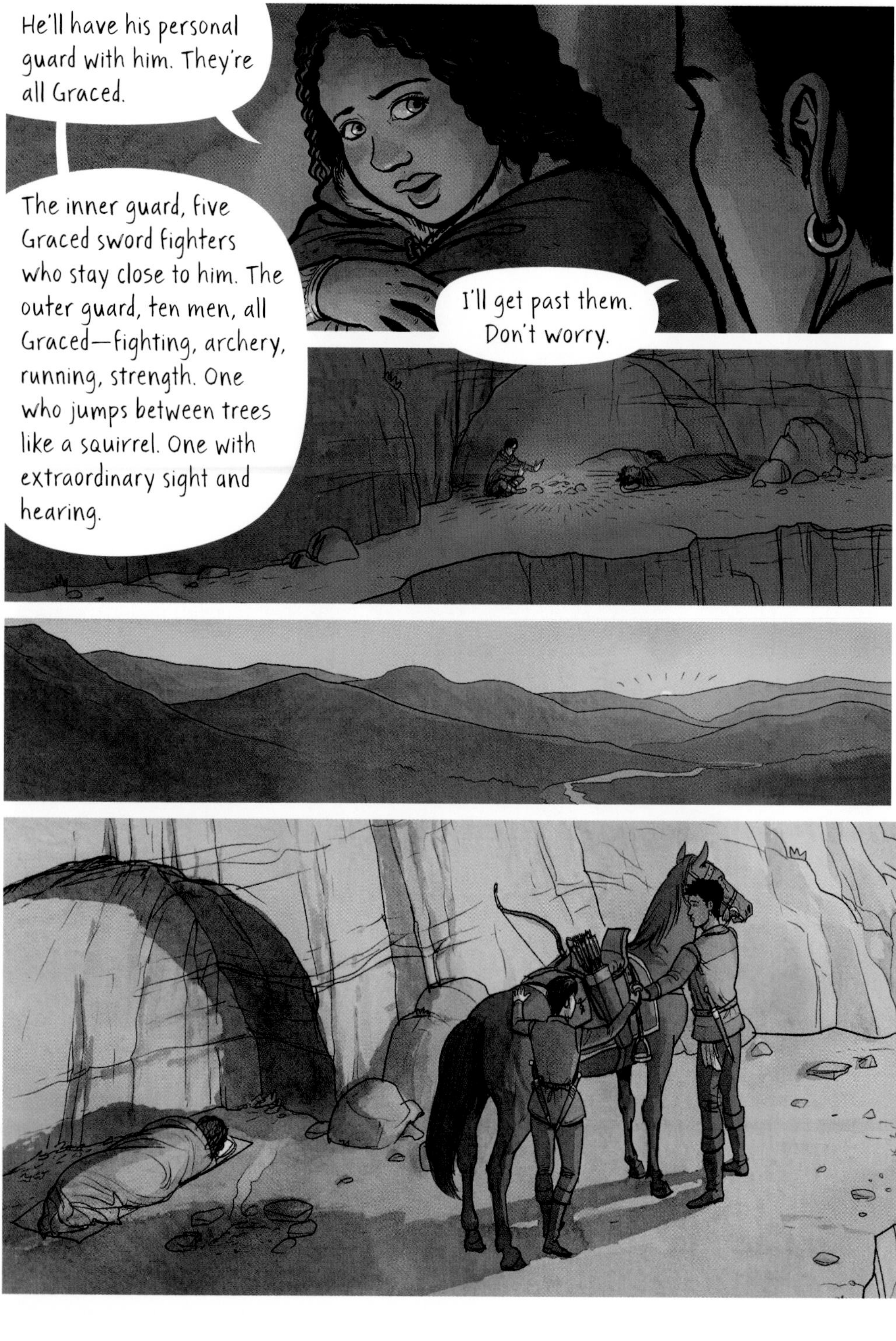
He'll have his personal guard with him. They're all Graced.
The inner guard, five Graced sword fighters who stay close to him. The outer guard, ten men, all Graced—fighting, archery, running, strength. One who jumps between trees like a squirrel. One with extraordinary sight and hearing.
I'll get past them. Don't worry.

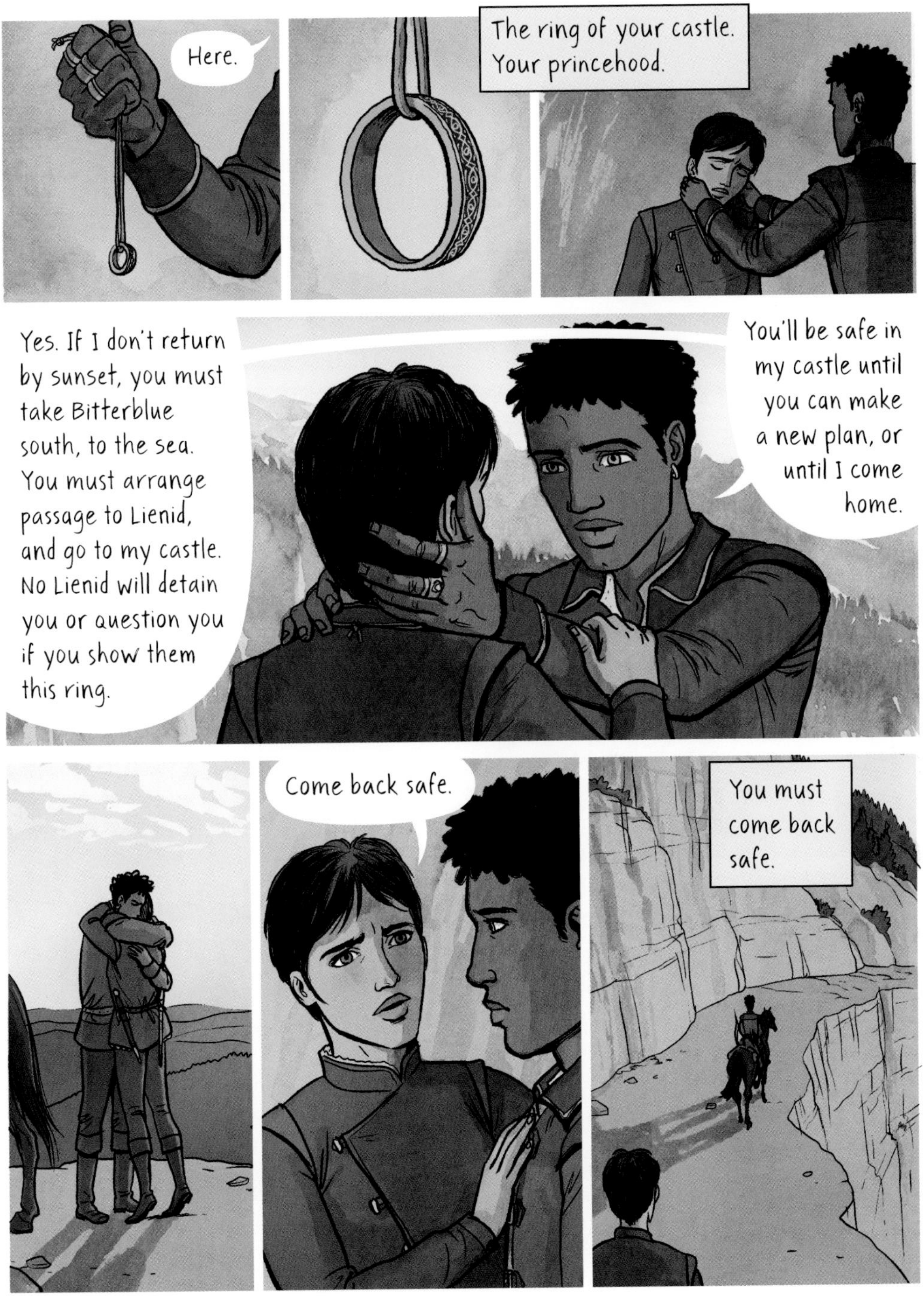
Here.
The ring of your castle. Your princehood.
Yes. If I don't return by sunset, you must take Bitterblue south, to the sea. You must arrange passage to Lienid, and go to my castle. No Lienid will detain you or question you if you show them this ring.
You'll be safe in my castle until you can make a new plan, or until I come home.
Come back safe.
You must come back safe.

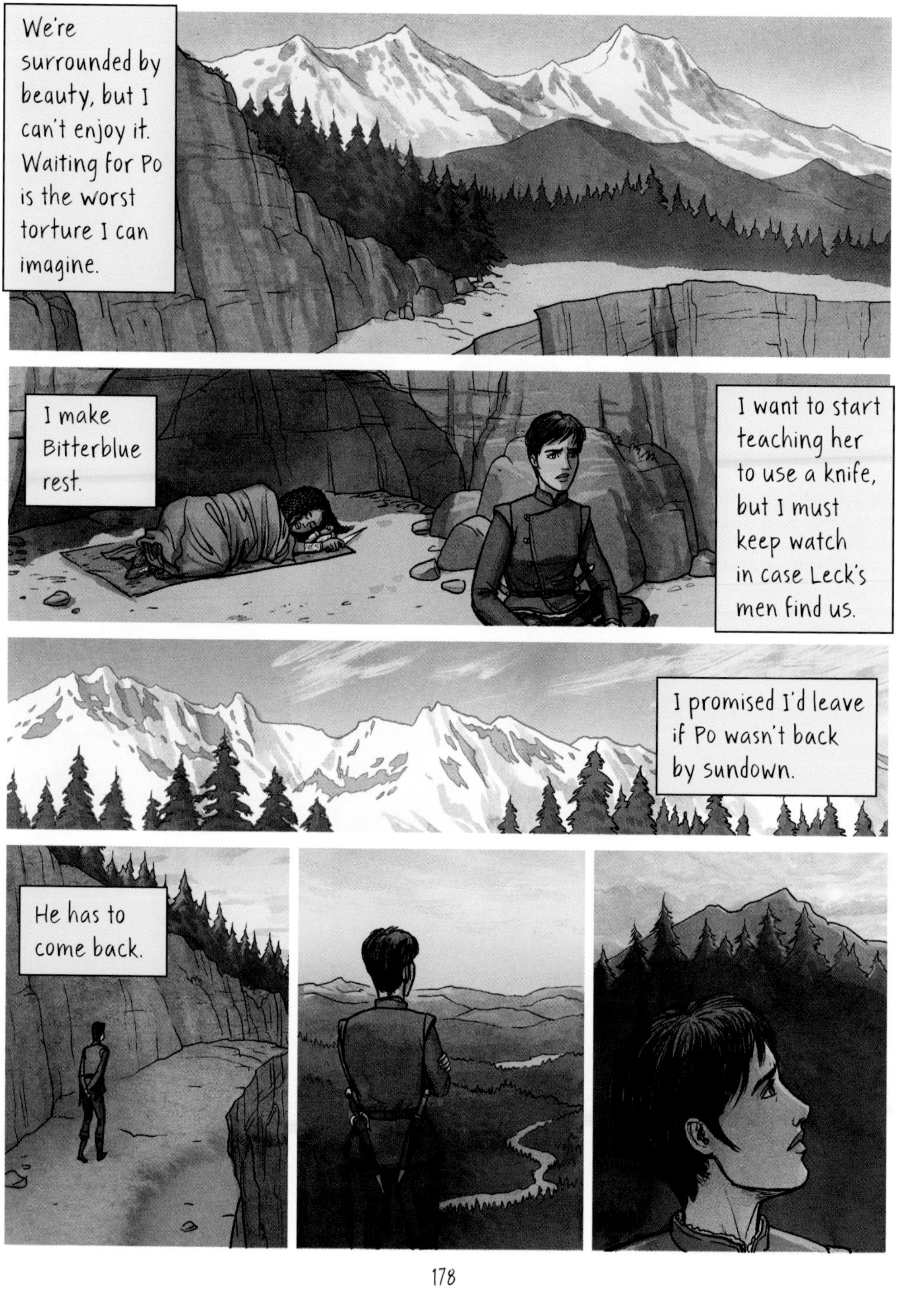
We're surrounded by beauty, but I can't enjoy it. Waiting for Po is the worst torture I can imagine.
I make Bitterblue rest.
I want to start teaching her to use a knife, but I must keep watch in case Leck's men find us.
I promised I'd leave if Po wasn't back by sundown.
He has to come back.

I can't leave. He could be close by, wounded, unable to get to us.

But I swore I'd leave.

Well, Princess, we'd better be going.

TAC, TAC

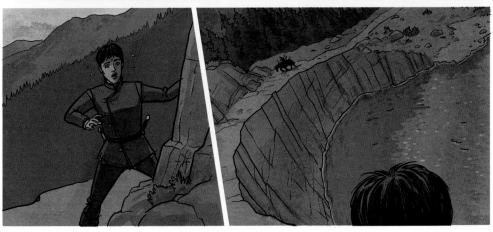

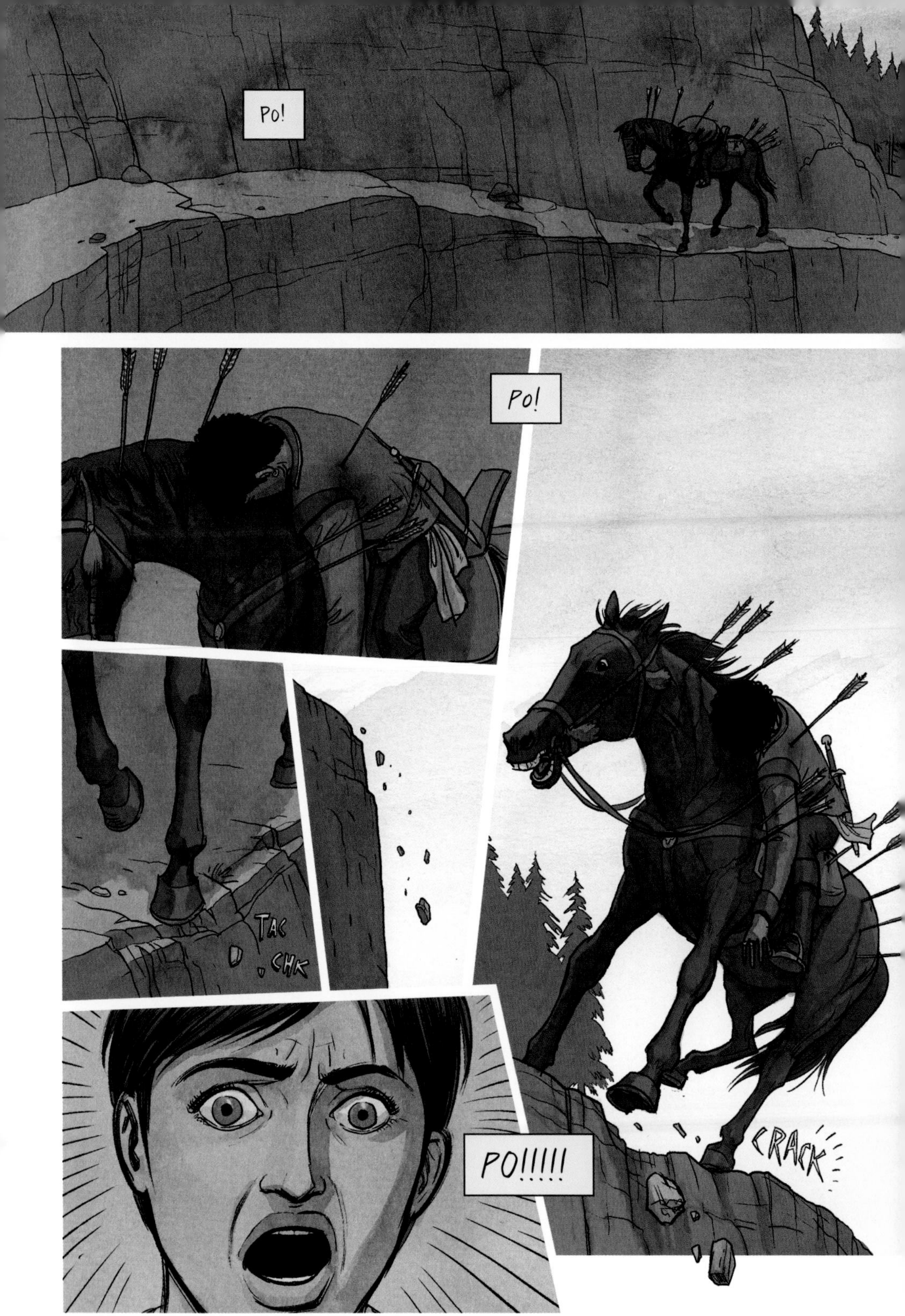
Po!
Po!
TAC
CHK
CRACK
PO!!!!!

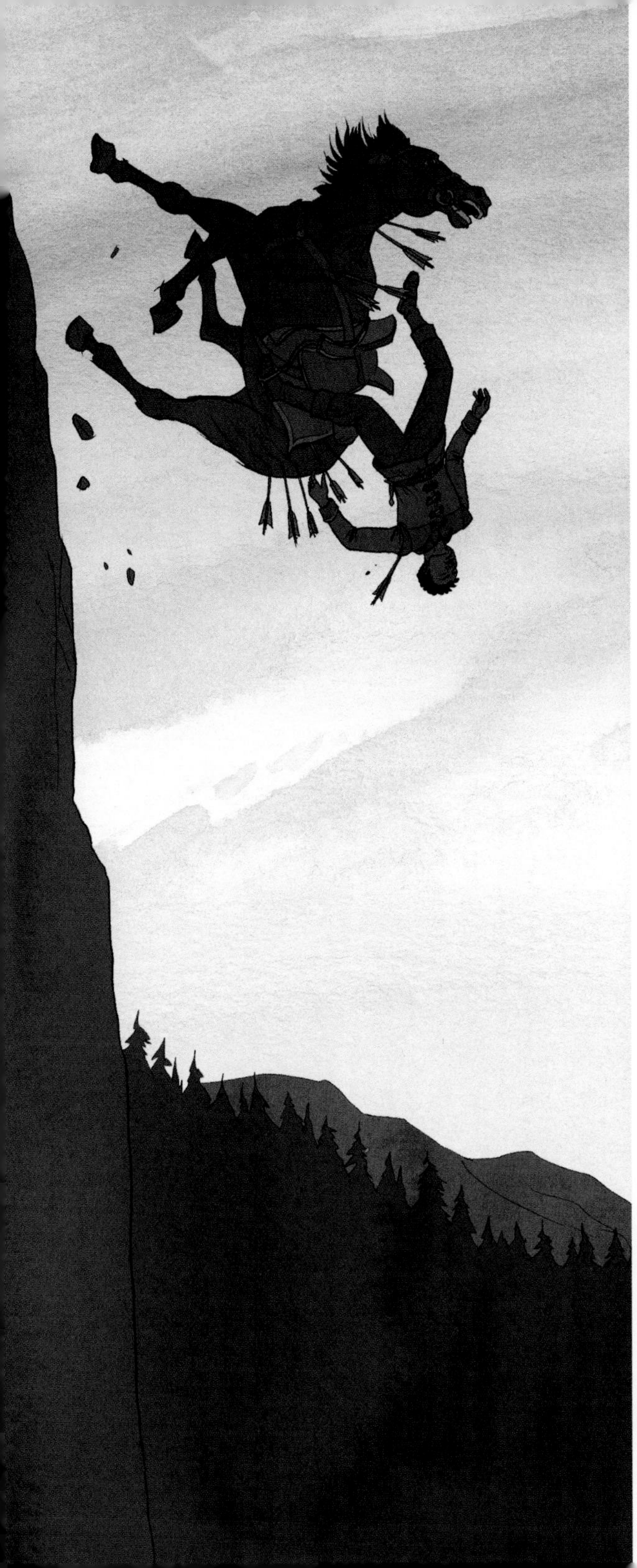
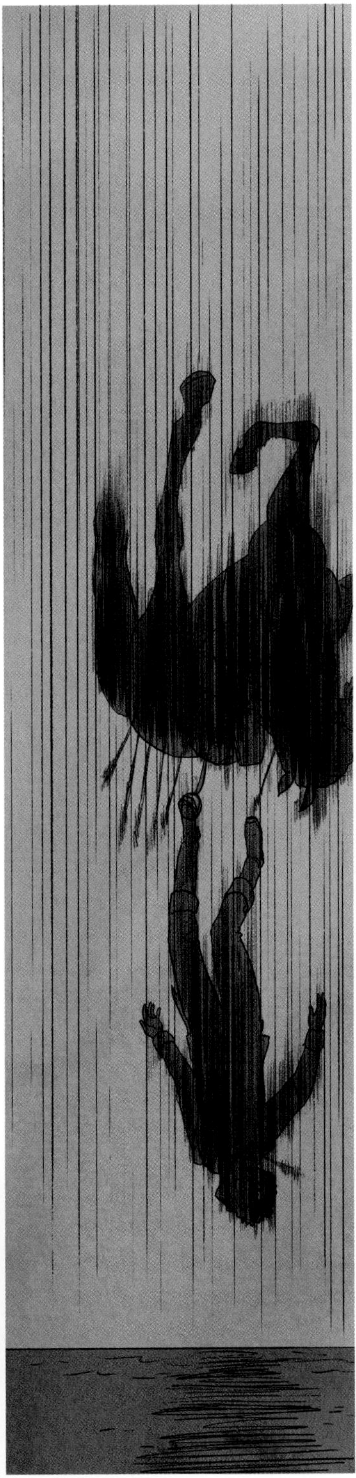

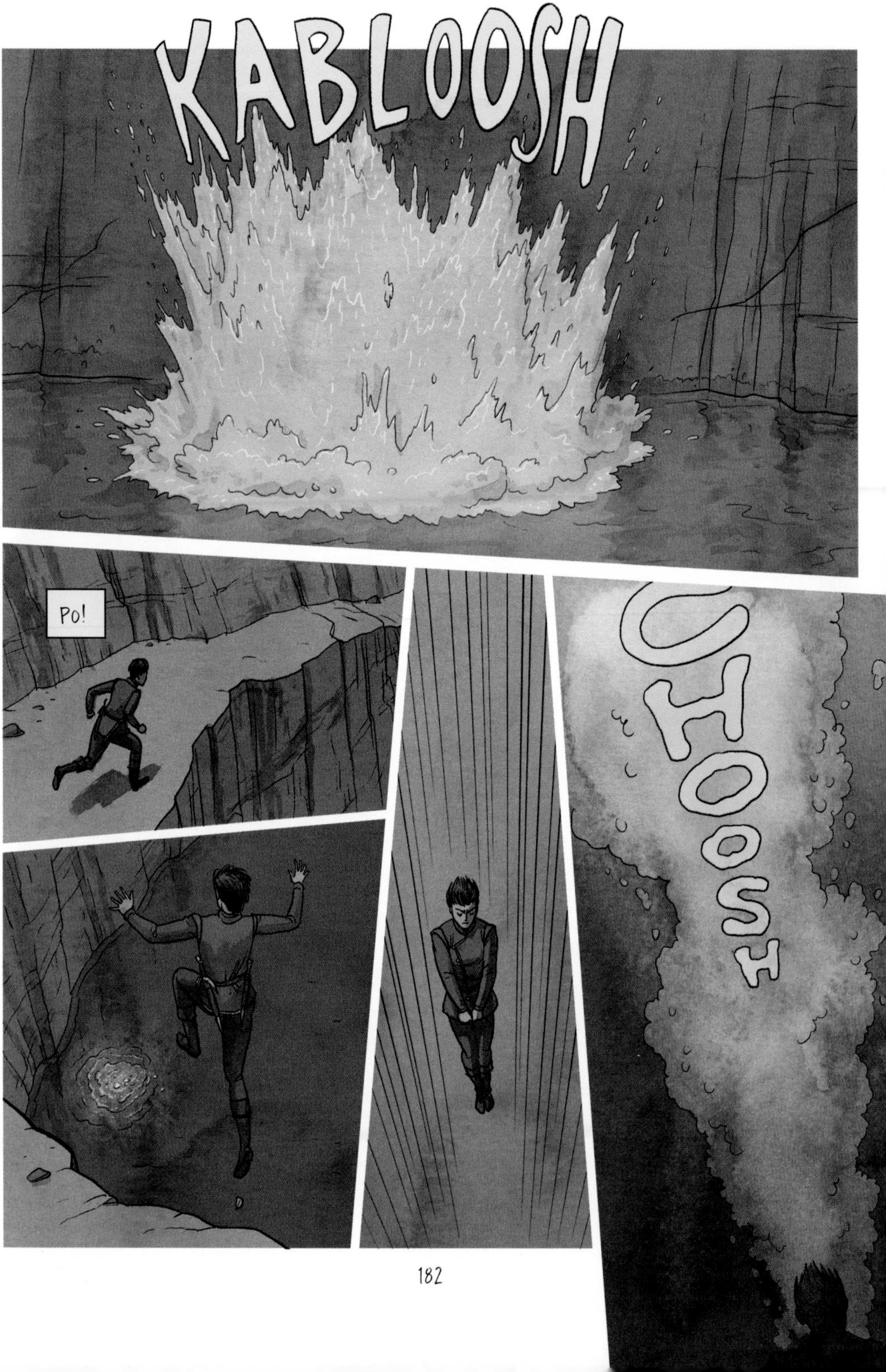
KABLOOSH
Po!
WHOOSH

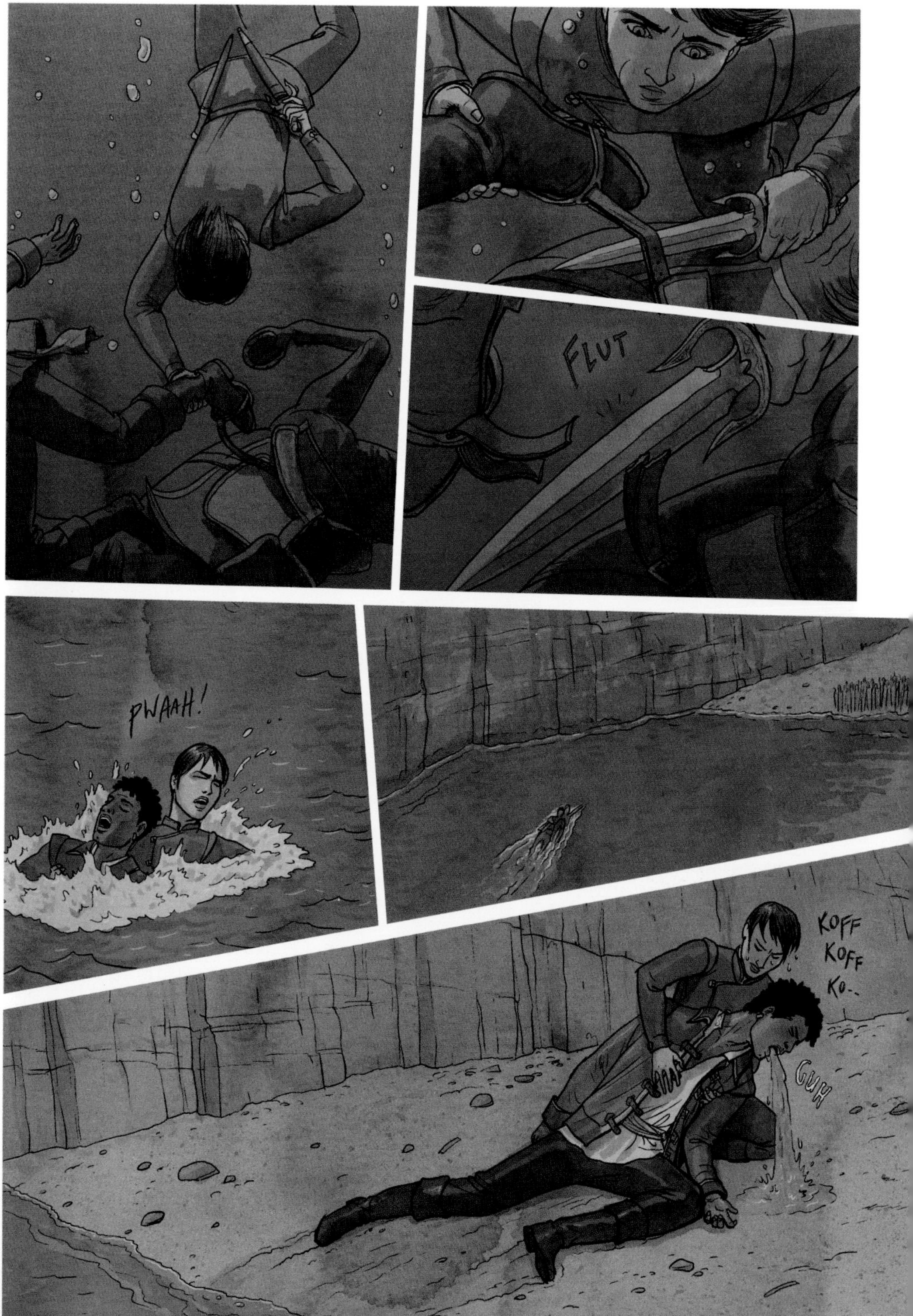
FLUT
PWAAH!
KOFF
KOFF
KO..
GUH

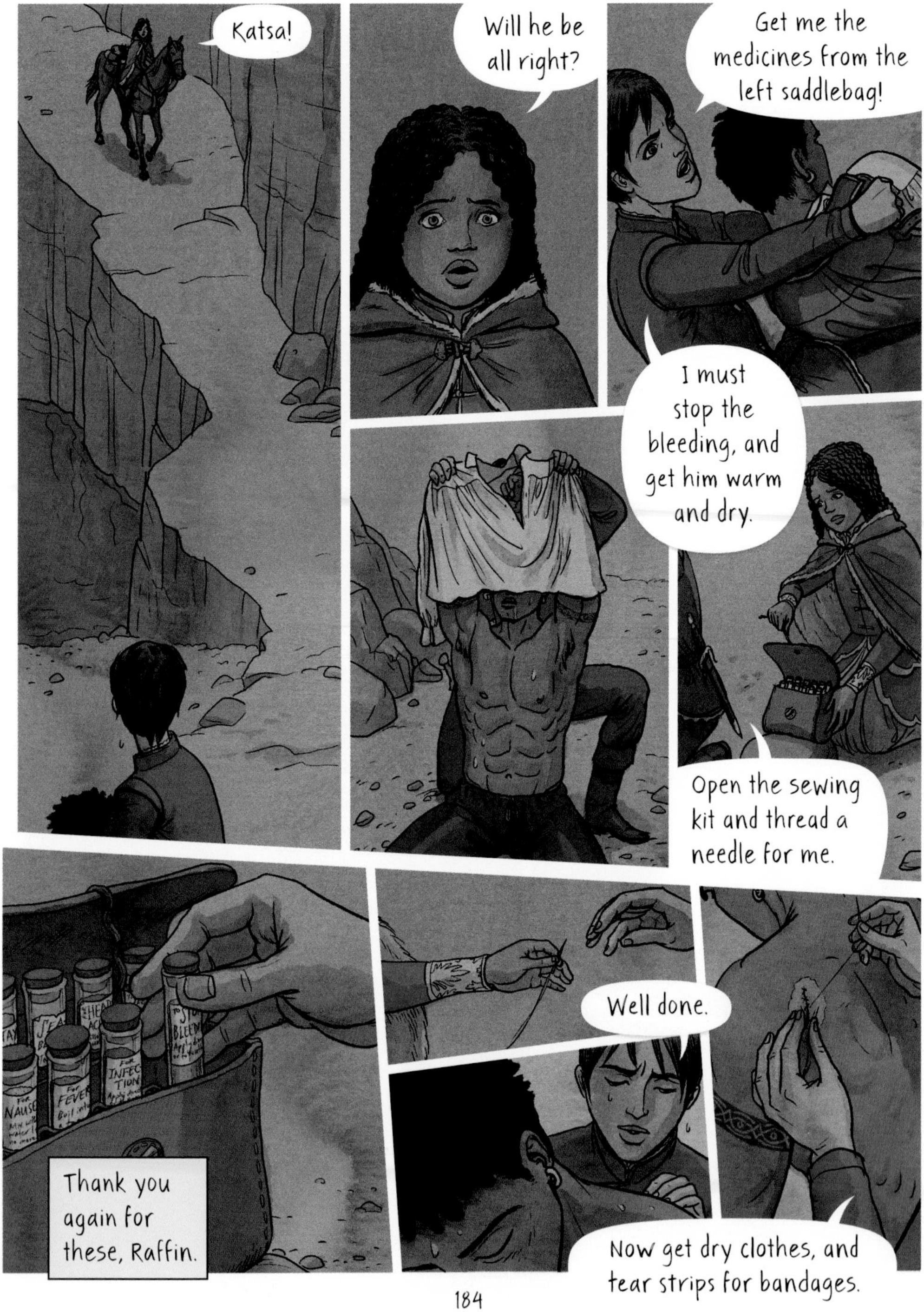

Katsa!
Will he be all right?
Get me the medicines from the left saddlebag!
I must stop the bleeding, and get him warm and dry.
Open the sewing kit and thread a needle for me.
Thank you again for these, Raffin.
Well done.
Now get dry clothes, and tear strips for bandages.

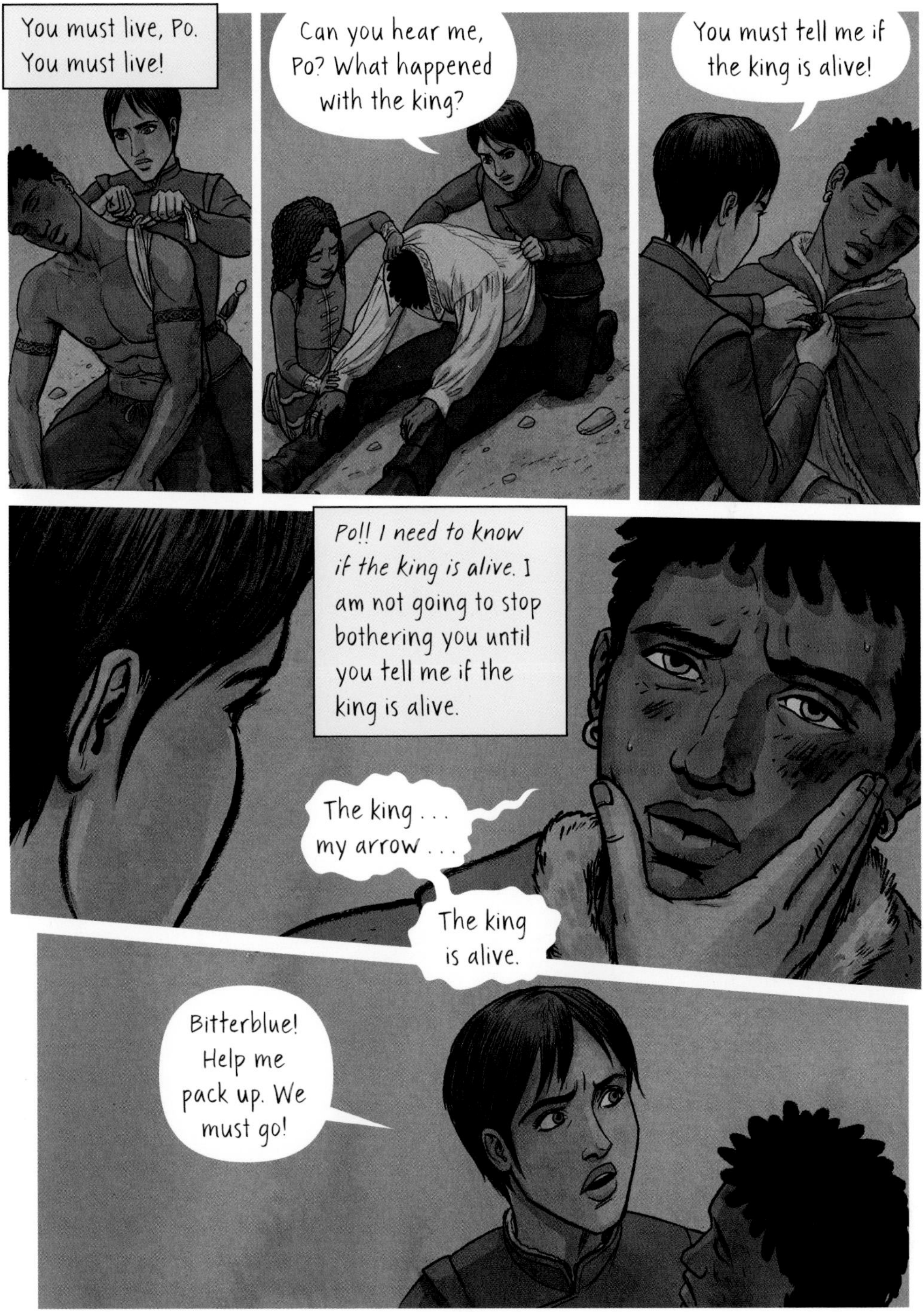
You must live, Po.
You must live!
Can you hear me, Po? What happened with the king?
You must tell me if the king is alive!
Po!! I need to know if the king is alive. I am not going to stop bothering you until you tell me if the king is alive.
The king . . . my arrow . . .
The king is alive.
Bitterblue! Help me pack up. We must go!

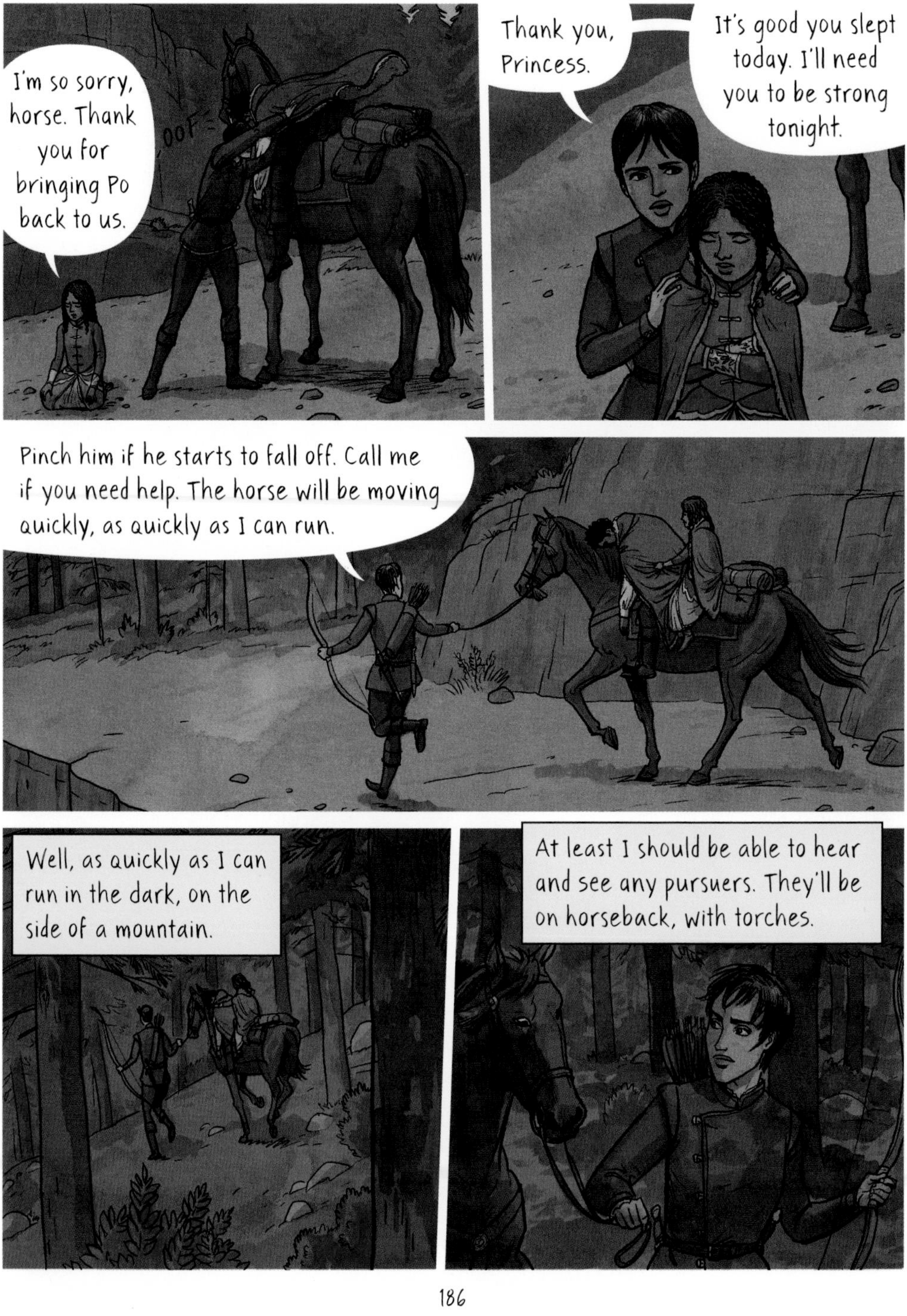
I'm so sorry, horse. Thank you for bringing Po back to us.
OOF
Thank you, Princess.
It's good you slept today. I'll need you to be strong tonight.
Pinch him if he starts to fall off. Call me if you need help. The horse will be moving quickly, as quickly as I can run.
Well, as quickly as I can run in the dark, on the side of a mountain.
At least I should be able to hear and see any pursuers. They'll be on horseback, with torches.

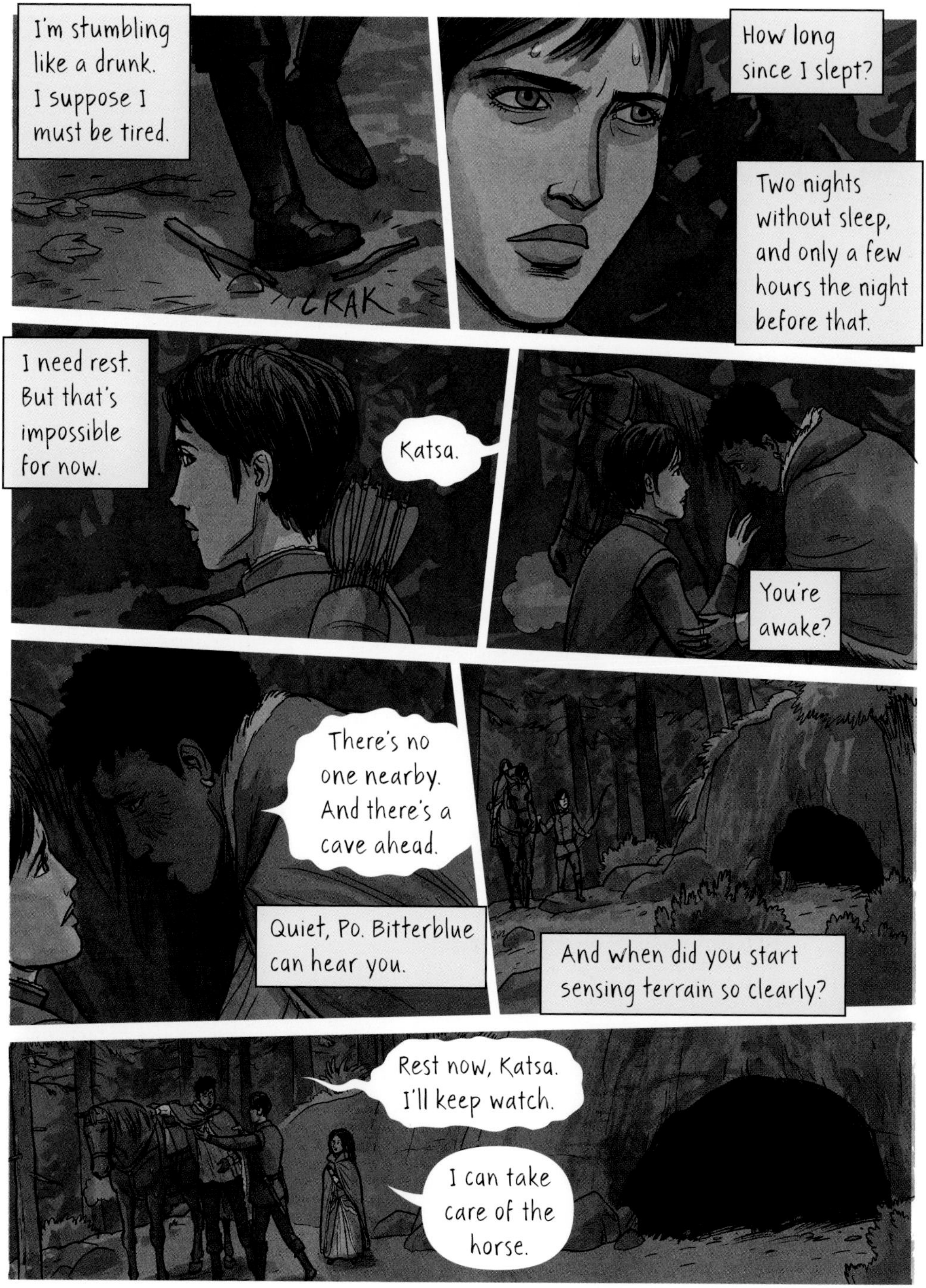
I'm stumbling like a drunk. I suppose I must be tired.
CRAK
How long since I slept?
Two nights without sleep, and only a few hours the night before that.
I need rest. But that's impossible for now.
Katsa.
You're awake?
There's no one nearby. And there's a cave ahead.
Quiet, Po. Bitterblue can hear you.
And when did you start sensing terrain so clearly?
Rest now, Katsa. I'll keep watch.
I can take care of the horse.

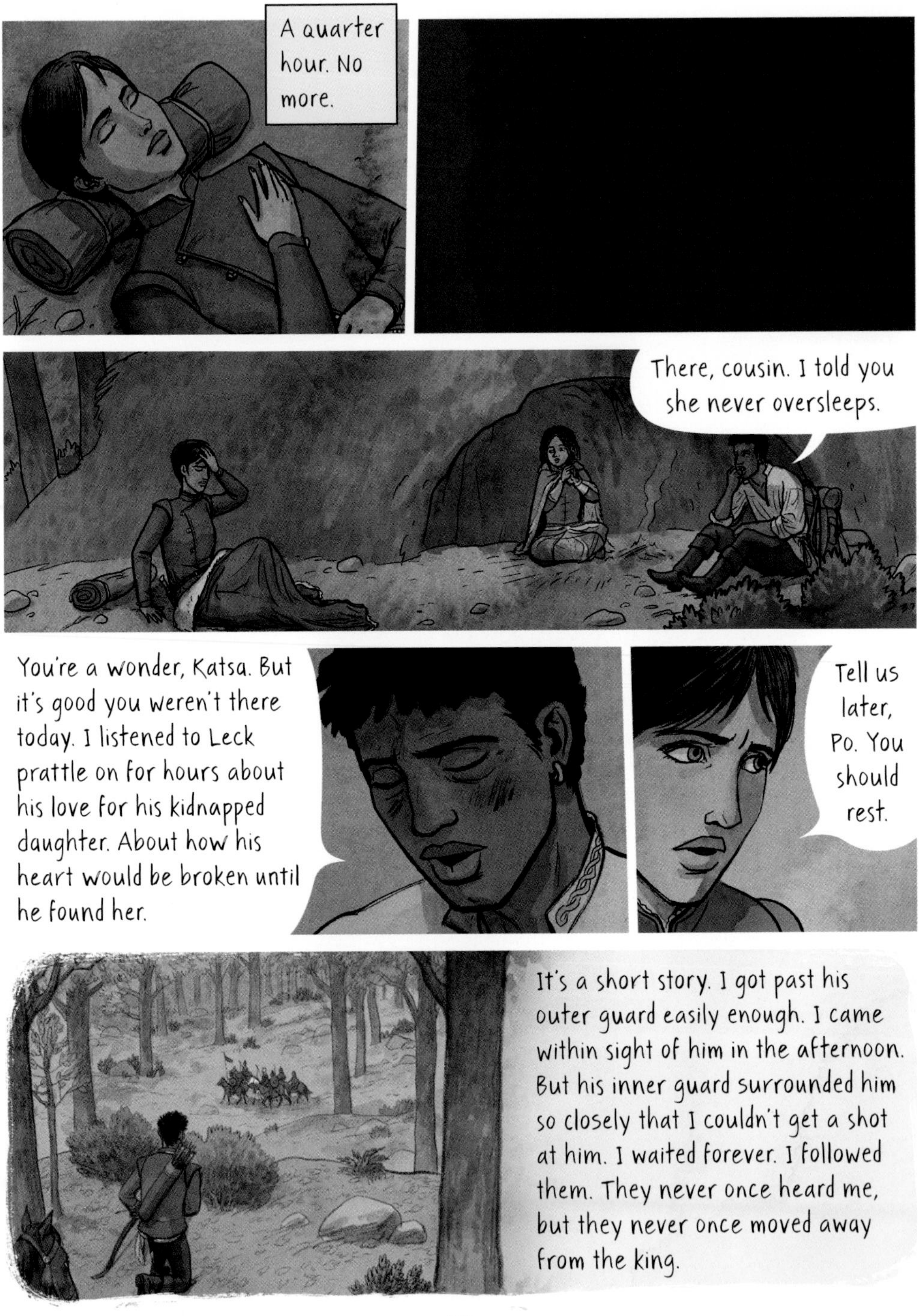
A quarter hour. No more.
There, cousin. I told you she never oversleeps.
You're a wonder, Katsa. But it's good you weren't there today. I listened to Leck prattle on for hours about his love for his kidnapped daughter. About how his heart would be broken until he found her.
Tell us later, Po. You should rest.
It's a short story. I got past his outer guard easily enough. I came within sight of him in the afternoon. But his inner guard surrounded him so closely that I couldn't get a shot at him. I waited forever. I followed them. They never once heard me, but they never once moved away from the king.

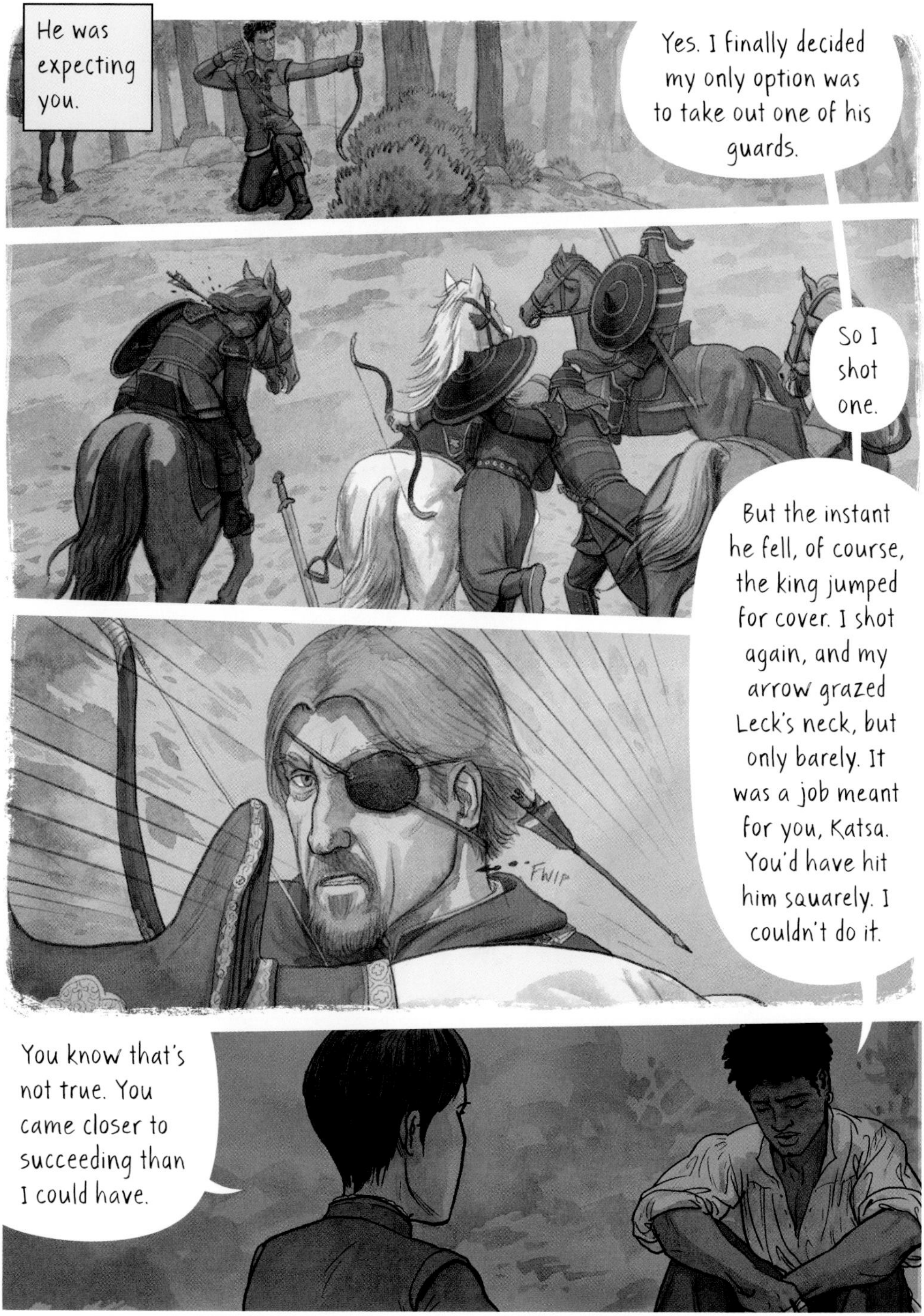
He was expecting you.
Yes. I finally decided my only option was to take out one of his guards.
So I shot one.
But the instant he fell, of course, the king jumped for cover. I shot again, and my arrow grazed Leck's neck, but only barely. It was a job meant for you, Katsa. You'd have hit him squarely. I couldn't do it.
FWIP
You know that's not true. You came closer to succeeding than I could have.

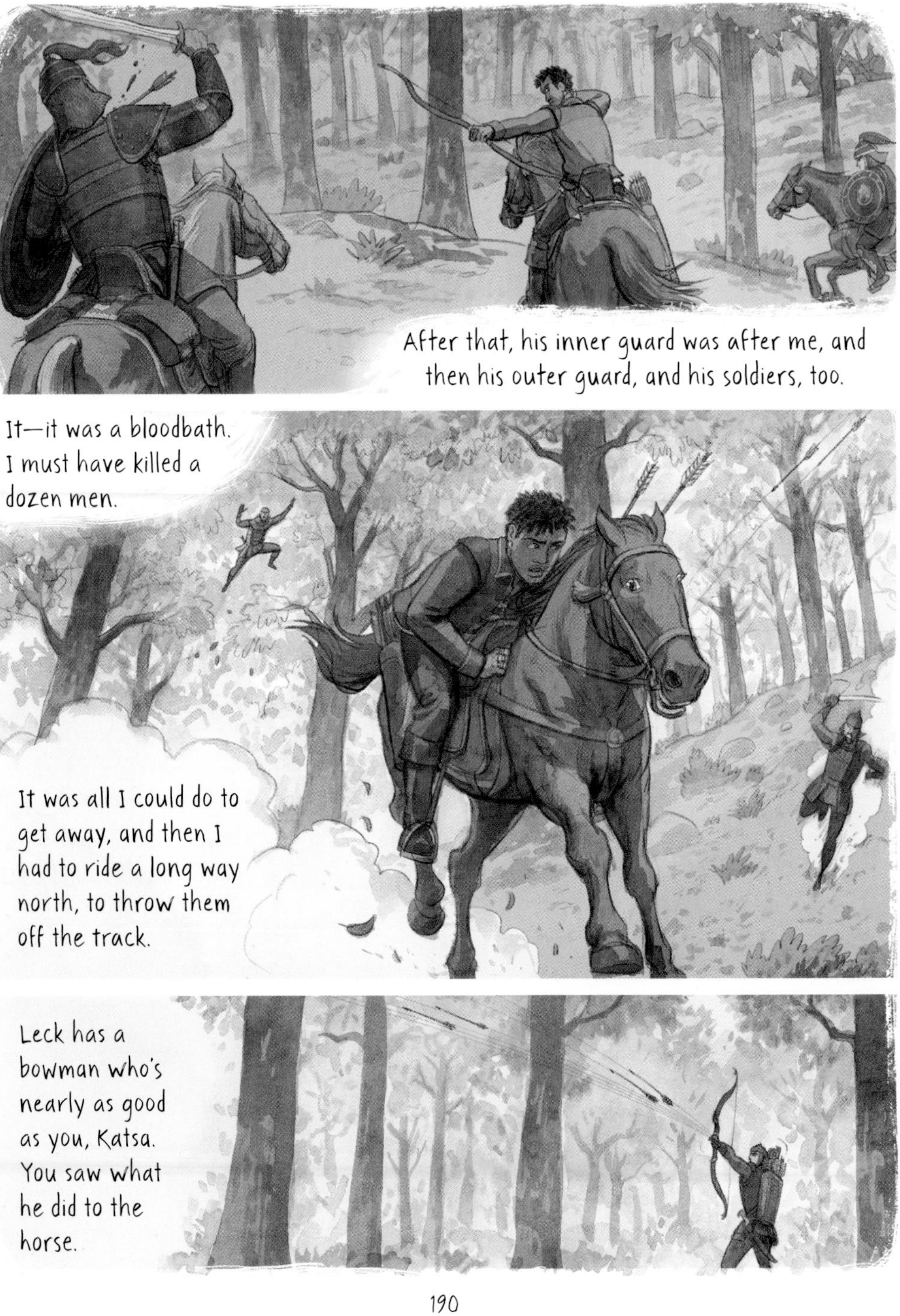
After that, his inner guard was after me, and then his outer guard, and his soldiers, too.
It—it was a bloodbath. I must have killed a dozen men.
It was all I could do to get away, and then I had to ride a long way north, to throw them off the track.
Leck has a bowman who's nearly as good as you, Katsa. You saw what he did to the horse.

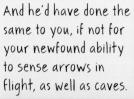And he'd have done the same to you, if not for your newfound ability to sense arrows in flight, as well as caves.

Come on. We must go.

Unh—!

There's something you need to do, Katsa.

And you're not going to like it.

What is it?

You need to leave me behind.

What? Have you lost your wits?

Katsa. Look at me. I can't even walk. The most important thing right now is speed, and I'm holding you back.

No. We need your Grace. I need you to keep my mind straight.

I can't keep your mind straight. The only way to do that is to stay far away from Leck and everyone he's poisoned. Running is the only hope for the child.

He will catch up with us, Katsa, if we continue at this pace. If you left me behind, you could ride fast. Faster than an army of soldiers.

I won't leave you helpless on this mountain.

Your head will feel better soon. You'll get your balance back, and we'll move faster.

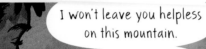

I won't get my balance back for some time, I think.

What do you mean?

It doesn't matter. Even if I woke up tomorrow completely healed, you'd have to leave me behind. We've only one horse.

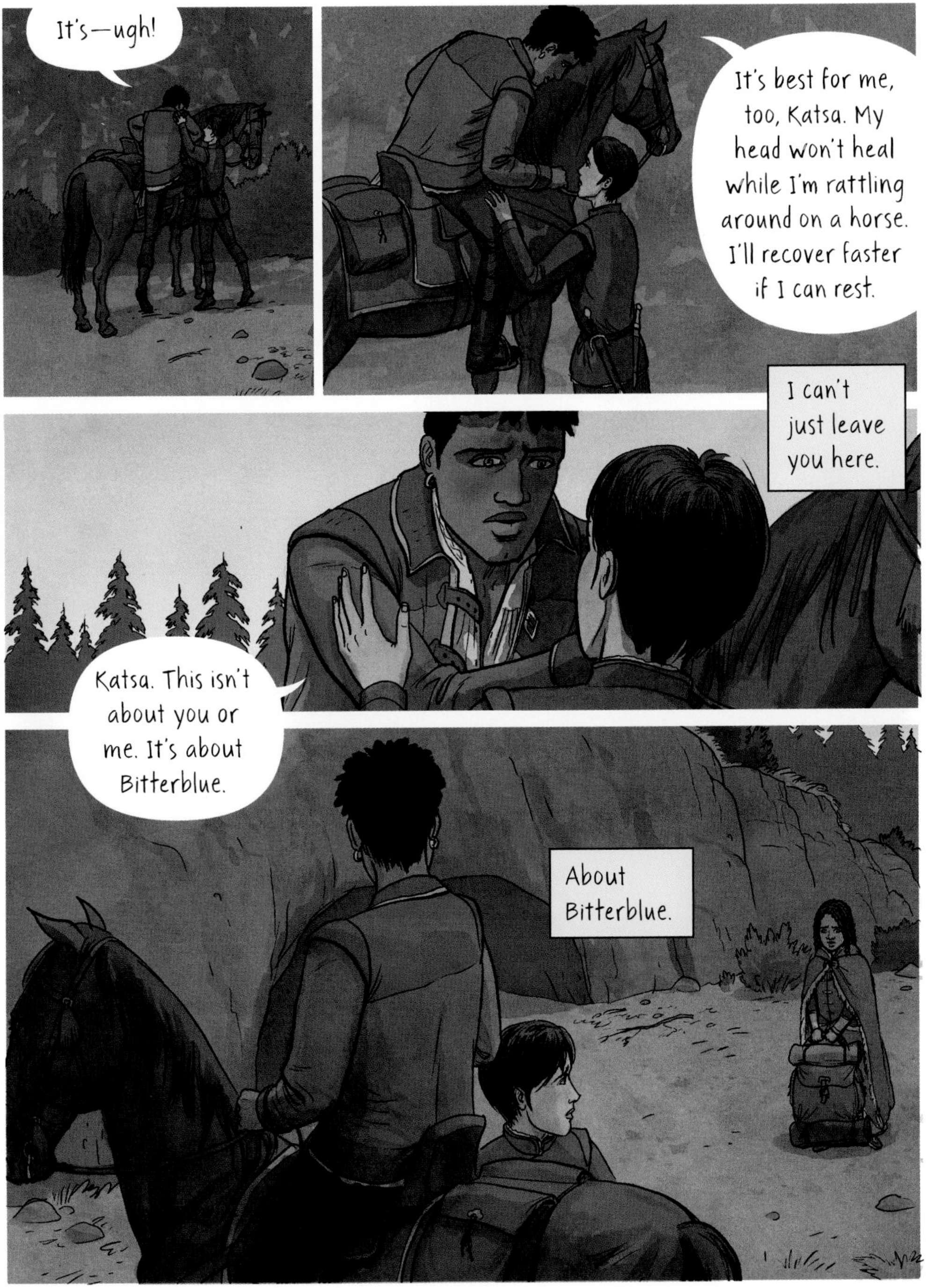
It's—ugh!
It's best for me, too, Katsa. My head won't heal while I'm rattling around on a horse. I'll recover faster if I can rest.
I can't just leave you here.
Katsa. This isn't about you or me. It's about Bitterblue.
About Bitterblue.

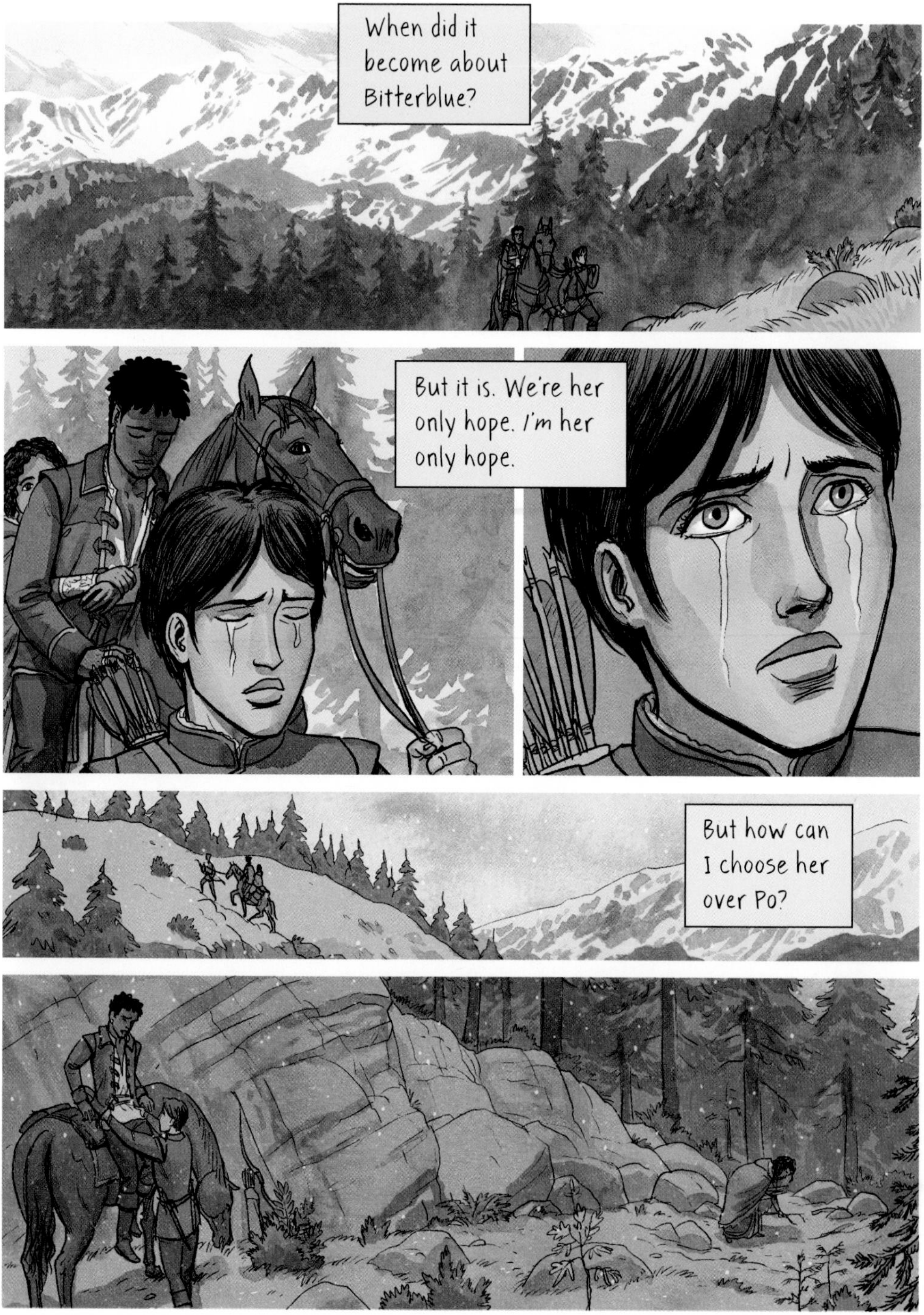
When did it become about Bitterblue?
But it is. We're her only hope. *I'm* her only hope.
But how can I choose her over Po?

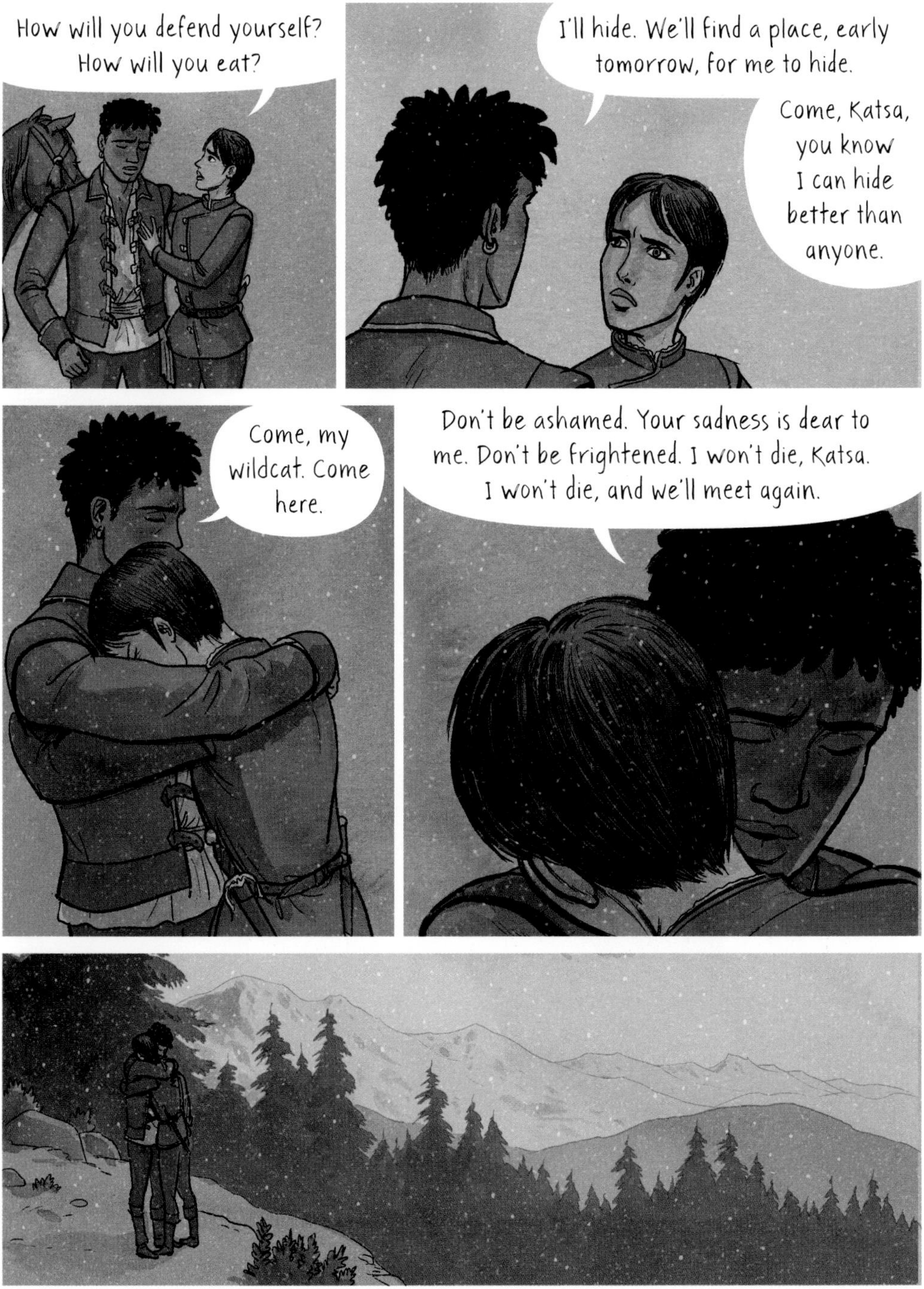
How will you defend yourself? How will you eat?
I'll hide. We'll find a place, early tomorrow, for me to hide.
Come, Katsa, you know I can hide better than anyone.
Come, my wildcat. Come here.
Don't be ashamed. Your sadness is dear to me. Don't be frightened. I won't die, Katsa. I won't die, and we'll meet again.

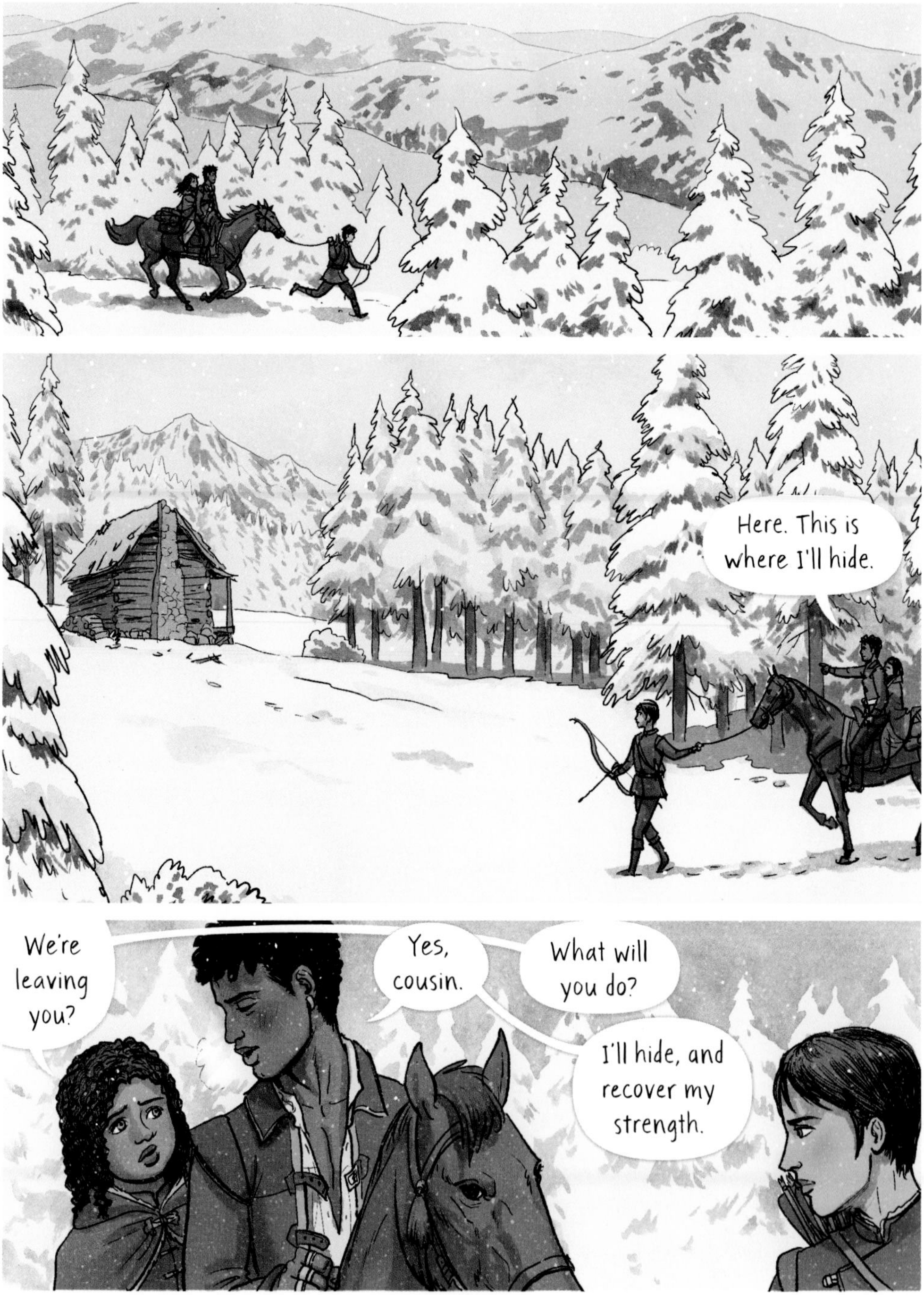
Here. This is where I'll hide.
We're leaving you?
Yes, cousin.
What will you do?
I'll hide, and recover my strength.

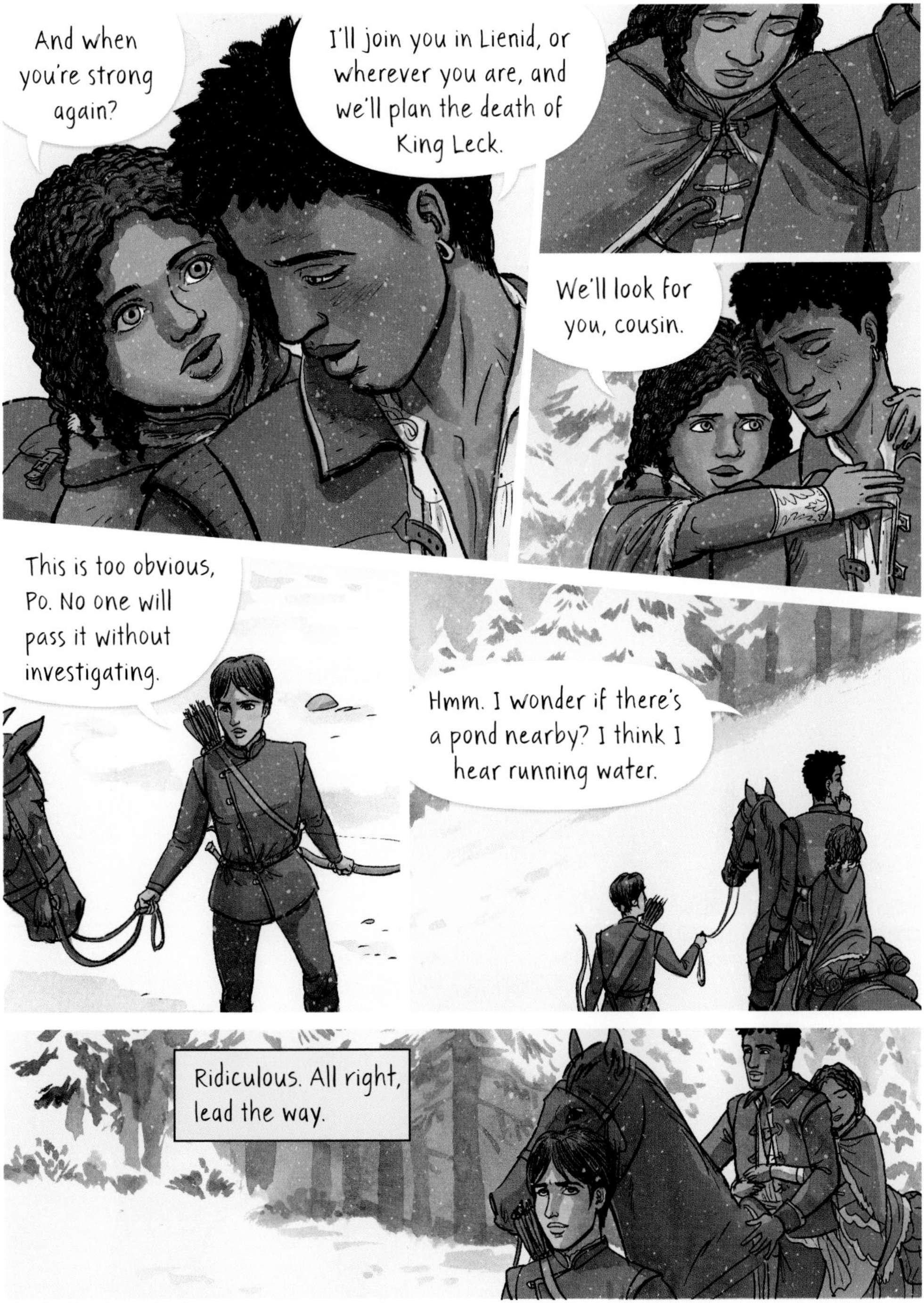
And when you're strong again?
I'll join you in Lienid, or wherever you are, and we'll plan the death of King Leck.
We'll look for you, cousin.
This is too obvious, Po. No one will pass it without investigating.
Hmm. I wonder if there's a pond nearby? I think I hear running water.
Ridiculous. All right, lead the way.

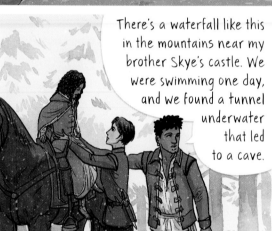

There's a waterfall like this in the mountains near my brother Skye's castle. We were swimming one day, and we found a tunnel underwater that led to a cave.

If there's a cave, I'll find it for you. But how will you get down here from the cabin? Crawl?

There's no shame in crawling when one can't walk. And swimming requires less balance.

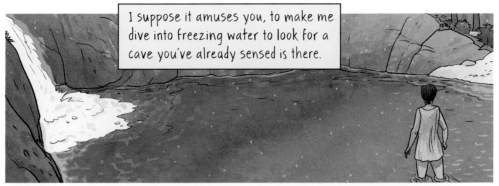

I suppose it amuses you, to make me dive into freezing water to look for a cave you've already sensed is there.

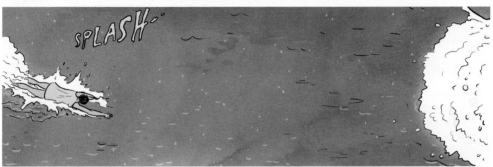

SPLASH·

This must be it.

It's deep.

And it's disorienting. Claustrophobic. And shockingly cold.

I'd turn back if not for Po's certainty. Can he tell for sure if there's air down here . . . ?

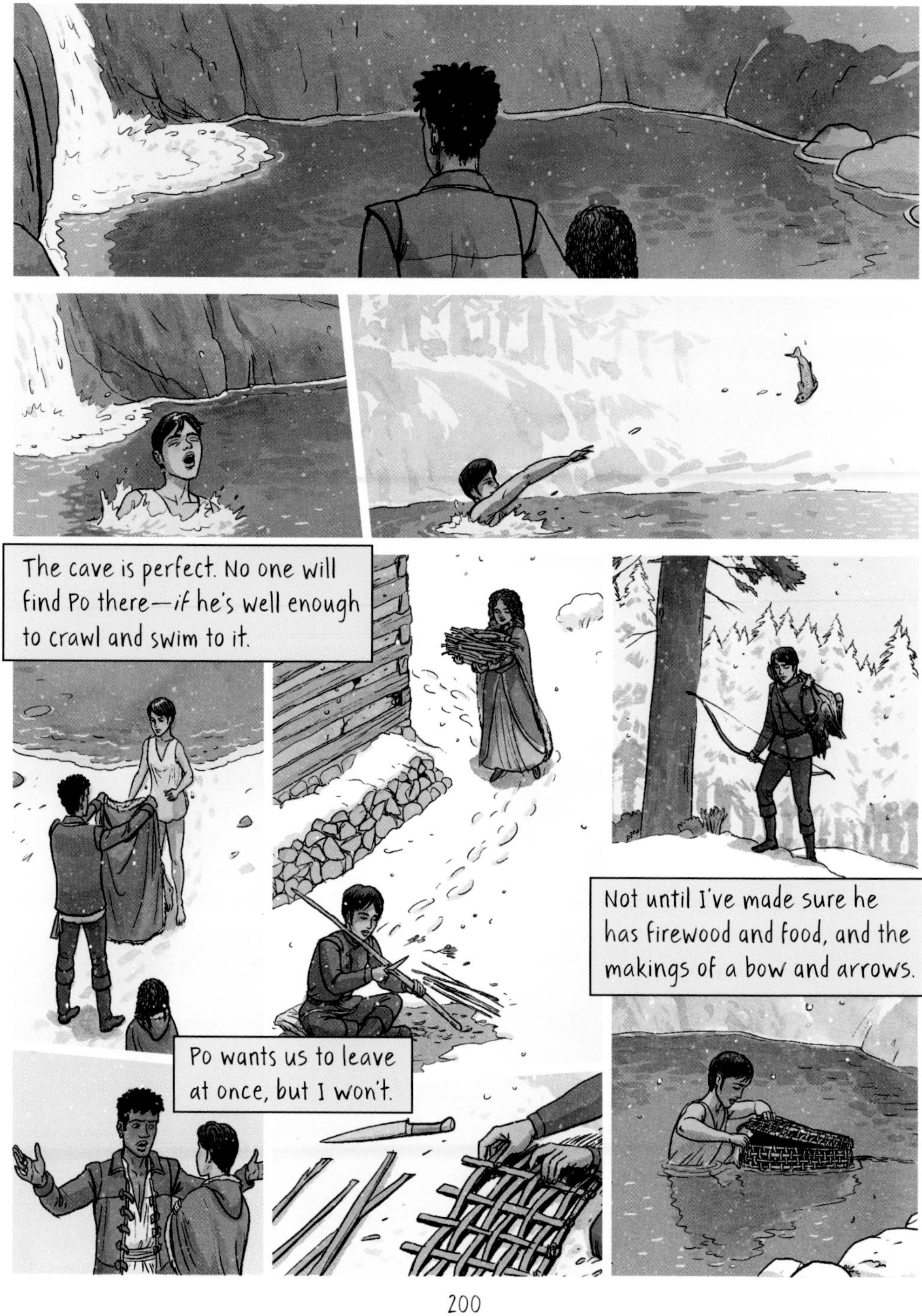
The cave is perfect. No one will find Po there—*if* he's well enough to crawl and swim to it.
Not until I've made sure he has firewood and food, and the makings of a bow and arrows.
Po wants us to leave at once, but I won't.

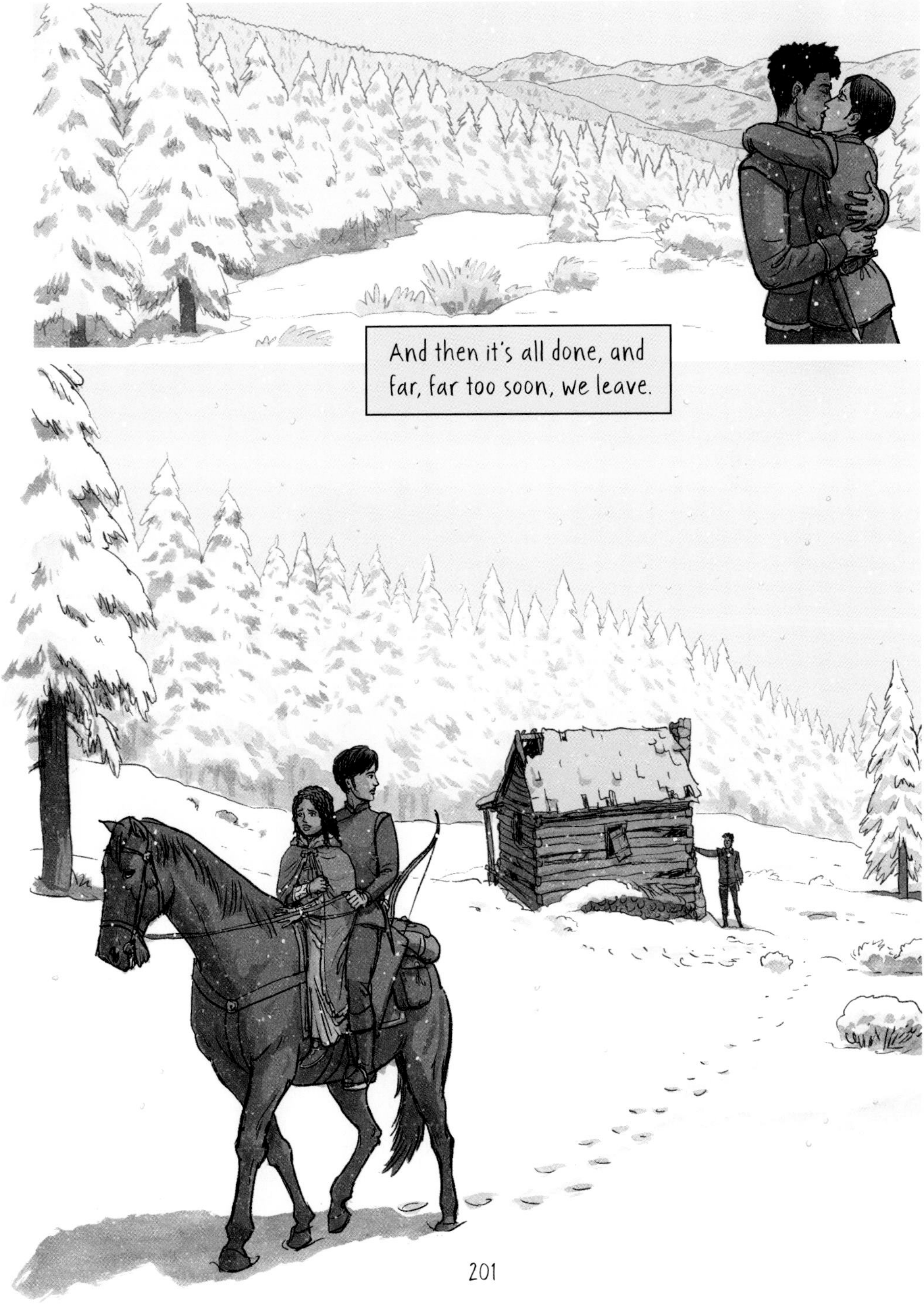
And then it's all done, and
far, far too soon, we leave.

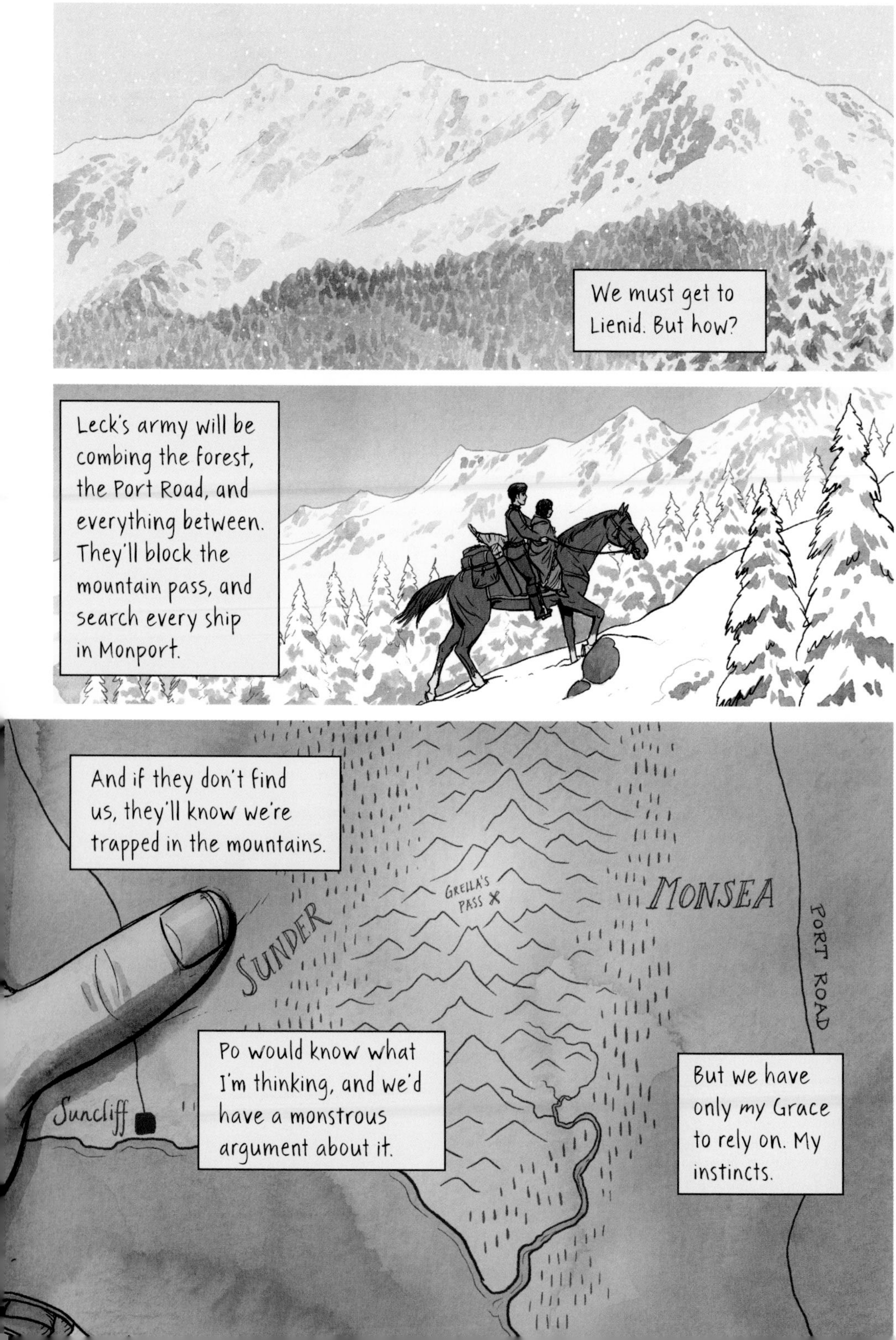
We must get to Lienid. But how?
Leck's army will be combing the forest, the Port Road, and everything between. They'll block the mountain pass, and search every ship in Monport.
And if they don't find us, they'll know we're trapped in the mountains.
GRELLA'S PASS
MONSEA
SUNDER
PORT ROAD
Suncliff
Po would know what I'm thinking, and we'd have a monstrous argument about it.
But we have only my Grace to rely on. My instincts.

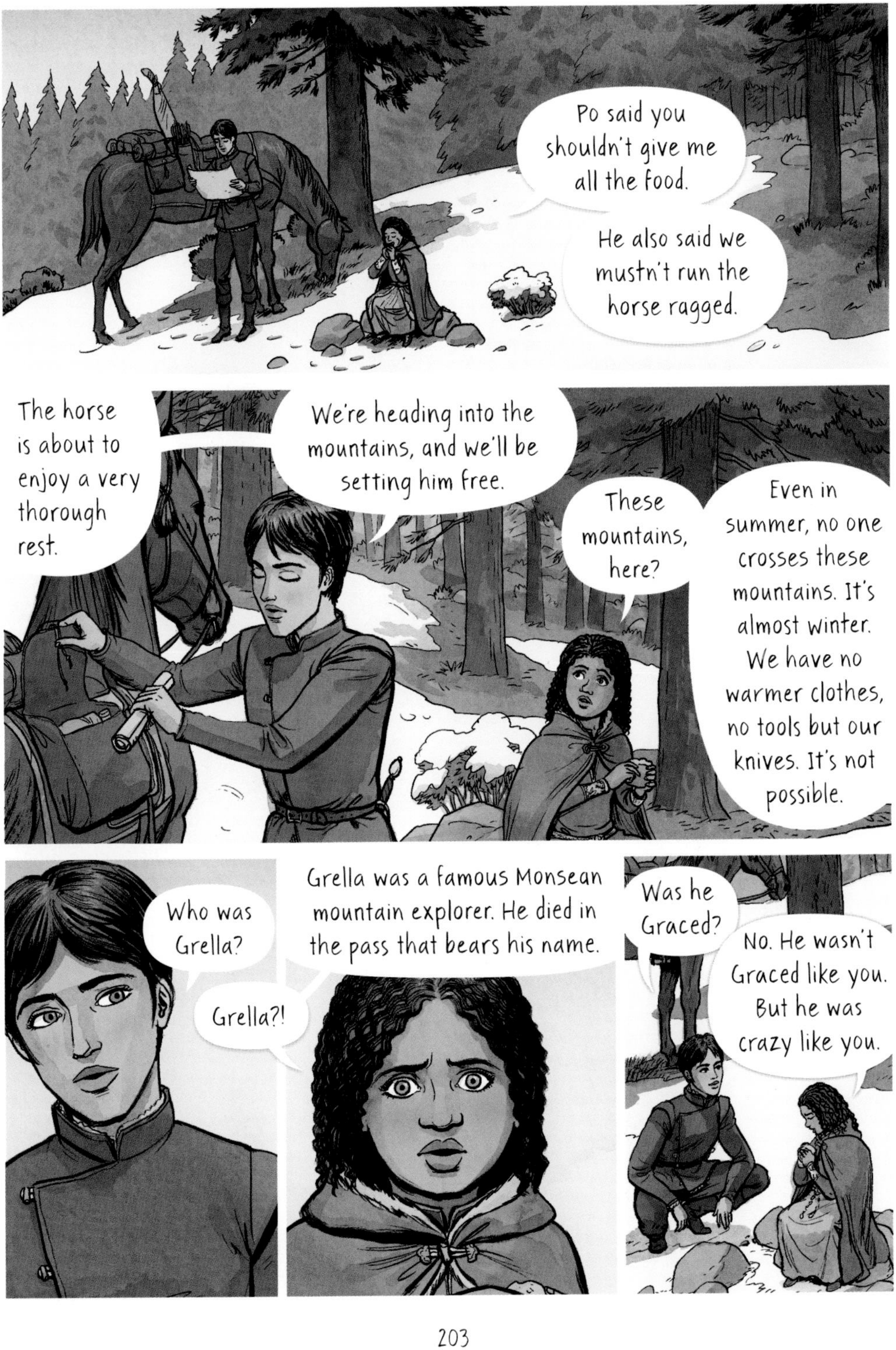
Po said you shouldn't give me all the food.
He also said we mustn't run the horse ragged.
The horse is about to enjoy a very thorough rest.
We're heading into the mountains, and we'll be setting him free.
These mountains, here?
Even in summer, no one crosses these mountains. It's almost winter. We have no warmer clothes, no tools but our knives. It's not possible.
Who was Grella?
Grella?!
Grella was a famous Monsean mountain explorer. He died in the pass that bears his name.
Was he Graced?
No. He wasn't Graced like you. But he was crazy like you.

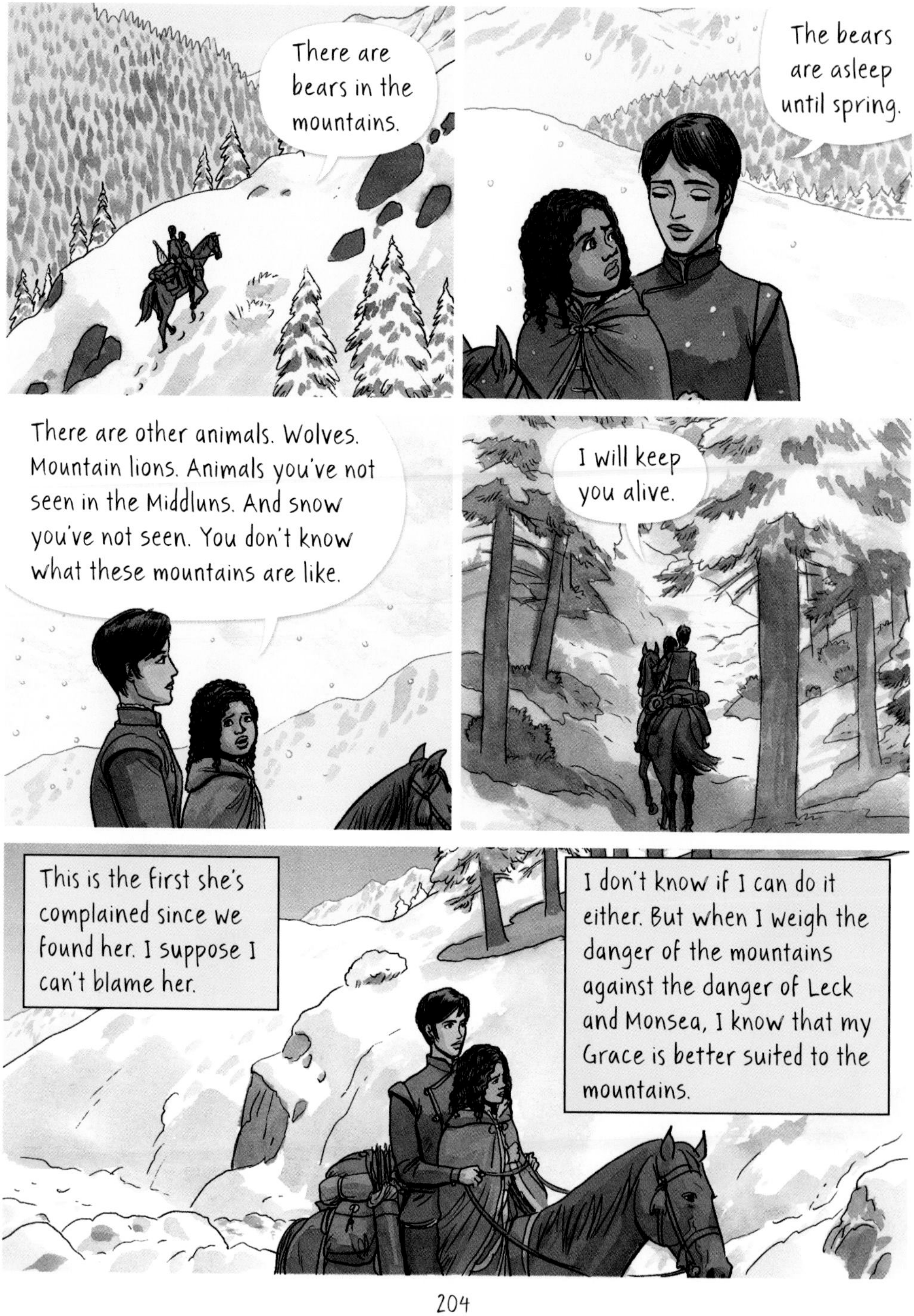
There are bears in the mountains.
The bears are asleep until spring.
There are other animals. Wolves. Mountain lions. Animals you've not seen in the Middluns. And snow you've not seen. You don't know what these mountains are like.
I will keep you alive.
This is the first she's complained since we found her. I suppose I can't blame her.
I don't know if I can do it either. But when I weigh the danger of the mountains against the danger of Leck and Monsea, I know that my Grace is better suited to the mountains.

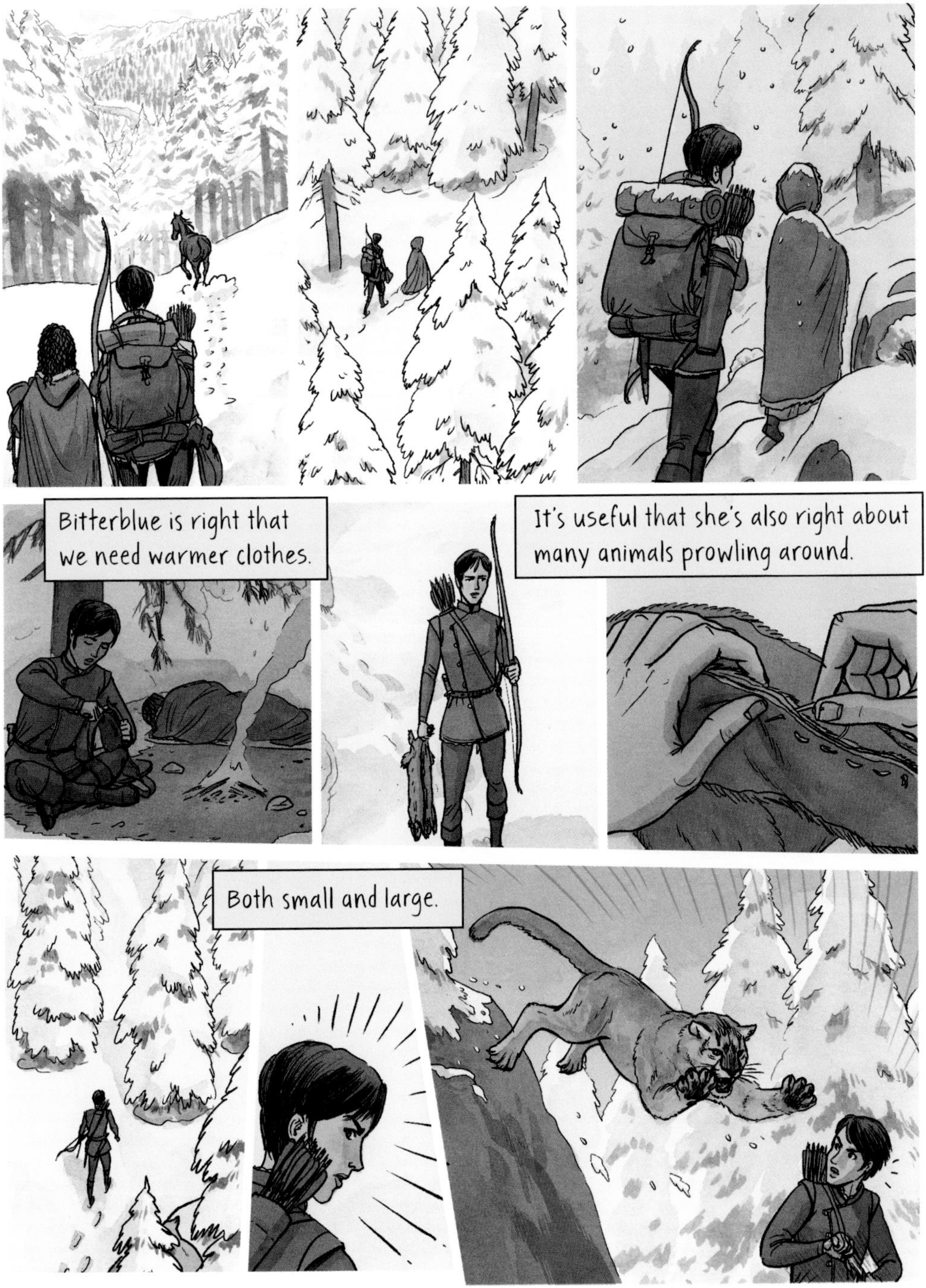
Bitterblue is right that we need warmer clothes.
It's useful that she's also right about many animals prowling around.
Both small and large.

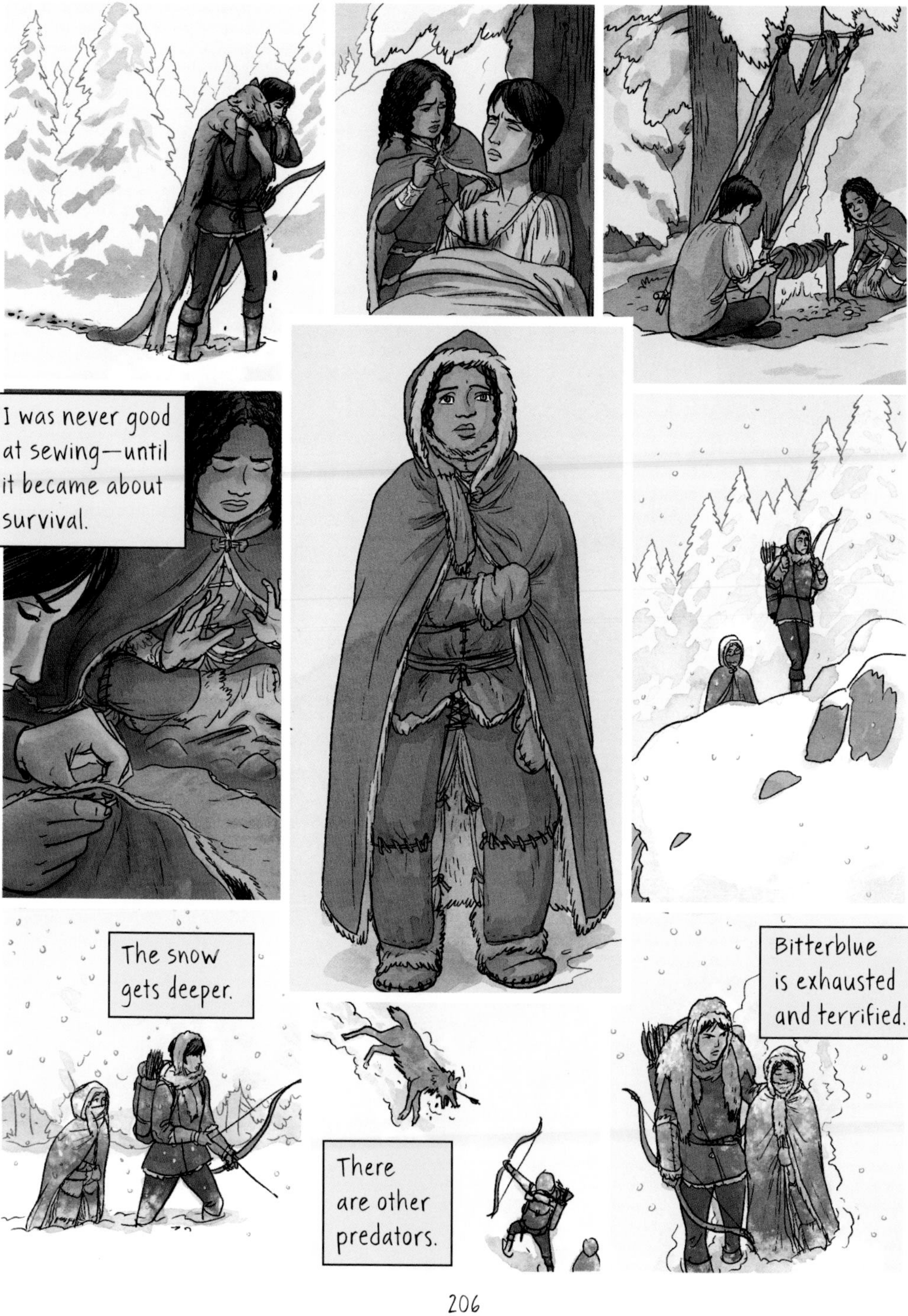
I was never good at sewing—until it became about survival.
The snow gets deeper.
There are other predators.
Bitterblue is exhausted and terrified.

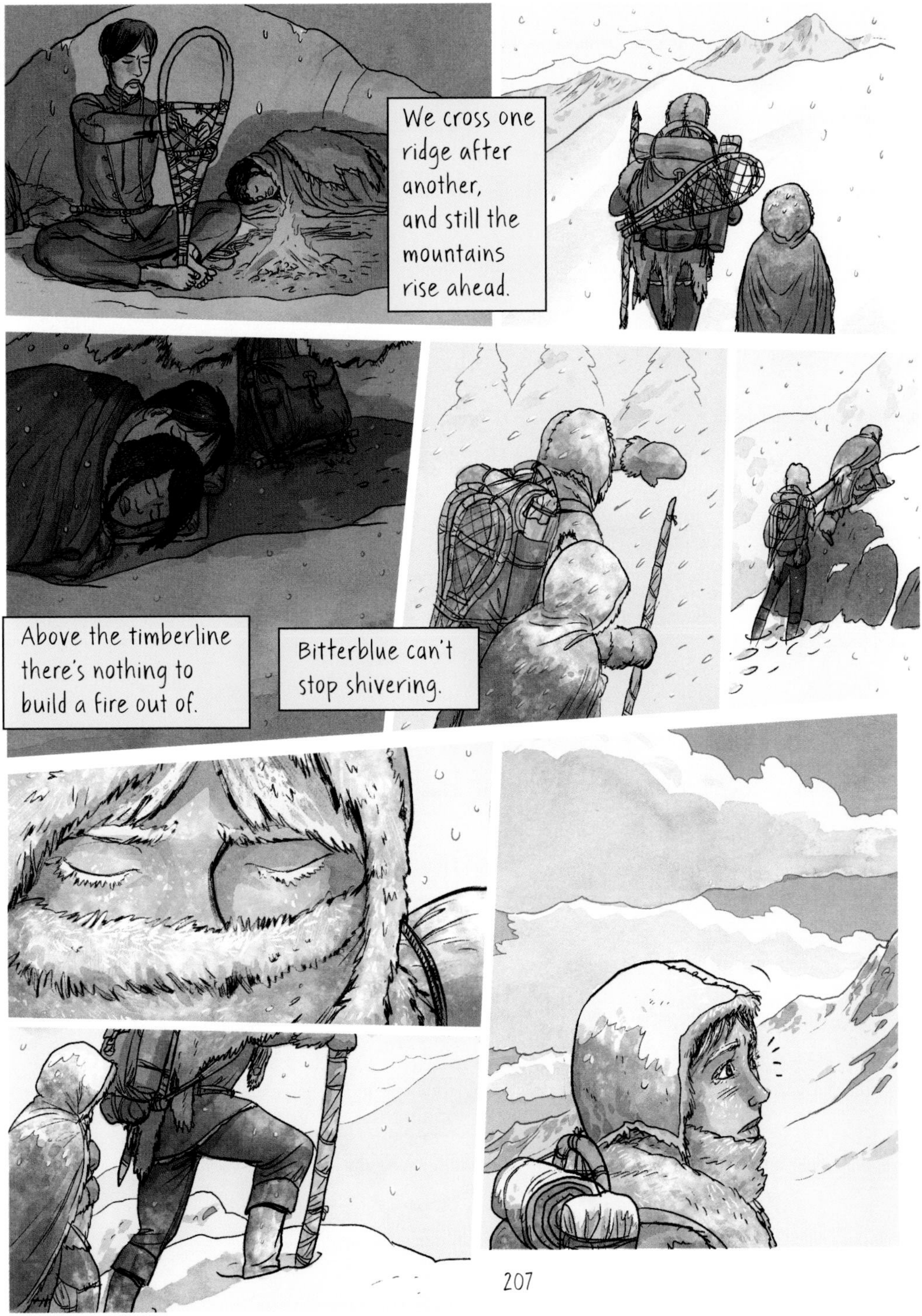
We cross one ridge after another, and still the mountains rise ahead.
Above the timberline there's nothing to build a fire out of.
Bitterblue can't stop shivering.

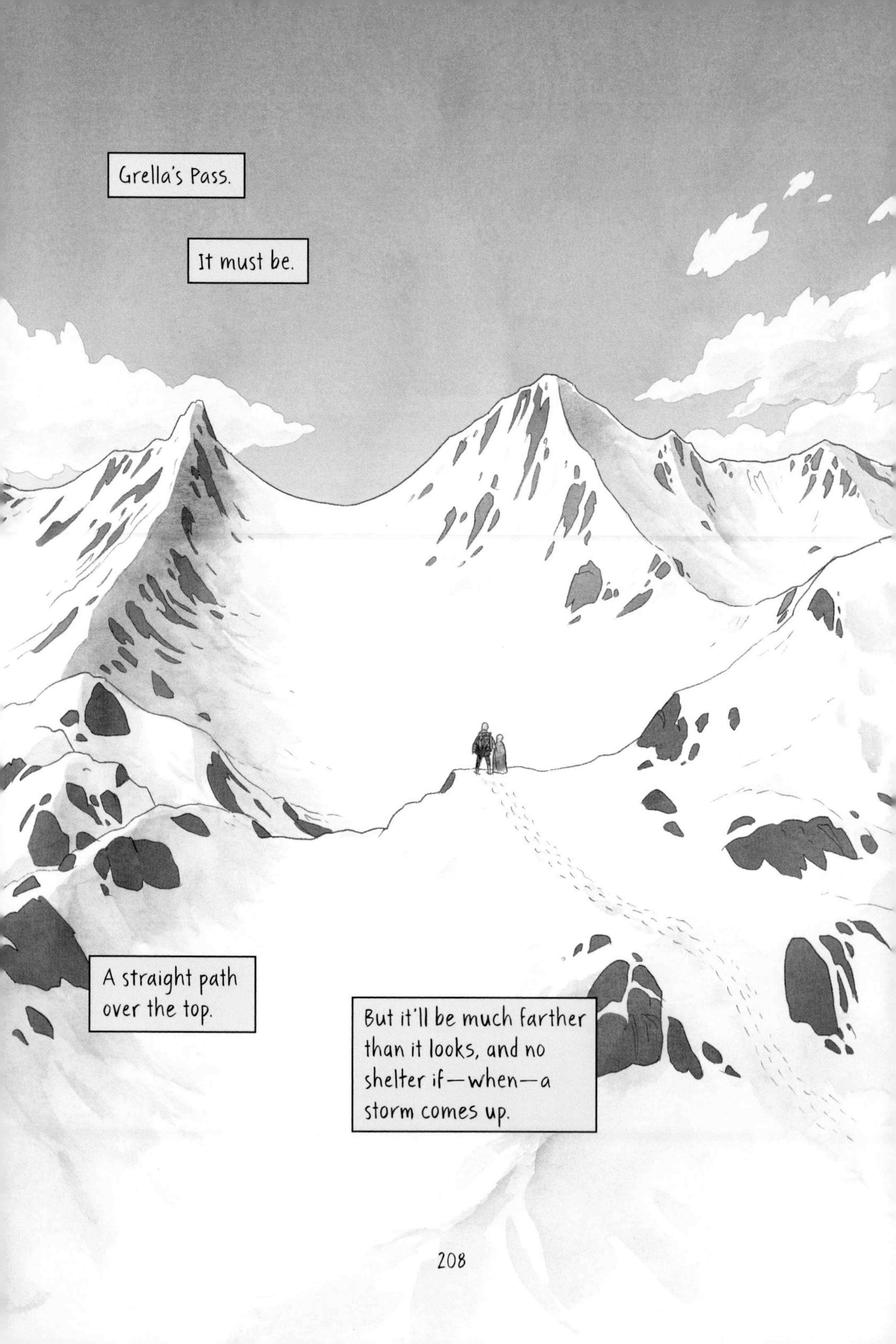
Grella's Pass.
It must be.
A straight path over the top.
But it'll be much farther than it looks, and no shelter if—when—a storm comes up.

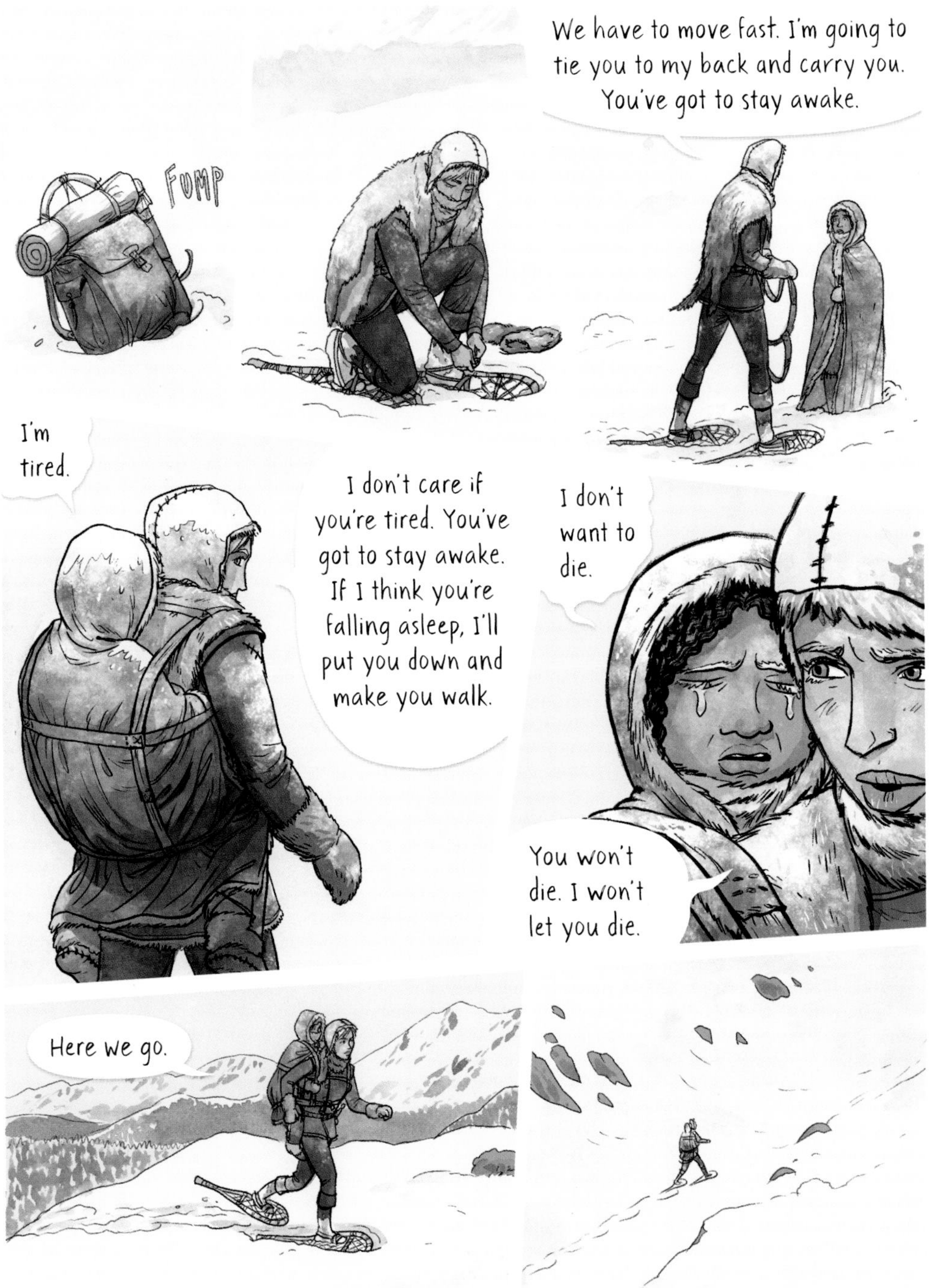
FUMP
We have to move fast. I'm going to tie you to my back and carry you. You've got to stay awake.
I'm tired.
I don't care if you're tired. You've got to stay awake. If I think you're falling asleep, I'll put you down and make you walk.
I don't want to die.
You won't die. I won't let you die.
Here we go.

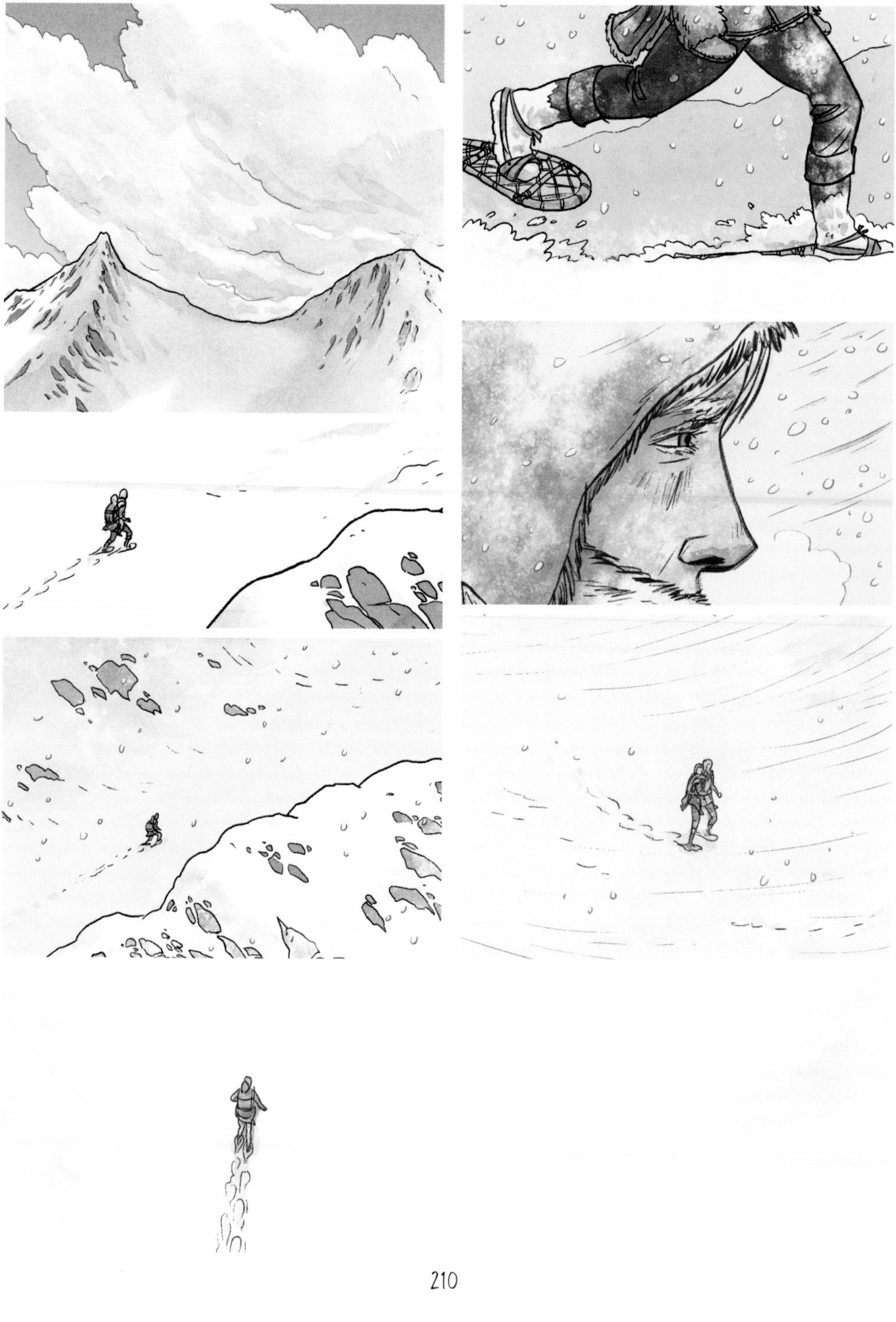

PART THREE
The Shifting World

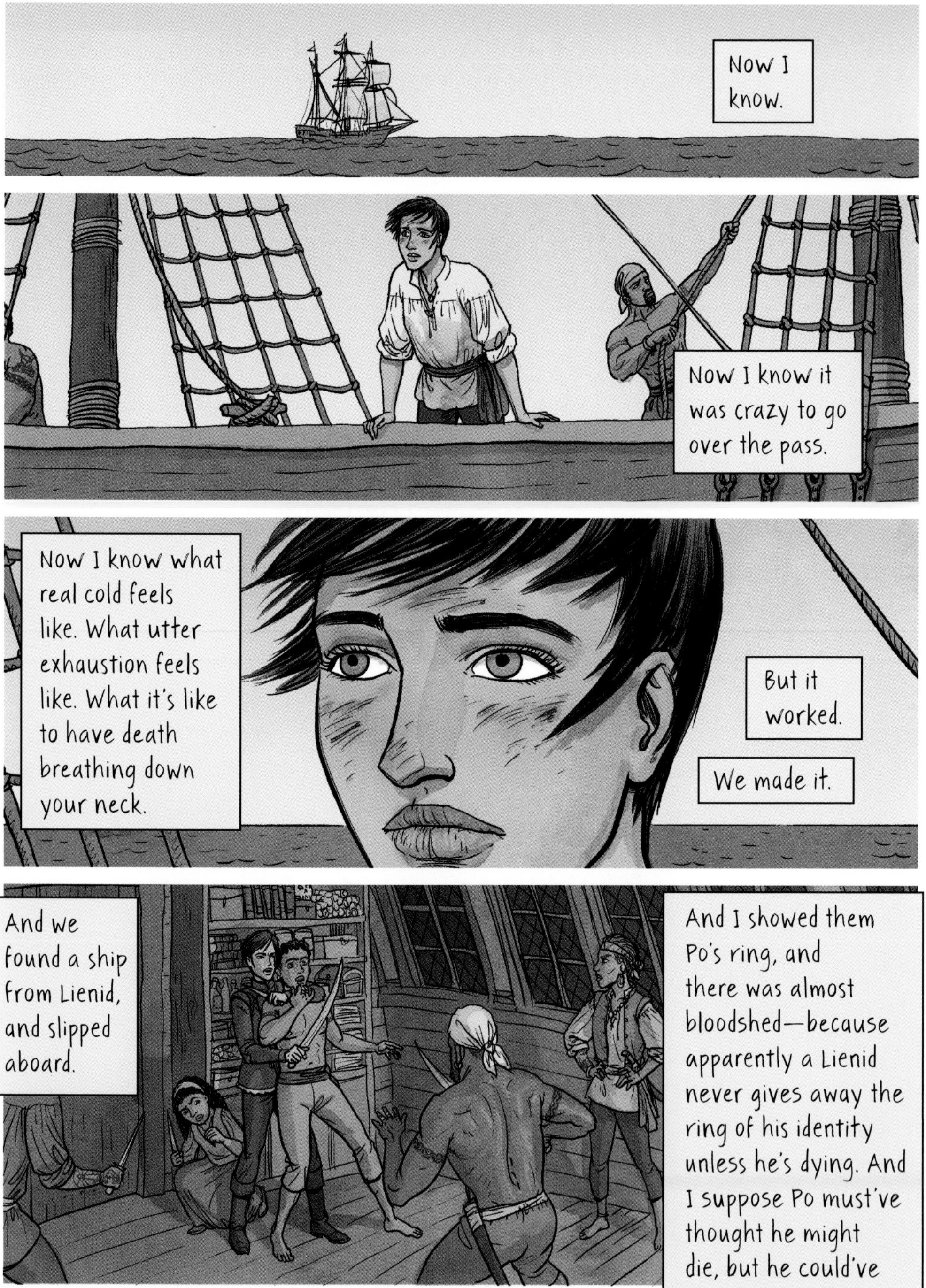
Now I know.
Now I know it was crazy to go over the pass.
Now I know what real cold feels like. What utter exhaustion feels like. What it's like to have death breathing down your neck.
But it worked.
We made it.
And we found a ship from Lienid, and slipped aboard.
And I showed them Po's ring, and there was almost bloodshed—because apparently a Lienid never gives away the ring of his identity unless he's dying. And I suppose Po must've thought he might die, but he could've warned me of this.

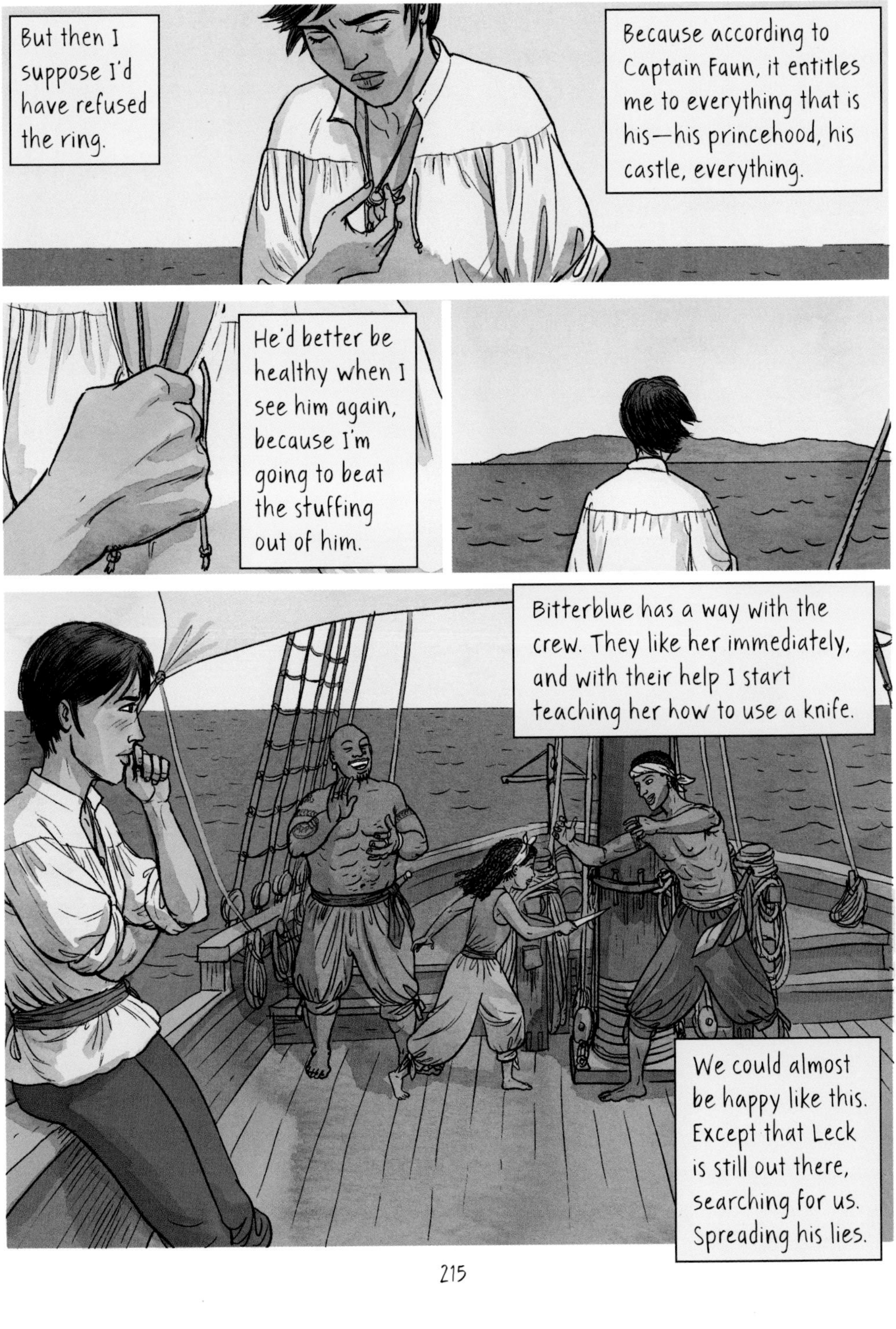
But then I suppose I'd have refused the ring.
Because according to Captain Faun, it entitles me to everything that is his—his princehood, his castle, everything.
He'd better be healthy when I see him again, because I'm going to beat the stuffing out of him.
Bitterblue has a way with the crew. They like her immediately, and with their help I start teaching her how to use a knife.
We could almost be happy like this. Except that Leck is still out there, searching for us. Spreading his lies.

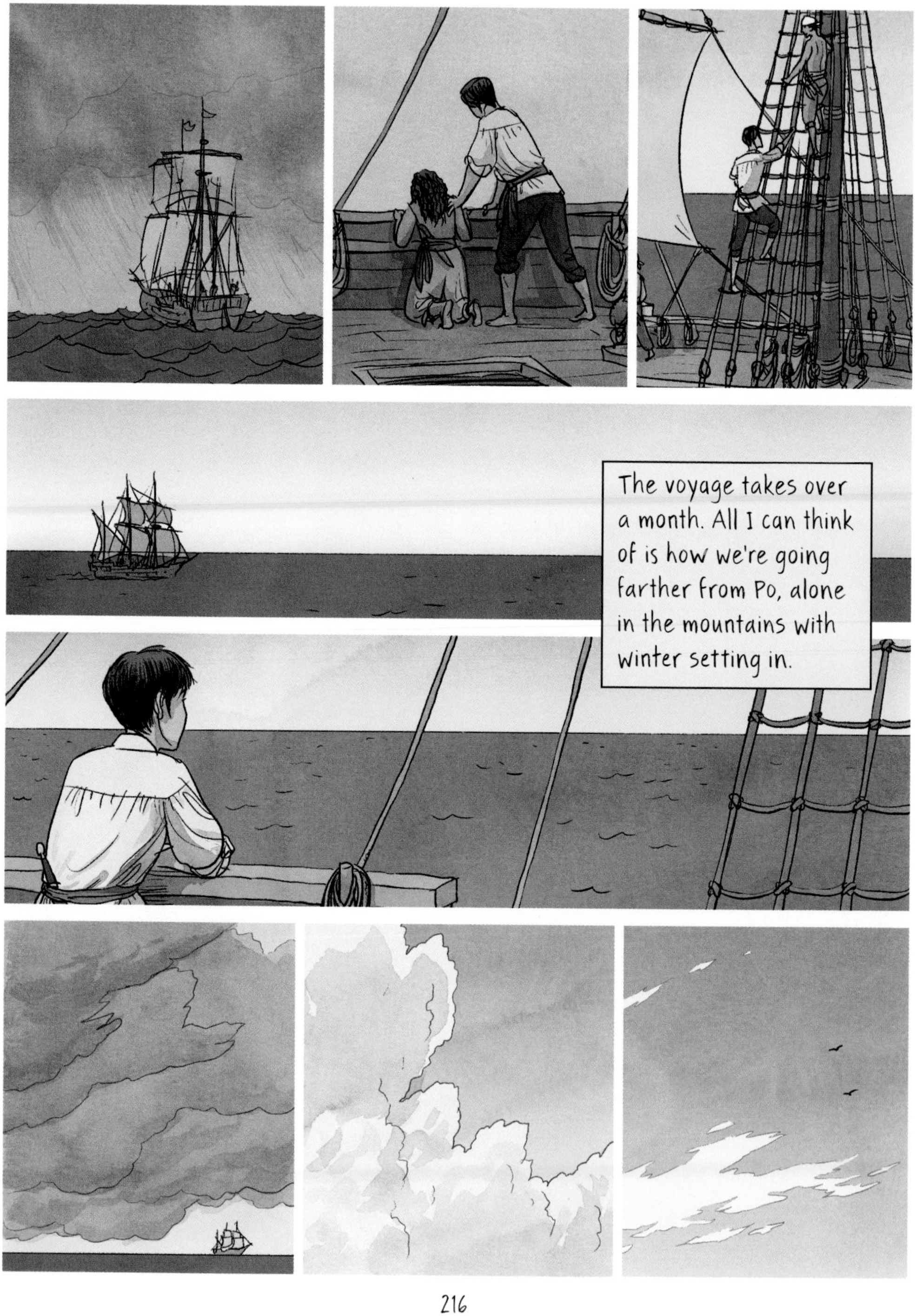
The voyage takes over a month. All I can think of is how we're going farther from Po, alone in the mountains with winter setting in.

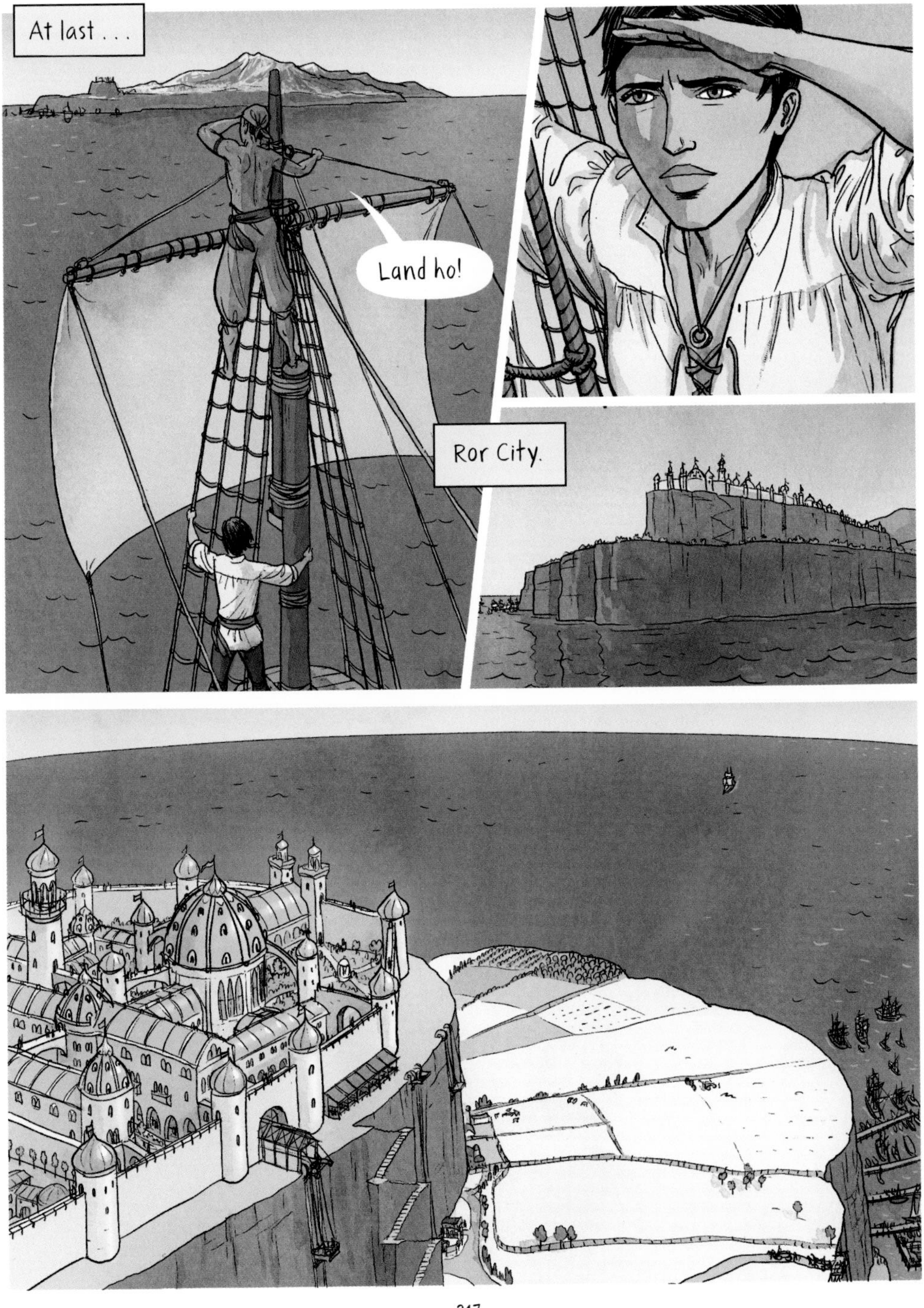
At last . . .
Land ho!
Ror City.

That's it.

Po's castle?

Your castle, Lady Princess, at least for now.

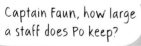

Captain Faun, how large a staff does Po keep?

Very few. It'll be quiet.

Good.

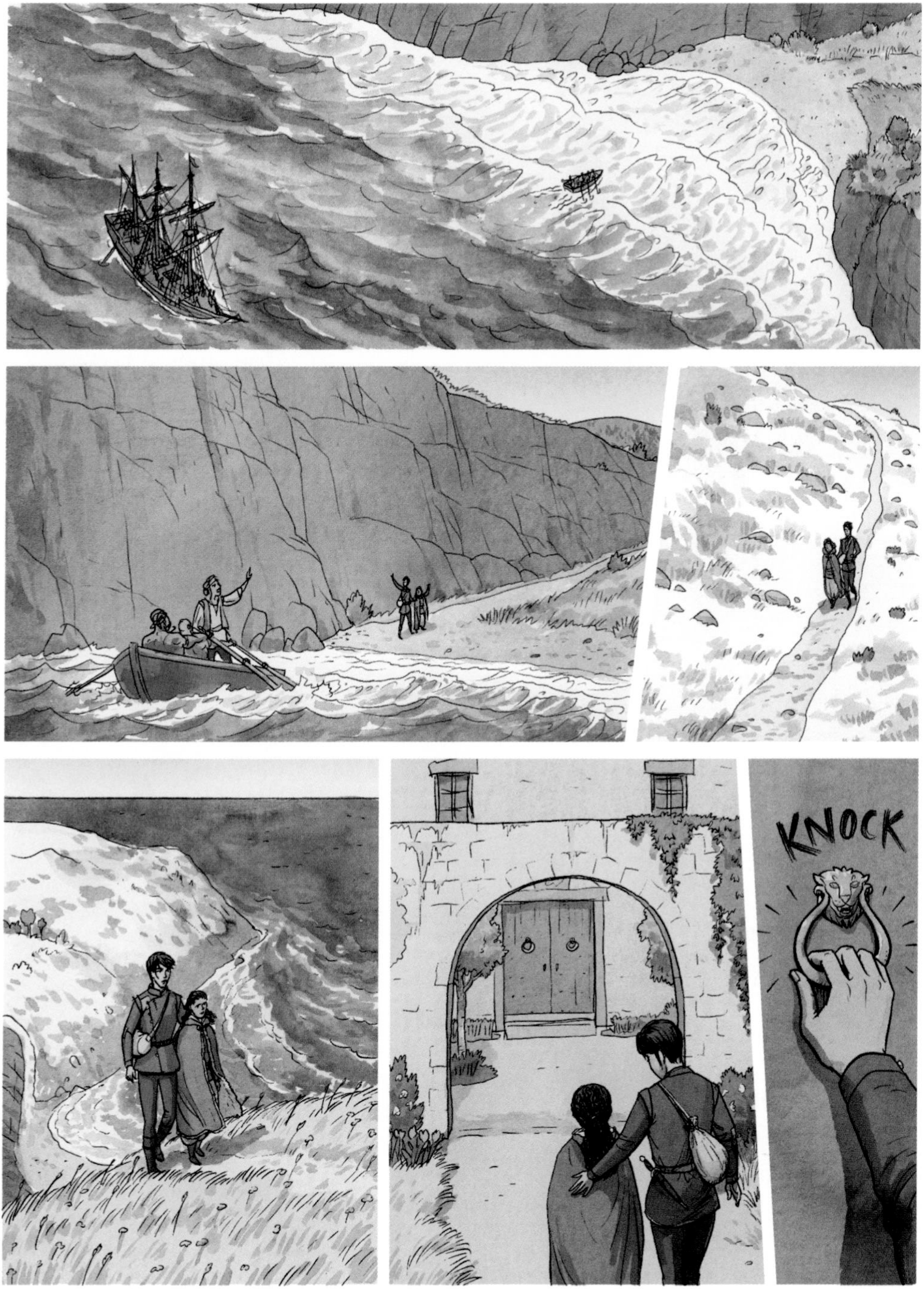
KNOCK

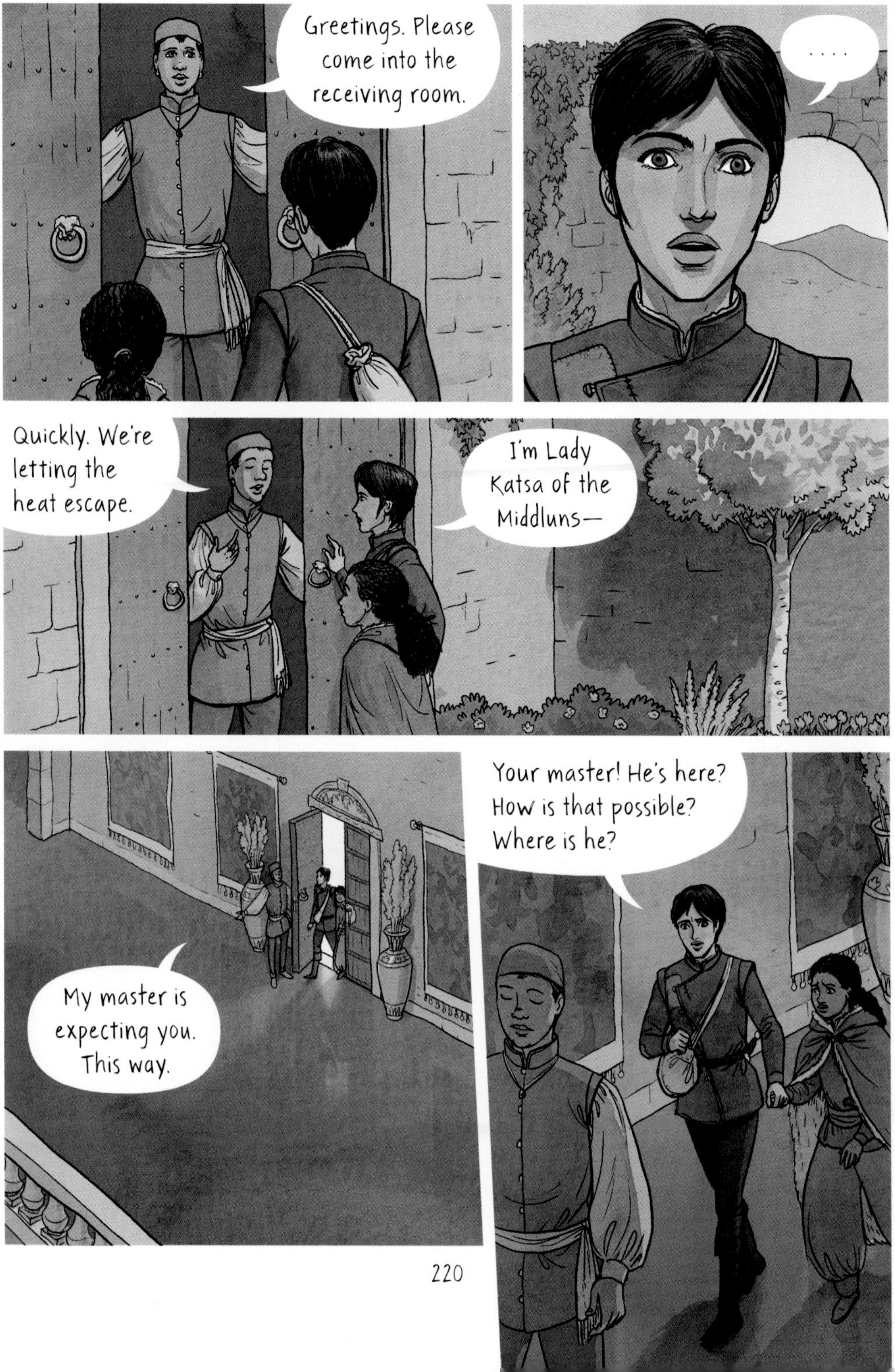
Greetings. Please come into the receiving room.
. . . .
Quickly. We're letting the heat escape.
I'm Lady Katsa of the Middluns—
My master is expecting you. This way.
Your master! He's here? How is that possible? Where is he?

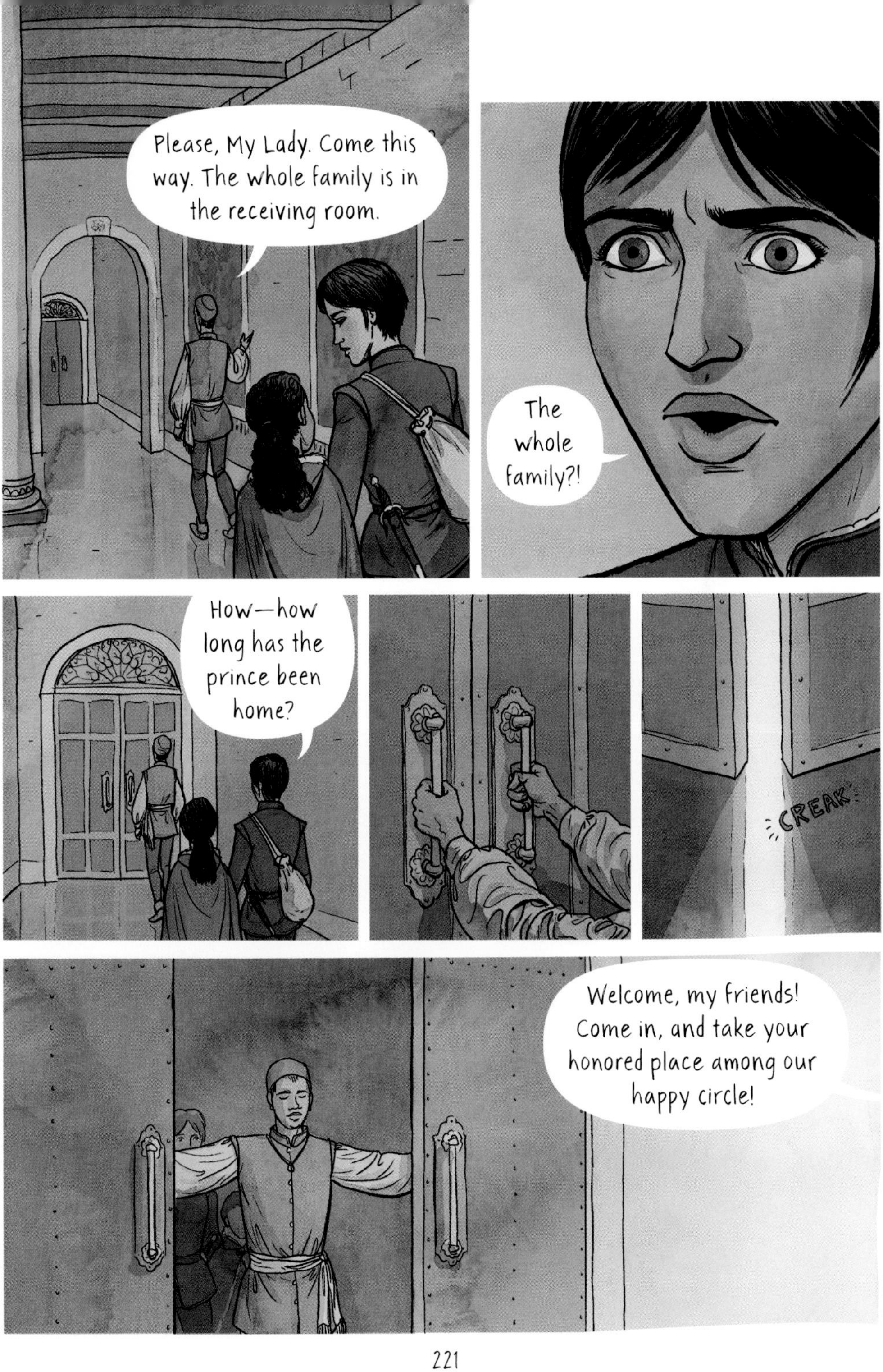

Please, My Lady. Come this way. The whole family is in the receiving room.
The whole family?!
How—how long has the prince been home?
CREAK
Welcome, my friends! Come in, and take your honored place among our happy circle!

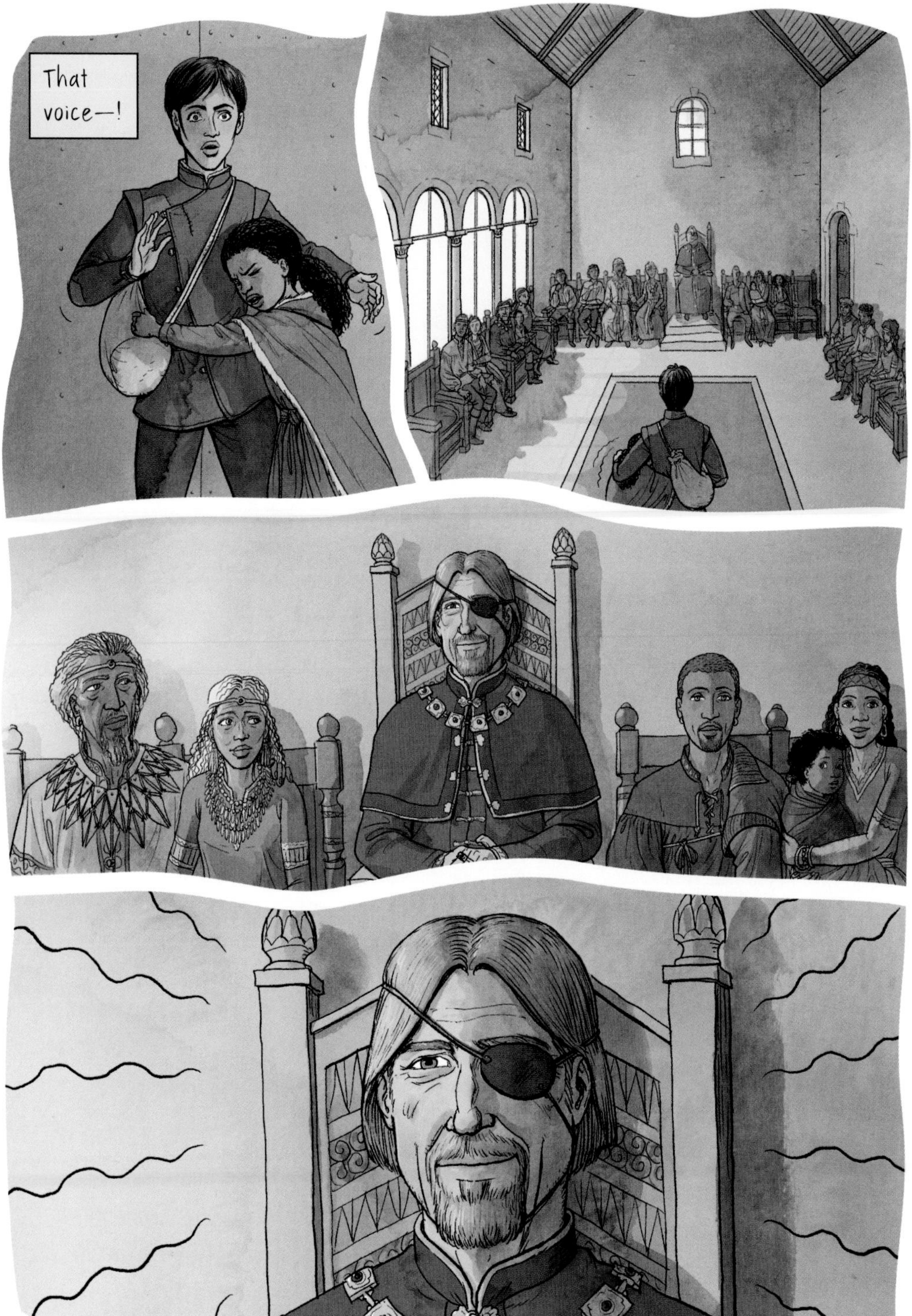
That voice—!

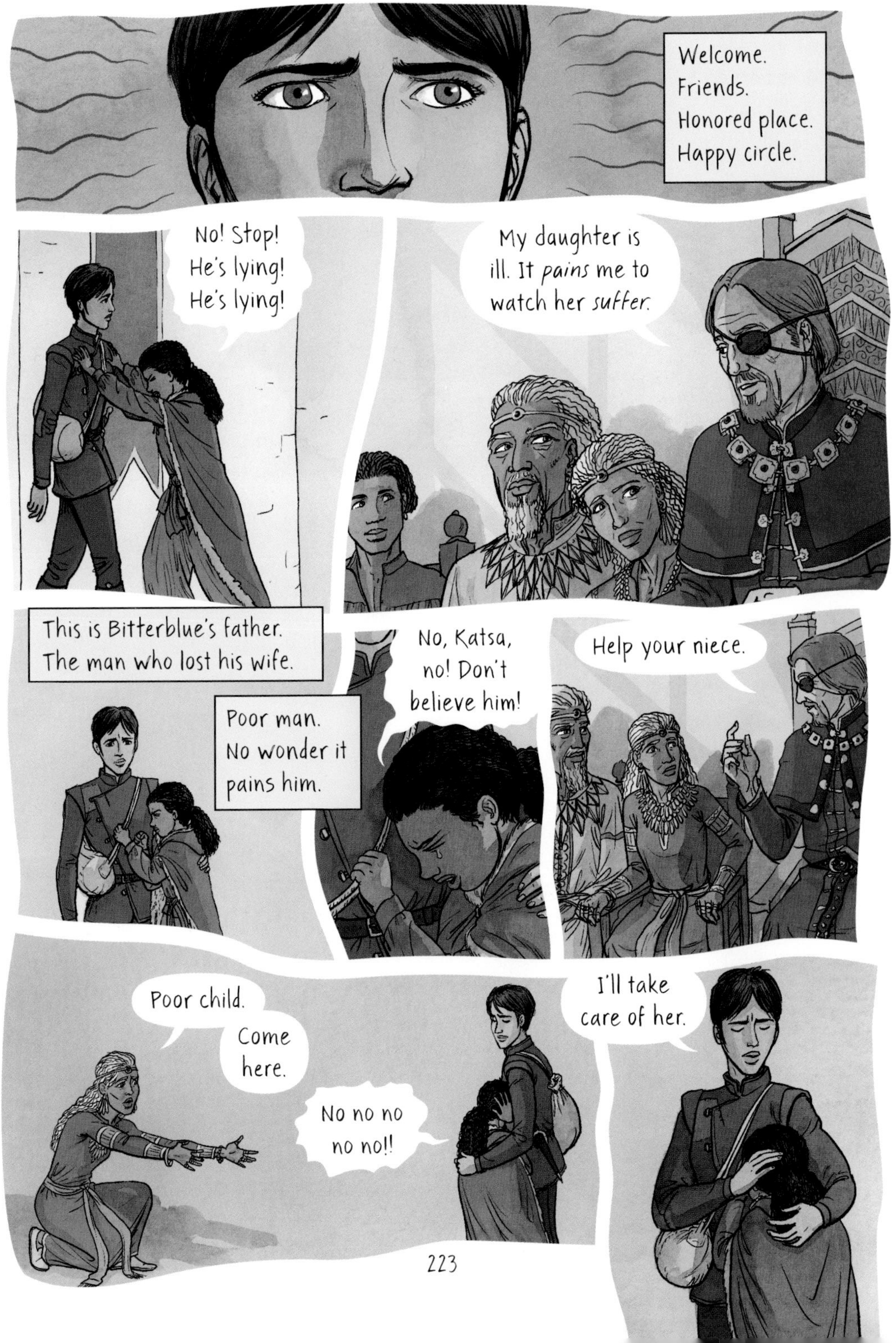

Welcome.
Friends.
Honored place.
Happy circle.
No! Stop! He's lying! He's lying!
My daughter is ill. It *pains* me to watch her *suffer.*
This is Bitterblue's father. The man who lost his wife.
Poor man. No wonder it pains him.
No, Katsa, no! Don't believe him!
Help your niece.
Poor child.
Come here.
No no no no no!!
I'll take care of her.

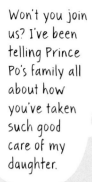

Won't you join us? I've been telling Prince Po's family all about how you've taken such good care of my daughter.

Po's family.

So this is Po's mother. Queen Zinnober.

My poor, sick, confused daughter.

I've been so worried about her. But you found her, and you brought her home, to my castle here in Lienid. Thank you.

I thought this was Po's castle.

Or was it mine?

No, that's a ridiculous idea.

224

How did you get here, by the way? Did you cross the mountains?

Yes.

Ha! I thought so, when you disappeared so completely.

And when I learned you're not welcome in your own court, I decided to take a chance and sail directly here.

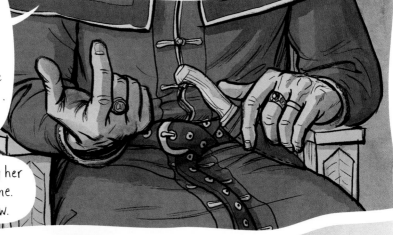

And now... I believe it's time for you to give my child back to me. We have a lot of... catching up to do.

Bring her to me. Now.

Yes, I...

No, no, don't, no, Katsa, no, no...!

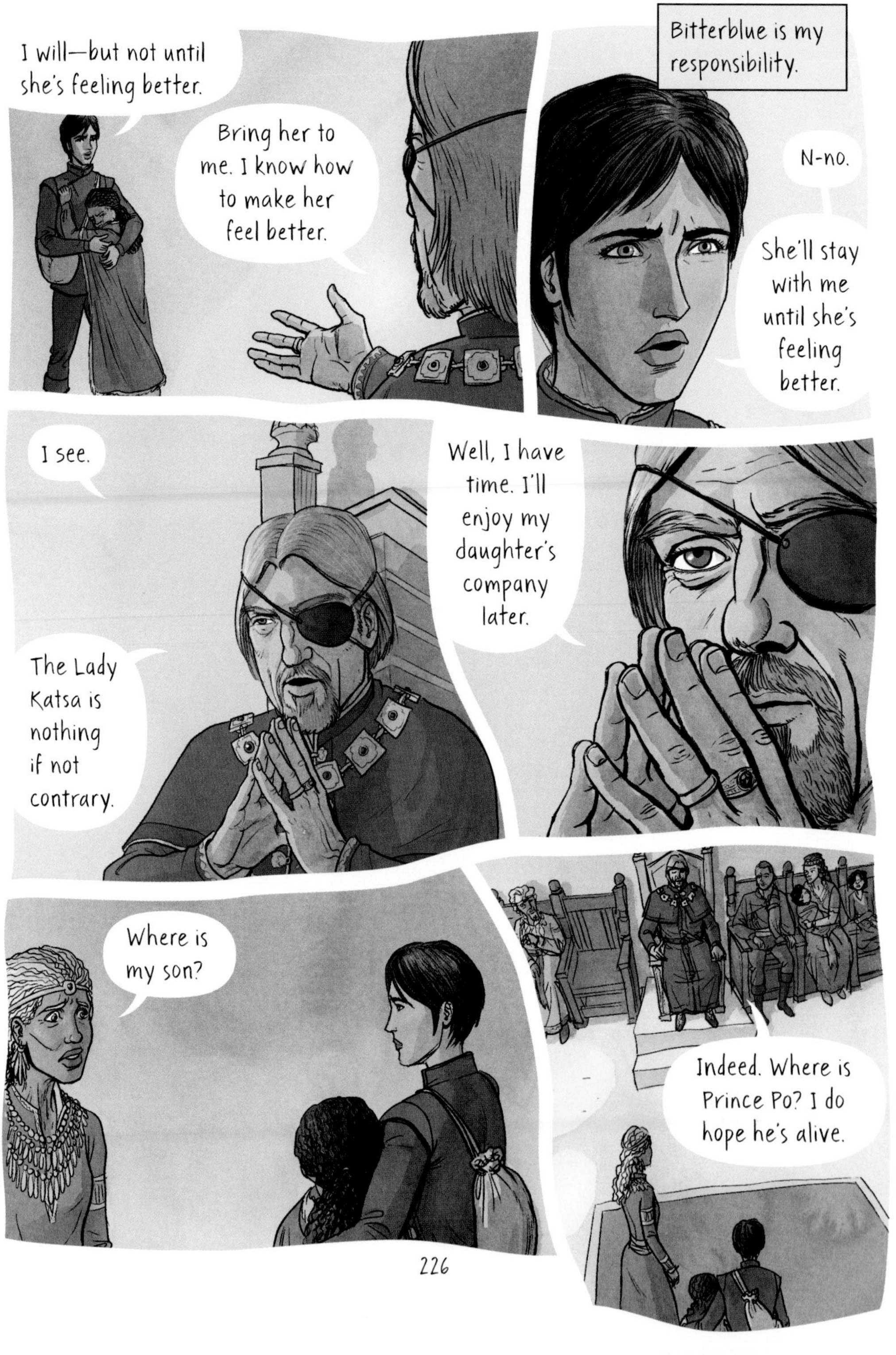

I will—but not until she's feeling better.
Bring her to me. I know how to make her feel better.
Bitterblue is my responsibility.
N-no.
She'll stay with me until she's feeling better.
I see.
The Lady Katsa is nothing if not contrary.
Well, I have time. I'll enjoy my daughter's company later.
Where is my son?
Indeed. Where is Prince Po? I do hope he's alive.

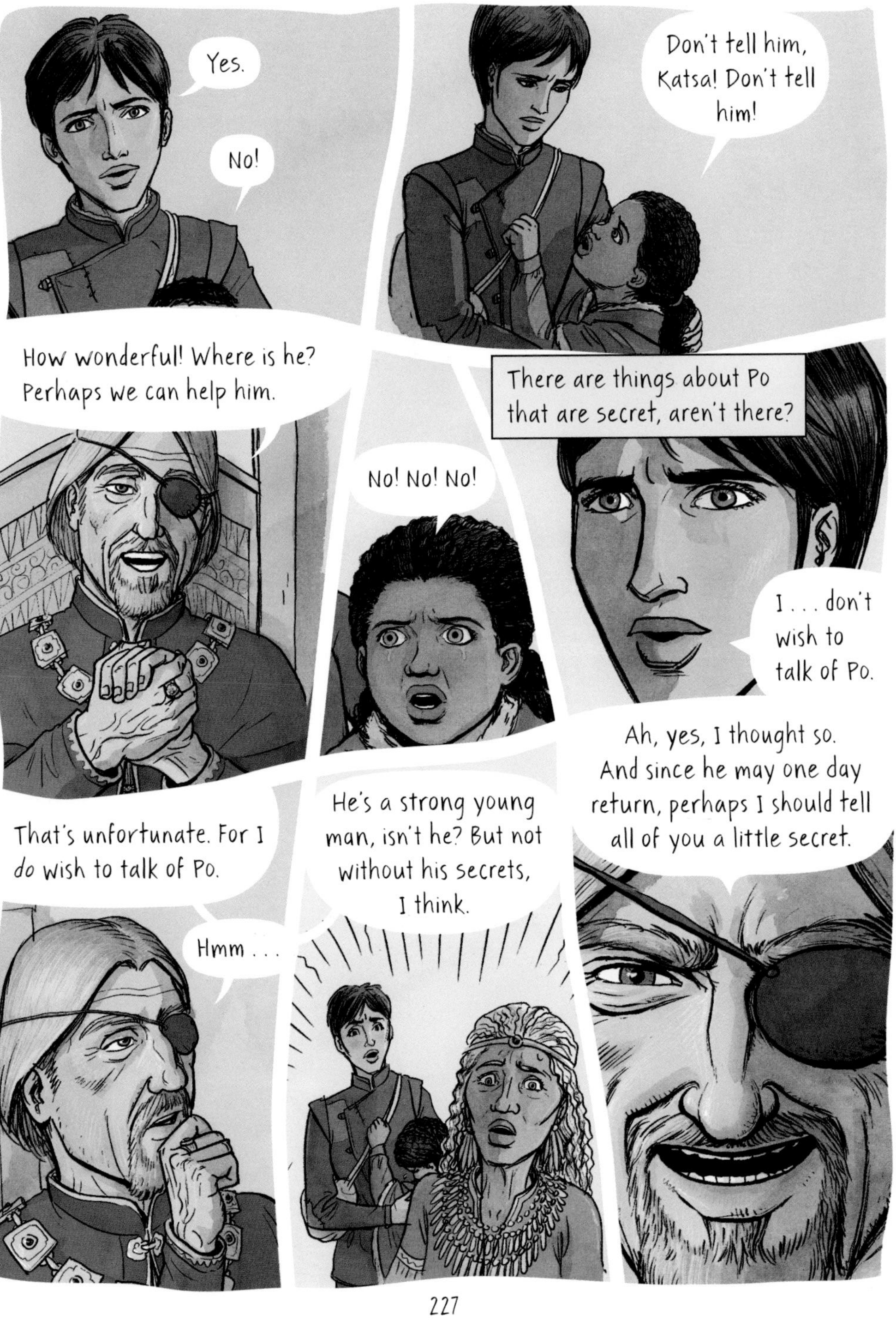
Yes.
No!
Don't tell him, Katsa! Don't tell him!
How wonderful! Where is he? Perhaps we can help him.
There are things about Po that are secret, aren't there?
No! No! No!
I . . . don't wish to talk of Po.
That's unfortunate. For I do wish to talk of Po.
Hmm . . .
He's a strong young man, isn't he? But not without his secrets, I think.
Ah, yes, I thought so. And since he may one day return, perhaps I should tell all of you a little secret.

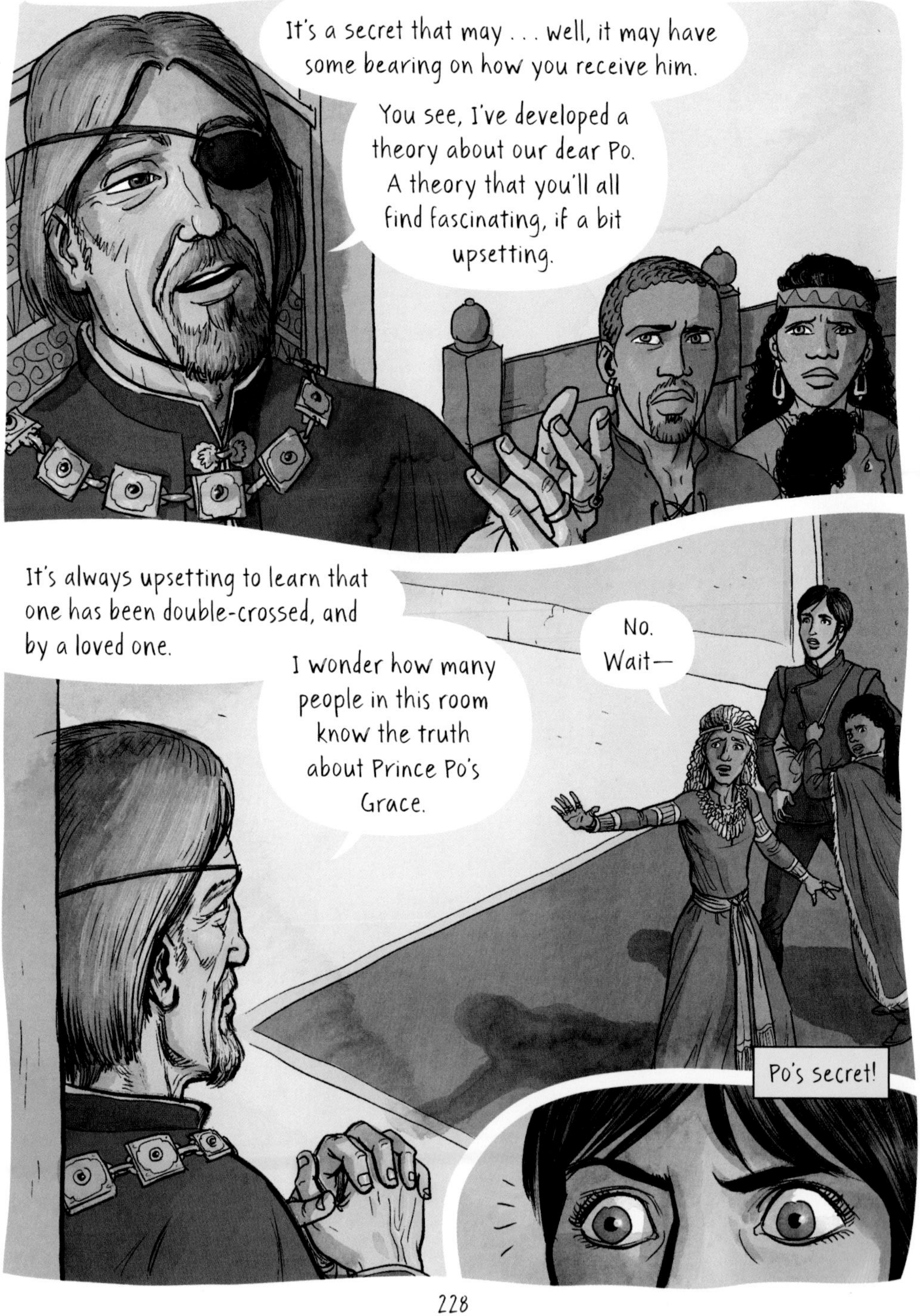
It's a secret that may . . . well, it may have some bearing on how you receive him.
You see, I've developed a theory about our dear Po. A theory that you'll all find fascinating, if a bit upsetting.
It's always upsetting to learn that one has been double-crossed, and by a loved one.
I wonder how many people in this room know the truth about Prince Po's Grace.
No. Wait—
Po's secret!

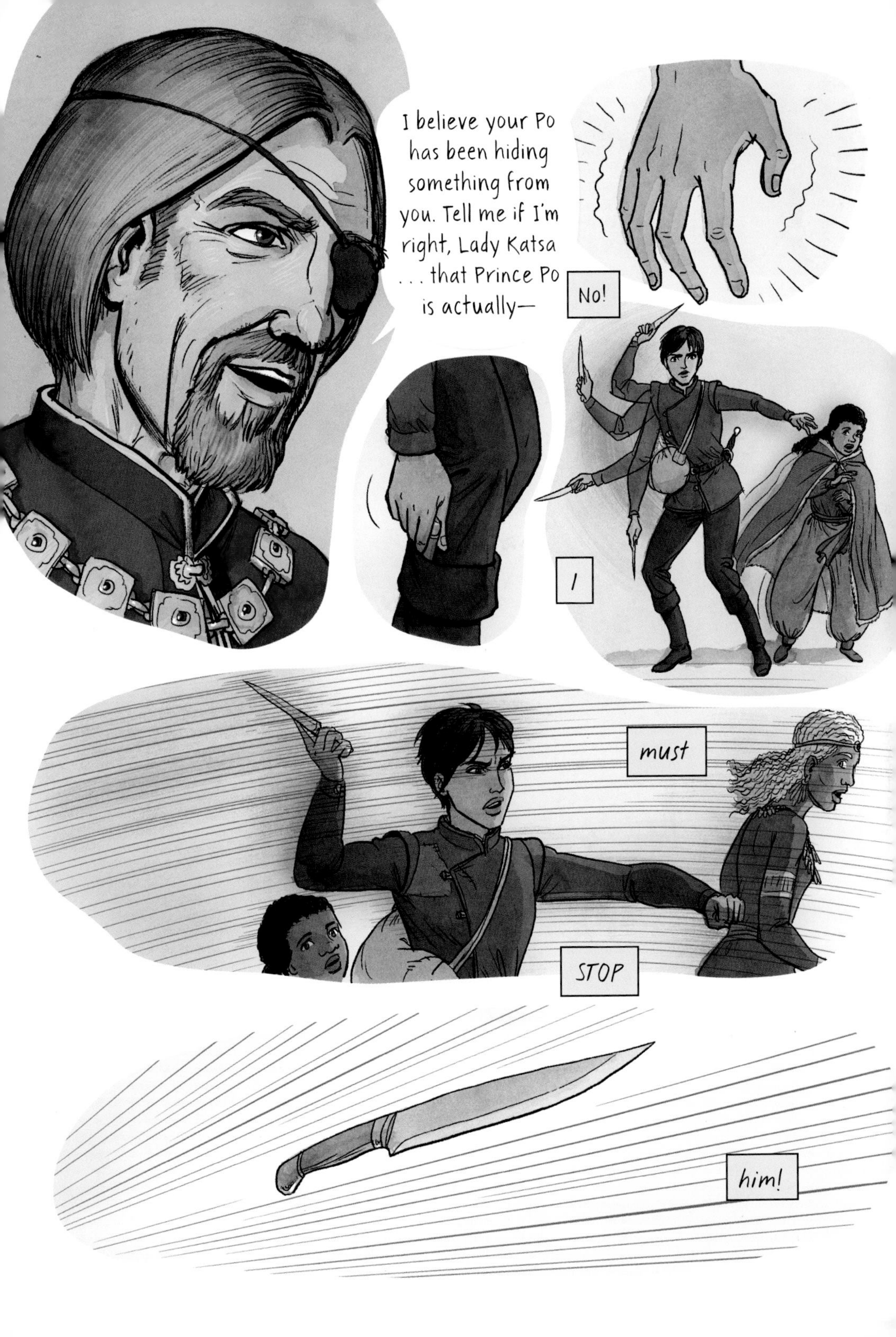
I believe your Po has been hiding something from you. Tell me if I'm right, Lady Katsa . . . that Prince Po is actually—
No!
I
must
STOP
him!

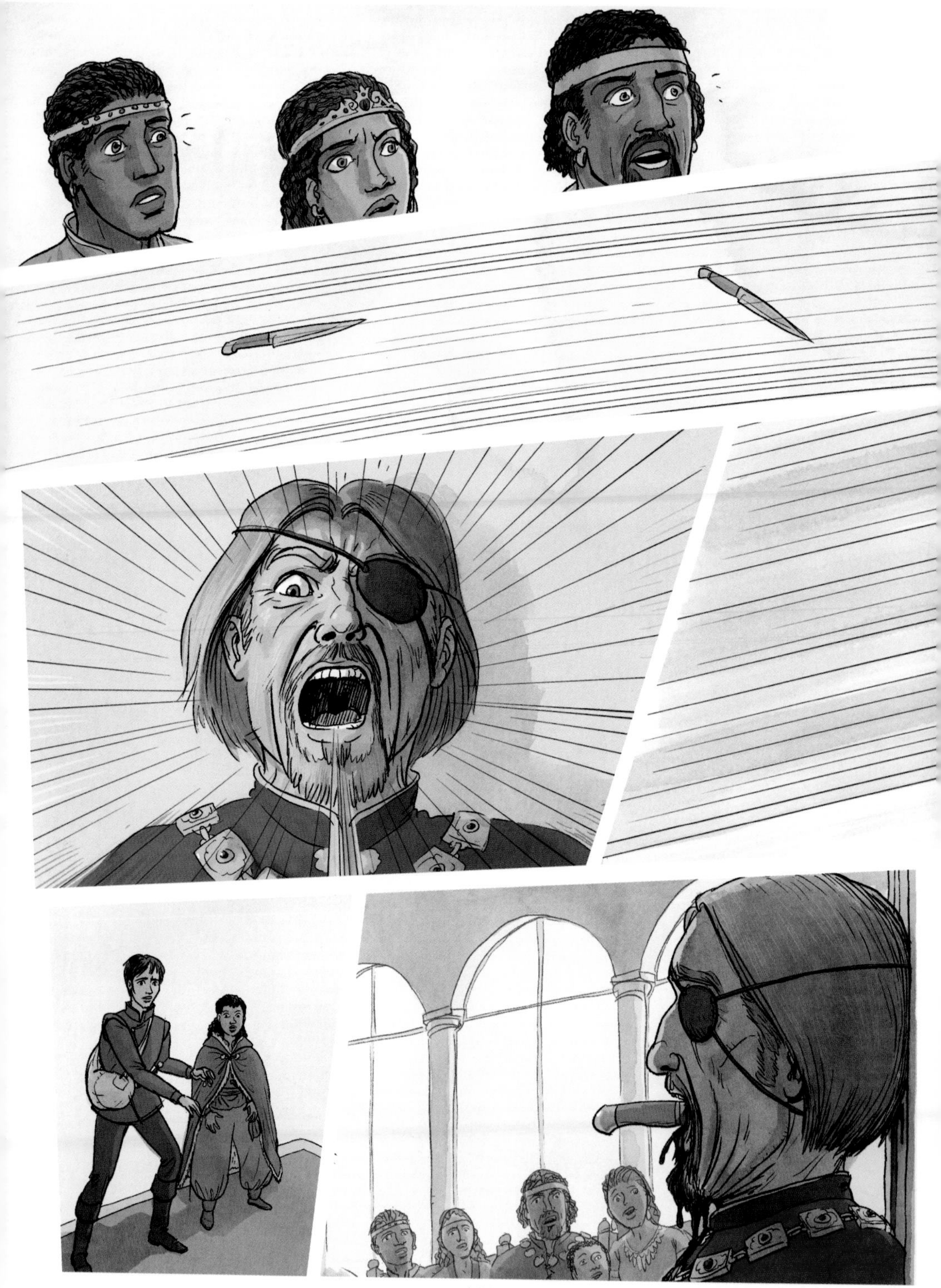

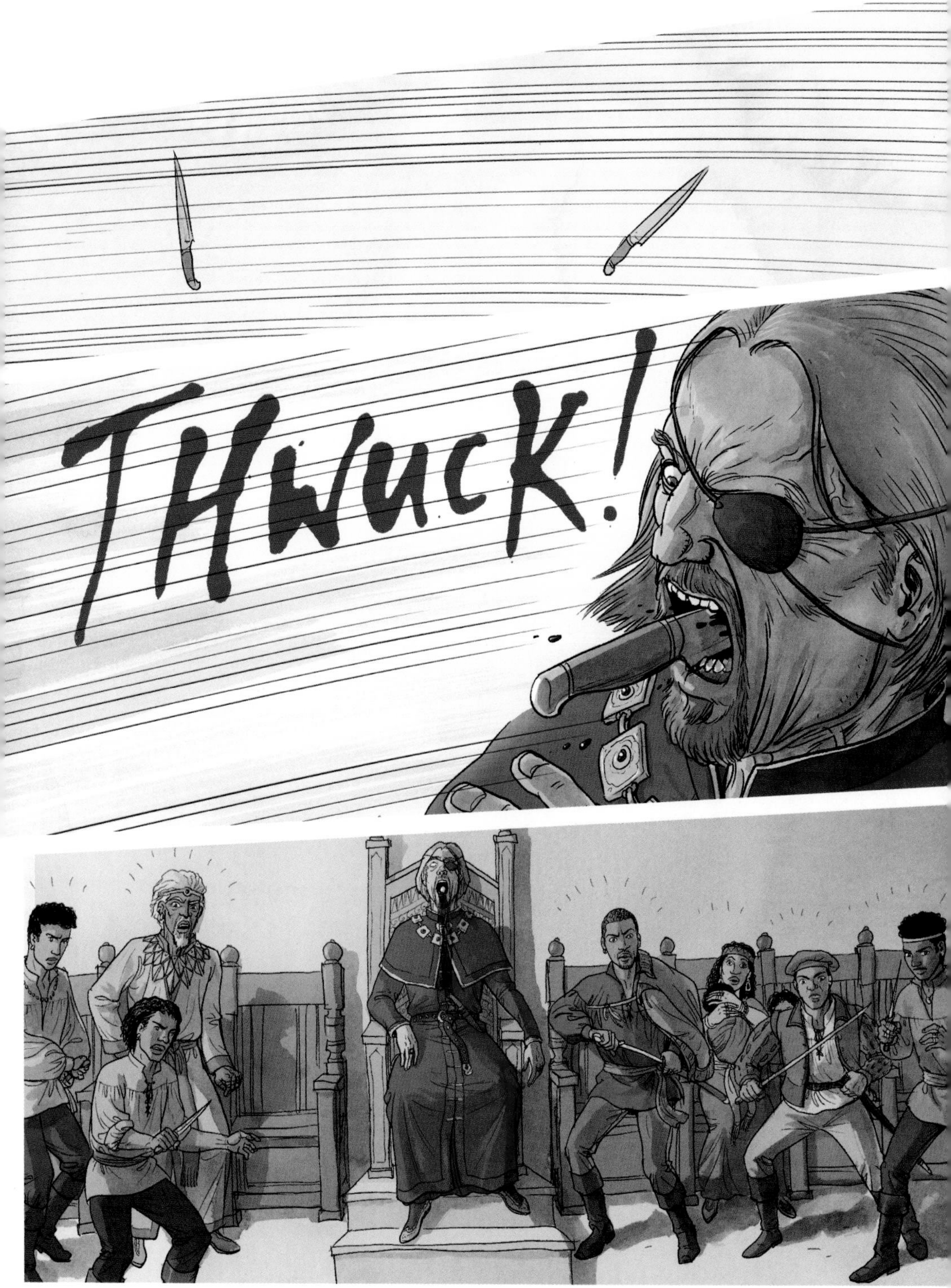
THWUCK!

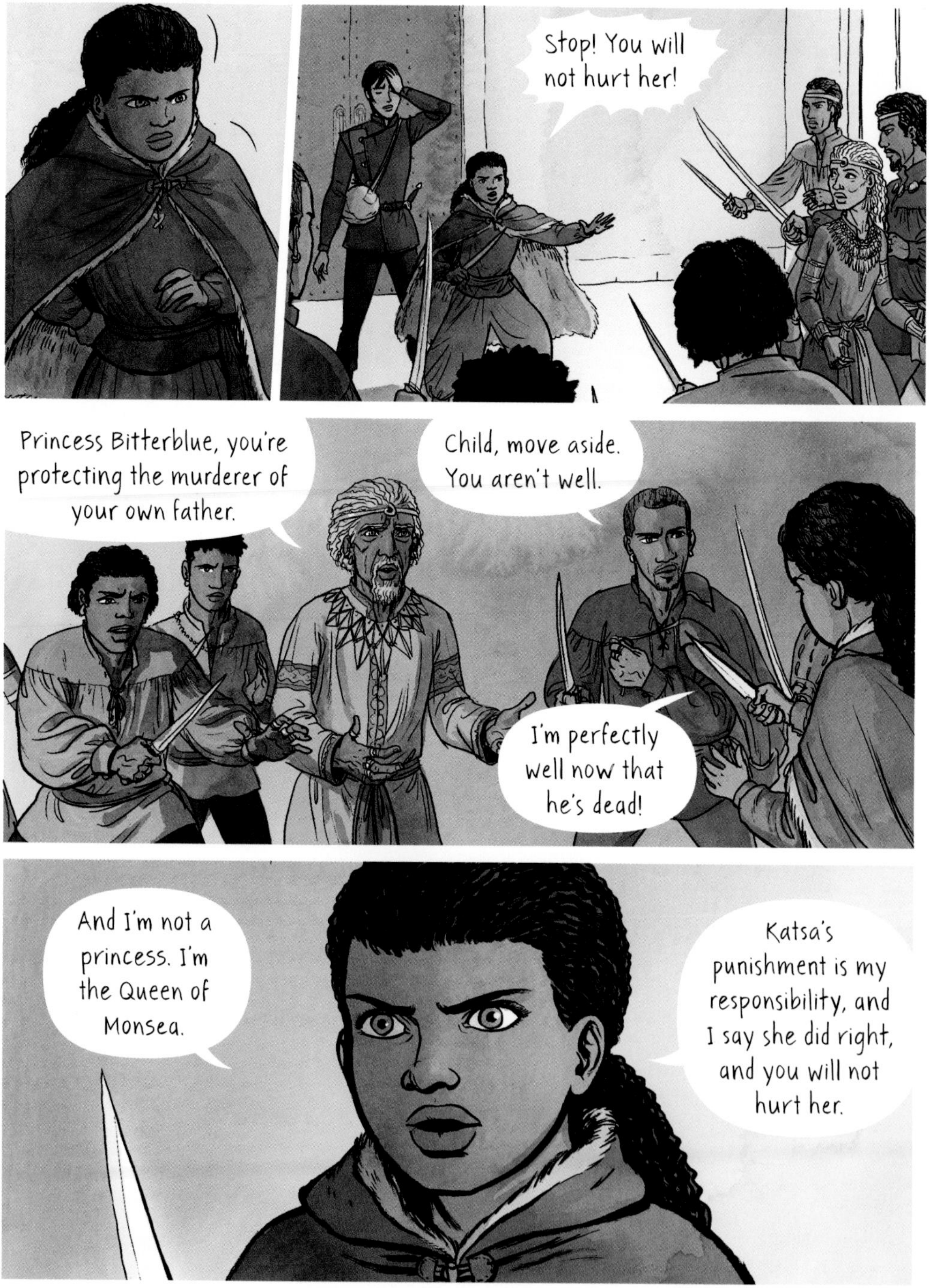
Stop! You will not hurt her!
Princess Bitterblue, you're protecting the murderer of your own father.
Child, move aside. You aren't well.
I'm perfectly well now that he's dead!
And I'm not a princess. I'm the Queen of Monsea.
Katsa's punishment is my responsibility, and I say she did right, and you will not hurt her.

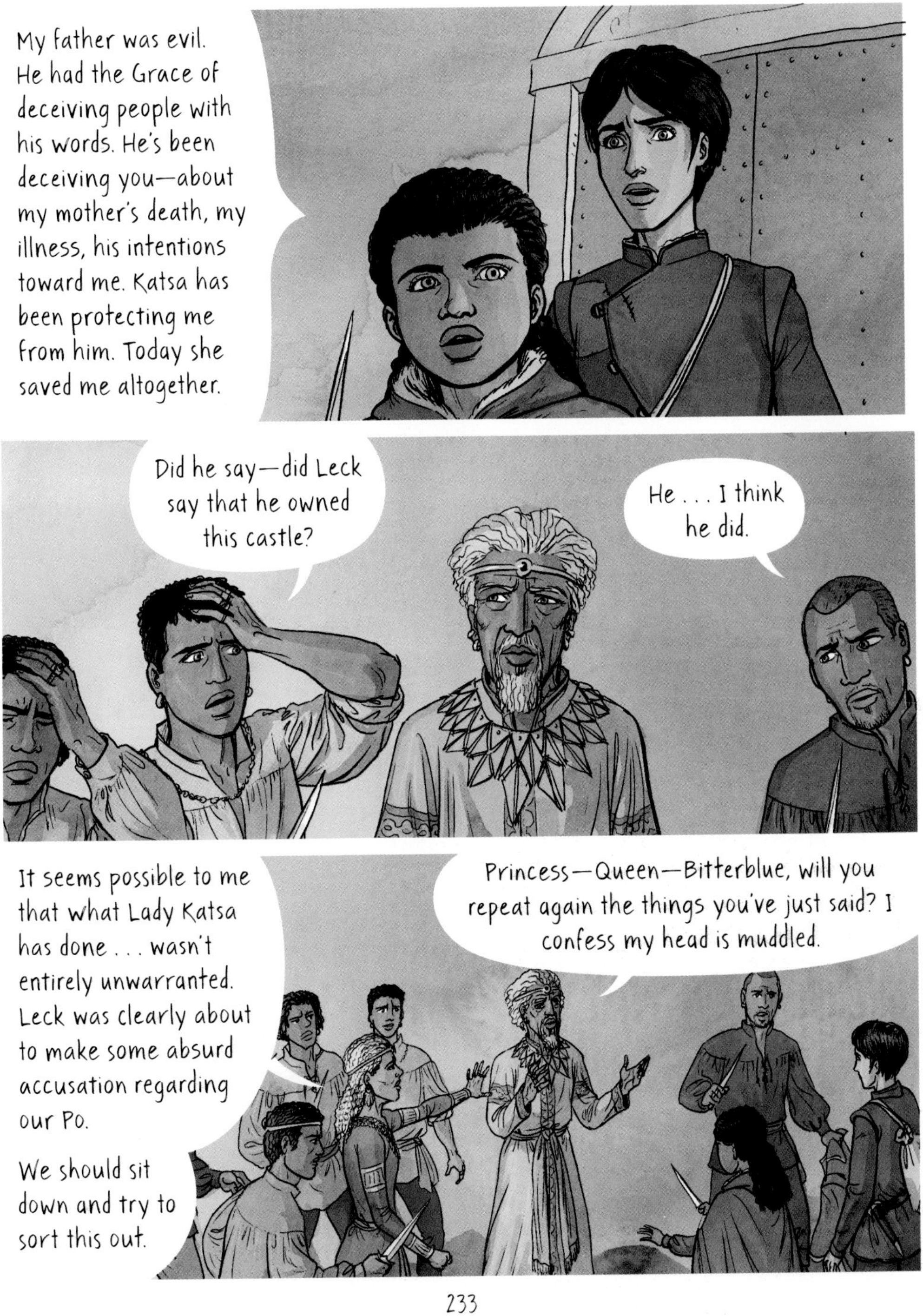
My father was evil. He had the Grace of deceiving people with his words. He's been deceiving you—about my mother's death, my illness, his intentions toward me. Katsa has been protecting me from him. Today she saved me altogether.
Did he say—did Leck say that he owned this castle?
He . . . I think he did.
It seems possible to me that what Lady Katsa has done . . . wasn't entirely unwarranted. Leck was clearly about to make some absurd accusation regarding our Po.
We should sit down and try to sort this out.
Princess—Queen—Bitterblue, will you repeat again the things you've just said? I confess my head is muddled.

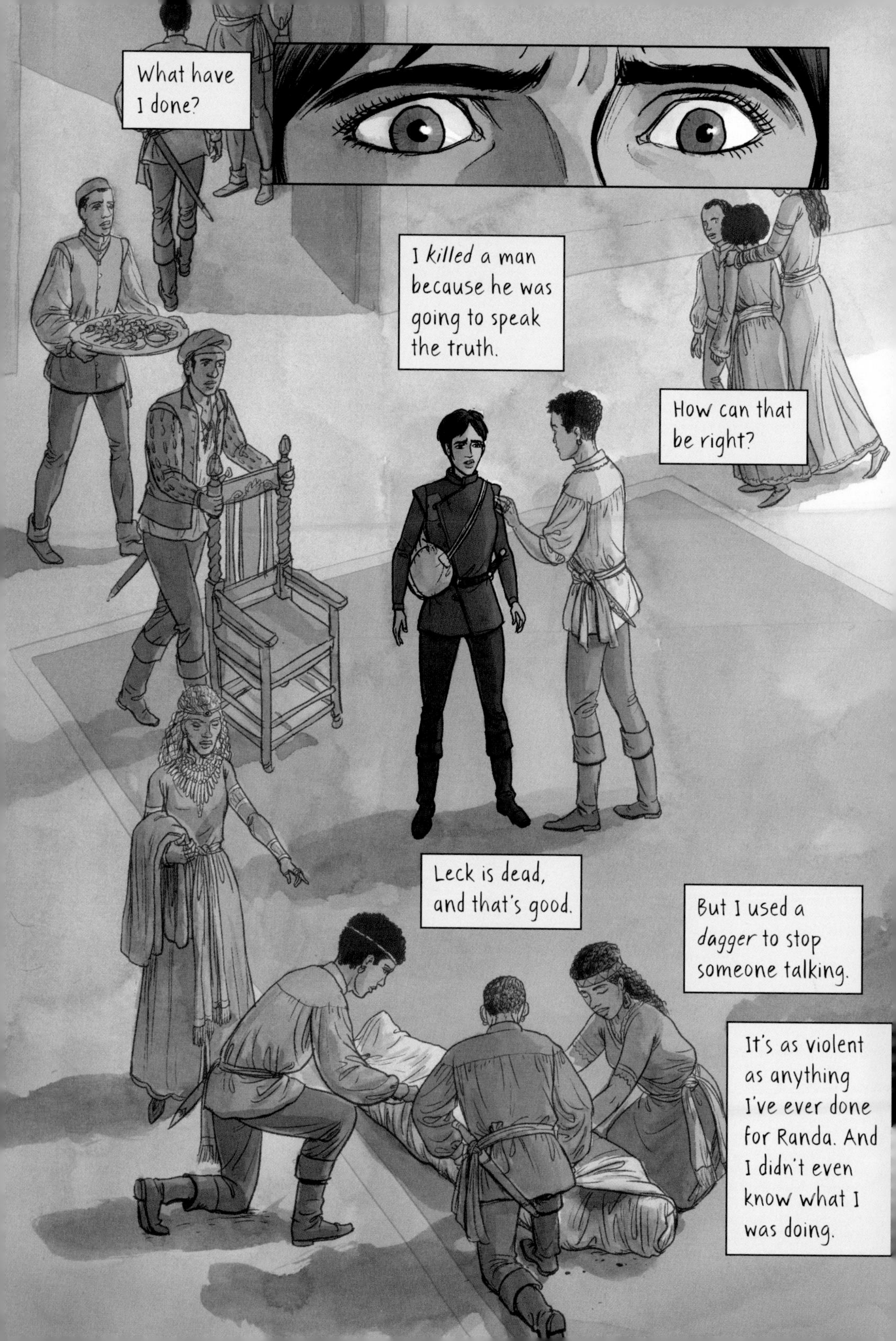
What have I done?
I *killed* a man because he was going to speak the truth.
How can that be right?
Leck is dead, and that's good.
But I used a *dagger* to stop someone talking.
It's as violent as anything I've ever done for Randa. And I didn't even know what I was doing.

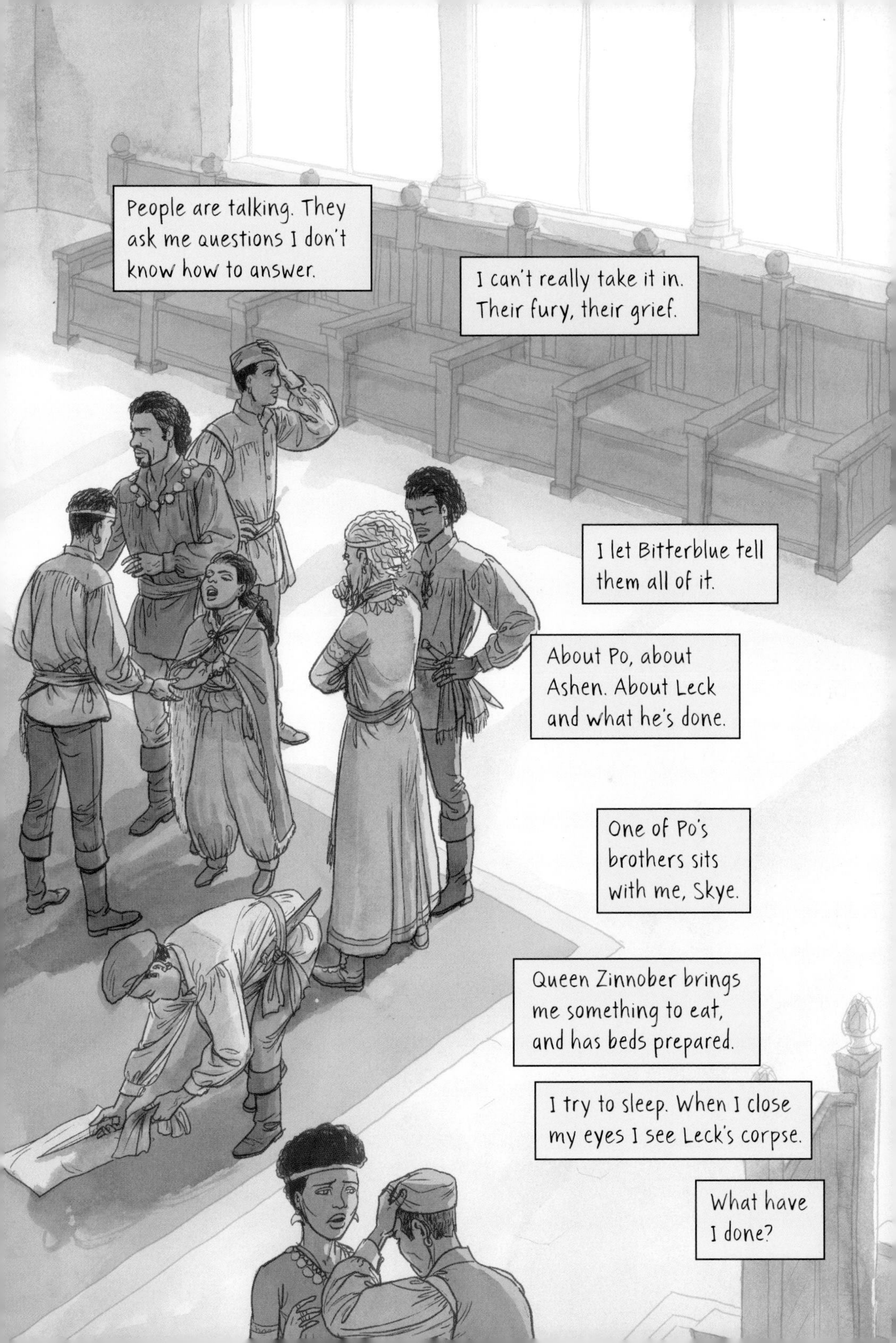
People are talking. They ask me questions I don't know how to answer.
I can't really take it in. Their fury, their grief.
I let Bitterblue tell them all of it.
About Po, about Ashen. About Leck and what he's done.
One of Po's brothers sits with me, Skye.
Queen Zinnober brings me something to eat, and has beds prepared.
I try to sleep. When I close my eyes I see Leck's corpse.
What have I done?

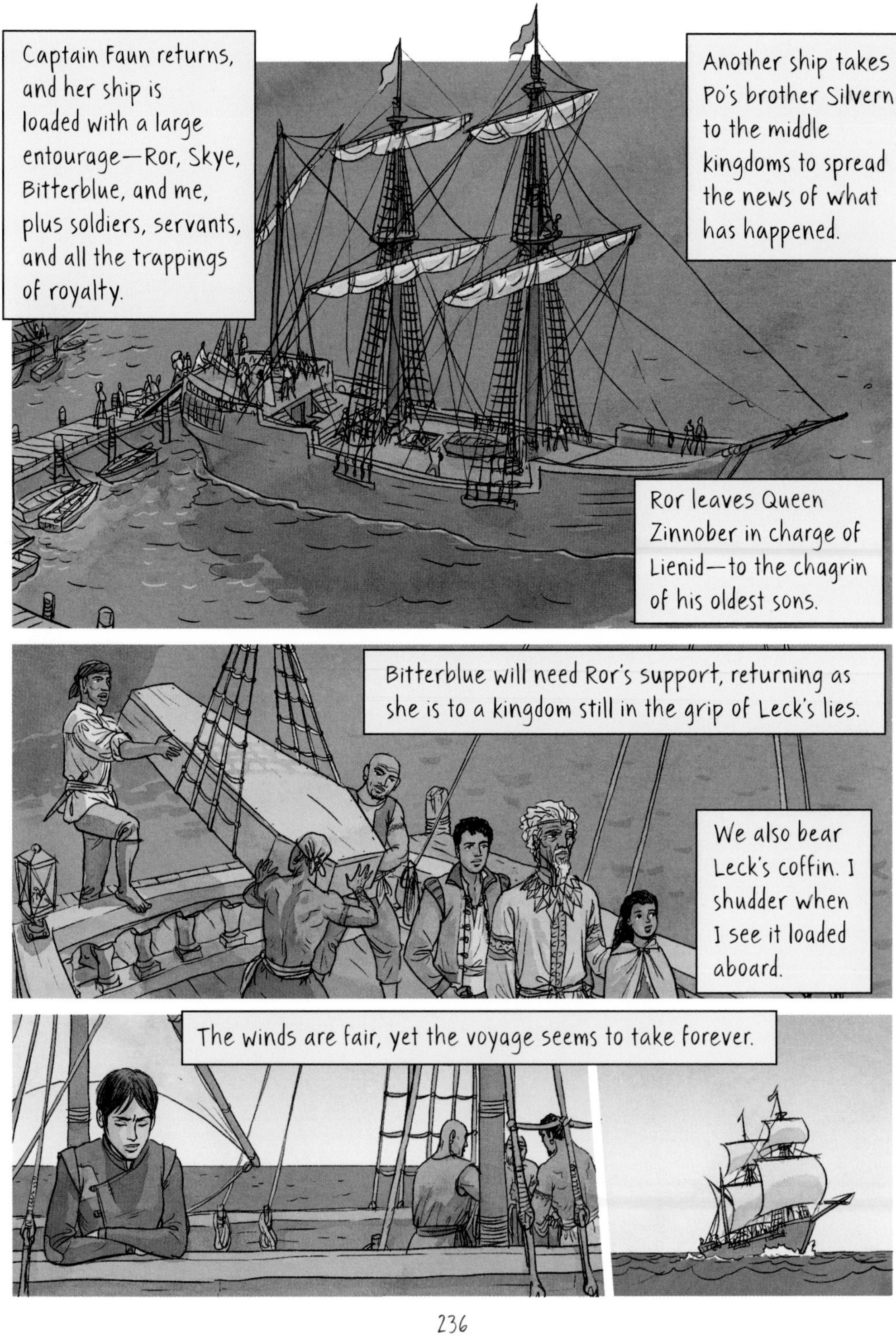
Captain Faun returns, and her ship is loaded with a large entourage—Ror, Skye, Bitterblue, and me, plus soldiers, servants, and all the trappings of royalty.
Another ship takes Po's brother Silvern to the middle kingdoms to spread the news of what has happened.
Ror leaves Queen Zinnober in charge of Lienid—to the chagrin of his oldest sons.
Bitterblue will need Ror's support, returning as she is to a kingdom still in the grip of Leck's lies.
We also bear Leck's coffin. I shudder when I see it loaded aboard.
The winds are fair, yet the voyage seems to take forever.

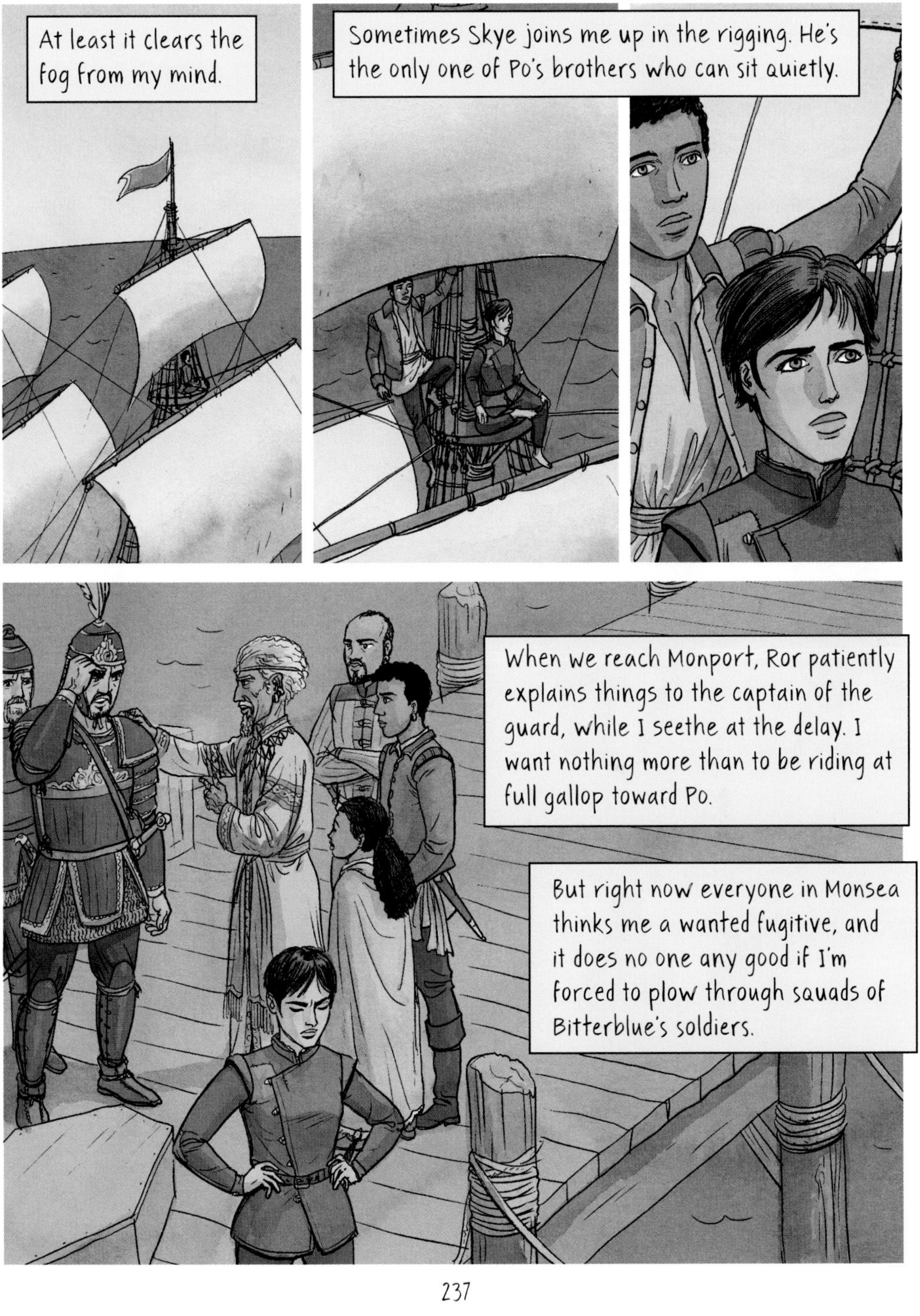
At least it clears the fog from my mind.
Sometimes Skye joins me up in the rigging. He's the only one of Po's brothers who can sit quietly.
When we reach Monport, Ror patiently explains things to the captain of the guard, while I seethe at the delay. I want nothing more than to be riding at full gallop toward Po.
But right now everyone in Monsea thinks me a wanted fugitive, and it does no one any good if I'm forced to plow through squads of Bitterblue's soldiers.

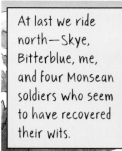

At last we ride north—Skye, Bitterblue, me, and four Monsean soldiers who seem to have recovered their wits.

Still I chafe at the slowness, but I hear Po's voice in my head, telling me not to lame the horses.

We're getting close.

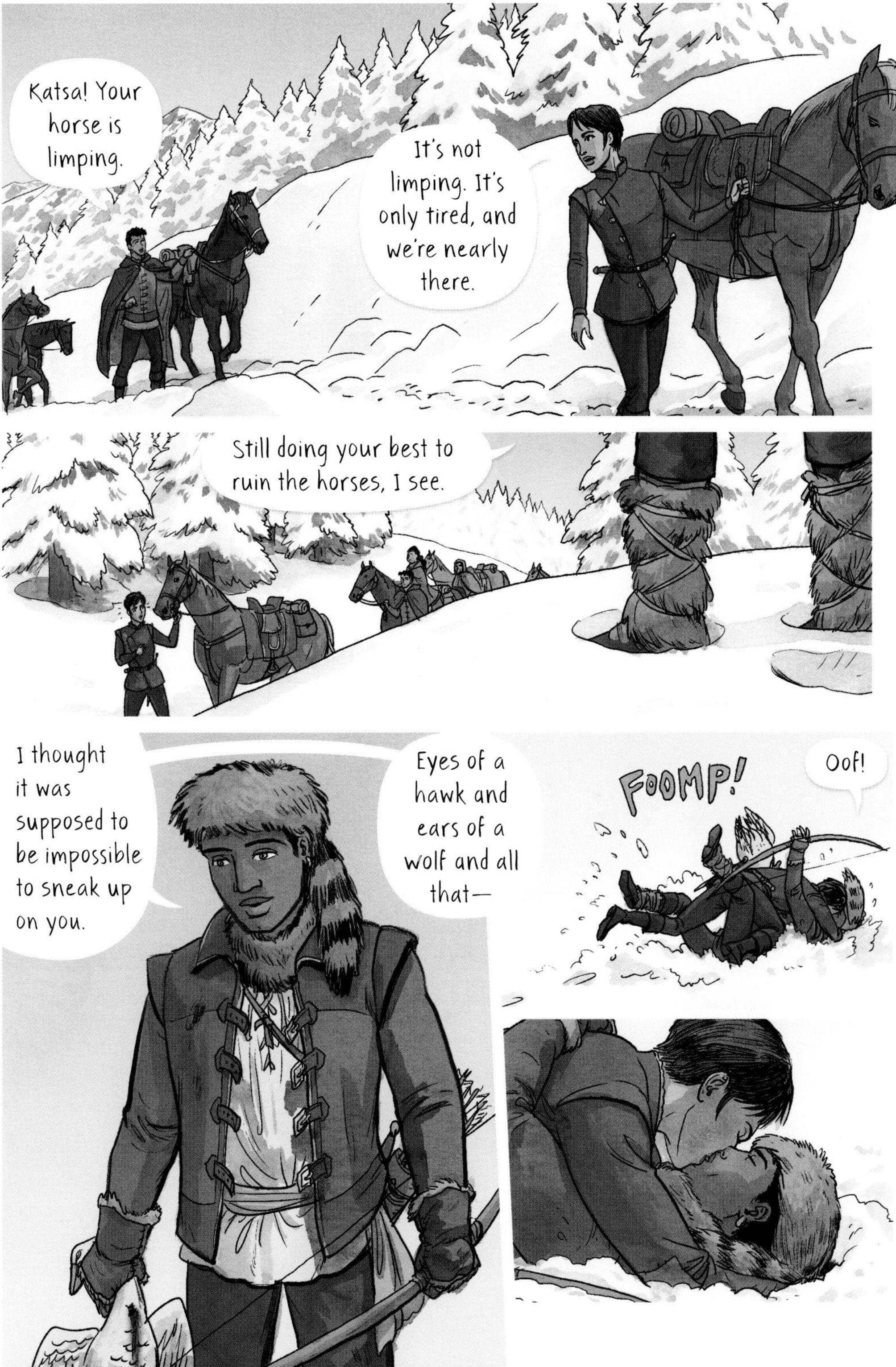
Katsa! Your horse is limping.
It's not limping. It's only tired, and we're nearly there.
Still doing your best to ruin the horses, I see.
I thought it was supposed to be impossible to sneak up on you.
Eyes of a hawk and ears of a wolf and all that—
FOOMP!
Oof!

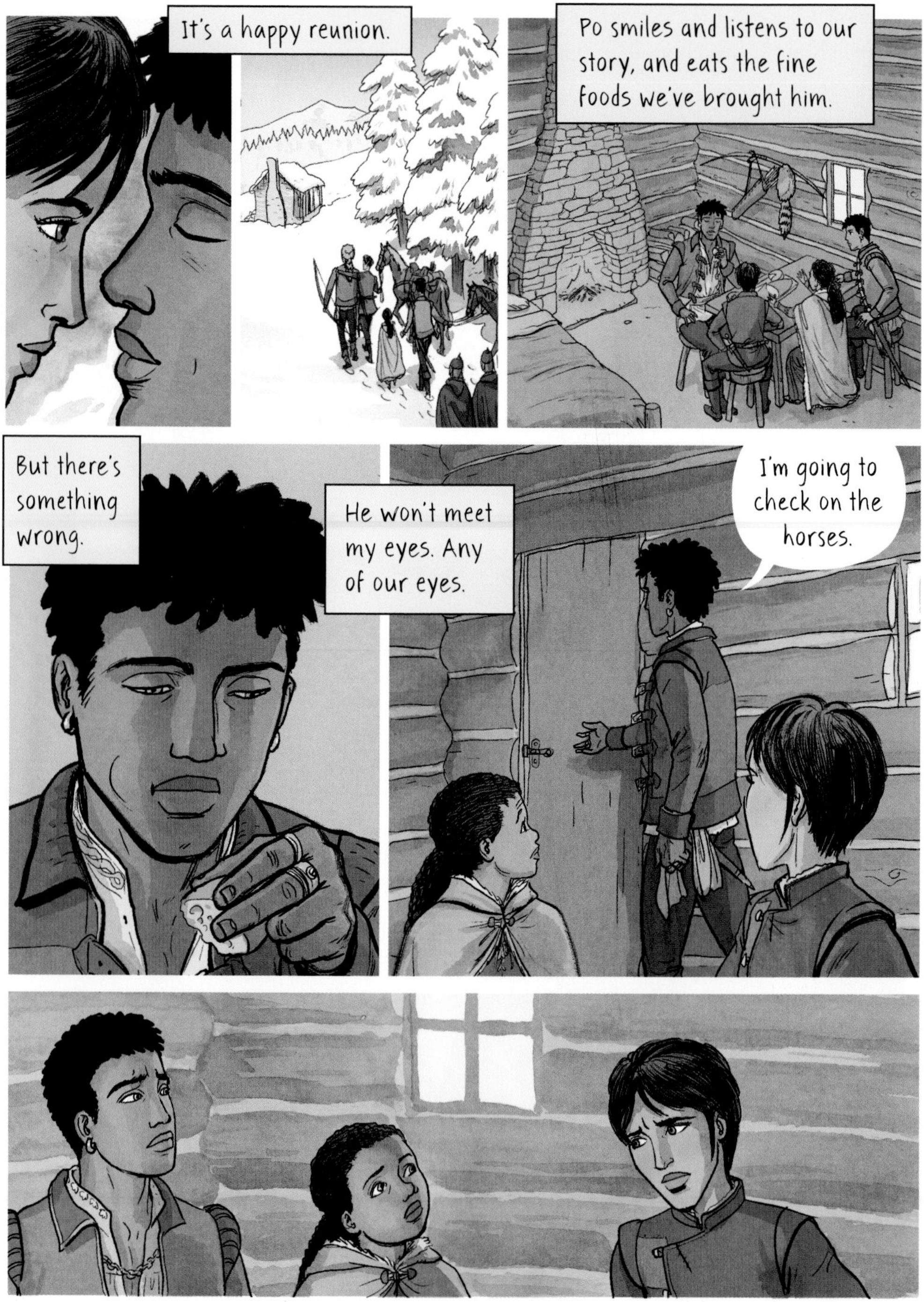
It's a happy reunion.
Po smiles and listens to our story, and eats the fine foods we've brought him.
But there's something wrong.
He won't meet my eyes. Any of our eyes.
I'm going to check on the horses.

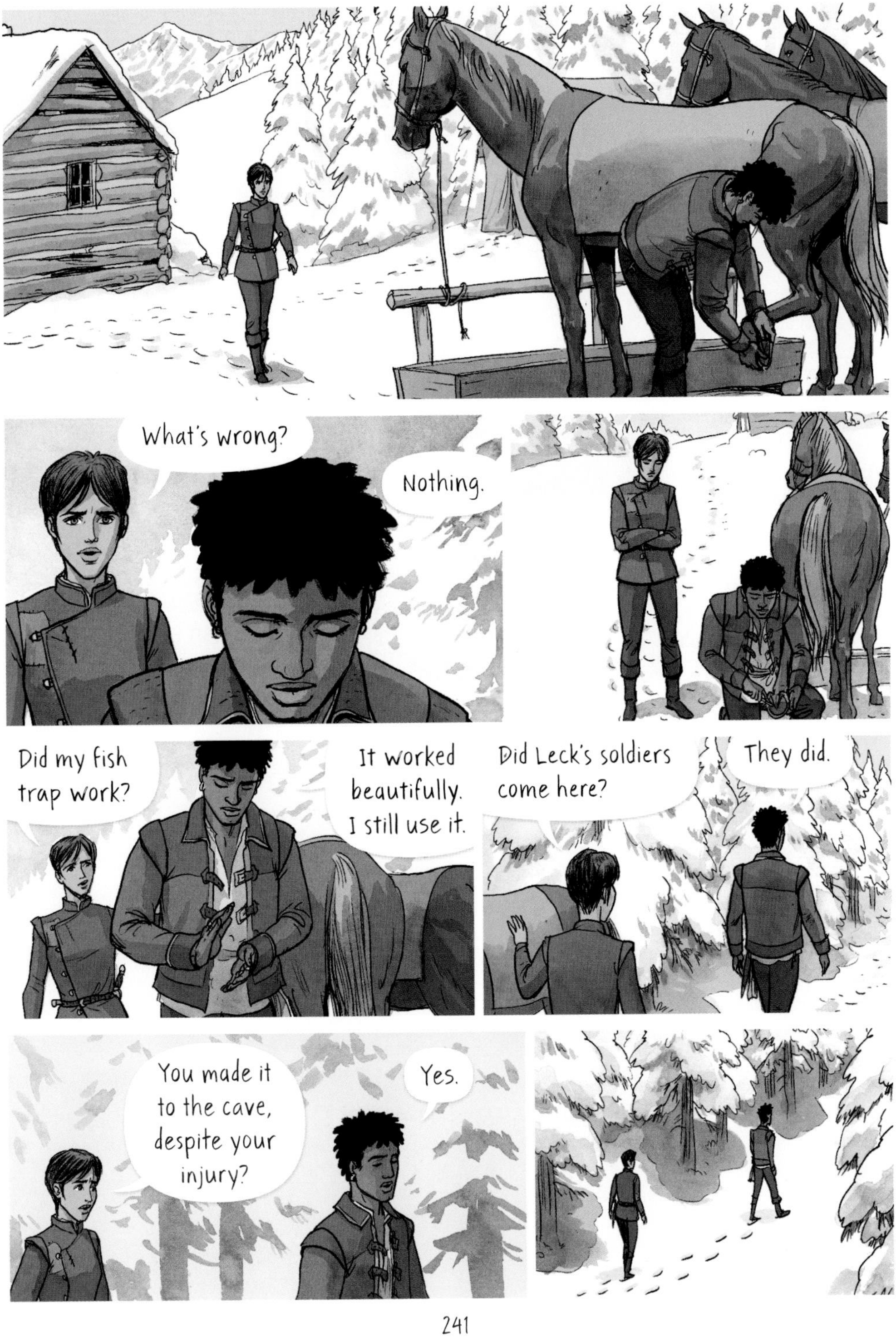
What's wrong?
Nothing.
Did my fish trap work?
It worked beautifully. I still use it.
Did Leck's soldiers come here?
They did.
You made it to the cave, despite your injury?
Yes.

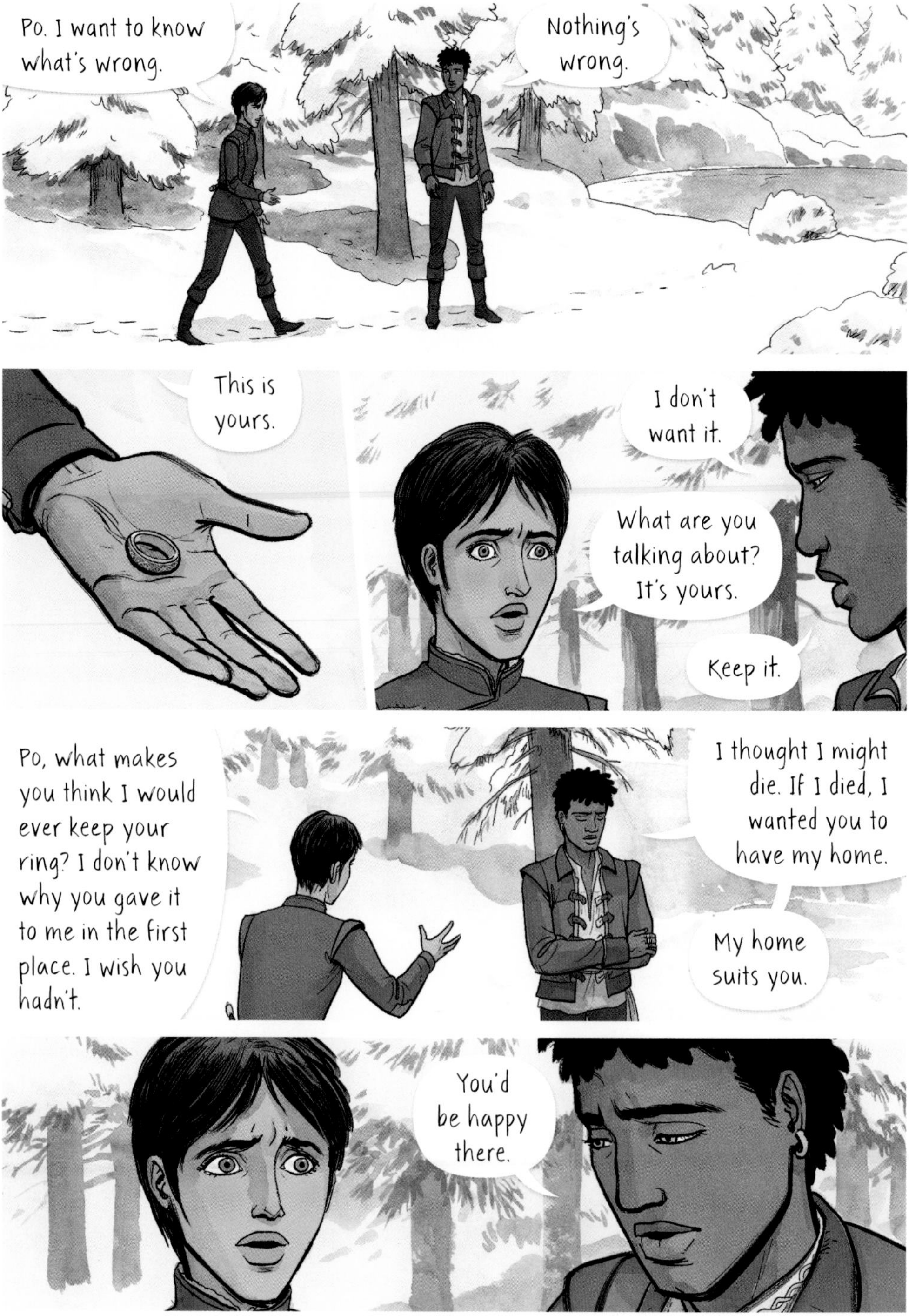
Po. I want to know what's wrong.
Nothing's wrong.
This is yours.
I don't want it.
What are you talking about? It's yours.
Keep it.
Po, what makes you think I would ever keep your ring? I don't know why you gave it to me in the first place. I wish you hadn't.
I thought I might die. If I died, I wanted you to have my home.
My home suits you.
You'd be happy there.

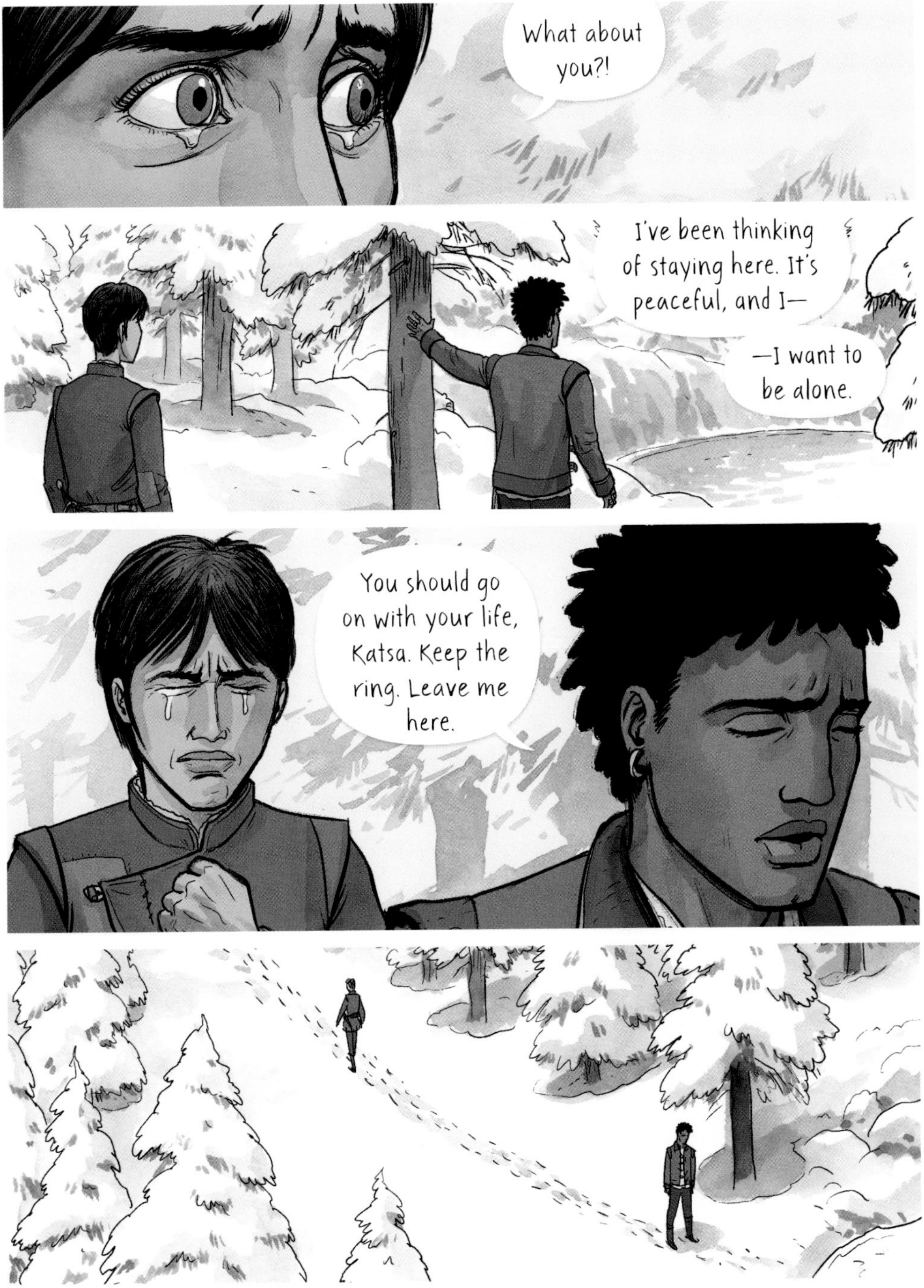
What about you?!
I've been thinking of staying here. It's peaceful, and I—
—I want to be alone.
You should go on with your life, Katsa. Keep the ring. Leave me here.

What's wrong with him?

I don't know. He won't tell me.

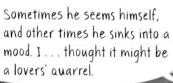

Sometimes he seems himself, and other times he sinks into a mood. I . . . thought it might be a lovers' quarrel.

If only it were that simple.

There's something strange about his eyes.

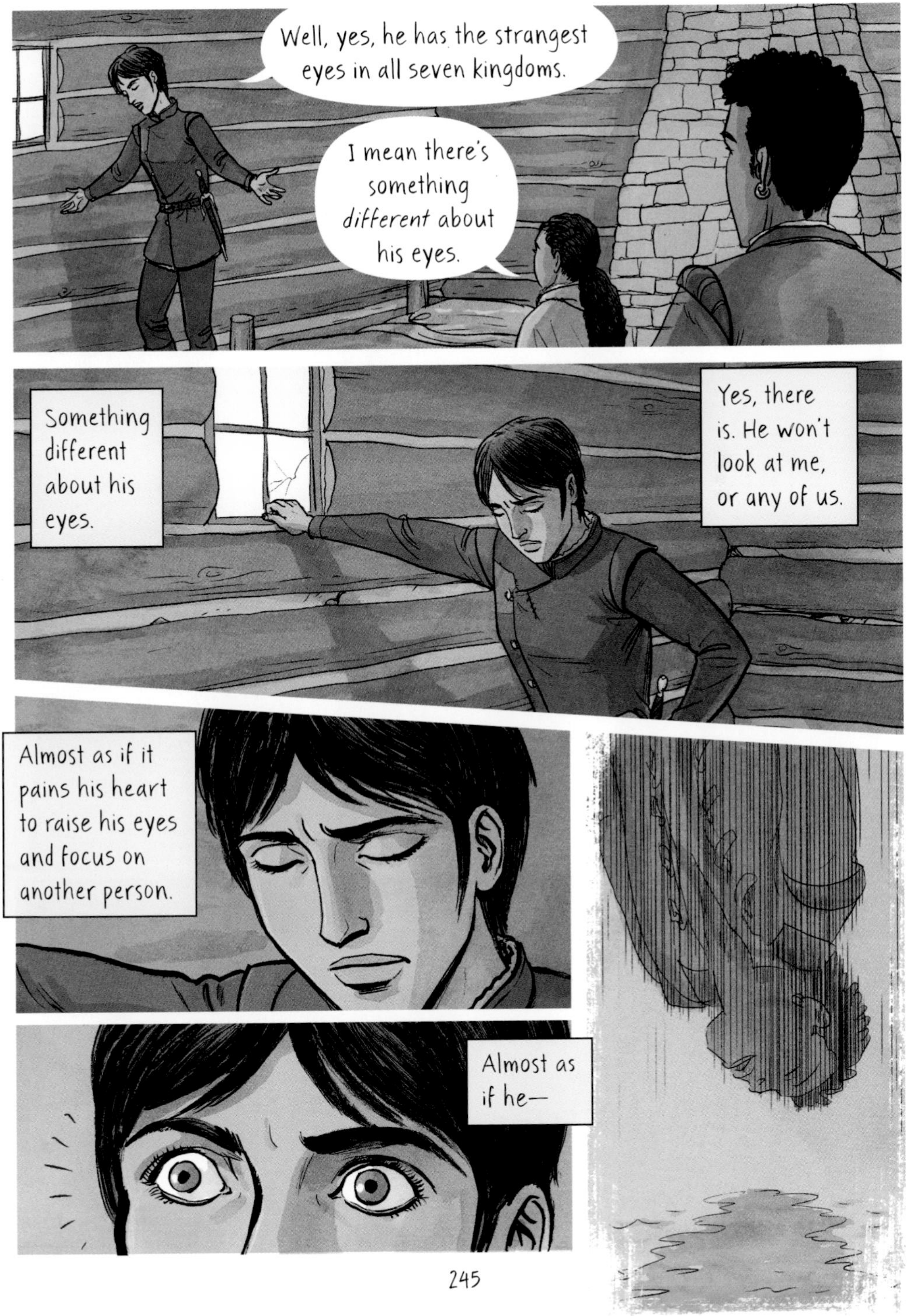
Well, yes, he has the strangest eyes in all seven kingdoms.
I mean there's something *different* about his eyes.
Something different about his eyes.
Yes, there is. He won't look at me, or any of us.
Almost as if it pains his heart to raise his eyes and focus on another person.
Almost as if he—

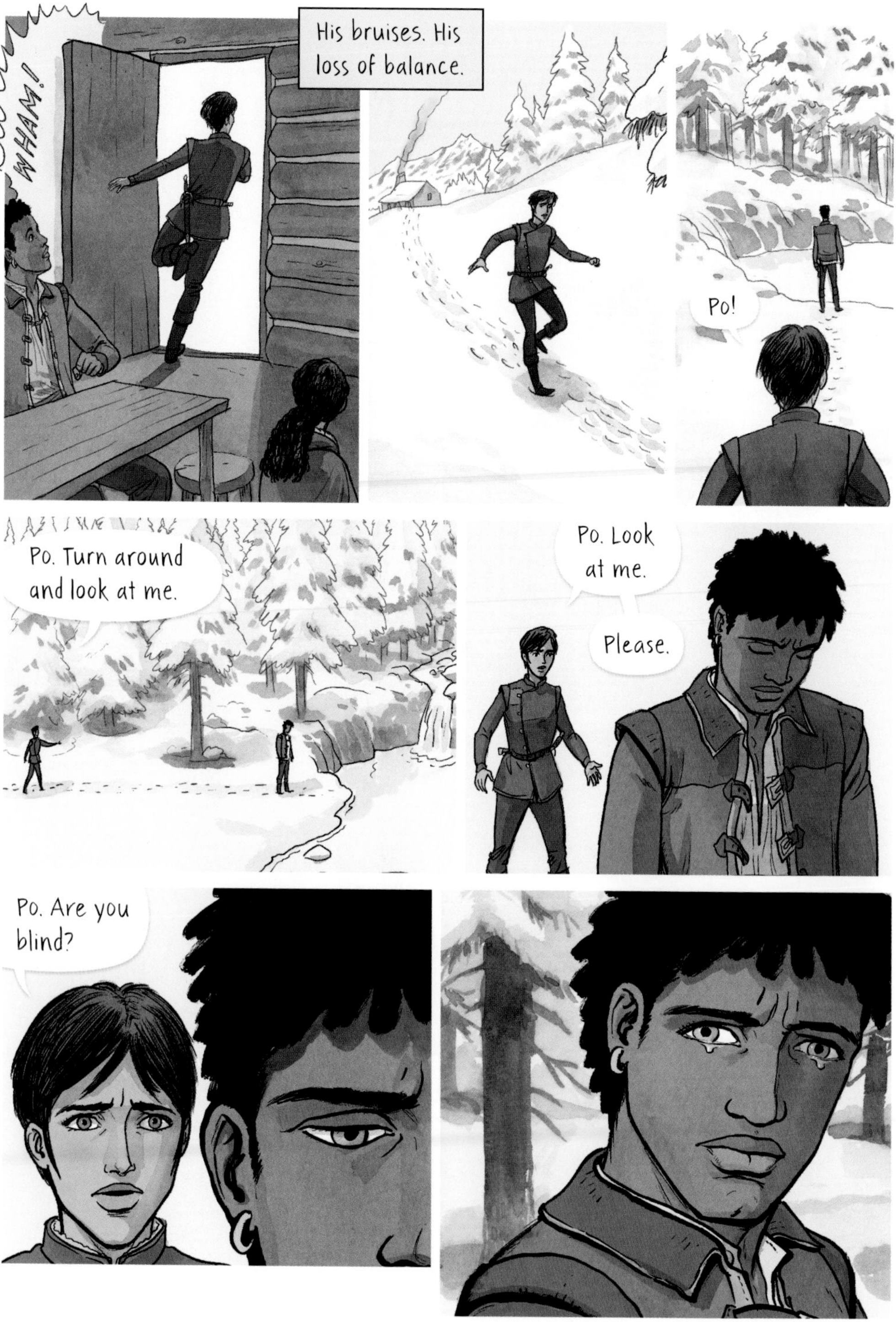
WHAM!
His bruises. His loss of balance.
Po!
Po. Turn around and look at me.
Po. Look at me.
Please.
Po. Are you blind?

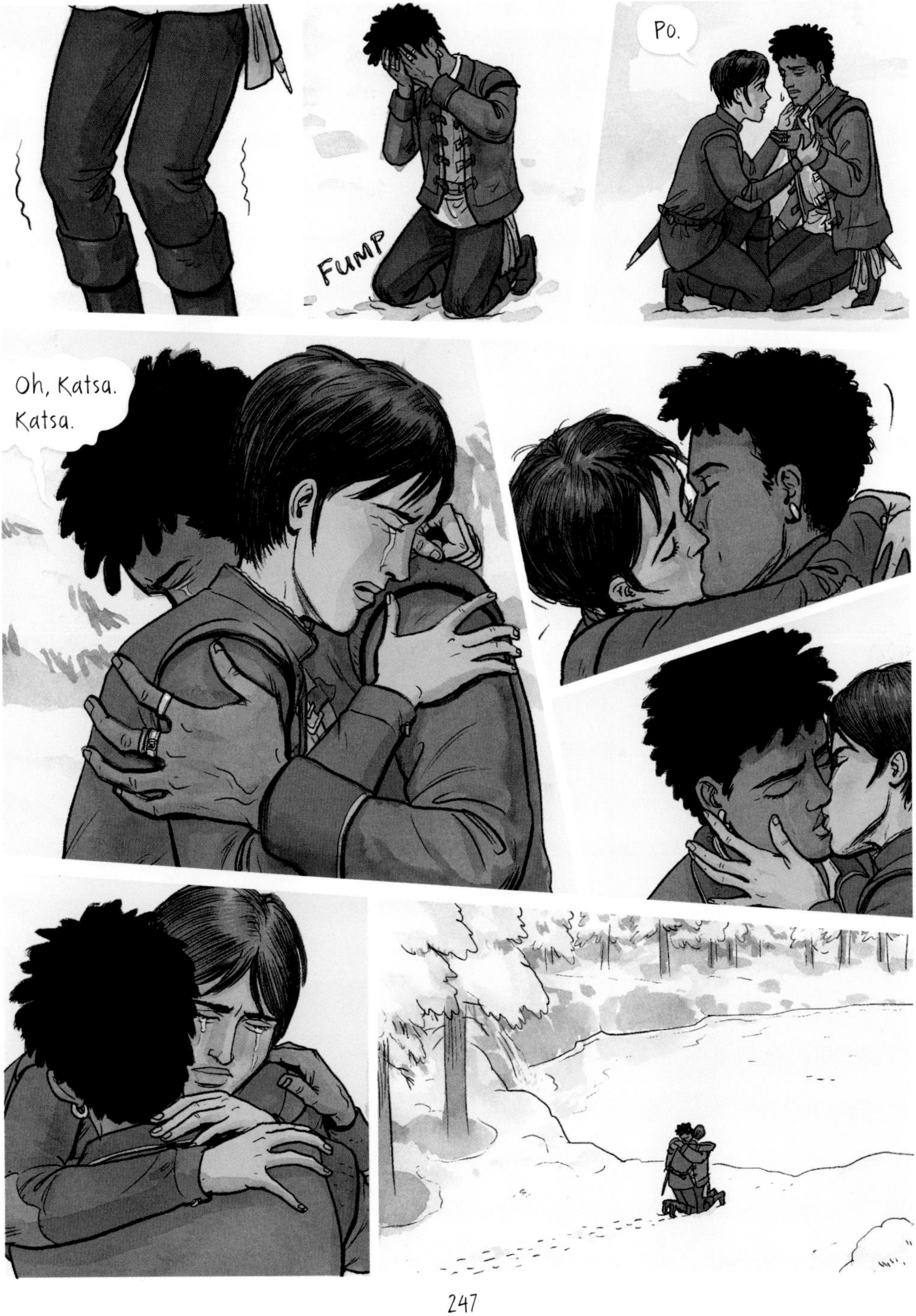
FUMP
Po.
Oh, Katsa.
Katsa.

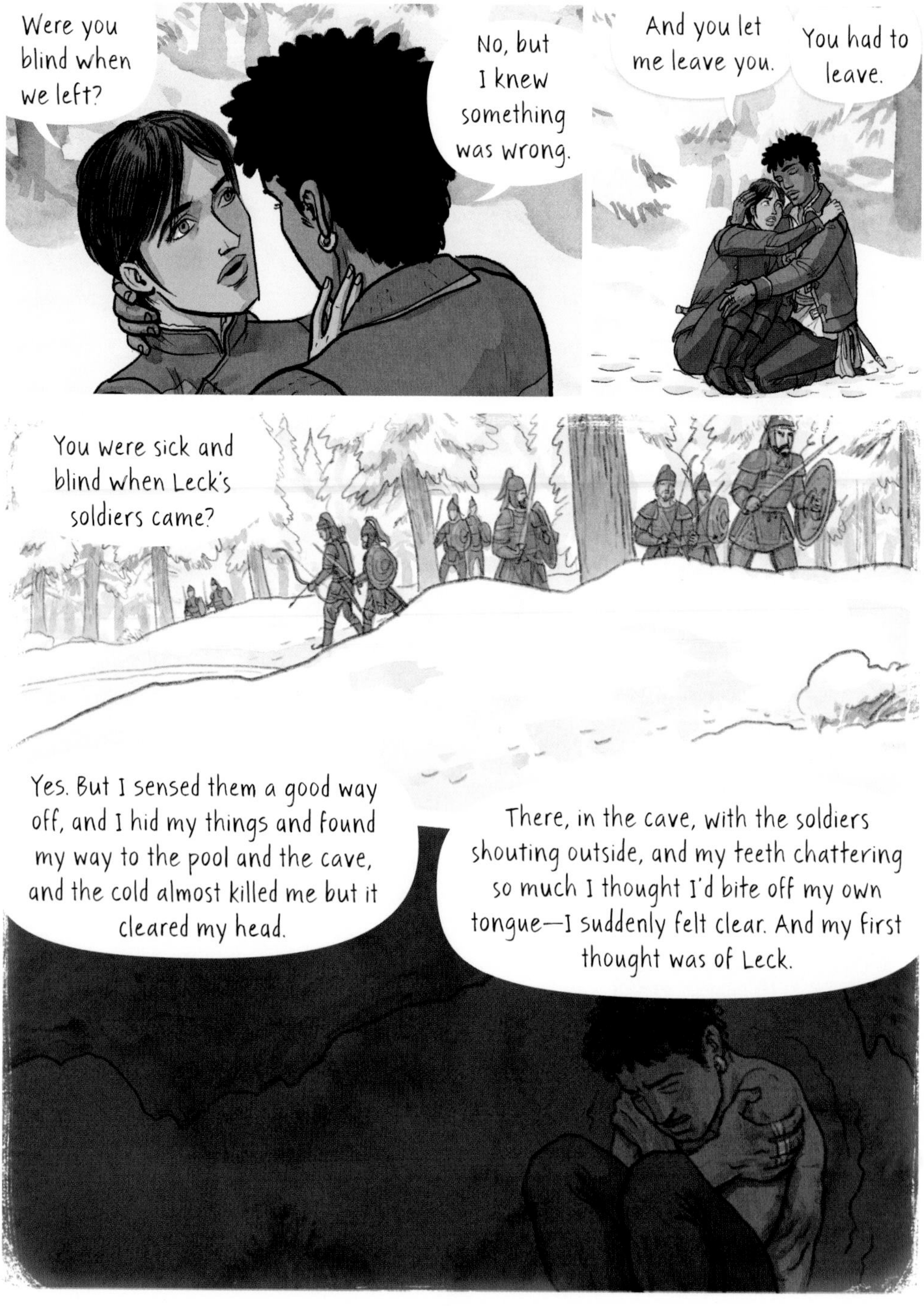
Were you blind when we left?
No, but I knew something was wrong.
And you let me leave you.
You had to leave.
You were sick and blind when Leck's soldiers came?
Yes. But I sensed them a good way off, and I hid my things and found my way to the pool and the cave, and the cold almost killed me but it cleared my head.
There, in the cave, with the soldiers shouting outside, and my teeth chattering so much I thought I'd bite off my own tongue—I suddenly felt clear. And my first thought was of Leck.

The thought of him still out there, spreading his lies, was what gave me the will to go back in that freezing water when the soldiers had gone, to go back to the cabin and start a fire with my numb hands.

To gather the fish and feed myself, and later, to build a bow and practice shooting it.

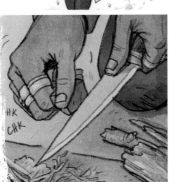

THK
CHK

Leck gave me a reason to go on.

THUK

And then we returned with the happy news that Leck was dead.

249

I've no right to feel sorry for myself. I see everything. I see things I shouldn't see. I'm wallowing in self-pity, when I've lost nothing.

Don't be stupid. You've lost something. And you've every right to feel sorrow for what you've lost.

Your Grace shows you the form of things, but it doesn't show you beauty.

Yes. I don't want to go back to my castle if I can't see it. And it's torture to be with you when I can't see you.

I can't read or write, either. How am I going to hide that?

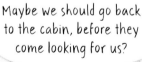

This is a good start. This is some excellent self-pity.

Maybe we should go back to the cabin, before they come looking for us?

Katsa.

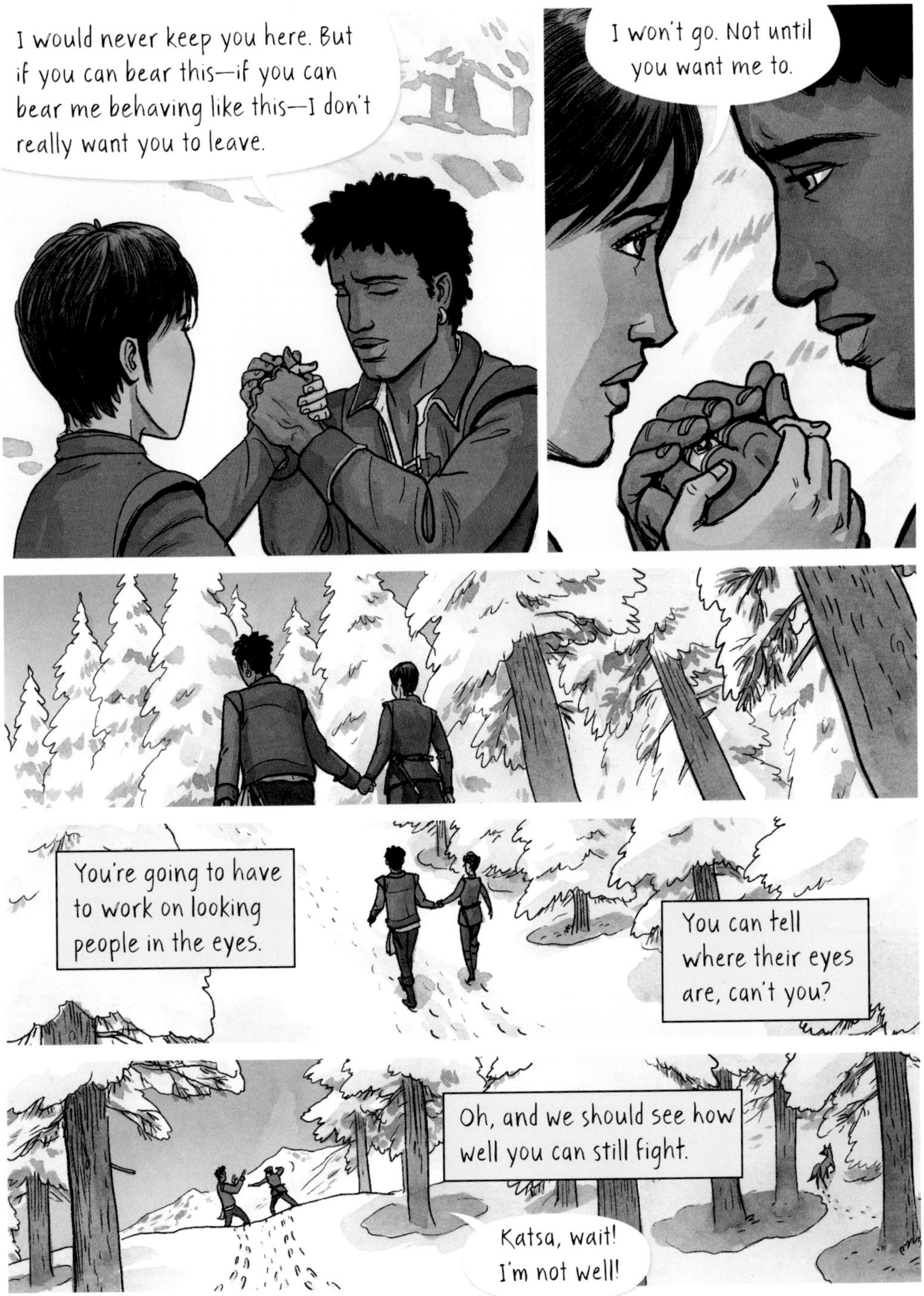
I would never keep you here. But if you can bear this—if you can bear me behaving like this—I don't really want you to leave.
I won't go. Not until you want me to.
You're going to have to work on looking people in the eyes.
You can tell where their eyes are, can't you?
Oh, and we should see how well you can still fight.
Katsa, wait! I'm not well!

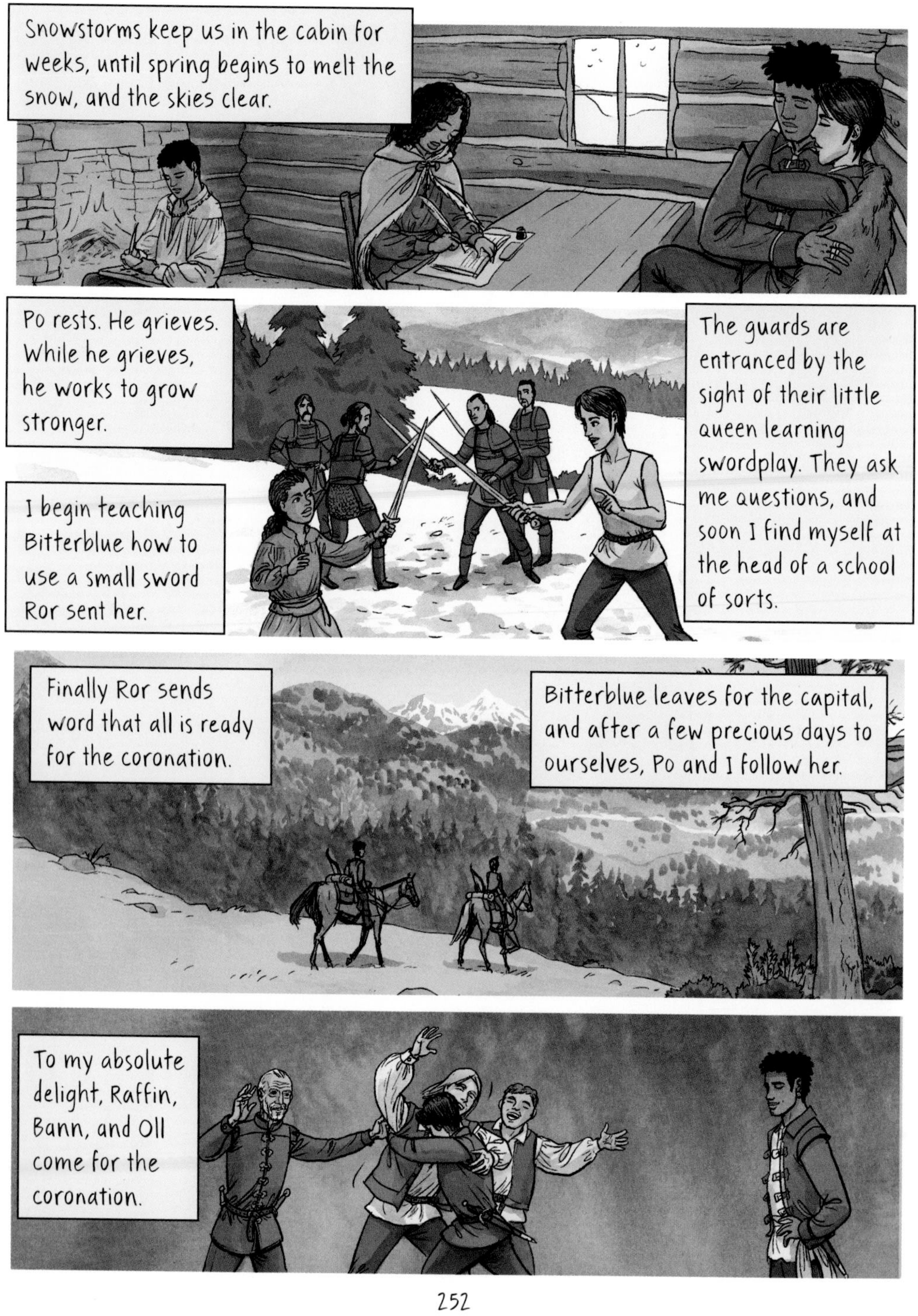
Snowstorms keep us in the cabin for weeks, until spring begins to melt the snow, and the skies clear.
Po rests. He grieves. While he grieves, he works to grow stronger.
The guards are entranced by the sight of their little queen learning swordplay. They ask me questions, and soon I find myself at the head of a school of sorts.
I begin teaching Bitterblue how to use a small sword Ror sent her.
Finally Ror sends word that all is ready for the coronation.
Bitterblue leaves for the capital, and after a few precious days to ourselves, Po and I follow her.
To my absolute delight, Raffin, Bann, and Oll come for the coronation.

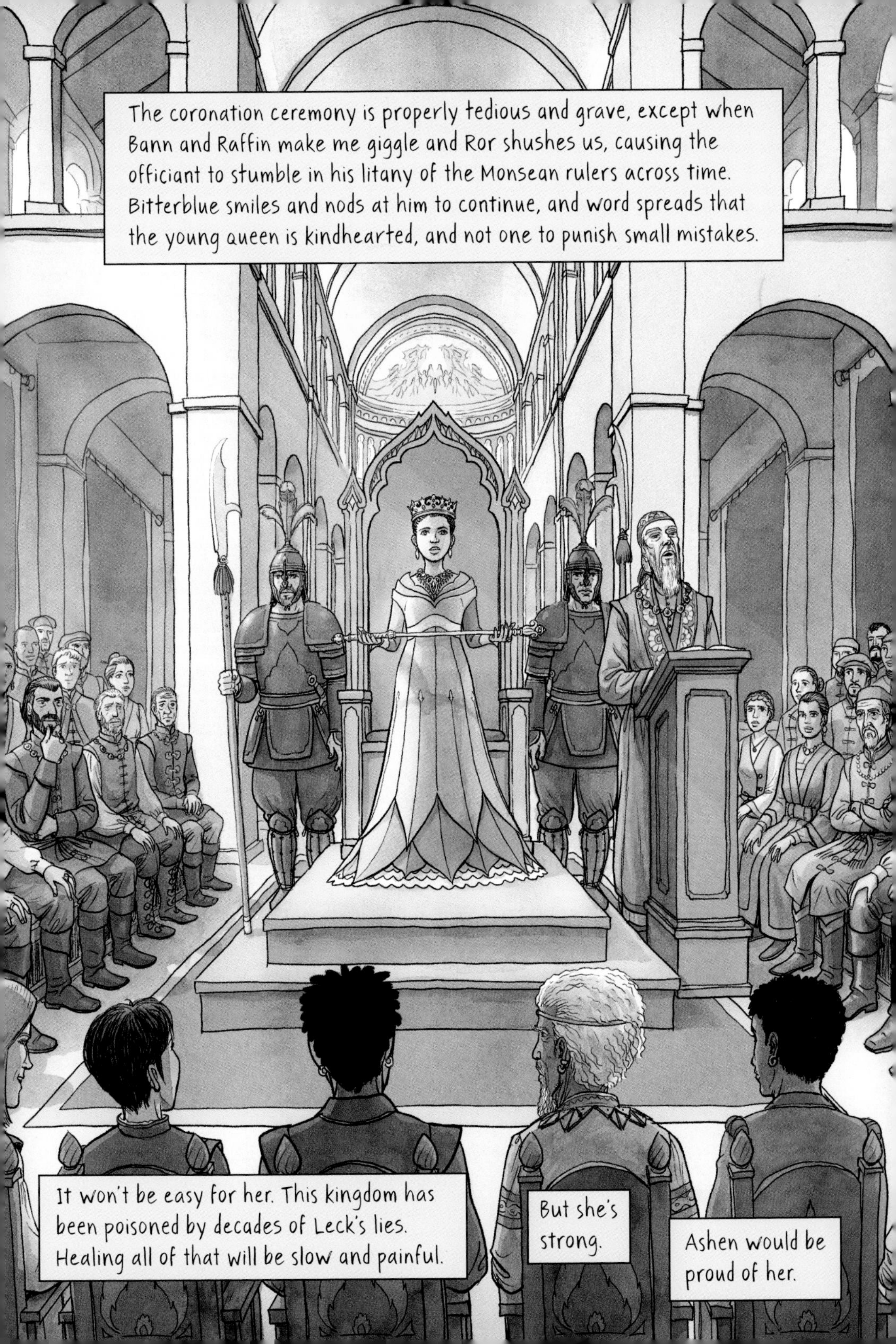
The coronation ceremony is properly tedious and grave, except when Bann and Raffin make me giggle and Ror shushes us, causing the officiant to stumble in his litany of the Monsean rulers across time. Bitterblue smiles and nods at him to continue, and word spreads that the young queen is kindhearted, and not one to punish small mistakes.
It won't be easy for her. This kingdom has been poisoned by decades of Leck's lies. Healing all of that will be slow and painful.
But she's strong.
Ashen would be proud of her.

Epilogue

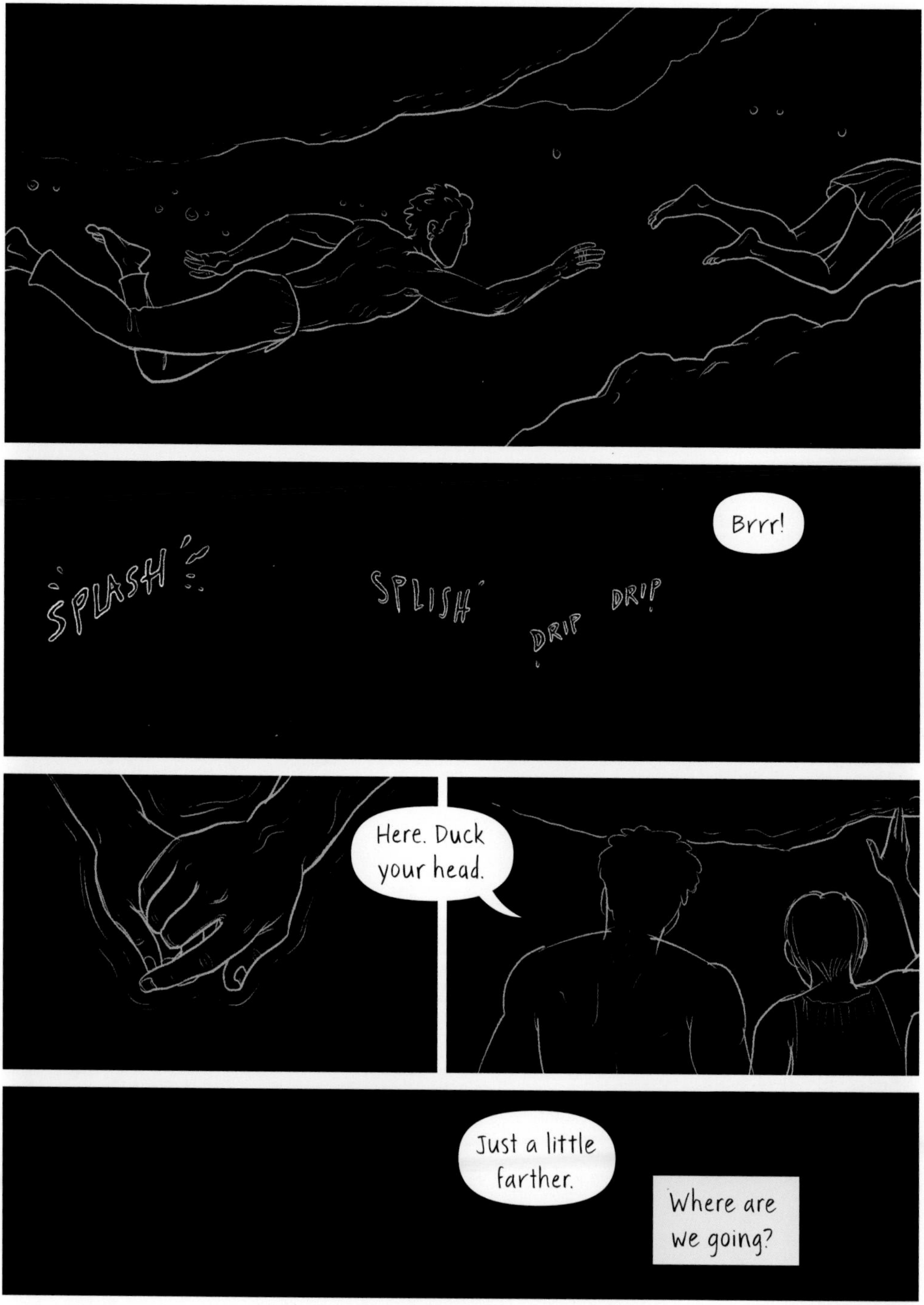
SPLASH
SPLISH
DRIP
DRIP
Brrr!
Here. Duck your head.
Just a little farther.
Where are we going?

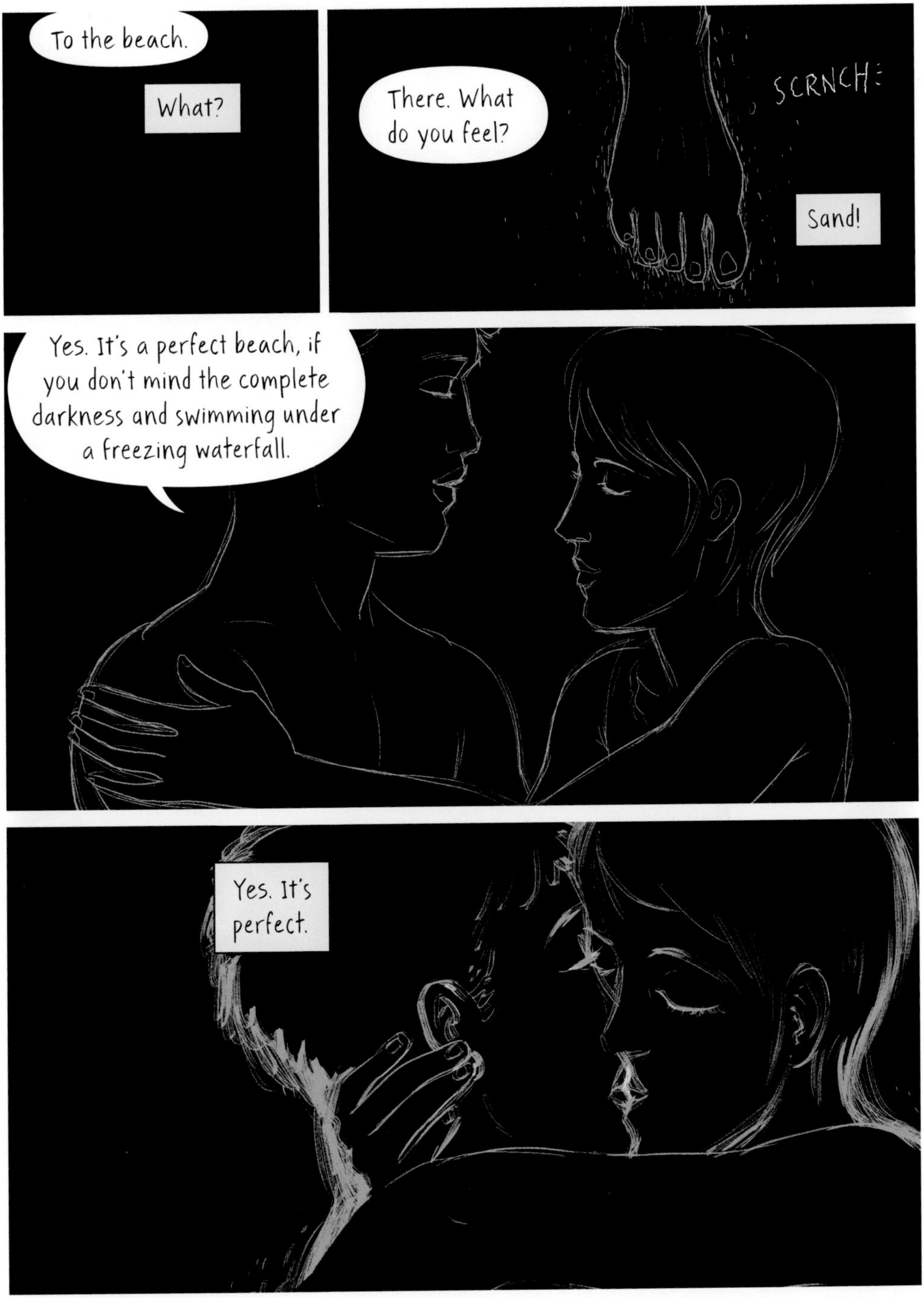
To the beach.
What?
There. What do you feel?
SCRNCH
Sand!
Yes. It's a perfect beach, if you don't mind the complete darkness and swimming under a freezing waterfall.
Yes. It's perfect.

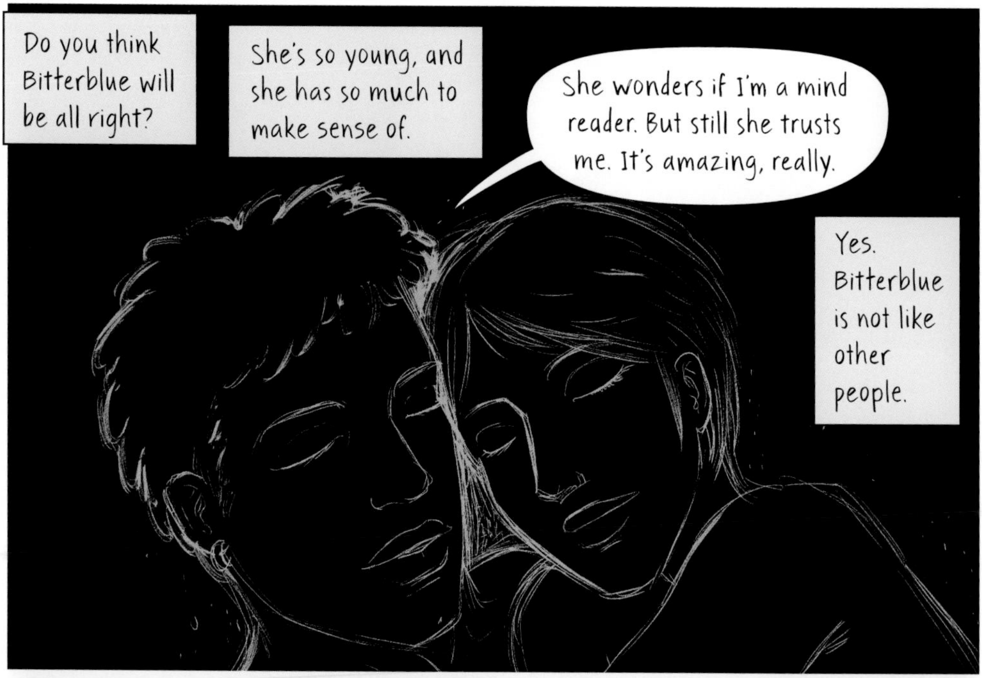
Do you think Bitterblue will be all right?
She's so young, and she has so much to make sense of.
She wonders if I'm a mind reader. But still she trusts me. It's amazing, really.
Yes. Bitterblue is not like other people.

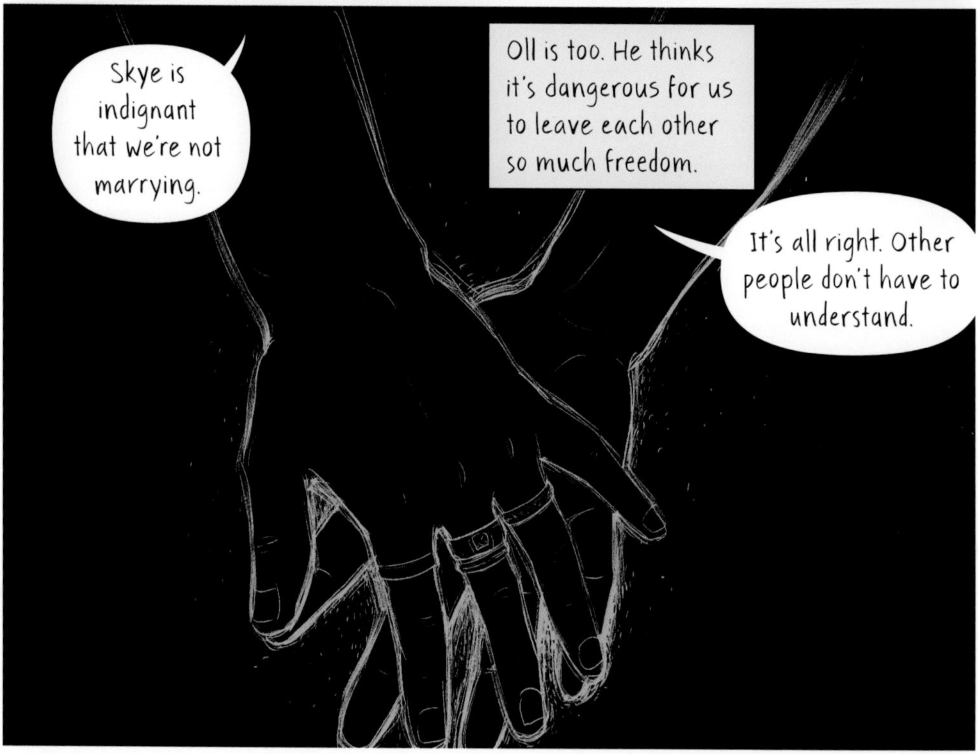
Skye is indignant that we're not marrying.
Oll is too. He thinks it's dangerous for us to leave each other so much freedom.
It's all right. Other people don't have to understand.

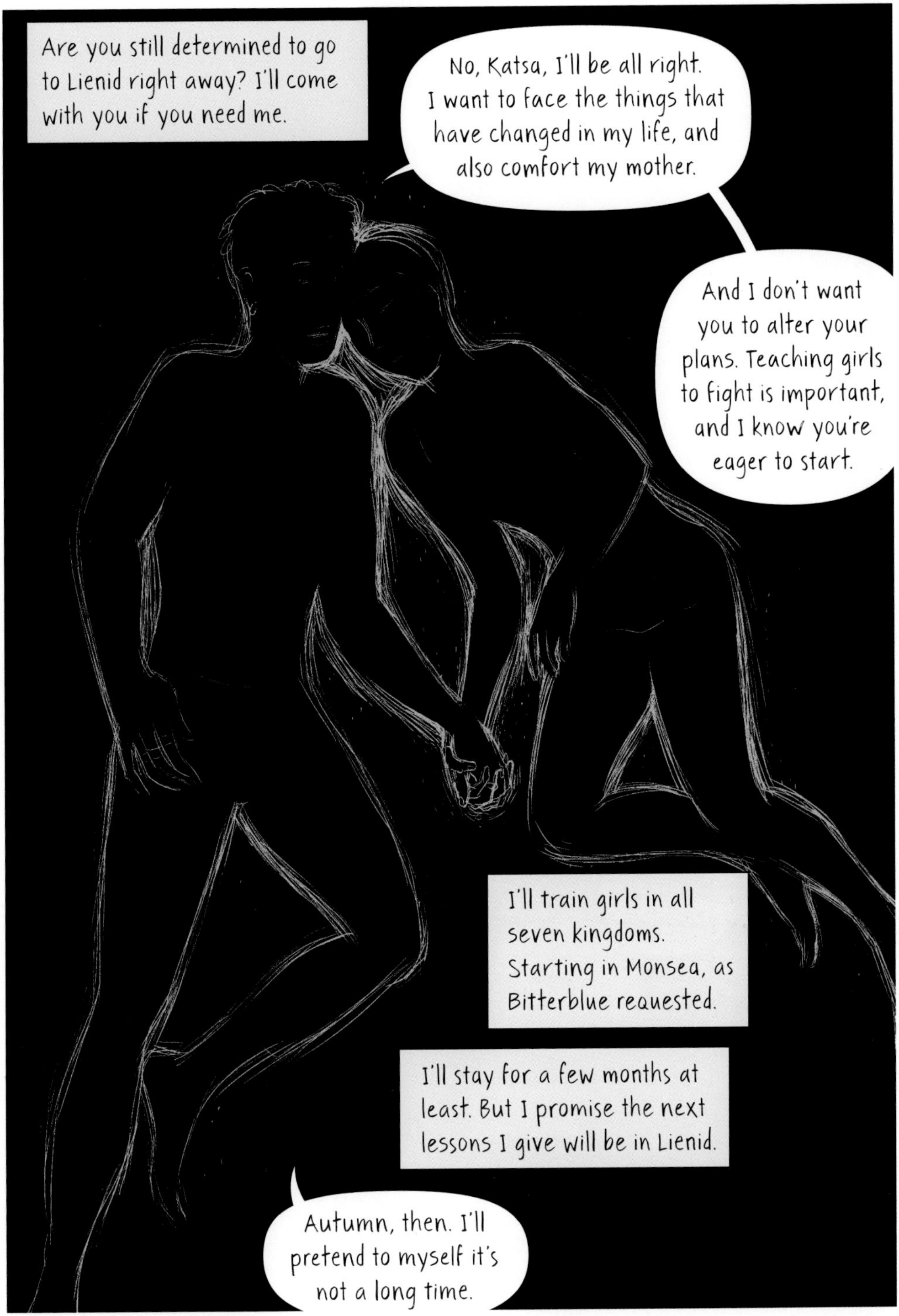
Are you still determined to go to Lienid right away? I'll come with you if you need me.
No, Katsa, I'll be all right. I want to face the things that have changed in my life, and also comfort my mother.
And I don't want you to alter your plans. Teaching girls to fight is important, and I know you're eager to start.
I'll train girls in all seven kingdoms. Starting in Monsea, as Bitterblue requested.
I'll stay for a few months at least. But I promise the next lessons I give will be in Lienid.
Autumn, then. I'll pretend to myself it's not a long time.

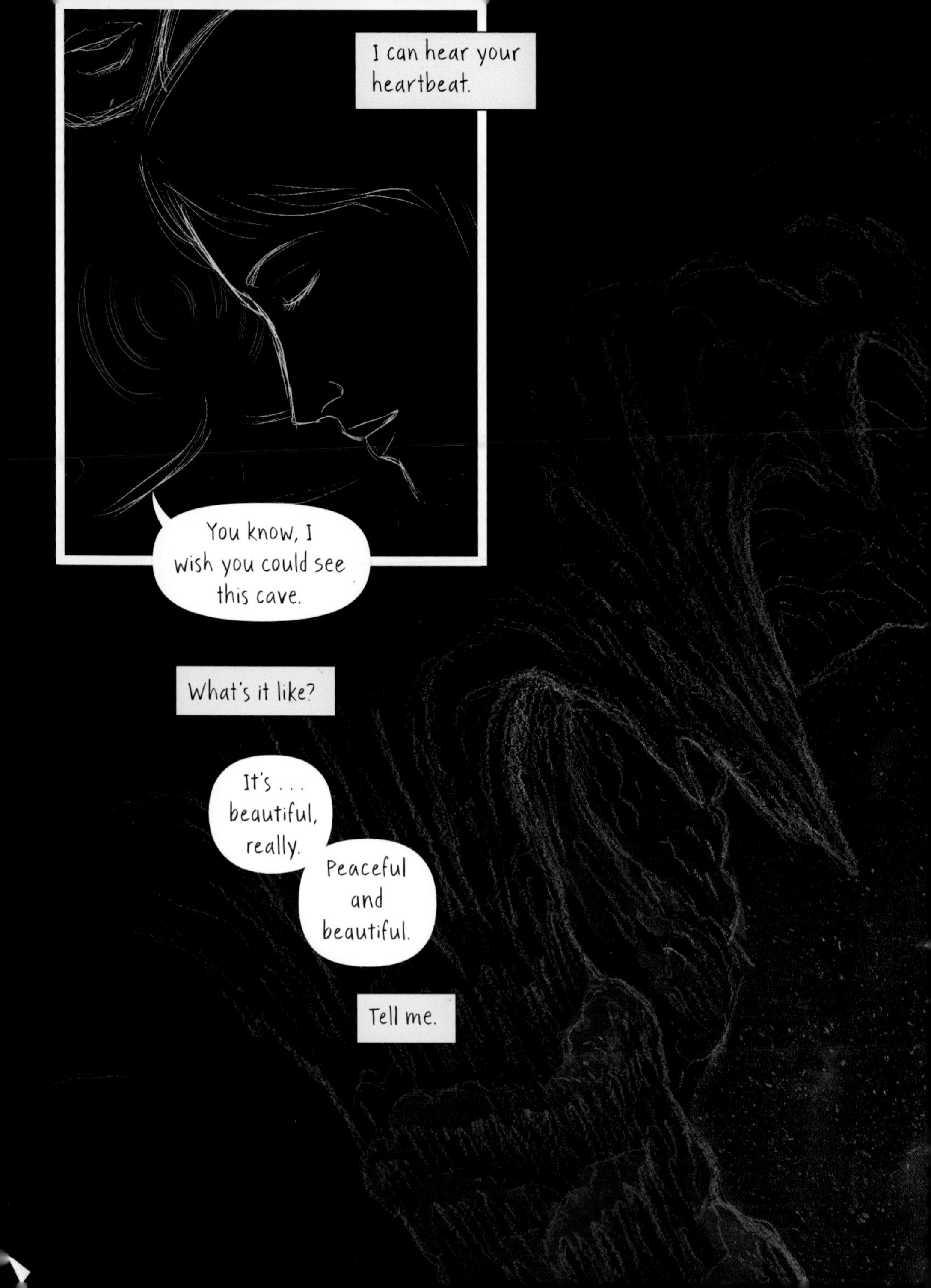
I can hear your heartbeat.
You know, I wish you could see this cave.
What's it like?
It's . . . beautiful, really.
Peaceful and beautiful.
Tell me.

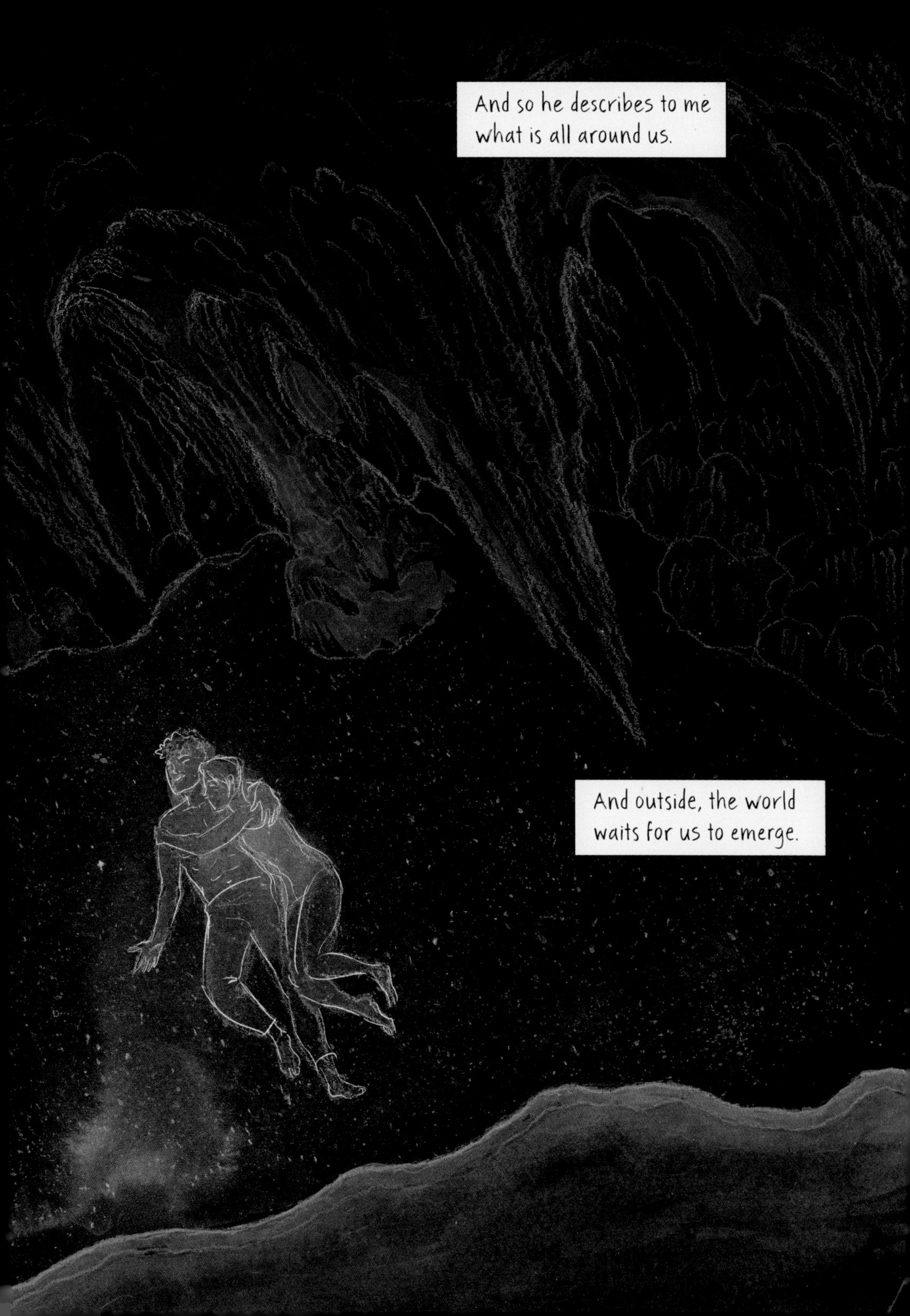
And so he describes to me what is all around us.
And outside, the world waits for us to emerge.

THE END

In loving memory of Fiona Heckscher,

whose flame burned bright,

whose Grace was spreading love and joy,

and whose light still shines

in all who knew her

—G. H.

A Note from the Adapter-Illustrator

My number one goal with this book was to honor and preserve Kristin's story and characters while making the most beautiful and compelling graphic novel I could. Having adapted Shakespeare and Homer, I expected *Graceling* would be relatively straightforward by comparison—but in many ways it was the most difficult adaptation I've done. The construction of the novel is intricate and precise, and I had to do some very tricky compositing of story elements in order to get it down to (believe it or not) about the same length as my adaptation of *The Iliad*! If you haven't already read the original novel, I hope you'll do so now, because it fills in a lot more detail about the world and the many wonderful characters who live there.

More than ten years after its publication, *Graceling* still resonates with readers not only because it is a great romance and action story, but because the evil in the story takes a form that is compelling, creepy, and still deeply relevant. Charismatic figures who can make masses of people believe outright lies will always be among us. They may not be able to fool everyone magically the way Leck does, but by manipulating human psychology and emotions they can create dangerous alternate realities that allow them to commit crimes with impunity and that encourage their followers to feel justified committing violence and atrocities against other human beings. This is not a new problem, but it is still current and urgent. Hate, fear, and lies can spread like a virus. But so can love, truth, and courage. I think our calling is to look clearly at our own choices and work every day to spread light instead of darkness.